THE CROWN OF EMBERS

THE CROWN OF EMBERS

RAE CARSON

GREENWILLOW BOOKS
An Imprint of HarperCollins*Publishers*

Crown of Embers

Copyright © 2012 by Rae Carson

All rights reserved. No part of this book may be used or reproduced in any manner whatsoever without written permission except in the case of brief quotations embodied in critical articles and reviews. Printed in the United States of America. For information address HarperCollins Children's Books, a division of HarperCollins Publishers, 10 East 53rd Street, New York, NY 10022.

www.epicreads.com

The text of this book is set in 11-point Bell.
Book design by Paul Zakris

Library of Congress Cataloging-in-Publication Data
Carson, Rae.
The crown of embers / by Rae Carson.
pages cm
ISBN 978-0-06-202651-4 (hardback)
[1. Kings, queens, rulers, etc.—Fiction. 2. Prophecies—Fiction. 3. Magic—Fiction. 4. Love—Fiction.] I. Title.
PZ7.C2423Cr 2012 [Fic]—dc23 2012014125

13 14 15 16 LP/RRDH 10 9 8 7 6 5 4 3 2
First Edition

 GREENWILLOW BOOKS

FOR CHARLIE,
MY FIRST READER AND BEST FRIEND

I

MY entourage of guards struggles to keep pace as I fly down the corridors of my palace. Servants in starched frocks and shined shoes line the way, bowing like dominoes as I pass. From far away comes a low thrum, filtering even through walls of stone and mortar, steady as falling water, hollow as distant thunder. It's the crowd outside, chanting my name.

I barrel around a corner and collide with a gleaming breastplate. Firm hands grasp my shoulders, saving me from tumbling backward. My crown is not so lucky. The monstrous thing clatters to the ground, yanking strands of hair painfully with it.

He releases my shoulders and rubs at red spot on his neck. "That crown of yours is a mighty weapon," says Lord-Commander Hector of the Royal Guard.

"Sorry," I say, blinking up at him. He and the other guards shaved their mustaches to mark our recent victory, and I've yet to adjust to this new, younger-looking Hector.

Ximena, my gray-haired nurse, bends to retrieve the crown and brushes it off. It's thick with gold and inlaid with a single cabochon ruby. No dainty queen's diadem for me. By tradition, I wear the crown of a fully empowered monarch.

"I expected you an hour ago," he says as I take his offered arm. We travel the corridor at a bruising pace.

"General Luz-Manuel kept me. He wanted to change the parade route again."

He stops cold, and I nearly trip. "Again?"

"He wants to avoid the bottleneck where the Avenida de la Serpiente crosses the merchant's alley. He says a stranger in the crowd could spear me too easily."

Ximena takes advantage of our stillness to reposition the crown on my head. I grimace as she shoves hairpins through the velvet loops to hold it in place.

Hector is shaking his head. "But the rooftops are low in that area. You'll be safer from arrows, which is the greater danger."

"Exactly what I said. He was . . . displeased." I tug on his arm to keep us moving.

"He should know better."

"I may have told him as much."

"I'm sure he appreciated that," he says dryly.

"I've no idea what advantage he thought to gain by it," I say. "Whatever it was, I was not going to give it to him."

Hector glances around at the people lining the corridors, then adds in a lowered voice, "Elisa, as your personal defender, I must beg you one last time to reconsider. The whole world knows you bear the Godstone."

I sigh against the truth of his words. Yes, I'm now the target of religious fanatics, Invierne spies, even black market gem traders. But my birthday parade is the one day each year when everyone—from laundress to stable boy to weather-worn sailor—can glimpse their ruling monarch. It's a national holiday, one they've been looking forward to for months. I won't deny them the opportunity.

And I refuse to be governed by fear. The life stretching before me is that of a queen. It's a life I chose. Fought for, even. I cannot—will not—squander it on dread.

"Hector, I won't hide in the sand like a frightened jerboa."

"Sometimes," Ximena cuts in, with her soft but deliberate voice, "protecting Elisa means protecting her interests. Elisa must show herself publicly. These early months are important as she consolidates her power. We'll keep her safe, you and I. And God. She has a great destiny. . . ."

I turn a deaf ear to her words. So much has happened in the last year, but I feel no closer to my appointment with destiny than I did when God first lodged his stone in my navel seventeen years ago. It still pulses with power, warms in response to my prayers, reminds me that I have not done *enough*, that God has plans for me yet.

And I am sick to death of hearing about it.

"I understand, my lady," Hector is saying. "But it would be safer—"

"Hector!" I snap. "I've made up my mind."

He stiffens. "Yes, Your Majesty."

Shame tightens my throat. Why did I snap at Hector? Ximena is the one I'm frustrated with.

Moments later we reach the carriage house, which reeks

of steaming manure and moldy straw on this especially hot day. My open carriage awaits, a marvel of polished mahogany and swirling bronze scrollwork. Banners of royal blue stream from the posts. The door panels display my royal crest—a ruby crown resting on a bed of sacrament roses.

Fernando, my best archer, stands on the rear platform, bow slung over his shoulder. He bows from the waist, his face grave. Four horses flick their tails and dance in their jeweled traces. I eye them warily while Hector helps me up.

Then he offers a hand to Ximena, and in spite of their recent disagreement, a look of fierce understanding passes between them. They are a formidable team, my guard and my guardian. Sometimes it's as though they plot my safety behind my back.

Hector gives the order, my driver whips the reins, and the carriage lurches forward. My Royal Guard, in its gleaming ceremonial armor, falls in around us. They march a deep one-two-one-two as we leave the shade of the carriage house for desert sunshine.

The moment we turn onto the Colonnade, the air erupts with cheering.

Thousands line the way, packed shoulder to shoulder, waving their hands, flags, tattered linens. Children sit on shoulders, tossing birdseed and rose petals into the air. A banner stretches the length of six people and reads, HAPPY BIRTHDAY TO HER MAJESTY QUEEN LUCERO-ELISA!

"Oh," I breathe.

Ximena grasps my hand and squeezes. "You're a war hero, remember?"

But I'm also a foreigner queen, ruling by an accident of marriage and war. Warmth and pride blossom in my chest, to see my people accepting me with their whole hearts.

Then Ximena's face sobers, and she leans over and whispers, "Remember this moment and treasure it, my sky. No sovereign remains popular forever."

I nod from respectful habit, but I can't keep the frown from creeping onto my face. My people are giving me a gift, and she takes it away so soon.

The steep Colonnade is lined on either side by decadent three-story townhomes. Their sculpted sandstone cornices sparkle in the sun, and silk standards swing from flat garden rooftops. But as we descend from the height of the city, cheered all the way, the townhomes gradually become less stately, until finally we reach the city's outer circle, where only a few humble buildings rise from the war rubble.

I ignore the destruction as long as I can, gazing instead at the city's great wall. It rises the height of several men, protecting us from the swirling desert beyond. I crane my neck and glimpse the soldiers posted between the wall's crenellations, bows held at the ready.

The main gate stands open for daytime commerce. Framed by the barbed portcullis is our cobbled highway. Beyond it are the sweeping dunes of my beautiful desert, wind smoothed and deceptively soft in the yellow light of midday. My gaze lingers too long on the sand as we turn onto the Avenida de la Serpiente.

When I can avoid it no longer, I finally take in the view that twists my heart. For Brisadulce's outer circle is a scar on the face of the world, blackened and crumbled and reeking of wet char. This is where the Invierne army broke through our gate, where their sorcerous animagi burned everything in sight with the blue-hot fire of their Godstone amulets.

A ceiling beam catches my eye, toppled across a pile of adobe rubble. At one end the wood grain shows pristine, but it blackens along its length, shrinking and shriveling until it ends in a ragged stump glowing red with embers. A wisp of smoke curls into the air.

The outer ring is rife with these glowing reminders of the war we won at such a cost. Months later, we still cannot wholly quench their fire. Father Nicandro, my head priest, says that since magic caused these fires, only magic can cool them. Either magic or time.

My city may burn for a hundred years.

So I smile and wave. I do it with ferocity, like my life depends on it, as if a whole glorious future lies before us and these sorcerous embers are not worth a passing irritation.

The crowd loves me for it. They scream and cheer, and it is like magic, a good magic, how after a while *they* win *me* over to hope, and my smile becomes genuine.

The street narrows, and the crowd presses in as we push forward. Hector's hand goes to his scabbard as he inches nearer to the carriage. I tell myself that I don't mind their proximity, that I love their smiling faces, their unrestrained energy.

But as we approach the massive amphitheater with its stone columns, I sense a subtle shift, a dampening of spirits—as if everyone has become distracted. The guards scan the crowd with suspicion.

"Something isn't right," Ximena whispers.

I glance at her with alarm. From long habit, my fingertips find the Godstone, seeking a clue; it heats up around friends and becomes ice when my life is in peril. Do I imagine that it is cooler than usual?

The theater is shaped like a giant horseshoe, its massive ends running perpendicular to the avenida. As we near it, movement draws my gaze upward. High above the crowd stands a man in a white wind-whipped robe.

My Godstone freezes—unhelpfully—and ice shoots through my limbs as I note his hair: lightest yellow, almost white, streaming to his waist. Sunlight catches on something embedded in the top of his wooden staff. *Oh, God.*

I'm too shocked to cry out, and by the time Hector notices the white figure, it's too late: My carriage is within range. The crowd is eerily silent, as if all the air has gotten sucked away, for everyone has heard descriptions of the animagi, Invierne's sorcerers.

The top of the animagus' staff begins to glow Godstone blue.

My terror is like the thick muck of a dream as I struggle to find my voice. "Fernando!" I yell. "Shoot him! Shoot to kill!"

An arrow whizzes toward the animagus in blurred relief against the crystal sky.

The animagus whips his staff toward it. A stream of blue-hot fire erupts from the tip, collides with the arrow, explodes it into a shower of splinters and sparks.

People scream. Hector gestures at the guards, barking orders. Half tighten formation around me; the rest sprint away to flank the sorcerer. But the crowd is panicked and thrashing, and my guards are trapped in a mill of bodies.

"Archers!" Hector yells. "Fire!"

Hundreds of arrows let fly in a giant *whoosh*.

The animagus spins in a circle, staff outstretched. The air around him bends to his will, and I catch the barest glimpse of a barrier forming—like glass, like a wavering desert mirage—before Ximena leaps across the bench and covers me with her own body.

"To the queen!" comes Hector's voice. "We must retreat!" But the carriage doesn't budge, for the milling crowd has hemmed us in.

"Queen Lucero-Elisa," comes a sibilant voice, magnified by the peculiar nature of the amphitheater. "Bearer of the only living Godstone, you belong to us, to us, to us."

He's coming down the stairway. I know he is. He's coming for *me*. He'll blaze a path through my people and—

"You think you've beaten us back, but we are as numerous as the desert sands. Next time we'll come at you like ghosts in a dream. And you will know the gate of your enemy!"

In the corner of my eye I catch the gleam of Hector's sword as he raises it high, and my stomach thuds with the realization that he'll cut through our own people if that's what it takes to whisk me away.

"Ximena!" I gasp. "Get off. Hector . . . he'll do anything. We can't let him—"

She understands instantly. "Stay down," she orders as she launches against the door and tumbles into the street.

Heart pounding, I peek over the edge of the carriage. The animagus stares at me hungrily as he descends the great stair, like I am a juicy mouse caught in his trap. My Godstone's icy warning is relentless.

He could have killed me by now if he wanted to; we've no way to stop his fire. So why doesn't he? Eyeing him carefully, I stand up in the carriage.

"Elisa, no!" cries Hector. Ximena has trapped his sword arm, but he flings her off and rushes toward me. He jerks to a stop midstride, and his face puckers with strain: The animagus has frozen him with magic.

But Hector is the strongest man I know. *Fight it, Hector.*

Shivering with bone-deep cold, I force myself to step from the carriage. *I* am what the sorcerer wants, so maybe I can distract him, buy enough time for my guards to flank him, give Hector a chance to break free.

Sun glints off a bit of armor creeping up on the animagus from above, so I keep my gaze steady, and my voice is steel when I say, "I burned your brothers to dust. I will do the same to you." The lie weighs heavy on my tongue. I've harnessed the power of my stone only once, and I'm not sure how.

The animagus' answering grin is feral and slick. "Surrender yourself. If you do, we will spare your people."

A guard is within range now. The animagus has not noticed him. The solider quietly feeds an arrow into his bow, aims.

Look strong, Elisa. Do not flinch. Hold his gaze.

The arrow zings through the air. The sorcerer whirls at the sound, but it is too late; the arrowhead buries itself in his ribs.

The animagus wobbles. He turns back to me, eyes flared with pain or zeal, one shoulder hanging lower than the other. Crimson spreads like spilled ink across his robe. "Watch closely, my queen," he says, and his voice is liquid with drowning. "This is what will happen to everyone in Joya d'Arena if you do not present yourself as a *willing sacrifice.*"

Hector reaches me at last, grabs my shoulders, and starts to pull me away, even as the guards rush the animagus. But his Godstone already glows like a tiny sun; they will not capture him in time. I expect fire to shoot toward us, to turn my people into craters of melt and char, and suddenly I'm grappling for purchase at the joints of Hector's armor, at his sword belt, pushing him along, for I can't bear to see another friend burn.

But the animagus turns the fire on himself.

He screams, "It is God's will!" He raises his arms to the sky, and his lips move as if in prayer while the conflagration melts his skin, blackens his hair, turns him into a living torch for the whole city to see.

The scent of burning flesh fills the air as the remaining crowd scatters. The horses rear and plunge away, trampling everyone in their path, the carriage rattling behind.

"To the queen!" Hector yells above my head.

A wind gusts through the amphitheater, extinguishing the biggest flames and flinging bits of hair and robe into the sky. The animagus' charred body topples off the stair and plunges to the ground, trailing smoke and sparks.

I turn to rest my forehead against Hector's breastplate and close my eyes as the chaos around us gradually dissipates. The chill of my Godstone fades, and I breathe deep of warm desert air and of relief.

Hector says, "We must get you back to the palace."

"Yes, of course," I say, pulling away from him and standing tall. "Let's go." Maybe if I pretend hard enough, I will feel strong in truth.

My guards form a wedge of clanking armor and drawn swords. As we begin the long, steep trek home, a bit of white robe, edged with glowing cinders, flutters to the ground at my feet.

2

I pray during the walk back, thanking God for my life and the lives of my guards, asking him to keep us safe just a little while longer. But as we approach the palace, Hector holds up a fist to halt our procession.

The portcullis is dropped and barred. Hundreds gather outside. Some yell and stomp, rattling the iron bars. Others stand quietly, carrying blankets, packs, small children. Their number swells as others trickle in from the adjoining streets and alleys.

"They think we're being attacked," I say, my voice catching. "They want protection within the palace walls."

"Maybe we are," Ximena says quietly. "Maybe it's war all over again."

"Back away quickly," Hector says. "But no sudden moves." I hear what he's not saying—if the desperate throng discovers me, I could be mobbed.

We crowd into a narrow alley between two townhomes. Hector whips off the bright red cloak marking him as a Royal Guard and turns it inside out so the softer, paler side shows.

"Put this on. That gown is much too noticeable."

The cloak smells of Hector—oiled steel and worn leather and spiced wine. After I fasten the claps at my neck, I gesture to the others. "All of you. Turn your cloaks inside out. Ximena, can you hide my crown?" I lift it from my head, and she untangles my hair from the various pins keeping it in place.

She holds it out for a moment, considering. She slips behind me, out of sight of the guards, and when she reveals herself again, the front of her skirt is lumpy and distended. "At least it doesn't look like a crown," she says with an apologetic shrug.

"Now what?" I say. "If the portcullis is barred, the stables are surely closed off as well."

"The kitchens?" a guard suggests.

"Or the receiving hall," says another.

Hector shakes his head. "The garrison is trained to lock down all entrances during drills."

Any member of the Royal Guard would be allowed admittance without question. There is a reason he's not sending someone to the palace to fetch a larger escort and a windowless carriage. "You think it's no accident," I say, "that someone ordered the palace locked down before I was safely inside. You think the crowd may not be the greater danger."

His gaze on me is solemn. "I'll take no chances with you."

"The escape tunnel!" I say. "Leading from the king's suite to the merchants' alley. Alejandro said only a few know of it." I swallow against the memory of long days spent in my husband's suite as he lay dying. I paid close attention to his every word, storing them up in my heart so I could someday pass them along to his son, Rosario.

Hector rubs at his jaw. "It's in disrepair. I haven't been inside since Alejandro and I were boys."

It will have to do. "Let's go," I order.

We leave the shadow of the brick alley and step into sunshine. From habit, the guards fall into perfect formation.

"No, no." I motion vaguely. "Relax. Don't look so . . . guardlike."

They drop formation at once, glancing at one another shamefaced. Hector drapes an arm around my shoulder as if we are out for a companionable stroll. He leans down and says, "So. Horrible heat we've had lately."

I can't help grinning, even as I note the tenseness of his shoulders, the way his eyes roam the street and his free hand wraps around the hilt of his sword. I say, "I'd prefer to discuss the latest fashion craze of jeweled stoles."

He laughs. "No, you wouldn't."

We reach the merchants' alley without incident. It's eerily silent, the booths vacant, the cobblestone street empty of rumbling carts. It's a national holiday. This place should be filled with shoppers, acrobats, and beggars, with coconut scones and sticky date pops and meat pies.

The news must have whipped through the city with the destructive force of a sandstorm. *The Inviernos are back! And they threatened the queen!*

All this emptiness makes us nothing if not noticeable. My neck prickles as I glance at the surrounding buildings, expecting furtive heads to appear in windowsills. But I see no one.

Quietly I say, "Alejandro said the entrance was through a blacksmith's home."

"Yes. Just around the corner . . . there." He indicates a large awning outside a two-story adobe building. The bellows beneath it is cold, and the traces dangle empty chains.

Hector's hand on my shoulder tightens as he peers under the awning. "Ho, blacksmith!" he calls.

The door creaks open. A bald man with a sooty leather apron and forearms like corded tree trunks steps over the threshold. His eyes widen.

"Goodman Rialto!" the blacksmith exclaims, and his cheer is a little too forced. "Your cauldron is ready. A beauty, I must say. Had some extra bronze sheeting lying around, which will reduce your total cost. Please come in!"

I look up at Hector for confirmation, and he nods, almost imperceptibly. We follow the blacksmith inside.

Every space of wall is used to display his work—swords, grates, animal traps, spoons, candlesticks, gauntlets. The scent of the place is biting, like copper gone sour. A low cooking fire crackles in a clay hearth. Only a blacksmith could stand to have a fire going on a day as hot as this. After we filter in, he closes the door behind us and drops the latch.

"This way, Your Majesty," he says, all trace of brightness evaporated. "Quickly." He pulls up the corner of a thick rug and reveals a trapdoor. With a grunt, he heaves on the brass ring. The trapdoor swings open to show rickety wooden stairs descending into darkness.

"We'll need light," I say.

He grabs a candle and a brass holder from a nearby table, reaches toward the hearth to light the wick, and hands it to me. "Be wary," he says. "The tunnel is reinforced with wooden beams. They're very old and very dry."

"I'll go first," Hector says, and the stair creaks under his weight. .

I start to follow but hesitate. "Ximena, take the rest of the guards and return to the palace through the main entrance. They'll let you in. People should be seen leaving here, just in case they saw us coming."

She frowns. "My place is by your side."

"I'm safe with Hector." Before she can protest, I turn and address the blacksmith. "Your name, sir?"

"Mandrano," he says proudly. "Formerly of His Majesty King Nicolao's Royal Guard, now retired."

I clasp his shoulder; it's as hard and round as a boulder. "Thank you, Mandrano. You have done your queen a great service today."

He bows low. I don't wait for him to rise, and I don't bother to see that Ximena and the guards have followed my orders. I step down quickly after Hector, holding my candle low to light my way.

His fingers reach out of the gloom, offering support, and I grab them. Just as my feet reach dry earth, the trapdoor bangs closed, making the darkness complete but for our puddle of candlelight.

I move close enough for the candle to illuminate us both. The flame casts strange shadows on his skin—blurring the scar on his cheek, softening his eyes, and rounding his features—and I am reminded how very young he is.

"Hector, who besides you and me has the authority to lock down—"

"Conde Eduardo, General Luz-Manuel, and the mayordomo." He rattles off the list so quickly that I realize he's been rehearsing it in his mind.

"You think someone *intended* to lock us out?"

Ximena would offer a kind inanity about it being an unfortunate misunderstanding. But Hector has nothing of dissembling in him. "Even after you're safely returned, we must tread strategically," he says.

I pass him the candle, nodding agreement. He leads the way, and I follow close enough that I can grab his sword belt if necessary. The tunnel is so tight that my shoulders brush the wood beams propping up the ceiling. I fight the urge to sneeze against the dust we kick up.

Something scuttles over my foot, glowing Godstone blue, and I squeal.

Hector whirls, but then he says, "Just a cave scorpion. They glow when frightened. Nearly harmless."

Nearly harmless is not harmless, and I open my mouth to point out as much, but I decide I'd rather be brave in front of him. "It startled me," I say calmly. "Please, continue."

He turns back around, but not before I catch the amused quirk of his lips. "Be glad it wasn't a Death Stalker," he says, pushing aside a thick cobweb.

"Oh?"

"They're much larger scorpions. Very poisonous. They live in the scrub desert around Basajuan. I'm surprised you didn't encounter them when you were leading the rebellion."

"I wish I *had* encountered Death Stalkers. They would have been marvelous weapons."

"What?" He stops short, and I nearly collide with him.

"One of the village boys kept vipers. I ordered him to toss them into an Invierno camp. He didn't stick around to see if anyone died, but he did report a lot of screaming. Scorpions would have been even better."

He is silent for so long that I'm worried I've offended him somehow. "Hector?"

"You always surprise me." And he moves off into the darkness.

We reach a crooked stair. The bottom step has collapsed with rot.

"This winds through the walls of the palace," Hector whispers. "We must go quietly."

He waits until I nod, then ventures upward. The wood-reinforced earthen walls cede to stone and mortar as the steps bend and creak with our weight. I notice signs of life—footsteps, muted voices, wash water running through pipes to the sewer below.

The stair dead-ends. Hector holds up the candle, exposing a wall too smooth for stone. He runs a finger across it, which leaves a rivulet of darkness in the dust-gray surface. Something clicks. The door slides soundlessly aside, revealing a slightly brighter gloom.

"The wardrobe," he whispers, stepping inside. "Stay here while I check the room."

Light floods our passageway as he pushes the double doors open, but then he closes them again, leaving me alone in the dull murk. My heart twists to sense the empty space around me. My husband's clothes used to hang here. I wonder what became of them all?

I wait the space of several heartbeats, listening hard for the sounds of a scuffle, wishing Hector had at least left me the candle.

Then he opens the doors, and I blink against the onslaught of brightness. "All clear," he says. I take his offered hand and step into the king's suite.

My late husband's bedchamber is huge and decadent, with marble floors and polished mahogany furniture. Tapestries the height of two men hang from gilded crown molding. An enormous bed looms in the room's center like a squat tower, its red silk canopy rising to a point.

I could live here if I wanted—it's my right, as monarch. But I hate this room. It feels garish and ridiculous. And because I've only ever been here to hold the hand of a wasted man and ease his passing, it also feels like death.

Just ahead is a smaller door that leads to my own chambers— and home. "I checked. No one there but Mara," Hector says when he sees me eyeing it with longing. "You're safe for now."

For now. *We must tread strategically,* he said in the tunnel. I clench my hands into fists, preparing for something, though I'm not sure what. "Let's go then."

We have returned ahead of Ximena and the guards. I pace in the bedchamber while Hector stands at the entrance, arms crossed, chin set.

"I have to *do* something," I say. "I can't just wait here."

Mara, my lady-in-waiting, beckons me toward the sun-drenched atrium. "But we need to change your gown," she says hurriedly. "It's covered in dust. And I should repowder your face and smooth your hair and . . . and . . ."

The soft desperation in her voice makes me study her carefully. She's as tall and slender as a palm—seventeen years old, like me. She won't look me in the eye as she adds, "And I just had the atrium pool cleaned! Wouldn't you like a bath?"

"Later. I have to figure out . . ." My protest dies when I see her trembling lip. I stride toward her and wrap her in a hug.

She draws in a surprised breath, then wraps her arms around me, squeezing tight.

"I'm fine, Mara," I say into her hair. "Truly."

"The animagus could have killed you," she whispers.

"But he didn't."

She's the first to pull away. When she straightens, her lips are pressed into a resolved line.

"Hector," I say.

He uncrosses his arms and stands at attention, but he regards me warily.

"I can't leave all those people out there. They'll work themselves into a terrified mob."

He frowns. "You want to open the gates."

"They should know that their queen will protect them, no matter what."

"To reverse the order of a Quorum lord, you must give the command in person." He puts up a hand to keep me from rushing out the door. "But you need a proper escort. We should wait until Lady Ximena and the other guards return."

"People are mobbing the gate *now*."

He considers a moment, then nods reluctantly.

To Mara, I say, "Will you check on Prince Rosario?" Treading strategically means protecting my heir.

She reaches for my hand and gives it a squeeze. "Of course. Please be careful." She doesn't let go until I squeeze back.

Hector and I hurry into the hallway and immediately stop short. Soldiers pour from an adjoining corridor and run off ahead of us, a cacophony of clanking armor and creaking leather. They wear the plain cloaks of palace garrison—General Luz-Manuel's men. "Hector? What—"

"I have no idea." But he draws his sword.

Another group approaches from behind, and we step aside to let them pass. They move with such haste that they fail to notice their queen staring at them as they go by.

The soldier bringing up the rear is a little younger, a little shorter than the others. I grab him by the collar and yank him backward. He whips his sword around to defend himself, but Hector blocks him neatly. My ears ring from the clash of steel on steel, but I manage not to flinch.

The soldier's face blanches when he recognizes me. "Your Majesty! I'm so sorry. I didn't see . . ." He drops to his knee and bows his head. Hector does not lower his sword.

"Where are you going?" I demand.

"The main gate, Your Majesty."

"Why?"

"We are under siege."

Hector and I exchange a startled glance. It must be the Inviernos. How did they sneak into the city unnoticed? How could so many—

"The citizens of Brisadulce are rioting," the soldier adds.

Oh, God. "You mean we're defending the palace against *our own people*? Tell me who gave the order to lock down the palace."

He folds in on himself a little. "It—it was Lord-Conde Eduardo."

"By sealed message or in person?" Hector asks, and it takes me a moment to understand: If it was a sealed message, the parchment might still exist.

"His adviser, Franco, relayed the message."

Franco. I've made it a point to memorize the names and positions of every person in my court, but I don't recognize this one.

"I require your escort to the palace gate," I tell him as Hector nods approval. "Quickly." I gesture for him to lead the way, preferring Hector at my back, and lift my skirts to keep pace.

The dusty yard teems with palace garrison—archers up along the palace wall, light infantry in a row, ten paces back from the gate. Spearmen stand at the portcullis, swatting at grappling hands with their spear points, barking warnings to the people on the other side. From the swelling noise, the crowd has at least tripled.

"Thank you," I tell the young soldier. "You may join your company." He bows and flees.

Hector points to the wall above the gate, to a space between crenellations. "It's Conde Eduardo."

Sure enough, a figure stands tall, hands on hips, observing the crowd beyond.

"Let's go."

Hector bellows, "Make way for the queen!"

Soldiers scurry out of the way as we rush forward and take the stairs to the top of the wall two at a time.

The conde's eyes widen slightly as I approach, but a blanket of composure drops across his features quickly. He's an almost-handsome man with broad shoulders, sharp eyes, and a black close-cropped beard that cedes to gray along his temples. "You shouldn't be here, Your Majesty," he says. "It isn't safe for you."

"Did you order the palace lockdown?" I ask, breathless from the quick climb.

"No. The mayordomo did."

I peer into the conde's face, trying to read any deception or nervousness there, but he is as preternaturally calm as always.

"I want the gate opened," I tell him.

"I'm not sure that's a good—"

"They're *our* people. Not our enemies."

"They're panicked. Panicked people do horrible things."

"Like dropping the gate against those we're supposed to protect?"

His nostrils flare as he takes a deep breath. He leans forward, eyes narrowed, and I resist the urge to flinch away. *Do not back down, Elisa.* Below, the mob has quieted. They have no doubt spotted me. They're waiting to see what I'll do.

Finally the conde straightens. "As Your Majesty wishes," he says.

I lift my chin to address the command toward the crowd. "The citizens of Brisadulce are most welcome. Raise the gate!"

The cry echoes throughout the yard. Gears shriek as the portcullis grinds upward. The garrison soldiers make way as the people of my city rush into the yard. But the initial panic blows itself out quickly, and after a moment, everyone filters through with orderly haste. My shoulders sag with relief. Until this moment, I was only *mostly* sure of my decision.

If the conde has a reaction to the quieting crowd, he does not show it, "There is much to discuss regarding today's events," he says.

"Indeed," I agree with equal calm. "I'm calling an emergency meeting of the Quorum."

He bows from the waist, then turns on his heel and strides away along the wall.

I watch him go, wondering about the flicker on his face when he first saw me, at his hesitation to follow my orders. Then I turn my back on him and the crowd gathering in the courtyard to look out over my city. I need to feel wide-open space, cleaner air.

I sense Hector beside me. He leans his elbows onto the wall so that our shoulders almost touch, and he says, "This is your first major crisis as sole monarch. You are weathering it well."

"Thank you." But I clutch the wall's edge with misgiving. I gaze out across the flat rooftops of Brisadulce. They hug the downslope like massive adobe stairs, lush with garden plants and trellises. Beyond them, the ocean horizon stretches and curves, as though someone has thumb-smeared the bottom of the sky with indigo paint. "Hector, you know how when clouds roll across the sky, everyone turns an eye toward the docks to see if the water will leap over them and flood the streets? To see if the coming storm is actually a hurricane?"

"Yes."

"I fear that's what this is. Merely the heralding surge."

3

I hate Quorum meetings.

Calling one is the right thing to do; we must deal with this incident decisively. But the lord-general and the lord-conde have been in power for decades. I'm the upstart—a seventeen-year-old queen reigning by royal decree rather than inheritance. On a good day, they talk over me as if I'm not there. On a bad one, I feel like a pesky sand chigger in danger of a swift swatting.

I'm the last to arrive. My entourage of ladies and guards stops at the threshold, for only Quorum members are allowed inside. Mara forces an encouraging smile as I swing the huge double doors shut and slide the bolt home to lock us in.

The Quorum chamber is low ceilinged and windowless, like a tomb. Candles flicker from sconces set in dusty mortar between gray stones. A squat oak table fills the center, surrounded by red cushions. The air is thick with unyielding silence, and I feel as though the ghosts of weighty decisions and secret councils press in around me, telling me to hush.

Hector is already seated on his cushion, looking stern. We always arrive separately, for it would be gauche to flaunt our close association. He lifts his chin in cold greeting, giving no hint that there is any warmth between us.

General Luz-Manuel, commander of my army, rises to welcome me, but his smile does not reach his eyes. He's a small, hunched man, unimposing enough that his rise to military prominence seems puzzling. Because of this, I know better than to underestimate him.

"You were right to call this meeting, Your Majesty," he says.

Beside him sits Lady Jada, who clasps her hands together and smiles as if in raptures. "Oh, Your Majesty, I'm so delighted the lord-general invited me again!"

I blink at her, marveling at her seeming unawareness of the moment's gravity. Jada is wife to Brisadulce's mayor and a temporary addition to the Quorum. We have been minus a member since I allowed the eastern holdings to secede, but we dare not meet with fewer than five, the holy number of perfection. Lady Jada is neither clever nor interesting, and therefore an unintimidating choice until we decide on a permanent replacement.

"I'm delighted you accepted," I tell her sincerely.

Conde Eduardo bows his head in greeting, then calls the meeting to order by quoting God's own words from the *Scriptura Sancta*: "Wherever five are gathered, there am I in their midst."

I settle onto a cushion at the head of the table.

The conde continues, his voice grave. "It concerns me deeply that an animagus could creep into our city unnoticed, much less climb to the top of the amphitheater. And his demand that we give the queen over to Invierne—"

"Is an empty threat," Hector says. "They were beaten badly. Her Majesty destroyed nine of their sorcerers that day."

"And yet one remained," says General Luz-Manuel. "Who knows how many others lurk in our city? How many more in their mountains? He claimed their population to be more numerous than the desert sands. Could they launch another army at us, even bigger than the last? We would not survive another such onslaught."

Hector frowns. "You don't actually believe we should give in to their demand, do you?"

I shift on my cushion, dreading the general's response.

After an awkward hesitation, he says, "Of course not."

"We should attempt some kind of diplomacy," Eduardo says. "Our greatest weakness has ever been that we know so little about them. And I'm sure our queen could charm them—"

"Their ambassadors were never forthcoming." I jump in, mostly because I'm already sick of being talked over as if I'm not here. "Short of sending a delegation to Invierne, I don't know how we'll find out what we need to know. But they always refused offers of a return delegation from my father."

"It was the same here," Hector says. "King Alejandro offered delegations several times, only to be rebuffed."

I know what my sister, Crown Princess Alodia, would counsel. "We need spies," I say.

General Luz-Manuel shakes his head. "We can't outfit spies over such a long distance. There's nothing left in the coffers.

And we'd have no way of communicating with them. It's too far, even for pigeons."

The helpless expression on everyone's face makes the chamber feel even tighter, even hotter. I wish I'd brought a fan with me.

"We have a more immediate problem," Conde Eduardo says. "Five months after the Battle of Brisadulce, our nation was finally beginning to heal. This is a terrible blow. Several people were killed today in the ensuing chaos."

My heart drops into my stomach. I remember the panic, the crowd, the runaway carriage. I hadn't realized people were dying around me. Maybe that was the Inviernos' plan all along, to frighten us into hurting ourselves.

Conde Eduardo adds, "Some misguided souls may even call for the queen's head."

"Surely not!" Lady Jada protests.

The conde shrugs. "If they believe giving Her Majesty over to Invierne will save their brothers and sons and wives, they will demand it be done. You saw how they nearly stormed the palace this morning."

The same people who cheered me along the parade, who chanted my name and hailed me as a hero. Ximena was right.

Lady Jada turns to me. "Can't you just"—she makes an obscure gesture with one hand—"do something with your Godstone? Defeat them like last time?"

I wilt a little on my cushion. "If only I could, my lady. I had an amulet then, and several old stones from long-dead bearers. Now I've only my own. Father Nicandro and I are working together to figure out how to channel its power." I choose not to mention that, aside from bringing a warm glow to the stone, I've accomplished nothing.

General Luz-Manuel leans forward, eyes gleaming. "I have an idea." He is a consummate politician, and he allows an exactly perfect stretch of silence before adding, "Your Majesty, we must discuss the issue of your regency."

I wipe my suddenly sweating palms on my knees. "I am not the prince's regent," I tell him, pretending to misunderstand. "It is wholly my choice whether or not to hand the throne over to Rosario when he comes of age. The king named me his unequivocal heir and Queen *Regnant*." I'm proud of my steady voice.

"The king was on his deathbed and suffering tremendously, perhaps not in his right mind. You are so young, Your Majesty; not yet come of age yourself. And foreign. Many doubt your worthiness to rule. Add to that today's terrifying incident, and you must consider that *you* need a regent. It would go a long way toward assuring the populace."

I do my best not to gape at him. "I fought for this nation as one born to it!"

He nods solemnly. "What you did was an important part of the whole effort." I curl my hands into fists against the condescension in his voice. "But you have difficult decisions coming up, like raising taxes to support rebuilding efforts. You will find that when people are tightening their belts, your heroics won't matter. They will blame you, Your Majesty, and you alone. They'll demand we hand you over to our enemy."

I knew my Quorum held little respect for me. But I didn't anticipate this. And his words cut hard because he is right. I am a child, and an inexperienced one. Leading a small desert rebellion, defeating Invierne's animagi with my Godstone—these things were impressive, certainly. But they were nothing like ruling.

Lady Jada's gaze shifts between the general and me, her eyes large and eager. She is a keen gossip, and I wonder if Luz-Manuel invited her specifically in the hope that she would spread the idea of my regency. Or the *reason* for my proposed regency—that I can't rule on my own.

Conde Eduardo stares into the distance, rubbing at his close-cropped beard. Finally he says, "There is another way." He leans his elbows onto the table and stares at each Quorum member in turn, settling finally on me. "My dear queen, it is time for you to choose a husband."

Ah, so that's it. The regency discussion was simply meant to introduce marriage as the more palatable alternative. They probably worked it out between themselves ahead of time.

"Oh, yes!" says Jada. "Someone whose counsel is widely respected. Everyone would accept your queenship with a strong prince consort at your side, even given today's events."

Softly Hector says, "The king has only been dead five months."

"The queen is beyond the ceremonial mourning period," Conde Eduardo says with a shrug. He turns to me. "I don't mean to speak ill of the dead, but our nation suffered weak rule under Alejandro and Nicolao. We were coming apart at the seams even before the war. Your Majesty, I beg you to put your people first. Please choose either a regent or a strong husband, and bring the stability we so desperately need."

"You would gain the most political advantage by choosing someone from the northern holdings," the general adds. "The north bore the brunt of the war."

"I'll compile an eligibility list," Lady Jada says. "We can look over it at our next meeting. Lord Liano of Altapalma comes to mind. And of course Conde Tristán of Selvarica, who is a southern lord but should not be discounted. Also . . ."

I can't bear to pay attention as Jada prattles on about every lordling in the entire kingdom. I've known for a while that I would marry for the good of Joya d'Arena. But now, faced with the prospect, I don't want to. I want to love someone again, the way I loved Humberto, or at the very least share a friendship, as Alejandro and I did in the end.

And I want to be queen of this great country not because someone is holding my hand, but because *I* can do it. Me. Elisa.

But I agree to look at Lady Jada's list at our next meeting, because I don't know what else to do or say. If nothing else, it buys me time to consider my options.

Our conversation moves to reconstruction. Whole villages along the desert caravan route still lie in ruins after the enemy's march. The cost to clean and rebuild is becoming enormous. The highway through Puerto Verde is near impassable after several years of unusually bad weather. The tanners' and weavers' guilds are close to rioting over the shortage of hide and wool, now that the seceded country of

Basajuan is no longer forced to trade sheep with the capital.

The nation is in shambles. Though we won the war, our coffers are drained, our army weakened, our people dispirited. Today's birthday parade was supposed to inspire hope, to demonstrate the safe normalcy our lives were returning to.

My ridiculous crown grows unbearable as I ponder the centuries of rulers who came before me and sat in this same room, at this same table. Did any of them inherit a mess this big? Were any of them mere children, like me?

I can't mask my relief when our meeting is over. I rise stiffly and thank everyone for coming; then Hector releases the bolt and opens the door. I bask in the fresher air that hits my face.

Once outside, my ladies press close. I yank off my crown and fling it at Ximena. Mara mops sweat along my hairline with a cloth and fluffs my skirt.

I say, "I need to walk." Mostly, I need to *think*, away from watchful eyes and weighty problems.

They clear a path, and Hector steps up to accompany me.

I shake my head. "I need to go alone."

"I'd rather you didn't."

"I'll just be a few minutes," I assure him. "I'm going to the catacombs to pray. I'll only walk where our own guards patrol. Come looking for me if I'm not back when the monastery bells ring the hour."

He reaches up as if to grasp my arm, but then changes his mind and lowers his hand. "Be wary, my queen."

I smile assurance, and then I'm off, away from the crowd.

The cobblestones beneath my feet are worn smooth, for

Brisadulce was built almost two thousand years ago, after God scooped up our ancestors from the dying world with his righteous right hand and deposited them onto this one.

As I walk, I run a finger along the rough stone wall, taking comfort in its solidness. I imagine the palace and its ancient capital, sprawling across its peninsula of limestone, surrounded by ocean on three sides and desert on one. My new home is such a determined place, unchanging despite being hemmed in by things that pound it with deadly sandstorms and hurricanes for a season each year, and the rest of the time are merely fluid and forceful.

The city's salvation is its underbelly. My old tutor used to tell me that long ago, before people arrived, our great sand desert was an inland sea. Something cataclysmic happened to drive all that water deep underground. Now it rushes out to meet the ocean in the caverns beneath my feet, providing plenty of fresh water for the beautiful oasis that is my capital city.

The catacombs, which were built to take advantage of the natural water-formed caverns, are my favorite place to find solitude.

The guard at the entrance is not surprised to see me. He greets me with a bow and a smile. "Glad to see you back safely, Your Majesty," he says. "I heard what happened."

"Thank you, Martín." But I don't want to talk about that. "How is your wife?"

He is one of the youngest among the Royal Guard, and it's hard to believe that someone barely older than me could be married and expecting a child already. "Approaching her ninth month of pregnancy. And cursing the desert heat every day." He lifts a torch from a wall sconce and hands it over. Martín's grin turns sheepish. "If it's a girl, she wants to name her Elisa."

I nearly drop the torch. "Oh. Well . . . er, I would be honored, of course. Either way, you must promise to introduce the child to me when it comes."

He knocks his chest with the flat of his fist—the gesture of a true oath. "I swear it, Your Majesty."

It's a strange thing to be a queen, to have one's every word given such import. I am a bit discomfited as I hold the torch high and descend the cool, tight stair. My gown drags on the steps behind me, but I don't care. I pray as I go, asking God's blessing for Martín's baby-who-might-be-Elisa, that she grow up to be charming and slender and beautiful.

An orange glow suffuses my path ahead. I duck through a low archway and enter the vast Hall of Skulls.

It's a cathedral of bones. Skulls layer like bricks, reach toward an arched ceiling so high as to be lost in shadow. A row of larger skulls juts out at the wall's midline, their gaping jaws plastered open and inset with glowing votive candles. Curving rib bones frame dark openings at regular intervals along the wall.

I am weary of death. When I close my eyes, I see blood leaching into the sand, flesh melting like wax beneath an anima-gus' fire, gangrenous wounds, lifeless eyes. But these beautiful skulls are free of their rotting flesh, preserved and smiling. I love this reminder that death is an important foundation of my great city, that something of the dead can remain forever.

I pass through the third entrance on the right and enter the tomb of King Alejandro de Vega. His chamber still smells of roses and incense. I sconce my torch in a brass holder and wait as my eyes adjust to the dim light. In the echoing distance, the underground river pounds through the caverns. It's near enough to stir the moist air, and my torch wavers.

Five stone caskets rest on giant pedestals, but the meager torchlight illuminates only the nearest three. One holds the remains of Alejandro's father. The second contains my husband's first wife, who died giving birth to our little prince, Rosario.

In the third is my husband.

A silk banner covers the casket, and I trace its smooth length with my forefinger. Banners cover the other caskets too, but they are tattered with time, or maybe with the moisture that pricks at my nostrils.

"Hello, Alejandro." My whisper echoes around me.

Talking to a dead man is likely foolish. Do those who cross the barrier into the next life see or hear what happens to those stuck in this one? The *Scriptura Sancta* is unclear on the point. But I talk to him anyway, because even foolish comfort is something.

"I watched a man set himself on fire today. I thought of you, the way they burned you." I place my palm against the casket, and for a crazy moment, I imagine Alejandro's heartbeat thrumming beneath the stone. I wrench my hand away.

"The Quorum wants me to remarry, and I think I must do as they ask. *Our* marriage was a jest, I know. Still, we started to become friends in the end. You even said we could have loved each other, given time. Or were those words simply your final kindness to me?"

I came close to death myself today; I embrace it fully, let the truth of it wash over me. The animagus could have turned his fire on me. I would have died young, like most of the bearers before me.

And once the idea has settled into my bones, I'm suddenly eager to say to Alejandro what I never could when he was alive.

"You were a good man but an awful king. Indecisive, frightened, unwise." I swallow hard against the still-unfamiliar sensation of missing him. "Oh, but now I wonder if I judged you too harshly. I must tell you, because I must tell someone, that I am . . . anxious. About being queen. I'm not sure I'm doing a good job of it so far. Ximena tells me I'm the only monarch in history who is also a bearer. But I'm only six . . . seventeen. What if I'm even worse than you were? Maybe—"

The Godstone freezes. I gasp as icy shards shoot through my blood, numbing my fingers and toes. I spin, seeking the source of danger.

Wind whips through the tomb. My torch winks out, leaving me in darkness.

Instinctively, I pray hard and fast, begging God to protect me from whatever lies ahead. The Godstone responds by easing warmth into my abdomen, just enough for my breath to come easier, to let me *think*.

I consider a strategic scream. But screaming would give away my exact location to whatever lies in ambush.

I need a weapon. I search frantically for something, anything. A silk banner flutters in the breeze. I grab the tassels and whisk the banner from its casket. Dust puffs into the air, and my chest lurches with the need to cough. The banner is long, nearly twice my height. Praying warmth into my limbs, I fold it in half, then once more.

I have no idea what to do with it. Venturing from the crypt armed with a silk banner is a ridiculous idea. And during my time in the desert, I learned it is stupid to fight when you can run and hide.

Two of the caskets are empty, awaiting their permanent residents. I have a sudden urge to crawl inside one, cross my arms over my chest, and close my eyes to the world. Instead, I creep behind the nearest and squat down so I can't be seen from the doorway. I only need to be invisible long enough for Hector to come looking for me.

A shape moves in the dark.

My stomach drops into my toes. Someone is here, has been in the crypt the whole time.

I lurch away, but I am too cold, too slow.

Light winks against a steel edge. I raise my banner against the wicked glimmer.

Something rams the silk, slides off, ricochets against my forearm. My skin parts; pain sluices up to my shoulder.

I drop the banner, scurry backward in a crab crawl, but I collide with a pedestal. The blade plunges again.

I scream as it glances off my Godstone, slips into my stomach as if I am made of butter.

The pain is like nothing I've experienced. I know I will burst from it.

Warmth glides across my belly, down my thighs. The blade is ripped from my body, and I crumple to the stone. My cheek splats into a pool of my own blood.

My last thought is of Alejandro, and how surprised he'll be to see me.

4

I awaken as if into a dream—a dream of light and heat and pain.

I should open my eyes, but I can't seem to find them in my head. I ought to cry out, but I'm too distant from my flesh to figure out how. I'm lost in the desert of my own mind, in a wilderness of sand and light.

. . . *dead soon,* I imagine the general's voice saying, distantly, as if from another world. . . . *the priest . . . final sacrament.* He wants me to die. I know it with surety, even from this bright, lost place.

But I refuse.

And later, maybe much later: *Elisa? . . . Hector. . . hand moved!* Rosario's high voice this time—someone who very much wants me to live. I focus hard on his words, cling to them as to a lifeline.

Warmth. Pressure. My hand! Someone squeezes it.

I make my hand my whole world. *Hand hand hand hand.* I push through the sand and light and heat, and with every bit of strength I have in me, I squeeze back.

·❖· ·❖· ·❖·

My next awakening is more real, my perception sharper, my pain so much more exquisite. My eyes are crusted closed, and I give up trying to open them.

My head is heavy and huge, like it has swollen to twice its normal size. The worst pain, though, is in my abdomen, just left of the Godstone.

I remember, and my breath comes in short gasps. The darkness, the gleaming steel edge, the dagger plummeting . . .

No. All this pain means that I am *alive*. I will think about that instead.

Even with my eyes closed, I know I'm in my bed. A cool night breeze caresses my fevered skin, bringing a sweet concoction of freesia and hibiscus. My balcony curtains whisper as they move; my bathing pool gurgles with a fresh infusion of water.

Someone found me, brought me here. Someone saved my life.

I sense movement against my shoulder. My stomach muscles clench involuntarily, which sends a wave of pain all the way to my breastbone. I force myself to relax, to breathe.

Then I turn my head to discover what rests at my shoulder. I get a noseful of soft, freshly washed hair, a blast of warm, sleeping breath.

I'd recognize his scent anywhere. It's Rosario, my little prince. I wonder if he's here by design or if he slipped his nurse again.

It makes my head swim to lift my neck, but I do it anyway,

just enough for my lips to find his forehead. He snuggles closer, which helps me focus. I'm awake a long time. In pain. Glad to be alive.

When I stir again, my eyes open easily. I start to sit up but abandon the effort. Pain aside, my stomach muscles simply do not cooperate. What if the assassin's dagger broke something inside me?

Rosario is gone, but I am surrounded by guards. One stands at the foot of my bed, two at my balcony, two at the entry door, one at the opening to my atrium.

I take a deep breath. "Morning," I say with enormous effort. My voice is that of a stranger, all cracked and dry.

They snap to attention.

One steps forward. My vision wavers with heat and dizziness, but I recognize Lord Hector by the broad set of his shoulders.

He whispers, "Elisa?"

Questions tumble in my mind, competing for attention. Who rescued me? Did they find the assassin? How badly am I hurt? Where are Mara and Ximena? Did I imagine Rosario cuddled beside me in the dead of night?

Bringing all this to my lips is impossible. I open my mouth, but nothing comes out.

"Your Majesty?" he says. "Are you able to tell me how you feel?"

My bedroom is taut with silence as everyone awaits my response. They *need* me to respond. They're afraid I can't.

So I try again. "Sandstorm," I manage.

It's not coming out right. The guards exchange worried glances.

I take an excruciating breath. "Sandstorm," I repeat. "Like I've been lost. And flayed alive."

Lord Hector wilts with relief. "You look it too."

The others gasp at his audacity, but I laugh. It sounds like a wheeze.

Hector turns to one of the guards. "Get word to General Luz-Manuel and Conde Eduardo *at once.* Tell them Her Majesty is awake and of sound mind."

Hearing his name, I'm tickled by a darkly distant memory of the general sitting my deathwatch. Or did I imagine it?

"I'll fetch Ximena and Mara," Hector says. "I forced them to eat and rest."

"Thank you." Already my vision clouds, and I want more than anything to close my eyes. "Wait! How long was I—"

"Three days."

It's like a punch to my already-aching gut. "And the assassin?" Words, at least, are coming more easily.

"Disappeared. We've searched everywhere."

I feared as much. Why else would I require so many sentries? "Was Invierne behind it? Was it related to the animagus' threat?"

"The other Quorum members think so. The people think so. Conde Eduardo posted notices throughout the city advising that no one go anywhere alone. Several districts have requested a stronger guard presence."

My mouth opens to ask if anyone has suggested giving me over to Invierne, but I can't bring myself to do it. Instead, I say, "Did you find me down there? Are you the person who saved my life?"

He freezes, and I wish my vision were clearer, for I would dearly love to read his face.

"I'll send your ladies," he says, and he strides away before I can respond.

I'm drifting in almost-sleep when Nurse Ximena and Lady Mara bustle inside, followed by a lanky man I recognize as the royal physician. Hector does not accompany them.

Ximena showers my face with kisses. "Oh, my sky," she says. "We thought ... we were worried that ... it's good to see you awake."

Mara fluffs my pillows. She doesn't meet my gaze, but I notice a tear in the corner of her eye, which she quickly scrapes away. "You remember Doctor Enzo?" she says.

"Of course. He took wonderful care of the king . . ." I almost say, *as he lay dying.* "After he was injured."

The ladies step aside, and Doctor Enzo leans forward to peer at me. He has a beakish nose and a razor-thin mustache that twitches with excitement as he absorbs information about my look and bearing. "I'm surprised to see you awake so soon. Your vision must be disastrous. Can you see at all?" Doctor Enzo was never one for niceties.

"It seems to be getting better."

"Nauseated?"

"Mostly dizzy. Doctor, please tell me—"

"Right here." He makes a stabbing gesture left of the

Godstone. My stomach clenches painfully in response. "Fortunately, the assassin missed. The knife slid in sideways. Didn't hit the important bits. There's a muscle here"—with his forefinger, he indicates an imaginary line alongside my navel— "that was nearly severed. If you remain very still for a couple of weeks, it may heal properly. As it is, you'll have a tremendous scar. May I document your recovery? It's such a *devastating* and *fascinating* injury."

"He didn't miss," I whisper.

"What was that?"

"The assassin didn't miss. The blade was deflected by my Godstone."

Someone gasps. The guards exchange looks of wonder, and I almost laugh. No sorcery was involved in the Godstone's interference, nothing divine. It was random luck.

"There's a slice across your forearm also," Doctor Enzo continues. "Bled a good bit, but stitched up beautifully. Some of my finest work. In a few years, you'll have only a faint scar."

"Why am I so dizzy?"

"You hit the back of your head. Your skull is intact, but your face swelled magnificently. You may have permanent damage."

I'm as taken aback by his emotionless delivery as the words themselves: *Permanent damage.* My heart squeezes at the thought. I am not beautiful. I am not a devotee of court politics. I'm not particularly queenly in bearing. What I *am* is well-studied and intelligent. My mind is my single advantage, the one thing I've allowed myself to take pride in. Any kind of damage is unacceptable.

"When will I know?" I ask in a shaky voice. "If there is . . . damage?" This conversation may be better had in private, away from the guards. Perhaps it is unwise to offer even the barest hint that the new queen is compromised.

Doctor Enzo pats my shoulder awkwardly. "The fact that you are awake and alert is a good sign."

I am not reassured. But I am too tired to think about it a moment more. Of their own volition, my eyes drift closed.

No. I snap them open. I've been asleep long enough. "Doctor, send someone to fetch my mayordomo." I need his report on the state of things immediately. Conde Eduardo and General Luz-Manuel have no doubt been ruling in my absence, and if they are willing to contest my worthiness in a face-to-face meeting, how much more will they undermine me while I am indisposed?

My mayordomo arrives within minutes. He is a decadent man prone to egregious ruffles and bright colors, but I admire his quiet dignity as my guards search him for weapons. It's probably the first time in his tenure as ranking palace official that he's been treated so abominably.

"Thank you for coming so quickly," I say in a warm voice, hoping to lessen some of the sting.

He has hardly risen from his bow when he blurts, "Your Majesty, the city garrison just put down another riot. They made several arrests."

I start to lurch to a sitting position, but the tearing at my abdomen sends me crashing back against my pillow. *"Another riot?"* I say weakly. "Why?"

"There have been three in protest of the tax increase. All were quickly put down by the garrison, but each riot has been progressively larger. . . ."

My head swims. Riots? Tax increase? How could I forget about a tax increase? Maybe this is what Doctor Enzo meant by "permanent damage."

"Remind me," I say carefully, "about the details of this tax increase."

"The Quorum pushed it through while you were indisposed."

I gape at him. "Can they do that?"

"According to article 67 of the *Concordancia*, when the monarch is physically unable to perform his duties, the longest-sitting member of the Quorum must vote on his behalf."

"So the general had two votes."

"Yes."

I clutch at my sheets until they are balled into my fists, but sharp pain darts up my forearm, so I force myself to unclench. *Maybe I would have voted for a tax increase*, I tell myself. *Maybe it's for the best.* We're desperate to refill the coffers for reconstruction. To rebuild our army before Invierne can mount another attack.

"And how did Hector vote?" I ask in a small voice.

"He abstained."

I sink into my bedcovers with relief, though I'm not sure why it's so important. "Thank you for your report," I tell him.

He turns to go.

"Wait!"

He spins and drops into a courtier's bow. "Your Majesty?"

"That day. When the animagus burned himself. Did you order the palace lockdown?"

"No, Your Majesty."

"Who did?"

"It was General Luz-Manuel."

The soldier told me it was the conde. The conde told me it was the mayordomo. What am I missing?

"Did you speak to the general in person?"

His eyebrows knit together thoughtfully. "I received word through His Grace the conde's emissary, Lord Franco. He is a much trusted adviser. Did I do wrong?"

Franco again. I must meet this person, and soon. "No, you did well. I assume the city has been searched thoroughly?"

"No other Inviernos have been discovered, though I'm sure the mere possibility of another attack contributed to this sudden spate of riots."

My city is splintering apart. I sense it as surely as if I still stood on the palace wall with Hector, watching it happen. "Thank you. You may go."

Doctor Enzo insists I'm in no shape to hold appointments or even make decisions, so the mayordomo clears my schedule. But I hate being useless. I lie awake for hours each day, trying to figure out how to rule effectively from my bed. First I summon Lord Franco, the man who reportedly ordered the palace lockdown, but I'm told that he has left for Conde Eduardo's southern holdings to oversee rebuilding projects.

I demand an accounting from General Luz-Manuel for

the tax increase. He insists that he couldn't wait. His queen was not expected to survive, and can he be blamed for acting quickly when so many of Brisadulce's unemployed citizens are desperate for the construction work the increase would provide?

Though I'm unable to find fault with his arguments, I can't shake the phantom memory of the general looming over my unconscious body, eager for my death. Something else is taking shape beneath his placid surface of diplomatic politeness. I'm sure of it.

Prince Rosario visits often at first, sneaking out of the nursery to be with me while the guards pretend not to notice. But once the boy has assured himself that I'm no longer in danger of dying like his father, his visits grow less frequent. I don't mind. It's hard to have him at my bedside without the freedom to ruffle his hair or play a quick game of cards.

Word has spread like wildfire that I seek a husband—even though I've made no official announcement. Gifts pour in from the nobility—especially potential suitors—and there's a disconcerting intimacy about them. "Sapphire earrings to match the blue of your Godstone," one note reads. "Since you are a scholar of holy scripture, here is a centuries-old copy of the *Belleza Guerra*," says another. So many strangers know so much about me, and they shower me with priceless gifts, just on the chance of catching my attention.

No one is sure what to do with the gifts, so Ximena shoves them into a corner of my atrium for later sorting.

I also get notes that are unnerving. A journeyman tanner

blames me for not having enough hide to practice his craft and calls for my abdication. A young widow with four children begs for a job. An acolyte from the Monastery-at-Puerto Verde sends a withered black rose, saying that the Godstone's blasphemous sorcery blackens my soul and makes a mockery of our most precious sacrament.

Several letters claim that because I allowed the eastern holdings to secede and form their own nation, I should do the same with the southern holdings. One letter boldly declares the south to be an independent nation.

General Luz-Manuel promises that each letter will be investigated for sedition and any true threat to my person will be dealt with. But even his assurances fill me with misgiving.

Every night, I dream of my assassin. In my nightmares, the catacombs are a huge black emptiness. I'm moving forward, arms outstretched against the dark, when I see a wicked glimmer. I have a flash of horrified understanding before the assassin becomes an inferno, and his flaming blade is plunging into my stomach, tearing me in half, and I scream and scream. . . .

Someone is always at my bedside when I wake. My ladies calm me with gentle words and cool, soothing hands, whispering that I'll heal faster if I don't try to leave the bed, that I'm safe now. But I can't return to sleep until Ximena has read to me from the *Scriptura Sancta*, or Mara has plied me with a cup of spiced wine, or Hector has checked the balcony for intruders.

One afternoon I'm startled by a commotion outside. I hear shouting, the ring of steel, tromping boots.

Beside me, Ximena continues to loop and pull with her

embroidery needle, but she meets my gaze with her own puzzled look.

Lord Hector bursts through the door. "Elisa! I need your help."

"What is it?" Fear shoots through me. The last time I saw him so wide-eyed and breathless, the animagi were burning down the city gate.

"It's an execution. I tried to stop it, but General Luz-Manuel—"

"Whose execution?" I demand. "Why?"

"Martín. General Luz-Manuel found him guilty of conspiring with Invierne to assassinate you. He sentenced him to death by beheading." He leans over and places his hands on the foot of my bed. "Elisa, he's one of my own men. I trained him myself. He would never harm you."

I try to rise from the bed. "Martín would never . . . he was going to name his baby—"

Ximena pushes me back down. "You're supposed to rest!"

I struggle against her. "Hector, help me up. Take me out there if you have to carry me yourself." The blood pumping through my veins makes my thoughts spin faster, and I revel in the clarity of it.

I could try to stop the execution with a missive, but there might not be time to authenticate the message. And Martín would forever be known as the man who *may* have allowed an assassin to attack the queen—unless I declare my belief in his innocence before the entire city.

Ximena steps out of the way, her face carved in stone, as

Hector reaches beneath my shoulders and knees and lifts me to his chest as if I am a small child. My boundless nightgown tangles at his knees.

My nightgown! I can't barrel into the courtyard dressed like this.

"Ximena, please bring my robe." I wrap my good arm around Hector's neck. "Hurry!"

He maneuvers me through the door and into the hallway, gesturing with a lift of his chin for the other guards to accompany us. Ximena trails behind, my robe in her hands.

"The assassin was already there when I arrived," I say as we rush through the palace corridors and down a flight of stairs. "I have no idea how long he was lying in wait. Maybe days. He could have sneaked down during anyone's shift."

His brisk pace brings knife pain to my abdomen. "I know," he says. "But the general outranks me, and when I scheduled a Quorum meeting to discuss it, he pushed up the date of the execution without telling—"

"Just get me there quickly."

We reach the entrance to the courtyard. Framed by the archway, a crowd gathers on the green, surrounding a wooden platform. On it, the hooded executioner stands tall and bare chested. Sun glints off the huge ax blade resting at his shoulder. My own crown-seal banner snaps in the wind above him.

"Put me down."

"Can you stand?"

"I must. Ximena, my robe."

Hector sets me down, so gently. My legs barely support my

weight, and I lean into the archway to keep my balance. The newly healed skin on my stitched stomach feels too tight, too thin. Ximena wraps the robe around my shoulders, ties it at my neck. It will have to do.

I whisper, "Catch me if I fall?" And I take a wobbly step into the sunshine.

My breath is ragged, my heart a drum in my head, as I look around for Martín. Surely the prison guards will make an entrance with him soon. But then the executioner raises the ax, and I know that beyond the wall of spectators, Martín must already be in place, his head on the block.

"No!" I shout as loud as I can, and a handful of people turn toward me, but it is not enough.

The executioner's voice booms, "In the name of Her Majesty, Queen Lucero-Elisa de—"

"Stop!" yells Lord Hector. "By order of the queen!"

The executioner's head comes up in surprise, but it is too late to stop the ax's descent. It whistles downward, disappears behind the crowd, and thwacks wetly into the wooden block below.

5

IT takes a moment for the crowd to register what has happened. As one, they turn a stunned gaze on me and my escort.

I am as still and silent as a stone. Ximena hurriedly adjusts my robe to cover more of my nightgown, but all I can think about is how an innocent man is dead in my name, beneath the waving emblem of my reign.

A few collect themselves enough to drop to their knees. The rest of the crowd follows, like an ocean wave, until finally the wooden stage and its broken body are revealed. It has fallen to the side, and the neck is a meaty, bloody stump. I can't see where the head rolled off to. And then I'm woozy with the understanding that I'm looking for the disembodied head of a man I considered a friend.

"Send General Luz-Manuel to my suite immediately," I say, in as cutting a voice as I can muster. I turn, intending to depart in dramatic fashion before everyone notices the tears streaming down my face, but my legs crumble. Ximena and Hector knock heads catching me. They half drag, half support me through the archway and into the shady corridor. Hector abandons all pretense of allowing me to walk and sweeps me up.

"I think I ripped my stitches," I say, as wet warmth blossoms beneath my bandages. I'm glad because it gives me something to think about other than the hole that seems to have opened up in my chest.

"Oh, my sky," Ximena says. "Oh, Elisa."

Doctor Enzo is already in my suite when we return. He glares at me.

Mara gives me an apologetic look. "I fetched him," she says.

After Hector lays me on the bed, he turns away so Enzo can lift my nightgown and examine my bandages. I hiss with pain as he peels them back.

Enzo says, "Surely nothing was so important that you couldn't—"

"I don't want to hear it."

He mumbles insincere apologies while pressing his fingertips against my abdomen. It hurts, but not terribly. "Fascinating. I must know, have you been gravely injured before?"

I once tried to cut the Godstone out of my stomach, but I don't want to talk about that. "I broke a couple of ribs," I say. "Ripped off a fingernail. Had a badly infected cut from the nails of an Invierno. They poison their nails, you know."

He squeezes the skin around the stitches and mops up the resulting ooze with a dry cloth. "How long after you broke your ribs until you could walk easily?"

I have to think about it. Humberto was the one who took care of me. I sigh at the memory of him slipping duerma leaf into my soup so I would be forced to sleep instead of travel. "A day. It hurt, but I could do it."

Enzo lifts his head to meet my gaze dead-on. "And how long until the pain went away?"

"Less than a week."

His nose twitches with excitement. He is like a hunting hound on the scent of his prey.

He stares at my abdomen, and I realize he's not looking at the wound, but at my Godstone. Tentatively, he reaches out with his forefinger, lets it hover above my navel.

"It's all right. You can touch it."

He does, reverently, drawing little circles with his forefinger against the topmost facet.

I sense the pressure of his finger, but the Godstone does not respond, just continues its usual mild pulsing. It's odd to feel someone else touching it. No one does that. Even Ximena and Mara barely brush it when they are dressing me.

"It's like a heartbeat," Enzo breathes in wonder.

Hector continues to face politely away, but he reaches for his sword. He grips the pommel, ready to unsheathe at a moment's need.

I'm growing uncomfortable. "What's this about, Enzo?"

He yanks back his finger as if stung. "Your Majesty, I believe, that is, I think, though I can't be sure, but it seems . . ." He takes a deep breath. "I mean to say that you heal too fast."

I frown. Though I have the benefit of a royal education, I am the least studied in the healing arts. I have to take his word for it. "And it has something to do with the Godstone?"

"I have no other explanation for why you show no sign of infection, how you were able to stand at all after having your abdominal wall severed, or for the fact that, even after your ill-conceived outing, I will only replace two stitches."

I'll have to think about it more later, when the blessed darkness of nighttime feels something like privacy. I grit my teeth against the pain as he stitches me up. Then Ximena ushers him out and pulls the covers up to my shoulders just in time to receive General Luz-Manuel.

"Your Majesty." He bows low but rises before I release him.

I inhale through my nose and tell myself to relax. The general is so slender and stooped, his hair thinning at the top, and once again I marvel that this insubstantial person commands my entire army. "General," I say in a cold voice. "I am displeased at the execution of someone I believed a loyal subject and ally." Displeased is an understatement, but I'm leery of being too forceful until I hear what he has to say.

"Indeed, Your Majesty, this has been unpleasant and disappointing for all of us."

I stare at him. Is he being deliberately obtuse? *Careful, Elisa. He is cleverer than he appears.*

"Forgive me for misspeaking, Lord-General. I did not mean to remark on the general unpleasantness so much as my specific disappointment with *your* decision to execute this man."

His gaze holds such concern. "You've been through so much, Your Majesty. First the animagus, and now this. It must be overwhelming. But I can assure you that the matter was thoroughly looked into."

"Not that thoroughly."

"My queen, we investigated every—"

"You never bothered to get details from the one witness to this crime."

He looks charmingly confused.

"You do realize, don't you, that *I* was present during the assassination attempt?" I snap.

Ximena gives me a warning look. Mocking the general may not be my best strategy, especially in front of the guards, who I am certain are intent on every word in spite of their carefully bland faces.

I force softness into my voice. "I don't mean to be curt, Lord-General, but I'm exhausted and deeply saddened. What's done is done, but do promise me that no one else will be punished in connection with the attempt on my life without my knowledge and consent. I'm sure you understand my wish to be personally involved?"

"Of course, Your Majesty," he says, bowing his head. "Anything to put your mind at rest and aid in your recovery."

I clench my jaw. He won't do as I ask because my input is valuable, or even because I am his queen. He'll only agree to consult me because it will make me *feel better*?

The general turns to go.

"Wait."

He whirls, and it's possible I imagine his flitting look of impatience.

God, what do I say to this man? How can I convey that I am the sovereign and he is not? That even though I come from a foreign land, these are my *people?*

The Godstone leaps in response to my prayer, and an answer floats to me gently on the afternoon breeze.

Sorrow comes easily to my voice when I say, "I lost so many people I loved in the war with Invierne. We all did. But the only reason we survive to mourn is because our army fought bravely and selflessly. And no one fought harder than my own Royal Guard, who held off the invaders at tremendous cost so I could have time to work the Godstone's magic." I hope he hears what I'm not saying: *Yes, General, we won the day because of* me, *remember?* "I'll not see them doubted or disrespected. In fact, I'll defend each one of them with my dying breath if I must, as they defended me. Am I clear?"

He stares at me as if deciding whether to protest further. But I know I've said the right thing because Hector and the guards stand a little straighter, and their eyes glow with pride. I hope they take this back to the barracks, the sure knowledge that their queen would die for them.

Finally the general bows, a little lower this time, and excuses himself.

The moment the door closes behind him, all the fight melts from my body. I cannot fathom why the general would do such a thing. Was he trying to discredit me on purpose? Is this his way of taking power for himself while I am unwell? Was he looking for a scapegoat to assuage the fear of palace residents? Or did he genuinely think Martín deserved to die? A single tear slides from the corner of my left eye. *Oh, Martín, I'm so sorry I couldn't save you.*

I am about to close my eyes and meet oblivion when Hector says, "My queen?"

I force myself to raise my head and meet his eye.

"I would like to inquire about Martín's wife and family. Make sure they are provided for." Emotion tinges his voice, and his face is gaunt with weariness.

Very few members of the Royal Guard are as young as their commander, were selected and trained by him the way Martín was. I've no doubt that Hector grieves deeply for him.

"Thank you. I would take it as a personal favor."

"I'll return as soon as I'm able," he says.

"Take your time. You deserve a respite from being at my side. Oh, speaking of being at my side . . . please tell me, did General Luz-Manuel visit when I was . . . indisposed?"

"Many times. He brought prayer candles and held vigil for hours."

I don't believe for a moment that the general wished for my recovery.

"I never left him alone with you," Hector adds softly, his face unreadable. "Not once."

I'm not sure what to say, so I just nod gratefully.

Tonight my dream changes. This time I carry a torch, and its warmth and light wrap around me. I think that I am *safe*.

The breeze is gentle at first, lifting strands of my hair, bringing a hint of brine. But the wind grows stronger; the gust becomes a gale. The torch dies, plunging me into darkness. The Godstone turns to ice.

I sob from sudden terror, knowing what comes next, waiting for it. The blade glimmers hot and cruel as it strikes. . . .

My own scream wakes me.

"Elisa?"

I grasp blindly for Hector. He clasps my hand in both of his, trying to squeeze the panic from my body by the force of his grip.

Gradually the pounding in my chest softens, my breathing slows. The high slant of sun through my balcony's glass doors indicates that I slept well into the morning.

When I can manage it, I say, "Did you find Martín's family?" I need to talk about something real and solid to shake the dream from my head.

"The Guard took up a collection. I delivered it this evening. In spite of everything, she was . . ." He swallows hard, then says with a touch of wonder, "She was *grateful*."

"I'm sorry I couldn't save him for you."

"Thank you for trying."

He gives my hand one last squeeze before letting it go. I snake it under my blankets, feeling vaguely disappointed. He has been stiff and uneasy with me since my brush with death. Ximena or Mara would have held my hand as long as I needed.

He leans back in his chair and crosses his arms, as if putting a wall between us. "It's very common for soldiers to experience nightmares after combat," he says. "Especially if they were injured."

My chest lurches just to think about it. "Oh?"

"And sometimes it helps to talk about them."

"Do you have nightmares?"

"Yes." His voice is hardly more than a whisper.

"And do you talk about them?"

He turns his head to avoid me. "No."

I study his profile. He usually looks so regal, even with the crisscross of scars on his left cheek. But the light pouring in from my balcony softens his features and makes him seem almost boyish. I say, "But you'd like me to talk about mine."

"Only if you want to."

"We could trade. A nightmare for a nightmare."

His gaze turns inward while he considers. When he finally looks at me, I catch the barest shift of his eyes as he studies every part of my face.

He opens his mouth. Closes it. At last he says, "I think it would be best if you discussed your dreams with Ximena or Mara."

The hurt that wells up my throat is unexpected and inexplicable. "Maybe I will," I whisper. "Thank you for your counsel."

During the next couple of days, I think hard about what Hector said. I try, twice, to talk to Ximena about my dreams. But the words clot in my mouth. It's not fear so much as shame that stills my tongue. I can't bear to be weak and frightened in front of everyone. I am queen now. I should be so much braver, so much stronger.

But then comes the night when the knife is so real, so cold and sharp against my skin for the barest instant before it is an exploding fire in my belly. Then the nightmare flashes to a different place, a different knife, a different terror. I am helpless, my limbs leaden, as the dagger pricks at Humberto's precious throat. "You could have stopped this, Elisa," he tells me, just before the blade whisks across his neck and Humberto's hot blood spurts all over my crown, which is suddenly in my hands.

This time, my waking screams are cut off by vomit spewing from my mouth.

Mara and Ximena rush to help me clean up. I try to rise, and they hold me down, insisting they will have me set to rights in no time. But I thrust them back with more strength than I ought to have. Clutching the bedpost, I drag myself over the side and gain my feet.

My legs quiver with disuse, but they do not betray me. "Find Hector," I order to no one in particular. The vomit is already a cold plaster gluing my nightgown to my skin, and my nose stings from the rotten-spice scent. "I'm going to wash," I tell them. "And then . . . and then . . ." I have no choice. I have to face this black monster of terror before it eats me from the inside out. "And then, I must return to the catacombs. Tonight."

I bathe quickly, with Mara's help. Ximena plies me with a gown, but I refuse. "Pants," I say. "And my linen blouse." I'll not be hampered by a skirt—it's all I can do to remain steady as it is—and I know I'll feel more comfortable, more capable, in my desert garb.

Hector arrives as Ximena finishes lacing my camel-hair boots, and I rise to greet him. "Sorry to rouse you," I say. I feel guilty that I've decided on an excursion during the one night he allows himself to rest.

"A queen needn't ever apologize to her guard. Where are we going?"

"The catacombs. I need to . . . to see the place again."

"We scoured it a dozen times. We found nothing."

Ximena weaves my hair into one long braid down my back. I have so much hair that she usually weaves two, one atop the other, but she senses my urgency. "*We* found nothing? Or the general?" I ask. "Forgive me if I don't trust him to be thorough."

Hector opens his mouth as if to say something, but changes his mind.

I wave off the question. "Also . . . there's something else. Like a memory that's almost there but not."

My nurse ties the end of my braid and gives my back a gentle pat. Hector says, "Then we go. But do let me carry you if you tire."

"Of course. Thank you." I turn away to hide my flushing face, remembering how he carried me in our failed rush to save Martín. It would be easy to let him do it again. For a moment, I consider pretending to be weaker than I am.

But I shake it off. I'm already in danger of being thought a feeble queen, and I will not pretend weakness. Not ever, not for anyone.

I hold my head high as my entourage—Hector, Ximena, Mara, and a handful of guards—array themselves in a protective circle around me. In careful formation, we exit the suite and hurry to the ground floor.

A sentry I've never met before stands in Martín's place. Anger at him boils up inside me, but I recognize the feeling as unfair and manage a nod as he bows low. Hector insists on leading us into the stairwell, and I let him. The steps are tricky, and my legs feel like date jelly, but I put a hand on Hector's shoulder and use him as a crutch as I descend.

The yawning jaws of the Hall of Skulls seem to pulse in the flickering candle flames. Mara is rigid beside me, and I find strange comfort in the fact that someone is as frightened as I am.

But the fear dissipates as we enter Alejandro's tomb. It's so different than in my nightmares, crowded with my companions this time, several bearing torches. It's bright and warm, the air still. I feel everyone's eyes on me as I wander through the caskets, my fingers brushing the silk banners. I'm not sure what I'm hoping to find, how this excursion will help. When the toes of my boots encounter a large dark stain on the stone floor, I freeze.

My blood.

My fingertips find the wound at my side, then the bump on my skull. I fell and hit my head, Doctor Enzo told me. But that's not right. I fell onto my side. Now that I'm staring at the exact spot, I remember my cheek splatting in my own blood. How, then, did I get such a terrible knot on the back of my head? What really happened here?

I mutter, "Something isn't . . . I don't remember . . ." I'm not sure what I'm trying to say. That I didn't hit my head? I obviously did. Maybe I tried to get up and then fell a second time. I lost so much blood, it's a wonder I remember as much as I do.

"Elisa?" Hector says.

I look up, startled by his voice. The torchlight makes

hollows of his cheeks. "I'm not sure. I . . ." Something about the light. The way it's moving. So different from my dream. My gaze moves to the torch he carries. "Your torch."

He waits for me to puzzle it out, familiar by now with the way my mind works.

Think, Elisa! And then I have it. "Your torch flame isn't moving."

"No," he agrees. "It's very still."

Everyone is watching us, watching me. Perhaps they're worried that my injuries have addled my mind, that, as Doctor Enzo suggested, there is permanent damage. But my thoughts are clearer than ever.

"In my dream—no, in my *memory*—there was a breeze." I close my eyes, listen to the underground river wash through the caverns. I remember the brush of air against my face before the torch winked out. "It was more than a breeze. It *gusted.* My torch was sconced in the wall. And when the wind blew, it died." I open my eyes.

It's such a small thing, the slightest sliver of strangeness, but I am queen and they must take me seriously.

"Maybe someone opened the entrance upstairs," Ximena suggests.

"Or what if someone walked by?" says one of the guards. "In a hurry."

"Her Majesty said it *gusted,*" Mara says. "Walking by would not cause a torch to go out."

"Maybe he had bad gas," says another. "Have you seen what they feed us in the barracks?"

"Fernando!" Hector snaps, but I chuckle. It's not particularly funny, but everyone joins me, and I allow myself to keep at it because in spite of the pain, it also feels really nice.

Finally I catch my breath and say what everyone is surely thinking: "I suppose we ought to consider that there is a hidden entrance to this chamber."

6

THINKING of the escape tunnel Hector and I used to reenter the palace, I realize that of course my new home would have other secrets, many of them forgotten, perhaps lost to centuries of restorations and additions.

Ximena brushes past me and begins searching the stone wall with her fingertips. "If there is another way in, we *must* find it," she mutters. She's right; we dare not leave any entrance to the palace unguarded.

Everyone jumps to help in the search, and my nurse directs them with strategic efficiency. Within moments, each section of wall and floor suffers the scrutiny of prying fingers. I itch to join them, but it's all I can do to prop myself upright against an empty casket.

"Search quietly," Ximena says. "Tell me if you hear something or feel air movement." It comes as no surprise that my guardian knows something of secret passageways. She probably knows as many ways to exit a fortress as she does to kill a man.

Mara is crawling on the floor when she says, "I feel something. A breeze maybe."

I start forward too quickly, and pain shoots down my side. Hector is at my elbow instantly. I lean into him.

"Which direction?" Ximena asks.

"Not sure." Mara looks up. "I felt it against my left cheek."

One of the guards crouches beside her with a torch.

"Watch the banner," Ximena says as the flame comes dangerously close to the casket's silk covering.

Mara and the guard run their fingers along the cobblestones, searching for cracks.

"Try pressing on them?" the guard suggests. "In my father's library, one of the hearthstones triggers a door."

So they press on all the nearest stones, from every different angle. Still nothing.

I say, "Try the pedestal." The casket resting upon it is empty, patiently awaiting a permanent resident, maybe me.

Everyone crowds around, torches held high, blocking my view. I loose an exasperated breath.

Hector whispers into my ear, "Everything all right?"

"Just frustrated. I hate being weak. And I may have dragged everyone down here in the middle of the night for noth—"

"A latch!" Ximena says. "Tucked under the base. Let me see if I can . . ."

The casket rises a finger's breadth. Several guards jump out of the way as the pedestal and its coffin pivot soundlessly to the side. Fresh air blasts the room, and a torch winks out. The others waver but hold.

Holding Hector's arm to steady myself, I peer over Mara's shoulder and almost sneeze from the cool, briny air pricking my nostrils. Where the pedestal stood is a gaping hole. Stone steps, edged with green moss, spiral into darkness. The guard shifts his torch, the light glints off the green stuff, and I see that it's actually a viscous mold.

"Ugh," says Mara.

"Ugh," Ximena agrees.

Hector says, "You were right, Majesty," and I get the feeling he's speaking for everyone else's benefit. "You were right to trust your instincts, and you were right to trust Martín."

His words warm me. Hector has always been my greatest ally. I catch his eye and nod slightly, hoping he understands how grateful I am to him right now.

"Well," I say. "Let's exonerate him by finding out where this leads."

The guards press toward the secret stairway, eager to step into the dangerous unknown.

"Wait a moment," I say. "Mara, return to my suite. Make excuses to any visitors. On your way, tell the sentry that I wish to be undisturbed as I pray."

She nods with obvious relief, and Hector gestures for two guards to accompany her.

As they depart, he turns to me. "Are you sure you're ready for this?"

"Doing something active is the best thing for my recovery."

"I knew you'd say that." The slightest smile curves his lips. "A walk in the monastery garden is something active. This is—"

"This is what I'm going to do."

He sighs, resigned. "Times like this, I miss Alejandro. He was malleable."

I choke back a startled laugh.

"Hold on to my shoulder. And if you change your mind—"

"Yes, let's *go.*"

I glance over at Ximena, expecting her to protest, but she just stares at Hector, her face unreadable.

Fernando steps into the hole first, holding the torch aloft, and Hector follows. When my turn comes, I'm careful to land squarely on the balls of my feet to avoid slipping on the green slime. Moist air tickles my face, lifting strands of hair from my temples. We are sure to encounter water on this expedition, for the underground river is nearby, its rushing steady and monstrous, so ever-present that it is almost like silence.

The stair spirals—tight and steep. The close-in walls are covered with the slime, and I'm reluctant to touch them, even for balance. I find it's easier to leave my hand at the crook of Hector's shoulder and trust him to keep us both upright.

"There are scuffs in the slime," Fernando says, and his voice echoes around us. "Someone passed this way."

"There were no footprints in the tomb," Hector asks.

"Did the floor look *too* clean, by chance?" I ask. "Who was first to investigate?"

Hector pauses on the step, and my knees bump the backs of his thighs. But he continues without answering. Maybe he doesn't want to name the general within hearing of his men.

My wounded abdomen throbs with strain by the time the

stair ends at a low tunnel. The sand floor is smoothly rippled, like a beach after the waves have retreated.

"It's flooded at high tide," Hector says as I'm drawing the same conclusion. "There's the water line." He points to the wall, where a wainscoting of barnacles reaches knee-high.

I swallow against disappointment. All trace of those who passed before will have washed away, and we are unlikely to find a clue here about my would-be assassin.

Fernando squeals, and we all jump. "Sorry," he says, breathless. "Crab." I'm suddenly very glad for my desert boots, which are impervious to slime and sand and scuttling creatures.

Something on the wall catches my eye—a carved rivulet in the stone. "What's that?" I point.

Fernando lifts his torch to reveal a line of script, each letter the height of my pinky finger. My Godstone warms with recognition.

"It's in the Lengua Classica," Ximena says, her voice breathy with wonder. "From the *Scriptura Sancta.*"

I translate. "The gate that leads to life is narrow and small so that few find it."

Ximena reaches out to trace the letters with her fingers. She was a scribe at the Monastery-at-Amalur before she became my nurse, and like me, she has a reverent interest in ancient texts and holy writings.

"Look at this loop here," she says. "And the flip at the end of the accent mark. This style of script hasn't been used for centuries."

"But is it meant for those coming or going?" I muse. "Which direction 'leads to life'?"

"Only one way to find out," Hector says, and it warms me to hear the anticipation in his voice.

The limestone squeezes tighter until the corridor is barely wide enough for the guards' armored shoulders. Though it's cool and breezy, I'm too aware of the weight of rock above. So huge, so heavy. A whole city goes about its business up there. I'm becoming very nervous when Fernando announces, "Another stair."

This one leads upward, straight instead of spiraled, and rough-hewn as if carved by a giant clumsy ax. I'm glad to note dry, mold-free steps.

"Fernando," says Hector. "Aim your torch away."

The guard puts the torch behind his back. Ximena does the same with hers, and it becomes apparent that a separate glow, faint but true, illuminates the stairway.

"Do you think it leads outside?" I ask.

"We've descended too far," Hector says. "Unless I've gotten turned around, I think we're beneath the Wallows."

The Wallows. The most dangerous quarter of my city, where I'm not to travel even with an armed escort. The place each monarch before me has vowed to improve, with mixed—mostly poor—results. Where prostitutes and beggars and black-market merchants band together to form a society within a society, outside of my rule.

Hector turns to me, his gaze fierce. "Majesty, if I sense danger, I'll hustle you away, against your will if necessary."

"And if that happens, I promise to be only temporarily enraged." It comes out more sharply than I intend, mostly out of pique that he has reverted to calling me Majesty even among friends. "Let's go."

Climbing yanks at my sore stomach, and I slow everyone down. The passage is so tight and steep that hanging on to Hector is more trouble than it's worth. The sound of rushing water gets louder, and the glow brightens. Soon we don't need the torches at all. I can't imagine what would cause such light so deep underground.

The stairway levels off. Fernando gasps, and I'm about to ask him what he sees, but speech leaves me when I step into brightness.

The stair has ended at a high ledge overlooking the most enormous cavern I've ever seen. The river curves against the sheer wall opposite our ledge. The water is as smooth and clear as glass, though a constant sound like rushing wind attests to rapids nearby. To our left, the wall is riddled with smaller caves, all connected to one another by swinging ladders and scalloping rope bridges. On the floor of the cavern are several large huts, cobbled together from driftwood and shipwreck scavenge.

People are everywhere, going about their lives as if this were any ordinary place. A woman sits framed in the entrance to one of the small caves, stirring something over a cook fire. Outside the largest hut, two bearded, wind-chapped men work together repairing a fishing net. Near the river, a group of barefoot children plays a game with sticks and a leather ball.

Light streams through cracks in the ceiling. These sunlit crevices are lush with plants: broad-leafed creepers, a few ferns, and hundreds of hanging vines that don't quite brush the tops of the huts.

"It's a whole village," I whisper, "right beneath our feet all this time."

"I've not even heard of this place," Hector whispers back.

But the peculiar nature of the cavern amplifies our voices, carries them to the huts below. Everyone freezes and looks up. I see my own shock mirrored in their faces.

Hector's hand flies to his scabbard. He and Fernando step up to shield me from view. But it is too late, for someone bellows, "It's the queen!"

I hear gasps of surprise, utensils clattering, running footsteps.

Hector whirls on me. "We need to get you out of here."

"Not yet! They're more afraid of us than we are of them, see?"

Fernando swings his bow over his shoulder and fits an arrow. He and Hector exchange a look, and Hector nods. The guard steps forward, draws the bow, aims toward the milieu below.

"Halt!" Hector booms. "In the name of the queen."

The sounds of humanity fade, leaving only the wind whistling above and the water rushing below. Now that everyone has stilled, I note bandages, a sling, a splinted leg, a head wrap stained brownish red.

"We have their attention, Your Majesty," Hector says. "Would you like to address them? Or do you wish to retreat? I recommend ret—"

"Hector, these people are wounded," I whisper.

"They were most likely involved in the riots," he says matter-of-factly.

They all stare up at me, half in terror, half in hope, and the sight is so familiar that my heart aches. Who would hurt these people? "They look like they've been to war."

"Riots *are* war."

Oh. My stomach thuds with the understanding that they were probably injured in my name. I am at war again. A nebulous, aimless kind, but a war nevertheless. These are my people. But maybe they're my enemy too.

"Do they have weapons?" I ask. "Can they reach us from down there?"

"I see none. We have the high ground and the advantage for now."

Maybe I should burn the place to the ground, force everyone to the surface. But the *Belleza Guerra* rings in my head. *Always cultivate allies. When that fails, cultivate fear in your enemies.*

I step forward. Hector moves aside to let me pass, but I know from the whisper of steel on steel that he has drawn his sword. Fernando's eyes roam the crowd, ready to shift his sights in the space of an instant.

My confidence grows, which seems strange until I realize that this secret cavern reminds me of the hidden desert camp where I spent months plotting our war against Invierne. Like my desert rebels, these people are ragged but clean, wounded but proud. I probably should not allow myself this feeling of kinship.

"This is a surprise," I say, and my voice echoes around me. I smile, hoping to put them at ease, but I see only fear reflected back. One woman reaches down and hooks a young boy with her arm, pulling him against her.

I decide honesty is the best approach. "I could send a company of soldiers to empty this place." Eyes widen, feet shift. "It's clear you've already caused some trouble, but I might be convinced to overlook that. If you're hiding here just to avoid the tax increase or to do some honest commerce away from the guilds' prying eyes, then I'm sure we can come to an arrangement."

Their collective wariness does not ebb in the slightest.

I try a different tack. "Do you have a leader I can speak with? If not, you must appoint a representative right away." I step back from the edge.

Ximena gives me a quick nod of approval, even as she bends over to pull a dagger from the inside of her boot. I watched her kill a man with a long hairpin once, in my defense. She slipped it under his jaw and into his brain with the ease of long practice and training.

A voice rings from below. "Your Majesty!"

Fernando trains his bow on an old man who has limped forward. He is weathered by wind chap, his hair thin and gray. A long piece of driftwood serves as his cane; it's polished smooth by waves but as gnarled as the hand clutching it.

"You lead these people?" I ask.

"No, Your Majesty. Lo Chato leads us, but he is not here. I expect him to return this evening."

The ground beneath me sways, and I grasp for Hector's arm to steady myself.

I've heard the name once before. Lo Chato was the animagus who interrogated me when I was a prisoner in the enemy's camp. Even months later I can imagine him with perfect clarity—his baby-smooth skin, Godstone-blue eyes, flowing white hair. I shudder to think of the preternatural grace of his movement, the way his sibilant voice managed to bury itself inside me. I thought I had killed him.

What are the chances of encountering the name of an old enemy only weeks after one of his brethren martyred himself in my city?

I ask the old man, "How long has this village been here?"

"Almost as long as Brisadulce itself. But we live and do business above ground too, in the Wallows. We are Your Majesty's loyal subjects."

"I'm glad to know it." I have so many questions. But my legs begin to tremble, and my breath comes too hard. I need to make an exit before my weakened state is too apparent. "When Lo Chato returns, tell him I require his presence in the palace. He will not be harmed. I wish only to speak with him. I'll leave word with my mayordomo that he is to be received at once."

The old man inclines his head in what I presume is the only kind of bow his body will manage. "You should know that he is a private, reclusive person. He will be wary of your summons."

"Then you must convince him. I would be *very* disappointed if he did not come." I pause long enough to see understanding in the faces below. Then I bid them good day and gesture for my entourage to retreat.

"Tyrant!" someone yells at my back, and I whirl.

The people shift uncomfortably, avoiding my gaze, and I can't tell who the heckler is. "Fernando," I say, clenching my fists. "Fire a warning shot."

He looses the arrow at once. It thuds into the ground at the old man's feet. Its fletched tail vibrates with impact, as the crowd recoils.

"Do *not*," I say, "add sedition to your transgressions."

I turn away and head into the tunnel, Hector and Ximena at my back. During our return journey, I nearly trip over myself more than once, so lost am I in thought. It was a small group—maybe sixty people. Why so few? Is the secret of the village so well guarded? Have they climbed the ledge and traveled this path to reach the catacombs? Was the heckler expressing the feelings of the whole group? Maybe the whole city?

Most disturbing of all is the mysterious man called Lo Chato. He could be my assassin. And I have invited him to my threshold. But the *Belleza Guerra* devotes a whole chapter to the art of keeping one's enemies close, and so long as I am cautious, I know I am doing the right thing.

By the time we reach Alejandro's tomb, my breath comes in gasps and pain shoots through my side. I want nothing more than a mug of spiced wine and a day of sleep.

Fernando asks permission to stay behind. "I'd like to experiment with this opening a bit," he says, gesturing toward the gaping hole we just climbed out of. "I want to see how it opens from beneath, determine how often it is used."

"Please do. We must keep it guarded from now on."

"I'll take care of it."

"I'll have breakfast sent to you. *Not* from the barracks."

He bows formally, but his lips twitch.

When we reach my suite, I don't bother changing into my nightgown. Ximena helps me shuck my boots, then I loosen the ties of my pants and collapse into bed, which is made up with freshly laundered sheets, thanks to Mara. They're still warm, and I burrow into my pillows, catching the faint scent of rosewater. Truly, my bed is the greatest place in the world.

I am drifting away when an idea startles me awake. "Hector?" I blink to fight off sleep.

"Here," he says from the foot of my bed.

"Do we have contacts in the Wallows? I'd like to pinpoint the cave's location from the surface, find out all we can about it."

"I'll look into it, Majesty."

"And please stop calling me Majesty in private. It makes me grit my teeth."

He nods with exaggerated solemnity. "I'd hate for you to ruin your teeth on my behalf."

"If that happened, I'd have no choice but to follow the general's lead and order your execution." I make a vague gesture and say, "Off with his head!" And then my face burns with my own crass inappropriateness.

But Hector chuckles deep in his throat, and I feel it all the way down to my toes. Softly he says, "My life has ever been yours, Elisa."

My limbs tingle and heat fills my cheeks as we stare at each other.

I snap back to myself. He's talking about his *duty*. Of course his life is mine. He is Queen's Guard, after all, sworn to jump in front of a crossbow bolt if that's what it takes to save me.

Carefully I say, "You're a good friend, Hector. And I'm grateful to have you at my side."

His gaze drops to the ground, and his chest rises and falls with a breath. "Always."

7

IT'S late evening, and sunset glows warmly through my balcony windows. Ximena and I sit cross-legged on my bed, surrounded by faded parchment and musty scrolls—old palace architectural plans, retrieved from the monastery archive by my request. We've been studying them for hours.

One shows the restoration of the throne room, another the monastery addition, but none give clues about secret tunnels or underground villages. I push them away with frustration.

Something slips from one of the scrolls—a tighter coil of vellum, blackening along its tips. Curious, I break the wax seal with my thumbnail, and my fingers smear with something dark—rot or mold?—as I unroll it onto my thigh.

It's a map of Joya d'Arena. My native county of Orovalle is unmarked—the beautiful valley that lies north of the Hinders was undiscovered when this map was drawn. Which means it is probably five hundred years old, a priceless treasure that I have now exposed to light and air. I should send it back to the archive immediately for treatment and safekeeping. But I can't make myself look away.

The eastern holdings beyond the desert—now the country of Basajuan, ruled by my friend Cosmé—are referred to as "territories." Only the northern and southern holdings are clearly defined. Much like my country appears now, I realize with a start. The arable land of Joya d'Arena is once again a crooked sort of hourglass—fat on the top and bottom, thin and fragile in the center where the desert and ocean push together right here at my capital.

But Joya d'Arena is not alone anymore. I have allies now, protecting my borders on two sides—my father and sister to the north, Cosmé to the east. It makes me feel a little safer.

"My sky, there's something I must tell you," Ximena says.

I look up at my nurse. Dust smudges her right cheek, and wisps of gray hair dangle from her usually neat bun.

She takes a deep breath, as if steeling herself. "I've been doing some research on the Godstone. Since you fell into a coma."

I straighten too fast, and several scrolls topple off my bed. "Oh?"

She runs a reverent forefinger across the parchment in her lap. "You know the prophecy in Homer's Afflatus, the one that says, 'He could not know what awaited at the gate of the enemy, and he was led, like a pig to the slaughter, into the realm of sorcery'?"

"Father Alentín thinks I fulfilled that prophecy when I was captured by Inviernos." I keep my tone and expression bland, afraid she'll change her mind about talking to me. Ximena spent years cultivating my ignorance on matters pertaining to the stone I bear. She believed it was the will of God. I know how much it costs her to turn her back on this tenet of a deeply personal faith.

"I'm not so sure you did."

I swallow hard. "Oh." I've been clinging to the hope that I am done with 'the realm of sorcery,' that being queen will be my great service to God.

She dumps the parchment off her lap and stands. "It's the word 'gate' that gave me pause," she says as she begins pacing at the foot of my bed. "In the Lengua Classica, it's an archaic usage that also sometimes translates to 'path.' As in, 'narrow is the path that restores the soul,' from the *Scriptura Sancta*."

"Go on."

"It's the same word we just found etched into the tunnel below the catacombs."

I whisper, "'The gate that leads to life is narrow and small so that few find it.'" I wrap my arms around myself. "I'm not sure what you're getting at," I say, but my heart patters and my limbs tingle. There is something to what she's saying. Something important.

"I made a study of that word when I was a scribe. I went through all four of the holy scriptures looking for usages. It occurs exactly ten times. Five times, it refers to the gate—or path—of the enemy. But the other five times, it refers to something positive. Like life, or restoration, or healing." Ximena pauses and grabs one of my bedposts. We lock gazes, and she says, "What are the chances of each reference occurring exactly five times?"

I shrug. "It's the holy number of perfection. Something will occur exactly five times if God wills it."

"Exactly. He must will it so. Such things do not happen by chance." She resumes pacing, and her face grows distant. "I always thought those verses were metaphorical. I thought the path that restores the soul was a way to live one's life. The way of faith, maybe. But what if . . ." She takes a deep breath. "What if it's a real place? What if they are both *real places*?"

The Godstone buzzes with affirmation, sending prickles up my spine. "Both of them, real places," I murmur. "The gate of the enemy, and the gate that leads to life."

"I don't know, my sky. But I'm looking into it."

"Father Nicandro might be able to help. He has provided quiet aid to me in the past. Also, he is fluent in the Lengua Classica, and I trust him with my life."

She nods. "I'll discuss it with him. I'm at the point where I need access to the restricted areas of the monastery archive anyway."

"Ximena," I whisper. "What if it *is* a real place? What if I still have to go there?"

A year ago, she would have offered meaningless platitudes—or maybe a pastry—in an attempt to brush away my fears. But now she just gazes at me, her small black eyes full of determination, maybe even excitement. I shiver.

Glass shatters. Something thumps to the ground.

Ximena rushes into the atrium. I follow as quickly as I can.

Mara is doubled over beside the bathing pool, hands clutching her stomach. Several items from the vanity lie strewn about the floor. The moist air is too thick and sweet with my freesia perfume.

"What's wrong?" I demand. "What happened?"

"I . . . shaking out your gown . . . my . . ."

"Her scar," Ximena says. "It split open again."

Her scar. From when the animagi burned her. Mara threw herself into the path of Invierne's sorcerers to allow me time to work the magic of my Godstone. She barely survived. I have hardly given a thought to her injuries since that day.

I yell for one of the guards to fetch Doctor Enzo.

Mara slips to the ground, legs stretched out. Ximena unlaces her bodice to reveal a white chemise dotted with bright blood. Then she gingerly peels the chemise from Mara's midriff.

I can't control the gasp that escapes me. A ropy scar, about four fingers wide, stretches across her stomach, ridged with peaks and valleys of skin where her navel ought to be. Blood wells along a line of split skin.

"It's deep this time," Ximena says, blotting gently with the edge of Mara's ruined chemise. "But it's clean and straight. Easily stitched."

"This time?" I ask. "It happens often?"

"I've been forgetting," Mara says between breaths, "to put salve on it."

"What salve? Where?" I demand.

"Small pot on the shelf by her bed," says Ximena, continuing to blot.

"I'll be right back." I hurry through the atrium to the maids' room.

It's much smaller than my own chamber, with one high window, four bunked beds, and a shelf next to each bed for personal items. A few simple gowns hang from pegs on the wall below the window, and beside them is a writing desk with several half-melted candles. Such a tiny place to live. I can't imagine how crowded it will feel when I finally acquiesce to my mayordomo's request to take on more attendants.

I spot the round clay pot on the shelf beside Mara's bed and grab it. Even without lifting the lid, I catch the strong scent of eucalyptus.

I'm hurrying back through the atrium when I step on something sharp. I nearly drop the pot as I lurch sideways to shift the weight from my foot. The effort tears at my abdomen, but I keep my balance. I peer down at the floor to see what nearly tripped me.

It's one of my ancient Godstones, detached from its long-dead bearer. After using it to magnify the power of my own living Godstone and defeating the animagi, I tossed it along with its used-up brothers into a jewelry box on my dressing table. Mara must have knocked it over.

I lift it up between thumb and forefinger. It's as blue-black as a bruise and jagged from its final devastating act. But in the wash of atrium light, I catch the hint of a spark, a tiny mote of untouched perfection deep inside the shattered jewel.

I hand the pot to Ximena, set the cracked Godstone on the vanity table, and crouch to face my lady-in-waiting.

"It's doesn't hurt that badly," Mara assures me. "It just caught me by surprise."

"She's being brave," Ximena says. "The rip is deep, and she shouldn't be moved until Doctor Enzo gets here. The salve will help keep the skin moist."

Someone pounds at my door, and with an apologetic shrug to Ximena and Mara, I hurry back to the bedchamber. A guard is peering through the peephole. "It's the mayordomo, on some urgency," he says.

His timing could not be worse. "Show him in." I smooth my rumpled pants, wishing I'd taken the time to bathe and change today.

The mayordomo has made a gallant attempt at elegance, with a velvet vest over a blouse with flared lace cuffs. But as always, his clothes are a size too small, and his belly strains the buttons near to popping. He dips into a courtier's bow.

"Rise."

"Forgive the intrusion, Your Majesty." He eyes the manuscripts strewn across my unmade bed. "I know you said to clear your schedule, but a delegation from Queen Cosmé of Basajuan has just arrived. I've assigned them to the dignitaries' suite. They expressed a strong desire to see you as soon as possible."

A delegation from Cosmé! I hope she sent friends, dear people I have not seen since my time in the desert. "You were right to inform me. See if they require food and drink. I'll be there as soon as I can."

Ximena appears in the doorway to the atrium, Mara's pot still clutched in her hand.

The mayordomo bows again. "Yes, Your Majesty. If you're ready to receive guests, does that mean we may discuss your

schedule? Several noblewomen have applied for the open attendant positions—a queen needs more than two ladies! And
I'm afraid you've acquired a long list of suitors; His Grace the
conde Tristán of Selvarica has been relentless in trying to
schedule an audience with you. There was a riot in the merchants' alley yesterday over the wheat shortage, so the mayor
would like to discuss increasing the guard presence there and
in the Wallows—"

I wave him silent. "Later. See to our guests."

He flees without another word. I frown at his back, unease
curling in my stomach. *Another riot.* I resolve to call him back
the moment I'm finished with the delegation.

"You'll need a quick bath and a change of clothes," Ximena
says.

"No time for a bath," I say, heading toward her.

"You can't dress yourself with that injury!"

I grab the pot from her hands. "I'll apply the salve while
you shake out my dress and undo the bodice." The stuff inside
is thick and brown, with the consistency of something between
wax and date jelly.

Ximena squeezes my shoulder and grabs my gown from the
floor where Mara dropped it.

I crouch beside Mara and dip two fingers in the pot.

"It's not right, Elisa," Mara protests. "You're my queen. You
shouldn't—"

"Oh, shut up. Should I avoid the tear itself?"

"No. It's also a disinfectant. It will sting, but . . . I'll be fine
if you want to wait—"

I hush her by touching a blob of the stuff directly to the tear. She hisses.

Her skin feels strange beneath my fingertips, so lumpy and stiff, hardly like skin at all. But it's as warm as normal flesh and bleeds just as easily. Gently I massage the salve along the edges of the wound, pretending not to notice when it mixes with seeping blood. I refuse to let myself feel revulsion, all the while thinking, *Mara is this way because of me. She did it for me.*

Mara makes no sound, but her head falls back against the wall as she squeezes her eyes closed.

"Your gown is ready," Ximena says.

I give Mara's arm a squeeze, then rinse my hands. Ximena dresses me with quick efficiency and then directs me to the edge of my bed. I'm not quite healed enough to bend over and reach my feet, so Ximena slides my stockings on. While she works, I pull out the pin holding up my braids and unravel my hair.

Thinking of Mara sitting alone on the floor of the atrium, I say, "The mayordomo is right, isn't he? I need more than two attendants."

"Serving you is an easy privilege, my sky. But once in a while, when we must hurry or when something goes a little wrong, like today, then yes, it would be nice to have one more person. Maybe two." She slips on a pair of soft leather slippers.

My world is already so crowded with guards and constant visitors. It's been nice to have a smidge of privacy in the atrium with only my two ladies, who are dear friends besides. I cannot imagine adding a stranger to the mix. But as Ximena sweeps up a layer of my hair and pins it with a mother-of-pearl comb, I say, "I'll speak to the mayordomo about it soon."

She plants a kiss on my cheek. "You'll do what is best." She helps me to my feet.

"Will you stay here with Mara?"

"I'm sure she'll be fine without me."

I open my mouth to snap that it's a command, not a question. But at the last moment, I decide on a softer tack. "It will bring me comfort to know you are with her." And I turn away, signaling the guards to accompany me.

We step into the corridor, and they center me in a tight formation of creaking leather and swinging swords.

Lord Hector hurries up as we round the first corner. The guards shift formation so he can walk beside me. "I just heard about the delegation," he says. "How are you feeling?"

"Healthy and hearty and eager to see old friends." We descend a wide stairway, and I gladly take his offered arm.

"It's strange to think of Cosmé as queen," he says. "I still picture her in her maid's cap."

Thinking of my friend brings an easy smile. "And I still see her in leather boots and a desert cloak, tending to the wounded and teaching the little ones to use their slings."

"She has always been exceedingly capable," he says.

"Indeed." Many times I have wished I were half so capable as Cosmé.

When we reach the dignitaries' suite, my guards clear a path so I can knock on the door myself. An older boy answers, and I don't recognize him until his face lights up upon seeing me. "It's Queen Elisa," he hollers over his shoulder.

I clasp his upper arm. "You've grown tall, Matteo."

His eyes are wide as he steps aside, and we have passed beyond him when he adds hurriedly, "I'll be fourteen next month!"

The suite is about the size of my own, with two large beds instead of one. The bathing area is partly blocked by a velvet curtain, but I see the edge of a garderobe and a large wooden tub with carrying handles.

A familiar voice says, "Hello, Elisa," as a figure pushes the curtain aside.

My breath catches as I look into the grinning face of Father Alentín, the one-armed rebel priest who became my mentor in the desert. He wears a traditional rough-woven tunic and robe, and as usual, his empty sleeve is tucked in at the shoulder.

Alentín wraps me in a hug. "Oh, my dear girl," he says. "It has been too long." He embraces me with such easy spontaneity, as if I'm merely a girl instead of a queen, and I melt into it.

I let myself cling to him, inhaling the dusty cook-fire scent of his woolen robe. I have to squeeze my eyes tight and swallow hard. "It's good to see you too," I manage.

He murmurs, "I have been praying for you every day."

I step back and hold him at arm's length. "And I you! How is Cosmé?"

"Struggling with limited funds to establish a stable government and build a garrison on the Invierne border. Growling at anyone who gets in her way. Putting nobles in their places."

"So, the usual."

"She sends her love. Actually, she said 'regards,' which amounts to the same thing."

I smile. There was a time when Cosmé held me in very low regard indeed.

Alentín's expression turns serious. "Elisa, there is something else. Something you should know."

"Oh?"

He turns toward the bathing area and hollers, "Come on out now."

"What?" I say. "Who are you—"

A young man steps from behind the curtain, and my throat squeezes. He is impossibly tall and reed thin, with a sharp jaw and hooked nose that make him austerely handsome. He wears a black leather patch over one eye.

It is Belén.

The betrayer. The boy who sold me to the Invierne army. He nearly ruined everything we had fought for, in his mistaken belief that he was doing God's will.

Softly he says, "Hello, Elisa."

I'm not sure what to say. It aches a little to see him, because before he betrayed me, he was my friend. And once he realized his mistake, he risked his own life to warn me of the animagi's plans.

But I can't force warmth into my voice when I say, "Why are you here, Belén?"

He opens his mouth but changes his mind about whatever he was going to say. Instead he hangs his head.

Alentín reaches out and gives Belén's shoulder a squeeze.

"This boy is quite reformed. But he remains unpopular in Basajuan, as you can imagine. The court demands his execution, but Cosmé can't bear to see him killed. She thought to make use of his scouting ability, sending him on forays into enemy territory. Alas, his reporting visits to the city have become increasingly challenging. There was a scuffle in the stables—"

"But why send him here? Why to me?"

"Because I asked her to," Belén says. He dares to hold my gaze. I catch myself looking back and forth between his eye and his patch before focusing determinedly on the bridge of his nose. "The *Scriptura Sancta* says that making amends is a holy and cleansing fire unto the soul. And that's what I want to do: to make amends, to pledge my life to your service."

I stare at him.

He whispers, "Please, Elisa."

"I'll think about it."

He hides his disappointment quickly. "Thank you."

I have a sudden urge to strike out at something, or maybe someone. Cosmé should not have sent Belén to me without regard for my wishes. Alentín should have known better than to support the plan. And yet I am forced to accept Belén's presence here, since he travels in a delegation.

I have trouble enough holding my own at court. How much worse is it to be manipulated by my allies and friends? To have them foist off their own problems on me? I glare coldly as I address them both. "From this point forward, you shall address us as Your Majesty."

They bow. "Of course, Your Majesty," the traitor says.

To Alentín I say, "Are you here in an official ambassadorial role?" Though I know the answer; it's the only way to ensure Belén's safety.

"I am," he says, and his bearing is suddenly stiff. "Queen Cosmé wishes you to know of an incident that occurred in her public marketplace and would like your view on it. In short, an animagus appeared, demanded that you give yourself over to Invierne as a willing sacrifice, and then burned himself alive."

I gape at him. "It was the same here!"

He nods gravely. "I was in your city not two minutes before I learned of the event."

But I hardly hear him for the pounding in my ears. Two similar occurrences in succession speak of planning, of deadly seriousness. What is so important as to be worth two martyrs? What could they possibly want with *me*?

You will know the gate of your enemy.

Frowning, I say, "Belén?"

"Yes, Your Majesty."

"Delegation or no, if I sense you are out to harm me or any of my people, I will have you imprisoned and tried for treason. If Hector does not kill you first."

If he has a response, I do not know or care, for I spin on my heel and head toward the door. My guards fall in around me.

I pause in the threshold and say to Alentín, "Weekly services will be held tomorrow in the monastery. You and Belén and Matteo should attend."

His eyes are wide. "Yes, Eli—Your Majesty."

They all regard me as if I am a stranger, and a creeping emptiness worms through my chest. I am nearly returned to my suite before I recognize the feeling as loneliness.

8

MARA is stretched out on my bed, Doctor Enzo hovering over her as he tucks in the edges of a bandage. The guards have turned politely away, as they do when I am dressing.

I grab her hand. "How do you feel?"

"Rather like I just split in half."

Enzo snorts. "Well short of half. Although stitching scar tissue is a complicated and delicate process. I used seven stitches this time, all quite small thanks to a new needle I commissioned."

Seven? This time? I'm about to ask about the other times when Ximena hurries in from the atrium. "I have everything set to rights. Mara made quite a mess when she fell."

Mara squeezes my hand. "Who was it? Anyone from Father Alentín's camp? I was so hoping—"

"Alentín himself is here." I hush her startled exclamation. "But there is more, which I will tell you in a moment."

Her eyes narrow, and she nods.

Doctor Enzo pulls Mara's chemise down over the bandage

and straightens. "Light work only for the girl," he tells me. "For a week. Bandages must be changed daily, the salve applied each time. Would you like me to look at you too, since I'm here?" He stares toward my abdomen, and his fingers twitch with eagerness. "I hear you've been up and about against my recommendation. I predict you have continued to heal anyway. I consulted some records in the archive of previous bearers, and—"

"Later, Enzo. You are dismissed."

He mutters disjointed grumblings as he exits the suite.

Mara struggles to sit up. I give her arm a gentle pull, and she slides from the bed onto her feet.

I relate my meeting with Alentín. Ximena's eyes narrow at the news that another animagus burned himself alive. And when Mara learns that Belén is in the palace, she collapses back onto the bed, looking dazed.

Ximena paces. "I don't like this," she murmurs. "Just how many animagi must there be for Invierne to sacrifice them so easily? And Belén. He needs to be watched. Which means we must assign some of the Royal Guard to their quarters. After the lockdown, I'm not sure we can trust the palace garrison."

"Which means," Hector says, "using some of the men who are assigned to your own protection."

Fernando, from his post at the door, clears his throat and says to Hector, "My lord?"

"Yes?"

"There is not one among us who would balk at a double watch." I gape at him, realizing he must have come straight here after poking around in the catacombs. Do my guards ever rest?

But they are all nodding agreement.

"I'm glad to know it," Hector says. "It may come to that."

In the silence that follows, I know what everyone is thinking: Before the war, the Royal Guard was a full garrison of sixty. Now, only thirty-two remain. No, I correct myself. Thirty-one, with the loss of Martín.

Determining the right size for a Royal Guard is a delicate balance. Too many, and my court would distrust me, fearing what I could do with my own personal army. But right now I don't have nearly enough. It makes me weak, vulnerable. And everyone knows it.

I tell my mayordomo that I'm ready to ease back into a schedule. The first thing I want to do is address the recent spate of riots, but he insists I begin by interviewing suitors, starting with Conde Tristán of Selvarica. The conde is here for next week's Deliverance Gala and has taken to accosting the mayordomo in the halls with regular requests for an audience.

I agree to see him first thing in the morning, telling myself that everything else can wait another day, and the mayordomo wilts with relief.

So I rise early, and while Mara sleeps in, I sit on my vanity stool while Ximena sculpts my hair into an elaborate coif of loops and curls. I'm holding up my neck curls so she can work the clasp of a sapphire-drop necklace—a piece I inherited from Queen Rosaura—when she says, "You're very nervous and fidgety this morning."

I hadn't noticed the fidgeting, but my stomach is indeed in knots. "Yes," I admit. She finishes clasping the necklace, and I drop the curls. Our eyes meet in the mirror. "Oh, Ximena, the appearance of the animagus, the assassination attempt—they have weakened my position greatly."

"Yes," she agrees solemnly.

"The way I see it, I have two bargaining chips right now: the vacant spot on the Quorum, which every noble house in the country is vying for, and my own marriage. My country is splintering apart. I *must* acquire strong allies with my choices. I can't make the wrong decisions!"

"Three bargaining chips," she says.

"Three? What do you mean?"

She gazes at me a moment, her eyes full of sympathy. "Hector, as second-highest ranking officer in the kingdom, has an automatic Quorum seat. He is young and handsome. He has the friendship of the queen. He is of modest but noble birth. He is, in short, the most eligible bachelor in your kingdom. You could marry him off to tremendous advantage."

"Oh." I blink at her, vaguely stunned. "Yes, of course." Why has this never occurred to me?

A knock sounds at the door to my bedroom, and moments later, a guard announces the presence of Lord-Conde Eduardo.

I fix a smile on my face as he enters the atrium. At least it's not the general.

"Ah, Your Majesty, I'm delighted to see you looking so well!"

My nose twitches against his sharp myrrh musk as I take

his outstretched hands and kiss his cheek. "It feels good to get back to a regular schedule," I say.

"Yes, I heard you would begin interviewing suitors today. I cleared my schedule so I could come and offer my support to you during your meetings."

My grin is so hard and stiff that my teeth ache. "Oh, you shouldn't have, Your Grace. I hate to think I'm keeping you from important matters."

He waves off my protest. "Our kingdom is desperate for stability. This might be the most important decision you make during your entire reign. Of *course* I will be there for you." He grasps my shoulder and squeezes tight, looking like a concerned father with his furrowed brow.

But every instinct screams against allowing him to accompany me. *Think, Elisa!*

I duck my head respectfully. "In that case, I am grateful for your presence and your counsel." He brightens visibly. "But I have a few more private preparations to make. Will you meet me in my office?"

"Of course, Your Majesty." His eyes sweep over me, taking note of my gown, my hair, my necklace. "You'll wear your crown, won't you?"

"I wasn't planning—"

"It's important you go into these interviews appropriately accessorized by the symbols of your office, don't you think?"

I groan inwardly, thinking of the headache I'll have by the time we break for the noon meal. "Of course you're right, Your Grace."

He smiles indulgently. "I'll see you soon." He bows and exits my bedchamber.

As soon as the door closes at his back, I say to no one in particular, "I want Conde Eduardo out of my office as soon as possible."

"I'll take care of it, my sky," Ximena says, and her soft voice has such a weight of authority that I have no doubt she can do as she promises. "I need some time—you'll have to suffer his company at first. But I'll have him away as soon as possible."

"Thank you."

When she places the crown on my head, it feels like a millstone. I fantasize about commissioning a new one, something delicate and feminine and light. But my coffers are drained, and a new crown would be an insulting extravagance when I can't even afford to hire and train more Royal Guards.

She pushes hairpins through the loops in the lining, but it doesn't matter—the crown lists to the right until the heavy edge presses against the top of my ear.

"I feel like I've grown an extra brow," I say, wrinkling my forehead experimentally. Sure enough, the crown slips even farther, and the cartilage of my ear starts to fold over. Ximena does some rearranging until the crown wobbles but stays put. *No sudden head movements*, I tell myself as she pronounces me ready to receive suitors.

I've hardly used my office since Alejandro's death. It's a bright room, with wood-paneled walls and two long windows whose deep ledges are lush with potted ferns. But I'm not yet at home here. Sitting at the desk, I feel like an imposter, like I'm playing at ruling. Still, it's better than my vast, echoing audience hall with its backache-inducing throne.

Hector takes his position at my right shoulder, Conde Eduardo at my left. Guards stand sentry at the windows and doorway. My secretary sits in a corner at a small desk, his quill poised to take notes. I can only see the top of his head because a small tower of documents sits at the edge of his desk, blocking my view. I'm supposed to review and sign them all. I force myself to ignore the stack; I can't think about it now.

My heart pounds with nervousness as we wait. How does a queen handle a suitor? When I was a princess of Orovalle, I was overweight and solitary, with an unnatural attraction to musty scrolls. Anyone who wished to court me did so behind the scenes, in negotiation with my father.

As queen, I must do my own negotiating. Everyone will want something—a new title, better trading opportunities, or maybe just power. Though they'll pretend otherwise, none will want *me*.

I don't know how I'll bear the polite dance of flirtation and innuendo that always precedes these agreements. Or even how to navigate the maze that is a royal marriage treaty. I certainly don't want to make any missteps that would cause Eduardo to feel he must jump in and help.

"He arrives," says a guard.

I straighten in my chair, trying to look regal.

A barrel-shaped man with thinning hair enters. His eyes are wide, his expression serious. Droplets of sweat collect on his protruding upper lip. He bows low.

"Your Majesty," says Conde Eduardo at my ear. "May I present Lord Liano of Altapalma?"

I look up at him sharply. I was expecting Conde Tristán.

"I took the liberty of making some slight changes to your receiving schedule so we could accommodate my good friend here," Eduardo explains. "I know how eager you are to make the acquaintance of some of the northern lords."

I'm not sure whether to protest or pretend gratitude. Is it a common practice here in Joya for everyone else to manage the monarch's schedule?

I force blandness to my face and say, "Welcome, Lord Liano. Thank you for coming."

He rises from his bow but says nothing. Am I supposed to direct our conversation?

"Lord Liano is heir to the countship of Altapalma until his older brother produces a son." Eduardo jumps in. "He's a devout observer of the holy sacraments and an accomplished hunter."

"Wild javelinas," Liano blurts out. "I've won the annual tournament three years in a row."

I can't stop staring at his wet upper lip. "Oh. That's . . . impressive," I manage.

His whole body shifts forward with eagerness. "And I tan javelina hides! My hides are soft enough to make riding garb for even the finest ladies. I make all my own hunting weapons. And . . ." He draws himself to full height. "I am Grand Master of the Society for the Advocacy of Javelinas as Livestock."

"So accomplished," I murmur, more than a little stunned. I

could not marry this man. Not ever. Not even to save my country. I'd rather abdicate.

Someone pounds on the door, and Lord Liano jumps.

A guard answers. After a muted conversation, he says, "Pardon me, Lord-Conde Eduardo, but Your Grace is summoned on a very urgent matter. Something about a letter from home?"

Eduardo's face blanches. He makes quick apologies and hurries out the door. I suddenly breathe easier. *Thank you, Ximena.*

I turn back to Lord Liano. "I am forced to cut our appointment short, my lord. I'm afraid my dear friend the conde was overly eager in scheduling you, as I have another appointment in moments."

His expression turns tragic, like that of a child who just had his favorite sweet taken away, and I hastily add, "But I'd love to discuss . . . javelina hunting further at some point. Are you in town awhile for the Deliverance Gala?"

He bows. "Of course, Your Majesty."

"Then I look forward to seeing you."

Once he is gone, I turn to Hector, who is trying very hard not to laugh.

"I can't, Hector. Not him."

"You can do better," he agrees.

Another knock, another murmured conversation, and my guard swings the door wide to receive Conde Tristán.

A small, foppish man with puffed sleeves and a plumed hat sweeps in and bows with a flourish. I am about to greet him, but he intones, "I present to you His Grace Conde Tristán, master equestrian, fighting man, and the pride of Selvarica."

Ah, just a herald then.

He steps aside as a second man strides through the door. He's of average height and lanky, and he moves with a dancer's purposed grace. His features are a touch too delicate for true handsomeness, the black hair gently curling at his nape a little too beautiful, but his eyes shine with warmth and intelligence. He looks younger than I imagined. I'm surprised to find myself returning his shy smile with one of my own.

He bows, straightens, stares.

"Um, hello," I say lamely. "Welcome."

"Thank you. Er, Your Majesty. It is . . . You are . . ." He shakes his head ruefully. "I'm sorry. I'm usually more articulate than this. It's just that you are so much more beautiful than I remember."

My eyes narrow as I try to discern his level of sincerity. In my peripheral vision, I notice Hector shift on his feet and cross his arms over his chest.

I decide to be frank. "Don't be ridiculous, Your Grace. You and I both know my court has pronounced me unlovely."

He decides to be frank right back. "True. Gossip has you pegged as portly, prone to uncouth wardrobe choices, and alarmingly blunt." His smile reveals straight white teeth. "I concur that you are blunt."

"I assure you they are correct about my fashion sense too. Were it not for my devoted attendants, I would be dressed in sand chaps and a goat-hair tunic."

"I'm certain you would be stunning in them."

I wait for him to make placating noises about the gossip regarding my reputed corpulence, and I'm a little disappointed, a little relieved, when he does not.

I'm not sure what to say next. From the corner comes the *scrape-scrape* of quill against parchment as the secretary feverishly records our meeting. I imagine him writing: . . . *goat-hair tunic.*

My head is now pounding from the relentless weight of my crown. Frustration boils over, and I say, "Conde Tristán, why are you here?"

He has the grace to seem flustered. He says, "I was hoping we could get to know each other. It is no secret that my people would benefit greatly if I were to . . . ally myself . . . with Your Majesty. But there is no hurry. I simply propose that we meet once in a while and see if we enjoy each other's company."

"That's it for now? No requests, no favors?"

"Well, there is one thing."

Of course there is. "What?"

"At the upcoming Deliverance Gala, would you be so kind as to honor me with two dances?"

Oh, God, I will have to dance. It hadn't occurred to me. I'm a terrible dancer.

The horror on my face must be apparent, for Conde Tristán takes a step backward, eyes wide with alarm. "I apologize, Your Majesty. Perhaps I am too forward—"

"Yes, you may have two dances. But it is my plan to test your devotion by stepping on your feet."

His eyes crinkle with genuine mirth. "I shall look forward

to it. You may find, though, that I am not so easy to step on."

I force myself to resist his smile, even as I admit to myself that I like him a little. I gesture to one of the guards and say, "Please escort the conde and his . . ." Herald? Assistant? ". . . and his man back to their rooms and make sure they have everything they need."

If the conde is discouraged by the dismissal, he doesn't show it. "Until the festival, Your Majesty." He executes a polished bow. His attendant does the same, and they leave with the guard.

After the door shuts, Hector says, "He thought you were joking about stepping on his feet," and we exchange a quick smile.

The secretary scribbles last-minute notations about the meeting. Will he record every single word spoken in this room?

"Mr. Secretary," I say.

He looks up, mid–pen stroke. A smudge of ink mars the tip of his nose. "Your Majesty?"

"I'm thirsty. Fetch me a glass of water, please?"

He frowns with the understanding that I'm getting rid of him but schools his expression quickly. "Yes, Your Majesty."

Once he's gone, I lean back in my chair and look up at Hector. "What did you think of the conde? An improvement on Liano, at least, yes?" I rub at my temples. The weight of this stupid crown is making it hard to think.

Hector's gaze turns inward as he ponders. I have always liked this about him, the way he mulls ideas over in his head.

He never feels obliged to speak until he has exactly the right words.

He says, "Conde Tristán is at the top of Lady Jada's list, but I think it has more to do with his general popularity and charm than it does his suitability. Selvarica is a small southern holding, consisting mostly of islands. It's difficult to access, not heavily populated. I'm not sure what the conde feels he can offer the throne. I think you can do better. And Eduardo and Luz-Manuel have both expressed a preference that you choose someone from the north."

He says it all without emotion, as if quoting an academic text. I look down at my lap. "But what of *him?*" I say softly. "What kind of man is he, do you think?"

Seconds pass. I feel his eyes on me, but I can't bring myself to meet his gaze, so I focus hard on the hands resting atop my skirt. My dark skin lies in sharp contrast to the blue of my gown. My right thumbnail is uneven from my habit of biting it. I should have Mara file it for me.

At last he says, "He inherited young, when his father died in a riding accident. By reputation, he is intelligent and charming. The ladies of the court consider him quite dashing. That's all I know."

His voice is so tight that I look up to try to read his face. It's hard and determined. We stare at each other for a long moment.

I need to fill the silence, to explain, so I say, "I know I'll marry for the benefit of Joya d'Arena, and my own feelings will not be a consideration. So it's silly to hope . . . but I can't help it. . . . That is, I hope I marry a good man. Like Alejandro.

I know he didn't love me, but he *was* my friend." The sigh that escapes is almost like a sob.

His eyes flash with something—pity, maybe—and he reaches down, grabs my hand. His thumb sweeps across my knuckles as he says in a gruff whisper, "I can't imagine there is a man in all of Joya who is good enough for our queen. But if such a man exists, we will find him. I swear it."

I swallow hard. "Thank you."

The mayordomo rushes unannounced through the doorway. Hector drops my hand and lurches to attention.

"Your Majesty!" the mayordomo pants. "He's here. Lo Chato from the Wallows. Do you still wish to grant immediate audience? You're scheduled to see Lady Jada next. I could ask her to wait."

My startled reaction has dislodged my crown, and it slips down my brow. I pull it off, wincing when strands of hair are yanked out by the roots. "Did Lo Chato come alone?" Even saying the name gives me a shiver.

"Yes, Your Majesty."

I set the crown on the edge of my desk. I hate that I am not big enough, not strong enough, to wear it. "Then send him in," I whisper.

He bows and exits the office.

"Be ready," Hector says to the guards, and hands move to scabbards; eyes shift toward the door. With a metallic *whisk*, Hector draws his gauntlet daggers. A smart choice, since his position between my desk and the wall gives him little range of motion for a sword.

The mayordomo enters and says in a clipped, formal voice, "Your Majesty, I present Lo Chato of the Wallows."

A figure glides into the room. He is impossibly tall, and he wears a long black cloak with a deep cowl that shadows his face. He drops to one knee, bows his head, and waits silently.

"Rise," I say, hoping he doesn't notice the tremor in my voice. I place a fingertip to the Godstone, hoping for a tickle of warmth, or even a chill—anything to indicate whether the person before me is friend or foe. But I feel nothing.

The cowled man straightens.

"Remove your hood."

He raises his hands, and I already know, even as he slides the hood back from his head—by the pale peach of his hands, the preternatural grace of his movement—what will be revealed.

Eyes as green as moss, a face so sharply delicate as to be catlike, waist-long hair the syrupy gold of honey.

It takes only a split second for my guards to ring him with swords. Hector steps in front of me, daggers in defensive position.

The man before me carries himself like an animagus. My forearm throbs with the phantom memory of a sorcerer's claws lashing into my skin, and I stare at his hands, expecting to see clawlike points embedded in his nails.

His nails are cracked and encrusted with dirt, but they are free of barbs. And unlike the uncannily perfect animagi I encountered, he has faint lines across his forehead; a patch of dry, peeling skin across his nose; and weary, bloodshot eyes. Not blue, those eyes. And his hair is not white.

Not a sorcerer, then. I breathe deeply through my nose, savoring this feeling of relief.

Still, an Invierno has been secretly living in my city, leading a group of my own people.

The mayordomo stands just out of range of the guards' swords, gaping at the creature he escorted in. I say with a steadiness that surprises me, "The secretary will return soon from an errand. Please head him off. And tell no one, not even Lady Jada, the nature of my current appointment."

"Yes, Your Majesty." He departs gratefully.

I gesture to one of the guards to close and bar the door.

The Invierno regards me calmly.

I'm not sure how to proceed, so I say, "Thank you for coming."

"Your Majesty commanded it, and I obeyed." He speaks perfect Plebeya, without even a trace of the clipped impatience I've heard from animagi.

"Why would an Invierno feel compelled to obey me?"

"I am Your Majesty's loyal subject."

Not likely. "Is Lo Chato your name?"

"A title."

"Do many Inviernos carry the title of 'Lo Chato'?" I ask, too tentatively.

"We have more Chatos than you have condes," he says.

I don't want to call him that. Not ever. "And your name?"

"My name, in God's language, means 'He Who Wafts Gently with the Wind Becomes as Mighty as the Thunderstorm.'"

One of the guards snorts.

He shrugs. "It's a common name in Invierne. But the people of my village call me Storm when they are being familiar."

"Ah, yes. Please explain why you live in a cavern beneath the Wallows."

"I first came to serve as ambassador to Joya d'Arena. I was a member of King Alejandro's court for several years. As the war began, I found it necessary to go into hiding."

The first part is easy enough to prove. "Hector, do you recognize this man?"

Hector is studying him, eyes narrowed. "No. Well, maybe."

"Maybe?"

"It *could* be him. There are similarities. The man I remember had darker hair."

"I see." I purse my lips, thinking hard. I can't read the Invierno's face, much less separate truth from falsehood. "You call yourself my loyal subject. That sounds more like defection than hiding."

"You are correct, Your Majesty. I was not hiding from the people of Joya, but from my own."

"Why?"

His face is void of feeling as he says, "I had failed, you see. After years of campaigning for port rights, I had nothing to show for my efforts. My life was forfeit, and my choice was to either go home in disgrace and face execution, or find a new home here."

"A harsh sentence."

"My kind embrace honorable death. I am wretched in my unusual desire to live beyond the shame of my failure."

I shudder, remembering the zeal with which the animagus atop the amphitheater burned himself. And before that, how dozens of Inviernos submitted themselves to the animagi's knives, the way their blood poured into the sand and fueled the fire magic that nearly burned our city to the ground. Did they all believe they were embracing honorable death?

Hector asks, "Why didn't you seek asylum? The king would have granted it."

"Your king could not have protected me. I had to disappear completely." Storm smiles for the first time—a slow, edged grin that sends shivers down my back. "Surely you realize? Your city is crawling with Invierne spies."

The guards exchange a startled glance.

I breathe deeply through my nose to keep steady. Though my pulse races, I wave a hand nonchalantly and say, "Everyone spies on everyone else. My own father, King Hitzedar of Orovalle, has several spies in my court."

Storm says, "Your Majesty, there are hundreds. Living right here in the city."

"Inviernos like you? Or are Joya's own citizens turning against her?"

"Both."

Hector says, "We would recognize Inviernos among us."

He just shrugs and looks off in the distance as if bored.

I lean forward. "Would we, Storm? Would we recognize them?"

His expression turns smug. "All of you Joyans and Orovalleños look exactly alike, with your dirty skin and dark hair and wood-rot eyes. You are like black rats crawling across the sand. But we Inviernos are a colorful people, and as numerous as the stars in the sky. It is rare to find some among us who resemble you enough to pass, but found them we have. Enough to make spies."

"You claim to be my loyal subject, yet you speak as though you hold my people in contempt." I should be angrier, but I find myself fascinated with his complete disregard for propriety.

"You are a contemptible people. I am loyal out of necessity, not love."

Strange that he does not make even the barest attempt at flattery. "Hard to believe you were unable to make diplomatic headway in my husband's court, charming as you are."

He nods knowingly. "This is the *sarcasm* your people are so fond of. When you say one thing but mean another. Inviernos value honesty too much for it, in accordance with God's will."

I don't have the time or energy for a doctrinal debate, so I let that go. "The animagus who burned himself alive . . . surely you heard about it?"

He nods. "Everyone within two weeks' journey has heard by now."

"Did you know him? Did you know what would happen?"

"No, and no. I was not surprised, though. The animagi are fond of such demonstrations."

"Are you the person who tried to kill me?"

He doesn't even flinch. "No."

"If your life is in such great danger, why answer my summons?"

His lips twist into that cruel smile. "I came to warn you, my queen. It occurred to me that a warning would be taken more seriously if it came from me rather than from an ignorant, impoverished denizen of the Wallows."

He's probably right about that. "And what is your warning?"

"You are in grave peril, Your Majesty. I have seen the signs, and I know Invierne will make another play. Soon. But this time, there will be no army to defend against. This time, they will come at you like spirits in the night, and you won't recognize the danger until it's too late."

The animagus uttered similar words. I swallow the panic that rises in my throat. "Why? Why warn me?"

"I like my life. My secret village turns a nice profit on river scavenge. The people I lead are stupid and filthy, but they treat me with respect, even worship. All my needs are tended to. I would like things to stay exactly the way they are, and I know the city of Brisadulce has its best chance of remaining stable if you are in power and well aware of the Invierne threat."

Hector leans forward, nostrils flared, face hard. I have never seen him so angry. "The Inviernos will find that Elisa is very difficult to kill," he says, making the dagger dance in the air by some gymnastic of wrist and fingers.

Storm laughs, and the sound is as brittle as breaking glass. "Did I say kill? I don't believe I did. Invierne wants her very much alive. Though I assure you that if one of Invierne's innumerable spies gets hold of her, she will wish herself dead."

It's possible that I hate this man after all. "This audience is over," I snap. "Take him to the prison tower."

My guards pin his arms and turn him around.

"Arresting me will mean my death, Your Majesty," he calls over his shoulder. "And once Invierne finds me and kills me, you'll learn nothing more. I know you're curious. About us. About what we want with that thing in your belly."

"Wait!" I say, and the guards halt. "And if I let you return to your village?"

"Visit any time and ask all the questions you want. As I said, I am your loyal subject. You have nothing to fear from me."

I pretend to consider for a long moment. "You may go free. But Storm, in accordance with God's will, I must be *honest* and tell you that I hope you will give me an excuse to kill you."

Something flits across his face. I hope it's fear. He bows. "Until we meet again, Your Majesty. Remember to watch your-self." The guards step aside. He flips the cowl over his head and sweeps from the room.

I whisper to the guards, "Follow him."

They nod, wait a few beats, and then one slips out the door after him.

"Well," says Hector, sheathing his daggers. "I believe that really was the former ambassador, different hair color notwith-standing. I remember him being deeply unpleasant."

"Arrogant superiority must be a cultural obsession. The animagi I encountered were much the same."

He crosses his arms and leans a hip against the desk. "You could simply make it known that he's here. If what he said is true, his own people will take care of him."

Seeing Hector in such a relaxed pose helps me force the

tension from my own limbs. I take a cleansing breath and say, "I'm glad you were here, Hector. I admit that was terrifying."

His sloppy grin makes my stomach clench, not unpleasantly. "You faced him down like a seasoned warrior," he says.

"Only because I had your daggers at my back."

"Always."

"Do you think he was telling the truth? About the spies? About why he wanted to warn me?"

Hector shrugs. "Alejandro and I used to speculate that the Inviernos are incapable of falsehood. They tend to go silent and refuse to speak rather than lie. He was wrong about one thing, though. *Someone* wants you dead, as your wounds attest."

Reflexively, my fingers find my Godstone. Then they shift left, skim my bodice. It's thin enough for me to feel the ridges of my new scar. Another possibility occurs to me, and I gasp in surprise.

"What is it?"

"Hector, what if it *wasn't* an assassination attempt. Is that possible? Did someone mean to take me *alive*?"

His dark eyes seem to whirl as his considerable intelligence chews on the idea. Without breaking my gaze, he says to the remaining guard, "Lucás, step outside and watch the hallway."

"Yes, my lord," comes the voice. The door creaks open, bangs closed.

Hector and I are alone.

9

I'M suddenly aware of the silence; no creak of armor, no footsteps, no quiet chatter. Just his breath and mine, steady and even. It's the first time I've been alone—truly alone—with anyone in weeks, and it feels as though we are sharing a secret.

He says, "I don't care to discuss what happened that day in front of my men."

"Why not?" Looking up at him is giving my neck and shoulders a crick, so I stand and stretch my arms to the ceiling, careful of my mending side. Softly, I say, "What *did* happen that day, Hector? Were you the one who found me?"

He turns, putting his back to me. "The general held me back after the Quorum meeting," he says. "I let myself get distracted. I didn't go after you right away." When he turns back around, his face is stricken. "Elisa, I'm so sorry."

"Just tell me."

He runs a hand through his hair. "You left, and I was about to go after you, but the general grabbed my arm. He wanted to discuss a new rotation near the amphitheater—a collaboration between the Royal Guard and his own soldiers. It was ten minutes or more before I followed you."

"I see."

"I let myself get distracted. It won't happen again."

"I'm not angry."

He sighs as if exasperated. "You're rarely angry. Even when you should be."

"I'm angry all the time!"

"Not at me."

"No, not at you. I told you I wanted to be alone that day, remember?"

"Yes."

"How can I be angry when I got my wish? I was the foolish one, not you. You warned me. And I'm sorry about that. I caused a lot of trouble, especially for you." He starts to protest, but I put up a hand and look him straight in the eye. "Do you think Luz-Manuel drew you away on purpose?"

"How could he know you would go to the catacombs?"

"Well, I *had* been making a regular habit of it. Maybe it was just a matter of waiting for the right opportunity."

He looks off into the distance, worrying the pommel of his sword with his fingertips. "A few weeks ago, I would never have considered it," he says. "I've always thought him a devoted Joyan who would give his life for his country."

"And now?"

"Now I'll make sure you are never unguarded, even in your own palace."

Again I touch my forefinger to my waist, to the scar there.

I shudder to remember the blade, how it felt plunging into my abdomen. "Were you the one who found me?"

He rubs the back of his head as if suddenly exhausted. "I called your name, but there was no response. Then I saw your foot, poking out from behind one of the pedestals. I ran over, and . . . God, Elisa, I thought you were dead."

I clasp my hands together to keep them steady.

"You had stopped bleeding," he continues. "I've seen it in battle; a wounded soldier often stops bleeding when he dies. But then . . . you breathed. A big, strong breath. So I gathered you up and got you to Doctor Enzo as quick as I could."

I whisper, "Thank you."

He stares at me, and I stare back. His lashes are short but thick, and he has a tiny freckle at the crease of his left eye. He has the deepest eyes I've ever seen on a person, like a whole world goes on inside his head.

He says, "I think the Godstone protected you. Or started to heal you. Enzo didn't realize how badly you'd been stabbed until he broke the scab and cleaned the wound. At first he thought it was just the bump to your head that had sent you into a coma."

Hearing his account, it seems as though I barely escaped death. But something about it feels strange. Something doesn't add up.

"Is it possible my assassin knew exactly how badly to wound me without killing me? Was there any indication that he didn't leave me for dead? That he planned to take me alive?"

"No. Wait. Maybe. There was blood all over your face, even

though your face wasn't anywhere near the pool of blood. And the floor was streaked. I thought you had managed to crawl away before collapsing. But what if—"

"What if I was dragged? What if by coming to look for me, you interrupted something?"

Hector moves to the windows, paces back and forth between them. "This might be a good thing," he says. "Kidnapping you requires planning. Finesse. Merely killing you is easy by comparison."

"Oh?" The last thing I want to hear is that killing me would be *easy*.

"An abduction requires getting very close to the victim," he muses. "Nothing long range. They'd have to draw you away from your protectors. . . ."

An idea slams me. I turn it over in my head, considering it from different angles.

"Elisa?"

I led a rebellion, defeated sorcerers, became queen. I can do this too. I push my shoulders back, raise my chin, and say in my best queen voice, "Teach me to defend myself." Before he can protest, I add, "I'm not saying make me into an elite soldier. Just teach me to survive a close-quarters encounter. Teach me to evade an attacker. I'm a *very* good student. I can learn anything if I study hard enough."

He nods. "I know you can. But what about your injury? Shouldn't you—"

"We'll start slow and easy."

He grasps the pommel of his sword. "If you had been raised

to the throne, you would have learned basic techniques anyway."

"We'll need space. Privacy." I don't want to be clumsy and awkward before my entire guard.

"Alejandro's suite?" he suggests. "It's quite large, especially if we moved the bed to the side."

"Good idea." I grin in anticipation.

His lips twitch as he fights very hard to not grin right back.

The next day, the guards rearrange everything in the king's suite to open up space, shoving the absurd tower bed against the wall. Several rugs cover the floor in an array of sunset colors and textures. The guards start to remove these, too, but Hector stops them.

"You're mostly likely to be assaulted in the palace," he says. "So we'll practice with the rugs underfoot at first. And it's not just assassins I'm worried about—a queen can just as easily be killed by a mob. So we're going to focus on close-quarters encounters."

Hector dismisses all the guards except for Fernando, telling them to take up their regular posts in my own rooms. He orders Fernando to guard the door outside the king's suite.

I've given Mara the hour off, but Ximena settles on the bed to watch. Hector eyes her warily but says nothing. I sense the tension between them, but it is right that Ximena be here.

Hector and I face each other. Nervousness patters in my chest. I know it's silly, but I'm afraid of looking like a fool in front of him.

He says, "If I were an enemy, and I started bearing down

on you like this"—he draws his sword, stretches the tip toward me, takes a single step in my direction—"what would you do?"

Possibilities race through my head. Should I look for a weapon? Dodge and come up behind his guard? Trip him? Insult his mother?

I decide to be honest. "I would run," I admit. "As fast as I could."

"Good! That's the right decision. Escaping should always be your first resort. Everything I teach you is a contingency, to be used only if your first resort fails. Clear?"

"Clear." I glance over at Ximena to find her nodding approval.

"So, to start, I'd like you to get accustomed to holding a knife." From a utility belt at his waist, he pulls a short, light dagger. It's plain, with a wooden handle, but the blade shimmers from constant polishing and sharpening.

The blade.

My mouth goes dry.

He flips it in the air so that the blade is pinched between his thumb and forefinger and holds it out to me, handle first. "Go ahead," he says. "Take it."

I wipe my hand on my breeches. Slowly, heart pounding, I grasp the handle. It feels cold in my palm.

"You should have a knife on you at all times," he says. "We may have to adjust your wardrobe to accommodate one. If you keep it hidden, you'll have the advantage of surprise in a close-quarters encounter."

I stare at the thing in my hand.

"I'll teach you where to stab someone to inflict maximum damage," he says.

I stabbed someone before. I hated it. So intimate, so destructive. Afterward, there was blood everywhere.

"You'll notice that the edge is slightly serrated." He points to a couple of indentions near the tip. "That way, the blade does damage when you withdraw it as well."

The dagger that slid across Humberto's throat had a serrated edge. I remember it as if a painter had captured the moment and stretched out the canvas before my eyes. I wonder if the blade that plunged into my own body was serrated. Is that why I required so many stitches? It certainly went in easily enough.

My stomach roils with nausea. I swallow hard against it even as my cheeks go clammy cold.

"And since you are not a large person, I'll teach you how to get maximum leverage and force for stabbing. There are a few tricks—"

I drop the knife. It bounces off a rug, clatters to the stone floor. I wipe my hand on my pants again, as if I can wipe away the sensation memory.

"Elisa? What—"

"I can't," I whisper, looking everywhere but at him. "I'm sorry."

"I don't understand. This was your idea. And a good one. You should learn—"

"I'm not sure I can use a knife." I stare at it on the floor. Maybe I could work up to it again. I just won't think about it plunging into my own stomach. I can do it. I can be strong.

"It's the best way to defend yourself," he insists.

I'm about to tell him I'll give it another try when Ximena says, "It's really not."

He turns on her, brow furrowed.

Ximena scoots off the bed and lands heavily on her feet. She lumbers toward us, and I marvel that this large older woman is capable of protecting me. I'm eager to see what she'll do.

She bends over to pick up the dagger and hands it to Hector, hilt first. "Attack me," she says calmly.

Hector's eyes narrow. "You're sure about this, my lady?"

She smiles. "Do be gentle on an old woman, though."

He shrugs. Then, with lightning speed, he feints left, but sweeps right with the blade, arching it toward her belly.

She shifts to avoid it, and her arm blurs in a flurry of ruffles. Hector grunts. The dagger clatters onto the floor again.

Their eyes lock. Ximena holds his wrist, pinching it in such a way that his grip has relaxed and his hand flops uselessly. The sleeve of her voluminous blouse is torn.

"The Royal Guard trains in hand-to-hand combat," she says, "so you know as well as I do how easy it is to disarm someone." She lets his wrist go and steps back. "It is especially easy to disarm someone who is not adept with knife work. Which means, in essence, that the enemy ends up holding an extra weapon."

Hector rubs his wrist, frowning. "I *did* go easy on you," he says.

"Thank you," she says solemnly, but her eyes twinkle.

He turns to me and says, "Your nurse has a good point. But

I insist on training you to defend against a knife attack, even if you don't choose to keep one."

It's a fair concession. "Agreed."

"I'd like to teach you to use some kind of weapon," he says. "Maybe a quarterstaff?"

"A quarterstaff is not very subtle," I say. "Or handy. If a kidnapper comes at me, what am I supposed to do? Say, 'Excuse me, my lord, while I pull my *enormous quarterstaff* out of my bodice?'"

Hector rubs his jaw. "You're right. I'll give it some thought. But for now, we'll start with the easiest escape maneuver." He gestures with his hand. "Come here and turn around."

Feeling suddenly unsure, I glance at Ximena, who gives a nod of approval.

I approach, turn around. He presses up behind me and wraps his left arm around my torso, across my breasts, trapping my own arms to my sides. My head fits snugly and perfectly beneath his chin. The mink-oil scent of his rawhide armor pricks at my nose.

"It's instinct," he says, his breath tickling my scalp, "for an attacker to think of your arms and hands as dangerous. He'll subdue them as soon as possible. And it's instinct for the victim thus subdued to feel powerless."

"I see." I don't feel powerless at all. Pulled tight against Hector, hearing his voice shift low, I feel safer than ever. "I could stomp on your foot," I tell him.

"That's exactly what you should do. The instep of the human foot is made up of hundreds of tiny bones. You can do immense damage with one good stomp. So try it. Gently, please."

I comply by halfheartedly sending my heel onto the top of his foot. The force can't possibly be enough to hurt him through his boot, but he releases me instantly.

I turn to find him grinning at me.

He says, "Now that you have momentarily incapacitated me, what do you do?"

"I run?"

"Like you're being chased by a sandstorm." I begin to think that maybe I should practice *running*. "Come back. Let's do it again."

This time, when his arm slides around me, it feels slower, more deliberate. "The trick," he says in my ear, "is to be wholly committed to your action. No hesitation." His arm tightens in a little jerk, and I catch my breath. "Do you understand, Elisa? You might have to stomp to *live*."

I swallow hard. "I understand."

"Lady Ximena, can you bring us a few pillows?"

My nurse rustles around on the bed. She must know exactly what Hector has in mind, for she strides into my field of vision and, without being asked, crouches down to cover Hector's right foot with cushions.

Hector says, "Now come down as hard as you can on my foot."

"No! I don't want to—"

"Do it."

I lift my knee high and slam my heel into his instep.

He gasps, releases me.

I spin to face him. He is bent over slightly, regarding me

with wide eyes. Then he says, "Well done!"

I wilt with relief. "It hurts," I admit, flexing my toes.

"That's why I had Ximena bring cushions. You must be willing to hurt yourself a little in the short term."

I laugh. "The cushions were for *your* protection. If not for them, I would have broken your foot."

He shrugs. "You'll have to stomp a lot harder than that."

My mouth opens in surprise. Then I realize he's trying to goad me. It's working.

Without breaking his gaze, I say, "Ximena, please fetch more pillows. Hector is going to need them."

As she hurries away, he says, "Think you can learn this faster than your seven-year-old heir did?"

"Watch me."

He grins.

We spend several more minutes stomping, with each foot, and then he teaches me to dislocate someone's kneecap. By the time Ximena calls a halt, my heels ache, the muscles in my calves and shins tremble, and the scar on my abdomen stings with overstretching.

I'm surprised to realize I enjoyed myself. I rotate my ankles experimentally, relishing the burn. I feel strong in spite of my fatigue. Powerful, even. And Hector has always been easy to be with, since that day more than a year ago when he took a lonely princess on a tour of the palace to help her feel at home. I hope we have our next lesson soon.

10

I'VE neglected Father Alentín and Queen Cosmé's delegation long enough to give offense. It's especially insulting given that he now quietly aids Ximena in researching the Godstone. So I decide to host a small dinner in my private dining room, hoping to relax in the company of friends, share stories, rediscover the ease of having close companions.

But the mayordomo insists I also invite Conde Tristán and his foppish attaché, along with Lady Jada, whose Quorum vote I may need if we do not find a permanent replacement soon. He's right—it's the strategic thing to do. But my anticipation is replaced by dread. I had so hoped to indulge in an evening of not being *queen.*

By design, I am the last to arrive, for I can't stomach the idea of making idle chatter while waiting to be served. As is tradition in Joya d'Arena, the table is low and surrounded by huge sitting cushions. Not for the first time, I consider drawing up a royal edict demanding the use of proper tables and chairs.

Hector and Ximena seat themselves on either side of me. I

frown to think that I can't even enjoy a small private dinner without their protective hedge.

I nod to Father Alentín and Belén, sitting at the other end. Lady Jada is directly across from me, and after greeting me warmly, she goes right back to gazing shamelessly at Conde Tristán sitting beside her. But the conde doesn't notice because *his* gaze fixed on me the moment I entered and now does not waver.

I sigh as I reach for my glass of rose-hip wine, anticipating a long and tedious evening. If it were just Alentín and Belén, I would know exactly what to say, exactly how to be. I find that my anger with them has faded, so eager am I for the familiar.

To my relief, Conde Tristán is the one to open conversation. "Lady Ximena, how goes the late-night studying in the monastery?"

Everyone freezes. Belén becomes as dark and coiled as a storm cloud.

The conde looks around at us in alarm. "I've said something, haven't I? Something wrong?"

Lady Jada says, "Oh, I'm sure it's nothing. We just need to get to know each other." She turns to me. "Isn't that right, Your Majesty?"

My voice is dead flat when I say, "Your Grace, do tell me how you came to know about Ximena's studies."

He and his herald exchange a confused glance. The conde says, "I often walk at night, after everyone has gone to sleep. Lately I've been going to the monastery to pray. Last night I saw Lady Ximena with the ambassador from Basajuan." He indicates Alentín with a lift of his chin. "I just thought . . . I know she used to be a scribe. . . . That is to say, I've started studying the scriptures myself lately, and I thought to chat about . . ."

I laugh the moment a good lie comes to mind. It's a forced sound that will fool no one who knows me, but the conde's face relaxes at once. "I didn't mean to alarm Your Grace," I say. "It's just that we've kept it quiet intentionally. You see, not many people know that Basajuan's monastery archive took some damage during the war. We've been working with them to restore what documents we can, even scribing new ones as necessary."

He nods. "I'm glad to hear it. Small gestures will go a long way toward building goodwill with Queen Cosmé. Which is vital now that her country stands between us and Invierne."

"Indeed." I raise my wineglass. "To continued goodwill between Basajuan and Joya d'Arena."

Everyone raises their glasses and echoes the sentiment with polite relief.

"Were I you, though," the conde muses, "I would be scouring the archive for clues about the Godstone."

I stare at him. Is he bringing up these things out of innocent coincidence? Or is there a purpose to his comments?

"Why is that?" Ximena asks, and I can't be the only one who recognizes the dangerous edge in her voice.

"Well, the animagus, for one. The one who martyred himself. Invierne still wants that stone desperately. I must confess that I am deeply curious as to why. And I'm not the only one.

The whole city is talking about it. Maybe the whole country."

"Maybe they're afraid of it?" Lady Jada offers. "Her Majesty destroyed several of their most powerful sorcerers with it."

Tristán shrugs. "There have been bearers, Godstones, every hundred years for two millennia. Why go to extremes only now?"

I feel I should interject something, though I don't know what. They're talking about me, the most important part of my life, as if I'm not even here. There are probably exchanges like this going on all over the country.

My Godstone. Me. A dinner-table conversation. I suppose that as queen, I belong to everyone a little.

"You know what I think?" Lady Jada says.

"I would love to know," I tell her sincerely.

She lifts her chin. "I think they want this land back."

"Oh?"

"I would be a poor mayor's wife if I didn't know my history," she says primly. "My tutor says that a few centuries after God dropped the first families onto this world, one family went mad with ambition, gobbling up land and resources through marriage and war. But the others united against them and drove them out. They fled into the wilderness, the curse of God upon them, and became the Inviernos.

"They were *driven* out," she continues. "Everyone knows Brisadulce is the most beautiful city in the world. I think the Inviernos want it back."

Her history is mostly right, but her assessment of our capital is not. Brisadulce is an isolated city, surrounded on all sides by natural disaster, forced to trade for the bulk of its supplies. It remains our capital from long tradition and history and maybe nostalgia. But the land itself is impractical, even useless. Why would the Inviernos want it when they could pursue Puerto Verde or the lush rolling hills of the southern holdings instead?

I say solemnly, "A well-conceived theory. Maybe you're right."

Ximena chokes on her wine.

The kitchen master enters, accompanied by wait staff carrying trays piled with shredded chicken, corn tortillas, and fresh fruit slices. My mouth waters to see honey-coconut scones, my favorite. They're still hot from the oven; the honey glaze melts down the sides.

Lady Jada claps her hands. "Pollo pibil! It was the king's favorite, I hear." She points to the plate of chicken.

"It was," Hector says. "He first encountered it in my father's hacienda." At my questioning look, he says, "One summer King Nicolao's ship got caught in a storm and ran onto the reef. He and Prince Alejandro took shelter with us while the hull was repaired. It's how we met."

I've never heard this story. I wonder how many other things I don't know about Hector.

Father Alentín says, "You must have impressed him greatly, to have been named his page. And later, to be appointed commander of the guard. You're the youngest in history."

Hector shrugs, looking sheepish. "It was mostly an accident."

"What do you mean?" the priest asks.

"I had two older brothers, and we used to spar with toy

swords in the courtyard. The morning Alejandro was there, one of them knocked me off my feet, and the other starting teasing me, poking at me with his sword. It was all good-natured, nothing that hadn't happened a hundred times before. But Alejandro observed the whole thing through his bedroom window, and he came barreling into the courtyard, yelling at them to back off, that he had just named me his personal page and *how dare they threaten the royal page?*"

"He thought he was saving you," I say.

Hector nods, his eyes warm with the memory. "I was only twelve years old at the time, so naturally I thought he was the most wonderful person who ever lived."

"But eventually the two of you became friends in truth," I say.

"Yes, quickly. He was lonely. An only child. It was good for him to have a younger boy around, someone he could easily whip in swordsmanship." He adds haughtily, "That only lasted a couple of years, of course."

I laugh. "Of course. He told me you were the most fearsome warrior he knew."

"He did?" A shield drops from his face, and I see its truer expression, as if he and sorrow are steady companions.

"He did," I say gently. "He spoke of you often while he lay in hospice. Becoming his page may have been an accident, but becoming lord-commander certainly was not. He said it was the easiest choice he ever made, even though you were so young."

Hector swallows hard, nodding, and turns away to hide his face.

"This is fabulous," says Lady Jada, and I jump. For a moment, it felt like Hector and I were alone. She adds, "The pollo pibil, I mean. Your kitchen master is to be commended."

I'd love to ignore her, to press Hector for more details about his childhood, but I invited Jada for a reason, so I force myself to pay attention to her. "Thank you." I glance around for the kitchen master, but he has already slipped away to put the finishing touches on dessert. "He makes pastries specially for me now, from a recipe I brought from Orovalle." I grab a corn tortilla and nibble on it.

"Yes, your love of pastries is well known."

I study her face, trying to determine if she insults me on purpose, but she chews blissfully on her pollo pibil.

It is the traitor Belén who says, "Her Majesty has an even greater passion for jerboa soup."

I almost choke on my tortilla. Jerboa soup was our daily repast when we traveled together through the deep desert. If I taste it again in this life, it will be too soon. I glance over to find his lips twitching with humor.

Jada says, "But jerboa soup is so . . . pedestrian."

"Sometimes." I swallow the lump of tortilla and say gravely, "Life's simpler foods have great poetry to them, don't you think?" I have no idea what that means, but she nods as if concurring with a profound truth.

Conde Tristán says, "The official dish of Selvarica is called the sendara de vida. It's made of starfruit soaked in honey and lime, then roasted over peppered coals. It's sublime. If any of you come for a visit, I'd be delighted to serve it."

Ximena and I exchange a startled look. Her face is white.

My nurse turns toward the conde and says, carefully, "The *sendara de vida*. That means 'the gate of life.'"

He nods. "Named after an old legend."

"Oh, do tell us!" I say, with what I hope is artless enthusiasm. "I'd love to hear more about Selvarica."

At the end of the table, Father Alentín leans forward, eyes narrowed. Beside me, Hector sets down his wineglass and places his hands casually on the table.

Conde Tristán looks around at his suddenly rapt audience, aware that once again he is on the outside of an ongoing conversation. But he proceeds gamely. "It's wholly apocryphal, but legend says God created two gates, one that leads to the enemy and one that leads to life. The gate that leads to life, *la sendara de vida*, is somewhere in Selvarica, and many a nobleman's younger son has set off in search of it, hoping to prove himself and make his fortune. No one has succeeded, of course. But many of my people believe in its existence. They say whoever finds it will find life eternal and perfect happiness."

Silence weighs like a heavy blanket over the dining room.

Finally Alentín says in a tight voice, "Strange that I have not heard of this legend."

The conde shrugs. "I barely knew of it growing up. But Iladro reminded me." He indicates the overdressed herald beside him. "Right, Iladro?"

The herald reddens at our sudden scrutiny. The plume of his hat wobbles as he nods. "Yes, Your Grace," he says in an understated tone that belies his announcing voice. "The legend remains popular in the remote island villages." He grabs a scone from the tray and shoves it into his mouth, possibly to discourage the conde from calling on him to speak further.

"Apocryphal," Ximena mutters to herself.

"An old manuscript or two alludes to it," the conde says. "But that's how we know there's no truth to the legend, right? None of the inspired holy scriptures mentions it once."

"Indeed," Ximena says, but I hear the doubt—or possibly wonder—in her voice.

"What is 'apocryphal'?" Lady Jada asks.

Hector says, "The Apocrypha is a group of documents that were put forward as being inspired by God, but were proved by scholars and priests to be merely legends. Nothing divine about them after all."

I look at him in surprise and delight. I had no idea he knew about such things.

He regards me sidelong, his eyes dancing. "But interesting as pseudohistorical documents," he says to Lady Jada. "They say much about the attitudes and customs of the time during which they were written."

"What about you, Lady Jada?" I say, still smiling. "As wife of the mayor, can you tell me about any spectacular dishes—or legends—from Brisadulce your queen should know of?"

Lady Jada throws her shoulders back and opens her mouth to launch into what I am certain will be a treatise of profound triviality. "Your Majesty should instruct the kitchen master to prepare—"

She freezes at the sound of retching.

"Iladro?" says Conde Tristán.

The herald bends over the table, his body convulsing. He looks up, his eyes oozing tears. His delicate face is a blotchy purple.

Ximena launches across the table, a blur of ruffled skirts. She grabs his fork with one hand, forces open his jaw with the other.

Hector yanks me to my feet. With his free hand, he whisks a dagger from his vambrace. "Elisa, spit out any food in your mouth. Now."

Poison. My skin goes clammy cold. "I . . . there's nothing."

Ximena shoves the handle of the fork down Iladro's throat, saying, "Let yourself vomit, my lord. It may save your life."

And he does, in great geysers of half-digested, red-tinged pollo pibil and pastry lumps, all over the table before me. Acid singes my nostrils.

"The scone!" Belén says. "He was the only person who had one."

The kitchen master bursts into the room, yelling, "Stop! Spit out your food! The taster just—" He sees the mess on the table, and his face drains of blood. "Too late."

"Lady Jada," I order. "Find Doctor Enzo at once." She launches to her feet and runs from the dining room.

"Will he—?" the conde asks in a wavery voice, stroking his herald's arm. "Oh, Iladro, what did you—"

Hector's arm wraps across my shoulders, pulling my back against his torso as he backs us away from the table. He still holds a dagger in his free hand, though I've no idea what he thinks he can do with it.

"Water!" Ximena yells to no one in particular, and a glass appears before her. She tips it down the herald's throat. He chokes, and water spews from his mouth, but she yells something at him and he starts to gulp it down like his life depends on it, which it might. And then she makes him throw up again.

"Let's go, Elisa," Hector says, and he starts to drag me from the dining room.

But I resist. "No."

"It's not safe! We need to—"

I whirl on him. "Your sword will *not* protect me from poison." To the rest, I say, "Ximena, stay with Iladro until Doctor Enzo comes. Everyone else, with me *now*." I stride through the door to the kitchen, and everyone tumbles after me.

The kitchen is chaos. People rush everywhere to dump food and clean bowls and utensils. I catch the acrid scents of vomit and of burning bread. On the stone floor beside the chopping table lies a man I've never seen before. He is clearly dead. His eyes bulge, frozen in terror and pain. Blood-tinged vomit leaks from the corner of his mouth and puddles beside him. A girl in a maid's frock stares at him from behind the roasting spit. Tears stream down her face. Belén and the guards move to block the entrances.

"Silence!" I yell. Quiet settles, even as eyes widen with dread. "Everyone against the wall, there." I gesture, but they do not move fast enough. "Now!"

They scramble all over one another in their hurry to comply, but manage to line up neatly.

I pace in front of them. "Who prepared the scones?" I ask.

Silence. Then a timid voice says, "I did, Your Majesty. Felipe and I."

I turn on the source of that voice. It's the crying maid. "Did you poison them?"

"Oh, no, Your Majesty, I would never—"

"Where is Felipe?"

"I don't know." She can't bring herself to meet my gaze, and her maid's cap has skewed forward. It bothers me that I can't see her expression to read it.

So I reach forward and tip up her chin with my fingers. "When did you last see him?"

She swallows hard and blinks wet eyes. "I'm not sure. Maybe . . . just before we served? He said he needed wine to . . . to soak the pears. But . . . oh, God."

"Oh, God, what?"

"Pears weren't on the menu. I didn't think . . . at the time . . . I was so busy. How could I know?" Her gaze is terrified and shaky but guileless. I find myself believing her.

Without breaking her gaze, I say, "Belén, please check the wine cellar."

"At once, Your Majesty."

I step back, clenching my hands into fists. This cannot go unpunished. What will happen when the city learns that poison entered my private dining room? They will see me as weak, unable to govern my own staff, much less a country. And they will be right.

I need a show of strength. Of wrath. Something memorable.

I pace, worrying my thumbnail with my teeth. I could dismiss them all, throw them out of the palace. That would certainly be memorable. But there can be no doubt that most of them—maybe all—are innocent. If had proof, I would not hesitate to have the poisoner beheaded.

I freeze in my tracks. Is this why General Luz-Manuel had Martín executed? Merely as a show of strength? Because it was politically prudent to cast the blame *somewhere*?

Belén appears in the stone archway leading to the cellar. "He is here," he says, and I know from his grave expression that the news is not good.

"No one is to leave this kitchen," I say, and receive a flurry of "Yes, Your Majesty"s in response. "Hector, Tristán, with me."

Together we enter the cellar stair. It's steep and cool and smells of wet wood and pitch. Alongside the stair is a smooth slope for rolling barrels.

Belén is at the bottom, standing over the body of another dead man. A boy, really. He lies on his side, his arm crooked beneath his torso in an unnatural position. Vomit soaks his shirt and puddles at the base of a wine barrel.

He clutches a scrap of leather.

Hector bends to pry it from his stiffening fingers. He spreads it open and says, "A note."

"Read it."

"'Death to tyrants.'" Hector looks up. "That's all it says."

"Oh, God."

With a cry of anguish, Tristán rushes forward and sends a hard kick into the boy's flank. The body lurches; a dead arm flops hard against the ground, and something inside it cracks.

"Tristán, control yourself," I say.

The conde whirls to face me, and for the first time, I notice the wet brownish stain on his linen blouse. "But . . . Iladro, my herald . . . he might . . . he could be . . ."

"I know. My own personal physician is attending him. We'll do all we can."

His shoulders shake with rage, but he nods. "Yes, Your Majesty. Thank you."

"I'm not convinced," Belén says in his quiet voice.

"What do you mean?"

"Did this Felipe know how to read and write? If so, is this his handwriting?"

"Belén is right," Hector says, and the two share a look of accord. "It's too convenient to find him with this note clutched in his hand."

I put my thumb and forefinger to the bridge of my nose. The note is not proof—not really. But maybe I have to pretend it is.

I say, "Hector, will you learn everything you can about this boy? Maybe his family knows something."

"Yes, of course."

"Thank you. I need a demonstration. A show of strength. Tristán, what counsel would you offer me?"

His eyes narrow with the understanding that I'm testing him. "I suggest you have the kitchen staff flogged for negligence," he says evenly. "I know it's harsh, but it will do no lasting harm. You must send a clear message that you are not weak, and that you can retaliate quickly and effectively."

I breathe deeply to steady myself. Yes, a flogging. It will be awful, but better than executions or dismissals. "Thank you, Your Grace. Why don't you attend to your man now?"

He bows quickly and flees.

Hector studies me. "*Can* you?" he says gently. "I'll give the order for you, if you like."

I smother the instant feeling of relief. "No. I should order it myself. It's a sign of strength, right?" Before I can change my mind, I hurry up the stairs, Hector and Belén following after.

My kitchen staff are still lined up against the wall, under the watch of my guards. Alentín sits on the edge of the hearth, praying. Lady Jada has returned from fetching Doctor Enzo. Her eyes are wide with excitement, no doubt anxious to relate these events to everyone she knows. I find I can't bear to look at her.

I address the staff. "Felipe is dead, by his own hand. I believe he was the poisoner. I don't know if any of you conspired with him. However, I do know that you were negligent in allowing the food to be served too soon after being tasted."

I wait a few beats for it to sink in. Hopefully, they will fear the worst, and my punishment will seem mild by comparison.

"And so, tomorrow morning, you will be brought to the palace green." Someone chokes out a sob. "There you will each be flogged, in sight of the entire court." I see flashes of terror, but a few exhale relief.

I clench my hands into fists so no one can see how badly they shake. I have just ordered that innocent people be hurt, for my own political advantage. What kind of person does that? Someone like General Luz-Manuel, I guess.

A guard clears his throat. "Your Majesty, how many lashes are you ordering?"

Oh, God, lashes. I don't know anything about that. I need to hurt, not harm. How many is too many? Too few, and the punishment lacks weight.

Hector jumps in. "I suggest ten each, Your Majesty," he says.

I could hug him. "Yes, of course. Ten each." I'll have to watch it happen. Display myself at the flogging. The space between my eyes stings with threatening tears.

I must leave this room before I lose control. I take another deep breath and lift my chin to address a guard. "Hold them in the prison tower until the flogging tomorrow. Everyone else is free to go." And with that I stride from the kitchen and into the hallway.

Hector hurries to catch up. "Please allow me to accompany you," he says.

"Of course," I say wearily. "I just had to get away."

"You did well."

I don't feel like I did well at all.

He says, "I'll send Doctor Enzo to you when he has a prognosis on the conde's man."

"Thank you."

Moments later, we arrive at the door to my suite. He looks down at me, not bothering to hide his concern. "Will you be all right?"

"I hate myself right now," I admit.

He reaches out as if to touch me, hesitates, lets his arm drop. He says, "I know. But I don't. Hate you, that is." And then he's gone.

11

I pace back and forth in my suite, awaiting word from Doctor Enzo. I pray as I pace, begging God to spare Iladro's life. The Godstone suffuses me with warmth, but I know from long experience that the warmth is only an acknowledgment of my prayers, not an answer.

Mara paces right along with me, wringing her hands. "This would not have happened if I hadn't injured myself," she mutters. "If I had been the one cooking—"

Ximena has been calmly watching us. But now she grabs Mara's shoulder and stops her midstride. "Injury aside, it isn't right that the queen's lady-in-waiting cooks for eight people. For the queen, occasionally. But you will *not* cook for state dinners. You're a lady now, Mara. A noblewoman."

I stare at my nurse. Why Ximena feels compelled to argue such a point at a time like this is beyond me.

Mara peers around her to give me a stricken look. "You could have died. The kitchen master's taster is *dead.*"

"Yes," I whisper. I hate this. My taster in Orovalle died too, when I was just a princess. Hundreds of my Malficio—my desert rebels—died because of the hope I gave them. Then Humberto. King Alejandro. The guard Martín. Will my continued existence carve a bloody path through the lives around me? Will my life's greatest legacy be a wake of bodies?

I wish Hector were here. I need his solid presence, his sure-burning intelligence. Then I chide myself for weakness. My personal comfort is not as important as finding answers, and Hector is best where he is.

The rotten-pepper scent of vomit precedes Doctor Enzo, and I look up even as the guards announce his arrival.

"The herald?" I demand. "How is he?"

"He'll live."

My breath leaves me in a *whoosh* of relief as I collapse onto the bed.

"He may have stomach pain the rest of his life. He vomited blood, which means the poison ate into the lining—"

I hold up a hand to forestall further details. "What kind of poison?"

"Duerma berries, I think," he says, and I gasp. "He'll probably sleep a day or two."

"I poisoned an animagus with duerma berries once," I tell him. "It was nothing like what happened to Iladro. After digesting them, the animagus toppled over, passed out."

"You used raw berries?"

I nod.

"They're more toxic when dried and pounded into a powder. Mashed into flour, it would be almost tasteless. I suspect the powder mixed with alcohol is incredibly corrosive."

"We had wine with our meal." *All* of us.

"That would do it."

"That's why it didn't take effect on the taster as quickly. No wine."

"Rather ingenious, isn't it?"

I don't appreciate his admiring tone. "Thank you, Enzo. Good work tonight, as usual." I dismiss him with a wave of my hand.

I resume pacing. Unlike the first attempt on my life, this one was clumsy and unfocused. Ill planned. Anyone could have eaten those pastries. Everyone in the dining room could have been poisoned. There is a clue here somewhere. *Think, Elisa!*

Crickets begin their nightly serenade, and the sun disappears behind the distant palace wall so that only the faintest glow seeps through my balcony doors. Ximena lights the candles on my bedside table. Mara retrieves my nightgown and lays it out on the bed, then fetches a brush to start working on my hair.

But I'm not ready for our nightly routine. I'm about to assign them useless tasks, just to keep them occupied and out of my pacing range, when Hector returns. His face is grave.

"The assassin's employer?" I ask.

"No sign. The family knew nothing."

Disappointment is like a rock in my gut. I am desperate for answers.

"A stranger gave them gold yesterday," he continues. "Tall, young, hair slicked back with olive oil. Said he owed Felipe a debt. They gave it up eagerly once they learned what had happened."

My sweaty hands grip my skirt. "He was paid to do it!"

Hector nods. "The note was meant to scare you—if you survived."

I force my hands to release the fabric, to relax. Without meeting his eye, I say, "Maybe the poison wasn't meant for me. Maybe it was meant for someone else. The conde. Or even Alentín. He's an ambassador now, you know."

"*Honey-coconut scones,* Elisa. Distilled duerma poison, according to Enzo. It's hard to come by in Brisadulce. You have to cross the desert to find it. Someone was making a statement."

I rub at the headache forming at the bridge of my nose. "Someone who knew I poisoned the animagus with duerma plant."

"You also poisoned half the Invierne army, remember?"

"Hector, if that poison was meant for me, then someone truly wants me dead. Not taken alive, like the Inviernos do."

"That has occurred to me."

"Which means I have more than one enemy."

He says nothing, just presses his lips into a firm line. For the first time, I notice a shadow of stubble along his jaw. He is always clean shaven, as befits the commander of the Royal Guard. Either he hasn't had time today, or he forgot. It makes him look darker, fiercer.

I jump when Ximena's hand settles on my shoulder. "I wish we could get you away," she mutters. "There are too many people in Brisadulce. Too many agendas, too many dark corners."

I round on her. "No!"

She recoils, black eyes wide.

"I won't run away again. You and Papá and Alodia sent me away to keep me safe, remember?" Anger I barely knew I was holding in check rises in my throat like bile. "You forced me to marry a man who didn't love me, who hardly even acknowledged me. It didn't work out very well, did it? He's dead. And I've had more brushes with death than I can count. Running away just made . . ." I hesitate, realizing how shrill my voice is, how awful I sound. Like maybe I hate this place and this life.

She regards me with endless calm.

"I don't regret anything," I tell her.

"I know."

"But I won't run away again."

She crosses her arms and leans against the bedpost, which creaks in response. "Would you consider running *to* something?"

"What do you mean?"

She glances around at the room. Besides Mara and Hector, three guards stand watch, and as usual, their faces betray nothing of the conversation they are overhearing. They are so still and silent as to be nearly—but not quite—invisible. Ximena says, "There is something to the, er, line of research I'm engaged in that might require a long outing." She forces cheer to her face. "Maybe we can incorporate it into that tour of the country the Quorum would like you to go on."

She's talking about the gate. The one that "leads to life." And she doesn't want to discuss details in front of the guards.

Hector says, "I thought the conde's conversation grew particularly interesting tonight at dinner, before his man took ill."

"Indeed," Ximena agrees.

In the silence that ensues, I know we are thinking the same thing. The words used by the conde to describe his legend were uncannily similar to the verse carved into the rock beneath my city. *The gate that leads to life is narrow and small so that few find it.*

I say, "Our friend in the Wallows might know something."

Ximena nods. "He also might have insight into this latest attack."

The thought of seeing Storm again gives me a shudder. I imagine his too-perfect face with such clarity, dread the arrogance in his sibilant voice. But I need to take him up on his offer for information as soon as possible.

With no small amount of reluctance, I say, "I'll pay him a visit tomorrow morning."

Hector looses an exasperated breath. "Please don't. I don't know the territory. I wouldn't know how to place the guards. And the way that cavern echoes . . . there's no way you could have a private conversation."

I open my mouth to protest, to remind him that I refuse to be governed by fear, but I pause. Ignoring his advice has gotten me nearly killed.

"You're about to insist, aren't you?" he says, looking pained.

"No. I was thinking I ought to let you do your job for a change."

He gapes at me for a split second before recovering his

usual poise. "In that case, I'll send my men to fetch him tomorrow morning."

"Thank you. And if he doesn't come willingly and immediately, arrest him and bring him anyway."

He smiles. "With pleasure."

Mara steps toward me, and her face is bright and fierce. "I didn't understand any of that, and I don't care." She brandishes my brush at me. "All I know is that I am going to make breakfast for you tomorrow, and you will eat every bite."

The next morning, after eating Mara's goat-cheese omelet with diced scallions and red peppers, I must face the punishment I ordered. It's a small consolation that with everyone on the green, Hector may be able to slip the Invierno into the tower unnoticed.

With my entourage of guards and ladies, I parade through the inner courtyard to the beat of a slow marching drum. A huge crowd has assembled, and they part to make way for me. I wear a gown with wine-red brocade and gold embroidery, and I regret the choice as sweat pools under my arms and between my breasts. I hold my head high, in spite of the weight of my crown.

It's the same place where Martín was killed, the same dais, the same large crowd. But this time, I am a willing participant.

The kitchen staff are already in place. They face inward in a circle, their hands tied above their heads to a thick pillory made from the massive trunk of a banyan tree. All twelve fit around it easily. They are naked from the waist up, even the maids.

I clench my jaw to keep it from trembling as I mount the dais and sit in its makeshift wooden throne. Ximena and Mara stand at either shoulder. From here, I have a perfect view of the accused and the sea of spectators beyond. Some jostle for a better look. A young boy sits on his father's shoulders. Everyone is wide-eyed with fear, or maybe excitement.

A man approaches, carrying a long red cushion, and kneels at my feet. Is he the same man who beheaded Martín?

Like the prisoners, he's naked from the waist up. A black shawl covers his head and sweeps around to shield his mouth and nose. Ridged white scars slash across his tautly muscled torso and shoulders. He holds out the cushion. On it are various flogging instruments: a rod, a willow switch, a cat-o'-nine-tails, and a leather whip coiled like a snake except for the jagged bit of steel tied to the end.

Tears prick at the back of my throat.

The executioner whispers, in a voice as scarred and used-up as his skin, "Your Majesty, you must choose the instrument of punishment."

It takes a moment for his words to sink in, and when they do, despair settles over me like a hot heavy blanket. Of course I must.

They are arranged in order of potential damage. I don't want these people harmed. But I also cannot choose the mildest punishment.

I say, in my best queen voice, "Use the switch."

The scarred man faces the audience and lifts the switch high; it bends slightly under its own weight. The crowd roars approval.

And then I force myself to watch unflinchingly as, slowly and methodically, he flogs my kitchen staff. The switch slaps wetly against bare skin, sending tears stinging to my eyes. Welts rise up on their backs, and they arch away from the blows, but the pillory leaves them nowhere to go. The scarred man is very thorough, his aim precise. He varies the switch's landing so that every part of their flesh suffers its brutality.

A few refuse to cry out, but not most, and their raw, anguished voices arrow straight into my heart. One boy, the youngest by far, weeps openly, his cheek pressed against the pillory.

I am a stone. I am ice. I feel nothing.

Only the kitchen master remains standing after the tenth lash. The others sag on their feet, held in place by the manacles at their wrists.

The scarred man returns to me and bows. The switch in his huge hand drips blood. "It is done, Your Majesty."

"Thank you," I choke out.

"Do you wish to address the people?" he asks.

No, of course not. I can't wait to get away, to toss off my crown and bury my head in my pillows.

But then the small boy at the edge of the crowd, the one on his father's shoulders, spits on the maid who prepared the scones with Felipe. A viscous wad slips down her sweaty cheek and plops onto her bared breast.

I launch to my feet and stride to the edge of the dais. The crowd hushes.

"We consider their crime of negligence to be paid in full," I call out. "There will be no more recriminations. Anyone who seeks to do them physical harm, or harass them, or even"—I look pointedly at the little boy—"spit on them, will be dealt with severely."

I whirl away from the crowd and move toward Ximena, whispering, "I am shaking quite a lot and could use your arm to aid my dramatic exit." I suddenly wish Hector were here. I always feel so much safer, stronger, when he is at my side.

But she offers it at once, and together we float down the dais in what I dare hope is a show of regal righteousness. We depart the green far more quickly than we came, which is good now that I'm tasting a more acrid version of Mara's omelet in the back of my throat.

12

Hector returns to my suite with the unsurprising news that the Invierno was reluctant to answer my summons and had to be arrested. I take just enough time to lose my crown and change into a simpler gown before rushing out again. I'm glad for the haste—it gives me little opportunity to dwell on the flogging.

I've never been inside the prison tower. It's the highest point of the palace, and I expect that from its topmost chamber, I could see everything from the great sand desert and the walls of Brisadulce, across the merchant's circle and the Wallows, to the docks and the blue horizon beyond.

The tower is made of gray limestone, a dull and dirty contrast to the coral sandstone of its shorter brothers. It rises like a blight on the sky, and I see how impossible it would be to escape such a place. There is only one way up or down, and that is the stairway inside its walls.

It's an odd group that accompanies me to interrogate our prisoner: a one-armed priest, an aging nurse, a Quorum lord, and, unexpectedly, a seven-year-old prince. Hector had to cancel their daily swordsmanship lesson, and little Rosario was determined to come from the moment he learned the reason.

Our group is nothing if not memorable, and I curse myself for thoughtlessness. The news that someone of vast import is being kept here will be palacewide by evening.

Before we step through the arched entryway, I bend down and grasp Rosario's shoulder. "You're sure you want to come, Highness? There's an Invierno up there. He looks a lot like . . ." *Like the animagi who killed your papa.* "Er, like those other Inviernos we saw."

He puts his hand to the wooden practice sword at his belt. He glares at me, saying, "I'm not afraid."

I know better than to smile. "Well, *I* am. Just a little."

"I'll protect you. Like Hector does."

The boy has always idolized my guard, but even more so since his father's death. "That does make me feel better. Thank you."

As I straighten, Hector catches my eye and shrugs. I nod in response. If Rosario thinks he is ready to face an Invierno again, it would feel cruel to forbid it.

The moment we leave the sunny courtyard for the shade of the tower, I am hit full in the face by the scents of sweat and urine and moldy straw. The tower guards lurch up from a rough table strewn with playing cards and snap to attention. They are Luz-Manuel's soldiers, not Royal Guard, and they eye us warily as we pass. I hope they will do as ordered and keep quiet about their latest prisoner.

Hector leads us to the creaking stair that zigzags up one side of the stone wall. The inner structure consists of a series of wooden platforms, with huge beams and smaller wooden trusses to hold each platform in place. The stairway opens up to the platforms at regular intervals, and in the dim light provided by long slits in the wall, I see people, ten or so to a platform. They are barely clothed, scrawny, filthy, hairy. I can't begin to guess their ages. Each is manacled to the wall, out of reach of the stairway.

One, a woman with wild hair, strains against her bonds and spits at me. The glob lands on the planking near my feet. Ximena moves toward her, but I put a hand to her forearm.

"She suffers enough," I say.

Another prisoner, a man with a gray beard that swallows his face, gives the spitting woman a swift kick to the ankle. "Some of us remember," he says to me, and his voice has the harsh accent of the dockworkers. "We remember what you did for us, Your Majesty."

As Hector hustles me away, I wish I'd had the presence of mind to thank the man, to let him know how much his words of support mean to me.

I can't help but wonder what they all did to wind up in this awful place. Surely something terrible. By the time we reach the top, I am breathless, nauseated, and wracked by uncertainty. Maybe I shouldn't have had the Invierno brought here. All he did was refuse a royal summons.

The final, highest platform is the least squalid, with several extra slits for light and air, a small cot, and a slop bucket instead of rushes. But Storm obviously does not appreciate the distinction. He paces back and forth like a restless cat, all lithe grace and hunting fury. Ankle manacles are hidden by his long black cloak, but they rattle with every step.

When he sees us, he growls deep inside his chest, which sends shivers across the back of my shoulders. It's not a sound I've heard a human make before.

A tiny hand slips into mine, and I glance down to make sure Rosario is all right. But the hand gripping mine is the only indication Rosario is frightened. He leans forward, eyes narrowed, glaring at his enemy. I give him a light squeeze.

"Hello, Storm," I say in an even voice.

He whirls, and his moss-green eyes snap to mine. "You rank cow," he spits, and Hector's sword whisks from its scabbard. "We had a bargain."

Without breaking the Invierno's gaze, I put my free hand to Hector's chest to forestall anything hasty. "And you broke it. You refused audience."

"I would have gladly accepted audience in my village."

I laugh, genuinely amused at his audacity. "Surely you realize my predicament? There have been two attempts on my life. One not far from the underground village you call home. Of course I couldn't risk it."

"And yet you would risk my life by bringing me here. I'll be dead within two days. You have surely killed me."

I decide to give him the honesty he claims his people value so much. "Given a choice between my life and yours, I will choose mine. Every time. Without hesitation."

Some of the fight fades from his eyes. "I would do the same," he concedes.

"I plan either to let you go or move you to a different location. I haven't decided yet."

With a lift of his sharp chin, he indicates my companions. "Who are these people? The cripple and the old woman? I recognize only the commander and the prince."

"The 'cripple' is my friend Alentín; the 'old woman' is my friend Ximena."

"They must be important for you to bring them." When he realizes I'm not going to tell him, he shrugs and says, "What must I do to be let go?"

"Tell us about the gate that leads to life."

His eyes widen. He uses hooked forefingers to tuck his honey-gold hair behind his ears, and the motion startles me for its normalcy, its humanity. He turns his back to us. I wish I could see his face.

Still facing the wall, he says, "Take me with you."

"What? Take you where?"

"South. When you go in search of it."

"Of what? We haven't decided to go any—"

He whirls, and his green eyes spark. "You'll go. Make no mistake. It is the will of God."

It's utterly infuriating, the number of people I've encountered in my life who claimed to be the authority on God's will.

"I'm losing patience, Storm. Tell me everything you know about it, or you will never leave this tower on your feet."

His lips purse as he weighs the options. Then: "The gate

that leads to life is a place of mystery and power across the sea. But it is impossible to navigate there. Only those chosen by God can find it, much less pass through."

"And why would anyone pass through?"

"Because it leads to the *zafira*."

The Godstone leaps. I double over with the intensity, gasping for breath, as the stone pounds wave after wave of heat through my body.

"Elisa!" Hector's arm wraps around my waist. "Ximena, help me—"

"I'm all right," I gasp out. "Just give me a moment." It reacted this way once before—when I destroyed the animagi with my Godstone amulet. *What is it, God? What are you trying to tell me?*

Hector loosens his hold with slow reluctance and steps away. I force breath into my body until I can straighten again. The Godstone continues to pulse, though with less power, and my bodice sticks, sweat soaked, to my skin. Rosario's hand now grips mine so tightly that I can hardly feel my fingers.

The Invierno regards me through the lidded eyes of a smug, well-fed kitten. "Oh, yes, you will go."

Ximena demands, "What is this *zafira*?"

He regards her contemptuously.

She repeats her question in the Lengua Classica, adding, "If you don't tell us, we will leave you here to rot or be assassinated, whichever comes first."

If he is surprised that she speaks his language, he doesn't show it, but he says, "The *zafira* is the soul of the world, the magic crawling beneath our feet. The animagi use it to power their amulets. But those who pass through the gate can harness the power of the *zafira* directly, without the barrier of the world's skin. And it is power beyond imagining."

My body tingles with the Godstone's heat, and maybe with curiosity. *Power beyond imagining.* "How do you know about this?" I demand. "Is it in a scripture? Is it legend?"

"My people have always known. But we have been cut off from it. For more than a thousand years, we have had to grasp at the *zafira* through the world's shell, our power a fraction of what it once was."

"So that's it," Hector says. "That's what the Inviernos want."

I look up to see his eyes narrowed and distant. "Hector?"

"They've been campaigning for port rights for years. They want to search for it."

"Is that true?" I ask Storm.

"It is."

"So why reveal it now?"

"It is as I told you. I am Your Majesty's loyal subject."

"It must be terrible to subject yourself to a rank cow."

He nods in solemn agreement. "Indeed."

I consider him a moment. He is too valuable to risk. "I'm going to let you go. I'll send guards to escort you in secrecy. But next time you *must* answer my summons."

He opens his mouth as if to protest, then snaps it closed. Instead, he bows. "Yes, Your Majesty."

I turn to go, and my companions follow my lead. I'm sure Alentín and Ximena are itching to get back to the archive and scour it for references to the *zafira*. But Rosario yanks on my hand, stopping me. I look down into pleading eyes and a trembling lower lip. "What is it, Highness?"

He gathers himself up, blinks a few times, turns to face the Invierno.

Rosario says, "You are a very, *very* bad man." And he releases my hand and flees down the stairs ahead of us.

Hector and I exchange a puzzled look. He says, "I think Rosario just needed to . . . say something?"

"I'm not, you know," says Storm. "A bad man. I've always tried to do right, to follow the path of God."

I shrug. *"From the mouths of innocents flows truth."* I head for the stairs, not bothering to gauge his response. We hurry down, past the startled soldiers at their card table, and after our prince.

We find him alone in the courtyard. The sun glints off tears streaming down his cheeks. He wipes at them furiously, and we all slow down to give him time to compose himself.

In the most casual tone I can muster, I say, "I have a lesson now with Hector, but Father Alentín might have a moment to take you to the kitchens for some coconut pie."

He nods, gulping. Then he wraps my waist in a quick hug. He lets me ruffle his hair for just a moment before pushing off and finding Alentín's hand. The priest winks at me over his shoulder, and I watch them saunter off together toward the kitchens.

"He's a remarkable boy," Ximena says.

"He is. I just worry sometimes that he is . . . damaged. He watched his father burn."

"Alejandro was damaged too," Hector says, his brow furrowed. He rubs the pommel of his sword with his thumb. "Perhaps it is the price of ruling."

As I head back to my suite, flanked by my guard and my guardian, I wonder at his words, afraid to ask if he thinks I am damaged too.

As I anticipated, instead of staying to observe my self-defense lesson with Hector, Ximena hurries off to the monastery archive. Fernando steps outside to guard the door to the king's suite. The rest take up their posts in my own chambers. Like last time, I am dressed in my desert garb: soft breeches, a loose blouse, leather boots.

Hector's brow is still furrowed, and he paces back and forth like a restless cat. I search for a way to break the silence. "Er . . . will I stomp on your foot again today?"

"No," he snaps, and I almost take an involuntary step back. "Today, you'll learn which body parts should be sacrificed in defense of others." His words are clipped and harsh, his gaze dark with intensity.

"For instance," he continues, "it's better to block a sword with your forearm and let the bones shatter than allow someone access to your throat. And I'll show you which part of your forearm to use so that you're less likely to bleed out. After that, I'll demonstrate some pressure points, places on the body where you can inflict great pain with very little effort. And then—"

"Hector."

"—we'll do some stretching exercises to give you better

range of motion, especially in your arms and shoulders. It's easier to slip from someone's grasp without injury if—"

"Hector!"

"—the muscles are already limber and flexible. We need to get you thinking of your elbows, the crown of your head, even your chin, as potential weapons at your disposal. After that—"

"HECTOR! Stop."

His mouth snaps closed.

"You can't possibly teach me all of that in one afternoon."

He resumes pacing. "In that case, we'll get as far as we can. I think it's best we start with pressure points and then move—"

Swiftly I close the distance between us and cup his face with my hands.

He freezes, inhaling sharply.

We regard each other for a long moment. His jaw is warm in my palms. My right ring finger trails into his soft hairline. I watch carefully as the mania fades from his eyes.

"I need you to be clear-headed, Hector. I need that from you more than anyone."

He whispers, "I can't fail to protect you too." With gentle fingers, he peels my hands from his face. They're so much bigger, rough with calluses. "He was my best friend. I let him die. I dream . . ." His voice trails off.

"That's your nightmare, isn't it? The one you wouldn't tell me about? You dream of Alejandro's death."

"No. Not him."

I expect him to drop my hands, to put distance between us the way he always does. But he merely changes the subject.

"Elisa, you take too many risks. Every day. Like just now, interviewing the Invierno yourself. The animagus who burned himself alive could have hurt you if he wanted to. We were helpless to stop him. You almost died in the catacombs. And the poison . . ."

"You saved my life in the catacombs."

"I shouldn't have had to."

No, he shouldn't have. My face grows hot with shame. Hector is the most honorable man I know, devoted to his country, to his duty, to me. And I have prevented him from doing what is most important to him. "You advised me to cancel the birthday parade. You advised me not to go to the catacombs alone. You can't be blamed for my stubbornness."

He looks down at our entwined hands and mumbles, "And yet I like your stubbornness."

And abruptly, he releases them. I let them fall to my sides, where they ache coldly.

He says, "Dismiss me."

"No."

"I've failed to protect you. Someone else should—"

"I don't want anyone else." My own words echo in the air around me, hammering me with their truth, and I can't contain my slight gasp. *I don't want anyone else.*

He runs a hand through his hair, looks everywhere but at me. Silence stretches between us.

"I've been a fool," I admit finally. "I've been so afraid of seeming weak. Of being like . . . like Alejandro. I've made bad decisions. Hector, you are the person I trust most in the world.

I would do better to heed your counsel. And from now on, I will. But I promise you . . ." I force a smile. "If I die? You are definitely dismissed." I hold my breath and await his response. I know the morbid joke will either infuriate him or put him at ease.

After a moment he shakes his head ruefully. He returns my forced smile with his own feeble attempt and says, "In that case, today I will teach you nothing more than the warm-up series practiced by the Royal Guard. In addition to strengthening and stretching your muscles, I think you'll find it meditative and calming."

I exhale my relief. "Good. I could use 'meditative and calming' right now."

"Turn around." From behind, he reaches for my right arm and gently lifts it to shoulder level. "I'll guide your movements."

But something in the air has changed. I am too deeply aware of the warmth of his nearness, the scents of mink oil and aloe shaving gel, the touch of his callused but gentle fingers. And I am forced to conclude that doing the slow, dancelike warm-up exercises of the Royal Guard with Hector as my partner is not calming at all.

13

That evening, I send Mara to bed early for some healing rest. Ximena helps me don my nightgown, then leaves for a late night of poring over musty documents with Fathers Nicandro and Alentín.

In spite of everything that has happened, in spite of my doubts about God and his will and his words, I still find the *Scriptura Sancta* to be a soothing balm to the day's stresses, and I look forward to reading each night by candlelight before sleeping.

But I am too restless tonight. The words blur on the page. After I've read the same sentence several times without comprehending, I toss the manuscript onto the quilt and swing my legs over the edge of my bed. I grab the candle and its brass holder from my bedside table and carry it toward the atrium.

In the archway, I say to the guards, "I would like some privacy, please." They oblige by turning their backs as I enter.

The water in my ever-circulating bathing pool shimmers blue, and I don't have to look up at the skylight to know that the moon is full or near to it. As I approach with my candle, shards of reflected flame-light dance on the surface.

I set the candle on the tiled edge of the pool.

Before me is my vanity mirror—and my own reflection. I wear a silk nightgown of pale lavender edged in delicate lace. The looseness of the gown drapes pleasantly, flatteringly, and my thick sleeping braid snakes around one shoulder almost to my waist. My skin glows in the candlelight. I feel almost beautiful.

I light the oil lamp on my vanity so I can see better.

The outline of my Godstone is sharp against the thin material. I slip the nightgown's straps from my shoulders and let it fall to the ground.

I study my naked reflection, curious. I try to see myself through someone else's eyes. Would someone else look past the welted red scar, the faceted blue of my Godstone to notice the slight softness in my lower belly? The way my inner thighs just brush when I stand? My legs will never be willowy and elegant like my older sister's, but they're straight and strong.

Finally I allow my gaze to drift toward my breasts. They are the softest part of me, heavy enough that during the day, it is more comfortable to have them bound in a bodice. Unbound, they swoop low and full, enough to balance my hips nicely. Staring at them, I become acutely aware of cool air against their dark tips.

Ximena always told me men would notice my breasts. I've never noticed anyone noticing. But maybe I wouldn't. Mara says I'm pathetically ignorant in matters of love.

Slowly, face flushing, I lift my right hand to cup my left breast. I squeeze gently, and it is a tiny battle to decide what I want to understand most: the feel of a hand on my breast or a breast in my hand.

"Elisa?"

I whirl, hand dropping.

It's Mara. She stands in the doorway to the attendants' quarters, her hair mussed, her eyes heavy with sleep.

"I thought I heard something. Are you all right?"

She's seen me naked a hundred times, but I have a vague sensation that I've been caught at something shameful. "I'm fine. Couldn't sleep."

She regards me a moment as if considering. Then she beckons with one hand. "Why don't you come sit with me awhile?"

I crouch to grab the puddle of silk at my feet and hurriedly slip my arms through the straps. I stand and follow Mara into her room.

Mindful of her wounded stomach, she lowers herself onto one of the bottom bunks and pats the mattress beside her. "Sit," she says, as if she were the queen and I the maid.

I sit.

"You can tell me anything, you know," she says.

"I know."

A shaft of moonlight edges through the high window and hits the opposite wall above our heads, leaving us in shadow. It is the darkness and her patient silence that give me the courage to ask, "Mara, have you ever had a lover?"

She doesn't hesitate. "Yes. Two."

"Oh." How can someone so young have had two lovers already? I'm desperate to ask about them, about what it was like, if either of them broke her heart. But I can't make my mouth say the words.

"I'll tell you about them, if you like," she says.

Oh, thank God. "All right. Yes."

"The first was when I was barely fifteen. He was two years older, a virgin like me. We flirted for a week or two. He was the handsomest boy I'd ever seen. One day I took my father's sheep to a high canyon to graze. He followed, and I thought it was the most romantic thing in the world. We started kissing, and then we were taking each other's clothes off, and then I realized that the rocky ground was poking into my back, and it was very cold outside, and the sheep started drifting away. . . . I changed my mind about what we were doing. But I didn't say anything. I just endured. It was over after a few painful seconds. The next day in the village, he ignored me. We hardly spoke to each other during the next year."

I stare at her shadowy outline in horror. "That . . . I'm so sorry. It sounds . . . terrifying."

She shrugs. "It wasn't so bad. You know, my father was the priest of our village. Very strict. He used to say he could tell when a girl had lost her virginity by the way she walked. And I walked around very carefully for days after, terrified that he would know. But he never did. I was exactly the same person after as I was before. Just, maybe, a little wiser."

My heart is pounding. "Was it awful afterward?" I ask. "To be ignored like that?"

"Yes. I wish I'd waited, had the courage to say no or push him away. But the awfulness didn't last. We both met someone else."

"Oh?"

She takes a deep breath, releases it. "Julio was a little older. Not as handsome, but so much kinder. I used to make a goat-milk scone with pine nuts that I smeared with honeyed apricots. I sold it at market every week. He always bought several, and he always lingered to talk. It was months before he kissed me. Months more before we made love, which by the way was wonderful. We made love a lot. As often as possible. He was going to ask my father for my hand."

Softly I ask, "What happened to him?" Though I think I know.

"He was killed when Inviernos burned our village. Just before I met you in Father Alentín's rebel camp."

I remember. She was so sad at first. Meeting God's chosen one seemed to bring her comfort. "Oh, Mara."

"I still miss him. But I also know how lucky I am. I could have been pregnant when he died, for we were careless. My father could have found out and beaten me for it." She points to the scar above her eyelid. "I have another scar like this one between my shoulder blades. But Julio saw past the scars and found me beautiful."

Her voice catches a little on the word "beautiful," so I reach an arm around her shoulder and give her a squeeze. "You *are* beautiful."

She laughs. "I know! Even with these awful scars. Julio

always said he loved my smile. And my nose! Admit it, my nose is perfect."

"Your nose is perfect."

She leans into me. Her soft hair smells of honeysuckle. Her voice trembles a little when she says, "I do worry sometimes, since being burned by the animagi, that maybe I'm *too* scarred now. And burn scars have a particular awfulness, all ridged and warped and oddly colored. I may never take a lover again. I couldn't bear for someone I cared about to . . . to be repulsed."

It's a feeling I understand well. I used to dread the moment when Alejandro would turn away from me in disgust. But he died before I found the courage—or maybe the desire—to be naked before him.

"And I worry that what I shared with Julio is something that only happens once to a person," Mara says. "Maybe I've used up my love luck." She shrugs.

"I worry about that too."

She sighs. "I liked Humberto. He was always smiling, always cheerful. I didn't realize you were lovers until you told me about him."

"We weren't."

"You never . . . ?"

"Never."

And somehow she understands that by saying "never," I'm not just talking about Humberto, for she says, "You will. As queen, it's inevitable. You will marry, and everyone will pressure you to have a child so that there is more than one heir to the throne."

"You make it sound so calculating."

"Oh, it often is. But after marrying you could take a lover. Most of the royals do, or so I've heard."

I'm glad the darkness hides my flushed face. "I couldn't. When I married Alejandro, he had a lover already. It was . . . hurtful. Even though there was no intimacy between us."

"I see." And I know she does. I grab her hand and squeeze tight. I could never say it aloud, but I hope she understands how glad I am that she is here with me tonight instead of Ximena.

Her voice turns mischievous. "Well, maybe you'll get lucky. Maybe you'll marry a man who is rich and powerful and wise *and* wonderful to be naked with."

I can't help the giggle that bubbles from my mouth.

"Maybe," she says, "you should ask all your suitors to drop their breeches so you can inspect the merchandise."

"Mara!"

"You could make it a royal command."

I toss a pillow at her.

She just laughs at my discomfort. But then she sobers and says, "You're beautiful too, you know. When you get intense, you *spark*. And you have the kind of hair any man would want to get tangled in."

Of its own accord, my hand goes to my braid, strokes it. I've always liked my hair. Would a man really notice it?

Mara adds, "You don't have to settle for a first time like mine."

I shift the subject. "Well, if I ever meet that young man, I'll . . . er . . . speak sternly to him."

"Oh, you have already. It was Belén."

I am stunned. "I thought . . . he and Cosmé . . ."

"Yes. But that was after."

I had no idea the two knew each other before we formed the Malficio. What must it be like for Mara to have him show up here in the palace? I say, "I can make sure you never encounter him while he is here."

"No need. I'm quite over it. We even got to be friends again when we stayed in Father Alentín's camp." She stands. "And *you*, my queen, need to get some rest. Full schedule tomorrow."

I stand. On impulse, I wrap my arms around her. She freezes for a split second, but then she returns my embrace. "Thank you," I whisper.

After I creep back to bed and blow out my candle, my thoughts are still too busy, my skin too warm, for easy sleep. It's terrifying to consider that I might someday share a bed with a man who is a stranger, a calculated alliance, someone who might not care for me at all.

The next evening, escorted by Hector and several guards, I am hurrying toward my office for appointments with a few more suitors when Conde Eduardo intercepts us.

"May I walk with you, Your Majesty?" he asks.

Ugh. "Please." Hector moves aside to give him room. I hope the conde is not planning to intrude on my meetings again.

Eduardo is formally dressed as always, with gold epaulets that mark him as both a high conde and a Quorum lord. My nose stings at the sharp mix of tallow and palm oil, which means his close-cropped black beard has suffered a recent repair.

"I hear you visited the prison tower yesterday," he says.

"Hmm," I say noncommittally.

"And that the young prince accompanied you."

Once again, I curse myself for thoughtlessness. I should not have sent Storm to the tower, no matter how much I wanted to put him in his place. Now I must give an account or raise further suspicions. And I must say something that satisfies Eduardo enough that he won't pursue little Rosario with his questions.

In response to my silence, he adds, "The prison guards say it was a man. Tall, cowled. He only stayed for a few hours before being escorted away by the Royal Guard."

"Yes, that's an accurate description." My mind races. What to tell him? The truth will only lead to more questions about where the Invierno came from and what I want with him. I'm not ready to reveal the cavern beneath the Wallows or the fact that I'm using Storm to learn more about the Godstone.

Which leads me to the disconcerting realization that I do not trust Conde Eduardo, that my distrust goes well beyond that of mere political machinations. He is my own Quorum lord, a man who was a great ally during our war with Invierne. But my every instinct screams caution.

"Your Majesty—"

"Eduardo, obviously there are things we must discuss, but I'm afraid a quick jaunt through the hallway will not do justice to all I have to tell you." I give him my winningest smile.

"Do you think we could call a special Quorum meeting soon? Maybe two days hence?"

He frowns. "That's the day of the Deliverance Gala."

I feign surprised disappointment. "Of course. Thank you for reminding me. And everyone will be exhausted from the festivities the day after. So perhaps four days from now?"

I've trapped him neatly. He can't push without seeming desperate or impolitic. Still frowning, he nods and says, "I'll let everyone know and make arrangements."

"Thank you, Your Grace."

"One last thing before I leave you to your errands."

"Oh?" *What now?* I slow down, realizing I had unconsciously increased my pace as if to get away.

"Lord Liano has expressed a strong desire to see you again. I would take it as a personal favor if you would grant him a dance or two at the gala."

I school my features into perfect pleasantness and say, "I would be happy to."

He bows. "Until the gala, Your Majesty."

I incline my head, and he strides away.

All my breath leaves me. I hadn't known I was holding it.

"That was well done," Hector whispers once we are a safe distance away.

Strange how I can brush off Ximena's praise as the ravings of a madly affectionate nurse, but kind words from Hector feel like drops of water in the desert. "Thank you. But Hector, *four days.* That's how long we have to come up with something plausible."

"We'll do it. Somehow."

"You and I should meet with—" My Godstone turns to ice.

"Elisa?"

"Hector! Something—"

He whirls with lightning speed, placing himself in my path, as an arrow meant for me impales the back of his shoulder.

He gasps. The blood drains from his face.

Heedless of the shaft sticking from his flesh, he grabs me, pushes me against the wall. "To the queen!" he yells, and my guards hem me in on all sides in a smooth maneuver that comes only from long practice.

Hector turns to face whatever is coming, sword drawn, and now I see that the arrow is lower than I thought. Below his shoulder blade. In his ribs. Bright blood spreads across his tunic. *Oh, God.*

An arrow whistles down the corridor and clatters harmlessly against a forearm shield. Another *thunks* into a guard's calf muscle. He cries out but does not break formation.

More arrows spear down the corridor from the opposite direction. We are trapped.

"Should I pursue?" a guard asks. "See if I can break through?"

"No!" Hector says. "They're trying to lure us into doing exactly that. Stay tight. They may not attack openly."

So we wait. Hector's back is to me, and I am lodged between him and the wall. Sweat breaks out at the nape of his neck. His skin is as white as an Invierno's.

Please, God, I pray furiously, my fingertips to my navel.

Not Hector. Keep him safe. Keep all my guards safe.

A crazy thought occurs to me. "Hector, shouldn't we yell for help?"

He actually laughs. "Yes, yes of course!"

So we do, every single one of us, and my voice soars over them all.

In moments, I hear running footsteps, the clang of steel on steel. Someone comes to our rescue.

The blood from Hector's wound drips to the floor now. My head swims at the sight. *Don't you dare faint, Elisa.*

Then something about the smell, metallic and hot, snaps me back to myself. It's familiar.

It's war.

I know exactly what Cosmé would do. "Hector, I need to break off the arrow shaft."

"Wait . . . what?" His voice is breathy with pain. I hope the arrowhead has not embedded itself in bone.

"You may need to use that arm. Can't risk the shaft getting knocked around. Please."

He twists to give me an easy grip. "Hurry."

Though I watched Cosmé do this a few times in our rebel camp, I never did it myself. My teeth are chattering and my hands shake, from the icy Godstone or from fear I cannot tell as I wrap both hands around it. Cosmé always braced the body part, snapped hard and fast.

He hisses from pain. "Snap lower," he says. "As close to my ribs as possible."

I move my hands until one rests against his back. The

sounds of fighting come closer. *Don't think, Elisa. Just do.*

With a grunt, I snap the shaft in two. The jagged end snags my palm, drawing blood. I toss the shaft to the ground and wipe my hand on my skirt.

Hector sways on his feet. Instinctively I wrap my arms around his waist to hold him up. He leans against me a moment, then straightens, breathing hard. "It's all right. I'm all right." But I'm not so sure. I know he can handle the pain, but his body could go into shock.

A flurry of bodies approaches. I see glinting blades, swinging limbs, a wooden shield. "To the queen!" calls a voice I recognize.

It's Conde Tristán. He works his way toward us, accompanied by men dressed in the sky blue and ivory of Selvarica. The assailants are no one I recognize. I count five, but in the chaos I can't be sure. They're dirty and unshaven and clothed in little more than rags, but they wield quality blades and bows.

Tristán cuts through attackers with astonishing speed, a short sword in one hand, a dagger in the other. His fighting style is beautiful, almost like a dance. He and his companions give no quarter, and the attackers cannot draw their bows.

Now that we have reinforcements, Hector gestures for three guards to investigate the opposite end of the corridor, and they take off running. The wounded guard is swaying on his feet, and Hector yanks him back toward me, saying, "Don't engage. Defend the queen."

Only two attackers remain. Hector lunges at one and pierces him cleanly through the breast. Tristán leaps, whipping his sword around toward the other as I yell, "I need him alive!"

The conde adjusts midair, lands easily, sends the hilt into the attacker's temple. The filthy man crumples to the ground. The Godstone's ice fades and is replaced by soft warmth.

My guards, Hector, Tristán, the men from Selvarica all look around at one another, in that shared moment of relief and triumph I've seen a dozen times before. Bodies litter the corridor. Tristán nudges one with the toe of his boot and watches for movement. Nothing.

"Mercenaries?" Tristán says.

Hector nods. "They fought poorly, and their attack was ill conceived. They might not even know their employer."

I point out, "There's no way men dressed like that can afford weapons like those."

"We'll need to question the one His Grace conked on the head," says Hector. "But he may not be able to tell us . . ." He sways.

I jump forward, lodge myself under his armpit, and wrap his arm around my shoulder. Blood soaks his shirt. It smears all over the skin of my neck, seeps into my bodice.

"Find Doctor Enzo!" I say to no one in particular. "Tell him to meet us in the commander's quarters."

Hector is almost limp in my arms. Fear stabs at my gut.

"Conde Tristán, can you escort us to the barracks?"

"Of course." He gestures to one of his own men. "Stay with the unconscious one. Tie his ankles and wrists. Roll him onto his side in case he vomits."

And we're off, down the corridor toward the barracks. Hector sags hard against my shoulder, and his feet drag. My thighs burn with effort as each step pounds a prayerful rhythm through my head: *Not Hector, not Hector, not Hector.*

14

HE is passed out by the time we reach his quarters, and Conde Tristán supports most of his weight as we drag him inside. The other guards help us lay him gently on his bed.

Doctor Enzo rushes in, followed by two assistants in gray frocks. "Too much blood," he murmurs. "Roll him onto his side and cut off his shirt," he orders one assistant. "And you," he says to a guard, "get me hot water and clean rags, as many as you can find. We need to clean him up so I can see exactly where he's bleeding from once I push the arrow through. Your Majesty, please step back."

I realize I'm hovering, but I don't move. "Is he . . . will he . . . ?"

He whirls and pushes me back by the shoulders until I hit the wall. "I suggest you start praying," he says.

Staring at Hector's pale form, I slide down the wall to the floor and pull my knees to my chest. Tristán settles beside me. He grabs my hand and says, "You care about him very much."

I nod. "Hector is . . . he's one of my dearest friends."

"Then I'll stay here and pray with you for a while."

"Thank you," I whisper. It's no use telling him I've prayed for people I care about before, that it didn't help.

Doctor Enzo yells at an assistant to light a fire in the hearth and heat the poker.

As Tristán murmurs a prayer beside me, my hand clasped in his, I can hardly focus on the words. I can only stare, horrified, as Doctor Enzo takes what looks like a man's razor with a long handle and begins to cut around the arrowhead.

"Interesting," the doctor says. "Very interesting."

"What?" I demand, interrupting Tristán's prayer.

"It almost split the rib," he says. "Right on the lung, so I can't push through. I'll have to pull it, but the arrowhead is scored. It will do some damage coming out."

But Hector's skin is too blanched, his breathing too shallow. Sweat sheens his cheeks. I don't know that he can survive more injury.

I find myself praying anyway; I don't know what else to do. I close my eyes, lean my forehead against Tristán's, and pray in earnest, letting the Godstone radiate its deceptive calm throughout my body. I refuse to cease praying, to open my eyes, even when Hector's unconscious grunt tells me Enzo has yanked the arrow out. Even when a hot poker hisses against flesh and the scent of burned blood fills the room.

The doctor and his assistants are cleaning up, removing blood-soaked rags and mopping the floor near Hector's bed when Tristán shakes my shoulder gently. "I must see to the man I knocked on the head," he says. "Find out what he knows."

I had forgotten about him. "Oh, yes, please do." He rises and heads for the door. "Tristán?" He turns back around. "Thank you. For coming to our rescue. For staying with me."

He bows low. "Is it all right to leave you here?"

"I'm safe in the barracks of my own Royal Guard."

"Of course. By your leave." And he exits Hector's quarters.

Hector's quarters. I've never been here before. I look around, unsurprised to find it austerely beautiful. His bed, his wardrobe, even the undyed woolen rug at my feet speak of elegant simplicity with their clean lines and subdued colors and perfect craftsmanship. On one wall hangs a painting, the only splash of true color in the place. It's of a vineyard, and rows of grapevines heavy with bloated grapes scallop over golden hills, fading into the sunset. Several manuscripts, even a few books, are piled haphazardly on his nightstand beside a half-melted candle—the only bit of disorderliness.

This is where Hector sleeps. And judging by the manuscripts, where he spends what little free time I allow him. I breathe deep. The place even smells of him—leather oil and aloe shaving jelly and a hint of sweat.

The doctor and his assistants head toward the door, arms laden with bloody rags. "Your Majesty, I need to see to the other guard. I hear he has a leg wound?"

"Wait. Tell me about Hector."

"He lost too much blood, and the arrow nicked his lungs. I couldn't keep him from going into shock. He is unlikely to survive, even with my considerable skill."

My vision tunnels and my bodice is suddenly too tight and hot.

"Are you staying awhile, Your Majesty?" he asks in an uncharacteristically soft voice.

"Yes," I hear myself say.

"In that case, I've left devil's nettle tea on the hearth. Make him drink it, in the unlikely event that he wakes. It will help the blood clot and relieve pain. I'm leaving orders for no one else to enter this room—he needs perfect rest. If you must leave, ask the guard outside to sit in here quietly to mark his . . . health. I'll return later to check the stitches and bandages."

I hardly notice when he closes the door behind him. I'm staring at Hector's face, at the eyelashes curling against his cheeks, his slightly open mouth, the dark stubble along his jawline.

My skin is flushed, from the still-glowing hearth, from the Godstone's responses to my prayers, from fear. *He is unlikely to survive.* I crawl to his bedside and kneel there. I reach for his hand and clasp it tight. He does not stir.

A great hollow has opened in my chest where my heart and lungs ought to be, and oh, it hurts. It's like the breath-stealing pain beneath my breastbone that comes of days walking the desert without enough to drink. It's like a dagger to the gut. It's like dying.

I rest my forehead on his knuckles. *Please, God, help him get better. Don't let him die.* My Godstone throbs, but I know it's not enough. How many times have I prayed for a life, only for God to turn away?

I will do anything. I'd give him my own life and health if I could.

He's a good man, the best man. He deserves to live. Please.

I imagine pouring my own life force out of my body, through our clasped hands, filling Hector, knitting his wound.

The Godstone becomes a fire. I cry out as white-hot pain zings up my spine.

After a moment the pain lessens. Something else takes its place, something like water or light or desert wind, leaching up from the ground, pouring into my Godstone. My body shivers with it until I feel like I will burst.

Hope dares to spark inside me, for I have felt this once before—when I killed the animagi with my Godstone amulet.

I don't know where the power came from or how I've managed to channel it again, but my body hums with possibility, with potential, as if the power building inside me is a huge boulder about to tumble off a cliff.

God, what do I do?

Hector's fingers twitch. I grip tighter, press my lips to the back of his hand, concentrating on the power inside me.

Live. Please live.

Nothing happens.

Think, Elisa! Last time, I quoted God's own words from holy scripture. It became a conduit for the power of my Godstone, focusing it where I needed.

Aloud, I say, "The gate that leads to life is narrow and small so that few find it." My Godstone lurches, and the force inside me begins a slow spin. Encouraged, I add, "For the righteous right hand of God is a healing hand; blessed is he who seeks renewal, for he shall be restored."

Power trickles out of me, from my hand into Hector's. My heart pounds with excitement, with hope. I wrack my mind for more.

The "Prayer of Service"! "Take my life, O God, as a consecrated offering, holy and pleasing. Make me your vessel of service . . ." The power begins to fade. "No! God, please no."

I gaze at Hector's face, memorizing every detail—his pale lips, the line of his jaw, the crisscross of scars on one cheek. And suddenly I have it. The perfect verse.

My heart swells with knowledge as certain as the tides. I whisper, "For love is more beautiful than rubies, sweeter than honey, finer than the king's wine. And no one has greater love than he who gives his own life for a friend. My love is like perfume poured out—"

The floodgates open. Power rushes out of me, into Hector. He arches his back, and his eyes fly open, showing nothing but bloodshot white. Then he crashes back to the bed.

I have just enough time to notice that his breathing is easier, that color returns to his face, before my vision blurs with exhaustion and dizziness. My heart slows to a single thunderous beat every few seconds. Too slow. Am I dying? Have I given my own life for Hector's?

A good trade, I think, as I collapse against the bed, my cheek thudding against his forearm.

I wake to a hand on my head, fingers tangling in my unraveling braid. A man's fingers, rough and thick. They trail down my cheek, stroke my jawline, brush my lips.

I raise my head and blink to clear my eyes. Hector is awake, staring at me with a strange expression. He does not move his hand from my face but lets it linger, his thumb gently tracing my chin.

My relief is so huge it feels like I can breathe again.

"You stayed," he says, and his voice is hoarse.

"And I'm not dead!" I say wonderingly. At the confusion on his face, I hastily add, "How do you feel?"

"Like I got punched in the back with Captain Lucio's gauntlet. Which is odd. I should feel worse."

"It worked!" His hand has still not left my face, and I have the urge to lean into it, kiss his fingers, maybe.

"What do you mean?"

"My Godstone. I knew it had healing properties, but I didn't know if it would work on someone else."

His hand drops, and he sits straight up, wincing. "You thought you were giving your life to me."

I open my mouth to deny it, but then I decide it's best to say nothing.

He swings his legs over to the side so that he faces me. "There's dried blood all over you," he whispers. "My blood, isn't it?"

I'm about to tell him that it's nothing that won't wash away, but speech leaves me when he cups my face with his hands. "Please, Elisa," he says, "don't ever, ever give *your* life for *mine*."

"I couldn't let you die. I'd rather—"

A knock sounds at the door, and we spring away from each other.

"Come in!" Hector calls, though he continues to hammer me with that unreadable stare.

Doctor Enzo bustles in, but he stops short, his mouth agape. "This is most unexpected."

After an awkward silence, I say, "Perhaps your skills are even more considerable than you realized?"

He looks back and forth between Hector and me, frowning. "I admit to a certain well-earned reputation," he says thoughtfully. "But this is not the result of my ministrations."

"A miracle?" I say weakly.

His gaze drifts to the general direction of my navel. "You healed him," he accuses. "Somehow."

I shrug, not wanting to talk about it. I do need to tell someone what happened. Father Alentín or Ximena. But not Enzo. "I fell asleep. Something happened before I woke up." Hector's eyes flash with understanding; he knows I'm not telling the whole truth. Before I can be pressed on the matter, I say, "I need to get back to my suite. I'm scheduled to be in preparations for the gala in the morning. Enzo, please make sure your patient rests. I'll find guards to escort me."

At my back, I hear Enzo say, "May I record this incident? The *Journal of Medical Anomalies* would be fascinated—"

As I close the door behind me, God's holy scripture echoes in my head. *My love is like perfume poured out . . .*

I bend over, hugging myself with relief, with unshed tears, with exhaustion, and with an understanding as bone-wrenching as it is pure: I am wholly and irreversibly in love with the commander of my Royal Guard.

Thank you, God. Thank you for saving him.

I straighten to find several guards staring at me. One is Fernando, who regards me with the helpless gaze of a frightened pup. "Lord Hector . . . ?" he says in a wavering voice.

"Will be fine," I say. "I require an escort to my rooms."

Fernando orders the others to accompany me, then takes up watch, his arms crossed, his face determined. I am not the only one who loves their commander.

Night has fallen, and I consider going to bed, but I know I won't manage any kind of sleep. "To the monastery," I say, and they fall into formation around me.

The corridors are empty and silent. Light from sconced torches shimmers against the glazed-tile pattern in the wall, but it also casts shadows over our cobbled path. I imagine assassins hiding in patches of darkness, behind corners. Every scuff of sound, every whisper, is an arrow flying through the air, a dagger whipped from its sheath.

I think of Hector, wishing he were here. And then I'm glad he isn't, for I have much to think about before I see him next.

We round a bend and enter the monastery, a place that never quite sleeps. Scattered petitioners kneel on prayer benches, and an acolyte in a gray robe quietly tends the candles on the altar. I breathe in the perfume of sacrament roses as comfort. Surely I am safe here, in this place of worship.

I open the door to the archive and find Ximena, Alentín, and Nicandro sitting on stools at the scribing table, bent over a piece of vellum so old that its edges are curled and black.

I thank the guards and ask them to watch the entrance, then I close the door behind me.

They look up, startled, and Ximena's face freezes with shock. "Elisa? Is that *blood* all over you?"

I had forgotten. "Yes. Hector's. We were attacked in the hallway outside my office. Hired mercenaries. Tristán came to our aid. But everyone is fine now." I came to tell her all about it, about healing him, but suddenly I don't want to. I need to think about something else for a bit, before I think on that.

"And the mercenaries?" she demands. "Do you know who hired them? Were they captured or killed? There may be more—"

I hold up a hand. "Later. Please distract me with moldy vellum and impenetrable wisdom. *Please.*"

The three of them exchange a glance, then Nicandro says, "I'll show you what we've found." He pats the stool next to him, then moves an oil lamp to the side to make a space for me at the table.

I hop up onto the stool, uneasy with the memory pricking at my thoughts. The last time I sat here late into the night with Father Nicandro, he revealed that I had been kept in ignorance of bearer lore, that a prophecy destined me to encounter the gate of my enemy.

And I thought I *had* encountered it, when I was captured by Inviernos and nearly tortured by an animagus. But maybe not. Maybe the worst is yet to come.

"This here," he says, pounding the vellum with a forefinger, "is the *Blasphemy of Lucero.*"

I gasp. "Lucero is my name."

He nods. "This document was presented for canonization as official scripture almost a century ago, but it was rejected by a council of priests."

"Not just rejected," Father Alentín cuts in. "It was *banned*."

"Wait. A century? That means . . ."

"He was your predecessor," Alentín confirms.

Lucero. The bearer before me. Though he lived a hundred years ago, I suddenly feel closer to him than anyone. My voice is shaky as I ask, "So why was this document banned?"

Ximena says, "The structure is atrocious, for one. It was penned by an uneducated hand; the original is rife with spelling and grammar errors. The council believed God would never allow his holy words to be anything less than pristine."

I stare down at the vellum. The script is faded with age, but the lines are even and precise, perfectly scribed. "So this is a copy."

Nicandro nods, "Of a copy of a copy, no doubt. The original is lost to us forever. No one felt it important to preserve it."

"And now you think the priests were wrong? Maybe it isn't blasphemy, but actual scripture?"

"No," Ximena says, even as Alentín says, "Definitely."

They exchange a friendly glare. Then Ximena sighs and says, "Adding to the cannon is no light matter. It could alter centuries of traditions. Of beliefs. I would have to be absolutely certain before I accepted it as God's own words."

Alentín says, "But you concede the possibility. We have compelling evidence."

"I concede the possibility."

"Aha!" he says, as if he's won a great victory, and then I'm shocked when Ximena rolls her eyes at him. I've never seen her resort to such impropriety.

"Tell me, then," I say. "Why you think it ought to be considered scripture? What does it say?"

Nicandro clears his throat. "Master Lucero was a poor village boy. He could neither read nor write. According to the introduction, he dictated his vision to a friend, who scribed it hastily on a sheep's hide. The friend, as it turned out, was also not very good at reading and writing. The manuscript, if you can call it that, was delivered to the nearest monastery, but the story was never verified. The boy disappeared. The monastery searched for him for years, to no avail."

"So the priests declared it blasphemy." I can see why. They would think it odd that God would speak through someone so poor and backward as to be totally illiterate. But I warm to the idea. It's nice to consider that God may not count imperfection as an obstacle to working out his will in the world.

"Seems a little convenient that he would disappear," Ximena grumbles. "Not available to answer questions or have his Godstone verified by the monastery."

Alentín leans forward, eyes bright. "But it's not unusual for a bearer to disappear. Three hundred years ago, for example. Another boy evaporated right out of the Monastery-at-Altapalma, his service undone. No one knows what happened."

I imagine that they fled—from expectations, from terror, from the constant barrage of others deciding the best way to accomplish God's will. Or maybe they died young, suddenly and unexpectedly, as most bearers seem to do. It's something I came to terms with when I lived in the desert—that I would likely die young in service to God.

I say, "Why do *you* think we should take the boy's message seriously?"

"Lucero knew things," Nicandro says. "Things an illiterate boy from a remote village could never know. I won't go into detail, but it was enough to give me pause. Enough to keep me reading eagerly. And then I reached this right here." He scrolls down with his finger until he finds the pertinent passage. "Go ahead, Your Majesty. Read it."

I lean forward, tingling with anticipation, with the possibility of discovery. "'The gate that leads to life is narrow and small so that few find it.'" I look up, puzzled. "Nothing new here. It says the same in the *Scriptura Sancta.*"

"Keep reading," Ximena says.

"'The champion alone shall traverse it and find the *zafira*, for this wellspring of his power shall beckon him. And all the power of this world shall come into him and he shall have life eternal in accordance with God's will. None shall stand against him, and his enemies shall crumble, verily a thousand shall fall before his might.'"

All the power of this world. My Godstone thrums in recognition, sending shivers of warmth up my spine.

"The *zafira*," Ximena says.

"Just like the Invierno said," Alentín points out.

"How would an uneducated village boy know that word?"

Nicandro asks, his voice soft with awe. "It hasn't been in use since the first families came to this world. It's older even than the Lengua Classica."

Darkness edges my vision, whether from dread or excitement or residual exhaustion from healing Hector I can't tell. I ask, "What, exactly, is the *zafira?*"

Alentín says, "The *Afflatus* says that magic crawls beneath the skin of this world and that once in every four generations, God raises up a champion to bear his mark and fight magic with magic." I love the way his voice falls into rhythm whenever he quotes scripture. It takes me right back to our desert cavern and our lessons together while sitting on gritty shale and drawing letters in the dust.

After a pause, he adds, "Scripture supports the Invierno's claim that the *zafira* is the magic of the world."

I narrow my eyes, thinking hard. "The animagi can call the magic to them from anywhere. All they have to do is feed the earth a bit of blood. But Storm made the *zafira* sound like a specific place."

He nods. "Storm also made it sound as though calling this magic takes no small effort. But Lucero's *Blasphemy* describes a crack in the world, where the wellspring of power bubbles to the surface. I think it refers to a place where the world's magic is more accessible, or maybe more concentrated."

They all regard me with expectation as I mull their words.

I say, "The champion alone shall find the *zafira* . . ." And as soon as the words leave my mouth, I know I want to. More than anything.

But how would I manage such a thing? A queen does not have the luxury of leaving everything behind in pursuit of a nebulous quest.

"You *are* the champion," Nicandro says. "It goes on to say that your determination will be tested. That you must prove your worth. But it also says that he who bears God's own stone shall pass through the gate." He shrugs, sighing. "Frankly, I think it sounds dangerous."

Prophecy is a tricky thing, I have learned, full of edges and secret meanings and mischief. Prophecy can feel like the betrayal of a dear friend, the disappointment of a lifetime, the hope of a nation.

"This could be it, Elisa," Ximena says, and her black eyes spark with something fierce. "What you need to rule. To finally grasp the destiny I know God has prepared for you."

I'm not sure why, but her words make me uncomfortable—even though she's a little bit right. With that kind of power, I would be able to discourage the machinations of the Quorum. Keep my enemies at bay. Make my kingdom whole again.

"And Elisa . . ." Nicandro's voice is dark with gravity. "It's best that you tell no one about the *Blasphemy*. It's a forbidden text, after all."

"And yet you had a copy lying around in the monastery."

He shifts on his stool. "Er . . . no. Father Alentín did."

A laugh bubbles in my throat, and Alentín flashes me a mischievous grin. This is the man who stole the oldest known copy of Homer's *Afflatus* when he fled the Monastery-at-Basajuan. *Of course* he has a copy of the forbidden *Blasphemy*.

"We should begin making arrangements, my sky," Ximena says. "We could leave—"

I hold up a hand to cut her off. It's crusted with Hector's dried blood. I say, "I'll think about it."

15

BUT I don't have time to think about it, for the day of the Deliverance Gala dawns hot and bright and busy. Everyone hurries through preparations sheened with a layer of sweat. I spend the morning approving last-minute changes to the menu and guest lists and practicing the blessing I will recite at the ball. That afternoon, I tell Mara and Ximena about healing Hector, though I leave out the most pertinent detail. Ximena is beside herself with excitement that I have found a way to tap into the Godstone's power.

"God has a great destiny for you, my sky," she says, her eyes shining.

If she realizes I'm keeping something to myself, she does not press. Still, I'm relieved when it's finally time to dress for the gala, for it means I'll have something to do besides avoid her zealous gaze.

I can't stop thinking about Hector. I can't wait to see him again, for Doctor Enzo has declared him well enough to escort me tonight.

Because of the attempts on my life, my own personal guard will be on my arm, soldiers will be stationed at every entrance and crossbowmen in the high cupolas overlooking the audience hall, and every guest will be thoroughly searched for weapons. Still Ximena insists on one further precaution.

She holds up a corset of leather nearly as stiff as rawhide. "I had it specially made," she says with a pleased look. She knocks it with a fist, and I wince at the hollow sound. "It should repulse a dagger, or at least minimize damage. And it's fitted, just flexible enough to wear under a gown."

I gaze at it in despair, already feeling suffocated. "All right," I say, resigned. When she fits it around me and begins to lace it, I try to convince myself it's not much worse than my regular corset with its thick stays.

Mara looks on with amused interest. "It looks like Hector's informal armor," she says. "Except with space for breasts."

"Funny," I say with a glare. But my glare dies when I see my reflection. I hardly recognize the girl looking back at me. She seems so strong in her corset armor. I throw my shoulders back and hold my head high.

My gown—made of aquamarine satin—slides over it with surprising ease. It's a bolder color than I usually prefer, but I like the way my skin glows next to it, the contrast of my dark skin and black hair. The gown is sleeveless but has two impossibly long chiffon ties that form a halter behind my neck and float down my back, all the way to the floor.

Ximena sweeps my hair up, leaving a few curls to trail down my neck. Mara lines my eyes with kohl and adds a little sweep at the corners, which enhances their cat shape and makes them look huge. She steps back, grinning smugly, and says, "I've been practicing on the laundress."

Tears fill Ximena's eyes. "You look like a queen, my sky."

Mara says, "You look like the most eligible marriage prospect in the country."

The face staring back is strange. More chiseled, less pudgy than it used to be. And the eyes—so dark and dramatic and large! They are the eyes of someone who has seen and lost much.

Softly I say, "I look like a widow."

They shift a bit closer, as if forming a protective hedge, and Mara settles an arm across my shoulder. I'm grateful for their sympathy, their understanding.

Mara squeezes my shoulder. "You'll find love again," she says.

I catch my breath. *But I already have. And I don't know that it matters.* Carefully I say, "Love is not for me. I'll marry for the good of my kingdom." But my words seem too hard and sharp. "Probably a northern lord," I continue, forcing nonchalance into my voice. "Approved by the Quorum."

Ximena regards me thoughtfully—she knows me too well. But she doesn't press the matter, just arranges the ties of my dress to drape more fluidly and says, "You're ready to go as soon as Hector gets here."

My heart does a little flip at the sound of his name, but I ignore it, saying, "First I have something for you." I gesture for them to follow me into my bedchamber. I reach into my nightstand to retrieve the gifts I've hidden there and hand each of them a packet wrapped in supple leather.

Mara beams as she opens hers but then gasps with astonishment. "A spice satchel. With marjoram, cinnamon—oh, Elisa. Saffron! How did you procure saffron?"

I'm so glad to have surprised her. "There are advantages to being queen. Now you, Ximena."

My nurse peels back the leather wrapping to reveal a bound book with a painted cover and gilded pages. *"The Common Man's Guide to Service,"* she breathes. "It must be two hundred years old."

"Look at the pages."

She opens it. "Oh, my sky."

I laugh, delighted with her reaction. "They're illuminated!"

Ximena runs a finger across the elaborate lettering, caresses the border painted in shimmering sacrament roses. Tears fill her eyes. "I've never owned something so valuable."

It takes so little to please my ladies, and my heart fills to see the happiness shining in their faces. I reach my arms out, and then the three of us are elbowing one another in an awkward hug. "Happy Deliverance Day," I whisper, and they respond in kind.

Someone's throat clears, and we separate. Mara moves from my field of vision to reveal Hector standing in the doorway.

My mouth goes dry.

For the first time since I have known him, he is dressed as a Quorum lord. He still wears the red cloak of the Royal Guard, but instead of combing back his black hair, he has let it curl naturally at his forehead, at the nape of his neck. In lieu of a breastplate and thigh guards, he wears a loose white blouse tucked into tight black breeches. A sword belt slings across narrow hips, but it's a smaller gentleman's sword. Without the bulk of his armor, I see how very broad his shoulders are, how tanned the skin of his neck and collarbone is.

He looks vulnerable. Exposed.

And yet he looks stronger than I've ever seen him. He's not beautiful like Alejandro, for there is nothing of delicacy about Hector. And he is not wild and unpolished like Humberto. Hector's jaw is too smooth and solid, his eyebrows too full and well shaped, his neck and shoulders hard with sculpted muscle. Everything about him speaks of elegant power.

I realize the silence has stretched forever. How long have I stood here gaping?

His pupils are huge, his gaze on me steady. He has watched me study him, and more than anything, I wish I could read his thoughts.

I find my voice at last. "Happy Deliverance Day."

"You are beautiful," he says simply.

Warmth floods my neck, and I swallow hard. "Thank you. You look very nice too."

"I brought something for you."

"Oh?" For the first time, I notice the package in his hand. It's box shaped, large enough that I will need two hands to hold it. "You didn't have to get me anything." Earlier, I had a page deliver a silver brooch for his cloak—the same gift I gave all my guards. I didn't know what else to do. There is still so much I don't know about him—about his childhood, his interests—and I couldn't think of a gift that felt personal enough for someone so important to me. Staring at the box in his hand, I wish I'd given it more effort.

"It's from all of us," he says. "The Royal Guard, Ximena, and Mara."

I whip my head around to stare at my ladies. Mara grins like a child about to eat naming-day pie. "Go ahead," Ximena says. "Open it."

Hector hands the box to me, and our fingers brush as I take it. I pull at the twine until it unravels, then peel away the decorative wrapping to reveal a hinged jewelry box of polished mahogany. The de Vega seal is burn etched onto the cover. My heart is in my throat as I tip the lid back.

Inside, resting on blue velvet, is a crown made of white gold with swirls and loops as intricate as lace. It's dainty enough to be light on my head, and yet so much more substantial than the tiaras I wore as a princess. Indeed, it is fit for a queen.

But what makes me draw breath sharply, what fills my eyes with tears, are the shattered Godstones set into the gold. They range from dark blue to black; some are no more than shards. In the center is the largest, the one Godstone that survived mostly intact, though a large spiderweb crack bursts across its surface just left of center.

Whoever designed the crown was inspired by the broken jewels and carried the theme through the whorls and spikes of gold. Though delicate, the overall impression is one of bold strength and jagged shimmering.

It's the crown of a warrior. Of someone who has faced destruction.

Because I am frozen in place, Ximena lifts it from the box and settles it on my head. It feels perfect. I step into the atrium to view my reflection in the vanity mirror. Tiny motes of untouched sapphire spark under the skylight.

"No one," I breathe, "in the history of all the world has worn a crown such as this."

"No one else could," Hector says over my shoulder. Our eyes meet in the mirror. I'm the first to look away.

"Thank you," I say. "Thank you all. But how—"

"All those gifts from your suitors," Ximena says. "When you were convalescing. We sold several items, melted the jewelry down. It was Hector's idea. Mara helped the jeweler design it. Each of the guards chipped in a few coins."

"It's amazing," I say. "It's magnificent."

"Go show it off, my sky," Ximena says with a soft smile.

I find I'm eager to do so. I look to Hector, and he holds out his arm.

The audience hall is transformed for the Deliverance Gala. Rose garlands swoop from crystal chandeliers, filling the hall with their heady scent. The casement of each high window holds a lighted candelabra, so that the room seems surrounded by stars. Low tables line the walls. They are covered with silk cloth and brimming with appetizers and drink served in silver dishes, all surrounded by sitting cushions for easy chatting.

Musicians play vihuelas and dulciáns from a wooden stage near the entry, and hundreds of people mill about, smiling and laughing, dressed in their yearly best. More trickle in through the entrance after being thoroughly searched for weapons, but even this does not damper the mood. They're as bright as a flower garden in their Deliverance colors—coral hibiscus and yellow night bloomers and sky-blue vine snaps. Women wear their hair up in jeweled nets; men wear long stoles trimmed in gold embroidery. It's a night for shimmering, for catching the light just so.

No one dances yet. It's up to me to begin the festivities.

The moment I enter, the hall goes silent. Hector pauses in the threshold, giving them a chance to size up their queen. I hold lightly to his arm, and he reaches with his other hand and gives mine a quick squeeze.

Everyone bows, but their collective gaze fixes on my new crown. I give them a defiant smile in return and wait the space of a few beats for them to fully understand what they see.

I gesture for everyone to rise, and Hector and I resume our procession. The crowd breaks into a flurry of low-voiced conversations. I catch the words "Godstone" and "sorcery." I hold my smile easily, knowing the crown has had its intended effect.

At the end of the hall, my throne dais has been rolled away to reveal the massive Hand of God, a masterwork of marble sculpture we gaze upon only once each year. My Godstone leaps in rapturous response. I calm it with my fingertips, mumbling, "Stop that."

The man who carved the hand, Lutián of the Rocks, spent his whole short life working on it. They say he was overcome with God's spirit, that he carved with fevered frenzy, stopping only for occasional food and drink and sleep. When he finished at the age of twenty-one, he pronounced it good and promptly collapsed of a burst heart. He bore a living Godstone, like me, and carving this giant hand was his great service.

With Hector's help, I climb the steps leading to God's cupped fingers. I step across them carefully, for they are as rounded and ridged as real fingers. I spread the skirt of my aquamarine gown around me, and lower myself so that I sit cross-legged in the giant palm.

The crowd hushes in expectation.

I close my eyes, lift my hands to the sky, and intone the Deliverance blessing.

In you our ancestors put their trust,
they cried out and you delivered them.
Yea, from the dying world they were saved;
in you they trusted and were not put to shame.
Bless us, O God, as we remember your hand;
your righteous right hand endures forever.

"Selah!" the crowd thunders.

The musicians resume, dancers float onto the center floor, and the Deliverance Gala has officially begun.

From below, Hector gestures for me to come down. Normally, the monarch would sit in the Hand of God for several dances, absorbing luck and blessing. But it is too dangerous for me to be exposed for so long.

Holding tight to his hand for support, I navigate the steps, mindful of my full skirt. My foot has barely reached the floor when I am accosted by my first partner.

"May I have this dance, Your Majesty?" asks Prince Rosario. He bows with the ease of long practice, his small fingers outstretched in gentlemanly supplication.

"Of course!" I say with genuine enthusiasm, taking the offered hand.

His head does not even reach my chest, and I'm tempted to lead him, but he seems determined to do the job credibly, so I let him.

"Did your nurse put you up to this?" I ask.

He peers up at me from beneath thick lashes—his cinnamon eyes are so like his father's—and says, "No, but Carilla wants to dance with me." With a quick tip of his chin, he indicates a young girl with wild curls and satin ruffles standing at the edge of the crowd, no more than nine years old. Rosario wrinkles his nose. "She tries to kiss me. It's awful."

I laugh. "So you told her you had to dance with me instead."

He nods solemnly. "Even though you are a terrible dancer. Dancing with you is better than dancing with Carilla."

With equal solemnity, I say, "Excellent decision. You will be a wise king one day."

"Yes," he agrees. "Wiser than Papá. Everyone says so."

My heart breaks for him a little. "We should drift across the hall so that you are far away from Carilla when the song ends."

He brightens. "Good idea!"

As we dance, I ask him about his studies, which he loathes, and his swordsmanship lessons with Hector, which he loves.

By the time our dance ends, we are laughing together over his favorite pony, who can nose his way to a syrupy date even through three layers of clothing. I don't step on Rosario's feet even once.

When we separate, he bows. "I thank you for the dance, Your Majesty," he intones.

"It was a pleasure, Your Highness," I respond. Several people around us applaud lightly, as if we have put on a bit of theater. And I suppose we have. I hope it has cheered them to see their queen and her heir having a good time together.

A hand grasps my elbow. I look up into Hector's worried face. He whispers, "*Please.* Do not drift through the crowd while dancing. Stay close to the edge, where I can see you."

The music changes to a slow, rhythmic bolero.

"I didn't realize . . . I'm sorry." He is very close, and my heart starts to pound. I remember our last lesson, the way his hands stroked up my bare forearm, showing me proper form, guiding my movements. The way the world dropped away as we moved effortlessly together, lost in the drill that was more like a dance.

I whisper, "Dance with me."

He pauses, as if considering. Then, "Yes, Your Majesty." And my heart sinks to think that dancing with me may be yet another *duty* for him. But then I can't think of anything at all, for his hand has slipped around my waist to pull me toward him. Holding my gaze, his left hand slides gently down my forearm to my fingers. He entwines them with his own and spins me into the center of the floor.

We are not close enough as we dance. I imagine myself pressed against him, my face buried in his neck. But this particular dance demands a certain choreographed distance, and we comply. I focus instead on the hand at the small of my back. The leather of my hidden corset protects me from daggers, but it protects me from Hector's touch too, and I find myself hating it. I can feel the pressure of his hand but no more. I want to feel his fingers, his warmth. I want to feel *everything*.

"How is your injury?" I ask, to distract myself.

"I have forgotten to notice it."

I have no idea how to respond. After a moment of my stunned silence, he says, "Of all your suitors, has any one caught your particular attention yet?"

His question startles me. It feels out of place. Forced.

I consider making a joke but abandon the idea. Instead I say, "I haven't encountered many yet, but Conde Tristán seems nice. He's intelligent and charming. And . . . and I think he likes me, too."

"You think he could be a good friend, then?"

"Maybe. I don't . . ." *I don't love him.* "I don't know that the Quorum will approve. He's southern, after all. But I think he's a good man."

I hear him sigh, and his arm squeezes my waist, pulling me a little closer. He says, "I'm glad. You could do much worse. And I'll always be grateful to him for coming to our aid."

I nod agreement, trying to keep the disappointment from my face. It's wrong of me, I know, but I don't want Hector to be glad about a potential suitor.

The dance floor is full now, and Hector is careful to keep us from brushing against anyone else. He leans down and whispers, "I'm not sure it's proper for a queen to dance with her guard."

My heart sinks a little more. Always the dutiful commander. I lift my head to whisper back at him, and my lips accidentally brush his jaw when I say, "I don't care."

"May I cut in, Your Majesty?"

I turn toward the intruder, angry.

It's Conde Tristán. He is so wide-eyed with nervousness that I soften at once.

Hector says, "Of course, Your Grace. Her Majesty and I were just discussing some of the finer points of security, but our conversation is finished." He spins me toward the conde, and I catch one last glimpse of his unreadable face before Tristán traps me in his arms and Hector drifts back into shadow.

The bolero is picking up speed now. "I can't imagine that anyone would risk God's wrath by trying to harm you during his own holiday," the conde says.

I don't care to discuss my safety anymore. "How is Iladro?"

He brightens. "Much better, thank you. He can only eat small portions, and he remains weak, but he's better every day. I pray for a full recovery. If God can heal Lord Hector so thoroughly, surely he has some mercy to spare for my herald."

"You are very devout then?" I crane my neck, looking for Hector, but I can't find him. I know he watches me, though. I can feel it.

"Only in recent years. Since my father's death, I've taken

great comfort in weekly services, most especially the holy sacrament of pain. The slight discomfort of a thorn prick is very meditative and calming. It helps me exist in the present moment, helps me forget the stresses of ruling a countship."

He could not have answered more perfectly if I had coached him myself, and I stare at him in suspicion.

"Does Selvarica have its own monastery?"

"No. But it would be my life's greatest legacy to establish a Monastery-at-Selvarica. I've been working on it. So far, we've been unable to attract a head priest to our tiny countship."

"Why not?"

"Honestly, I can't imagine. We're remote, I suppose. But Selvarica is the most beautiful place in the world. A lush green island, surrounded by sea the color of blue quartz. Never too warm, never too cold. The mountain peaks trap enough rain-clouds to provide water year-round. Waterfalls tumble from verdant cliffs into icy pools. Flowers grow everywhere. Truly, Selvarica is God's own garden."

"It sounds lovely."

His voice grows husky. "I would love to show it to you someday."

I return his intent gaze without flinching. We are the same height, which is a nice change. Hector and Mara and Ximena are all unusually tall, and it seems as though I'm always craning my neck.

I say, "I may pay a state visit. The Quorum has suggested I tour the country after hurricane season. They would like to make a very big deal of it. Lots of fanfare."

He laughs. "You sound as though you despise the idea."

I grin. "I've considered making unreasonable demands. Just to punish them for the thought. Like refusing to ride in a mere carriage. Only a litter will do!"

"And trumpets. A queen should be heralded for the entirety of her journey."

"And chilled fruit, which would be near impossible to provide during a long journey. Imagine the fit I could have."

"Also, a change of clothes every two hours. A queen should stay fresh at all times."

The song ends, and I'm surprised to realize that I enjoyed our dance.

Conde Tristán raises my fingers to his lips and kisses them. "Thank you, Your Majesty." Before dropping my hand, his gaze turns mischievous. "You are not as terrible a dancer as your reputation indicates."

I laugh. "Just a little bit terrible, then."

He has a wonderful smile, with eyes that shine. "A little bit," he agrees. "But you forgot to step on my feet." With that, he whirls away and disappears into the crowd.

I look around for Hector again and spot him near a drink table. He chats easily with a young woman I don't recognize. She wears a soft green gown, and her clear skin sparkles with metallic powder. A long black lock drapes from the mound of luxuriant hair piled on her head, across her bare shoulder.

I stare at her with dejection. I'll never be so lovely.

Lord Liano claims me next. He is oafish and wide gazed, his sweaty lip as protuberant as ever, which makes him appear stunningly stupid. I listen with heroic patience as he regales me with the tale of an epic hunt for wild javelinas, which he lovingly describes as piglike creatures that roam the scrub desert of his brother's countship. When he attempts to mimic the chattering noise that javelinas make by rubbing their tusks together, I am forced to conclude that, indeed, sometimes the impression of a man's look and bearing holds true.

I hope Conde Tristán will claim me next—he asked me for two dances, after all—but Conde Eduardo finds me first. He is rough and jerky, and his hand on mine is too tight, his beard oil too pungent. I plaster a game smile on my face, but it wavers when I notice Hector dancing beside us, the lovely green-gowned creature in his arms. They seem to have an easy conversation interspersed with much laughing, though he looks over her head occasionally to check on me, always the devoted guard. I can't mask my relief when the song ends.

After thanking Eduardo, I catch Hector's eye and gesture toward the nearest refreshment table to let him know where I'm headed. Though it lies only a few steps away, I decline three offers to dance during the short journey, saying that I'm still healing from my ordeal and need to pace myself, but thank you so very much for the invitation.

A servant offers a glass of chilled wine, and I accept with grateful despair, knowing that a new taster now risks his life for me. Everything at the gala has been thoroughly tasted, hours earlier, and then again right before bringing it out.

As I sip, I glimpse Mara between dancing pairs. She twirls, laughing, and I smile to see her having such a good time. She is beautiful in a light yellow gown that sweeps into a slight train behind her. It's the plainest gown in the hall, without a stitch of embroidery or even a tiny pearl. But the simplicity suits her well, and the women around her seem gaudy by comparison.

"Mara seems to be enjoying herself," says Hector in my ear, and I hope he doesn't notice my tiny jump.

"She deserves to have a good time. As do you." I gesture toward the floor. "You should dance. Have fun. If your injury allows it, I mean." I can't deny him a little celebration. He works so tirelessly on my behalf.

He starts to protest, but I cut him off. "Don't worry," I say. "I'll protect you from harm. I stand ready to jump to your defense."

He laughs, and I love the sound. "I'm very content to enjoy the festivities from here," he says. "Is that Belén dancing with Mara?"

I crane my neck just as the pair shifts, revealing the face of her partner. Even from a distance, there can be no mistaking the patch over his eye. "Yes, that's him." I have a sudden urge to march over there and throw my wine in his face for what he did to my friend years ago.

"Well, they seem to be familiar," Hector says. "They're easy with each other."

His words check me. Hector is right. Mara chatters, and Belén laughs in response. Then the two glide behind a wall of dancers, obscuring my view.

"They are very old friends," I tell him. I suppose that if Mara can forgive Belén so thoroughly, maybe I can too.

I catch a movement in the corner of my eye and turn to see Lord Liano bearing down on me, his purposed stride a stark contrast to his vacuous gaze. Again I look around for Tristán, hoping he can save me from another disastrous turn with Liano, but he is nowhere to be found. "Oh, God," I mutter.

"What is it?" Hector asks.

"Please walk with me. I need some air. The gardens, maybe?"

16

HECTOR offers an arm, and I accept gratefully. We turn at the same moment Lord Liano calls out, "Your Majesty!"

"Keep walking," I say under my breath.

Hector snickers. "I take it your first dance together did not go well?"

"I learned that the best place to spear a javelina is in the throat, just above its chest."

"Aahh. Well, if you ever find yourself needing to ignore him, ask him about the time he stumbled upon a mother puma in her den. He's good for half an hour, uninterrupted."

"I'll remember that. Thank you."

The double doors to the gardens stand open for fresh air. As we step into the night, onto the winding paver path, I breathe deep of the sweet scent of yellow night bloomers. They are like a weed, the way they twine around trellises and ferns. Unchecked, they'd choke everything around them. But we tolerate them, cultivate them even, because at night they spread their weblike petals wide, proudly showing off stamens that glow brighter than fireflies.

"Hector, would you mind . . . that is, do you think it's safe for me to walk alone for a bit?"

"I think so, yes," he says with obvious reluctance. "It's an interior garden, and I have guards stationed around its perimeter. It's also best for propriety's sake that I stand guard where everyone can see me. But promise you'll remain within yelling range?"

"Of course."

He squeezes my arm and lets me go. And as I meander through the garden of tiny stars, I feel heady—from my glass of wine, from the cool breeze on my skin, from the touch and scent of the man I just left behind. A fountain tinkles nearby. Dimmed laughter and music curl around me.

The palm beside me rustles unnaturally. I hear hurried whispers, heavy breathing.

Surely there is no danger. Everyone was searched for weapons, and guards watch every entrance. But my mouth is dry and a slight tremor sets my fingers twitching as I check my Godstone for telltale cold. Nothing.

I reach out, and with the tip of my finger I move the palm fronds aside.

A man stands in a cavern of star-pricked foliage, his back to me. He is locked in a passionate embrace with someone else, someone smaller whose delicate arms ring his neck.

I can't help the giggle that bubbles from my mouth.

They whirl at the sound, and their faces are pale and stark among the dark greenery. I gasp with recognition.

It's Conde Tristán. Encircled in his arms is the herald, Iladro.

They stare at me, horrified. I want more than anything to run away, but shock freezes my feet.

The conde's features soften into resignation. Without breaking my gaze, he says, "Iladro, dear, why don't you go calm your stomach with a glass of water?"

The herald disengages himself, manages a panicked half bow in my direction, and flees toward the audience hall.

We are silent for what seems like an eternity. Finally Conde Tristán says, "Your Majesty, I swear on the *Scriptura Sancta* that everything I have told you is true."

Indignation helps me find my voice. "That I am stunningly beautiful? That you intend to court me?"

"Yes."

"Do you even *like* women?"

"Not in that way, no. But one doesn't have to be a lover of women to understand your quality."

I'm shaking my head. "Everything you said is a lie. Maybe not the words themselves, but your intent has been to deceive me." And deceive me he has. I'm so naive.

The conde lowers his head, whispering, "I'm sorry, Your Majesty. Truly." He sighs hugely. "Iladro is the love of my life. But Conde Eduardo has been gradually annexing my land, and my countship is in desperate need—"

"I suggest you retire for the evening."

The conde starts to protest but changes his mind. He nods instead. Then he slips out of the grotto and disappears.

Suddenly I'm not just alone but lonely. I stand there a long time, swallowing against tears, taking deep breaths to calm the fluttering humiliation in my breast. I don't blame Tristán for wanting to help his people during hard times. But it does sting to know that a man can't find me desirable. Maybe no one will. Maybe not ever.

Certainly not Hector.

I wipe under my eyes to make sure my kohl has not smeared. Then I throw my shoulders back and lift my head high. Thus collected, I return to the entrance and to my personal guard.

He makes no effort to disguise his relief at seeing me. "I saw Conde Tristán," he says. "He left in quite a hurry. Didn't even notice I stood here."

"We . . . we quarreled."

"I'm so sorry."

I can't bear to be pitiable before him, so I wave it off. "It was nothing."

But he is not fooled. When I take his offered arm, his free hand settles atop mine and squeezes gently. "Go back inside and dance," he insists.

"What?"

"Have a good time. Dance with as many suitors as possible. Let them flatter you outrageously." He's so intent, his voice urgent.

"But none of it will be real. None of them will want *me*. My throne, yes. Prestige. A conquest. But not me."

Silence stretches between us, and I realize I could not have given him a better opening to pay me ridiculous compliments.

It probably sounded like I was begging for them.

"Elisa . . . I—"

"You're right. I'll go back inside and do my queenly duty." I force brightness into my voice. "Who knows? Maybe Lord Liano has hidden depth of character."

He sighs. "I hear he once chose a short spear for the hunt instead of the crossbow, just to give the javelina a fighting chance."

"A man of true compassion!"

"He'd be glad to tell you about it."

For the rest of the evening, I play the role of queen. I down another glass of wine to dull the sharpness in my chest, fix a smile on my face, and work hard to not step on anyone's toes. I dance with everyone who asks, and I never lack partners. I'm told that I am radiant, that I have a beautiful smile, that I am a gifted dancer. They compliment me on my choice of gown, my speedy recovery, my political savvy. They extend condolences on my recent ordeal. They offer their personal services, suggest trade policy, beg me to raise taxes further, beg me to lower taxes.

Later, when I am finally back in my suite, Ximena helps me out of my gown. "How was it?" she asks. "Did you have a good time?"

I have run out of banalities and niceness. I have nothing to spare. "Fine," I snap. "It was *fine*."

"Will it cheer you up to know you have a letter from home?" She pulls a tiny leather canister from her apron pocket and waves it at me. "Just delivered from the dovecote."

She drops it into my palm, and my heart does a little flip when I recognize the de Riqueza sunburst stamped into the leather. From Papá. Or maybe my sister. I haven't spoken to either in over a year, except for a few brief messages like this one, via pigeon. I'm eager for news of home.

No, I correct myself. Joya d'Arena is my home now. My time in Orovalle feels like it happened to another girl, a different Elisa.

I open the canister, break the wax seal with a fingernail, and unroll the parchment. I'm glad to see my sister's careful and lovely script.

Dearest Elisa,

Word reached me of your grave injuries. I'm glad to know you are recovering well. I pray for you every day.

I write because Papá's council has asked that I begin seeking a husband in earnest. They suggest I choose from among Joya d'Arena's most influential nobility to further strengthen ties between us. Ximena has written to me about Lord-Commander Hector of the Royal Guard and has suggested I consider him. There is no opinion I trust more than yours. Please tell me: What kind of man is he? Would I do well to open negotiations with him? Your earliest reply is most appreciated.

Papá sends his love.

Alodia

It feels as though someone is standing on my chest.

"Elisa?"

I look up from the parchment now crushed in my fist. Ximena studies me carefully while the guards exchange worried glances.

I can't force the proper platitudes to my lips.

You knew this was coming, Elisa. Of course he will marry, and marry well. It is right and good that he become a prince consort. Would you rather Alodia marry someone who does not *feel like family already?*

"I need parchment," I whisper. "And quill and ink." I can't seem to remember where I put them.

Fernando rushes to fetch the items from my writing desk. Ximena takes a step toward me, but I back into the atrium, shaking my head. I can't even bear to look at her for wondering if she knew all along that I was falling in love with him.

By the time Fernando enters with the writing implements, my fist is to my lips, as if it can tramp down the nausea roiling in my belly. *Get control of yourself.* I take a deep breath. Then another. I force my jaw to unclench. Then I grab the ink and parchment and set them on the vanity.

But my fingers tremble and my script is jerky as I write.

Dearest Alodia,
Hector is the best man I know. You could not do better.
Elisa

I roll it tight and slide it inside Alodia's canister. I hand the canister to Fernando with instructions to send it immediately.

As he leaves, Ximena says, "Do you need to lie down for a moment? Maybe a glass of wine?"

"I'd like to be alone, Ximena," I say in the deadliest whisper, and she lowers her head and backs away.

But alone is such a nebulous state when one is queen. Knowing the guards surround me, I pull the canopy closed and cry as softly as I can manage it.

It is near morning when an idea finally dams the flood of tears.

17

I scoot off the bed and throw a robe around my shoulders. Ximena is already awake, though her long gray braid is sleep mussed. She sits near the balcony, taking advantage of the morning light to work on a tapestry. She looks up at me. "Is everything all right now?"

"I need to dress quickly. No time for a bath."

"We need to wash your face. With luck, people will think you had too much to drink and will not guess you spent the night crying."

At least she doesn't ask me why. "Fine. Is Mara awake yet?"

"She didn't get back until very late." She gathers the material in her lap and plops it into a basket near her chair.

"Let her sleep a few more minutes, but we'll have to wake her soon."

"Are you going to tell me—"

"Soon." I don't even want my own Royal Guard to know what will transpire next. My idea hinges on secrecy.

I send a guard to fetch the mayorodomo while Ximena

begins sifting through my wardrobe. She holds up a riding gown; it has a split skirt and a tight black vest. I never ride, but I sometimes wear it when I need to feel strong.

I nod approval. Ximena has read my mood well.

I have just finished dressing, and Ximena is combing my hair in the atrium, when the mayordomo arrives. His dressing robe hangs crooked, and the left side of his head is sleep plastered into a solid wall of hair.

"Your Majesty?" he says, out of breath. "The guard said your summons was urgent."

"Thank you for coming so quickly. Tell me, is Conde Tristán of Selvarica still here in the palace?" Ximena's face in the vanity mirror shows perfect composure, but I sense increasing tension in her brushstrokes.

"He filed a departure notice very late last night." He shakes his head with disgust. "Who departs during Deliverance week? And on the night of the gala! It was most untoward, and I—"

"But Tristán is still here? He hasn't left yet?" I realize I'm wringing my skirt in my right fist. I release it and flex my fingers.

"I don't know."

"Find out. *Now.* If he hasn't yet departed, tell him I require his presence immediately in my chambers."

"Yes, Your Majesty." He executes a quick bow and hurries away on slippered feet.

Ximena puts her hands on my shoulders and makes eye contact with me in the mirror.

"I'll explain soon," I whisper. I just hope the conde has not had time to gather his entourage and flee from last night's encounter.

Fortunately, I do not wait long.

When a guard escorts the conde into the atrium, Tristán drops to one knee and bows his head, refusing to meet my eyes.

"Rise."

He does, and I note his traveling clothes: leather breeches, a loose blouse, a utility belt.

"Going somewhere so soon?"

He focuses on a point just above my head. "Yes, Your Majesty. I thought it prudent."

"You were going to leave without saying good-bye."

He looks sharply at me, really looks, not bothering to hide his confused suspicion.

I press on. "I had thought . . . or maybe just *hoped* that we had found a sort of connection, you and I."

"Your Majesty, I . . . I'm sorry, but I thought . . . last night . . ."

"Your Grace." I stand from my stool and offer him my arm. "Let's go somewhere private where we can talk." To Ximena, I say, "Wake Mara. I need that room."

She hurries away. The conde and I follow at a slower pace.

When we enter the austere attendant's room, Mara is sitting up in bed, rubbing bleary eyes. She and Ximena start to leave, but I hold up a hand. "Stay." I close the door behind me.

"Keep your voices low," I say. "My Royal Guard listens close for danger, and I do not care for them to know about this."

"About what, Your Majesty?" the conde says wearily, looking at the floor. "Why am I here? If you're going to punish me, or exact some kind of revenge, please get it over with."

Ximena and Mara exchange a puzzled look.

Something about his frankness pleases me. I say, "Conde, I need your help."

His gaze snaps to mine. "Oh?"

"How many people know about you and Iladro?"

"Not many. My mother. A few attendants."

"Good. I need a reason to . . ." I almost say "escape." "To leave the city and go south. I also need the Quorum—no, the whole country—to believe I am very serious about selecting a husband."

His eyes flash with understanding. "You want to pretend we are betrothed."

"Or at least pretend to begin negotiations. Which, of course, would require that I visit Selvarica and inspect your holdings."

"Of course. I assume that, after an acceptable period of time, we would regretfully conclude that we are not as compatible as we had hoped?"

"It might be a long period of time. But yes."

"And if I don't agree to this? Will you expose me for the liar I am?"

"No."

He stares at me.

"I'm not interested in that. If you don't want to help me, you are free to go." I shrug nonchalantly. "Though if you tell anyone about this conversation, I will destroy you."

He cracks a relieved smile in response to my threat, which also pleases me. But then he leans against the frame of Mara's bunk, and his eyes turn thoughtful. "You do realize that a broken betrothal would be a huge blow to my countship's status? Everyone would assume the worst, that you found me lacking in some way."

"I am prepared to offer something in exchange."

"I'm listening."

"Despite our incompatibility in marriage, you and I will discover a deep mutual respect and affection. I will be so taken with the good people of Selvarica, with their character, their potential to evolve into a great countship, that immediately upon returning to Brisadulce I will nominate your house to the open Quorum position."

He gapes at me. "I . . . I hardly know what to say."

"I also want two votes once you are a Quorum lord. Two separate occasions of my choosing when you *must* vote with me on an issue, regardless of your own feeling on the matter."

He begins to pace. I force myself to remain silent and still, giving him time to consider. I glance at my ladies. Mara is wide-eyed, whether from surprise or alarm I cannot tell. But Ximena wears a soft, approving smile, and when I catch her eye, she gives me a barely perceptible nod.

At last he says, "This seat on the Quorum. It will be permanent, yes?"

I nod. "To be passed down through your heirs. Only the military seats are not inherited."

"You think you can get the votes to approve my nomination?"

"I have one vote assured. I only need one more, and I have a few ideas on how to get it."

"So you can't guarantee that I will have a seat on the Quorum."

"I guarantee that I will try my best. Even if my nomination does not pass—which is unlikely—you will be forever marked as one who has the queen's favor."

He stops pacing, runs a hand through his hair, looking suddenly sheepish. "We could marry in truth, you know," he says. "You needn't offer me the concession of a Quorum position. I think . . . I think we could be good friends, you and I. Marriages are built on less."

Softly I ask, "Could you give me another heir?"

"Probably?"

I stare at him.

He sighs. "So, a fake betrothal in exchange for a Quorum nomination. And two votes if I take office."

"That is my bargain."

"Done."

I reach out and clasp his offered hand. He returns my smile with a delighted grin that lights up his whole face, and I think, briefly, what a tragedy it is for women everywhere that he cannot love them.

Then I add, "This is a secret bargain, witnessed only by my two ladies. It's fair that you be allowed two witnesses as well. Would you like me to repeat my offer in front of anyone?"

He doesn't even think about it. "I trust you."

"Then we are agreed. Would you mind postponing your departure? I would like to inform the Quorum of our imminent betrothal and give the nobility the opportunity to fawn over you."

He bows. "Of course, Your Majesty."

"Please. Call me Elisa."

We make preparations quickly. Tristán's people and mine will travel together in state. But there are certain precautions we must take, and Hector and Tristán spend long hours together, going over routes and formations and personnel.

Hector alone of the Royal Guard knows our betrothal to be a pretense.

We have a heated discussion about whether Storm the Invierno should accompany us. Ximena insists that he is too easily recognizable. But Father Alentín believes his knowledge could be useful. I point out that I would rather have him where we can keep an eye on him. When Hector promises to keep him cowled and hidden in a carriage, and Tristán vouches for the discretion of everyone in his entourage, we agree that Storm will come.

He is only too willing. He knows the truth of it: that I go in search of the *zafira*.

I cancel the Quorum meeting, the one I would have used to explain my foray into the prison tower, pleading eagerness to spend time with my potential husband. I tell Conde Eduardo that Tristán and I used the prison tower to begin negotiations, that with so many visiting the palace for Deliverance week, we both preferred privacy. It's a weak lie, and by the narrowing of his black eyes, I know the conde does not believe me.

But he does not press. He merely says, "It's not too late to change your mind and do what is best for our kingdom. I'm confident you'll come to understand that one of the northern lords would be more suitable."

I thank him for his counsel and assure him that I will make a considered choice.

The night before our journey, I am grateful for the darkness and solitude. I lie awake a long time, thinking of Alejandro. Though I've no intention of marrying Tristán, everyone *thinks* I do. A tear trickles down my cheek to think how easily displaced my late husband is. His presence touches everything around me. I see him in the dark woods and jeweled tones of his chamber, in the newly commissioned portrait in the Hall of Kings, in the face of his son. But the court gives him up so easily. When I do finally marry, it feels as though even the phantom memory will be well and truly gone.

"Elisa?" I feel the mattress dip as a tiny form crawls toward me on the bed.

I lift the blankets to let Rosario slip underneath. He worms close, and I wrap an arm around him.

"Does your nurse know you're here?"

He shrugs against me, which means she does not. I press my lips to his forehead.

"You're going away again," he accuses.

"Yes."

"I want to come."

Excuses run through my head. But I settle on the truth, as I always seem to, with him. "Bad people are trying to hurt me. So I can't have my heir travel with me. I need you to stay here and be safe."

"Are they going to kill you?"

"I hope not. I'm going to try my hardest to live."

"Hector will protect you."

I smile. "Yes, he definitely will."

"Will you come back?"

"I'll try my hardest to do that too. I promise."

He shifts, and his cold bare feet knock my leg, but I know better than to pull away. He says, "You always keep your promises."

I catch my breath. It's something I told him long ago. Little did I know at the time how important it would be to him, a boy to whom promises had never been kept. "I do."

He is quiet for such a long time that I think he must be sleeping, but then he whispers, so softly that I have to strain to hear, "I don't want to be king."

It's like a dagger in my chest, because if feels like failure. Of course he doesn't. Of course he's terrified. I know how hard it is to be frightened for so long. *I'm so sorry, Rosario.*

After a moment spent collecting myself, I say, "I think that if you decide you want to be king, you will be the greatest king in the history of Joya d'Arena. But I won't make you. You don't have to." My court would have collective apoplexy if they heard me say this, but I could never force the boy.

He sniffs. "Promise."

"I promise. But you have to promise me something too."

"What?"

"Promise me you won't discuss this with anyone until I get back." The last thing I need is for the country to start rumbling about an abdication. "Not a word. Also, if anything goes wrong, or if anything scares you while I'm gone, I want you to find Captain Lucio, Hector's second-in-command, and do exactly what he says. He will help you. If you can't find Lucio, go to Matteo. He's with Queen Cosmé's delegation in the dignitaries' suite."

His wide eyes gleam in the dark. "I promise."

I don't want to frighten him, but this is important. So I ask, "Who did I just say to find if something goes wrong?"

"Captain Lucio or Matteo."

"That's my boy." I pull the quilt up over his small shoulders. "How about you sleep here tonight?"

"Oh, all right," he says, as if it wasn't his grand plan all along.

The entire palace sees us off—servants, resident nobles, the city garrison. Conde Tristán's carriage leads the procession, followed by several guards on horseback, another carriage for my servants and supplies, and finally the queen's carriage, larger and more elaborate than the others, surrounded by even more guards on foot. The royal crest streams behind on pennants, and almost-sheer curtains hang in the gilt-framed windows.

But I am not in the queen's carriage.

I walk just behind it, surrounded by the conde's servants. I wear a rough cotton skirt and a shapeless blouse, a maid's cap pulled low on my brow. My skin is powdered to appear lighter, and my hair—my most distinctive trait—is plaited tight against my head and hidden under my cap.

General Luz-Manuel and Conde Eduardo stand on a balcony overlooking the main gate. The general is as cold and unreadable as always, but the conde seethes blackly. His eyes are narrowed, his jaw taut, his arms crossed. It's obvious that my last-minute excursion to Selvarica is not part of his plan, whatever it is. As we pass beneath him, under the palace portcullis, I force myself to look straight ahead lest I catch his eye.

Hector walks nearby, and from the crowd's perspective, I hope it appears as though he guards the queen's carriage. Through the almost-sheer curtains is the shape of a young woman sitting inside, a large crown on her head—my ruby crown, not my new one. The one made of shattered Godstones rides comfortably in my pack beneath the carriage bench.

Hector hired her. I don't know who she is or where he found her. And I don't want to know. She waves enthusiastically at the crowd, and I'm terrified for her, this decoy Elisa. I scan the onlookers for danger, thinking of all the ways to kill a person. It would be so easy.

Just like the day of my ill-fated birthday parade, we make our way down the Colonnade toward the city gate. To my left, a townhome towers above us, its high windows sparkling in the sunshine. An archer could hide up there, send an arrow spearing into the carriage, and then slip away in the chaos. And though the crowd is not as thick as it was for my birthday parade, enough strangers press close that I find myself flinching away. Any one of them could be carrying a dagger.

This is what it's like to be Hector and Ximena, I realize. Always terrified for someone else, always distrusting, imagining weapons and foul intentions where there are none. Is that why Hector is so stoic and hard? Why Ximena keeps so many thoughts to herself? Because it's the only way to deal with existing forever on the cusp of disaster?

My guard and my guardian.

Hector said that damage is the price of royalty, but maybe my price is so high that others will be forced to pay it. Maybe he and Ximena are the damaged ones. And Mara. And Rosario, who is afraid to be king.

It's a very long walk.

But when the gate and the desert beyond come into view, my heart starts to pound, not with terror but with excitement, maybe even happiness. I'm desperate to get beyond these walls, into open air and sunshine. I can't wait to feel the crush of sand beneath my boots, for the dry air to whip my hair against my cheeks. I hope we trade our horses for camels somewhere along the way. I miss their soft, long-lashed gazes and their resolute plodding. I even miss the scent of camel-dung campfires.

At last we pass through the shadow of the great wall and into the light. Our road leads south along the coastline, but to our left stretches my desert, vast and golden and shimmering with heat. Looking at it, my heart is so full I can hardly stand it. I feel freer, lighter, with each step we take away from the city. I want to skip or run or reach my arms wide to the openness of the sky and breathe it all in. I settle for kicking at bits of sand and gravel on the highway.

Hector sidles over and peers down, an odd look on his face. "I've never seen you smile like that before," he says.

I hadn't realized I was smiling. "Just glad to be outside, I guess. And look at that desert! Isn't it beautiful?"

"Yes," he says softly. "Beautiful."

"Did you know that some nights, if you time it just right, you can glimpse the Sierra Sangre at sunset? As the sun dips below the ocean, the eastern horizon flashes red, bright as blood. It's amazing."

"No, I didn't know that."

"You should look for it tonight. And in the afternoon, when it's the hottest, all the colors of the world coalesce where the sand edges up against the sky. Like a ripple of light."

"You don't say."

I look up at him sharply, wary of the amusement in his voice. Is he mocking me? "Surely there's a place you love too? Somewhere you're always happy to go back to? Where you feel more yourself than anywhere else?"

As Hector considers, our procession shifts to the right to allow the steady stream of oncoming traffic—a few dusty riders, both on camelback and horseback, one small merchant caravan. They view the queen's carriage with wide eyes and keep their distance. Up ahead, Mara swings out of the servants' carriage to walk beside it. I don't blame her; I wouldn't want to be ensconced with Storm for any length of time either.

"Yes, there is such a place," Hector says at last.

"As your queen, I command you to tell me about it." I want to whip off my maid's cap, to expose my head to the sun and sky, but I don't dare. Everyone in our group knows who I am—their participation in the plan is crucial—

but the highway is too busy this close to the city.

"Well, since you command it," Hector says wryly, "I'll tell you about Ventierra, my father's countship."

For some reason, I'm feeling the need to tease. "Oh? Surely that tiny patch of dirt is nothing compared to this." I gesture toward the dunes.

He takes it in stride. "'That tiny patch of dirt' is made up of rolling hills, bright green during the rainy season, golden when dry. The grass is like an ocean, so long that it ripples on a windy day. From a distance, it shimmers like velvet." His eyes grow distant as he speaks, and the planes of his face soften. "Waves crash against the coastal cliffs, spewing geysers of white water into the air. Near the mouth of the river are tide pools—I spent hours and hours playing there as a boy. But nothing is more beautiful than a vineyard ready for harvest. Rows and rows of grapevines, dripping with frosty purple . . ."

"Ah," I say. "That painting in your quarters."

"Yes. I used to steal grapes off the vine when my father wasn't looking. I felt sorry for them, getting beaten and pressed, rotting into something that smelled bad. It seemed to me that grapes would rather be grapes than wine."

I laugh.

"What did I say?"

"Nothing. It's just that I've never seen *you* smile like that before."

Our gazes lock. The rest of the world drops away, and all I can think is, *God, I love his smile.* It melts the last few years off of his face, and I see the boy underneath, the one who scampered among tide pools and rescued helpless grapes. What happened to that boy? Alejandro, I suppose. And war. And me.

I say, "I'd like to see Ventierra someday."

His smile fades. "I would too."

"You miss it, then?"

He just shrugs.

I stare at his profile, which has gone flinty. It's his way, when he's trying not to feel too much.

"I didn't realize you were so homesick."

He whips his head around. "I didn't say—"

"You didn't have to."

He shrugs sheepishly. "I like my home in Brisadulce too."

"I'm glad."

Up ahead, the curtains of the queen's carriage part, and Ximena peeks out. I smile and wink. She starts to smile back, but then she sees Hector beside me and her smile fades. The curtain swishes back into place. I frown at the spot her head just vacated, wondering what she is thinking.

As evening burnishes the sand to copper, we bypass a busy way station of scattered adobe huts and palm-roofed stables in favor of making camp alone, well off the road and in the sand.

I peer into the queen's carriage for my pack and tent. Ximena sits beside decoy Elisa, looking stiff and out of sorts. The girl herself has wilted beneath her veil and crown, and pools of sweat collect under her arms. I wince in sympathy. "I don't think the crown is still necessary," I tell her. "Or the veil. This far from the road, why don't you open the curtains and cool off?" She and Ximena will sleep in the carriage, presenting a tempting target for any would-be assassin.

"Thank you, Your Majesty," she says in a shy voice. I haven't bothered to learn her name. I don't want her to become too real to me.

I spot my pack and tent beneath the bench and grab them. I call out to Hector, "Where do you want me to set up?"

He gestures toward a flat spot, saying, "We'll make a perimeter around you."

I flip open the tent roll, pull out the poles, and get to work. My fingers fly with motion memory, and I revel in the feel of it, the crunch of sand as I bear down with my poles, the sound of fabric flapping in the wind. I leave the entrance open, tied up at the side with loops for that purpose. I rummage through my pack for flint and steel, then toss the rest of the pack inside my tent. Time to get a cook fire started, if Mara hasn't already.

A shape looms before me, and I nearly drop my flint and steel.

Conde Tristán is staring at me, his eyes wide. "I don't think I've ever seen someone set up a tent so fast. I didn't know you could do that." Other tents are going up around mine, including a larger one to be shared by Belén and Alentín.

My grin is smug. "Did you think I spent my days as leader of the Malficio embroidering? Composing odes to the desert sunset, maybe?"

He runs his hand through his hair. "No. I guess I just imagined more . . . administrative tasks."

"I can also start a fire, skin a rabbit, forage for edible plants, tend minor wounds." It feels good to brag shamelessly. "Oh, and I can definitely scare something off by flinging a rock in its general direction with a sling."

Several paces away, Hector has removed the saddle from an antsy bay gelding and is toweling him down. He looks up from his work and catches my eye, a smug look on his face. Hector, at least, is unsurprised to find me so capable. He might even be a bit proud. It makes me feel warm all over.

Later as we sit around the campfire sipping Mara's soup—not jerboa, but a light broth made with lentils and dried vegetables—the sun dips into the distant sea. I'm not paying attention to see if the sky flashes red on the opposite horizon because I'm staring north instead. Though we are too far from Brisadulce to see its walls, a soft sphere of radiance against the black sky marks the spot. I think of the thousands of lanterns and candles now brightening my capital city. And I think, with a twist of despair, how I feel so much happier, safer, *abler* away from it.

But we haven't gone far the next day when Hector mutters, "I think we're being followed."

I snap my head up to look at him, then force myself to stare straight ahead. If indeed we are being followed, then it wouldn't do for the queen's Guard to be seen talking to a maid who looks uncannily like the queen.

I say, "Are you sure? This road is highly traveled."

"No. Just something to watch for now. But a group of riders has kept a steady distance behind us since we set off. They don't have carriages, and no one is on foot. So they should be traveling much faster than we are."

"Everyone knows I journey south. Maybe someone is curious. In fact we may attract quite a caravan along the way."

"Maybe." But his tone is unconvinced.

"Would it help for me to walk in front of the queen's carriage instead of behind it?" I say hopefully. I'm choking on dust, and I've had to tie my shawl across my nose on several occasions.

"It might," he says. "Though I hate to give up the advantage of having you covered in filth. No one would recognize you like that."

I can't help turning to glare at him. His lips twitch, but the amusement fades quickly. "We'll keep an eye on them," he says.

"No." I'm in the desert now. I know exactly what to do. "We'll do better than that."

"Oh?"

"If they're still behind us when we camp tonight, I'll send Belén to scout them."

"You've decided to trust him, then?"

"I trust his ability to scout." I think back to the day of Iladro's poisoning. It felt so natural to call on Belén for help. The moment required it, and we slipped back into our old roles as if nothing had happened. "And I dare hope the other kind of trust will come in time."

When we make camp, the riding party Hector spotted is still there, tiny black figures near the horizon. Other travelers come and go, but these riders stop when we do, make camp when we do. Their campfire glows as dusk fades to night.

I order everyone to forego campfires tonight, and we dine on jerky, dried dates, and flatbread. I don't want anyone to see us from a distance, to know that we hold council.

We sit in a rough circle with only the moon and stars for light. There are almost thirty of us, including Tristán's people, all of whom were personally vouched for. Even Storm dares exit the carriage to join us. The others eye him warily but make a space for him. He does not remove his cowl.

I stand and say, "Belén, come here."

He approaches without hesitation and drops to one knee.

I ask, "Do you still wish to swear fealty to me?"

His soft indrawn breath is the only indication that I've taken him by surprise. "I do," he says evenly.

"Then I would accept you into my service."

He reaches up with both hands and clutches the fabric at my waist, quickly, as if he's afraid I'll change my mind. It's intimate and unnerving, especially when the side of his thumb brushes across my Godstone, and I hear the whisper of drawn daggers somewhere nearby. But it's the traditional gesture of a newly sworn vassal, and it must be allowed.

Belén intones, "I swear my life and service unto you. I swear to protect you and to honor you. I am yours to command in all things. For as long as I live, your people shall be my people, your ways my ways, your God my God."

I take his hands and pull him to his feet while everyone in the group mutters, "Selah."

He towers over me. I can't help but stare at his eye patch. He was tortured. For me. Because he refused to give me up once he realized his mistake. On impulse, I pull him close and hug him tight.

He whispers, "Thank you, Elisa."

Behind him, I glimpse Mara's face. Her cheeks shine with moonlit tears.

I pull away, hoping I have not forgiven too easily. But it feels right to do it. "I need your help," I tell him. "Tonight."

"Anything."

When I explain about the riders following us, he nods, unsurprised. I don't even have to tell him what to do. He simply says, "I'll be back by morning." And he slips away into the darkness.

"Who do you think it is?" Mara asks, once he is gone.

I sit back down and cross my legs. "I suspect Conde Eduardo. He was displeased to hear of this journey and its purpose. He is set on me marrying a northern lord. And he knows I've been keeping things from him."

"He does not know about me, yes?" Storm says in his sibilant voice.

"That is one of the things I've been keeping from him."

"If they are the conde's people," Ximena says, "we might be able to use them to our advantage. Set a false trail, maybe."

"Exactly what I was thinking," I say.

"What if they're thieves?" says a female voice I don't recognize.

Hector barks a laugh. "Then they are poor thieves indeed," he says. "Five against all of us?"

He is right to be amused. He and Tristán could probably defeat five common thieves alone. What I worry about, what I don't say, is that they might be assassins. They might be observing, patient and cold, waiting for the right moment to creep into our camp.

Perhaps Hector is thinking the same thing, because he says, "Until we know for sure, we're doubling our watch. Elisa, will you ride in the servants' carriage tomorrow, out of sight?"

I open my mouth to protest, to say that I prefer my own two feet to a hot, bumpy carriage, but then I remember that I've decided to trust his judgment in these matters. "All right," I say. And it really is.

18

I'M awakened by a hand pressing across my mouth. I arch away
from the intruder, pulse pounding, drawing breath through my
nose. It's happening at last, what I have feared—

"Elisa!" comes Belén's whispered voice. "It's me."

I go limp with relief. He removes his hand, saying, "Shh!"

"What do you think you're doing?" I whisper furiously.

"I wanted to see if I could sneak past Tristán's sentries and
the Royal Guard and into your tent."

"Oh." I push back my bedroll and sit up, then rub warmth
into my arms. My guard is the most elite force in the country.
Surely not just anyone could slip by them. Weakly I say, "Well,
you *are* one of the sneakiest people I've ever known."

"I don't deny it." I can't see him in the dark, but I hear the
smile in his voice.

"What did you find?"

My tent tilts precariously as he knocks the wall crossing his
legs. "Five men trying to pass as desert nomads. By their clothing, you'd think they came from my own village. But the hair

isn't right. It's too . . . careful. Coifed, even. And their horses are stout and sea bred. No colors, no markings, but their tack is high quality. Even the weave of their saddle blankets testifies to wealth."

"So they might be Conde Eduardo's men after all. Or the general's."

"I recognized one. I don't know his name, but I've seen him at the conde's shoulder. A very tall man, taller than me. Fine, straight hair slicked back with oil. He seems young at first glance, but I'd wager not. He has the look of experience about him."

I search my memory, cataloging the conde's advisers and attendants. There is only one I've never encountered. "You may be describing Franco," I say. "An elusive man. I don't know that I've ever spoken to him."

He pauses, shifts in his rear. "Elisa . . . you should know. If Humberto were alive, he would be very proud of you."

The hurt that wells up is so unexpected that it's a moment before I can speak. "Thank you," I manage. I have to redirect the subject. I'm not sure I want to talk about Humberto. "Did you overhear anything?"

"A tasteless observation about one of their mothers and her goat, which I will not repeat. One suggested they allow themselves to drop farther behind tomorrow. 'Out of sight,' he said. But the tall one—Franco?—said, 'We have to keep her in view. She'll make a move soon enough.'"

I loose a breath I didn't realize I'd been holding. "So we can reasonably conclude that they follow us, most likely on the conde's orders."

"I think so, yes."

I lie back down and pull the blanket up over my shoulders. "Go get some sleep. We'll let the others know in the morning."

"Yes, Your Majesty." He turns over on his knees, no longer bothering with stealth.

"And Belén?"

"Yes, Your Majesty?"

Maybe I *do* want to talk about him. A little. "Humberto would be proud of you, too. He always believed you'd come back to us." Saying his name aloud doesn't hurt as much as I thought it would. *Humberto*, I practice silently. *Humberto*.

A soft catch of breath. Then: "He had a way of believing in people long before they believed in themselves, didn't he?"

The entrance to my tent flaps closes, and he is gone.

As we breakfast on corn cakes fried in olive oil, Ximena and Hector argue about whether or not to split the group apart. Everyone else listens to their discussion, shifting awkwardly in the sand, trying to be invisible.

Only Storm has not joined us for breakfast; he does not dare leave the carriage in daylight.

"There is safety in numbers," Ximena insists. "Five men against our guard and Conde Tristán's warriors? It's no contest. And I'm not convinced they're out to cause trouble. It's likely the conde just sent them to keep an eye on Elisa. This journey does not play into his plans, and he's desperate to feel like he has some sort of control over the situation. The best thing we can do is stick together. Go to Selvarica as planned.

The more expectations we meet, the less suspicious we become to observers. But if we separate, Elisa is even more vulnerable."

Conde Eduardo is not the only one desperate to feel some sort of control, I muse as I chew on my corn cake. Ximena seethes with the frustration of being stuck in the carriage with the decoy queen, unable to keep close watch over me. She hates ceding complete responsibility to Hector.

"I hope you're right, Lady Ximena," Hector says. "But if he merely wanted to keep an eye on the queen, why didn't he insist on letting his own delegation travel with us? It doesn't make sense. And the presence of Franco has me concerned. He's a shadow adviser. No one knows anything about him. My instincts say all is not as it seems."

"We should have traveled with a larger party," Ximena says.

Hector shakes his head. "I don't trust enough people to form a larger party. Better the enemy out there than here among us."

Tristán has been listening quietly, sipping from a waterskin at regular intervals. He ties it off, sets it in the sand, and gains his feet. He does it gracefully, in such a way that all our eyes are drawn to him. His beautiful face is grave when he says, "My father was killed on a journey such as this. It's the perfect opportunity, you see. Anyone can be blamed. So no one ever really is. I still don't know who killed my father."

Everyone is silent. I say, "What do *you* advise?"

He shrugs. "I don't know. Caution, I guess. I think the Lady Ximena is overly optimistic to hope the conde merely wants you observed. But I'm also not convinced that splitting off would be safer for you."

I take a deep breath. I have to make a decision. And it's one that could lead to someone's death. Mine, or decoy Elisa's, or someone I care about. I used to make these kinds of decisions all the time, when I was only a desert rebel. I would have expected to become accustomed to it.

"We have a plan for splitting the group if necessary, right?" I say.

Hector nods. "We do. But we can't do it in open desert. We need to reach a village or trading post. Better yet, a large port like Puerto Verde."

"Then we continue on as we are for now. Belén, you will observe them every night, so long as you feel you can get there and back undetected."

He ducks his head obediently. "I can do it."

"I'll reevaluate when we reach a trading post."

We break off to pack up camp. Ximena glowers as she returns to the decoy carriage.

As I'm rolling up my tent, Hector comes up beside me. "Tonight," he says, "I'll sleep outside your door. We'll see if Belén can get by *me*."

I freeze, and my fingers dig into the tent fabric. Humberto used to do the same thing, to protect me from the others. I look into Hector's eyes. They're steady and fierce, but I can't tell what he's thinking. I could always tell what Humberto was thinking.

Hector is so much more complicated, and though he is less a mystery to me than he used to be, it feels like I could spend years peeling back the layers, trying to learn his whole person.

When I don't answer right away, he says, "Please let me do this."

One thing I am certain of: I trust him utterly. "Thank you," I say at last. "I'll sleep easier knowing you're there." And it's the truth.

Riding in the servants' carriage is as awful as I anticipated. In no time, my back and rear ache from being jostled against the wooden bench, and I am crazy with heat, for we deliberately chose carriages with only small, curtained windows. Sweat pools between my breasts and soaks my hairline, curling wisps of hair that have escaped my plaits.

There are two nice things about the arrangement, though. One is that Hector sits beside me, and our thighs brush with every jolt of the carriage. When one wheel hits a large stone, the carriage lurches to the side and I slide along the bench until our hips collide. The carriage rights itself quickly, but neither of us bothers to move away.

The second nice thing is that it gives me a chance to talk with Storm for the first time in days. He sits on the bench across from us, and he is so tall his head nearly brushes the roof. He has pushed back his cowl, and sweat glistens on his near-perfect skin. He fans himself with a dried palm frond.

"Are you enjoying our journey so far?" I ask with no small amount of amusement.

He hisses, and his green eyes spark with fury, or maybe loathing. I feel Hector's body go taut.

But I am no longer afraid of the Invierno. Logic tells me to consider him a threat, to remember that he might even be the assassin who stabbed me in the catacombs. But my instincts say otherwise. Perhaps it's his transparency that makes me feel safe with him. He is one of the few who never bothers to hide his true thoughts from me. Maybe the only.

"This desert is God cursed," he says.

"Your people do not seem well suited to it," I observe.

"Indeed not. Our skin cracks and dries; our feet blister. There are days it feels like my blood is boiling. I found much relief from the wretched climate in my cavern hideout."

I scowl at him. "And yet you marched an army of thousands across the desert to try to overrun us."

"Well, we skirted it to the north and south, but yes. It was a difficult journey. Hundreds perished from the heat alone."

"Your own country is much cooler by comparison?"

"Cooler. Wetter. Lovelier. Better, really, in every possible way than this forsaken blight that you rule."

I surprise myself by laughing.

I'm further surprised to see his lips twitch with a hint of a smile. He says, "So tell me, Your Majesty. Why do I have the displeasure of your company today?"

"I yearned to bask in the light of your empathy and good cheer."

"Sarcasm again. I thought you would tell me you had decided to hide like a frightened rabbit from the group following us."

"I'm hiding like a wise rabbit."

"Do you think they are the conde's men?"

"I do, though I can't be sure. One of them, a tall, quiet

man, has been seen with the conde before."

He starts forward so abruptly that our knees collide.

Hector's dagger is at his throat in an instant. "Back. Away."

Storm edges back, resumes fanning himself with the palm frond. His face becomes a mask of calm, even as he keeps a careful eye on Hector's dagger. He says, "Describe this person to me."

So I do, trying to remember Belén's description exactly: Tall, hair slicked back, young looking, a close adviser. Storm coils in on himself, growing tighter and tighter with the telling until he looks like a cornered cat.

"What is it? Do you know this man?"

"I have to get away," he says. "At the soonest opportunity. Leave me at the next trading post. No, leave me when we get to a large port. I'll need a place big enough to disappear in. I can make my way back—"

"Storm! Do you know this man?"

He inhales deeply, and the mask of calm settles over his uncanny features once again. "I do know him. Franco, right? That's not his real name. His real name, in God's language, is Listen to the Falling Water, for Her Secrets Carve Canyons into Hearts of Stone."

I gasp. "An Invierno!"

"A spy," Hector says.

Storm says, "If Franco learns I am here, he will kill me."

"Conde Eduardo has an Invierne spy working for him," I say, as though sending the words aloud into the world will help me believe them. "Does the conde know that Franco is an Invierno?"

Storm shrugs. "I don't know."

"Why didn't you tell me there was an Invierne spy in the employ of one of my own Quorum lords?"

"You didn't ask. Also, I've been underground for more than a year. I didn't know he had worked his way into the conde's inner circle."

"Have any others infiltrated my court?"

"Not that I know of. Your Majesty, you *must* let me go at the nearest port."

The carriage lurches again, and I grab Hector's knee instinctively. Storm's gaze drops to my hand, and he allows himself a secret smile. I draw my hand back, curl it into a fist in my lap.

"If I let you go," I tell him, "you would miss your chance to accompany us to the *zafira*. You won't get another. Only someone who bears a living Godstone can navigate there, remember?"

He runs a hand through his golden hair, considering. Now that I've become a bit used to the odd color, I find it more beautiful than alarming. "You make a good point," he admits.

"We could leave Storm behind," Hector suggests, and his gaze on our companion is unwavering. "It might distract Franco, give us a chance to put some distance between us."

That will never happen. I don't care to show my hand to Eduardo or the Invierne spy by revealing that I'm harboring the former ambassador. But the alarm on the Invierno's face is so satisfying that I pretend to consider it.

"If we left you behind, do you think you could get away?"

"No! Not if Franco sees me and recognizes me. He would stop at nothing to have me killed."

"So it *would* be sufficient distraction. They would abandon us for a while to chase after you."

He opens his mouth, closes it. I see the exact instant he recognizes that I've trapped him on purpose.

"This Franco. He must be very capable for you to be so frightened of him."

Fury rolls off him in waves. He says, "Your Majesty, he is a trained assassin."

I gasp. An Invierne assassin in my own palace all this time. In the employ of a Quorum lord. I never even suspected. What if he's the one responsible for the attempts on my life? If so, he will surely try again.

I say to Storm, "I suppose you ought to stay hidden in the carriage. Like a frightened rabbit."

He scowls.

"Don't worry," I add. "I'm sure I can find someone to keep you company."

"I'd rather be alone."

I turn my lips into what I hope is a decent approximation of his own smug grin. "I know."

"You would do well to hide, too," he says. "Franco is cunning and skilled. He is to murder what an animagus is to magic."

"Oh." I let my face fall into my hands, not caring that Storm will see and be amused. "Hector, we have to tell everyone about this."

He reaches over and gives my knee a squeeze. "Yes," he

murmurs, and I close my eyes to savor the sensation.

When we break for the noon meal, I tell everyone else what I learned from Storm. No one is more surprised and terrified than decoy Elisa, who clings to Ximena's arm with a white-knuckled grip. Her veil blurs her eyes and nose, and I'm relieved that I can't see the fear sparking there, even more relieved that we cannot make eye contact. Because I'm terrified for her, too.

"I can take care of him," Belén says. "Tonight. I'll slip into his camp and put a dagger to his throat."

"Storm said Franco is specially trained," I remind him. "He might be your match."

"I can take care of him," Belén repeats.

I know what Belén can do. Cosmé once told me the story of how she watched from a ridge as he snuck into an Invierno scout camp, slit the throats of three of their warriors, and disappeared like fog. Should I send an assassin to kill an assassin? I know so little about Invierne. Is this Franco an anomaly of their world? Or does he come from a long tradition of elite selection and training, like my own Royal Guard? I must ask Storm about it before deciding.

Tristán says, "I'd like to change my vote."

"Vote? What do you mean?" I ask.

"I think our company should split up," he says. "At the next port, you and a few others should go off in search of the *zafira* without the rest of us. We'll try to draw the assassin away. It's an opportunity you shouldn't pass up. They'll eventually figure out what happened, but you could buy yourself days, even weeks, of safety."

I nod, considering.

Ximena says, "I agree. It was one thing to be followed by the servants of a pouting Quorum lord. An assassin is another thing entirely." She looks down pityingly at the creature clinging to her.

"Hector, when is the soonest we could split off?" I ask.

"If we can make Puerto Verde, a few days south of here, I might be able to commission a ship. I know a captain who's scheduled to be in port soon with a batch of early-harvest wine."

Probably wine from his home in Ventierra. "Someone you trust, then?" I ask.

He nods. "With my life and honor."

"Then we continue on to Puerto Verde and split off there. We'll keep a close eye on Franco and his group until then and adapt as necessary." I look around at everyone. "Unless I hear convincing counsel otherwise?"

No one has anything to add.

"Then let's get moving."

As Hector and I climb back into the carriage, I glance northward, along the shimmering highway. It's strangely devoid of travelers, except for the small group following us. They are barely more than motes on the horizon. So there is no reason, I tell myself, no reason at all, to feel as if the assassin's gaze is boring holes into my back.

19

AFTER an evening meal of dried tilapia and dates, I sit cross-legged just inside the threshold of my tent while Ximena unpins my hair to let it down into a more comfortable sleeping braid. While she works, Hector comes over and flips out his bedroll in front of my door. He sets his pack beside it, shoving it down into the sand so that it doesn't tip over. I watch him carefully, fascinated by the way he moves. Every motion is so strong and sure.

When he pulls off his overshirt, my heart speeds up. His bare shoulders flex as he reaches beneath one arm to unlace his breastplate, and I swallow hard against the sudden moisture in my mouth as he lifts his breastplate over his head and sets it on top of his pack. His back is broad and taut with muscle, his waist trim. His sun-darkened skin shimmers faintly, and even though our camp is dimly lit, I see his scars, several of them. Most are tiny white lines, but one is larger and jagged, running diagonally across his lower back. I have an overwhelming urge to trace its length.

Instead I place my fingertips to my own mark, just left of the Godstone. Both of us, scarred. I wonder how he got his? I want to know about it more than anything. I want him to share that part of himself with me. I want—

Ximena's fingers grip my chin. She forces my gaze to hers and regards me sternly for a long moment. "It is a hard thing to be queen, my sky," she says.

I blink up at her. She's warning me. She wants him for Alodia, after all. And she's right. It would be a smart match.

But the very thought hollows out my chest, leaving me empty and aching.

Not trusting my voice, I just nod. She kisses my forehead, then goes off to attend her fake queen.

Ignoring Hector, I crawl into my tent and lie down on my bedroll with my head at the door. I lie there a long time, listening to him breathe.

Minutes later, or maybe an hour, I raise my head and whisper, "Hector?"

"Yes?" he whispers back.

His face is so near. Just the space of a breath away. I swallow hard. "My sister. Alodia. She has . . ." Oh, God, it's so hard to say, but I can't bear to pretend away such a huge thing. I inhale through my nose and try again. "My sister has made inquiries about you. In regards to a potential marriage agreement."

A long pause. Then, "Well, that would explain why she opened correspondence with me."

"Oh!" Pain, sharp and hard, squeezes my chest. Alodia already made her move then, before writing to me.

"She's like you, you know," he says. "Intelligent. Beautiful. But . . ."

"And will you . . . that is, are you considering . . ." I can't finish. I'm not sure I want to know.

He looses a shuddering breath. Then he says, "I will do whatever my queen commands."

Of course he will.

Something overtakes me, desperation maybe, and before I know it I'm slipping my hand past the tent flap. My fingers find his wrist. It shifts, and suddenly my hand is wrapped in one of Hector's much larger ones. Something about his gentle strength brings tears to my eyes.

It's on the tip of my tongue to tell him I love him. Instead I say, waveringly, "I told Alodia that you are the best man I know."

He gives my hand a squeeze. "Thank you," he whispers.

I fall asleep like that, my fingers woven with Hector's. Belén does not visit me. Or if he does, he chooses not to intrude.

Two days later, the desert cedes to rolling coastal hills. The sand still stretches east as far as the eye can see, but the hills along the coast mark the beginning of the southern holdings, the most temperate part of my kingdom. As we climb, the land beside the road turns from sand to hard dirt that is dotted with dry grass and the occasional scrub tree.

A day after that, we reach Puerto Verde. We crest a hill and there it is, laid out before us, a deep crescent bay the color of turquoise, carved into cliffs that protect the port from heavy surf. Cargo ships dot the water; I stop counting at twenty. There are even more small boats; dinghies and fishing vessels predominate, with a handful of flat pleasure barges.

A medium-size city hugs the cliffs, spills into the water on stilted buildings and docks. It seems that docks are everywhere, sending crooked fingers well into the bay. It's such a boisterous place, and from this distance, it takes a few moments for me to make sense of the bustle. Traders haggle and yell. Sailors load and unload ships. Clerks catalog piles of items. Everyone is busy, fast moving, loud. It's so different from the easy rhythm of Brisadulce.

My people, I think. I rule this city as surely as any other, and yet this will be my first time setting foot in it.

The road zags down the cliffs, and we hug the walls tight as we travel. I've never been afraid of heights, but I still can't bring myself to peer out the carriage window and over the edge to the bay far below. I gaze out the opposite window instead, and I catch glimpses of wooden platforms jutting out over our heads, of elaborate pulleys and winches used to haul cargo up the cliff face.

By the time we reach the bottom, word has gone out that the queen's carriage approaches, and the city goes still with reverent silence. We made no secret of our journey. Wasn't that the whole point of this excursion? To be openly courted by Conde Tristán? To explore a remote part of my kingdom in search of the *zafira* without raising unwanted questions? But my teeth clench and my neck and shoulders ache with strain. Everyone stares as we pass.

We reach an inn called the Sailor's Knot. A small crowd gathers on the porch to greet us—the inn staff, no doubt. I see smiles and nervous shifting and a few flags hastily embroidered with my royal crest. Our official itinerary declares a two-day recess here.

But our official itinerary, like my decoy queen, is meant to throw off potential ambushes. I'm glad. The place looks creaky, with a porch made of poorly joined driftwood and sandstone walls that drip random stains. As we pass by, though, I twinge with self-reproach, for the faces in the crowd deflate, then gaze after us with confusion and disappointment.

A block farther, we turn a corner and arrive at our actual destination, the King's Inn. Conde Tristán chose it specifically because its high third-story provides a good view of the surrounding buildings, and because its location one block from the main street makes the entrances less visible.

Our caravan noses into an alley that leads to a wide, dark stable. Hector and I jump from the carriage—Storm will stay inside until nightfall—and my guard moves quickly to establish a perimeter at our rear while Tristán's men unhitch the horses and begin unloading. When decoy Elisa steps from the queen's carriage, a cry of greeting goes up, from the few stubborn souls have followed us here. "Queen Elisa!" a voice calls. "Your Majesty!" yells another. Someone jostles my guard for a better view, but my men hold firm.

Decoy Elisa doesn't react, except to clutch her veil close to her throat. Led by Belén and Alentín, my ladies hustle her through the stables and into the back entrance of the inn.

I sling my pack over my shoulder, then grab a trunk from the queen's carriage, just like a real maid. I follow my decoy into the inn, feeling darkly wrong about leaving my people outside, ignored and unacknowledged. "I'll make it up to you," I whisper. Someday, I'll come back when I can be *me*.

The innkeeper, a gnarled man with a bald patch and a nervous smile, falls all over himself to accommodate us, arranging for hot baths and meals in our rooms. Decoy Elisa smiles vaguely at him and manages a few thank yous. When he finally leaves, she lies down for a nap, and I have my first bath in days.

"I do love baths," I say with a luxuriant sigh.

Mara laughs. "I know. Though truly, Elisa, you hardly need pampering out here. You seem perfectly happy to tramp about the desert in your nomad clothes, sweaty and dusty and sun darkened."

My smile dies on my face before fully formed. "I would be, if I weren't terrified for my life and the lives of those around me."

She doesn't say anything to that, just grabs my hand and squeezes.

Ximena approaches armed with a brush and several hairpins, but I put up a hand to ward her off. "Can we leave my hair down, please? Just for tonight? It's been tightly plaited the last few days, and my head *aches* from it."

She frowns and puts the hairpins and brush away with obvious reluctance. I stare at my nurse while Mara towels my hair dry and finger brushes it. Ximena has always been unperturbedly calm and stoic—I suppose she and Hector have that in common. But lately she seems downright surly.

Awhile later, my hair has dried in waves down to my waist, and I am dressed in a clean linen tunic belted over soft leather pants when the rest of our group files quietly into my suite. Two guards will remain outside to watch the door, but everyone else squeezes inside and finds a spot on the rugs or the beds to sit.

Hector is the last to arrive, and when he sees me, he freezes, then moves quickly to an empty space at the foot of decoy Elisa's bed, where he plunks down and stretches out his long legs.

Mara leans over and whispers in my ear, "I know you're charmingly naive when it comes to matters of the heart, but you just stopped him in his tracks."

I bring my knees to my chest, reach down to finger the hem of my pants. I whisper back, "I was about to tell myself I had imagined it."

She rolls her eyes at me.

Tristán moves to the center of the room to address everyone. "We're scheduled to be in town for two days," he says. "I'll meet officially with Puerto Verde's mayor tomorrow. The dowager queen, Rosario's grandmother, is also in residence here, on an estate in the hills, but reportedly in failing health and unable to offer us hospitality. I'll make an attempt to see her, for appearances' sake. Her Majesty Queen Elisa has unfortunately taken ill from a bad batch of oysters and will be unable to make any appointments."

Everyone titters with amusement.

"But we need to be prepared for contingencies, which

means lengthening our stay, or even cutting it short. I expect everyone to be alert at all times for changes in plan. Understood?"

I find myself nodding along with everyone else. Tristán has such a nice presence about him. Commanding, intelligent, worthy of my trust.

"Hector?" Tristán cedes the floor to the commander of my guard and sits down beside Iladro, who gazes at him with unabashed admiration. Now that I know they're lovers, it's so painfully obvious to me that I wonder how I didn't notice before.

Hector stands, saying, "I've confirmed that a ship is scheduled to dock here this week. It could be tomorrow or a week from now, depending on weather. The ship is well known to me, and I trust its captain and crew to protect the queen with their lives. So I suggest we wait for it before splitting off. Alternately, we could hire a different ship, or even a caravan."

As one, everyone turns to me for the ultimate decision. I say, "Belén, can you scout again tonight? I'd like to know if our new friends have followed us into the city and whether they take lodgings nearby."

"I can," he says.

"Then we will wait for Hector's ship, unless Franco makes a move."

"Or if he disappears entirely," Hector adds.

I nod. "If he is able to slip Belén's careful eye, I will consider that making a move."

"My offer to kill him stands," Belén says. "Just say the word."

"Thank you," I say, and it gives me a strange, twisty feeling to know I'm grateful for someone's willingness to kill for me. "But focusing Conde Eduaro's efforts in the wrong direction is too good an opportunity to pass up."

Tristán says, "Majesty, have you decided who goes with you when we split off?"

I take a deep breath. I have been dreading this moment. "Tristán, you and Iladro will of course continue with the caravan."

He bows his head. "Of course."

I need people who are used to rough travel, people I trust with my life. "There will be five of us, the holy number of perfection," I say. "Mara, you will come with me. And Belén. I confess I'm not sure what to do about you, Father Alentín. I'd like to have a priest with me as we track down the *zafira*. Your knowledge, your ability to sense the Godstone, could be crucial. But as Cosmé's ambassador, your absence would be noted."

The priest nods wearily, rubbing at his stumped shoulder as if aching with phantom pain. "I want to help you find the *zafira* more than anything," he says. "But I'm an old man now. And Her Majesty Queen Cosmé will be disappointed if I do not travel in state with false you and your soon-to-be betrothed. My ultimate loyalty must be to Basajuan now, you see."

I manage a sad smile. This is it, then, for us. Truly, he will never again be *my* priest. "Then I insist you go with the caravan," I tell him.

"I will pray for you every day," he says softly.

I swallow the lump in my throat. "Thank you."

"What about Storm?" Ximena asks.

"His knowledge may be useful. And he'll behave, so long as he's on the track of the *zafira*. He comes with me."

Ximena's eyes narrow. "He is nothing if not noticeable."

I nod. "I'll order him to cut and dye his hair tonight. That should help him pass cursory glances, at least." It will also give him something harmless to focus his fury on. I smile just thinking about it.

"I will go with you, of course," she says. "As your guardian—"

"No." There. I've said it.

Her black eyes fly wide. Not with surprise, I note carefully, but frustration and anger. She knew it was coming as much as I did.

"You are the queen's most visible attendant," I explain. "Mara has been my lady-in-waiting for less than a year. But you've been with me my whole life, and everyone knows it. You *must* be seen with my decoy."

"I have to go with you," she whispers. "Always. It is my duty. I was ordained for it by the Monastery-at-Amalur. Elisa, *it is God's will.*"

And that is exactly the wrong thing to say to me, because anger boils up in my throat, so thick I almost choke on it. "You will attend my decoy as if she were me." I enunciate each word, my voice sharp and hard. "You will protect her with your life."

Her chest rises as she draws breath to argue further, but Tristán wisely interjects. "So, you, Mara, Belén, and Storm. Lord Commander Hector too, I presume?"

"Yes. Hector. He's the one with the plan." I meet Hector's eye and note the slightest softening of his features. "The five of us."

Hector says, "We'll slip away at dusk disguised as highway traders. A small wagon waits for us in the stables, packed with a few odds and ends. We'll take it to the docks, ostensibly to trade with one of the ships there, but of course, we will never disembark. If something goes wrong, I have an alternate escape prepared through the sewer beneath the inn."

"Ugh," Mara says.

"We'll hope it doesn't come to that," Hector says. "And a few weeks from now, we'll rendezvous in Selvarica after finding the *zafira*."

"That's it, then," I say. "Everyone get a good night's sleep. Except Belén."

Belén's answering grin is as quick and bright as lightning. He is the first to slip out the door. Everyone else follows at a more leisurely pace.

I overhear Ximena saying, "Hector, a word with you, please?"

His face is expressionless as he follows her to a dark corner of my suite. She speaks softly to him, but her gaze is intent, her fists clenched at her sides.

Mara whispers, "You made the right decision."

"Yes." But I press my fingertips to the Godstone and pray. *Oh, God,* did *I make the right decision?* Ximena is the closest thing I've ever had to a mother. She has always wanted what is best for me. It feels strange to have pushed her away, like pushing away an extra limb or a small part of my soul.

It also feels a little bit like freedom.

"What do you think she's telling him?" I ask.

Mara covers her mouth to mute soft laughter, and I look at her, startled. "I'd bet all the saffron in my spice satchel," she says, "that she's threatening to hang him upside down by his toes if he ever takes your clothes off."

"Oh!" Mara talks about these matters with such casual ease, and I'm not sure I'm ready to hear it. Still, I study Hector's reaction very, very carefully. He has drawn himself to full height, chin raised, eyes hard.

"You could order her to tell you," Mara suggests.

"She would lie if she thought it necessary." As the words leave my mouth, their truth hits me full force. She has not always wanted what is best for me. She has always wanted what *she thinks* is best for me. And she has never hesitated to work around me or anyone else to accomplish it.

Hector is shaking his head. Ximena sticks a finger in his chest and hisses something at him. His eyes narrow, and he spits something in response. Then he turns his back on her, sweeps past Mara and me, and exits the chamber.

Ximena's cheeks are flushed, and her breath comes fast. I've never seen her so angry, so lacking composure.

A year ago, this would have terrified me. I stand and approach her.

Her gaze on me turns soft with longing, and I wish there was a way to convince her that separating myself from her doesn't mean I love her less. I give her the only peace offering I know. "Ximena, I'm ready for you to braid my hair now, if you don't mind."

She nods, swallowing. "Yes, my sky."

I wake to someone jostling my shoulder. My eyes fly open. A forefinger presses against my lips, and I hear, "Shh, Elisa."

"Belén?"

"Franco is coming here," he whispers. "Now."

Oh, God.

"The others accompany him, but at a distance," he adds. "He'll slip inside the inn, and his companions will block the entrances to prevent escape. Majesty, it's a siege."

I fling the covers away and sit up. "Where is Storm?"

"He came in not long after our meeting."

"And how long until sunrise?"

"About three hours."

My heart thumps in my chest. This is it. We have to make it happen now, or never. I glance at decoy Elisa, sleeping in the narrow bed against the opposite wall. She could die tonight. *I* could die tonight. *Please, God, keep us all safe.* The Godstone responds to my wispy prayer by sending dry heat up my spine. At least it has not yet gone cold. "Get Hector. I'll wake the ladies."

"Stay away from the windows." And then he's gone, as quickly and easily as a breeze.

I shake Ximena awake first and explain. She dives into her pack and pulls out a gleaming stiletto. I gulp back a wave of nausea. A stiletto is useless for cutting; its only purpose is to stab, hard and deep, even through armor. She grips the hilt with the ease of long familiarity.

"Wake Mara," she says. "And get into the corner beside the dresser."

"The girl?" I indicate decoy Elisa, who is softly snoring.

"Let her sleep." *Let her be a target*, she means.

"How . . . will you be able . . ."

"Rope ladder out the window, but we have to draw them toward this room first, and you must be gone by then."

I'm shaking Mara awake when the doorknob twists. Ximena strides unerringly toward the door, elbow bent to plunge her stiletto. But it is only Hector, followed close behind by Tristán.

Hector says, "Storm and Belén will meet us in the cellar. Do you have your things?"

"At the door beside you." I indicate Mara's and my packs propped against the wall. They are always ready to go, a habit from our time as desert rebels.

Tristán pushes past Hector and heads toward my sleeping decoy. To my shock, he crawls into bed with her. She startles awake, but he shushes her, drapes an arm around her shoulders, says, "I'm here to protect you, my lady."

But I realize the truth of it: They've brought an extra warrior to protect her, yes, and who would be surprised to learn that the queen's betrothed is sneaking into her bed?

"Tristán," I say. "Thank you. And please be careful. Eduardo opposes our match; I'm sure of it. If he can't kill me, he may go after you." And with those words, I fully embrace the staggering possibility that I am at war with my own Quorum lord.

"Just find the *zafira*," Tristán responds. "Joya d'Arena needs it."

Ximena hugs me close. "Be safe, my sky. Be wise. Remember God's words from the *Common Man's Guide to Service*: 'Blessed is he who puts the sake of others before his own desires.'"

Even now she can't help but warn me away from Hector. I pitch my voice low so that only she can hear. "I know you want him for Alodia."

Ximena goes rigid in my arms. "It's a good match," she whispers back.

"Elisa!" Hector hisses from the doorway. "We must go *now!*"

"Yes. A good match. Ximena, be well." I push her away. "Protect the girl."

Then Mara and I grab our packs and hurry out the door.

20

WE are met outside by four of my Royal Guard. "Go with God, Your Majesty," one says, and I barely have a chance to nod before Hector is hustling me down the corridor.

"Wait." I freeze in my tracks.

"Elisa, we must go!"

But it's not right. Too much depends on sleight of hand, on stealth, on chance.

I turn back up the corridor toward the guards. "You!" I say to the one who addressed me. "Find the mayor of Puerto Verde. Rouse him from sleep. Tell him his queen demands his presence right now. Tell him to bring his entire household. Tell him I expect him here within minutes."

"Yes, Your Majesty." He flees.

"And you, rouse every single person in this inn. Make noise. We want chaos. Lots of it. You two, stay and guard this door with your lives. Where are Tristán's guards?"

"One floor below," Hector says.

"Let's go." I jog down the hallway toward the stair, my pack bouncing at my back. Hector and Mara hurry after me. When we reach the floor below, I bang on doors and walls as we pass. Hector follows my lead, pounding with the pommel of his sword, producing a shocking, hollow boom that no one could possibly sleep through.

Belén intercepts us, gliding up like a wraith. "I lost track of Franco," he says. "He may be inside." Doors swing open, people spill into the hallway, sleep mussed and startled. "Is this your doing?" he asks, looking around in alarm.

"We need chaos. A reason to be in the corridor, more obstacles for an assassin."

He nods. Then he bangs on the nearest door and yells, "Fire!"

I take up the cry. "The stable is on fire!" Then, softer, to Belén, "Go light the stable on fire. Bring the whole city down on us."

His answering grin gives me shivers. "Meet you in the cellar," he says, and then he's gone.

We rush down the stairs, through another corridor, into the kitchens. We duck to avoid hanging brassware, skirt a huge stone bread oven, and find the trapdoor leading to the cellar. Hector grabs the iron ring and heaves it open, revealing steps that lead into dank gloom. It smells of pickled fish and spilled wine.

"Mara, you first," he says, and as she descends my heart is in my throat, for he has ordered her to go first in case danger lies in wait at the bottom.

After a moment comes her clear whisper: "No one here but Storm!"

Hector nudges me down and follows after, closing the trap-door over our heads. We are left in utter darkness. I step carefully, feeling with my toes for the edge of each step.

I hear the strike of flint and steel, and brightness sears my vision. It dies, then light flares again, softer and surer. Storm stands at the bottom of the stair holding a torch aloft, Mara beside him. His cowled head nearly brushes the ceiling.

He scowls. "You made me cut and dye my hair."

Surely he understands that we face greater problems? "I thought it would greatly improve your looks," I snap.

"Shorn hair is a sign of shame. You humiliate me greatly."

"I'll light a candle tonight in honor of your dead tresses."

His frown deepens. "Where is Belén?"

"Causing chaos. We wait for him."

It seems that we wait forever, and the space grows tight and hot. Food stores surround us—a few wine barrels, hundreds of tightly sealed ceramic jars, slabs of raw meat hanging from ceiling hooks. Opposite the stair is a low, dark hole in the wall, a trash chute, I presume, that leads to the sewer and the sea.

"Hector, has the ship you were expecting made port yet?"

"No. But her colors were seen yesterday evening. As soon as the wind picks up, she'll be here."

"So we row out there and hope for the best?" It seems like too tenuous a plan to me. One of the hardest things about being queen is determining when to trust someone to take care of things for you and when to take charge yourself. I have trusted Hector and Tristán to handle all the arrangements and contingencies for this journey. They are good men, natural leaders. I hope they have thought of everything.

"I can signal them from a distance," he says cryptically. "We'll head out to sea and keep going until we intercept them. It will be fine so long as the waters are calm."

I study his face. "You must know this ship and crew *very* well. To be able to exchange signals. To know their exact route."

"Yes." This time I'm looking for it, so I catch the twitch in his jaw that tells me he is being taciturn in order to keep from feeling something too much.

The trapdoor above us groans open.

"Snuff the torch!" Hector says.

The cellar goes black. Hector fills the space before me, backs me up with the press of his body. "Back," he whispers in my ear. "Behind the stair." I catch a glint of light along his sword edge, held at the ready.

I hear no footsteps, not even a breath of movement, but the trapdoor shuts with a soft *clunk*, and Belén says, "The inn is in an uproar, but I haven't been able to find Franco. We must assume he will follow."

Storm relights his torch. "He may be able to sense Her Majesty's Godstone," he says.

A panicked prayer flies unbidden to my lips, and as my belly warms in response, I realize that praying is the last thing I should do. I slam my mouth closed.

Activity has always made the Godstone easier for others to sense. Prayer comes so naturally to me, and I will need to focus hard to keep from doing it.

Hector gestures toward the barrels along the wall. "Belén, roll them in front of the trash chute while I get everyone down into the sewer. It might buy us a few seconds."

"Trash chute?" Mara asks quaveringly.

"You first, my lady," he says. "You'll slide a bit, then drop into the water. It's about waist deep. If you go under, don't panic. You'll be able to stand up. Now go!"

She closes her eyes a moment, then, holding her precious spice satchel above her head, she slides neatly inside, feet first.

Belén rolls a barrel up to obscure the view of the entrance to the chute as Hector takes the torch from Storm. "Now you. Go!"

Storm growls, low and deep, but he follows Mara's lead and plunges into the hole. His disappearance is quickly followed by a distant, echoing splash.

"Elisa? Your turn."

Oh, God.

The Godstone leaps, and I curse myself for stupidity. I dangle my legs into the hole. It reeks of dead fish and rotting vegetables. I place my hands beneath my thighs and push off.

I slide, but not quickly. My pants catch in muck, slowing me down. I reach out for the walls of the tight tunnel to push myself forward. My fingertips sink into sludge. I refuse to think about what I am touching.

I slither a bit farther, and suddenly I'm surrounded by air, and falling. I've no time to be surprised before my heels hit the water, then my rear. My feet hit bottom but slip out from under me, and ice-cold water closes over my head. I gather my feet and shoot to the surface, sputtering. "Mara?" I call.

"Here."

I wade toward her voice, wiping water from my eyes and nose. The surface reaches just past my Godstone. It's cold, but not as bad as I feared. Wading is going to be difficult in my boots and thick desert garb. I hope we reach a boat soon.

A splash behind me brings light with it. Another splash sounds quickly after.

"All here and uninjured?" Hector asks. He looks everyone over quickly.

"My cloak is ruined," Storm says. His cowl has fallen back, and in the torchlight, I finally glimpse his new hair. It's cropped close and inky black. It makes his cheeks appear even more gaunt, like a feral cat's.

"You'll live," I tell him. "And when we get back to—" I gasp as my Godstone becomes ice.

"We must go!" I whisper. "Now. He is very near."

"Belén, guard the queen's back," Hector says, grabbing the torch from him and starting down the sewer tunnel at an impossible pace. There is a slight hiss as he dunks the torch in the water. The tunnel goes black.

Pushing through waist-deep water at a near run while fully clothed and booted is one of the hardest things I've ever done. It's as hard as wading through sand, as hard as climbing cliffs. My lungs burn with effort and my limbs become leaden with cold, for the Godstone continues to pulse icy warnings through my veins. But I don't dare pray myself warm. I imagine Franco searching the cellar above, hoping to feel the tickle of warmth that tells him the Godstone is near.

I take comfort in the fact that if Franco is following us, it means he is not following Ximena. Maybe they'll get away. Maybe they'll be safe. I hope the entire city has descended upon the inn by now.

The arching ceiling of the tunnel begins to appear, dark and blurred as a ghost; we must be approaching the exit to the bay and open sky. But I don't know how I'll make it that far. My teeth chatter and my lips have gone numb. My limbs move too slowly. Hector's form grows distant.

"Hec . . ." My mouth can hardly form words. "Hec . . . tor."

He spins, and water laps against the sides of the tunnel as he rushes toward me. "What is it?" His whisper is frantic. "Are you . . ." His hand reaches blindly for me, connects with my cheek. "Your skin is ice." He grabs my shoulders and pulls me against him, saying, "Belén. Do it now."

In my peripheral vision, I catch a faint gleam as Belén clamps the blade of his dagger between his teeth, breathes deep through his nose, and then slips below the surface of the water.

I bury my face in Hector's neck, seeking his heat. He rubs up and down along my arms. "Is it the Godstone?" he whispers.

"Can't. Pray."

Storm and Mara are silent in the space beside us as we wait for Belén. What if more than one person pursues us? How will Belén be able to see what to do?

Hector's grip on me tightens, and my soaked body molds to his. Warmth sparks in the pit of my stomach, something wholly separate from the Godstone. Of their own volition, my arms snake around him, slide beneath his pack. My hands splay against his broad back, and I pull him close, closer. It would be the easiest thing in the world to press my lips to his throat, the line of his jaw. It would almost be like an accident.

A grunt. A splash.

Hector releases me and pulls fighting daggers from the vambraces at his forearms.

But the ice is fading from my blood. "It's all right," I say, laying a hand on his wrist. "The cold is gone." I send out a quick prayer, just enough for a smidge of warmth and a bit of gratitude.

A moment later, Belén's shape appears. Something dark and glittering streams across his face. "There was only one," he says. "Not Franco, but definitely one of his men." Beside me, Storm looses a ragged sigh. "If we are very lucky," Belén continues, "they'll never find the body. But only if we are very lucky. I suggest we go quickly."

"Elisa, can you move?" Hector asks.

In answer, I push forward through the black water. Behind me, I hear Mara whisper, "Are you hurt?"

"No," Belén says, and she breathes soft relief.

The tunnel stinks more and more, like a rotting privy or meat gone sour. Odds and ends float in the water beside us, and I try to avoid touching anything. My inner thighs chafe from the wet fabric of my pants, and my boots sink into sludge with each step. I feel like I'll never be clean again.

The details of my companions' faces are beginning to show

when we reach an iron grate. I glimpse a shimmer of moon-light on the water beyond.

"We have to swim under," Hector says. "There's a hole on the bottom left. Mara?"

Looking resigned, she says, "Hand the satchel to me through the grate?"

He takes it from her, saying, "There's room enough if you dive low."

Mara gulps air, then sinks below the surface. She kicks hard, connecting with my shin underwater, and then nothing. I count. *One, two, three, four, five, six . . .*

Her head breaks the surface on the other side. "Easy," she says, gasping. Hector pokes her satchel through the grate, and she grabs it.

Storm goes next, then Belén. Hector and I are alone. He hooks me around the waist and pulls me back, into the dark.

"Hector? What—"

"Quickly," he whispers, and his face is very close. "This may be our last chance to speak alone for a long time." I'm acutely aware of the pressure of his hand on the small of my back. The buzzing warmth returns to the pit of my stomach. "Last night Ximena warned me that you have a tendency to form strong attachments to people in close proximity to you."

"People like you," I say flatly.

"I told her you were stronger and smarter than she real-ized," he says, and his gaze drops to my lips. "She wanted me to promise that I would be wary of getting too close."

Did you? I want to ask. *Did you promise?*

"We argued right in front of you. It was a terrible breach, and I'm sorry."

"Hector? Your Majesty?" comes a whispering voice.

I can't stop staring at his lips. "Ximena's right, you know. Do you think it weakens me? To care so much?"

"No," he says without hesitation. "I don't think that at all." Our bodies are a hand's breadth apart, separated only by a cushion of heat.

"Me neither," I whisper. "It just hurts more."

Suddenly, he yanks me against him and bends his head to kiss me.

I melt into him as his fingers tangle in my wet hair. My mouth opens to his, and our tongues meet for the briefest instance before he pulls away.

We stare at each other. I read dismay in his face, as if he can't believe he did such a thing.

"Elisa?" It's Mara's worried voice.

Before I can think about anything else, before the pain of his regret can bloom in my own chest, I take a deep breath and sink. Water closes over my head, and I reach blindly for the grate. My fingers grasp slick algae. I leverage myself down, down . . . there! I find the gap and kick through. My pack snags on a jagged end, and I have a moment of panic and struggle, and then I'm free. I shoot to the surface.

I wipe water from my eyes and note that we are in a narrow inlet, sheltered by stone breakwalls on each side. The ocean lies just beyond. The water is as calm as a mirror, and the low moon paints a stream of light across its surface. To our right looms the dark shape of a long, high dock meant for mooring large ships. The water must drop off quickly, to accommodate their deep hulls.

Hector surfaces beside me. He shakes the water from his eyes and points toward the dock. "A boat there," he whispers. "Tied to the pilings beneath. We must go quietly; every sound carries on a calm night such as this."

He sets off and we follow, edging along the breakwall toward the dock. It's getting easier to see, as though all the candles and lamps in Puerto Verde illuminate the water. Maybe they do, after the ruckus we caused. I hope Ximena is safe. And Tristán. And the girl pretending to be me.

The end of the breakwall crumbles with disrepair. As we skirt it, I stub my toes on chunks of rock or mortar or brick that have fallen into the water. I step carefully, wary of a twisted ankle.

We slip beneath the shelter of the dock. Sure enough, the plunge of the ground is precipitous; it feels like walking along the side of a very steep hill. I clutch the pilings for support, and barnacles slice at my fingertips.

We weave through the pilings into chest-deep water. At last a shape manifests in the gloom. It looks like a small fishing boat—or maybe a large rowboat—with enough benched seating for eight people.

Hector lifts Mara over the edge, and the boat tips treacherously as she topples over the bench before gaining her seat. Hector pulls me in front of him.

"Hands on the side," he says in my ear, gripping my hips.

"When I lift, push up and swing your legs over."

He lifts; I scramble. My left knee knocks hard against the edge, but I make it in. I slide over on the bench to make room for Storm, who grumbles as Hector gives him a boost. Then Hector and Belén vault over the side.

Hector unties the thick rope holding us to the piling and coils it into the prow. He pulls one oar from the floor; Belén grabs the other. With a dip and a swish, Hector maneuvers us away. Belén follows his lead, using his oar as a pole against the pilings. Together they weave us out from under the dock and into open sea.

I take a deep breath, relieved to have gotten this far. The night is warm, and I know my chill will be gone soon, even wet as I am. Before us, the moonlit harbor is dotted with ships and smaller boats. Surely one more won't cause a second glance?

At my feet is a rolled-up sailcloth, a large net, a floppy wide-brimmed hat, and a wooden crate filled with fishing supplies: a dagger, bone hooks, twine, weights. We've commandeered a trawling boat.

I whisper, "Should we pretend to fish or something?"

"In deeper water, maybe," Hector says. "If we're out here for a long time."

I'm about to ask him just how long he thinks we'll be trapped in this boat when my nose pricks with something sharp and my neck itches, as if I'm being watched. I twist around to look at the city we leave behind. My hand flies to my mouth.

It's in flames. Clouds of grungy smoke roll into the sky, their bottom edges glowing red-orange.

No wonder the sky was so bright. No wonder we got away so easily. My plan to create chaos worked too well. "What have I done?" I whisper. Mara turns to see what has caught my attention and lets out a little "Oh!" of dismay.

"We did what we had to do to get away," Belén says. "It's just a few buildings."

Looking closer, it seems that only three, maybe four, structures are on fire. Still, I worry for the people who lived and worked there. Are they burning in the flames? Choking on smoke? Even if they did get out safely, I have destroyed their livelihoods. The King's Inn has stood on that spot for over a century.

Is it really worth it, to destroy someone's life to save my own? Even if I am the queen?

I turn my back to the flames and squeeze my eyes closed. Now that we are away from the shelter of the breakwall and the dock, I hear shouting, maybe screaming. What if they can't contain the blaze?

I consider ordering Hector to turn us around, to face this thing I've done, to make it right. But now is not the time. I must find the way that leads to life and the *zafira*; my country depends on it. I just hope that once we've found it, my list of wrongs to right is not too long.

We row through the bay, weaving between hulking ships. Figures move around on decks and climb through the rigging, even though it is not yet dawn. Shadowy shapes stand at the rails, gazing toward the conflagration. Surely they will turn toward us at any moment, notice that we don't belong.

But they don't. As we leave the bay and aim south along the shore, the sky brightens to dark indigo, still fading to deepest black along the watery horizon. Shadowy but glorious estates dot the rolling hills and cliffs above us, with vined trellises and marble statues and sandstone terraces. Soon we pass beyond even these. The waters are calm, and not a single ship goes by. We are alone, and very small.

Hector's breathing grows labored. As the sun peeks over the hills, its light catches on the sweat of his brow and shoulders. He closes his eyes, hardens his jaw, and keeps rowing.

Belén struggles too. Sweat runs from his hairline, mixes with dried blood and dirt, coating his face in a gruesome patina of red and black. There must have been a lot of blood. Cauldrons of it, for some to remain even after his dip under the sewer grate.

I wonder when they last slept? Certainly not last night; Belén was tracking an Invierne spy, and Hector was making arrangements for an escape that came too soon.

"Hector." I lean forward and put a hand on his wrist.

He looks up, startled, blinking sweat from his eyes.

"Rest," I say. "Both of you. We are alone and safe for now."

"We have to keep going," he says. "Felix's ship will—"

"On my order, you will rest. I need you sharp. Mara and I will row for a bit. And if a ship comes into view, we'll rouse you."

He lifts his shirt to wipe his eyes, and I can't help notice his stomach, taut and tanned from the training yard. I swallow hard.

Hector rests the oar on his lap and rolls his shoulders to loosen them. "Have you rowed before?"

"No."

"Mara?"

"Me neither," she says.

"I refuse to row," Storm says.

I say, "We'll figure it out. Close your eyes so you don't see how embarrassingly awkward we are at it." I'm gratified to see his glimmer of a smile.

"Trade places with me," Hector says.

We both stand, and the boat lurches. He grabs me to keep me steady, and we manage to squeeze past each other. I settle on the bench and grab the oar, saying, "There's plenty of water in my pack. Help yourself. You should probably rinse the water skin first, though; it's covered in sewage."

He does exactly that while Mara and Belén trade places; then, using my pack as a pillow, he slides under the bench and closes his eyes. Belén stretches out beside him. Mara takes up her oar, and after some useless splashing and a few hard knocks against the side of the boat, we slowly push south.

As the sun rises, the surface of the water becomes so bright hot as to be blinding. How will we ever find a single ship out here? What if it takes us days? Will our drinking water last that long? Though surrounded by water, we are as alone and barren as if we traveled the deep desert.

In no time, everything burns with effort; my back, my shoulders, my wrists. My palms and fingertips are rubbed raw. Every stroke makes me gasp for breath. Mara and I switch sides so we can abuse a different set of muscles, but even that mild reprieve does not last long.

To keep my mind off the pain, I gaze at Hector. He sleeps soundly, his chest rising and falling with deep, even breaths. His features have softened, and the hair at his temples curls loosely as it dries. His mouth is slightly parted.

My lips tingle to remember his kiss. It was desperate and tender and wholly unexpected—and as easy as breathing.

Later, when we've found this mysterious ship of Hector's and are safely away, when I have time to rest and worry and a quiet corner to hide in, I will coldly remember that being a queen means being strategic. And I will imagine sending off the man I love to marry my sister. I'll rehearse it in my head, maybe. Get used to the feeling.

But not now. Now, as I row toward an uncertain destination, his kiss still throbbing on my lips, I luxuriate in watching him sleep.

21

STORM is the one who spots the ship. "There!" He points.

I twist and shade my face to peer through the brightness. The coast curls southeast, hiding the bulk of the ship, but I can see a long bowsprit, a beak head painted red, and what might be a foresail, hanging limply in the windless morning. I'm caught between hope and alarm.

Please, God, let it be the right ship.

I lean forward to shake Hector. He startles awake, whipping his hand to his scabbard.

"Watch your head," I tell him, putting my hand between his forehead and the bench above. "There's a ship, just south of us. I doubt they've seen us."

He blinks sleep from his eyes and frowns at the blisters on my hand.

I pull my hand back. "Is it the right ship?"

Still frowning, he slides out from under the bench to peer southward. He is quiet a long time. "I think so," he says, and for some reason the raw hope on his face is hard to look at.

"We'll have to get a little closer to be sure."

I grab the floppy, wide-brimmed hat and toss it to Storm. "Put that on."

He shoves it onto his head and hunches over. I don't blame him for being afraid; in the close quarters of a ship, anyone would recognize him for an Invierno, even with his falsely darkened hair.

Hector and Belén take up the oars again, and we cut through the water with relative ease and speed. Mara and I exchange a scowl.

Gradually the ship comes into view. It's a gorgeous *caravela* with three masts and wickedly curved lines of burnished mahogany and bright red trim. Painted sacrament roses twist along the bow, and it seems as though their petals fall, become drops of blood, before disappearing into the sea.

"That's her," Hector says. "The *Aracely*."

My heart thumps. I have a feeling I'm going to learn something very important about Hector. "Should we signal?" I ask.

He throws back his head and laughs. As we all gape at him, he explains, "I had this system all worked out to signal them from afar. But with the sea so calm, all we have to do is row right alongside."

Storm mutters, "It's about time *something* on this accursed journey proved easier than expected."

"The captain and the crew," I say. "Are they to know who I am?"

"The captain, yes," Hector says. "We'll speak to him first and then decide."

As we approach, Storm crouches lower and lower on the bench. My own misgivings swirl in my thoughts, but I'm also a little bit excited. I've studied about ships and seafaring, but I've never been on a ship before.

Figures appear on deck as we close the distance. Two others hang fearlessly from the rigging; another watches us from the top castle above the main sail. I shudder to think of him so high up, tossed this way and that by wind and water.

The curving bow looms over us when Hector waves his hands. "Ho, *Aracely*!" he calls.

A bell rings across the water, letting the crew know they've been hailed, and they respond with a flurry of footsteps. More heads peek over the rails. They're a ragged, weathered bunch, with long hair tied back, two-week beard growth, and suspicious eyes.

"Ho, trawler!" The speaker's voice races across the water. "We're short on supplies and have little to trade. Best to be rowing back toward Puerto Verde."

"We wish to treat with Captain Felix," Hector yells.

Some of the heads disappear. The others exchange wary glances. A moment later, another man appears, more finely dressed than the rest in a clean linen blouse and thick black vest tight across his barrel chest. The whites of his eyes are uncannily bright next to his sun-dark skin. Beads are woven into his enormous beard; they catch the sunlight and return sparks of amethyst and aquamarine. His neck is thick and corded. He places huge hands on the rail above us; he's missing the first two joints of his right pinky.

He scowls deeply when he sees us. "I was afraid that would be you," he growls in a voice black as night. He turns to the crew. "Winch them up onto the quarterdeck!"

Hector is grinning like a little boy as he and Belén maneuver us to the front of the ship. The crew lowers thick hemp ropes. Hector grabs one and dives neatly into the sea, which sets us to rocking wildly. A moment later, he comes up on the other side, rope in hand.

They wrap the boat three times and tie off in a flurry of twisting knots. Hector gives the signal, and after a loud count and a "Heave!" we are sucked out of the water and left swinging in the air.

When we are halfway up, Hector leaps from the boat to the netting hanging over the side and climbs up. Belén follows, and the lightened load allows us to be hauled up more quickly. When we are close enough to touch the gunwale, Hector is already there, looking down at me, his hand outstretched. His hand clasped in mine feels relaxed, which surprises me. With his help, I pull myself over the rail and land on the quarterdeck.

As he reaches to help Mara and Storm, I look around. Most of the crew are busy hauling up the boat, their forearms veined and straining at the knotted ropes. But the others eye me with obvious interest. Some warily, some hungrily, as if I am a delicate cream puff with honey glaze. Instinct forces me to back away, but my rear hits the rail and I realize I've nowhere to go.

"A lady!" one whispers loudly.

"Two ladies," says another as Mara clambers over the side.

"I don't see any ladies here," the captain bellows. "And neither do you. Get back to work."

The crewmen on the ropes flip the boat onto the stern and tie it down through iron loops that I realize are for that exact purpose.

The others stare unabashedly at Mara and me, even as they resume their tasks. I stare right back, trying to seem unafraid. At least they're staring at us rather than Storm. Maybe they won't notice his uncanny height or that his eyes shine like emeralds.

The dark captain herds us with his vast arms. "This way. To my quarters *now*." His urgent voice rumbles, like empty barrels rolled across cobblestone.

We take the steep steps to the main deck at a near run, then twist under the quarterdeck and through double doors hung with real glass. He closes the doors behind us and swings the latch closed.

The chamber is low ceilinged and made entirely of polished mahogany. Light pours in from portholes, two on each side. A large desk rife with paper and ink and small metal instruments I don't begin to understand takes up most of one wall. Jutting out from the other is a huge bed covered in silk the shade of pomegranate fruit. A thick rug covers the floor, woven to show a cluster of purple grapes in a circle of green vines—the seal of Ventierra.

The captain turns to us, and a huge smile lights his face. I gasp in recognition. I know that smile. I've seen another version of it many times.

"Hector!" he says, opening his arms wide, and the commander of my Royal Guard rushes into the embrace and endures a fierce back thumping.

The captain grabs Hector's upper arms and pushes him back to study him while Hector grins like a little boy. "Look at you," the captain mutters. "A Quorum lord."

I say, "You're Hector's brother."

His gaze whips to me, and his eyes narrow. He studies every part of me: my dirty face, my unraveling braid, my breasts, legs, and feet. Something sparks in his black eyes, as if he has learned something. My face grows hot, but I refuse to flinch.

Softly he says, "And you are his young queen." And he drops to one knee with more grace than a man his size ought to have. "Welcome aboard the *Aracely*, Your Majesty."

"Thank you. Please rise."

He stands and turns an accusing look toward Hector. "This is a very dangerous thing you ask me to do, little brother. Our hold is full and we sit low in the water. We should not be so near the coast. I trust you have a good reason?"

Hector nods. "You may have heard that Her Majesty is on her way south to negotiate a betrothal with Selvarica?"

"Yes, the whole country speaks of nothing else."

"It's a fabrication."

Captain Felix raises his eyebrows.

"We were heading south, it's true," Hector continues. "But we were followed by an Invierne spy, a trained assassin. Given the recent attempts on Her Majesty's life, we thought it prudent to slip away."

I gape at Hector. He must trust his brother indeed to share all these details with him. Mara shifts uncomfortably in the space beside me.

The captain steps out of Hector's reach and crosses his arms. "You want me to take you south," he says.

"Yes."

"I can't." He turns to me. "I'm so sorry, Your Majesty, but I have a hold full of early harvest wine, the first decent harvest since the hurricane three years ago. I *must* get it to port so I can pay my men and bring home much-needed supplies."

At first, Hector's face is cast in stone and unreadable. But I see the exact moment he resigns himself to his next course of action. He's going to commandeer his own brother's ship. He has the right, as a Quorum lord. But not even brotherly affection could survive something like that. And I can't bear to see it happen. Not because of me.

He opens his mouth to give the order, but I jump in. "Can you sell your cargo at Puerto Verde?"

Hector slams his mouth closed and stares at me. I give my head what I hope is a near-imperceptible shake. *Please don't do it.*

"Yes," the captain says. "But we'd only get half price. It's the Orovalleños who pay top coin."

I smile with remembrance. "I don't doubt it. Ventierra wine was a favorite in my father's court. Do you mind if we sit down?"

"Please," he gestures with a flip of his hand. "Anywhere."

I plunk down on the nearest cushion and say, "It's a long

journey to Orovalle and back. You'll overlap with hurricane season."

He grins with the understanding that we are about to haggle. "It's one of the many reasons I love the life of a sailor," he says. "Don't you find, Your Majesty, that when you and death are bedmates, *that* is when you feel most alive?"

"I wouldn't know."

His eyes widen. He expected to put me off balance by referring to the attempts on my life.

"I'm always in bed with death. Since the moment I left my father's palace. I've nearly died more times than I can count. And I'm a bearer, which means I'm likely to die very young. So, you see"—I shrug with purposed nonchalance—"I wouldn't know the difference."

His beard hides any turning of his lips, but his eyes crinkle with amusement. "What do you propose?"

I have a hunch about him, about the person he is. What kind of man leaves the soft life of a conde's son to embrace the open water? Sacrifices his youth to endless sun and wind, his fingers to the sea? Someone who loves open space and danger, I'd bet my Godstone crown. Someone who can't wait to see what lies just over the horizon.

"My honor compels me to warn you," I say, "that our journey is dangerous and our destination uncertain."

Sure enough, one eyebrow raises high, and the expression is so familiar, so endearing, that it's hard not to smile. "Oh?" he says.

"I need a captain and crew I can trust absolutely. For it is a secret journey. Outside this room, only a small handful of people know its purpose."

He raises his chin and looks down at me through lidded eyes. "Seems to me that someone would pay top price for such a venture."

"Seems to me that the kind of discretion I need cannot be bought for any price. I hardly know where to start."

His eyes glow, and he's practically salivating over what I'm about to offer. Good. "Let's start with my lost cargo. I'll need to be compensated for the difference in price."

I nod. "That's fair."

"And I'll need extra supplies."

"You'll need the same supplies as if you were traveling to Orovalle," I point out. "You'll just be going in a different direction."

"I'll need compensation for this *danger* you speak of, and to ensure crew loyalty."

"So the crew is loyal to coin but not to you?"

"They're loyal to me because I make good on my word to give them coin. Did you bring any to give me?"

I hesitate.

He glances at Hector, then throws up his hands in a show of frustration that may be a bit exaggerated.

I've intrigued him, certainly, but here I am at a loss. I'd hoped to trade on royal credit. But I have no coin on hand, no horses or—

"I have saffron," Mara says. "Enough to line the pockets of your crew and then some."

I twist to face her, remembering how carefully she has preserved her satchel throughout our journey so far. "Mara, are you sure?"

In answer, she pulls a small porcelain phial from her satchel and hands it to Felix for inspection. He feigns disinterest, but his eyes light up when he raises it to his nose.

"I suggest you sell your cargo in Puerto Verde," I say. "Get what you can for it. The saffron will more than make up for the rest."

But how do I compensate the captain for risking his ship and his crew? I purse my lips, thinking hard, while Captain Felix unstoppers the phial and examines the contents carefully.

I get an idea. Though I don't have money to bargain with, as queen I possess something much more valuable. I add, "And for the service of taking us where we need to go, fearlessly and loyally, I'll write a letter to my kitchen master and stamp it with my own seal, declaring Ventierra the official Royal Vintner."

His mouth drops open before he can school his expression, and his breathless voice belies his nonchalant demeanor as he turns to Hector and says, "We'd have to pull out all our stores to meet demand. We'd have to sell the oldest barrels at premium prices to keep from running out. We'd have to replant the southern vineyard."

"Yes," Hector says. "We would have to do all that." But he's staring at me, a little perplexed.

"Do we have a bargain?" I ask. "Because if not, your men

should lower our boat before we're too far from shore."

The captain crouches down to take my hands in his huge ones. He pauses, noticing the burst blisters from my disastrous attempt at rowing. I'm determined not to wince. Instead, I squeeze his hand hard, and the expression on his face takes on a measure of respect.

"Your Majesty, we have a bargain." His beard tickles my knuckles as he kisses them.

"You haven't even asked where we're going!"

"Later," he says, his nose wrinkling in disgust. "First, baths for everyone. I can only offer seawater for baths, but I must insist. You all reek of something terrible."

"I can't smell anything except the fish oil in your beard," Hector says, straight-faced.

Felix laughs free and easy, so unlike his younger brother. On his way out the door, he clasps Hector's shoulder and says, "That queen of yours played me like a *vihuela*, didn't she?"

"Yes," Hector agrees, and though his face is solemn, his eyes shine.

"Please stay here while I make arrangements," the captain says to the rest of us. "I need to evaluate my crew and see if anyone should be quietly disembarked before you start making regular appearances on deck."

As the doors close behind him, Hector says, "Thank you, Elisa."

"You're welcome."

"I don't think he noticed Storm," Mara says.

The Invierno is huddled on a cushion behind me, partly

hidden by the corner of Captain Felix's enormous desk.

"Oh, he noticed," Belén murmurs. He is using a small knife to clean under his fingernails.

"Felix trusts me," Hector explains. But the look he gives Storm is one of suspicion. Or maybe regret that he brought the Invierno onto his brother's ship.

22

AFTER baths and a quick meal of salted pork with too-hard bread dipped in onion broth, we agree that Felix will give up the captain's quarters for me and Mara. He and the men will share the largest passenger cabin below deck.

The next day at midmorning, I'm trying to make sense of the captain's navigation charts when the crew sends up a raucous cheer, followed by much pattering across the decks. The ship lurches. I rush to the nearest porthole and am delighted to see choppy water pass by. We have caught a wind.

It takes two whole days to unload and sell the wine cargo and acquire a new batch of supplies. I spend the time pacing in the captain's quarters, trapped and antsy, frustrated at having to backtrack, even for a short distance.

When Felix returns from his final negotiation, he brings back news.

"The queen and the conde are safely on their way to Selvarica," he says, his eyes dancing. "Apparently it is the city's greatest shame that the inn she was staying in burned down around her, but no amount of apologies could convince her to stay. They're already calling it The Great Embarrassment."

The relief is so overwhelming that I have to sit down. "They're safe, then. No word about an assassin?"

"Nothing."

"Good. That's good." *Thank you, God.*

"So, where to, Majesty?"

I look up at him and return his grin. "South, toward the island countships. I'll know more . . . eventually."

But as he takes his leave, I wonder, *Will I?* If God's holy scripture has thus far proved unreliable in matters pertaining to the Godstone, how much less should I trust the apocryphal writings?

I pinch the bridge of my nose and whisper experimentally: *"Zafira."*

My Godstone vibrates joyfully in response.

I'm standing in the prow, gripping the rail, fascinated by the way the *Aracely* slices the water below. Wind has whipped my braid into a tangled mess. Spray stings my eyes and chaps my lips. The foresail above me bulges with air.

The crewmen have accepted Hector and Belén easily enough, and they gawk at Mara whenever she passes. Storm stays hidden in the passenger cabin. But they give me wide berth, too frightened or shy to approach their queen. Or maybe the captain has warned them off. I don't mind. It's nice to feel a little bit alone on this tiny ship.

I sense a dark presence and look up to find Captain Felix

studying me thoughtfully. "You've found your sea legs," he observes.

"Not really," I say. "It seems like they were always there, not needing to be found." It's been nice to have something come naturally for once. Storm, on the other hand, can barely get out of bed without vomiting, though we've been assured it will pass eventually.

"It's like that sometimes," he says. "It was like that for me."

"Is that why you became a sea captain?"

"Partly."

"I'm quite interested in the other part. You gave up the life of a conde's son in favor of a dangerous career running cargo. But from what little I know of Hector's family, I doubt they threw you out in the street. I'm guessing you ran away."

He laughs. "Hector warned me that you are the cleverest girl I would ever meet." My face flushes at the praise. "I understand now," he adds.

"Understand what?"

"Why Hector stayed with you."

I stare at him blankly as my grip on the wet rail tightens.

"You really don't know, do you?"

I force myself to relax my hold. If I squeeze any tighter, I'll hurt my healing blisters. Wearily, I say, "Please explain."

He leans over and rests his forearms on the edge, gazes out to sea as if soaking up the sight of a lover. "I was set to inherit the countship of Ventierra," he says, his voice distant with remembering. "But I hated it. The pageantry, the polite warring between houses, and sweet holy sacraments, the paperwork. One day, when I was seventeen, my father and I fought. I don't even remember why, but yes, you're right. I ran away to the shipyards. Offered my services as a deckhand on a merchant ship for no pay except food to eat and a hammock to sleep in."

"And you fell in love with the sea."

"Among other things."

I don't know what this has to do with Hector. "Why not go back? You could still inherit, couldn't you?"

"Well, no. You see, I also fell in love with a lady of the docks and had a son with her."

It takes me a split second to realize that a "lady of the docks" must be a prostitute, a split second more to remember how the crewmen referred to Mara and me as "ladies" when we first boarded.

"When my father heard," he continues, oblivious to my flushing face, "he journeyed to Brisadulce to rescue me from what he was certain were monumentally bad decisions." His smile breaks wide. "So when I heard my father was in town, I rushed Aracely to the nearest priest and married her."

"You named the ship after her!"

He nods. "Well, yes. When you tell your wife you're going to be gone sailing for several months, and by the way, have fun with our screaming newborn, it helps to make a grand gesture."

I chuckle. "You are a wise man."

"Funny, I tell my wife that exact thing all the time!"

"What does this have to do with Hector?"

He sobers. "When I married Aracely, my father gave up

trying to groom me to be a conde and turned instead to his next son, my brother Ronin." Pain flashes across his features, so aching and fresh that I almost recoil. Softly he says, "Ronin died in the war with Invierne. On the day you defeated their sorcerers. He went with Conde Eduardo to defend the southern front and was cut down with an arrow to the chest."

"Oh." Hector lost a brother in the war. Barely seven months ago. And I never knew. *Why didn't he tell me?* "I'm so sorry," I choke out.

"So that left Hector," he said. "To inherit Ventierra."

I gape at him.

Felix says, "My parents wrote to him, begging him to come home. *I* wrote to him. His king was dead, after all, and Hector has always been the best of us. Born to lead, to rule. He wrote back. Said he would come home as soon as possible. That he missed Ventierra more than words could say, that he would resign his position as commander of the Royal Guard and give up his seat on the Quorum. But something happened."

It feels like someone is standing on my shoulders, and I'm frozen with the weight of it.

I happened. I changed his mind. I remember the day well. He came into my office and laid a letter of resignation on my desk. I asked him to reconsider, to become my own personal guard.

"I had no idea," I whisper. "None at all." And more recently, after visiting Storm in the tower, he asked me to dismiss him. He thought he had failed me. But maybe, just maybe, he also wanted desperately to go home.

"He gave up a countship for you, Majesty. And the home he loves. I've always wondered why. But now I understand."

I open my mouth to protest but change my mind.

Is it possible? Could Hector love me as much as I love him? Is it cruel of me to wish that he would, when there is no chance for us? *Something* made him kiss me in the sewer tunnel, at a time when we should have been fleeing.

After too long a silence, I say, "Hector is naturally loyal, with a strong sense of duty. He'll stay in whatever position he feels will be in best service to his country." Would he, though? If I gave him the choice, would he stay with me?

"You know him well," he says.

"No one knows Hector well."

He says something else, but I don't hear because my Godstone leaps. I gasp.

"Your Majesty?"

"I'm not sure . . ." The stone tingles, and then I feel the slightest brush across my belly, like butterfly wings. "My Godstone! It . . ." The butterfly wings coalesce into something more solid, poking, prodding, and like ghost fingers, they reach painlessly into my stomach, wrap around my Godstone, and *pull.* "Oh," I breathe. "Oh, my."

"Should I fetch Hector?"

"No. It's all right." The sensation eases, but it's still there, tugging gently. Tugging in a very specific direction. "I think I've found it. The way." I turn to him. "I know which way to go."

He gives me a skeptical look. I don't blame him. It seems ridiculous. Maybe I've imagined it.

But I close my eyes, let the tugging sensation guide me. It's faint but sure. I pivot slightly to my right, lining up my toes with the exact direction. I raise my arm and point into the endless watery horizon.

"That way."

He shakes his head, resigned. "Of course it's that way. Right into the wind." He turns toward his crew, cupping his hands to his mouth. "Beat to windward!"

I return to quarters, knowing it's best to keep out of the way as they work to adjust our course. The *Aracely* is a warren of ropes and hooks and beams and swinging things, but I seem to have an instinct for it all, and I navigate it with ease. And so much glorious wood! Always kept in polish. Never have I seen so much wood in one place, for it is hard to come by in my desert.

Mara is alone, sitting on the huge bed, her satchel opened and spread out before her. She looks up when I enter.

"I found it, Mara. The *zafira*. My Godstone sensed it."

"That's wonderful news!" she says, closing up the satchel. "I felt us shift course, but I didn't know why."

"I'm sorry we had to sell your saffron," I say, eyeing the leather in her hands. "You took such care to keep it from getting wet, even in the sewer."

She laughs. "It wasn't the saffron I was worried about. Something much more valuable."

"Oh?"

Hector bursts in, and we look up, surprised.

"Felix said you gave him a new course," he says.

"Yes! Hector, I sensed the way. It called to me. Just like the *Blasphemy* said."

He takes a deep breath, whether from relief or trepidation I cannot tell. "That's good," he says.

"It's good," I agree. I turn to Mara and say, "There's something I'd like to discuss with Hector—"

"I'll go visit Storm," she says. "He'll hate that." She gathers up her satchel, and at my curious look, she mouths, "Later."

After she shuts the door behind her, I turn to face my guard. Neither of us moves to close the distance.

He leans against his brother's desk and crosses his ankles. His fingers thrum against the beveled edge. It's the tiniest break in his usual composure, but it's enough to make me study him closely. He stares wide-eyed at his brother's rug as if it contains all the wisdom of the world. He's nervous, I realize. Why?

Ah. Our kiss. He thinks I want to talk about it.

I clear my throat. "Felix told me . . ." This is going to be harder than I thought. But I can't bear to think that he might be with me against his will. I plop onto the bed, lean my head against the bed post, and try again. "After Alejandro died, you could have inherited Ventierra."

The words come out wrong, like I'm accusing him of something. They hang in the air between us, and he is silent for so long that I worry I've offended him.

At last he says, "I chose not to."

My fingers dig into the silk bedspread as I softly ask, "And do you regret that choice?"

He hesitates, which tells me all I need to know. "It was the right choice," he says.

"That's not what I asked."

"No," he agrees, "it's not."

I steel myself, force steadiness into my voice. "Hector, I'm so glad you stayed. There is no one I trust the way I trust you. And . . . and whose company I enjoy as much." Surely my heart is in my eyes, saying all the things I really shouldn't. "But when this is over, after we've found the *zafira*, I'm going to give you the option to go home. To be free of me. So think about it."

His mouth parts and his eyebrows lift. After a long moment, he says, "I thought you might marry me to your sister and pack me off to Orovalle. I'm quite the bargaining piece, or so Ximena tells me." I'm certain I don't imagine the edge of bitterness in his voice.

I sigh, too loudly. When I see Ximena next, we will have a very long talk about . . . a lot of things. Carefully I say, "It *is* important that we find a good match for you." Now my hands are clenched so tightly in my lap that my knuckles hurt. "But only in consultation with your own feelings on the matter. I know what it's like to not be consulted. I could never do that to you."

He nods, though he looks everywhere but at me. "It would be very nice to see home again," he muses, staring out one of the starboard-side portholes. Toward Ventierra.

I smile sadly. "So you already know, then, what your choice will be?"

"No. But I thank you for giving it to me."

The sun drops below the horizon. Mara and I are alone in Captain Felix's quarters.

"Storm said something you should know about," she says as she unravels my braid.

"Oh?" I say, feeling my muscles slacken as she works.

"He said that the gatekeeper would sense you coming. That he would test you."

The relaxation disappears and I sit straight up. "What does that mean?"

"I don't know. But it makes sense that the gate would have a gatekeeper, yes?"

"Maybe so." I frown, wishing I had thought to bring my own copy of the *Blasphemy* to study. Ximena was the one who packed it into the queen's carriage. I never even saw it. Perhaps she *meant* for me never to see it.

"Father Alentín said something about a test, about proving myself worthy, but nothing about a gatekeeper."

She pulls the brush through my hair. "Maybe you should pay Storm a visit. Ask him about it."

"I will, yes. But right now I want to know what's in that spice satchel. Mara, what could you possibly be carrying that is more valuable than saffron?"

She moves around to face me. Her eyes sparkle. "Just a little something I brought for us."

I watch, wildly curious, as she retrieves it and lays it out on the bed. She reaches into a pocket and pulls out a clay figurine. It's ochre-colored, shaped like a naked woman from the knees up. She's voluptuous, and she crosses her arms over her stomach, as if protecting it.

Mara pulls off its head; it comes uncorked with a popping sound. She tips it, and a few tiny grains spill into her palm.

"Lady's shroud," she says. "I have two bottles, one for each of us. Had to sneak it past Ximena. I knew she wouldn't look in my spice satchel."

At my confused look, she sighs. "Ximena never told you about lady's shroud, did she?"

"No." There are many things Ximena never told me about.

"Take eight to ten of these seeds once per day. No more. Chew them well and swallow." She pours them back inside the bottle and stoppers it, then shoves it into my hand. "It will keep you from getting pregnant."

My hand closes around the bottle like a fist. "Oh," I breathe.

"You don't have to take it, of course. But I just thought, well, we were going on this journey, and there was so much talk of splitting off, and I knew Hector would be with us, and sometimes the look you two share could liquefy sand, and . . . I wasn't too presumptuous, was I?"

"No. Well, I don't know." I stare at the figurine. She is lush in my hands. Naked. Shameless.

Mara's voice is softer when she says, "You could have a first time with someone you trust and love."

I look up at her, startled. So she knows how I feel. If she knows, then Ximena assuredly does too. "He might not have me," I admit.

"Elisa, he wants you desperately."

Warmth floods my neck. "I think he regrets staying on as my guard. He may leave after we find the *zafira*. To go home. And my sister, Crown Princess Alodia, has expressed an interest in betrothal with him. So, you see, it would go nowhere. There is no future for us."

She moves the satchel aside and sits next to me on the bed. "But you love him," she says, and at her simple acceptance, the last of my barriers crumbles away.

"Oh, Mara, I do. I love everything about him. I love that he cares so much about honor and duty. I love how, when he's working hardest to mask his feelings, they're actually leaking out all over the place. I love the way his hair curls when it gets wet, his slightly crooked smile, the way he smells. When he laughs, I feel it in my toes." I let my forehead drop onto her shoulder. "I sound like an idiot."

"Yes," she says, and I hear the smile in her voice. "You do."

"He kissed me. In the sewer."

"Holy God," she says. "That was very bad timing."

"The worst."

"And very unlike Hector."

"Very unlike him, yes."

"I really think you should start taking the lady's shroud. Just in case."

I straighten, take a deep breath, look calculatingly at the figurine in my hand. "Ximena wanted him to promise not to form an attachment with me."

She wraps an arm around me and hugs me tight. "Ximena

is a wonderful woman, and she loves you very much, but she is a meddlesome fishwife."

I choke on surprise and laughter.

"You have to be the one to decide, Elisa. Not Ximena. What do *you* want?"

"I want Hector." There. I've said it.

"Even if it means you can only have him for a short time?"

"I don't know."

"Fair enough." She scoots behind me and reaches for my hair to put it in its sleeping braid. We sway a little as the wind picks up and rocks the ship. It's comforting, like being rocked in a cradle.

"You said you brought two," I say. "One for each of us."

Her fingers on my hair still. "Yes. Belén and I . . . He is so handsome. And capable. Quiet and fiery, both at once." She sighs. "We've both changed a lot. He's scarred too, now. So maybe he won't mind that I . . . even after everything that happened between us, I thought . . . maybe . . ."

"Just in case," I say.

"Just in case," she agrees.

Tonight, I decide not to take the lady's shroud. But I wrap it carefully in my spare blouse and stash it in my pack. I lie awake a long time, wondering which would be more foolish, to prepare for something that may never happen, or not to prepare for something that might.

23

THE waves grow playful. They toss the *Aracely* about, and I clutch the rail as I descend the stair on my way to the passenger cabin to visit Storm.

I knock, and I hear what might be permission to enter, but I can't be sure. I open the door anyway.

The scent of stale vomit makes me gag.

"You really need to let some fresh air in here."

"Go away," he mutters. He lies on the bottom bunk, one long leg dangling over the side, his arm over his eyes. Footsteps patter across the deck above us. A single fly executes lazy circles around the slop bucket near the head of his bed.

"Maybe you should go up on deck. At least you'd be able to throw up over the side instead of in that bucket."

The ship tilts on a sudden wave, and he groans.

"I sensed the *zafira*," I tell him. "We're heading toward it now."

He lurches to a sitting position. "You're sure?"

"It feels like it's calling—"

He heaves into the bucket. It hasn't been dumped in a while, and a bit splashes over the side. I jerk my feet away just in time. "Ugh," I say. "I could get someone to clean that up."

He wipes his mouth with a sleeve. "No. It keeps Hector and the captain out of my room. They've been sleeping in the hold."

I'm torn between laughter and disgust.

"You'll be tested," he says. "The closer we get, the harder it will be."

"That's what I came to talk to you about. You said something to Mara about a gatekeeper."

He nods. "I did, yes."

I sigh, exasperated at how he makes me work for every bit of information. "Tell me everything you know about the gatekeeper."

He lies back down. "Fetch me some water. Throwing up is thirsty work."

"Information first, water later."

I catch the faint hint of a smile before he says, "It's an ancient Invierne legend. The gatekeeper was selected from among the animagi. Only the most powerful applied. There was a contest of sorts, and the winner was sent to watch over and protect the *zafira*."

I frown. "You've never mentioned any of this before."

"You never asked. Also, I'm not sure he really exists. But I *am* certain that my people would have erected some kind of defense around their greatest resource. Why not use the most powerful animagus in our nation to do it? And since the *zafira* conveys life and power, someone in close proximity could live a very long time."

I stare at him in disbelief. "But your people have been cut off from the *zafira* for so long. He'd have to be hundreds of years old."

"More like thousands."

I laugh. "Not that old. After God brought humans to this world, it was a long time before we split off into separate nations."

He gapes at me. "You're a very stupid girl," he says.

"What? Why?"

The ship lurches, and he covers his mouth as he gags. I ease away from the bucket before repeating my question. "Why do you think I'm—"

The ship's bells peal, starting high and faint at the top castle, gaining strength as the other bells pick up the signal. A voice booms down the hallway. "All hands! All hands!"

Crewmen hurry past Storm's doorway. "I'll be back!" I say to the Invierno before rushing out after them. Have we been hailed? Have we sighted land already? Has someone gone overboard?

I burst onto the main deck and into blinding daylight. Sailors mill about with tasks I hardly understand. Two scurry up the rigging, daggers in their teeth. Why would we be preparing to cut the sails?

"Elisa!" It's Hector. He stands at the bottom of the stair leading to the beakhead, gesturing for me to hurry.

I jog across the main deck. He grabs my hand and yanks me up the stairs. Captain Felix is already there, staring southeast. I follow his gaze.

A blue-black cloud bank curls along the horizon, a rolling

darkness in an otherwise crystal sky.

"It's a huge storm," Hector says. "Maybe even a hurricane. We'll know more in a few hours."

The air feels different. Charged. Like it holds its breath.

"It's too early in the year for hurricanes," I protest, even as the storm bank flashes, turning the clouds a sickly green. *Please, God, not a hurricane.*

"By a month at least," Felix agrees, staring out to sea. A gust of wind lifts his hair from his temples. "And from the wrong direction. In all my years on the water, I've never seen one come from the south. It's unnatural."

His words chill me. "Can we make for land?" I ask, even as I realize that we've been sailing away from the coast. We'd never make it back in time.

He shakes his head. "There's no port for days. The *Aracely* has ridden out some rough storms, but a hurricane would swamp us. If we can last long enough, we may be able to harness it, get it to push us onto the reefs. We'd wreck her for sure, but some of us might be able to get to shore." He skims his hand along the railing, caressing it like a lover. "She's been a good ship," he says quietly. "The best ship."

I squeeze my eyes closed, unable to face his brave resignation. As I do, the *zafira* lurches into focus, pulling me forward like I'm a fish on the line. I have a sudden urge to dive off the prow and swim in the direction it bids me, straight into the roiling storm.

I open my eyes to find the clouds bearing down on us, already larger and darker than moments ago. And as the rising wind presses my garments against the shape of my body and my Godstone begins to twitch with telltale cold, I decide that Captain Felix is absolutely right. The swelling storm is unnatural.

To no one in particular, I mutter, "Storm said I would be tested."

Hector raises an eyebrow. "You think God is sending a tempest to test your mettle? Surely he knows you better than that by now."

I appreciate his attempt at humor, but I can't bring a smile to my lips. "Not God. The gatekeeper." The most powerful animagus in the world. Someone who has lived maybe thousands of years. "And Father Nicandro said I would have to prove my determination. He said there would be a test of faith."

"What exactly are you saying, Your Majesty?" says Felix in a cold voice.

I loose a breath that is nearly a sob. It's one thing to be God's chosen, to be put in danger at every turn, made to fulfill some nebulous destiny. It's another thing entirely to endanger a ship full of good people to do it.

I do my best to explain, even though I know it won't be good enough for Felix. "I am the champion, according to Homer's *Afflatus*. And I must not waver. I'm sure you've heard it? 'He could not know what awaited at the gates of the enemy, and he was led, like a pig to the slaughter, into the realm of sorcery.' The passage promises that if the champion stays the course, he will be victorious by the power of God's righteous right hand."

Hector pinches the bridge of his nose and groans.

"What?" Felix says, looking back and forth between us. "What am I missing?"

I point toward the storm. "We need to go through that. Straight through. No wavering in our resolve."

The captain gawks at me. "You can't be serious."

Instead of answering, I place my fingertips to the Godstone and allow its warm pulse to comfort me. It's so familiar. I can't imagine being without it.

My faith has been greatly shaken in the last year, but not broken. I have this conduit, after all, this constant reminder that someone or something listens to my prayers, grants me strange power in trying circumstances, warns me of danger. So I know to trust where it leads.

Hector turns to Felix and says, "Not two weeks ago, I was hit with an assassin's arrow." Hector pulls up his shirt and twists around to reveal a thin white scar just beneath his shoulder blade. It looks like the injury happened years ago. Felix studies it with interest. "The arrowhead nicked my lung," Hector says before letting the hem drop. "I had to fight through it, so I bled everywhere. By the time I got help, it was too late. I was a dead man."

Though I know how the story goes, I'm intent on his every word, hoping for a glimpse into his mind.

"Elisa healed me," Hector says. "With the power of her Godstone. It was sore for a few days"—he curls his arm and straightens it again—"but it's fine now. Not even a twinge."

Now he looks at *me*, dead-on. "She saved my life," he says. "It took a lot out of her, more than she'll tell me, but she did it. So if she says we must steer into the storm, I believe her."

I could almost forget about the storm, about my Godstone, about everything, when he looks at me like this, like I'm the only thing in the world.

Felix says, "You're asking me to risk more than twenty lives. Not to mention my ship. If we ran aground on the reef, I could at least salvage part of her. Maybe a lot of her. I don't know if you've noticed, Majesty, but your country is in shambles. Good work is hard to come by. This ship means life for a lot of families—not just my sailors, but the coopers who make our wine barrels, the seamstress who mends our sails every year, the pig farmer who sells salted meat for our long hauls."

I tear my eyes from Hector's with reluctance. "Oh, I know," I say to Felix. "I know all that and more. There were four riots in Brisadulce during the last month alone, thanks to a tax increase I was maneuvered into. The people are right to be angry. The Wallows is in more desperate condition than ever, mostly because the blue marlin ran so poorly last season. And did you know the output of the tanners' guild was reduced by thirty-one percent? My fault, you see. I let Basajuan secede, and now we don't have access to their sheep hides until we work out a trade agreement with Cosmé." I turn my back on the storm and lean against the railing. Felix regards me with undisguised alarm. Maybe he's worried I'll commandeer his ship after all. Maybe I will.

But I'd rather convince him. "Joya d'Arena needs to heal. And we could. We're in desperate need of timber for rebuilding, for instance. Someone could make a fortune hauling mangrove and cypress from the southern islands. But no one will take on the venture. Because of the recent war, because of the animagus' threat, and because"—it hurts to say it, but I'm going to anyway—"and because I have been a weak ruler. Everyone is frightened. They're holed up in their homes, the curtains closed, growing hungrier and more desperate.

"I *need* the *zafira*. It's the only way I know to neutralize the Invierne threat once and for all and consolidate my own power. So while I appreciate the sentiment you feel for your crew and the livelihoods of those connected with the *Aracely*'s commerce, please understand that I have a whole kingdom on my shoulders. And yes, your ship is worth the risk."

He sighs, fingering one of the beads in his beard. "You really think we should steer straight into a hurricane."

"I do."

"Can you guarantee that no one will be harmed? That God will see us through?"

I shake my head. "I won't lie to you. There is always a cost. All I can guarantee is that it will be the right thing."

"It's insane," he says, but without vehemence.

"It's faith," I say.

He caresses the gunwale with his fingertips. "If we do this, I insist on telling the crew everything, about the *zafira*, about your Invierno refugee. They should know why we risk so much."

I hesitate only a moment. "Agreed."

He bows from the waist. "By your leave, Your Majesty." And he hurries down to the main deck to speak with his men.

Hector leans forward onto the rail, and we gaze out to sea

together, our shoulders not quite brushing. "I won't let anything happen to you," he says. "You'll survive this."

"You will too," I tell him, and my voice is fierce. "I order you to. I didn't go to so much trouble to heal you only to let you die."

He traces a whorled pattern in the wood with his fingertip. "What trouble exactly, Elisa? What happened that day?"

"I . . ." It's on the tip of my tongue to tell him everything, to tell him how I feel. "I wasn't harmed in any way, if that's what you're worried about."

"You thought you were going to die to save me, so yes, I'm worried about that."

I hate keeping something from him. I've trusted him with everything, always. But I couldn't bear it if he didn't return the sentiment. Or maybe I couldn't bear it if he did.

Thunder rumbles in the distance as I slide my hand along the rail toward him. I find his fingers and clutch them tight. He squeezes back.

I say, "I hope that I am . . ." Foolish enough? Courageous enough? ". . . able to tell you someday."

He sweeps his thumb across my knuckles. "I shouldn't press the matter. You're not obligated to tell me anything. You're my queen."

For some reason his words sting, and I find myself fighting tears. I pull my hand away. Lightning spears the horizon as I say, "I need to tell Mara what's happening."

I feel his watchful eyes on me as I descend the stair. Ever the dutiful guard.

24

NIGHT comes early with the mounting clouds. Crewmen
light the ship's lanterns and quietly go about the tasks of tying
down cargo and checking and rechecking the rigging. I marvel
at their brave acceptance. They continue to avoid me, but after
watching them at work for a bit, I can't help it: I have to seek
them out. Accompanied by Hector, I pat each one on the shoulder, ask his name, tell him "Thank you." Up close, it's easier
to see the fear in their weathered faces. But they still manage
to duck their heads and mutter a few clumsy "Your Majesty"s.

There can be no doubt that we face a hurricane. Already
the lanterns swing violently as we dip and plunge through
the sea. White water gushes over the prow at irregular intervals, soaking everything. We've shortened the sails to take
less wind, and several crewmen have lashed themselves to the
rigging, ready to cut the sails completely if the masts start to
give way.

I stand with Felix and Hector near the ship's wheel, for we
are sure to go off course. No ship can sail directly into a storm.

The best we can do is tack through the water, pushing directly into the waves whenever possible to avoid being capsized. My Godstone and I will be the ship's compass, pointing us in the right direction as we do our best to make corrections. Hector holds thickly coiled rope in his hands, ready to tie me down if the waves threaten to wash us overboard.

I have trouble keeping my feet as we climb and dive. In the night, the waves are a huge black darkness tipped in foamy white, swelling higher than the gunwale, but always, at the last moment, our prow breaks through and my stomach drops as we slip down the other side.

Felix tells me it's too early to be afraid, that they've survived harsher weather than this. "We are barely at the edge of the storm, Your Majesty," he says with a grin that holds more mania than humor. "The worst is yet to come."

An older man with a gray beard and a missing earlobe rushes up to the captain and yells, "Bilge is halfway to the first mark."

"What does that mean?" I holler through the wind.

"Some of the water coming over the side filters down to the bilge," Hector yells back. The wind has whipped his hair into a wild, curly mess. "Someone mans the pump at all times, but if the water gets high enough, we'll have to use buckets too. If it goes past the third mark, the ship is lost."

And then it begins to rain in great stinging sheets.

The deck is slick and chilled. I cling to a bit of rail stretching across middeck that seems to be made for that purpose. The sky flashes brighter than daylight a split second before thunder crashes around us.

God, please show us the way and keep us safe.

A smidge of warmth snakes through me, bringing the sensation, stronger than ever, of tugging at my navel.

Hector bends close. "You just prayed, didn't you?"

I look up at him, surprised.

"I can always tell," he says. "Your face changes." He wears a slight smile, as if we're sharing a secret. Lamplight shines against the planes of his sea-soaked face.

The ship rolls sideways, flinging me against him. He wraps one arm around me, braces us against the railing with the other. "Maybe having you on deck is not such a good idea," he says in my ear. "You heard what Felix said. Things are going to get worse."

"I have to help navigate!"

"There will come a point when it doesn't matter anymore, when we just have to survive."

I stare up at him, acutely aware in spite of everything of the way our bodies are pressed together. What if I *don't* survive? It would surprise no one if I died young, like most of the bearers before me.

Or worse, what if *he* doesn't survive? I lost Humberto before I could tell him how I felt. I can't bear to do it again.

"Hector, I need to tell you—"

"Oh, no, you don't," he says, putting a finger to my lips. "No good-byes, no confessions. Because we are going to live. Both of us. It's faith, right?"

Lightning streaks the sky behind him, as if in punctuation.

"Yes," I say. "Faith." He's right. I need to prepare to *live*, not to die.

Maybe I've been preparing to die for too long—ever since that day in the desert when I decided it would be better to die in service to God than to live uselessly. And maybe I will. Maybe tonight.

But I'm suddenly frantic to do something—anything—to prove to myself that I won't, to feel some kind of power over my predestined future. Hector's face is very close. It would be so easy to wrap my arms around his neck, force his lips to mine, and kiss him until we are both breathless.

I want more from Hector than a single ill-timed kiss. No, I want more from life. I clench my fists, and my nails bite into my palms as I think, *My supposed* destiny *can drown itself in the deepest part of the sea. Along with everyone else's plans for me.*

"Elisa?"

"I'll be right back!" I yell, and dash across the deck to Captain Felix's quarters.

I bang open the doors, and Mara looks up, startled. She's huddled on the floor at the foot of the bed, knees to chest, and her cheeks are streaked with tears. "Elisa?" she says waveringly.

I shed water everywhere as I grab my pack and drop down beside her. The ship rolls while I reach inside for the naked figurine that holds the lady's shroud.

"What are you doing?" she asks.

"Preparing to live." I put my hand to the stopper.

Mara grabs my wrist. "Wait." She reaches for her satchel

and retrieves a matching figurine. "Me too," she says with a shaky grin. "Ready?"

In answer, I pull the stopper and upend a few seeds into my palm. She does the same. In unison, we toss them back and start chewing. They're bitter and hard and taste faintly of lemon rind.

The ship rolls again, and I almost choke on the seeds. The captain's chair slides across the planking and tips over at our feet. Mara whimpers. I wrap my arms around her, and she does the same right back, mindless of my soaked state. I shouldn't linger, but I revel in the luxury of stealing these precious moments with my friend.

"You should go," she says, disengaging.

I rise to my feet, and though the floor sways beneath me, I feel steadier than I have in a while. "Stay here. I won't risk you getting washed overboard."

She nods. "Be safe, Elisa."

I open the doors to a dark deluge. Water pours from the frame, soaking the entrance. Hector is there already, as if standing watch, and he helps me fight the wind to pull the doors closed.

My thanks are whipped away as we lurch and slide across the deck. Captain Felix mans the wheel himself. "I need a bearing, Majesty," he shouts.

I grab the rail and close my eyes. Wind sends rain stinging into my face, and it's a moment before I can focus enough to feel the tug, but it's there, steady and sure. I point toward starboard. "That way."

What I don't tell him is that the Godstone has gone ice cold.

Felix gives the order and swings the wheel while others adjust the sails, and slowly, gradually, we fight through wind and waves toward a new heading.

During the next hour, the waves grow higher. The deck tips precariously as we climb and plunge. My hands become stiff with cold, and my grip on the rail slips. I slide to the deck and wrap a leg around the rail instead. Hector takes it as a cue to tie me down. He wraps the rope once around my waist and ties off with a quick but sturdy knot.

Then he pulls a long dagger from one of his vambraces and plunges it into the planking beside my knee. "If something happens to me," he yells, "you may need to cut yourself free."

I nod, praying, *Please don't let anything happen to Hector.*

Lightning streaks the sky ahead, illuminating the strangest cloud I've ever seen. It's a long, crooked finger poking at the ocean's writhing surface, sending spray in all directions.

I tug on Hector's pants and point. But there is only darkness, and he looks at me, confused. "Wait for the lightning. Watch!"

The next time lightning cracks the sky, the finger cloud is even closer, close enough for me to understand its Godlike power, how even the mighty sea tossing us about like driftwood is helpless against it.

"Tornado!" Hector yells, and others take up the cry, but their syllables are washed away by driving wind and stinging rain.

The ship rolls, so hard and fast that Hector falls hard to the deck. He slips across the planking, toward the edge.

"Hector!" I reach for him, but the rope at my waist holds me fast.

He grapples against the planking, finds purchase with his fingertips, but the *Aracely* continues to tip. Water pours by him, and I know he can't hold on for long.

"Felix, help!" I scream, but thunder booms all around us, and he does not hear. He fights with the wheel, straining to turn the ship into the wave before we capsize.

I grab for the knife at my knee. It takes both hands to pry it from the deck. I start to saw at the rope around my waist, but then I get a better idea.

"Hector!" I wave the knife to make sure I have his attention, then pantomime what I plan to do. He nods once, his face veined with strain.

I aim carefully, then let the knife slide toward him. He hangs by one hand as he reaches out to catch it, flips it around, slams the blade hard into the deck.

I breathe easier, knowing he'll last longer holding to a knife grip. Hopefully long enough to crest this wave.

All available deckhands are at the opposite side of the boat, clinging to the rail, trying to use the weight of their bodies to keep the *Aracely* from going over. Felix continues to battle with the wheel, gesturing wildly to adjust the sails.

I look toward the masts and see the problem: the mizzen sail has not turned like the others. Something must have broken; it's dragging us, keeping us from steering into the wave. Two figures hang like spiders from the rigging, sawing at the ropes to cut the sail free.

Hector has begun a stomach crawl toward me, using the dagger to pull himself up, which means that for the split second it takes to reposition the dagger, he must hang by the fingertips of one hand. I shout at him to stop, but a blast of seawater fills my mouth and chokes me.

Something claps, like a drumbeat, and the mizzen sail drops for a split second before being snatched away by the wind. Only one man remains in the tattered rigging near the mast. Where is the other?

Realization dawns. *Oh, God. He's gone.*

But now the ship turns, with agonizing slowness. The prow rises. Water gushes over my face, up my nostrils. I'm hacking and gasping for air as the bowsprit pierces the wave's crest.

And then we're falling, falling into the trough. I feel Hector's arms wrap around me as we level off at last.

Thank you, God. Thank you. Hector leans against my shoulder in exhaustion, and his chest lurches against me as he coughs water from his lungs. He clings to me, taking strength instead of giving it for once.

"Majesty!" Captain Felix yells. "A bearing!"

The tug is stronger than ever. I point, to port this time, as lightning flashes a portrait of the sky.

I am pointing directly at the tornado, which is nearly upon us.

The captain gapes at me, frozen with shock. His beard is plastered to his face, and it seems as though I stare down a darker, wilder version of Hector. He starts to protest, but a deckhand plunges across the deck to the wheel. "Bilge is to the third mark," he yells. "We cannot bail fast enough."

Felix's features soften as he nods acknowledgment, and the deckhand disappears as quickly as he came. The captain closes his eyes, caresses a spoke of the wheel. His lips move with prayer, and I know he is preparing to die.

One arm still wrapped around Hector, I put my free hand to my stomach. The rope at my waist is in the way. I wrestle it downward to reveal my Godstone, and the effort scrapes my skin through my saltwater-soaked blouse.

I place my fingertips to the stone. *What am I supposed to do? I know I should have faith, but this, God, this is impossible.*

The boat is suddenly steady, though spray comes at us from all sides. It's the tornado, more powerful than even the waves, forcing calm to the nearby water before sucking it up.

Hector shifts so that I sit between his legs. He wraps one arm around the railing, the other around me, as if he can protect me from the monster bearing down on us.

I lean back and lift my lips toward his ear. "Pray with me," I say.

"I have been."

I find his hand, guide it toward my navel, press his fingertips over my blouse to my Godstone. I hold it there as I intone, "Blessed is he who walks the path of God. He shall stray neither to the left nor the right, for the righteous right hand guides him for all his days."

Hector is muttering too, urgently, though I can't make out the words. There's power in this, something about the two of us praying together; it builds inside me.

"The champion must not waver," I say, as warmth floods

me until my body sings with it, until I am a goblet about to overflow. "The champion must stay the course. Yea, though he pass through the shadows of darkness he shall not fear, for God's righteous—"

A crack, even louder than the storm. I open my eyes to see that the tornado has snapped the bowsprit in two. Needles of water sting my cheeks and eyes. In moments, we'll be ripped apart and washed away.

Hector's hand slips beneath my soaked blouse, his fingers slide across my skin, find the Godstone. He presses down gently. I cover his hand with my own. "The champion must not waver," he says in my ear. "Yea, though *she* pass through the shadow of darkness, *she* shall not fear, for God's righteous right hand shall sustain her and give her new life triumphant."

The warmth inside me becomes an inferno. My body blazes with heat, with desire, with desperation. The Godstone is riotous with it, pulsing with unused power. *God, I want to live. I want all of us to live. What should I do? Why did you lead us here?*

Another snap, a sail ripped asunder. The ship begins to pivot.

And then I sense it, tiny tendrils curling into me. I can't see them, but I feel them, like will-o'-the-wisps on the wind, coming from every direction. I know them well, for I've been living with them my whole life.

Prayers.

Everyone on this ship is praying right now, I'm sure of it. And their broken, desperate thoughts flit toward me and feed my stone with even more power.

The tornado rips into the side of the ship. Planking and splinters fly everywhere.

Hector's prayer falters. His grip on me freezes for an instant before tightening, even more fiercely than before. Then his cold, wet lips press against my cheek, just in front of my earlobe.

He says, "I love you, Elisa."

Something breaks inside me. The world flashes brighter than daylight for the briefest moment—debris from the ship spins in the air, and beyond it, the largest wave I've ever known looms wicked and black—and then there is nothing but darkness and calm and a stillness like death.

I can't see. I can't feel my limbs. I can't hear. It's as though I've ceased to exist, save for my thoughts in a vast emptiness.

And then a heartbeat, true and steady. No, it's two heartbeats, mine and Hector's, beating almost as one.

And then nothing at all.

25

I'M lying on my side, my cheek mashed into the planking. Hector's body curls protectively around me.

Everything is still and bright, so bright that I blink against the pain of it. A soft breeze caresses my face, bringing the scent of hibiscus. A gull cries, a slide of sound from low to high.

A gull!

Gasping, I sit up.

Crewmen lie prone all around me. I worry they might be dead, but then my eye catches movement at the wheel. It's Felix. His great beard twitches as he mutters and stirs from the place he fell. Others stir around us.

Alive. All of us, alive.

I look down at Hector. Sleep has softened his features. He seems so peaceful. So young. Before I realize what I'm doing, I'm tracing the line of his eyebrow with my fingertips, trailing down his cheek, to the shadow of his cheekbone, where a drop of blood has welled. It's caused by a splinter; it must have speared into him when the tornado hit.

Alarmed, I look closer to make sure he breathes. Where there is one splinter, there could be more. There could be a whole plank, impaled in . . .

His eyelids flutter.

"Hector?"

When he sees me, he shudders with relief. "We're alive," he whispers.

"I did order you to live, after all."

He sits up and looks around. "How?"

"I have no idea. Something to do with everyone's prayers, I think, channeled by my Godstone. Be still. I have to pull this out." I brace his chin with one hand and reach for the splinter with the other. Just enough protrudes for me to grip it with my fingertips. I pull gently but steadily, trying to keep to the exact angle of entry.

He gazes at me without flinching.

The splinter is longer than I thought—the length of the first joint of my forefinger—and a good bit of blood wells up after it. I toss it to the deck.

I'm about to wipe the blood away with my fingers but he traps them, lifts them to his mouth, kisses them. "I thought we were going to die after all," he says. "Right there at the end."

I think about the way he held me, the way we prayed. I remember his fingers on my Godstone, on my *skin*. And I remember what he said.

I blink hard against tears. "You might have saved me. Saved us all. I don't know how the Godstone's power works yet, or how we survived, but you kept me focused."

His gaze drops to my lips. "I shouldn't do this—"

"You really should." And I close the distance between us.

His lips on mine are so sweet, so gentle, like he's savoring me. Learning me. But he doesn't linger there. Instead he kisses the corner of my mouth, my cheek, the tip of my nose. Then he leans back to regard me. His eyes are steady and frank when he says, "I don't regret telling you what I did."

"That's good, because you did say it, and I can't unknow it."

He lifts an eyebrow, smugly amused, and I marvel that for all his usual stoicism, he seems unashamed to have exposed something so personal. "And I can't unfeel it," he says. "I won't let it interfere with my work. Even though I expect things will be . . . difficult."

"Oh, yes," I agree. "Very difficult."

"Land!" someone yells. "Dead ahead!"

We jump to our feet. People stir all around us. There is no sign of the storm. The sky is beautiful and clear, and the water dances lightly, teased by a breeze. I could almost convince myself I imagined the whole thing.

Except that the *Aracely* is a disaster, especially the port side, which has a huge, uneven gouge in the hull where planking was ripped away. Only one sail remains intact, and we sit much too low in the water. In the distance a bluish lump looms on the horizon, and the tug on my Godstone is stronger than ever, pulling me toward it. I just hope the ship holds together long enough to get there.

"We should check on everyone," I say.

He nods. "See to Mara. I'll look for Storm and Belén."

We part, reluctantly, me for the captain's quarters, Hector for the lower deck.

The quarters are in shambles. Paintings and bits of furniture litter the floor, water streaks the walls, and the glass in one of the portholes is shattered, its jagged edges sparking in the sunlight.

Mara huddles on her side in the middle of the bed, her knees curled to her chest.

She looks up when I enter but does not move. "You're alive," she says, and it's almost like a sob.

Something is wrong. I rush over to her. "What is it, Mara? Are you hurt?" I brush the hair away from her face. "We hit a tornado, and—"

"Belén? Is he all right?"

"Hector is checking on him. Mara, tell me."

"My scar. It split open again. The ship tipped so far that I had to hang from the side of the bed. . . ."

"Let me see."

"I'm afraid to move. Elisa, I think it's bad." She lifts the hand cradling her stomach and shows it to me. It's covered in blood.

My heart sinks. "I might be able to stitch it. I watched Cosmé do it often enough. Or Belén! He's done it lots of times. Did you bring your salve?"

She nods. "In the satchel."

I look around frantically for it. Who knows where it ended up after the storm, or if its contents are still intact? I note my own pack, lodged between the fallen chair and a broken shelf. I give a worried thought to the figurine, hoping it didn't break.

"Do you remember where you saw it last? I can't . . ." Then I get another idea.

I take a deep breath against the audacity of it. Could I heal her? The way I did Hector? That was sort of an accident. Actually, everything I've ever done with the Godstone has been sort of an accident. But I came here, put everyone to extraordinary risk, on the chance that I could figure out how to channel its power deliberately.

"Mara, give me your hands. I'm going to try something."

She does, her gaze trusting. I grab them, trying to ignore how cold and slick they are with her blood.

"Er . . . close your eyes and relax. Hector was unconscious when I did it to him."

She closes them.

Think, Elisa!

When I healed Hector, I felt the power stir inside me, sucked in from the world around us through my Godstone. I try to imagine it, the sensation of something flowing, filling me up. *Please, God. Help me.*

The power surges into me like a flood, and I gasp, delighted. So easy this time. So natural and right.

I say, "For the righteous right hand of God is a healing hand; blessed is he who seeks renewal, for he shall be restored."

Nothing.

Last time, it happened out of desperation and need. Out of love. Maybe love is the trick.

I focus hard, thinking about what Mara means to me. I consider her brave acceptance of the danger we share, her determination to learn everything she needs to be a good lady's maid. I've watched her edge away from the shy, broken girl whose village had just been destroyed to become a cheerful, laughing person, resolved to embrace her new life.

Mara is precious to me. I love her.

I whisper, "For love is more beautiful than rubies, sweeter than honey, finer than the king's wine. And no one has greater love than he who gives his own life for a friend."

The power is rushing out of me even before I finish. Mara stretches out her legs, arches her back as her face contorts in agony, and I lurch forward, worried that I've made things worse. But then her body goes limp. After a few panting breaths, her face relaxes into an easy smile.

"I think it worked," she says. Gently she probes her stomach with her fingertips. "It hurt, but it worked."

My breath catches with relief. So much easier this time. Maybe it's my proximity to the *zafira*. Or maybe I *am* finally learning to channel my stone's power. "That's good," I say. "That's very . . ." My head swims. "Just need to lie . . ." I collapse onto the bed.

I wake to a sea of faces. I blink up at them, recognizing Hector, Felix, Mara, Belén. "Stop hovering," I growl sleepily.

They lurch away, except for Hector, who says, "Are you all right?"

His hair is mussed, his eyes huge. He seems so young all of a sudden, so unsure. It's definitely not a good idea to wrap my arms around his neck and force him to kiss me in front of the others. "I'm fine. Tired but fine." I sit up and swing my legs over the side of the bed. "Mara?"

"The wound closed up perfectly," she says, her voice breathy with wonder. "And my scar . . . it's still there, but it's softer. Healthier, I think."

The relief is so powerful that my knees shake. Or maybe I'm just that fatigued.

The captain rubs at his beard and asks, "You think you could heal everyone on board? We have a broken leg, a few bad scrapes. One of my men can't get the water out of his lungs."

"Absolutely not," Hector says. "You've seen how it exhausts her."

"I'm not sure I could," I admit. "I think it only works when . . . for people I . . ." *For people I love.* I hesitate to say it straight out, because returning his sentiment would just make it worse, in the end. "It only works for people who are very dear to me," I finish lamely.

But hope flashes across Hector's face, so raw and exquisite. Maybe I ought to tell him anyway. I could lie to him, tell him that our future has a happy ending.

Instead, I scoot off the bed and step away, putting distance between us. "How is Storm?" I ask, refusing to look in Hector's direction.

"Uninjured," Belén says. "More interestingly, I haven't heard him complain in hours."

Hours. "How long was I—"

"Hours," Mara confirms. "We were very worried. We're almost to the island."

I rush out the double doors and take the steps to the beakhead two at a time.

The view makes my hands fly to my mouth in awe.

We approach a crescent harbor of aquamarine water, ringed with crystal-white sand. Beyond the sand is a forest of coconut palms, whipping in the breeze. And beyond them are impossibly steep mountains, or towers, or maybe the fingers of God, jutting into the sky, trapping clouds with their fingertips. They seem verdant and alive, smothered in green, veined by shimmering waterfalls. White birds with pointed wings dive and soar among them, giving scale to their vastness.

The tug at my navel is stronger than ever. I press my fingers to the Godstone, as if to keep it from leaping out of my body and into the sea.

"I've never seen this place before," says a voice beside me, and I jump. It's Felix. He rests his forearms on the rail. "No one has. It's not on any of my charts. My best guess is that we are somewhere south and slightly west of Selvarica, but I'm not sure I could navigate here a second time."

"Perhaps," I say, "the only way to get here is through a sorcerous hurricane."

"Perhaps. I just hope we don't have the same trouble when we leave."

I look down at the water, so clear and beautiful. Silvery fish dart away from the ship as we sail forward, and patches of dark green plants wave with the current. They seem to be just below the surface, but our draft is deep, so I know it is only an illusion.

"How is the *Aracely*?" I ask. "Can we repair her?"

"We're not taking on any more water, so the bilge will empty soon enough. I'll send divers down to inspect the hull when we anchor to be sure. The bowsprit is lost. We've only the main sail left. I've a small spare in the hold we could unroll and use as a mizzen. Looks like there's timber to be found on the island, enough to patch the port side. It will take a couple of weeks, but I expect we'll limp away from this place just fine, so long as the weather holds. Another storm and we're done for, so pray for sunshine."

A couple of weeks. That's far too long. Ximena and Tristán can't keep up a pretense with decoy Elisa forever. Our ruse is sure to be discovered, and a queen can only go missing for so long before everything degenerates into chaos, before ambitious condes—like Eduardo—begin wrestling for power in the wake of my disappearance.

"Our biggest problem," Felix says, "is supplies. Looks like we'll have plenty of fresh water, but we lost an entire barrel of salted pork, and one of the grain bins is soaked. We'll have to forage and fish, not just for our stay here, but for the return journey."

I'm about to ask after his wounded crewmen when Hector saunters up and leans against the railing. "It's beautiful, isn't it?" he says.

I nod, gazing at a sparkling stream pouring from the jungle and into the sea. From here it looks like a silver ribbon winding through green velvet. "All that water! The place looks *alive*. It's unnatural."

He laughs. "You've been in the desert too long."

I grin up at him. "I look at those waterfalls and see the wealth of a thousand nations."

"Maybe that's exactly what they are. Do you sense anything? Is it still guiding you?" He glances toward my navel, and my stomach does a little flip to remember his hands on my skin.

"It's very strong now," I tell him. "And when I healed Mara, it was a lot easier. The power was right there when I called it, even though . . . even though . . . I . . ."

He studies me, letting me struggle for words. Then, "Even though the need was not as great?" he offers softly. "She wasn't injured as badly."

I nod.

A crewman's head appears at the stair. "Captain!" he calls. "Eight and a half fathoms at last sounding."

"Drop anchor!" Felix booms.

"Ready to go ashore?" Hector asks.

I stare at the island; it's so wild and foreign and foreboding. "Ready," I lie.

26

I hurry back to the captain's quarters to grab my pack. I peek inside and find, to my immense relief, that my bottle of lady's shroud is intact. Mara holds up her satchel and nods, which I take to mean that hers survived too.

The *Aracely*'s dinghy was lost to the hurricane, but by some miracle our trawler stayed tied down on the quarterdeck. I'm eager to get to shore, but Hector insists on letting another group go first. "Let them scout around, make sure it's safe," he says, and I agree reluctantly.

I pace back and forth across the deck as a group of eight men with supplies rows toward the beach. Once they are close enough, they jump out and pull the boat onto shore, unload, and then disappear into the jungle. It seems like forever passes before they reemerge, waving with a signal that all is well. Finally two men push off and hop back into the boat, leaving the rest behind to start setting up a camp.

Mara, Belén, Storm, Hector, and I are in the second group to ferry over. As we settle in the boat, the tug on my Godstone is so insistent as to be nearly painful. To distract myself from the discomfort, I trail my fingers in the warm, clear water as we skim the bay. The fish astound me. I see brightest gold, flashes of red, even Godstone blue. I'm tempted to dive in for a swim.

Once we reach the shallows, I jump from the boat and splash through water, heedless of soaking my clothes. We drag the boat onto the sand, and I'm surprised when my legs waver, as if the land leaps and rolls like an ocean.

Hector notices my teetering and grins. "You'll adjust to solid ground soon enough."

The sailors who disembarked before us have begun setting up a haphazard camp. They've already lined a fire pit and erected one tent—but they're doing it all wrong. I suppose that, as seamen, they've had few opportunities to organize encampments on land. On the other hand, I've had plenty.

"You there," I call. "Haul the supplies farther into the trees. We need shelter from wind and surf. And you, would you move the fire pit, please? Find a spot where sparks won't catch on dried palm fronds overhead." I tap my fingers to my lips. If we're to be here for weeks, then we need a latrine pit, far away from our water source. "Belén, do you see a good spot for digging a—"

"Latrine? Against the cliff face, there," he says, pointing. "It's downwind and far enough from the stream."

"Yes, perfect." I gesture toward a man I've seen in Felix's confidence on several occasions. "Do you read and write?"

"Yes, Your Majesty."

"Compile an inventory of all our supplies—fishing gear, foodstuffs, tools, material we could use for repair, everything you can think of."

"Yes, Your Majesty."

I eye the stream critically. The silt has created a small sandbar that protects it at low tide and keeps the mouth narrow. I mutter, mostly to myself, "We may have enough undamaged netting to stretch all the way across, which would take care of our fishing needs even if we come up short on other tackle."

I look up to find Hector staring at me thoughtfully.

"Anything I haven't thought of yet?" I ask him.

He closes the distance between us. My breath catches as he grasps my upper arm. In a low voice meant for my ears only, he says, "If you were like this, with this kind of confidence, this clarity of thought, while in Brisadulce, no one would dare challenge your rule."

My heart sinks a little. He means it as encouragement more than criticism, and the thumb sweeping across my shoulder attests to how much he cares. But it stings because he's right. A whole country is so much vaster, more complicated, more important, than a village of desert refugees or a temporary island camp. That's why I'm here, after all. Because I need something more than just me to do a good job of it. *I* haven't been enough.

"Perhaps I spoke out of turn," Hector says. "But I truly believe you have it in you to be a great queen."

I lift my chin. "Thank you for saying so."

"I'll get started on that latrine." He turns to go.

"Hector, wait."

He whirls. Sand clings to the bottom of his soaked breeches, and the moisture in the air has turned his hair into a mass of waves.

I say, "You have *never* said anything to me that is out of turn."

He knows I'm speaking of a different moment entirely, for he allows himself a slow, satisfied smile that turns my insides to date pudding.

I add, "I expect honesty and truth from you always."

He nods once, firmly. "And you shall have it."

We end up making camp in a small clearing well back from shore, where the coconut palms are interspersed with rambling pink bougainvillea bushes and thick banyan trees with sprawling roots. Morning-glory vines wind up their trunks, dripping purple flowers. Their close cousins, the yellow night bloomers, twine in sync with them, and it's hard to see where one ends and the other begins. But when evening falls, the morning glories will twist closed as the night bloomers unfurl, bathing our campsite in soft light.

After a late-afternoon meal of dried jerky, pistachios, and fresh mango, I announce that I will begin searching for the *zafira* first thing in the morning, while Felix's men make repairs to the ship.

"You know which direction to go?" Hector asks.

"Oh, yes," I say, pressing my fingertips to the Godstone. "It's very . . . compelling."

"I'd rather explore a bit first," he says. "The island seems to be deserted, but I'd like to be sure."

I sigh. Of course he would. "The day after tomorrow, then?"

"I think it would be best."

I nod, but I avoid his gaze as I come to a decision.

The hurricane is not the only test I will face; I'm certain of it. Storm said it will get harder as I get closer, and I've put everyone else at risk enough as it is. We have lost two men overboard already. I could not bear to lose Mara or Belén. Or Hector.

I have demanded his honesty but not given him mine, for tomorrow I will deceive him. While he's out exploring, I will slip away—alone.

When I finally dare glance at him, he is studying me through narrowed eyes.

Beside me, Mara wipes her fingers on her pants and says, with a mouth still full of mango, "I need a bath. And to wash my clothes. Maybe we could find a good place upstream?"

I'm glad for the excuse to turn away from Hector. "That sounds lovely. My boots still stink of sewer."

"Belén and I will scout first," Hector says. "We'll need to sweep the area."

Mara and I make no effort to disguise our shared eye roll.

We tell Captain Felix where we're going, and then the four of us make our way upstream. It's a rough hike through thick jungle and slippery mud. The farther inland we go, the rockier and steeper it gets, and I step carefully.

At last the stream widens into a pool, hemmed in by black boulders and curving palms. In the middle of the pool, just slightly off center, is a large bean-shaped rock with a flat top. "It's perfect!" Mara exclaims.

While Hector and Belén scout around, we empty our packs and rinse everything—spare clothes, knives, water skins—of any leftover sewage. I even pull out my crown box. The wood is warped and streaked with salt, the cushion a soggy mess. But the Godstone crown is as pristine as ever. I dunk it in the pool, wipe it down carefully with my spare blouse, and then set it atop my pack to dry.

When they are out of sight, when we can't even hear them rustling through the jungle, we pull out our bottles of lady's shroud and quickly down the appropriate dose. Mara grins all the while, delighted with our little intrigue. But I feel awkward and strange. I'm still not sure what I'm going to do. And Hector feels far too important to be merely the object of two giggling girls playing at love.

But maybe that's how it's supposed to be. Perhaps by forcing smallness onto this thing that is so huge in my heart, I'll be able to manage it.

They return and declare the area safe. "We'll be within earshot," Hector says as he and Belén retreat downstream.

"I just bet you will," Mara mutters.

I look at her, startled. "You really think they would . . . peek?"

She sighs. "Just wishing. Neither of them would. Too honorable." She waggles a finger at me. "But don't think it hasn't crossed their minds."

I manage a wan smile in return. The thought of being so exposed fills me with a little excitement and a lot of dismay. I don't despair of my body the way I used to. But it's still worrying.

Being naked before Mara, however, is another matter; she's my lady-in-waiting, after all. "Race you," I say.

Together we struggle with the laces of our blouses, shuck our boots and our pants, and jump in. It's deep, and when I break the surface, I gasp from the cold shock. But it's clean and clear and wonderful, and soon Mara and I are splashing and laughing and forgetting to wash anything.

We swim for a long time before Mara finally grabs soap from her pack and we lather everything—our skin, our hair, our clothes. We hang the clothes to dry, then lie side by side on the flat rock, soaking up the warmth of late afternoon.

"Your scar," I say. "It really is better." It's less angry, less puckered.

"Yours too," she says, and then she laughs. "We're an oddly matched pair, aren't we?"

The sun is dipping behind the giant peaks and tree frogs are beginning to chorus by the time we swim to shore and don our still-damp clothes. We find Hector and Belén downstream a ways, and it's obvious they did some washing up of their own, for they are scrubbed clean and smell faintly of soap.

"Sorry to keep you waiting so long," I say to Hector as we begin the trek back. "We lost track of time."

"It's not a problem," he says, but his voice is curt. I glance up to find his face has gone flinty cold.

I look away, feeling vaguely hurt. But I won't ask if I've done something to anger him in front of the others. The four of us hike through the jungle in silence.

The night bloomers have unfurled by the time we return

to camp. Our tents float in a garden of stars, reflecting palest blue in their soft light. A breeze rustles the palm fronds above us.

After a quick meal of whitefish baked on sticks over the fire pit, I unravel the hasty braid Mara did for me after our swim. I'm beginning to loose the laces of my blouse when the import of what I'll do tomorrow hits me. My fingers pause on the ties.

I know so little about the *zafira*. I have no idea what will happen or what I'll find. I don't even know if I'll make it back. What if I never see him again?

I crawl from my tent and go in search of Hector.

I find him on the beach, just outside the line of palm trees. He sits on a hollowed-out log, one knee bent, the other long leg stretched out in the sand. He grips a tall stick, which he whittles with his dagger. It takes me a moment to realize he's making a spear.

He looks up as I approach, his face unreadable.

"Do you mind company?" I ask.

With a lift of his chin, he indicates the space on the log next to him. I settle beside him, careful to avoid the end of his stick, and lean forward to rest my elbows on my knees. The sea glows with the light of a half moon. I lift my face to the breeze and listen to the gentle lap and suck of the surf and the *whisk-whisk* sound of Hector's knife against the wood.

"What are you doing here, Elisa?" he asks in a weary voice.

I flinch away. "I . . . I didn't mean to intrude. If you'd rather be al—"

"Did you come to torment me?"

"What?" Well, yes, maybe a little. "I know you're angry at me, but I'm not sure why."

He's gripping his dagger too tightly, and his next stroke lops off the tip of his spear. He sighs. Dagger still in hand, he wipes his brow with his wrist. He says, "I'm not angry at you. Mostly at myself."

"Oh?"

He opens his mouth to say something but changes his mind. Instead he whittles at his ruined stick, and I recognize the expression as the one he wears when chewing on a particularly tough problem.

Finally he says, "Honesty in all things, right?"

"Yes, please." But I'm coiling in on myself, trying to make my heart a stone, because I have no idea what he's going to say.

He stares out across the moon-glass bay. "It was difficult for me today," he says, "to stand guard for you. To hear you laughing and splashing with Mara, knowing you were . . . bathing. Very . . ."

"Oh," I breathe. "I see."

"The most important thing I do is protect you. I would die to keep you safe." He's gripping his dagger so tightly his knuckles are turning white. "But you make it very difficult. Sometimes you can't help it, of course. But sometimes you can."

"I don't understand." I don't know why, but my chest tightens with shame. "I've been taking your advice. I'm taking fewer risks. . . ."

He lets the dagger and spear drop into the sand and twists

to straddle the log. His eyes are very close when he says, "I can't defend against *you.*"

My heart is a drum in my chest.

His forefinger reaches toward me, to my cheek, gently sweeps a strand of hair behind my ear. From there his finger trails along my jawline, up to my mouth.

My lips part. My whole body buzzes.

"I told you I wouldn't let it interfere with my work. But every time you smile at me, and especially when you look at me the way you're looking at me right now, everything disappears." His thumb sweeps across my bottom lip, down my chin. His voice is low and dark as he says, "When it happens, I'm not guarding you anymore. Your enemy could come up behind me, and I would never know, because all I'm thinking about is how badly I want you."

My heart sings. I stare at his mouth. It's beautiful, with full pale lips set off by his sun-darkened skin. I would only have to lean the tiniest bit to close the distance between us.

He starts to back away.

In desperation, I blurt, "Mara says I should take you as my lover."

His indrawn breath is as sharp and hard as if I've wounded him. My face fills with heat, and I can't bear to look at his face. I'm embarrassed at my own weakness, unable to say such an important thing straight out. *I want you as my lover,* I should have said. But I can't bring the words to my lips, because if he says no, he'll be saying no to me, instead of merely to Mara's idea.

But he'll have none of that. "Elisa. Are you asking?"

Panic and hope war inside me. It's up to me, as it has always been. I can ask him or not. Asking him is terrifying. But not asking would be so much worse.

"Yes, I'm asking. Hector, I—"

With a swift motion, he cups the back of my head and presses his warm lips to mine. The pit of my stomach drops away as I open my mouth to his.

He groans, wrapping his other arm around my waist, pulling me toward him until I am almost in his lap. I arch against him; my breath comes fast as he explores my mouth. Before, his kisses were patient and sweet. But there is nothing of sweetness in him now, just heat and desperate need.

He tangles his fingers in my hair and yanks my head back, breaking our kiss. I let out a little "Oh!" of disappointment, but then he's sliding his mouth along my jaw, to the pulse at my throat. "Elisa," he murmurs. "I've wanted to do this for a long, long time."

His words send me spiraling with dizzy gladness. I clutch at his hair—it's even softer than I imagined—and press my lips to the top of his head. I close my eyes, wanting to memorize this perfect moment, and I breathe deeply of leather oil and fresh-washed jungle and something a little sharper, something distinctly Hector.

His lips brush my collarbone and then dip lower, toward my breasts. I slide my hands to the hem of his shirt and start to pull, desperate for more, more skin, more *him*.

He freezes. Then he pushes me away.

"Hector?" I gasp out, suddenly aching and bereft.

He closes his eyes tight, takes a deep breath. Opens them. They are huge and warm and . . . wet? as he whispers, "Elisa . . . I . . ."

Why did he stop? Did I do something wrong?

He tries again. "I can't. I won't." He slides back, putting cold hard space between us.

I pull my knees to my chest, curl into a tight ball. This is what I've feared, why it was so hard to ask. I find myself shaking my head against whatever comes next.

"I need to explain," he says.

I find a tatter of pride and say, "No, you don't owe me an—"

"I said I need to explain."

I rest my chin on my knee to steady myself. "All right."

He says, "You have every possible power over me."

"What?"

"You have the power of a dear friend, you have all the power that a beautiful woman has over a man who loves her, and most importantly, you are my sovereign. You have the power to command me in everything."

Something about his choice of words makes me angry. "You have plenty of power over me too," I say.

But it's like a dam of control has burst, and he hardly hears me for needing to get out all the thoughts that have been spinning in his head.

"Have I told you about my parents?" he asks. "They're best friends. Partners in everything." His eyes grow distant as he talks, and his mouth curves into a sad smile. "I've watched them my whole life, the way they are with each other. So easy and natural. They finish each other's sentences. They can exchange a look across the dining table and instantly know what the other is thinking."

The gaze he turns on me is fierce, like he's desperate for me to understand. "Neither is subject to the other; they're more like two halves of a whole. And that intertwining of lives, of *being*, it's amazing to see. Being lovers . . . it feels like it would be such a big thing, yes?"

God, yes.

"But it's only the littlest bit of who they are together. And theirs is the only kind of love I could have with you. Anything else makes me *less*." He takes a deep breath, as if steeling himself. "I won't become a helpless marionette or a temporary diversion for my queen."

Pain blooms beneath my breastbone, because I'm starting to understand.

He grabs my hands. I lower my knees and let him draw me toward him until our foreheads touch. "I understand how careful you have to be with your alliances right now. So when we get back from this, you'll marry someone else. I will too. Maybe your sister. We might be able to arrange a tryst on occasion, and God, part of me thinks I should do anything, *anything*, if it means having you once in a while. But it wouldn't be enough." His thumbs caress my knuckles. "Don't you see, Elisa? I love you the way a drowning man loves air. And it would destroy me to have you just a little."

I choke on a sob, and tears leak from my eyes. It's the cruelest of cruelties, for him to love me so deeply but refuse to have me.

He lifts his fingers toward my face and gently, so gently, wipes a tear from my cheek. He says, "I'm glad to know, though, that you think of me that way. I'll always remember that."

Grief threatens to strangle me. I have to push it away before I dissolve into a puddle of despair.

I blurt, "I just started taking lady's shroud. Isn't that silly of me?" I mean to sound cavalier, like I'm ready to laugh at myself and move on. But my face flames as soon as the words are in the air.

He grasps my hands and rises, pulling me to my feet. "You've been thinking about this a lot," he says, a touch of wonder in his voice.

I nod, swallowing against further tears. "At least as much as you have."

"Oh, I doubt that very much." And suddenly he's kissing me again, a deeper, longer kiss, and it's a good thing our arms are wrapped around each other, because I don't think I could stand on my own.

I want the moment to last forever, but of course it can't. This time, when he pushes me away, I'm ready for it. I slide my arms from his shoulders, let them fall to my sides.

He takes a step back. We regard each other solemnly.

He says, "I won't kiss you again."

My vision wavers and the world tilts beneath my feet. *I won't kiss you again.* Humberto said that to me once. It proved prophetic, for he died not long after.

Hector is turning his back, walking away from me. How

can he, when my head still swims with his words and my skin still hums with his touch? When my heart feels as jagged as Godstone shards?

Something wells up inside me. Desperation, maybe, that I have loved and lost yet again. Or terror; people have a tendency to die after kissing me.

But no, neither of those. It's rage.

I clench my hands into fists and yell, "Hector!"

He whips around.

"You were never, *never*, going to be just a diversion to me."

He sighs, nodding. "That was unfair of me," he says. "I'm sorr—"

"And you *will* kiss me again. That and *more*. Count on it."

His mouth slams closed, and his eyes flare like a starving man's.

I whirl and stride away.

27

MORNING brings a light shower, but the skies clear quickly, and our tents steam with the scent of wet goat hair in the rising sun. Hector scurries easily up a nearby palm, using both feet and hands for leverage. He twists off several coconuts, which he drops to the ground. Mara bores holes in them and spices them with cinnamon and honey, and we sit around our too-damp fire pits and drink coconut milk for breakfast.

A group of sailors laden with axes sets off for a grove of acacia trees to cut timber for repairs, while Hector and Belén organize others to explore the island. Hector is shoving a water skin inside his pack when he says to me, "Stay within sight of someone at all times. Don't go anywhere alone. If you sense danger, have someone row you out to the ship. I'll be back by nightfall."

I nod up at him helplessly, knowing I'm going to do the exact opposite of all those things, wishing I could kiss him one last time, or at least tell him how I feel. He deserves to know.

"Hector, I . . ." I'm not sure what stills my tongue. Guilt, maybe. "Be safe," I finish lamely.

"You too." His gaze drops to my lips. And then he hurries away, slinging his pack over his shoulder.

I sense Storm's impossibly tall form at my back. He whispers, "Take me with you."

I whirl on him, glaring.

"Please." For once, his face is devoid of mockery or smugness. "I can sense it too, you know. Not like you can, I'm sure. But it's close. We could find it by nightfall."

"What makes you think I'm—"

"You love your people too much, little queen," he says. "You won't risk them. This is your only opportunity to slip away. He always watches you, you know. Like he's a man dying of thirst in the desert and you're his wavering mirage that stays just out of reach."

"Storm!" I hate hearing it from him. He makes it sound so cheap and ridiculous.

"It must be hard for you. To do what you're planning, knowing he may never forgive you when he finds out."

I'm torn between the desire to strangle him and gratitude that there is at least one person I needn't deceive. "Haven't you ever loved someone, Storm? Besides yourself, I mean."

His head lowers with something that might be regret. "Yes. Oh, yes."

Something about his tone makes me soften toward him. "Then maybe you do know how hard this will be."

"Does this mean you'll take me with you?"

"Hector doesn't trust you."

"But you do."

I sigh. It's true, mostly. And if he can sense the *zafira*, nothing would stop him from sneaking away without me. "Yes, you can come." At least this way, if one of us slips and breaks an ankle, the other can go get help. "No packs," I tell him. "Gather as much food as you can carry in your pockets. I'll meet you upstream in a bit. Try not to let anyone see you."

I have as much right to walk through our campsite as anyone, but it feels as though every eye is on me as I return to my tent. From my pack, I grab my water skin, which I hook through the loop in my utility belt; pouches of dried jerky and dates, which go into the pocket of my pants; and my knife, which I shove down into my boot. I grab my crown too. It's made of Godstones, after all. Maybe it will prove useful. No place to hide it, though. Reluctantly I put it back into my pack.

I feel bulgy and obvious as I make my way to the stream.

Mara sits on the edge atop a rocky outcropping. She holds a smooth gray stone in one hand and is grinding away at a thick brown root. Something spicy-sweet pricks at my nose. She looks up at me and says, "Ginger! A whole patch of it across the stream. I'm going to dry it out and take some home with us."

"It will be a wonderful addition to your satchel," I say.

Something about my tone sobers her. "Is something wrong?"

"No," I'm quick to say. "But I haven't spent much time praying lately, so I'm going upstream a ways for privacy. I'll keep the camp in sight."

"I'll come find you when lunch is ready."

"No! I mean, I might be longer than that. I have a lot on my mind." Truly, I am the worst liar in all of Joya d'Arena.

But she just shrugs. "In that case, I'll save some for you."

"Thank you." I wish I could lean down and hug her, but I dare not arouse suspicion by making a big deal out of what should be a very small good-bye. As I turn my back, I hear the *scrape-scrape* of her grinding stone.

I'm barely out of sight of the camp when Storm melts from the trees to join me. Wordlessly we clamber upstream, and we navigate the jungle trash with agonizing slowness because of our need for stealth. Eventually we pass the pool where Mara and I bathed, and the terrain grows rocky and steep until we are scrambling over moss-covered boulders, using palm trees for leverage that have found stubborn rootholds in deep crevices and patches of mud.

The *zafira* calls to me; I feel it as surely as a lasso around the waist, pulling tighter and more agonizingly with every step. I pray as I walk, and soothing warmth spreads through my abdomen to take the edge off the pain.

The stream dead-ends at a small lake shadowed at the base of one of the mountains. A waterfall rushes down the side of the mountain and crashes into the lake, a faint rainbow shimmering in its white spray. I look up, up, up—but the source of the waterfall is hidden in the clouds.

I stare at the cliffs ahead of us, dismayed, for there is nowhere to go. Yet the *zafira* continues to tug at me.

"Another test," Storm says.

"I've climbed cliffs before, but those are impossible. Too slick and steep. Too high."

"Don't be stupid," he says.

I open my mouth to insult him right back, but hesitate. He's right. I need to think differently.

I take a deep breath and focus hard on the tug. It leads straight across the lake to the cliffs. The base is blurred by mist. Just maybe, a ledge lurks behind the water fog. Or boulders. Something we can use to get a better look.

"We need to go around the lake," I say. "Get to the other side."

"Yes," he says, his eyes distant. "I think so too." Surrounded by jungle foliage, his eyes are greener than ever, like the sun shining through emeralds. I shudder as I turn to lead the way.

The boulders edging the lake are black and porous and sharp, and as I use my hands to climb, the soft pads of my fingers are scraped raw. Movement catches my eye. I peer into the crystal water—it's deep and shadowy, but something swims down there, something large.

I lean closer. It darts away and disappears beneath an underwater overhang. I stare at the spot it vacated, puzzled, as the silt it churned up diffuses to the bottom. The creature was larger than a tuna, but I could have sworn I saw stubby legs and a long, whipping tail. Maybe I imagined it.

"Something wrong?" Storm asks.

"This is a very strange place," I say as I continue on. But I keep a close eye on the water's edge.

Mist from the waterfall settles in my hair, on my clothes, on times around my forearm. Storm understands instantly and does the same. Then we step into the cave.

The noise of the waterfall becomes echoing and hollow and so, so much louder. A few more steps take us behind a wall of white water. Soft daylight barely penetrates, giving the fall a crystal sheen, and I'm suddenly thinking of Hector, wishing he was here to see something so beautiful.

I clench my jaw and turn away from the waterfall, into the tunnel. The light grows dimmer as we walk. The tunnel is just high enough for me to stand upright, which means Storm has to stoop. Gradually, though, the night bloomers wrapped around my arms unfurl and begin to glow, faintly at first but with increasing determination, until we can see several paces in every direction.

The tunnel is obviously unnatural. The walls are too perfect, too polished, the floor too even. It slopes slightly upward, and rivulets of water trickle past us to empty into the lake.

Our path curves to the left. We round the corner, and the light from our vines catches on a bit of unevenness in the wall. My heart hammers with a sense of familiarity.

Lichen grows over the unevenness, fanning out in rings of yellow and brown. I reach up with my fingers and scrape it away to reveal script carved into the wall. The Lengua Classica. An ancient style of writing. *The gate that leads to life is narrow and small so that few find it.*

"It's the same," I say to Storm, and my voice echoes. "The same as the tunnel leading to your cavern in the Wallows."

"Yes," he says. "That holy passage has long been associated

my skin. As we approach, the mist turns to spray, then stinging needles of water, and the air is so drenched that I can't see but a few hand spans in front of me. The waterfall booms around us, whipping up a fierce wind. I'm careful to place my hands and feet just so on the slippery rocks, testing each step, each handhold, before taking another.

And finally we can go no farther. We stand on a slight lip between the cliff and the lake, the waterfall before us. There are not enough handholds. No way to climb. Storm yells something, but his voice is whisked away by the merciless water.

Think, Elisa.

I gaze at the cliff face, blinking through water. It's black with wetness, save for a few mossy outcroppings. Stubborn ferns curl out of rocky grooves, straining for sunshine. Vines, choking in parasitic night bloomers, drip down the side and swish back and forth in the water-churned wind, brushing the surface of the lake.

The vines. I peer closer. A darkness lies behind them—something darker than wet rock. I push the vines aside.

It's a cave, or maybe a tunnel, curving behind the waterfall into utter blackness. The tugging at my Godstone leaves no doubt that we must go inside.

I curse myself for not bringing my tinderbox, but then I realize that in this wetness, nothing would catch fire anyway. We'll have to feel our way along in the dark and trust my stone to guide us. It's a test, after all. It's supposed to be difficult.

But no, we *do* have a source of light. I grab a handful of vines and yank hard until they pull free. I wrap them several with the *zafira*. I used to climb up to the tunnel and look at it. I would sit there for hours, hoping God would reveal something to me."

I look at him sharply. He just admitted that he climbed up into the tunnel.

He returns my gaze, his eyes wide with wonder, and I notice, unaccountably, how the roots of his falsely dark hair shimmer gold in the soft light. "Yes, I know the tunnel leads up to the catacombs," he says. "But no, I'm not the one who tried to kill you that day. Truly, I am Your Majesty's loyal subject."

"Do you know who did?"

"No."

"But you've been pursuing the *zafira* for a long time. Even in your exile, you thought about it."

"Yes."

Something clicks into place. "Is this your redemption, Storm? Do you hope that by finding the *zafira*, you can be reconciled to your people? Hailed as a hero? Your death sentence commuted?"

He turns away. "I don't know," he whispers. "Maybe."

"And would you betray me for the same purpose? If you handed over the only living Godstone, would you receive a hero's welcome?"

He shoves me aside and continues down the tunnel. But I understand him a little now, and I've observed he avoids answering to keep from telling a lie.

Chilled—and maybe a little relieved to finally know for sure—I hurry after him.

Our path grows steep, steep, steeper. The smooth floor gives way to perfectly sculpted steps and sudden switchbacks. My thighs burn, my heart pounds, and my breath comes fast as we climb ever upward. It's drier now, and creatures scuttle away at irregular intervals as we approach. I imagine crabs. Or cave scorpions. Or maybe rats with nails long enough to scrape the stone. Whatever they are, they disappear before the arc of our fading light can reach them.

It seems that hours pass, or days. I find myself stepping in time to my heartbeat, which is huge in my chest and throat. My lungs burn, and the tug on my Godstone has become a fire in my belly. Surely we are near the top of the spire by now. Surely we are at the top of the world.

We round another switchback to find the vaguest hint of light. As one, we hurry forward, desperate to lose these walls. The light strengthens. One more corner, and light explodes full in our faces. I blink and raise my forearm against it.

The night bloomers snap closed. Gradually my eyes adjust, and I lower my arm.

We look out over a high mountain valley, green and gently rolling, hemmed in by summits that catch the clouds. They are the same mountains I saw from the ship, I'm sure of it. But now I view them from the other side, and from so much higher up.

Exactly five narrow peaks jut into the sky—the holy number of perfection. One is a little shorter and squatter than the others, like a thumb, and with a start I realize that from a certain angle, I could almost imagine I'm staring at God's righteous right hand, and the streams cutting through the valley are the creases of his cupped palm.

It's a huger, greener version of Lutián's Hand of God sculpture in Brisadulce.

Storm clutches at his chest, and his breathing comes hard, but not, I think, from exertion. The astonishment in his face is stunning to see; it shifts his angled lines into something a little wilder and nearly beautiful.

"You're sensing it very strongly now," I observe.

"Oh, yes. It's almost painful. We're supposed to go down into that valley."

I peer down at the incline in dismay. It's too steep to descend safely. Maybe by using the vines and ferns that hug the slope, we can lower ourselves gradually.

"There," Storm says. "Steps cut into the rock."

I look in the direction he's pointing and decide that calling them "steps" is generous. They are more like handholds, overgrown with moss. After scraping the dying night-bloomer vines from my forearms, I scoot down, lodging my heels into the indentions, clutching plants for support.

Sharp pain pierces my finger, and I yank my hand back. A drop of blood wells on my forefinger. With my other hand, I push aside a fern frond to see what pricked me.

A rose vine, not quite blooming. Deepest red peeks from budding green tips. Thorns wrap around the stems, much longer and harder than those of common roses.

Tears spring to my eyes, for I feel like God has given me a gift.

I have no priest to guide my prayer, no sizzling altar to

accept my blood, no acolyte to bathe my wound with witch hazel. But I can't help but feel that this moment was meant to be, somehow, and so I decide to do what I always do when I am pricked by a sacrament rose: pray and ask a blessing.

In the past, I have asked for courage. Or wisdom. This time, I close my eyes and mutter, "Please, God. Give me *power.*"

I open my eyes, turn my finger over, and let the drop of blood fall to the earth.

Something rumbles—whether it is the world around me or the prayer inside me I cannot tell—and the earth tilts. The air shifts, like a desert mirage, and for the briefest instance, I see lines of shimmering light, Godstone blue and thin as threads. They race from all directions through the mountain peaks, across the valley, to meet at a central point where they are sucked into the ground.

I blink, and the vision is gone, leaving me breathless and puzzled and frightened.

"What just happened?" Storm demands. "You fed the earth a bit of your blood. I felt it move."

"I'm not sure. I saw something strange. Lines of power. But they're gone now."

He stares at me suspiciously. "Let's go. I become impatient."

It doesn't take long to reach the valley floor, which is a good thing given how my legs are shaking from exertion. There are no palm trees here, just sprawling cypress and towering eucalyptus and a tree I've never seen before, with such huge broad leaves that a single leaf would cover my whole body. Birds flit among the branches; dappled light catches on them and shoots away in prismatic facets. It's so startlingly odd that I peer closer.

No, not birds. They're giant insects, as large as ospreys, with downy white abdomens and gossamer wings.

Misgiving thumps in my chest. This valley has a wrongness to it. It is alien. *Other.*

And there is something about it that inspires silence. We move quietly, as if in expectation, or perhaps reverence. Piles of stone like crumbling altars litter the forest floor, some as tall as I am, covered in green lichen and dust. A cypress tree clings stubbornly to the side of one, its roots prying open cracks in stone.

We round a bend and find another pile, but this one is as tall as a tree and square shaped, with arched openings for windows. A ruined building. I look around in awe at the other piles. Ruins, all of them. This was once a city of stone, its shape now worn down by sun and wind and tree roots and time.

"This must be centuries old," I breathe.

"Several millennia," Storm says, and there is a quiet sadness in his voice I've never heard before.

I regard him sharply. "That's impossible. God brought people to this world—"

"Yes, yes, he rescued you from the dying world with his righteous right hand less than two thousand years ago. I've heard you tell it." The anger in his voice is palpable. "Little queen, don't you realize? We Inviernos have *always* been here."

I stare at him agape, even as the rightness of his words spark inside me. Behind him, one of the insect birds flits through the branches of a eucalyptus, alights atop the ruined building, and begins to groom its rainbow wing with a spindly black leg.

"Your people came, bearing magic we'd never seen," he continues. "They changed us, made us less than we were. Changed themselves too, the legend goes, though I don't know how or why. They scattered across the land now called Joya d'Arena, and we fled before them into the mountains. After that, *they changed the whole world.* Your country wasn't always a desert, you know."

I'm shaking my head, with uneasiness rather than denial. If what he says is true, then my ancestors were interlopers. No, thieves. But surely one cannot be considered a thief when one is taking only what God gives? God offered us this world. All the scriptures say so.

My old tutor did tell me our great desert was an inland sea before a mysterious cataclysm forced the water deep below ground. So maybe what Storm says is partly true. Maybe we *created* the desert somehow. But how? "That makes no sense," I say aloud. "God wouldn't—"

My Godstone leaps, and the tugging on my navel becomes a dagger in my gut.

Storms gasps. "I don't like pain."

I bend over, clutching at my stomach with one hand, even as I grab Storm's shoulder with the other and push him forward down our path. "Just . . . keep . . . moving." I can hardly put one foot in front of the other. All I want to do is drop to the ground and curl up, knees to chest. Maybe this is what Father Nicandro meant when he said my determination would be tested.

I have a lot of determination.

But a few steps farther and the vise on my abdomen twists suddenly, and I tumble to my knees, panting. I will crawl if I have to. I will—

"It's worse for you, isn't it?" Storm says, looking down at me with irritation.

I nod, unable to speak.

He stares at me a moment. Then he sighs, squats down, grabs one of my arms, and loops it over his shoulder. He stands, pulling me to my feet. "Just a bit farther, Your Majesty."

I swallow my surprise and concentrate on moving my feet as he drags me down the path.

Just when I think the pain can't get any worse, when my body wavers between vomiting and passing out, we break into a small clearing. In the center is another ruined building, as perfectly round as a tower. But its summit has long since crumbled, leaving it merely the height of a man.

Chains rattle.

A pale face with eyes the color of a hazy sky peeks out from behind the tower. White hair streams from a middle part on his sunburned scalp, all the way to the ground. It's the gatekeeper.

28

HE has the flawless face of an animagus, but his stooped shoulders and rheumy eyes make him seem as old as the mountains themselves.

"Two!" he squeals. "Two apprentices!" His Lengua Classica is thick and muddled, like he has a mouthful of pebbles. "I must be one of God's favorites," he says, "to be so blessed." He steps from behind the tower to reveal tattered clothes of indeterminate color and filthy bare feet in rusty manacles. The skin of his ankles bulges up around the manacles so that it is impossible to see where iron ends and flesh begins. I have to look away.

"Who are you?" he asks. "I've felt you coming for hours now. Or years?"

I try to speak, but I can't. I am nothing but pain and that awful tugging.

"Oh, yes, that," he says. He flicks his fingers, and the pain disappears.

Relief floods me, and desperate gratitude starts to bubble

on my lips, but I bite it back. I straighten cautiously.

"Are you the gatekeeper?" I ask.

"You first!" he says, clapping. "Tell me who you are. And come here, come here. Let me get a better look at you."

I edge forward. He lunges toward me, and I recoil, but his manacles have caught him. He is chained, I see now, to the tower. He cries out in frustration, stomping on the ground like a child throwing a tantrum. Then he collects himself, and the frustration melts from his face as quickly as it came. "I believe you were about to tell me who you are?" he says with preternatural calm.

I'm careful to stay just beyond the reach of his chains when I say, "I am the bearer." And after a moment of silence: "And a queen."

He taps his lip with a crooked, dirty finger. "Not very good at either, are you? Your heart screams your inadequacy." He turns to Storm. "And you?"

Storm draws himself up to full height. "A prince of the realm," he says.

I gape at him.

He shrugs. "You never asked."

The strange man leans toward us conspiratorially. "But not much of a prince anymore, yes? A shadow of what you were." He grins, like it is all a great game, and I shudder to see his teeth, pointed like canines and brown with rot. "Would you like to see the *zafira*? I can show it to you, yes, I can. It will have a bit of your blood, and then it will decide whether you live or die."

Storm and I exchange an alarmed look.

I say, "So you *are* the gatekeeper? What's your name?"

His teeth snap in the air. "I've told you a thousand times and you never listen! I am Heed the Fallen Leaf That Grows Dank with Rot, for It Shall Feed Spring Tulips."

"Of course. Apologies." He is insane. Totally and completely insane. "I think I'll just call you . . ." *Rot.* "Er, Leaf."

"Leaf! Yes, I'll be Leaf. Let me see your stones." When I hesitate, he barks, "Now! I must see them to let you inside."

Reluctantly I lift the edge of my blouse to reveal my stomach and its resident jewel.

And then Storm reaches beneath his shirt and pulls out a leather cord that dangles a Godstone of his very own, in a tiny iron cage.

I gape at him. "How did you . . . When did you . . . ?"

"I've always had it. Since birth."

Too many possibilities compete for attention in my head. Was it given to him? Was he born with it? "My Godstone never warmed to it," I protest. "Never reacted. It always senses another Godstone nearby. *Always.*"

Storm wilts a little. "It's quite dead. It fell out at the age of four. I trained to be an animagus, to learn to eke some power out of it. But I never could. I failed."

Understanding hits like a rock in the gut. "The Inviernos are born with Godstones."

Storm shakes his head. "Only a few of us. They fall out very early. And we've been separated from the source of their power for so long that they are mostly useless."

"The animagi burned my city, burned my husband. That's hardly useless."

Storm shrugs. "That's destruction magic. Easy, for an animagus. It's creation magic, like barrier shields or growing plants or healing, that's difficult."

"*I* can heal." The words are out of my mouth before I think to censor them.

"What? You can?" His green eyes narrow. "You never said."

I stick a finger in his chest. "You. Never. Asked."

His brief moment of startlement dissolves into desperate laughter. "And yet you can't even call your stone's fire, which is the easiest, most basic power. You might be a worse failure than even me."

Leaf has been looking back and forth between us, grinning all the while. "You are enemies!" he says, clapping with delight. "So much fun. Look, here's mine." He parts the rags hanging from his shoulders to reveal petal-white skin and protruding ribs.

A Godstone is sewn into his navel. Threads of hemp or dried grass crisscross over the top, holding it in place. The skin around the edges is puckered and scarred from so many piercings. One thread dangles, wisping back and forth in the breeze. I avert my gaze, sickened.

"Will you take us now?" Storm asks. He leans forward and his face twitches, as if he's about to crawl out of his own skin in anticipation.

"This way," Leaf says, and disappears behind the tower, his chains clattering with each step. After exchanging a troubled look, Storm and I follow.

An archway on the opposite side leads into darkness. Leaf reaches down and grabs his chain, which seems to have a little slack now, and hoists it over his shoulder. "Ready?" And he steps inside.

I remember the way he lunged at me. I debate the wisdom of following. I put my fingertips to my Godstone and whisper a quick prayer for safety. It nearly scalds my fingers with its sudden heat, and I gasp with the sensation of power flowing into me.

So much! It's what brought me here, after all. I take a deep breath and step inside the ruined tower.

My eyes adjust quickly to the gloom. A spiral stairway bores into the earth. It smells of wet earth and mold. A few twists down, and our path begins to glow faintly, bluely, as if from night bloomers. The glow brightens as we descend, until the colorless walls have taken on its tint, until my skin is bathed in it. My Godstone thrums softly, as if crooning to a lover.

When the stair opens into a vast cavern, I fall to my knees, gasping in amazement.

The walls are lined with Godstones. Thousands. Tens of thousands. A river flows against the far wall, but not of water. It's a slow-moving course of light and fog and power, glowing blue, as nebulous as a cloud. Its light reflects off the Godstone walls so that the cavern seems under a barrage of sapphire sparks.

My own Godstone sings in greeting. A finger of glowing fog creeps from the river, slithers across the damp ground like a searching tentacle, glides over my knee and up to the Godstone, where it presses gently.

There is an audible *click*, like pieces of a puzzle coming together. The energy inside me flares joyously, and suddenly I feel connected to the whole world as the *zafira* feeds me life and energy through the siphon of my Godstone. My head swims, my limbs tingle, and I'm a little bit delighted, a little bit horrified.

"Oh, it loves you, yes, it does," murmurs Leaf. "Have you fed the earth a bit of your blood already, then?"

"I . . . yes. On the way down. I found a sacrament rose bush, and prayed for . . ." Power. I prayed for power. And here I am, connected to the source of all magic, but I feel no closer to my goal than before. My body buzzes with energy, certainly, like I could do anything. I could heal a thousand people. Bring down a hurricane. But can I take that power with me to help me rule a kingdom? Or does it only work here, in this cavern?

Storm is gazing at the walls, his mouth agape. "It's a grave," he says. "A catacomb of animagi."

"Oh, yes," Leaf says. "They used to come here to die. Or if they died too soon, they would have their bodies brought here. But only their stones remain. No one has come here to die in a very long time. Until now!" He claps, showing his rotting teeth.

Fear shoots through me. I jump to my feet, eyeing the opening to the stairway, wondering if Storm and I could outrun him if he turned on us. But no, I won't run. I can't. "We came to learn about the *zafira*," I say firmly. "Not to die."

"Oh, no one minds being dead!" he assures us. "But some people mind being alive. Like me. I've lived far too long." He rattles his chains, which now lie coiled like a snake at his feet. The opposite end drops over the lip of the riverbank, into the vast blueness. "One of you will take my place as the *zafira's* gatekeeper, its living sacrifice. God is so kind; he gave me two to choose from!"

The wonder on Storm's face cedes to misgiving.

"One of you, *if* you survive, will leave here a true sorcerer," Leaf explains, "having made the pilgrimage and tasted of the *zafira*. And oh, she is fickle. It's fun to guess if someone will live or die. I only get it right some of the time. But the other . . ." He dances a joyful jig, blood oozing around his swollen ankles. "The other must stay so that I can sleep. Oh, I am so tired. Let's begin, shall we?" He lifts his arms above his head and mutters something unintelligible. A stream of light rises from the river of fog and rushes to the space between his hands, where it grows, coalesces, begins to spin.

I gasp with recognition. I know what this is, for I've done it myself, when I destroyed the animagi with my Godstone amulet. He is drawing the power to himself, storing it up, readying it to explode into a wave of energy.

Panic builds in my throat. I have to do something. But what? The force he gathers brightens. It illuminates the whole cavern, showing a roof gnarled with the roots of trees from the valley above.

Storm sprints for the doorway.

"Trying to get away, little mouse?" says Leaf. A tendril of blue fire whips from the river, shoots toward Storm, wraps his torso like a snake, and yanks him to the ground. He lands hard on his back, where he gasps like a beached fish, the wind knocked out of him.

Think, Elisa! I have channeled this power before. I've won a war with it. I've healed people. I pushed the *Aracely*, somehow, through a massive hurricane. I can *do* this.

I close my eyes, place my fingertips to the Godstone, and imagine the *zafira's* power pouring into me.

It does, like a flood, like a hurricane, until I'm spinning with it, mad with it. My hair lifts from the nape of my neck, and my fingers tingle with power that feels so natural, so easy. The earth beneath me disappears.

I open my eyes to discover that I float several inches above the ground and the *zafira's* soothing flame has wrapped around me like a lover's arms. But what to do with all this power?

"Interesting," Leaf says as his ball of blue fire begins to shoot white sparks. "You may be a worthy opponent, with your living stone." And from his spinning sun, he sends a bolt of blue fire spearing toward me.

I imagine Hector's forearm shield, the way it sheltered me when arrows flew down the hallway of my palace. A shimmering barrier materializes out of thin air before me, and the bolt of fire bounces harmlessly against it. So easy! The power, drawn directly from its source. Exactly what I've been looking for. Exactly what I need.

Leaf giggles with delight. He sends more bolts, so fast they are blurs of streaking light, but I continue to pull the *zafira's* energy into me, and they bounce away from my barrier.

"And now I try to kill your enemy!" he yells, and he turns toward Storm, who lies defenseless on the ground, still gasping for air.

"No!" I send my barrier flying toward him, but it is too late—a bolt of energy plunges into his leg. He screams as the fabric of his robe sears away in a widening, blackening circle, and I catch the agonizingly familiar scent of burning flesh.

I clench my fists with frustration. I have all this power, but I lack the skill, the finesse, to channel it properly. I can't defend both of us. I close my eyes, racking my brain for an idea.

I've never been able to destroy, save for the one time. But I can create. I can knit flesh and renew life. I focus on the tree roots over our heads. I think about their bark, their soft insides. I imagine them growing.

Another bolt shoots toward Storm, but he rolls away just in time. Leaf bends his elbows behind his head, readying to fling the ball of light at Storm. I know what will happen next—it will explode in a wave so powerful that nothing can stand in its way.

Grow. Please grow.

Light tendrils whisk up my arms toward the ceiling. They wrap around the roots, untwisting them, pulling them down. And suddenly I *am* the roots, reaching as if with massive fingers. I grasp for Leaf, coil around him, yank him from the ground and dangle him in the air.

His light ball blinks out. He gapes at me for a moment, then kicks his legs in the air, which sets his chain rattling.

"Well, all right, then," he says. "Your apprenticeship is

complete. You're a sorcerer now. I declare it so." He closes his eyes and mutters intelligibly. Something jerks in my chest as my roots release him. He falls to the ground, lands with a great *crack* beside Storm. I drop to the ground a moment later. My knees buckle, but I keep my feet.

Leaf sprawls, his knee bent at an unnatural angle. "Ah, broke that leg again," he says, as if it's hardly worth his notice. "But no healing for me this time." He cocks his head at me. "Would you like to be my replacement?"

I take a step back. "Er, no thank you."

"I thought as much. You are a queen, after all. Things to do, things to do, yes? Also, I probably could not make you, living stone that you have. No matter. I'll take this little mouse, weak as he is." Leaf reaches out with a spindly hand and splays his fingers across Storm's horrified face. "And now, my weak prince, all the power you've ever wanted is yours."

"No!" I shout, grasping for more of the *zafira*. I sling tendrils of light toward Storm to pull him away, even as the manacles around Leaf's ankles dissipate into fog.

Storm begins sliding toward me, but it doesn't matter. Shadows form around his ankles, darkening until they are as hard and true as iron.

Leaf sways; then his cheek hits the ground, hard. He gasps in the dirt, a smile on his face. "Free!" he whispers. "You'll put my stone into the wall, yes? With the others?"

His face caves in on itself until he is little more than a grinning skeleton. His hair turns black as he shrinks, dissolving into a cloud of dust. The dust coalesces in the air, then rains to the ground, forming an ashy pile. A single glittering Godstone winks from the pile's center.

"I'll be here forever," Storm whispers. "Forever."

I tear my gaze from the pile of dust that used to be Leaf and say, "No. We'll find a way to free you. Maybe an ax? I'm sure Captain Felix has a blacksmith in his crew."

Storm's face falls into his hands. "The chains are formed by magic. No blacksmith can break them."

"Maybe I can—"

"You can only do creation magic, remember? You can't destroy these chains."

"I'm very good at figuring things out."

He clambers to his feet, and his features suddenly calm with resignation. "Majesty, go. Leave me here. Even if you could figure out a way to free me, you won't do it. The *zafira* connected with you. I saw it. You'll be able to call on its power forevermore. No matter where in the world you are. Just like the animagi of old, when we had our full strength. You truly are the chosen one."

He's right. Even now, I hum with strength, like I can do anything. It's wonderful to feel such breathtaking power. I'm almost dizzy with it.

"But the *zafira* needs a living sacrifice, a conduit," he says. "Without a gatekeeper, it's useless to you."

All I do is walk away from this place, and I become the most powerful sovereign who ever lived. "Storm, I never meant—"

"You told me you would choose your own life over mine, remember? So do it. Choose now and leave me alone. You know I prefer to be alone than in your miserable company."

Tears prick at my eyes, and I suck in air through my nose to keep steady. "Will you . . . How will you . . . ?"

"The *zafira* will sustain me. Even now it heals my burns. Just promise me that when you face Invierne—and you will face them—that you'll tell them about me."

"What do you want me to say?" I ask in a small voice.

"Tell them that the man who failed as an animagi, who failed as a prince, and who failed as an ambassador, found the *zafira* and restored his honor by becoming its living sacrifice. Will you do that?"

"You never cared about honor! You've been content to live without it, so long as it meant you could *live.*"

"It's all that's left to me. Please?"

I nod, voiceless.

He lowers himself to the ground, crosses his legs, and closes his eyes. "Go now, Elisa. Go be the queen you couldn't be on your own."

I turn away, even as his words bore into my chest, twisting like barbs. *Go be the queen you couldn't be on your own.* I have what I came for. Power beyond imagining.

Why then, with it coursing though me, filling me to over-flowing, do I feel like a hollow shell of a girl?

I have passed through the doorway, and my foot is on the first step leading out of the cavern when I freeze.

Channeling all the magic of the world is no different from choosing a regent or making a desperate marriage alliance. It's just an instrument. A crutch.

Hector's voice, low and intimate, echoes in my head. *If you were like this, with this kind of confidence, this clarity of thought, no one would dare challenge your rule.*

The *zafira* is not what I need.

What I need is to be a better queen.

29

I turn back around. My heart flutters and my knees tremble at what I might do. *Is this the right choice?* But there is no response, or if there is, it is so overwhelmed by the rush of the *zafira* that I can't detect it. I must make a choice wholly independent from God's voice, from his stone, from his power.

I take a deep breath. "Storm."

His head whips up.

"Come with me."

"What?"

"To the surface. Now, before I change my mind."

He bolts to his feet and hobbles toward me as quickly as his manacles will allow. "How will you get the chains off? And if you do, the *zafira* will be lost to you forever. To all of us. What if—"

"Do you *want* to stay here for thousands of years?"

"No."

"Then shut up and follow me."

Before we enter the archway, I cast my gaze around for one

last look at this catacomb of Godstones. So beautiful. So much history and remembrance and even worship, so much magic.

Think like a sorcerer, Storm said. But what I need to do is think like a queen.

And as the stones shine brighter than the brightest sapphire, I think: *so much* value.

Quickly I pry a Godstone out of the wall. It comes loose with a soft *plink,* and I shove it into my pocket. I grab a few more, until my pocket bulges.

"Let's go." Together, chains clanking behind us, we spiral up the steps and into the sunshine.

"Now what?" he asks, gasping for breath.

I look around the tiny clearing. The trees are very close.

"Keep still," I order.

I gather power into myself until my muscles thrum with it. I cast my awareness into the earth, to everything growing there—tiny grass roots, a colony of ants milling about in oddly organized industry, a worm. I feel them all, as if they're an extension of myself. With the *zafira* coursing through me, perhaps they are.

There. A mass of cypress roots, twisting together like a nest of snakes, perfectly sized.

I coax them toward us. They writhe through the ground, poke out of the grass, weave through the links of Storm's chains. I shove them hard, and their widening girths strain the links. Something groans like a dying animal as I torque them mercilessly.

The links snap.

"Run!" I yell. I have no idea if the chains will reform, if the *zafira* will grab him back with a relentless light tentacle.

Storm sprints away, and I dash to keep up. His manacles rattle with each step, dangling lengths of broken chain that threaten to catch in the foliage and yank him down.

For the first time since entering this valley, my Godstone turns to ice. The earth begins to rumble, and Storm freezes, but I shove him on. "Just go!" I hope I have not broken the world.

We scramble up the footholds toward the entrance to the cavern, chased by the sounds of grinding rocks and splitting earth. I tell myself not to look back, to concentrate on moving forward, but when we gain the top, I can't help it. I turn around and gasp.

Trees slowly lean toward the center of the valley like they're bowing to God. Then a series of massive *pops* echoes all around as roots rip from their moorings and the trees topple over. Clouds of dust explode into the air.

The valley is caving in on itself, forming a giant sinkhole where Leaf's tower used to be.

I press shaking fingers to my lips. *What have I done?*

A stream diverts, collides with another in a thunderous spray of water and mud. Their joined force is relentless as it sweeps boulders and uprooted trees into the gaping sinkhole.

My teeth rattle in my jaw as the valley booms, again and again. No, it's not just the valley. The sound comes from above too. The mountain is about to tumble down on us.

"We need to move," Storm says. "Fast."

His words spur me to action, and I sprint toward the cavern. It gapes darkly before us. "We need light!" We don't have time to feel our way down the dark stairs. But by traveling in haste, we will surely fall to our deaths. "Do you see night bloomers? Anywhere?"

"Just the ones we discarded. Nearly dead."

"They'll do." I grab the wilting vines from where I dropped them. Drawing on the *zafira*, I reach inside their stems and coax them to life. But the power bleeds away from me even as their leaves straighten with health, as the petals unfurl. By the time their stamens have brightened into a steady glow, the power is gone.

I allow myself the tiniest moment of grief. I brush the night bloomers against my cheeks, breathing in their honeysuckle-like scent. Then I step into the booming mountain.

Dust and pebbles rain down on us, urging us on as we descend. Our way becomes slick with mud. Twice I slip on my heel, but Storm is quick at my elbow, shoring me up with a strength that belies his delicate frame.

We dare not stop when we reach the waterfall, for we are still too close to the shaking mountain. Dusk has fallen, and as we clamber across the boulders lining the lake I find it nearly impossible to distinguish between cracks and sinkholes and shadows.

It is nearly full dark when we reach the stream, and living night bloomers unfurl in the trees all around us. The noise of the collapsing valley fades, and I dare to hope that we are safe.

We stop to catch our breath. Storm bends over, hands on his

knees, heaving for air. His face and robe are covered in drying mud, tinged gruesomely blue in the night bloomers' light. I imagine I look the same. "Why?" he manages between gasps. "Why did you save me? My own people would not have done so much. Stupid queen. You are powerless now."

"You are my loyal subject."

He stares at me.

"But I'm not powerless." I continue. "I've always had my Godstone and its minor magic. I healed Hector in Brisadulce, you know, so there are things I can still do just by reaching through the skin of the earth." It would be useless to tell him that I'm done sacrificing other people for my own gain. I won't whip innocent kitchen workers, I won't burn down buildings, I won't ask anyone to give up an inheritance for me, and I certainly won't leave a friend at the mercy of a mysterious magical force—merely for the sake of my own power. I press my fingers to the stone at my navel, taking comfort in its familiar pulsing. What I tell him is, "And I have me. *I* will be enough."

The camp is silent and somber and half emptied when Storm and I step from the trees. Mara sits alone near the fire pit. She holds up a steaming fish speared on a stick and is about to take a bite, but she sees us and lets it drop into the embers, jumping to her feet. "Elisa?" she whispers, and then she's running toward me, wrapping me in her arms. "Oh, God, I knew you had probably gone off alone, that you weren't *taken*, but when I heard all that rumbling a bit ago, I thought that . . . I thought maybe . . ."

I return her hug fiercely. "I'm sorry," I say.

She steps back. "Did you find it?"

"Yes."

"And what happened? Did you . . ." she makes a vague gesture with her hand.

"Can I tell you about that a little later, maybe? I need to . . . think."

Her eyes drift to Storm's shackles, then back to my face. "All right," she says, but her gaze is troubled, maybe a little bit wounded.

"Where is everyone?" I ask, though I think I know.

"Looking for you. Hector is sick with worry."

I wince, dreading the moment I will face him. I say, "I need to walk. I'll be at the beach."

"Do you want something to eat first?"

"No, thank you." I feel her puzzled gaze at my back as I step away.

The half moon sends ripples of gold across the water. In the distance floats the black, battered shape of the *Aracely*, her main sail hanging limp in the windless night. The air is hot, the water calm.

On impulse, I shuck my filthy boots and blouse. Wearing nothing but my linen pants and a sleeveless undershirt, I wade out into the warm water.

A strange thing happens. Where the water touches me, it glows, Godstone blue. I lie back and float, waving my arms experimentally. The glow is like a shield wrapping around my body, a clinging aura of power. I laugh, delighted, thinking about all the things I've seen lately that glow in this way: my Godstone, when I'm about to release its power. The river of energy. The night bloomers. And now this luminescing bay.

And I realize that the *zafira* is everywhere. I may have destroyed access to its purest form, but it leaks out all over the world.

I see movement along the shore. A dark shape materializes out of the trees, and I catch my breath. I know him from so far away, just by the way he walks. I'm suddenly desperate to see him up close, to look into his eyes, to hear his low, soft voice, even though I know whatever we say to each other next cannot end well.

I swim toward shore until my feet touch bottom; then I walk from the glowing water to meet him.

He stares at me as I approach, his face unreadable to me again, the way it used to be. When he is only an arm's length away, I say, "Hector, I'm sorry."

He studies me thoughtfully. Then my whole body goes hot as his gaze travels—slowly, deliberately—from my neck, to my breasts, my hips, down to my feet, and all the way up again. My clothes cling to me like a second skin, leaving little to the imagination.

At last he says, "Sorry for what, exactly?" and his voice is cold, cold, cold.

I swallow hard. "For leaving without telling you."

"A queen need never apologize to a mere guard." He makes it sound like an insult, and I gasp from the pain of it.

"Still, I should have—"

"You're my queen, Elisa. You can do whatever you want. You never owe me an explanation."

He is reminding me, with patient and lethal efficiency, of how much power I have over him, of why we could never be together.

"Now, if we were *lovers,*" he says, "I might feel angry that you demanded my honesty but refused me yours. I might feel insulted that you slinked away to do something dangerous knowing full well that the most important thing I do is protect you. And I might feel perplexed that you lacked the courage to face me, when all you had to do was give the order."

I've never felt so contemptible and small. Part of me wants to flee, to escape his ruthless gaze. Another part wants to wrap my arms around him and beg forgiveness, for there can be no doubt that I have hurt him deeply.

He can't help adding, "It's a good thing, then, that we are not lovers, yes?"

It's like a dagger to the gut. He means it to be his final rejection. He means to hurt me, and maybe to grasp on to some power of his own. It's cruel of him, and unworthy of the Hector I've come to know. And yet the anger melts out of me as quickly as it forms.

I reach up and cup his face with one hand. It shocks some feeling into his eyes, and I watch carefully as he considers whether or not to recoil from my touch. He doesn't.

I say, "What I did was weak. Cowardly. Unqueenly. But I learned some things about power when I went to the *zafira,* and you were right. About everything." I brush across his cheek, memorizing the texture of his skin, the feel of slight stubble against the pad of my thumb. "I do have power. Enough that I don't need you. But I will miss you awfully."

He lurches away, and my heart aches to see the torment on his face. He looks everywhere but at me, running his hands through his hair as if to keep them busy. He says, "How do you *do* that? You always disarm me. You have from the day I . . . And I hate it. I truly hate it."

From a place of knowledge as old as the *zafira* itself, from the depths of a feminine power I'm only beginning to understand, I say with conviction: "No, you don't."

I want to tell him how much I love him. He deserves to know. But it would be too perilous in this moment. It would sound like I was begging, or saying what he wanted to hear just to diffuse his anger.

So I leave him alone with his thoughts. I return to camp, resolved to face Mara and tell her everything, hoping I can salvage at least one friendship.

30

WE spend the next week repairing the ship and gathering foodstuffs. We make a rack of mangrove roots and set it in the sun to dry fish. A pile of coconuts becomes a mountain as we forage. I've always been handy with a needle, so I volunteer to repair a rip in one of the smaller sails. All the while, we are surrounded by the sounds of ax and mallet.

Hector is unfailingly polite to me, but I miss the way his warm gaze used to linger on my face, the way his lips would quirk when I said something that amused him. We renew our lessons in self-defense, carving out a space on the beach to work. He demonstrates the places on the human body that are most subject to pain. He shows me how to use my own body weight to throw an opponent to the ground. He explains how to shove a man's nose into his brain with the base of my palm to kill him instantly and has me practice the motion on an unlucky coconut.

He does all this while managing to never touch me.

And though he says nothing, I'm certain he has decided

to leave my service and go home to Ventierra. There's a desperate focus to his teaching, as if he's shoring me up with as much knowledge as possible before we part ways.

I dread leaving this place, for it means returning to all the problems I left behind, problems that have inevitably worsened. Our ruse has certainly been discovered by now. I hope decoy Elisa has survived and that Ximena is well. I worry for Rosario and his safety. And I cannot doubt that Conde Eduardo has maneuvered in my absence, that he has found a way to turn the situation to his advantage.

Too soon, Captain Felix declares us prepped and ready, and we weigh anchor and set sail for our rendezvous point in Selvarica. I stand on the quarterdeck, the wind whipping hair into my eyes, watching the island grow small. From this vantage, I can see that one of the mountains is shorter now, with a jagged peak, its zenith a crumbling ruin in the valley I destroyed.

During the voyage, we try to remove the manacles from Storm's ankles. But the blacksmith cannot forge them open, the cooper cannot pry them open, and though I can make them glow warmly, I cannot force them open by magic. Storm grumbles at our efforts and finally snaps at us to leave well enough alone. "To all my other failures, I must add my failure as gatekeeper to the *zafira*." He sighs dramatically.

"I don't believe you mind so much," I point out.

He cracks a rare grin. "Truly, I do not." He pulls himself up to full height. "In fact, I will wear these chains proudly. However, I require salve and a bit of cloth to use as cushioning around my ankles. Silk, of course."

"I think it's an improvement," I tell him. "I'll never again worry about you sneaking up on me."

"I hate you."

I reach up to squeeze his shoulder. "I know."

The wind holds, and it takes less than two weeks to make port in Selvarica. The land is as Tristán described it: lush and green and gorgeous, not unlike the island we come from.

As soon as we dock, we are greeted by a large complement of solemn-looking soldiers in full armor.

"What's going on?" I demand.

"Conde Tristán sent us to escort you, Your Majesty," says one. "This way, please. Quickly."

Hector and Belén flank me as we hurry down the dock. Mara and Storm, who is cowled once again, follow behind, and Storm's clattering steps cause dockworkers and fishermen to pause and stare. We reach a waiting carriage, and a soldier assures us our belongings will be collected and sent to us. Then he smacks the horse's flank and waves the driver off.

A group of soldiers jogs alongside as we travel up a steep drive. I peer out the window and notice fortifications along the road. Temporary walls with arrow slits. A blockade on the side that could be moved quickly to block traffic.

"Tristán is preparing for war," I say to no one in particular, and my heart thuds. I thought I was done with war. Forever done.

"I see Conde Eduardo's colors too," Hector says in a grave voice. "Tristán may no longer be in command of his own garrison."

We reach a carriage house, where we are quickly unloaded and ushered through a servants' wing, across an inner courtyard with marble fountains and tiled pathways and hanging plants, and into a long dining hall with an enormous low table, much like the one in my own council chamber where the Quorum meets.

A handful of people already sit on cushions around the table, and they look up when we enter. I am so very glad to see Tristán, Iladro, a few of my own Royal Guard, and . . . my eyes sweep the room looking for her. There! Ximena leaps to her feet and barrels toward me, arms outstretched for an embrace. I fall into the hug easily and gratefully.

She pushes me back to arm's length, and her eyes are wet with tears when she says, "I'm so glad you're safe and well, my sky."

A puckered redness slashes across her cheekbone—a clumsily stitched wound that will leave a large scar. I point to my own cheek. "Ximena, what happened?"

"Later." She guides me by the shoulders toward the table.

"And the girl?"

"Dead." She sighs. "I'm sorry."

I swallow hard against the sudden knot in my throat. Another innocent person added to my wake of bodies. I'm torn between writhing guilt, and gladness that Ximena survived.

Hector and his men greet one another in a fierce demonstration of backslapping. Then Hector and Tristán clasp forearms while Mara and Ximena embrace. Finally we all settle onto our cushions.

I lean forward, elbows on the table. "Tell me at once what is going on."

Tristán rubs wearily at his temples. "Franco came after the girl," he says. "It happened very publicly, with an arrow to the neck. We had no choice but to reveal that she was not you, that the queen still lived. As planned, Father Alentín began circulating the rumor among the priests that you were on a mission from God himself."

"And Franco?" I ask.

"Disappeared."

"Was he working alone or on Eduardo's orders?"

"We don't know.

Ximena says, "Conde Eduardo came south not long after we left Brisadulce. He began asking, in the politest way possible, of course, if you had abandoned Joya d'Arena. He claimed distress over your choice to pretend to court a southern lord, only to disappear. Without ever saying it straight out, he convinced a lot of people that the south had been dealt an insulting blow."

All the decisions of the last few months are like a millstone about my neck. I don't need them to explain the rest, because it all clicks together in my head until I am sick with it.

"The southern holdings were already in tumult," I say. "They blame the arid north for draining the country's resources. There has been talk of seceding, like the eastern holdings did."

"Yes," Tristán says.

"Eduardo wants a civil war." I hide my hands under the table so no one can see how much they tremble. "He wants to be king of his own nation. It's what he wanted all along. He tried to have me killed. When that didn't work, he did everything he could to weaken me, especially in the eyes of the southern holdings. That's why he was so set on me marrying a northern lord—to keep my southern alliances thin. That's why General Luz-Manuel had Martín executed—to weaken and dispirit my guard. The two of them must be working together." My heart pounds with certainty and dismay. "The general is the one who has ordered these fortifications, yes?"

The ensuing silence is heavy and thick.

I whisper, "What about Rosario? Is he all right?"

"We don't know, Your Majesty," Tristán says.

I'll never forgive myself if something happens to the boy.

"Captain Lucio will have gotten him to safety," Hector says. "At the first sign of trouble."

Even as I meet his gaze and nod my thanks, I pray to God that he is right.

"So, Your Majesty, what do we do?" Tristán asks.

This is it, then. The moment I must think like the girl who led a desert rebellion and won a war for her husband. Like a queen.

I rise to my feet and begin pacing, worrying at my thumbnail with my teeth. I need allies. Resources. I must turn sentiment in my favor, at least long enough to stall the conde's inciting efforts, long enough to prepare my own fortifications.

My pacing quickens. The first thing I'll do is announce Conde Tristán's nomination to the Quorum. Maybe it will bury the "insult" a little, bely Eduardo's claim that I have abandoned the south. But that will only go so far.

Then what, Elisa? You need a demonstration of your commit-
ment to the south. Something permanent. You need . . .

My head whips up.

I need . . .

I almost choke on grief and gladness and terror as my gaze
snaps to Hector's.

I need to marry Hector.

Inheritor of a southern holding much more powerful than
Tristán's. A war hero. The best leader I know. Before, marrying him would have been foolish, for he was already my
staunchest supporter. But now that my kingdom is about to
split apart, a very public alliance with him could be the thing
that holds it together.

"Elisa?" he says softly. "What is it?"

I stare at him, at his precious face. I love his dark eyes, the
way his hair curls slightly around his ears, his strong jaw, his
beautiful lips. I know exactly what those lips feel like against
mine.

I could ask him. Right now. But he might say no. Or I could
command, and he would obey, but he would never forgive me.

But maybe, just maybe, I will ask and he will say yes.

How, exactly, does a queen propose? Is there an etiquette to
observe? A document to sign? I look around the room in panic.
Everyone gazes back, puzzled.

I hear shouting. Stomping footsteps, the ring of steel on steel.

Soldiers pour into the dining hall from all three entrances.
They are dressed in the crimson and gold of Conde Eduardo's
countship.

Everyone at the table shoots to their feet, drawing their weapons, even as a strong arm wraps around my shoulders and the cold point of a dagger presses against my throat.

Eduardo's soldiers ring the room. We are outnumbered three to one.

"Drop your weapons," says a sibilant voice in my ear.

Hector looks to me for instruction, and more than the arm holding me captive, more even than the dagger at my throat, the desperation in his face sends terror shooting through me. Never have I seen him so frightened and helpless.

If they defend me, we will all die. But if the assassin kills me without a fight, maybe he'll let them live. "Do what he says," I say calmly. "Lower your weapons."

They do, reluctantly, plunking them onto the dining table.

Without turning to face my captor, I say, "Hello, Franco."

"Well met, Your Majesty," he says with equal calm. "You have given me an enjoyable and challenging chase. Thank you for that."

"How did you find me?"

"We followed the old lady." Ximena's mouth drops open. "We knew you'd rendezvous eventually."

"Are you going to kill me, then?" I ask, preparing to send my heel into his instep, the way Hector taught me.

"Possibly not." He steps back and lets me go.

I turn to face him. Up close, I don't know why no one saw him for an Invierno. He is too tall, too preternaturally beautiful, to be anything else. His slicked-back hair is a shade or two lighter at the roots, and his eyes are a startling gold—a rare color among Joyans.

But maybe that's why we never met, why he conveniently absented himself when I summoned him. Because more than anyone, I was likely to recognize an Invierno among us.

"Then what *do* you want?" I ask, even as I pray silently, drawing power through the earth, into the Godstone. It comes slowly, a mere trickle, but it comes.

"Don't you dare," says Franco. "If you try to work the magic of your stone, I'll kill every single person in this room."

And just like that, the power dribbles away, leaving me empty and hollow.

"Better. Now, if you want your people to live, you must come with me."

"Come where?"

"Invierne, of course. As a willing sacrifice. It is very important that you come willingly, in accordance with God's will. Failing that, my secondary objective has always been to kill you, which I did attempt, but you have proved wily."

I don't understand what my willingness has to do with anything, though I can't help but note the eerie similarity to Leaf's words about the gatekeeper. *A living sacrifice.* I'll have to think about it later.

"You've been pulling the strings the whole time, haven't you?" I ask. "Invierne meant to weaken me with a very public martyr and set the stage for a civil war. You want us to tear ourselves apart so you don't have to."

His edged grin gives me shivers. "We did say we would come at you like a ghost in a dream."

"Does Eduardo know you're an Invierne spy? Does he know he's being manipulated?"

He shrugs. "He knows. But his ambition allows it. I have promised to rid him of you, another weak ruler in a long line of them. The rank fool thinks he betrays you in service to his country. So, Your Majesty, will you come?"

Ximena rises to her feet. Swords ring her neck instantly, but she puts her hands out, palms up, to show that she means no harm. "I have a better idea," she says.

"Ximena? What are you—"

"The queen still has supporters. If you take her now, Joya d'Arena will rise up against Invierne. So take him instead," she says, pointing to Hector. "If you let everyone go and take him, she will follow. Willingly. She loves him."

I stare at my nurse, shocked and sick. What is she doing? What is she thinking?

"Is it true, little queen?" Franco asks eagerly. "Do you love that man? Such a thing would be even more pleasing to God— for you to follow, intending to give yourself up for him. *No one has greater love than he who gives his own life.*"

I hate Franco for quoting that verse, the one I used to heal Hector. Swords ring Hector's neck now. His eyes on mine are steady but dark with fear—for me, not himself. He nods once, almost imperceptibly. He wants me to say yes. He hopes they'll take him away, leaving me alone and safe. *Don't ever give your life for mine,* he once told me.

Without breaking his gaze, I whisper, "Yes. I love him. Enough to follow him anywhere."

And then Hector realizes his mistake because he gasps like a dying man and closes his eyes against the pain of it.

I turn to Franco, and my voice is clear and cutting when I say, "Hector is a Quorum lord. Taking him hostage is an act of war."

Franco grins. "Stupid queen. We never stopped being at war, your country and mine. Invierne merely retreated." He gestures to the men surrounding Hector, and they grab his arms and haul him roughly away from the table. Hector does not resist.

"You have two months," Franco says. "I expect to see you in our capital by then. Come with no thought to returning, for this is pleasing to God. You may bring a very small escort, but no soldiers. Otherwise, he dies."

"If you kill him, I'll destroy you." Actually, I think I'll destroy him anyway. Yes, I most definitely will.

But Franco ignores me. "Let's go," he says to his men. To Tristán he says, "If your soldiers follow, he dies."

They are halfway out the door when I cry out, "Wait!"

Franco whirls.

My anger, my resolve . . . it has melted into anguish, and all I can do is beg. "Let me say good-bye? Please?"

Franco looks back and forth between us, amused. He shrugs permission, and the soldiers loosen their grip on Hector.

I fly into his arms. He holds me close, stroking my hair, pressing his lips to my temples, murmuring words I can't take in.

"I'll come for you," I whisper.

"Elisa, no." He pushes me away, holds me at arm's length. "Let me do my job this one last time. Take my advice."

"I need you to survive this. Stay alive for me, Hector. Please? *And be ready.*"

And then they're dragging him away, and it feels like I've been gut punched, for I can't force my lungs to draw breath. I fall to my knees, clutching my stomach. *God, how did everything turn out so wrong?*

A hand squeezes my shoulder. It snakes around my neck, pulls me close. "I'm so sorry, my sky," says Ximena. She draws me against her breast, the way she did when I was a little girl. I clutch at her bodice, taking in her familiar scent as she strokes my hair.

"I hope you find comfort in the fact that he sacrificed himself for you," she murmurs. "As I always knew he would. He loved you very much."

I lurch away from her and stare, puzzled, my skin crawling.

"Oh, my sky, the pain will fade. I promise. Just like it did with that boy from the desert. I know it's hard to understand now, but your destiny is so glorious, Elisa. You are a bearer *and* a sovereign. Twice chosen by God. And someday, all this will pale in your memory." She holds her arms out for another embrace.

I rise to my feet, wiping at tears I don't remember shedding. I look down at my nurse. My guardian. The closest thing I've ever had to a mother. It seems as though she kneels at my feet.

"Ximena," I say with imperturbable calm. "You have killed

for me. You have kept things from me. You have sacrificed one of my dearest friends. You did all this without consideration for my will."

Her black eyes are hot with conviction. "I have only ever done what is best. You're just seventeen! You need—"

"I am a grown woman and a queen. And *you* are dismissed."

She gapes at me.

"Go home, Ximena. To Orovalle. I'm sure Papá and Alodia can find a post for you."

"No! I'm your guardian! Elisa, my sky, I love—"

"Tristán, would you please have my former nurse escorted to the nearest passenger ship?"

"At once, Your Majesty," he says coolly, and he gestures toward a handful of men.

Ximena rises, smooths her skirt, then folds her hands together in perfect composure. As they lead her away, she glances over her shoulder at me and says, "I'll always be your guardian. No matter what. It is God's will."

I turn my back on her, sickened and sad, but well and truly ready to be the queen my people need.

"Tristán. Are you still willing to take a position as Quorum lord?"

"Yes, Your Majesty."

I fish one of the Godstones from my pocket. It glitters more deeply than any jewel, in spite of its lifelessness. "Take it. It should fetch a high enough price for a whole garrison. I'll validate it as an authentic Godstone from my personal collection, with a document bearing my royal seal."

His fingers pause in the air above my hand for a moment before he takes it. "Thank you."

I gesture for Fernando to approach, and then I pull out another Godstone and lay it in his palm. "Take this to Captain Lucio. Recruit more guards to defend the palace, if it is not overrun already. If it is, you must go into hiding and rebuild the Guard in secret." I close his fingers around the stone. "Fernando, make me an army of my very own."

"Yes, Your Majesty." He stares at his fisted hand.

"Belén!"

He approaches, his face dark.

"You are now my personal guard. You will see to my safety above all else."

He nods acceptance, then peers down into my eyes. "You're planning something dangerous and brilliant again."

In spite of everything, I smile up at him. Indeed, the threads of a strategy are patterning together in my mind, and I'm heady with the power of it. The kind of power I really need.

"I want messages sent to Crown Princess Alodia and Queen Cosmé," I say to no one in particular. "Multiple copies, to be safe. See if they'll agree to meet me in exactly three months' time in Basajuan, for the world's first parliament of queens."

I resume pacing, right where I left off when Franco's men barged in. "I'll send a message to Ventierra, to Hector's father, commanding that he reinstate Hector as his sole heir. And I need a proclamation—Mara, did my wax and seal survive our journey?" When she nods, I say, "A proclamation announcing my betrothal to Lord-Commander Hector, heir to the countship of Ventierra." That should stall Conde Eduardo's efforts to discredit me with the southern lords. All I need is a little time.

Mara hurries over and takes my hands. "Er, congratulations on your pending nuptials?"

I whisper, "He'll be so angry when he learns I have engaged us without his knowledge."

"Yes," she says. "Definitely. But you'll convince him."

Belén says, "When do we all leave?"

"We all?"

"We're going to Invierne with you, of course," Mara says.

Of course, she says. As if journeying deep into enemy territory is no more than a quick jaunt through the market. I blink against tears. "I need a few days to make arrangements and set things in motion. Then we go."

Clanking chains echo through the dining hall as Storm rises to his feet. "I'm going, too," he says. He has been near invisible the whole time, huddled beneath his cowl. "You need a guide. And it's time I stopped hiding like a frightened rabbit."

I nod, knowing he offers in friendship this time, that he truly is my loyal subject. "The four of us, then."

"You should have five!" Tristán protests. "For blessing and protection. It's the holy number."

I draw myself to full height, and my voice rings clear when I say, "The fifth place is for Hector."

In a Moment

Caroline Finnerty

POOLBEG

Published 2012
by Poolbeg Press Ltd
123 Grange Hill, Baldoyle
Dublin 13, Ireland
E-mail: poolbeg@poolbeg.com
www.poolbeg.com

© Caroline Finnerty 2012

Copyright for typesetting, layout, design
© Poolbeg Press Ltd

1

A catalogue record for this book is available from the British Library.

ISBN 978-1-84223-527-0

Typeset by Patricia Hope in Sabon 11.3/16
Printed and bound by CPI Group (UK) Ltd, Croydon, CR0 4YY

www.poolbeg.com

About the author

Caroline Finnerty lives in County Kildare with her husband Simon, daughter Lila, twins Tom and Bea, and their two dogs. *In a Moment* is her first novel.

Acknowledgements

Firstly a huge thank you to Paula Campbell in Poolbeg for the phone call that made my dreams come true. Paula, I will say it again – I don't know how you do it! I am delighted to come on board with you and all the team.

Also thank you to Gaye Shortland for your amazing eye, your encouraging words and also your enthusiasm for the characters, which means a lot to me. I look forward to working together on future books.

To Simon, thank you for taking the children off at weekends to give me time to write. I can't think of anyone else I would rather share this life with. I love our little family. xx

Thank you to Mam and Dad – everyone should have parents like you. Thank you for everything throughout the years and all that you still do for me now. I couldn't even begin to mention how much I appreciate this. Mam – this book would not have happened without your unwavering belief in me and your constant encouragement. Dad – thank you for instilling a love of books from a young age.

To Dee Finnerty for your help on all kinds of things, from being a spare pair of hands for the twins, to your knowledge of all things photography-related and of weird computer glitches.

For my parents-in-law Mary and Neil for all that you do for us, from child-minding to dinner-making, but above all for your support.

To the staff on St Peter's Ward in Our Lady's Children's Hospital, Crumlin for taking such good care of my babies.

Thanks also to Elaine and Darren for the play-dates when you already have your hands full.

To Daisy Cummins for your advice.

To my wonderful friends for the chats, fun and laughter.

And, of course, thank you, reader, for choosing this book from all the great titles that are out there. I really do appreciate it. I hope you enjoy reading it and I would love to hear from you on my website www.carolinefinnerty.ie or on www.facebook.com/carolinefinnertywriter.

With much love, Caroline xxx

For Simon, Lila, Tom & Bea,
my beautiful family
xxxx

Prologue

She felt her knees buckle beneath her and she reached out to grab onto the post of the staircase. She used it to guide herself downwards so that she was sitting on the bottom step. Just as she thought she might be starting to heal, taking tentative steps forward, this had come and knocked her off balance again. She wasn't expecting it – it was like a below-the-belt punch coming at her, leaving her reeling in its wake. She needed to see his face, as if somehow by looking at him it would confirm that he had been a real person. She ran upstairs and into her bedroom. Pulling out the drawer of her bedside table, she reached for his photo.

Part I

1

Winter, 2010

The lift doors separated and Adam White stepped out into the bright reception of Parker & Associates. As he walked across the high-glaze cream travertine tiles he was almost overpowered by the scent emanating from the two extravagant conical vases standing on either side of the reception desk. They were brimming with fresh metre-high arrangements of snapdragons, burnt-orange birds of paradise and fuchsia-toned orchids. The area was minimally furnished with only a simple Scandinavian-style bench, which was more for show than functionality.

Parker & Associates was a young firm of business analysts located just off the Grand Canal on the south side of Dublin City. Their ultra-modern headquarters took over the entire top floor of the building and consisted of floor-to-ceiling glazed offices surrounding a central roof garden. Depending on which end of the office you went to, the view extended all the way up to Howth Head on the north side of the city or down to Killiney Hill on the south side.

By the time Adam had grabbed himself a coffee, sat at his desk and switched on his PC, his rising in the small hours of the morning seemed like eons ago. He rubbed his eyes for the umpteenth time. He felt fuzzy with tiredness, he found it hard even to think straight, his reactions were slow and his whole body felt heavy as if he was lugging two huge suitcases on either side of him whenever he walked. As he tried to concentrate on a spreadsheet on the screen in front of him, the rows seemed to merge together.

Although it was eight thirty, it was very early by Parker's standards and the office was still largely empty. On any given day the majority of people wouldn't arrive in until nine at the earliest but normally on Friday people didn't show their faces until much later after the ritual of Thursday-night drinks. Fridays were a write-off as far as work was concerned; it was generally accepted that you did only the bare minimum to get by and then spent Monday to Thursday making up for it. The company prided itself on its 'relaxed and casual' culture. The open-plan office was decorated with leafy, tropical foliage and beanbags were interspersed randomly to help soften the corporate feel. Croissants and pastries were delivered fresh from the local bakery every morning and there were always baskets scattered arbitrarily around the place, brimming with sweets and chocolate. Employees were also welcome to help themselves to the fully stocked fridge which was laden with ice-cream and soft drinks. It was lamented by all who worked there that once you joined Parker & Associates, there was no avoiding gaining the 'Parker-stone'.

A while later Adam's colleagues started arriving in. He greeted them and watched as one by one they dropped their bags at their desks before heading straight to the staff room for a pecan-nut pie, the only pastry deemed suitable for the hangover of Fridays.

* * *

Emma made her way with slow footsteps down the grey vinyled corridor. As she walked, she couldn't help but think

6

what a contagious shade of grey it was; it wasn't the soft dove-grey of a cashmere sweater or the inky grey of a storm cloud before it burst – it was that awful shade of grey that sucked the life out of you just from merely looking at it. As she rounded the corner, she could hear the high-pitched screeches coming from behind the canteen door. Well, 'canteen' was probably stretching it – it was a room barely six metres square. The floor was covered with worn lino and it was sparsely furnished with a Formica table, six red shiny plastic-backed chairs, a cork noticeboard and a dire fridge where, no matter how many group emails were sent warning users to discard their foods after their best-before date, no one ever seemed to lay claim to the mouldy ham.

You could almost tell the day of the week it was by the roars that filtered out into the corridor. Fridays were full of raucous laughter; Mondays were a more sombre, almost silent affair.

Emma pushed open the door and glanced around at the usual posse of girls sitting at the table scattered with takeaway sandwich-wrappers and foil crisp-bags. The roars from two seconds earlier disappeared almost like someone had twisted a volume-switch on the whole room. Nothing new there, she thought to herself. She was used to having this effect on people recently. The stench from some rice-and-ham dish that Dan from IT was reheating in the microwave almost made her gag.

"Hiya, Emma. Busy?" Helen the receptionist chimed, in an overly cheery voice.

"Y'know yourself, kept going."

Helen nodded. "Tell me about it."

What would you know about being busy unless it's trying to stick your gel nail back on and answer the phone at the same time?

"That won't keep you going!" Helen nodded to the teabag that Emma was taking out of the jar above the microwave.

"I'm not hungry just now, I'll grab something later."

Emma knew her tone sounded defensive, but she felt self-conscious in front of the group about her lack of lunch – but she just couldn't stomach anything right now. She turned away from Helen and her cronies and as soon as the kettle had boiled she busied herself by pouring boiling water onto her teabag.

Helen turned back around to her gang and proceeded to moan about how her bridesmaid had put on weight since the last dress fitting and that now she would have to get the dress altered for her. Her audience tutted in sympathy and agreed that her friend had some cheek to gain a few pounds. One of them even added that if she were a real friend she would *at least* offer to do the cabbage-soup diet to fit back into the dress. Emma wasn't included in the conversation, nor did she want to be.

Emma worked on the creative team for A1 Adverts but A1 Adverts was not your typical glamorous advertising agency residing in beautiful glazed offices with a sea view and bountiful budgets. Rather A1 specialised in bright and zingy 'can't get it out of your head' type adverts for their clients. A1's specialty was the discount market; they didn't do the high-end adverts that won awards. How she would love to work on campaigns such as those! A1's customers were discount furniture stores, tile shops, budget airlines and basically anyone in the business of discount retailing in Ireland. All their adverts were the same: flashing bubble-text on a neon-coloured background and always backed with shouty voices. In fairness to A1 Adverts, it was a model that worked; they were cheaper than their competitors and they were tailored to that end of the market. But it was a long, long way from the glossy editorials with their subtle imaging that she had spent so much time analysing in college. Emma was a 'campaign developer' – in other words, she had to come up with new ideas for their clients' adverts.

She went back, sat at her desk and sighed wearily as she

scrolled down to the next red-flagged email from her overflowing inbox. No matter how hard she tried, she never seemed to be able to get on top of the work that was piling up around her. At the moment she was working on a pitch for a company called Sofa World which had asked Dublin's top advertising agencies to come up with a tag line for their Christmas campaign. Oh, she was a long way from Chanel adverts starring Keira Knightley! It was very late for launching a Christmas campaign. A1 suspected Sofa World had rejected other advertisers' efforts before turning to them at the last minute.

Moments later, Emma's boss Maureen Hanley popped her head around the screen of her cubicle. Her frizzy hair was tied back with a scrunchy in a manner that made Emma wonder if the woman even possessed a hairbrush.

"Hi, Emma – can you come in for a chat in five?"

Emma felt herself redden as if Maureen could read her mind about what she had just been thinking. "Sure."

"Don't worry, it's nothing major," Maureen added, obviously noticing Emma's red face.

Emma hated her high colouring; it always betrayed her innermost feelings. At the drop of a hat her cheeks would go red for almost any reason: embarrassment, frustration, alcohol, spicy food, and God forbid she should try to tell a lie. Emma just had to accept it was part and parcel of the raw deal of having fair skin.

She watched as Maureen walked back to her office in her black pencil-leg trousers that didn't quite meet her court shoes and revealed her white cotton socks. On top she wore a brown tweed blazer buttoned entirely up to the top so that it was puckered across her large bust; she'd had that blazer ever since Emma had started working there seven years ago and Emma imagined she had probably had it at least seven years before that. Maureen was a harmless enough sort of woman – well, as much as a boss can be harmless. She had never married; she'd been too busy sacrificing her life for A1 Adverts. The woman lived and breathed A1, so Emma suspected that the only reason she wanted a meeting was probably because she wanted her to jump up and down about the chance to pitch to Sofa World. But Emma would not be doing any jumping.

Five minutes later Emma grabbed her A4 refill pad so she could scribble down any ideas that would be thrown at her and walked back down the life-sucking, grey-vinyled corridor towards Maureen's office. She knocked on her door and let herself in. Maureen looked up from her computer, almost in confusion.

Don't tell me she doesn't remember asking me to come in five minutes ago?

"Oh yes, of course, Emma – come in and sit down." She let out a heavy sigh as she set about clearing bundles of paper and mugs with coffee stains running down the sides off the messy desk in front of her.

Emma did as she was told and sat opposite her.

Emma cut to the chase. "Did you see the email from Sofa World?"

"What?" Maureen was distracted. "Oh yes, I saw that. You might draft something up and send it on and we can sit down then and have a look, yes?"

Emma was taken aback. What did Maureen want her for if not that?

"Well, Emma . . ." Maureen paused.

Well, Maureen. Emma felt she should say something but Maureen's tone told her it wasn't her place to speak.

"Well . . . God, Emma I'm not sure how to broach this . . ." She breathed in deeply through her nostrils, so that they flared slightly. "Well, it's just I've noticed you've been putting in a lot of hours here lately. Some of the times on your emails have me worried – eleven p.m., midnight – there was even one at two a.m. last week! Now don't get me wrong, I'm all too happy for

people to show their commitment to A1 Adverts but well . . ."
She hesitated. "Just with everything going on, I'm a bit worried
about you, that's all." She was starting to get flustered. "What
I'm trying to say is – and I'm not doing a very good job of it –
I know you're a good worker, I've never had a problem with
your work. I just want you to make sure you're looking after
yourself? That's all."

Emma was stunned; she wasn't used to such public displays
of concern from Maureen. She instantly felt the heat creep into
her cheeks. *I don't want to talk about this.*

"I'm okay, Maureen," she said coolly so that Maureen would
know it wasn't a discussion she wished to get into.

"Well, that's good then," Maureen added nervously. "It's
just, you're not long back and well . . . well, I think you should
ease yourself in a bit, that's all."

Emma shifted in her seat and the discomfort between the
two was palpable.

"Okay, so you'll send me on your proposal for Sofa World
then?" Maureen said in an obvious decision to change the
subject.

"I'll have something for you by Monday afternoon," Emma
replied curtly.

"Great, so."

"Right, if that's all?"

Maureen gestured to the door, indicating Emma was free to
go. Emma stood up to leave. She wanted to get the hell out of
there. She wasn't a person who liked discussing her feelings at
the best of times, least of all with her boss.

She went back and sat at her desk and the more she thought
about the conversation she'd just had, the more she felt rage
building inside her. Why were people so nosy, always trying to
push it with her to see if they could be the one to make her
crack and fall apart into a mess? It was nobody's business what
time she worked until. If she was skiving off, they'd be on her

back – she couldn't win! She was used to Helen and the rest of them pushing her buttons, trying their best to see if they could be the one to elicit a reaction. But Maureen? She had expected more from her boss. They had always had a perfectly healthy standoffish relationship, so what the hell was Maureen doing trying to change the playing field?

Jesus, what had got into the woman? Surely she was too old for the menopause?

2

Come three o'clock and as the hangovers began to ease, Parker's entire workforce were already planning where they would head later on that night and at five to five they began to pack up to leave.

Adam was just heading for the lift when Ronan from Accounts joined him.

"Are you coming for one?"

"Nah, I should probably be heading home." Adam was hesitant. Not that it would make any difference, he thought bitterly to himself. She barely spoke to him anyway.

"C'mon for one!"

"I'd better not – maybe next time, yeah?"

"Are you sure?"

"Yeah."

"No worries."

They took the lift down.

"See you Monday, so," said Ronan.

"Have a good one!"

Ronan joined some of the others and Adam stood watching as

they walked over to McCormack's bar, carefree and untroubled. How he wished he could join them – he would rather be going anywhere else but home.

He took his bike from the shelter and headed for Rathmines. He pedalled slowly and allowed the cool evening air to fill his lungs, feeling his chest rise in fullness before falling again. He felt his thigh muscles work hard as he pedalled up the steep incline before turning left over Harold's Cross Bridge. His cycle to and from work was the only time of day he had with his thoughts to himself. It was his time when he got to think about everything that had happened and try and make sense of it all. It was still so fresh. He only had to look at himself to see angry reminders criss-crossing his skin. Usually when he cycled he racked his head trying to remember the exact sequence of events but his brain would only allow him to go so far.

When he reached their house, he pushed open the wrought-iron gate and wheeled his bike up the path. He could see the lights were all off downstairs. He fumbled with his keys in the lock for a few moments before he was finally able to get into his house. Today's post sat waiting for him on the mat inside the door. He stooped to pick it up. The envelopes told him it was nothing more interesting than bills, junk mail and a bank statement. He placed them unopened on the hall table. He shouted out to see if Emma was home but no voice answered his call. He hardly knew why he did that as he knew she wouldn't answer anyway. He went into the kitchen and took a cool beer out of the fridge. He pulled off the metal top and gulped it back.

* * *

Emma's head hadn't been up to much for the rest of the day. She'd tried her best to think of some winning tag lines for the Sofa World campaign but she didn't have much luck.

The office began to empty out after four with everyone

14

heading off to various parts of the country for the weekend and by seven she was alone in the open-plan office. She preferred it that way; she could concentrate better without the constant drone of voices. She tried putting some words onto her notepad but nothing was coming. Eventually, after nine, she admitted defeat and knew that stupid tag lines for springy sofas would be swimming around in her head all weekend long.

In keeping with their low-cost strategy, A1's offices were located on Rosses Street, in a dingy part of Dublin City, which was long overdue rejuvenation. It was a notorious area for muggers, so she made her way hurriedly down towards the quays. She watched as hordes of teenagers, hen and stag parties, already bladdered, made their way towards the city's current hot-spots, gearing themselves up for a heavy night of drinking.

She didn't want to go home just yet so she decided to keep walking and headed down towards Dawson Street. The narrow paths were crowded with gangs of smokers standing outside so she turned onto a cobble-locked side-street where crowds were sitting along the outdoor terraces under café-bar awnings, protected from the cold evening air by patio heaters. By immersing herself amongst these people, she didn't feel so alone.

She wandered aimlessly for a while until she felt her stomach growl and she suddenly realised she was hungry. After skipping lunch, she had forgotten to eat anything for the rest of the day. She looked at her watch and it was nearly eleven o'clock so she hailed a taxi and headed home to Rathmines. She climbed into the back, stated her destination and sank into the leatherette upholstery. She sat listening to the constant buzzing and conversation over and back on the radio between the base station and the different drivers. The driver made half-hearted chit-chat with her – well, he talked and she made occasional sounds of agreement, which seemed to be enough for him to keep rambling on. By the time they turned onto Rathmines Road, she could feel her stomach begin twisting into its familiar knot and, as the car pulled up outside her home, Emma felt her heart lurch. She took her time to locate her money in her wallet before paying him and slamming the door shut.

At least the lights were off.

With trepidation and slow steps she walked up the driveway to her home. No matter how hard she tried and how successfully she carried it off at work, once she was on her own doorstep, she couldn't push the reality of her life out of her head any more.

3

Emma put on her heavy wool coat over her work suit and gloves and wrapped her thick-knit scarf twice around her neck. The day was cool and crisp and as she left the office block and walked briskly towards St Stephen's Green she watched her breath turn white on the air in front of her. Although it was lunchtime, the weak sunlight still hadn't managed to melt the morning's frost. She made her way to the bench where she had arranged to meet Zoe.

Zoe and Emma had been friends since they had met at Irish dancing classes at the age of eight. The two of them would be thrown into class every Saturday morning and Emma (who had zero co-ordination and could never keep up with all the steps) and Zoe (who was too busy being the class clown to learn how to do a reel) became firm friends. They were the weakest link of their class so were usually left to their own devices, playing together at the back of the hall.

They had attended the same primary school but were in different classes so would only get to meet at break-times in the school-yard. It wasn't until secondary school that they managed to persuade their teachers to put them into the same class and it was then that their friendship flourished. Where Emma was a serious soul, Zoe was a messer. Anne Fitzpatrick had lit many holy candles and said many novenas over the years in worry about Zoe's influence on her daughter, but still Emma would get yet another letter home for talking or for sniggering at a note that Zoe had passed to her in class.

Emma used to have a great circle of friends. They had all met in secondary school, gravitating towards each other because they were neither the popular girls nor the geeks. They had managed to stay close even when they all had gone to universities and colleges scattered all over the country. Throughout their twenties they would meet for dinner once a week and have a great natter over a few bottles of wine about what they were up to in their lives: about who had just got a promotion, who was getting married, who was being tormented by having to watch their ex getting loved up by his new girlfriend. They would spend hours chatting until they were the last ones left in the restaurant. But that had all gone by the wayside now and one by one the visits had become less frequent until they had petered out altogether. She knew it was probably the deadly combination of looking at a broken woman – when they looked at her she was a reminder of how cruel life could be – that and the fact she was hardly 'Exuberant Emma' these days. The last few months had been the litmus test for most of her friendships and in the end it was only her best friend Zoe still left flying the flag solo for the former group of schoolfriends.

A few minutes later, a panting Zoe wearing a cream baker-boy cap on top of her sleek black bob came running up.

"Sorry I'm late – I got called into a design meeting. Fucking directors wondering how thin we can make the fabric before the dress becomes completely see-through! Bloody tight-arses!"

"No worries. I've only just arrived myself."

Zoe had studied fashion design in college and now worked in the rag-trade for a company that ripped off catwalk designs and sold them on to low-cost retailers. It was a job that allowed her a limited amount of creativity but not nearly the amount that a person like her needed. It was constantly drilled into her that she needed to be more commercially astute; she needed to be aware of fabric costs and whether she could substitute a particular fabric for a cheaper one instead. Did she really need to use six buttons down the front of a cardigan or would they get away with five? She hated having to be so cost-conscious and she would argue that the cardigan would "look shit" with five buttons but, inevitably, her bosses would win out.

"So how're you doing today?" Zoe asked, her face showing her concern.

"Same as all the other days."

"Stupid question, isn't it?"

Emma smiled. "I know, but what else can you say?"

"True."

"So how was the date with 'The Accountant'?" Emma asked, changing the subject. It was great just to switch off and get a break from her thoughts and get caught up in Zoe's world instead.

"Disastrous. The man is potentially deranged."

"Why?"

"What kind of man bores a girl to tears about the size of his diversified stock portfolio? The only question he asked about me was whether I was worried about my pension provision! Do I look like the kind of girl losing sleep over a pension? *Then* he nearly lost his life when I ordered a cocktail! He checked the menu to see the price and then he kept on exclaiming 'Nine euro, *nine euro* for one of them!' He tried to talk me out of it by saying that they wouldn't use full measures and that maybe I should just get a vodka and Coke!"

Emma had to laugh.

"Oh, it gets worse, Emma – when the bill arrived he totted up who had eaten what and made me pay the extra because I had ordered the bloody cocktail!"

"He did not!" Emma said in horror.

"Oh yes! You see what I have to deal with? This is what is left on the Dublin dating scene!"

Zoe had spent her twenties, and now her early thirties too, plunging from one disastrous relationship to the next. She had stories that made Emma, who had been in a relationship for almost her entire twenties, wince with wide-eyed disbelief at the dating game. The Accountant had been a blind date set up for Zoe by her cousin but, as she said, she had to wonder which was the blind one – herself or her cousin?

Emma's theory was that Zoe's inability to take life seriously stemmed from the fact that her father had walked out on her mother when she was only four years old. Her mother had gone on a year later to have a nervous breakdown when she learned that her ex-husband's new girlfriend was now pregnant with his baby. It was all too much for her to take and she ended up spending three months in the psychiatric unit in St Anne's Hospital. Zoe had been shipped off to her grandmother who at the age of seventy-five wasn't able to devote the attention to her that a spirited five-year-old required. This had resulted in Zoe being passed around to various aunties and friends of her mother's until her mother was well enough to care for her again. To this day, Zoe always had that fear of people leaving her and Emma believed that humour was Zoe's internal defence mechanism. She could imagine the five-year-old Zoe acting the joker just to put a smile on her mother's face and believing that if she could stop her mother from feeling sad, then perhaps she wouldn't need to go back into hospital.

After Zoe filled her in on her escapades, Emma checked her watch and it was just gone two.

"Jesus – where does the time go? It's gone two. I'd better head back before Maureen starts trying to track me down."

"Shit, I'd better run too – I'll mail you tomorrow."

They walked back through the park together and hugged warmly before heading off to their respective office blocks.

4

Behind the spare-bedroom door, Emma lay wide awake; sleep had forsaken her in the early hours of the morning. She listened to the sounds of the house breathing at night, the rattling pipe in the attic, cars whirring past on the road outside. She was plagued by her own thoughts; they kept on swirling over and over, sloshing around inside her head, spinning like a top until she could no longer keep up with them. She could hear the sound of contented slumber brimming from the bedroom next door. *Well for some, being able to sleep,* she thought bitterly.

She lay there looking around the familiar room. Its high ceilings were adorned with the original cornicing and the sash windows still retained the folding wooden shutters. It had been one of the main reasons that they had fallen in love with the house: to think that over one hundred years ago someone had chosen to decorate the house in this way and the features remained to this day! They had spent so long agonising over the shade of grey for this room; they had tried at least ten different samples before eventually settling on a shade called 'Elephant's Breath', but now the grey walls just made the room feel cold.

She must have drifted back to sleep at some stage because she woke to find her alarm blaring beside her. She never slept through her alarm; she was normally awake before it even had time to sound. She jolted upright and tried to silence the bleeping. It took her a few seconds to register what day it was and, when she realised she didn't have to get up for work, she eased herself back down onto the pillows again for a few moments. But it was already after eight and she knew she would need to hurry on if she wanted to be gone before Adam got up. She wondered where she would go today. Emma didn't like weekends; the constant feeling of trying to avoid her own husband wore her out. At least when he was in work, she didn't come into contact with him. But at the weekends the day was stretched out ahead of her in an endless field of time that would have to be killed and she felt weary even thinking about it. But she had no choice; it had to be done.

She had a quick shower and got dressed in black leggings, black leather riding boots and a black and white silk tunic with a butterfly print. It was almost nine when she finally sat into her car, wondering where she was going to go. It was too early to call in on anyone; most of her friends had a life and would be enjoying their Saturday morning lie-ins. And she was *sick* of shopping centres. Normally these were her usual port of call but at this stage she had seen all the clothes in every shop. She decided to go to Dee's coffee shop on Gregory Street, which was the only café that would be open at this hour. That would kill time until ten o'clock and then she would call in to her parents. Ten was a safe time; if she went too early they would start to worry.

She cut a lonely figure in Dee's. She was obviously their first customer of the day and the wiry dark-haired girl working there resented actually having to be functional at that time on a Saturday morning. The radio was blaring something that sounded like an eastern European Eurovision entry backed by

23

a techno beat. Emma ordered a black coffee and sat down at a small circular laminated table in the corner, out of the way. Out of the way of what she wasn't sure because there wasn't a soul in the place – but that was how she felt, almost like she wanted to hide away from the world. She stirred the spoon around in circular movements so that the coffee swirled around inside the mug. She took a few sips but it tasted smoky and scalded. She took out her notebook and tried to come up with tag lines for the Sofa World campaign. She scribbled down a few words – *'snugly'*, *'comfort'* – but nothing was jumping out at her, every sofa retailer was using the same straplines. She wanted to create a warm-feeling advert, especially as it was targeted at the Christmas market. Frustrated at her efforts, she shut her notebook again.

After a while she looked at her watch, it was almost ten. She could call in to her parents now, without too much suspicion. She knew that they would be up at this stage; they didn't have that hectic a social life that they'd need a lie-in. She finished the last of her coffee and moved her chair back with such force that it caused the waitress to jump up from where she had been perched on a stool, sleeping with her head resting on her folded arms.

* * *

When she arrived into their driveway, she opened the creaking, rusty gate that had been there since before she was born. Rounding the corner to the back door, she met her dad pottering around the back yard with two pieces of pipe in his hands.

"Hi there, Dad!" She forced herself to sound cheery but it didn't ring true in her voice.

"Emma, love! How're you keeping?" He sounded surprised but thrilled to see her.

"Not bad, Dad, thanks. How're you?"

"Aragh, you know yourself. You're over early?"

It wasn't a statement, it was a question.

"Yeah, I was passing out this way anyway so I said I'd drop in for a cuppa."

"Well, it's great to see you. Your mother's inside – go on in and get yourself a cup of tea and I'll be in shortly."

She let herself into the house and found her mother standing over the cooker, busy frying sausages and rashers.

"Hi, Mam!"

"Emma, darling! Come in, come in, love, here, sit down here." She flustered around the place, acting like Emma was a very important visitor. She started scattering magazines and newspapers off chairs and clearing bundles of clothes from the table. "Here, sit here, love. Here you are now." She patted the armchair.

Emma did as she was told, happy to let her mam make a fuss of her. Even though she was the eldest daughter, her mam still treated her like she was her baby.

"Will you have a fry, love? I've one on for your dad and your brother. He's still in bed – it was after four when he got in last night – I was listening out for him. Twenty-five years of age and he still has no sense, that fella!"

"Okay, if you're cooking for everyone I'll have just a small one so."

"Well now, love, you're looking a bit frail to me. Do you know, I was just looking at you there when you came through the door and you look like you've lost even more weight."

"I'm fine, Mam," she said curtly. Her mother was always harping on about her weight and it irritated the hell out of her.

"But you're a bag of bones, love! Look at your collarbone, jutting out, and your cheekbones – you look almost, well – almost malnourished!"

Emma automatically put her hand to her collarbone.

"Jesus, Mam, will you give me a break!"

"Well, I'm just saying every time I see you you're thinner than the last time – a few sausages will do you all the good in the world!"

Oh yeah, a few sausages will solve everything.

"I said I'd have a fry, didn't I?"

Her mother looked at her, hurt by her harsh tone.

"Sorry, Mam," she said contritely.

"No problem, dear."

"So, any news?"

"Well, I got new shrubs in the garden centre, that's what your father's doing now. He's going to plant them in the rockery – you know, there beside the laurel bush at the front of the house."

Emma tried to feign interest. "Oh really?"

"Yes, it'll look lovely when it's all done. Then I met your Auntie Wendy afterwards and we went for coffee. I had a slice of apple tart with cream but Wendy's on a diet so she wouldn't have cream on her rhubarb crumble. I said, Wendy, if you're going to have the crumble you might as well have the cream but she wouldn't hear any of it!"

Emma groaned inwardly. She could imagine her mother giving her younger sister Wendy the same lecture about not eating.

While the fry hissed in the pan, Anne moved away from the cooker, placed two mugs of tea on the table and sat down opposite her daughter. They sat in silence for a few moments.

"So how's Adam?" Anne Fitzpatrick broached cautiously.

Emma felt herself tense up at the mere mention of his name. "He's fine." The words felt prickly and awkward coming from her throat.

"Oh love, it's not easy, God love you. I pray for you both every night. It's going to take a while but time is a great healer." Her hands fluttered anxiously towards her throat and she began to fidget with her gold cross.

If one more person says that to me, I won't be accountable for my actions.

Time wasn't helping. She knew her mam meant well. When she considered things calmly, everyone *meant* well.

Her mother stood up from her chair and walked over to where her daughter was sitting and wrapped her in a warm hug. Emma was glad she couldn't see her face because she was afraid what might happen if she looked her in the eye. She wished she could stay in her mother's arms forever where things like this didn't happen. Even though a year had passed, some days it all seemed so fresh, the hurt so raw, that every day she felt like she was reliving it all over again. Time wasn't helping.

5

When Emma got home from her parents' house that evening, she was relieved to find that Adam had gone out. She went up to the spare room and drew the curtains. She kicked off her boots and flopped onto the bed. As she lay there her hand automatically reached out and she found herself opening the drawer beneath her bedside table and taking out the book which fell open at the pages where the photo had been slotted in the last time. Even though she knew it wasn't going to do her any good, she couldn't help herself. It was a compulsion; she needed to see his face. She held the photograph firm in her hands and just stared at it like she had done so many times since. She pored over the face, her finger tracing the outline in a well-worn gesture. The smile beaming back at her made her feel like someone had twisted her heart with both their hands and then wrung it out again, leaving it void.

The longer she stared, the more her eyes were starting to play tricks on her and the photo didn't look right. She held it away from herself and stared hard at it to see if that helped but it still looked wrong. She began to panic. She forced herself to try and recall the face as she remembered it but it wouldn't come to mind. She told herself to stay calm, she tried to breathe in but it wouldn't come. *Please, please, please let me remember.* She noticed that the pillow under her cheek felt damp and she realised that fat tears were running down the side of her face, dropping onto the brushed-cotton pillowcase beneath her. She chastised herself. *What am I doing thinking about these things?* It was futile. Crying wouldn't change anything.

She heard the key twist in the lock downstairs and started. She listened as his boots thudded across the wooden floorboards of their hallway, making their way across the kitchen tiles. They then walked back down the hallway, *thud, thud, thud,* and made their way upstairs, getting ever closer until the thuds were right outside her door. The continuously present feeling of dread that haunted her every waking moment intensified until she could feel it rising up from her stomach and burning the inside of her throat.

The door opened inwards and his head appeared around it.

* * *

Adam had noticed her coat hanging on the stand and her keys on the hall table. As he climbed the stairs he saw a soft light coming from underneath her bedroom door. He knocked softly. No answer. He took a deep breath and pushed it back. His wife was lying in her usual position on her side under the glow of her lamp. He noticed that the photograph lay beside her. It caught him off guard, a wobble that he wasn't expecting. He had to stop a moment to catch his breath and swallow back hard.

"Hi there . . . How are you doing today?"

"Hi," she said back, tilting her face at an awkward angle because she couldn't quite make eye contact with her husband.

Her voice was unsteady and he knew by her face that she had been crying. He watched her eyes move towards his rolled-up shirt sleeves until they fixed upon the pinky-red keloid scar that ran vertically down the inside of his left forearm – a lumpy mass of knitted skin, still raw. It only stopped where his wrist met the soft flesh of his palm. His eyes automatically followed Emma's and he rolled down his sleeves self-consciously.

"Are you hungry? I'm going to get a takeaway." He tried to divert her attention from his arm but his voice sounded shaky and was a tell-tale sign of his desperation.

She shook her head. No words uttered.

"Right." The silence filled the space between them. "Okay, well, I'll be downstairs if you want me, yeah?" *Jesus, this is bad.*

He turned and left the room, pulling the door behind him, thus effectively sealing them into their separate quarters of the house. He made his way downstairs and, storming into the kitchen, jerked open the fridge and reached for a can of Heineken. He put it up to his lips and gulped a large mouthful back before swallowing hard. He wiped a dribble from the edge of his mouth. *Fuck dinner*, he was no longer hungry. Things were getting worse, if that was possible. He had believed that by now the pain of the last year should be starting to ease for her – but no.

He went into the living room and threw himself wearily onto the sofa. He flicked through the channels and eventually stopped on a *Top Gear* re-run. Sometime later he nodded off in the armchair, still with the remote in his hand, but no sooner had he drifted off than he was jolted awake again. It felt as though he had been asleep only for minutes. His neck was stiff – he stretched it out. The dream had been back again.

He forced himself to recall exactly what had happened. He could always remember the start of it – it always started off the same way. He was driving along with one hand on his grey-leather steering wheel and the other hand resting on the gearstick. The sun was always strong, almost white with brightness. He knew it was chilly because the frost had covered the evergreen trees in its velvety white coat and there were patches of ice here and there on the road. But this time there was more, he had remembered more. There was a house too: a two-storey white-washed farmhouse with old-style wrought-iron gates marking the start of the path leading to the red front door. He remembered a bend in the road and a crossroads beyond. He needed to remember more but somehow his body managed to wake him up at just this point each time.

It was really starting to get to him now; the dreams were becoming too frequent. They were getting in under his skin and leaving him with an uneasy aftertaste each time, a constant reminder from which he couldn't escape.

He went up to bed a while later, tip-toeing past Emma's bedroom door. He lay in bed alone, desperately wishing she was beside him. He needed her. He longed for the closeness of holding her; it had been so long since they had even touched. He needed to tell her about the dreams. They needed to talk but when he had called into her room earlier on, he had been a coward as usual. Confrontation had never been his strong point – in fact, that had been Emma's forte. If there was something to be said, she wasn't one for beating around the bush, but now it was as if she didn't care enough to fight for what they had. One of them was going to have to do something to get things back on track between them and it sure as hell wasn't going to be Emma.

6

Emma poured herself a glass of red wine, allowing it to fill up the glass almost to the top. Taking a sip, she instantly started to relax. She had arranged to meet Zoe for a drink in Taylor's Bar. As per usual Zoe was late but for once Emma wasn't looking at her watch – in fact, it was nice to sit and people-watch while sipping her glass of wine in a dark, wooden-clad alcove.

After a little while a blur could be seen making its way down towards her at the back of the bar.

"Here, pour me some of that, I'm parched," Zoe said, out of breath, while she took her coat off.

Emma filled Zoe's glass and Zoe grabbed it from her and knocked it back like water.

"Sorry I'm late – I won't even bore you with the reason," she said. "Let's just say, who knew that some shades of cream could be cheaper than others?"

Emma laughed. They chatted easily about work and other things before Zoe broached the awkward question.

"So how's Adam? Are things any better?" she asked softly.

Emma could feel herself bristle at the mere mention of his name.

"Well, we're still not really talking," she said quietly.

"Still? I hoped things might have improved a little?"

Emma shook her head. "It's not easy, Zoe – whenever I look at him I feel like shouting at him, lashing out at him."

"But it wasn't his fault, Emma."

"I know but what if he hadn't gone or if he had done something differently? I can't help it, that's all I can think about."

"You shouldn't think about things like that, it won't change anything."

"Easier said than done."

"But the 'what ifs?' will just consume you – they'll eat you up!"

"I know all this," Emma said wearily. "I know . . ." She paused. "I'm just so angry – so angry. I want him to feel like I do. To hurt like I do. How is he just able to move on like that, as if nothing has happened and life still goes on?"

"But why don't you try talking to him about your feelings?" Zoe kept her tone gentle, as she always did, though at times she felt weary to the point of exasperation – they had been over this ground so many times.

"I can't," Emma whispered, shifting uncomfortably under her friend's gaze.

"I don't think he has forgotten, Emma – he's just coping the only way he knows how to – everyone reacts differently."

"I can't help it, Zoe, I really can't. I'm trying so hard but the rage builds up inside me and it just takes over." She started to cry. "I'm sorry."

"Don't be sorry. God, don't be sorry at all. Here –" Zoe took a tissue from a packet inside her bag and passed it to Emma. "You know I'm here for you, you know that, don't you?" She put her arm around Emma's shoulders and hugged her hard.

"Sometimes the pain is so awful and Adam is just like this looming reminder of everything that has been taken away from me."

"It's only natural, after all you've been through. It is so unfair and nothing you can do will change it. I can only imagine how you're feeling."

When they left Taylor's bar, they walked home together. Reaching Emma's gate, they stood there chatting for a few moments under the street-lamp.

"Talk to him, Emma."

"I'll try," she said half-heartedly and Zoe knew she wouldn't.

7

Summer, 2000

Adam and Emma had first met in San Francisco. It was the year of the millennium and they had both come over on J1 student working visas. It seemed that the entire student population of Ireland had decamped to California that summer, spreading themselves out across infamous cities such as San Diego, Los Angeles and Santa Cruz.

Emma had come over with two of her friends and, after searching the city high and low, they had found a bijou apartment on the top floor of a three-storey slatted wooden house right on Union Square in the heart of the city. The rent was a bit on the steep side but it was their first time living away from home and they had wanted to do it properly. They had been saving up for this trip for the last year, using the money they earned from their part-time jobs. They wanted to experience real city living – the buzzing streets, being able to walk everywhere, having myriad shops and cafés on their doorstep – so they had overlooked the astronomical rent and signed the lease.

Before they even came over, Emma and her friends had jobs

lined up in a call centre that handled the customer-service operations for several large corporations. The company was going through a period of rapid expansion. It could not keep up with the volume of new business coming its way and the disposable workforce of students was perfect to meet their needs.

They had been working there for a month when Adam joined. He had come over with a large crowd of the lads from college. Rather than waste money that could be used for beer on renting an apartment, they had gone for the cheaper option and were staying in a live-in hostel in the Tenderloin district. Every day when they stepped outside the hostel they were met with the stench of urine rising up off the street in the heat and they had to step over drunks and homeless people to get outside their door. The four of them had squashed into a double room, so small that the door couldn't be opened fully because there wasn't enough room between the wall and the ends of the bed. They had to squeeze through a small gap to get in and out. Their room was next door to a guy called Mike who had been living in the hostel since the sixties and was growing a small garden-centre worth of marijuana in his room – sometimes he had to sit outside in the hall in a canvas deckchair because he couldn't move for the amount of plants in the place. But the novelty of the free grass soon wore thin when they realised that they and their room permanently smelt of weed. When all the money that they had come over with was spent and they finally had to face up to the fact that they needed to get jobs, they had heard about this call-centre that was in desperate need of more bodies, so that had been their first port of call. The human resources manager, who was coming under pressure from the directors to get more bodies to fill the short-term requirements of their clients, decided to overlook the fact that they all smelt of grass and no one was more surprised than they were to find themselves hired that same day.

On his first day they had paired Adam up with Emma. She was to be his 'buddy' but within five minutes Emma had already shown him everything he needed to know about the job. They had clicked straight away. She told him that all they had to do was follow a flowchart which had every conceivable answer built into a script so you could do it with your eyes closed.

Adam was intrigued by this willowy girl, with skin so pale that it was almost translucent, showing a network of bluey-green veins underneath. Her white-blonde hair was long with small springy curls and she had a fine, delicate bone structure. Only for her striking height, she would have almost seemed fragile. When she smiled her whole face was illuminated and her eyes lit up. The more he got to know her, the more he liked her cool and calm demeanour. She was so different to the usual girls he went for, with their fake-tanned midriffs permanently on show, voluminous hair extensions and gel-nails. Emma was classy, the antithesis of the other girls, and for some reason he couldn't help but be drawn to her. She was all he could think about and the more he got to know her, the more he found himself needing to know.

When Emma was finished training him in, he had pretended to their team-leader that he was still a bit unsure of how the whole thing worked and would feel more confident if he knew that his 'buddy' was nearby. Their team-leader had given him a despairing look and had made a mental note to speak with HR about the calibre of the candidates they were taking on recently. Reluctantly she had put him sitting at the desk beside Emma's.

By choice the students worked late most evenings. There were no supervisors on duty so they got paid time-and-a-half and would sit around drinking cans. So that they wouldn't be disturbed, they would push a button on their phone to divert incoming calls back to the end of the queue again. Then they would clock off around nine and head to whatever bar was running a dollar-a-beer promotion that night. Adam and Emma would always spend the whole night talking together, with everyone else blending into the periphery. Their focus was on each other but he was still too afraid to make a move on her. He knew she wouldn't be one for his usual charms.

Emma couldn't wait to get into work every day to see Adam; she had never enjoyed a job so much. They spent all day talking around their partition and taking the mick out of customers on the other end of the phone. Of course it helped that he was good-looking: six foot one and broad-chested, with messy dark hair. He had a cheeky smile and white even teeth but he always had girls fawning all over him and she didn't want to be just another one of his conquests. Her friends had told her that he looked at her in 'that' way but she wasn't sure. They were very different people. He was a complete alpha-male, always the centre of attention, whereas she was quieter and was more comfortable with one-on-ones than large groups.

One evening as they were walking home together after work, they had stood for a moment on the steps outside Emma's front door, looking at life busying on around them. They watched Crazy Vinnie, an amputee who had lost both of his legs in Vietnam but managed to get around the place by putting his trunk on a skateboard and pushing himself along with his hands. He got his kicks from shouting at people in the street and then laughing at them as they screamed when they turned around to see him whizzing past them on his skateboard.

They stayed talking for hours, only sitting down on the

steps when it was dusk, and even though they were both starting to get chilly, neither one wanted to move. Eventually Adam knew he needed to seize the moment. It was now or never, so with a wildly beating heart he had leant across mid-conversation and kissed Emma with firm lips, showing the strength of his feelings for her. She had kissed him back with the same intensity, all the passion that had been building for months between them finally released.

Things had moved pretty quickly after that evening. They spent all their time together. They would go for picnics in the park, cycle across the Golden Gate Bridge to Sausalito or spend a leisurely few hours just having brunch. Adam would stay at hers most nights. They would lie beside each other, bodies entwined, talking all night long. She had braved the live-in hostel in the Tenderloin once but once was enough.

The rest of the summer passed wrapped up in each other until the inevitable time came when they had to go home. After three months, they had fallen in love not just with each other but with this city too. They felt as though they had become like San Franciscans themselves; they now belonged in this pulsing city with its micro-climate and the fog over the bay every morning, where artists, homeless war veterans and careerists hurrying along to the financial district all co-existed to bring the city to life. They felt different to the tourists who swarmed around Pier 49, queuing to get a boat out to Alcatraz; now tourists asked *them* for directions. They both knew that the combination of coming from opposite ends of Dublin city, him a southsider and her from the north side, and the pressures of their studies meant they wouldn't have the luxury of so much time together back home.

So when the summer of fun was over, they had sadly said goodbye to the city that had brought them together and wondered how their relationship would survive against the backdrop of the reality of their lives at home. They had made a pact that they would do everything in their power to make it work and to the amazement of their friends and families, who assumed it was just another holiday romance, that was what they had done.

8

As Zoe walked home after meeting Emma she thought over the conversation they'd just had. It was painful to watch her friend. She seemed so lost. She was going through the motions and getting on with her life but there was still a deep sadness in her eyes. Even when she smiled, it wasn't a real smile – there was still an unmistakable pain lurking behind it. Zoe could understand why Emma felt the need to lash out; life had been very cruel to her. People reacted in different ways and she supposed that Adam must be a painful reminder to Emma of all that had happened. He mirrored her grief and it was impossible to be around him without dredging up all the hurt again. Zoe hoped that in time it would pass because, although Emma didn't realise it, she needed Adam.

As she strolled down the well-lit street, suddenly a car pulled up a little way ahead of her, jolting her out of her thoughts. She watched as the driver threw something out from the window which landed onto the footpath ahead of her. As quickly as it had stopped, the car screeched off again. She ran up the path to see what it was and she was completely shocked to discover it was a puppy. He lay whimpering on the footpath.

"Hey!" she roared after the car. "Come back here!"

A jeep pulled up on the footpath beside her moments later and a man hopped out.

"Did you see that?" she asked in disbelief.

"I tried to get the registration but they were gone too quick," he said.

Zoe bent down to the puppy who was now crying in distress. His brown eyes pleaded with her to help. He was so tiny; he was definitely no more than a few weeks old. She bundled him up into her arms.

"Oh God – we have to help him."

"There's a vet down on Charles Street – they're probably still open," the man said. "Here, get in!"

Zoe looked at the man for a second; for all she knew he could be a serial killer.

"Sorry, I should introduce myself – I'm Steve." He held out his hand to shake hers. His blue eyes seemed kind and trustworthy.

"Zoe." She shook his hand tentatively. She climbed up into his battered jeep. Putting the puppy on her lap, she listened to him crying while Steve drove towards the vet.

When they got there, they both jumped out quickly and ran into the surgery where they explained breathlessly to the nurse what had happened. Gingerly the nurse whose name was Carla, took the pup from Zoe's arms.

"Unfortunately we're seeing a lot more of this type of behaviour. Some people blame the recession for the rise in animal cruelty but there's no excuse for that!" She shook her head at them.

"God, that is awful – people are sick!" Steve said.

"I'll bring him in to the vet straightaway. He has most likely broken something from the fall. He's still quite young to be apart from his mother as well so we'll give him a good check-up, poor little mite."

"Will he be okay?"

"It's too early to say but we'll do our best for him – poor fella. If you want to leave me one of your numbers, I'll give you a call and let you know how he is."

"Oh, thank you," Zoe scribbled her number on a piece of paper.

"Now – I hate having to do this but I do need to know who is going to cover the bill?"

"Oh God, of course – sorry, I wasn't thinking," Steve said quickly. "I'll take care of it."

They both went outside and stood in the yard.

"I can't believe the bastards did that to a poor defenceless animal – I'm sorry, I shouldn't use language like that but that's how I feel about them."

Zoe shook her head in disbelieving agreement.

"Here, look, there's a little café around the corner," he said. "Do you – well, do you want to go for a coffee – I need something to settle my nerves after that."

Zoe looked at her watch and tried to think of an excuse. Yes, he had helped her get the puppy to a vet but he was a complete stranger she had literally met on the street. Plus she really wasn't in the mood for this – she was upset after seeing Emma, she was worried about her.

"Well, I –"

"C'mon, I could do with something to calm me down." His smile was broad and easy.

"Okay . . ." she said hesitantly. "Well, I suppose I could go for a quick one . . ."

"Great!"

They walked into the café and took seats. The waitress brought them over the evening menu. Zoe shook her head but was appalled when, instead of ordering coffee, Steve proceeded to order a steak and chips.

"Sorry, you don't mind, do you? I'm starving – it's been a long day."

"No, work away." She forced a smile. It would be at least an hour now before she could leave. All she wanted to do this evening was just to go home, have a nice soak in the bath and then sit on the couch in her PJs with a glass of wine.

"You might as well order something – no point looking at me stuffing my gob." He smiled at her.

"Sure," she said through gritted teeth as she scanned the menu. "Okay . . . lasagne, please."

The waitress took the menus and left.

Zoe's thoughts flipped back to the puppy. "That was awful, wasn't it? To do that to a poor little creature like that!"

"What kind of people throw a dog out of a car window? Jesus, there's plenty of animal shelters around!"

"I hope to God he'll be okay. What a crappy introduction to the world!"

He nodded in agreement. "I've had dogs all my life. The best pet you'll ever have – loyal to the last. I grew up on a farm."

He looked like the farming type, Zoe thought to herself. He was wearing a green wax jacket over a maroon-coloured sweater and navy cords. He stood out amongst all the office types seated around them in the café.

"I always wanted a dog when I was growing up," Zoe said.

"You *never* had a dog?" he asked, incredulous.

She had to smile at his surprise. "My mother could barely take care of me – let alone a dog."

"I see," he said quietly. "So, Zoe, what do you do with yourself – when you're not rescuing injured puppies?"

"I work in fashion design."

"Wow – now that's impressive!"

"Not really, we just rip off catwalk designs and sell them on to the high street – it's pretty mundane actually."

"It sounds exciting to me!"

"Believe me, it really isn't."

"Now I can't tell you what I do – my job is so boring in comparison."

"Go on!"

"I'm warning you, it's not very glamorous!"

"Tell me!"

"I work for myself actually. I have a small food company. I make bread, cheeses, pâtés, jams, chutneys, that kind of stuff. All organic, of course – then I travel the country selling them at Farmers' Markets."

"Wow, that's pretty cool!"

"Why?"

"Making your own produce and selling it – it must be great seeing people buying something you have made."

"Are you into food?"

"I love food – I just don't have the patience for cooking it."

"Well, I should give you some of my pâté. I'm told it's good."

Zoe could tell that, although he didn't think his job was glamorous, he was still very passionate about it.

"Well, I'd love to try it." She was really starting to warm to him now. His open nature made him very appealing.

When they were finished eating, Steve offered to drop her home. Somewhat hesitantly she agreed. He seemed like a nice guy.

They chatted away easily on the trip home and when they pulled up outside Zoe's apartment block, they stayed talking until eventually Steve said he'd better get on the road because he had to be up early to bake bread for the market in the morning.

"Can I leave you my number – you might give me a call as soon as you get an update from the surgery on the little fella?"

"Oh yeah – of course I will."

"Great, thanks for that. Well, Zoe, goodnight – and it was lovely to meet you even if the circumstances weren't the best."

"And you too."

"Goodnight, Zoe."

"Goodnight, Steve."

She walked off towards the foyer of her apartment block, wondering if she would ever see him again.

9

Adam woke up saturated again. Beads of sweat were coursing down his forehead, neck and back but he still felt chilly. He took a deep breath. The frost-covered hedgerows, the sunlight so low in the sky that it was glinting in through the car window, his grey-leather steering wheel, the farmhouse with the red door. The bend in the road. The crossroads. *Why couldn't he remember more?* The dream constantly haunted him during the night hours as if mocking his attempts at sleeping. He needed to do something. *Anything.* He lay there in the darkness listening to the traffic going up and down the road, the sound of footsteps on the pavement outside, a dog barking somewhere in the distance.

* * *

Adam moved noisily around the kitchen, tidying up things that had gathered on the worktops. He roughly lined up glass bottles for recycling so that they clattered together, threatening to smash. He opened the fridge and took packages of food past their sell-by date off the shelves and fired them into the bin. He had got up early, having spent most of the night lying awake in the aftermath of the dream. *Bloody stupid fucking nightmare! Why the fuck will it not leave me alone?*

The lack of sleep was really starting to get to him. The dreams were now occurring almost every night and even the heavy slumber of alcohol couldn't ward them off; drink only allowed him to forget temporarily. When he was awake, he constantly felt detached from the world that surrounded him. When he was in work he found it difficult to concentrate; if he tried to focus on a task his mind could often just go blank. His brain didn't even have the energy to daydream. He was constantly feeling foggy and was afraid that one of these days he might just keel over onto his keyboard in work and fall into a deep sleep. The thoughts kept swirling around and about his head. *What if he hadn't gone? What if . . .?* He was bloody sick of *'what ifs?'* He tried to suppress them because they weren't going to help him but like all bad thoughts that invade in the middle of the night, they were always the hardest to push away. It was gone to the stage that he was like a small child who was too scared to go to bed, scared of the nightmares that lay waiting for him in his sleep.

Although it was the weekend, Adam almost wished he could go to work – anything that would distract him from the misery of his home life. No matter how hard he tried and how successfully he carried it off at work, once he was within the four walls of his own home, he couldn't push the reality of his life out of his head any more.

He had heard Emma creep out of the house after eight, like she did every weekend. She hadn't even bothered to come into the kitchen and say she was going, he thought angrily, though she must have heard him.

He heard the electronic buzz of their doorbell, jolting him out of his thoughts. It had better not be the goddamn Jehovah's Witnesses again, he thought as he stormed out towards the front door. If it was them, he swore he would take their end-of-the-world-inferno pile of crap and stuff it down their own throats instead. In fact, on second thoughts, he hoped it *was* the Jehovah's Witnesses; it would do him good to take his anger out on someone. He pulled their heavy front door back with force and was almost disappointed to see the diminutive figure of his mother standing there with her back to him.

"Mam?" he exclaimed in surprise as his mother, who was dressed in a camel-coloured mohair coat that was swamping her petite frame, turned around to face him. When he was a child she had taught him that whenever you rang the bell you should always face away from the door and you should only turn around when it was opened. It never made any sense to him even now but Ita White obviously still adhered to her teaching.

"Hi there, love."

"I wasn't expecting you, come in."

"Surely your own mother doesn't need an invitation to drop by?"

"No, of course you don't – sorry, Mam. Come in."

He showed her into the living room and cleared off a space for her on the sofa.

"Will you have a cup of tea?" he asked.

"I won't, thanks, dear – it's only a quick visit to see how you both are."

He sat down next to her.

"Where's Emma?" She peered around the room as if Emma might magically appear from behind the couch or jump down from the bookshelves.

"She's gone out."

"Oh, I see." Silence. "Again?"

Adam nodded.

"Look, I don't want to speak out of turn but . . . is everything all right?"

"Of course it is. Why?" Adam tried to keep his voice level but he knew he didn't sound very convincing.

"Well, it's just that I haven't seen Emma in ages. Every time I call she's gone out and you haven't been over to the house together since . . . well, since . . ." She started to get flustered. "I'm just a bit concerned, that's all."

"We're working through it, Mam."

"Really, Adam?"

He couldn't lie to his own mother so he just said nothing. He couldn't meet her eyes.

She reached across and took her son's hand in hers and stroked it like she would a child's. When Adam looked at her, her eyes were brimming with tears and her face etched with worry.

The silence stretched itself out between them. Tension mounted in Adam as he steeled himself for the questions to come.

Then suddenly she relinquished his hand and stood up.

"Look, I'd better go . . . your father will be wondering where I got to. You look after yourself, love, won't you?"

"Of course I will, Mam." Adam tried to disguise his relief but it showed in his voice.

"And you know where I am if you need a chat? Any time of the day or night – y'know that, don't you, love?"

"I know, Mam. Thanks for calling in."

"All right, love. Tell Emma I was asking for her."

"I will," he replied even though they both knew it was a blatant lie.

10

Zoe couldn't sleep that night worrying about the poor dog and thinking about the strange evening she'd had. One minute she was walking down the road on her way home after meeting Emma and the next she was in the vet's with a strange man with an injured puppy and then they were having dinner. Life was bizarre.

The next morning she waited for news from the surgery. She was still upset at the thought of the fate of the poor puppy, only a few weeks old and already suffering at the hands of humans. Some people had no heart. Finally she got the call she had been waiting for all morning.

"Zoe – hi, it's Carla from Southside Surgery."

"Oh hi, Carla – how is he doing?"

"Well, the poor little guy had a broken leg from the fall and he's quite malnourished but he's responding well and we would expect him to make a full recovery."

"Oh thank God – I didn't sleep a wink worrying about him!"

"Well, he's in good hands here. He's a little dote actually. We're all mad about him."

"What are you going to do with him when he's better?" Zoe asked.

"How do you mean?"

"Well, are you going to find a home for him?"

"Well, unfortunately we have no control over that. We'll give the animal shelters a call – hopefully they'll be able to take him – but they are inundated with strays at the moment."

"Hopefully? But – but, what if they're not – you're not going to put him down are you?" She was horrified.

"I'm sorry, Zoe, it's not my call."

"Right." Zoe swallowed. She hung up feeling desperate. The poor little guy, his worries were only just beginning. If she didn't live in an apartment she would keep him herself.

She checked in her notebook and found Steve's number where he had scribbled it down. Even his handwriting seemed friendly and confident.

"Hello?" he answered cheerily.

"Hi, Steve – it's Zoe – the girl you met last night – we rescued the puppy?"

"Ah, Zoe – how are you? Have you any news on the poor little creature?"

She could hear the windy noise of the outdoors in the background. "He's going to be okay – he's broken his leg and he's quite malnourished but the nurse, Carla, said he is doing well. She said he's a gorgeous little thing."

"Well, thank God for that, I was worried sick about him. I hate seeing an animal in pain like that."

"But, Steve –"

"What?"

"Well, if the animal shelters can't take him because of overcrowding, they might have to put him down!"

"Jesus – that's awful."

"I'd take him myself but I live in an apartment and he looks like he could be a big dog but I'm going to ask around everyone I know to see if they would give him a home. I couldn't bear the thought of him being put to sleep. Maybe you could put the word out as well?"

"We can't let that happen to him! I'll ask around the farmers at the market – surely one of them would take him in."

"Oh, I hope so! I'm going to put fliers up on the way home too. Okay, well, let me know how it goes. It's my mission now to help him."

"You're a good sort, Zoe."

She was taken aback with the surprise compliment. "Thanks! So are you!"

When she got off the phone to Steve, she felt marginally better. Surely between the two of them they could find a home for the puppy, especially him with all his farming contacts – he would have to know someone out there who would take him in. She sent an email around to all her friends to let them know and she designed some posters to put in the local supermarket and shops to look for a home for him.

When she came in from work that evening, she had got changed into her tracksuit and Ugg boots and was just putting her feet up when the buzzer on her apartment door went. She looked through the peephole and saw Steve's face smiling back at her. *Oh God*, what the hell was he doing calling to her apartment? He'd better not be a psycho – she'd enough drama in her life now without having to deal with a lunatic nut-bar that thought it was okay to call on her because they had rescued a dog together. She cursed herself for being so stupid – what had she been doing going for dinner with a complete stranger anyway?

She pulled back the door, making sure the security chain was kept on.

"Steve?" she said cautiously.

"Surprise!" Steve was grinning from ear to ear.

She looked down and he was holding the rescued puppy in his arms.

"Sorry for calling unexpectedly but I wanted to surprise you. Say hello to my new dog!"

"Your new dog!"

"Well, after you told me that he could end up in a dog pound or worse, I couldn't let that happen to him. And, sure, I've been meaning to get a dog for a while now anyway – I've loads of space. And then this little guy happens to come along. Sure, I couldn't not take him!"

"Oh that's wonderful news, I'm so happy he's found a home!" Zoe said as she undid the security chain and opened the door. "Do you want to come in?" In fairness he seemed like a harmless sort.

"Sure, I've loads of fields around the house for him to roam in and he can keep me company driving around the country," Steve said as he stepped inside.

He was dressed the same way as the last time, wearing his wax jacket again, but this time with a navy sweater and beige cords. The look suited him – she could imagine him standing behind his table at the markets, selling his produce.

He followed Zoe into the kitchen and sat himself on one of the highchairs at her breakfast bar.

"He looks better already." Zoe stroked the chocolate-brown fur of the dog. His front left leg was bandaged up but other than that he looked quite content where he was snuggled in Steve's arms. "What breed do you think he is?"

"Well, I definitely think there's a bit of a Labrador in him – especially around his face, but God only knows what else."

"He's gorgeous!"

"Well, what are we going to call him?"

"We?"

"Sure – as his honorary mother, I thought you should be involved in the naming ceremony."

"Well, I think he should have a proper name – not Lucky or Patch, a real name."

"I completely agree – how about Dave?"

"*Dave?* Where on earth did you come up with that from?"

"He looks like a Dave, don't you think?"

Zoe looked at the sleeping puppy. "Mmmh, I actually think you're right. It suits him. Hello, Dave!" She cooed to the sleeping puppy. "He is so cute – I just love him!"

"Well, you know you can have visitation rights whenever you want."

Zoe laughed. "That's good to know!"

11

Today was the day that Arthur Pilkington, the managing director of Sofa World and his senior management team were coming into the offices of A1 Adverts to listen to Emma pitch for their business. Somehow she had managed to converge all the words that had been swimming around in her head for the last few weeks and put them together into what she hoped would be a winning presentation. She had tried to put her heart and soul into it like she did for every one of A1's clients but this time she just couldn't get enthusiastic about the pitch at all. Maureen had asked her if she was sure she was okay to do the presentation, saying that she had no problem stepping in herself, but Emma was determined to do it. She had gone through the pitch with Maureen already and she had given her the thumbs-up, so she supposed it was as good as it ever was going to be.

She had a black coffee in hand as she read and re-read the presentation. She visualised in her head the level of her intonation and pitch. She tried to cover all the angles that Arthur might pick to come at her with questions: budgets, target markets, efficacy of TV ads over radio. She was making sure that she had every detail engrained on her brain. She would be prepared.

Five minutes before they were due to start, Maureen popped her head over her desk partition.

"All set?"

"Uh-huh, think so."

"As I said before, I have no problem stepping in – are you sure you're okay to do this?"

"I'm fine," Emma replied through gritted teeth.

"Okay, well, deep breaths then – I've every confidence in you, Emma."

Emma walked into the board room with her shoulders squared. She was wearing her favourite red-suede stiletto heels and grey-tweed pencil-skirt with matching jacket. That was a trick she always used: she knew if she felt good about her appearance it would give her that extra edge of confidence. She took a deep breath and greeted the rotund Arthur Pilkington and his team with a warm smile and a firm handshake and introduced herself and Maureen to the group. Her calm, collected, composed exterior belied her racing heart.

Maureen initiated some general chit-chat for a few minutes about how times were hard for businesses at the moment, while Emma nodded sympathetically. Soon, though, all eyes were on her as they waited for her to start. She stood up and turned on the projector. Her heart was beating nineteen to the dozen, so loud she was sure everyone in the room could hear it.

"Gentlemen, thank you so much for coming here today and for giving A1 Adverts the opportunity to pitch for your business. We appreciate in these cost-conscious times that now more than ever customers need to see value for their money, or as the Americans say 'bang for their buck'."

She knew it was weak but the men laughed and she was grateful.

"So we are going to present to you now what A1 Adverts can do for Sofa World and how we can work together to ensure Sofa World is the number-one sofa-store of choice in the Irish furniture market."

Maureen flashed her an encouraging smile.

"We've looked at how all Sofa World sofas are designed by a team of in-house designers but the main competitive advantage you have over other sofa retailers is the fact that these designs are so competitive on price. Quality at the right price. So without further ado I would like to introduce you to the concept we believe sums up the core values of the Sofa World Christmas campaign."

She could hear an intake of breath from Arthur Pilkington as he waited with bated breath to see what tag line she had come up with. He was sweating profusely and removed the handkerchief that decorated the breast-pocket of his suit and used it to mop his brow. She could almost physically feel his sense of anticipation.

Stated simply on a slide with a black background in gold lettering – the colour of Sofa World's company logo – was the tag line: **"Quality Money *Can* Buy"**

There was silence in the room, no one even dared to breathe. She looked at Arthur whose forehead was creased downwards as he contemplated the tag line.

Oh shit, he hates it.

She looked at Maureen who was looking back at her with the same worried expression.

Everyone stayed silent, all waiting for Arthur to utter his verdict. After what seemed like an age, he eventually spoke.

"I like it!"

Arthur was smiling and looking around at his team to make sure they were too. His team of yes-men instantly perked up and began agreeing with him. Whispers of "fantastic" and "perfect" crept around the room.

"'Quality Money *Can* Buy!'" he repeated. "Yeah, I think it captures the essence of Sofa World perfectly. Quality Money *Can* Buy. Yes, indeed. I do – I like it."

The relief was palpable, not just between Maureen and Emma, but between Arthur and his team. It was obvious that the team didn't like it when Mr Pilkington was in a bad mood. If he was happy, their lives were easier.

"And what about the TV campaign?" Arthur shouted boisterously at Emma.

Emma's confidence was now buoyed up by their reactions. "Of course, Mr Pilkington. I will now show you our proposed TV campaign." She thanked Jesus and all the saints in heaven that she had done this. Normally it wasn't required in an initial pitch but she had learned from Arthur's ad manager's emails that he was a demanding individual and she had dealt with his type before. 'Expect the unexpected' was her motto when it came to these sorts.

She pressed play on the projector, which flashed to a thirty-second film showing a homely mother, maybe 5 feet 5 inches in height, with a shapely figure. She was dressed in a cashmere cardigan and beige slacks, and she cuddled a five-year-old blond-haired angel in the crook of her arm as they both leant back into a plush sofa. A beautifully decorated Christmas tree twinkled in the corner and the log fire crackled. The mother was reading a story to the child before his heavy lids closed for the Land of Nod. Then it cut to a full-screen image where a voice-over in a reassuring tone stated: 'Quality Money *Can* Buy.'

Arthur punched the air with his fist. "That's it, *that's it*!"

His team, now having the sign they needed, also started to whoop and holler in agreement.

Emma stared up at the screen for a few seconds too long after the clip had finished. She had played this video over and over when she was preparing her pitch but suddenly now she felt her throat go dry. All the men in the room plus Maureen were staring at her expectantly. She wasn't sure whether it was because she felt vulnerable in front of these people or stressed about doing the pitch, but her eyes began to fill with tears. She could see Maureen mouthing at her to continue.

"Well, gentlemen, has –" She tried her best to sound normal but her voice was too high and threatened to break. "I'm sorry – I have to . . ." She couldn't keep it together. Running out of the room, she left Maureen and the team from Sofa World stunned in her wake. She could hear Maureen apologising profusely behind her.

She ran back down the corridor towards the bathroom where she stood in front of the sink sobbing. She splashed cold water on her face as she stood there crying. Thank God the rest of the cubicles were empty.

Moments later, she heard the door swing open. It was Maureen.

"Look, I'm sorry, Maureen – I should have let you do it. I'm sorry I ruined it," she whispered.

"No, it's okay – it's only to be expected – I knew I shouldn't have left you on your own to do it – I should have stepped in and given you a hand."

Emma shook her head. "I should have been able to do it – I don't know – I had gone over it a thousand times in the last week and I was fine with it but the video clip just got me there. I'm sorry – I don't know what happened."

"Look, you were doing a fantastic job and I could see they were impressed – in fact, you had practically done the whole thing – the only thing remaining was the questions and I could handle them."

"I'm sorry for landing you in it."

"Nonsense, he had a few general ones about the cost of a TV campaign and whether I felt the price point was right for the target market. Nothing I wasn't able for. They seemed impressed, and Arthur nearly shook the hand off me on the way out so that's a good sign." Maureen put her arm around her shoulders. "C'mon, Emma, it's only to be expected."

Maureen handed her a tissue and Emma blew her nose.

"Do you want to head home early – maybe have an early night?" She smiled kindly.

Emma shook her head defiantly. "No, I'm better off in here, keeping busy. But thanks anyway." She sniffed and dabbed at her nose.

"Are you sure?"

Emma nodded.

After six Maureen turned off the lights in her office and came by Emma's cubicle, while wrapping her scarf double around her neck.

"Emma, love, I really think you should be heading home now. You've had a tough day."

"Yeah, I'm just finishing up now."

It was a lie but it was easier to pacify Maureen than start up her concern again.

She killed time surfing the web and eventually, around eight, when there was no one else left in A1 Adverts, she decided she'd better call it a night and head home.

12

Some days after, Steve rang Zoe with an update on how Dave was doing. He told her how it was like having a small baby in the house and that now he knew what new parents were talking about when they complained about sleepless nights. He had tucked Dave up in a basket with a hot-water bottle wrapped in a blanket but he could still hear him whimpering from the kitchen. He didn't have the heart to leave him like that so he had ended up taking him into his bed. The toilet training was also a bit hit-and-miss but all in all they were getting on well. Then nervously he asked her if she wanted to meet up at the weekend to see Dave.

"You can try some of my pâté and tell me what you think?" he added.

"Sure," Zoe agreed while thinking in her head again how strange the whole situation was. But after she had hung up the phone and was thinking about him, she found herself wanting to see him. His personality was infectious, being around him made you feel good about yourself. He had a natural way with people and he was charming without being smarmy. He was easy-going too, like nothing would ever faze him. He had a funny way about him – you couldn't not like him.

Over dinner the next evening she told Emma the whole story about Dave being thrown out of a car window, their trip to the vet and their dinner afterwards. Emma had been amazed by the irony of meeting someone in the street.

"He must like you," Emma said.

"Why do you say that?"

"Well, he wouldn't be asking you to meet up again at the weekend if he wasn't interested."

"I'm not sure, Emma. I'd say he's the kind of person that would be like that with everyone he meets, y'know."

"Are you going to go?"

"I think so – I know it sounds mad but he seems like a genuine sort."

"Well, who knows where it could lead."

Zoe laughed.

* * *

Zoe set off on Saturday morning with the directions that Steve had given her. She turned off the main road onto a narrow winding back road with only room for the width of one car. She could see the sea in the distance with foamy white waves topping it. The land rose up as she drove down the winding roads which weaved through the stone-walled fields. The place was so remote she hadn't passed a house for miles. Not for the first time, she began to doubt herself: what was she doing going driving out into the middle of nowhere to meet up with a man she had only met for the first time last week? She pulled over into a gateway at the side of the road and rang Steve.

"Hi there, are you on your way?" His voice was friendly and instantly she felt better.

"Well, I think I might be a bit lost – I followed the directions you gave me but it just seems a bit . . . remote?"

"Oh, people always think they've gone wrong – but keep following the road straight until the headland dips down to the sea and you'll see a turn up to the right, with my sign on it."

"Okay, well, I don't think I'm too far away then."

"Great, I'll put the kettle on so."

She pulled out in her car again and continued along the road. It really was beautiful out here, so quiet and peaceful. Living in the city she often forgot just how loud and in your face it could be. She finally saw a swinging sign for '*McCredden's Artisan Foods*' and she turned up an impossibly narrow track that had grass growing up the middle. Finally, a whitewashed cottage with small blue-painted windows came into view on the headland. When she looked down to the right she could see the sun glistening off the calm sea beneath her. It was amazing. She swung into the gravel driveway and Steve came out of the door to greet her.

"You found me okay, then?" he said, grinning at her.

"Just about," she smiled back.

"Come on in. Dave is dying to see you."

Zoe noted that he was dressed even more casually today – he was wearing jeans and a pair of green Hunter Wellington boots and the wax jacket was now replaced with a fleece, under which he wore a red check shirt. His blue eyes twinkled as he spoke and his dark hair was long but it suited him like that. His skin had a shadow of stubble. She had to admit he looked quite handsome, in a rugged kind of way.

Zoe walked into the country kitchen. Pots of herbs were scattered randomly on the windowsills, with jugs of wild flowers decorating the place. There was a big farmhouse table with mismatched chairs.

Dave was curled up in his basket in front of an Aga on which a kettle was boiling. When she stroked his ears, he opened up his brown eyes and wagged his tail. She was amazed to see how much he had grown. She had brought him some doggy treats and a red collar with his name on it. She played with him while he tried to nip her fingers with his razor-sharp teeth. As Steve recounted his antics during the week, she could tell that he had already grown very attached to him.

"Ah, the kettle is boiled." Steve made tea in a blue-and-white teapot and then left it to draw while he laid out a loaf of rustic bread and an earthenware dish of his homemade pâté.

He poured two mugs of tea – one mug was spotty and the other had a picture of a pig.

"Spots or pig?" he asked, holding up both mugs.

"Erm – oh, go on, I'll go for the pig!" she laughed. She sat at the table while Dave snuggled blissfully in her arms.

He sawed through the loaf of rustic bread and served it to her spread thickly with his pâté.

She picked up the thick crusted bread and bit a piece off.

"Well?" he asked after she had chewed the mouthful.

"You made this yourself?" Zoe said.

"Of course!"

"It tastes really good . . . mmmm . . ." She chewed some more. "It's completely different to the supermarket brands."

"That's because I only use locally sourced ingredients – everything I use comes from the farmers around here." He gestured in a circular motion.

When she had finished that, he took out a grey slate cheeseboard with a selection of smoked cheeses that he had cured himself and a small bowl of pitted olives for her to nibble on. She loved everything and made sure he knew it.

After lunch they strolled along the deserted beach, with Steve carrying Dave in his arms. She was amazed they had so much to talk about.

"How long have you lived here?" she asked.

"I bought it a few years back – I always used to come walking down here at the weekends when I was working in the bank up in Dublin."

"You used to work in a bank?" Zoe was genuinely shocked. He looked nothing like the slick banker types with their polished shoes and tailored suits.

"Uh-huh," he nodded. "But I got tired of the rat race. I was sick of losing sleep over shareholder dividends and hedge funds – I wanted to do something I enjoyed. I'm a great believer in the saying 'Do a job you love and you'll never do a day's work in your life' so that's what I did."

"What, you just handed in your notice and moved out here?"

"Well, not quite as dramatic as that – I had always loved food and cooking. My mother was a great one for the family dinners when we were growing up. And as I grew up on a farm I loved how everything grown on the land had a use. So I got the idea of starting my own small business. I started small, just making some chutneys and jams first and selling them on the weekends while I still worked in the bank during the week. But I got a great reaction so I began adding more produce, bread and scones and then the pâté and it just grew from there. So two years ago, I decided to take the plunge. I handed in my notice to the bank, put my apartment in the IFSC up for sale and started looking around for somewhere to live. One day I was walking down here and looked up at the derelict cottage and thought it was a beautiful setting, out on its own like that with nobody next or near you. But you should have seen the state of it! There were holes in the roof and grass growing out of the chimney! So I approached the farmer whose land it was on and he agreed to sell it to me but even the solicitor told me not to buy it, it was that rundown. I've spent the last few years doing it up in bits and pieces – I love that pottering around doing jobs, planning what project I'll take on next. Last year I extended the kitchen – that's where I make all my produce and I've sown a herb garden and vegetable patch."

"It really is the most amazing place I've ever seen. Dave is going to love exploring all around here when his leg is mended."

When they walked back up the dunes to the house, Steve put a snoozing Dave into his basket beside the Aga.

"C'mon till I show you the rest of the place."

He led her around the cosy rooms, all simply decorated with wooden floorboards and cream-painted walls. The bedrooms had cast-iron beds and small wooden dressing-tables.

After he had stuffed her with more of his food and chatted some more, Zoe reluctantly said her goodbyes. It was getting dark out and she didn't want to get lost on these roads with no signposts.

As soon as she had pulled out of his laneway, she knew she was seriously starting to like him but she really didn't want that to happen. As soon as she opened herself up to people, things never went her way. So she tried to tell herself to stop getting her hopes up. It was all just for Dave anyway. Plus he was so different to her usual type. Normally she went for the on-trend men, usually creative types from the fashion industry or the Dublin art scene. It wasn't that she chose these men – rather, because of her job, it meant these were normally the type she socialised with. But Steve was the antithesis of them. When she had first met him he had been wearing cords and a bottle-green wax jacket; she could no more imagine any of her exes in that get-up than she could imagine herself running a marathon. All her exes either had smooth baby's-bottom cheeks or carefully maintained designer stubble, but Steve looked as though he didn't shave from one end of the week to the next. He was what you might describe as a 'man's man', rough and ready. She knew he would also probably wrap you in his strong arms and hold you tight against his chest all night.

She dialled Emma's number.

"Well, is he a psycho killer?" Emma asked.

"No!" Zoe laughed. "Oh Emma, he's great – the more I get to know him the more I know I'm falling for him. I'm so scared though."

"Of what?"

"The unknown . . . letting go . . . seeing where life takes me . . ."

"Zoe, you have to let your guard down sometime," Emma said gently.

"I know, Em, I know."

* * *

On Sunday morning, Zoe's phone buzzed on her bedside locker. Sleepily she picked it up and saw it was Steve. She quickly answered it.

"Hello?"

"Good morning to you, Zoe."

Even the way he said good morning was full of infectious cheer.

"Morning, Steve. How's Dave?"

"He's doing great altogether – but he's getting a bit fond of my bed now."

Zoe laughed.

"I'm just ringing to check that you got home all right last night but I'm guessing you did?"

"Uh-huh, it's actually a lot closer to the city than I had thought but yet it feels like you're on the edge of the world out there."

"That's the beauty of it. Look, Zoe, I hope you don't mind but I was also calling to ask you something. Now tell me if you think I'm being a bit presumptuous but – well, I was wondering – well, y'see, there's this ball on – Irish Food Producers Association – it's an annual thing. Now I hate the bloody thing but, well, I was wondering if you would like to accompany me?"

"I would love that."

"Oh, thank God!" He breathed a sigh of relief. "I was worried the only reason you stayed in contact was because of Dave."

Zoe was taken aback by his honesty. "I actually thought you were doing the same thing!" she said, laughing. "When is it on?"

"This Friday."

"This Friday! Talk about short notice. I'll have to get a *gúna* sorted!"

"I know, I'm sorry. It's black-tie too. I wasn't even going to go this year and then, I thought, well . . . I thought it would be nice to go together."

"I'd like that."

"It's in Dublin anyway so you won't have to go too far – I have a friend who will look after Dave for me so at least he's sorted. If I pick you up about eight, is that okay?"

"I look forward to it."

Zoe lay back on the pillow and smiled. She felt like a giddy teenager. He had said he liked her. He really liked her back and not just because of Dave. She would make sure she looked fantastic on Friday so that he would be glad he brought her. She would need to call around to Emma and see if she had any great dresses – she used to be always going to weddings and fancy black-tie things so she should have something. She couldn't imagine him in a tux though. She tried to picture him but nothing was coming. She wanted to jump up and down and scream.

13

Zoe rooted through Emma's wardrobe while Emma sat on edge of the bed chatting to her.

"What do you think of this one?" Zoe took out a crimson crêpe-de-chine dress and held it up against her.

"I wore that to the Snow Ball myself and Adam went to three years ago – it's gorgeous on."

"I remember seeing photos of it on you – it was fab. Do you think it will fit me though?" Zoe was looking at the narrow bodice doubtfully.

"Of course it will – sure we're the same size."

Zoe looked at Emma's tiny frame and, knowing full well that they weren't, she decided not to say anything. "I'll try it on."

She got undressed and Emma helped her into the dress and zipped it up the back.

"There – it's stunning on you."

"I don't know – look at my tummy – it does nothing to disguise it."

"What tummy? You're ridiculous."

"I'd feel too self-conscious – sorry."

She got out of the dress and looked through some more on the rail.

"This one is beautiful – so elegant." She held out a black satin, strapless number.

"I wore that to a black-tie wedding – I just clipped on a wine corsage to decorate it. I'm sure I still have it somewhere."

As Zoe thumbed through the dresses Emma had a flash of the way her life used to be. Each dress marked a different occasion in their life. There was the dress she wore to their engagement party. She even had held onto the jersey summer dress she was wearing the night she and Adam had first kissed in San Francisco.

It's like my life in dresses. She smiled sadly.

"Oh my God – this one is beautiful!"

It was an empire-line full-length lace gown. The delicate lace was champagne in colour but it was spun with a fine gold thread and it had tiny beads sewn on all over.

"I think I got that one in a vintage shop actually – it's very *Pride and Prejudice.* It would be fabulous on your dark colouring."

Zoe slipped into the dress and stood in front of the full-length mirror.

"It's perfect on you," Emma said.

Zoe held her hair up messily with her hand and twirled in front of the mirror. The delicate shoulders of the dress and the empire line made her feel so feminine.

"It is amazing, Em! Are you sure you don't mind me wearing it?"

"Of course not – sure, when am I going to wear it again?"

Zoe said nothing.

"So you really like him?" Emma asked.

"Well, it is still early days but yeah – I don't know what it is – wait until you see him, Em, he's the complete opposite of my usual type but, I don't know, every time I think about him

71

I feel all – all tingly and I get flutters in my tummy. I just get so excited!"

"Well, he's going to be blown away when he sees you in that dress."

"I hope to God you're right, Em!"

She took off the dress then and folded it up neatly so as not to crease it. Emma loaned her a pair of shoes and pearl earrings.

"You're a star!"

"Not at all – I'm just glad to see you happy."

"I'm sorry, Emma – I'm being really thoughtless, amn't I?" Zoe said seriously.

"On the contrary, it's great to see you smiling and happy – you deserve it."

"Are things any better with you and Adam?" Zoe asked carefully.

Emma shook her head.

"Oh, Emma!" Zoe hugged her tight while Emma did her best to try to keep back the tears that were springing into her eyes.

14

While the rest of their friends were still living the helter-skelter single life – getting pissed most nights of the week, stumbling out of sweaty night-clubs and spending the rest of their time hung over – Adam and Emma were busy playing grown-ups. Both held down proper jobs, rented an apartment in the city centre and saved whatever money wasn't used to pay bills for a deposit on a house.

The spare room in their apartment was stuffed full of bits of furniture and antiques that Emma had bought over the years, just waiting on her dream home to put them into. When they had finally saved up enough for the deposit they thought the hard part was over, but finding the right house for them proved more difficult than they had originally anticipated. Inevitably, there were none that were right for them. Any that they liked were either too expensive or miles away from anywhere, with no public transport. Then there were those that looked fine from the outside but once you set foot inside you could see the rising damp and floorboards crawling with woodworm and there were so many with teeny tiny gardens where two people couldn't fit together at the same time, let alone a deck-chair. But they weren't prepared to settle – this wasn't to be just a starter home for them – this would be the house that they would live in for the rest of their lives, so they had to get it right.

Just as they were starting to question themselves, wondering if they were being too picky and if they would ever find their elusive dream home, Zoe had mentioned that an old lady living near her mother on Cherry Tree Road had passed away recently and that the house was now up for sale. Emma knew the house she was talking about. She had always loved it. It was an old two-storey red-brick Victorian house with white sash windows. The front door was painted submarine yellow with a white wooden surround and a semi-circular overhead stained-glass pane. The garden at the front of the house had a small wrought-iron railing and during the summer months it was always blooming with hydrangeas, hyacinths and sweet peas so the scent lifted you up as you walked past. Emma's heart had somersaulted when she had heard it was for sale and she knew in her bones this house was for them. She had phoned the estate agent straight away to arrange a viewing for that evening.

As Adam and Emma had walked through the house with the estate agent, their excitement began to build. So far it had ticked all their boxes plus more. It still retained all the original features, like the shutters on the windows and the ceiling cornicing. Each bedroom still had its tiled fireplace. They could see it was in need of some modernisation but that would be just cosmetic. They had to hold their breath as the agent led them out into the south-facing back garden. It had a long rolling lawn, with a small greenhouse on one side and a fragrant herb garden on the other, and as they walked down the winding path they saw there were two old apple trees, rhubarb plants and a blackcurrant bush. They could see themselves living in this house and had to try hard to suppress their eagerness in front of the estate agent. The agent had told them that the deceased lady's son was looking for a quick sale as he didn't live in Ireland and had no intention of trying to manage the house from overseas so they had put an offer in on the spot and they were thrilled to hear that it was accepted that very same day. Once the legals had gone through and the paperwork was signed they had picked up the keys to their new home and had moved in a few weeks after.

They instantly set about stripping down the floral wallpapers and had repainted the whole house from top to bottom, splashing out a small fortune on Farrow & Ball paint. They pulled up the carpets to expose the original oak floorboards. Adam had sanded down the wood and varnished them himself and they scattered rugs across them to create warmth in the room. They replaced the dated velvet curtains in each room with modern damask fabrics. In the kitchen they kept the original Belfast sink and black-and-white chequered tiles. As they couldn't afford to replace the kitchen, they painted the cupboard doors in duck-egg blue to brighten the place up. Emma now had a home for all the bits and bobs she had built up over the years. She was delighted when a small cross-legged writing bureau that she had found in a salvage yard fitted neatly into the alcove in their dining room and they now had room in their bedroom for the polished mahogany chest of drawers that she had come across in a car-boot sale.

They were so proud of their home; all their hard work had made it all come together and now it had their stamp firmly on it. 59 Cherry Tree Road quickly became the focal point for all their friends; its central location meant they would usually all meet there first before heading into town or else would come home for a night-cap after a heavy night out. There was always someone coming and going; calling in for tea or dropping by on their way into town.

Unbeknownst to Emma, as well as saving up to buy a house, Adam had been putting a little bit of money aside each month to buy the perfect engagement ring for Emma. He had been scouting in jewellers' windows and had fallen in love with a vintage solitaire dating from the 1940s. The diamond was held in place with four small clasps and was set onto a delicate white-gold band. It was breathtakingly stunning and when the stone caught the light, its clarity allowed it to shine straight through. On being told how much it was he nearly died on the spot, but after he had left the shop he couldn't stop thinking about it. The ring epitomised Emma, it was elegant and timeless, a perfect match for the woman he loved. So every week he checked back in the window praying it wasn't sold until eventually he had saved up enough for it. Coming out of the jewellers that day he couldn't keep the grin from his face. He had been so careful walking down the street, keeping his hand over the box inside his jacket pocket. His excitement was written all over his face and he was petrified that Emma would guess what was up.

He had also bought a fancy wicker picnic basket, with a red-and-white check cloth lining, in an overpriced lifestyle store. It had an inbuilt cooler bucket, proper cutlery and champagne glasses. He had stocked it with Emma's favourite foods – a salad with olives and goats' cheese, a smoked salmon and ricotta quiche – and he had also brought chilled champagne and strawberries.

They had set off for the Wicklow countryside early the next morning. They often went walking there so nothing seemed out of the ordinary to Emma. They had trampled through the long meadow grass, speckled red in places with wild poppies, walking for ages until there was no one around them. Eventually they came to the edge of the field, where the land sloped gently down towards the water's edge. They had sat up against a knobbly oak tree and Adam served up the picnic.

Emma was so impressed with the picnic basket that she hadn't noticed that he had been too nervous to eat anything. His heart had been pounding manically against his ribcage; he couldn't ever remember being this nervous before. He had swallowed hard and asked Emma Fitzpatrick to be his wife, listening to his shaky voice as if it was coming from someone else entirely. He had watched her stunned face, as her mind caught up with what was happening, change into an expression of pure joy. He opened back the lid on the small, black jeweller's box which contained the vintage solitaire and when he saw it again glistening in the sunlight, he knew he had made the right choice. With trembling hands, he had slid the ring onto the fourth finger of her left hand.

"Yes, of course. Yes. Yes. *Yes, of course I will marry you!*" she had screamed at him before throwing her arms around his neck.

He would never forget that moment as he had thought he might burst with happiness. They had sipped their champagne and admired the ring on Emma's slender finger. They laughed and cried and hugged and then cried some more.

They had wasted no time in setting a date. Emma had always dreamed of a Christmas wedding and although it was only six months away they managed to find an old manor house in County Kildare that was available. They had kept it small and intimate – she didn't want a large wedding, so it was just their family and close friends.

The night before the wedding, Adam found himself at home alone. Emma had followed tradition and had stayed in her parents' house, sleeping in her childhood bedroom. Adam had missed her in that short space of time; the house felt empty without her and the bed was cold on her side. He hated being away from her and, even if it was only for one night, he couldn't wait to see her again. After only a few hours apart, he already felt like he had so much to tell her.

He had stood nervously at the altar, shifting from foot to foot, zoning out on the conversation that his groomsmen were having. He barely registered the flowers decorating the pew ends or the organist warming up with Bach's 'Jesu, Joy of Man's Desiring' in the background. He shook hands with and greeted their guests as they came in and took their seats but his mind was elsewhere. Then he had heard the organist begin to play Pachelbel's 'Canon in D', which was the piece that they had chosen as their processional, as a hush fell on the congregation. When he had turned around and seen her standing at the back of the church linking her father, framed by the parted doors, looking serene and more beautiful than he had ever seen, he had lit up with happiness and pride. Her tall slender frame was enhanced by the delicate lace of the dress. He had felt so alive, so in love, so physically brimming with joy that it felt as though it was bubbling up inside of him and spilling out over their guests in the church. He watched in awe as she walked gracefully towards him with careful strides. They shared a smile and he had felt his eyes prick with tears.

When her father had handed her over to him, he had squeezed her hand tight to assure her that they would have a wonderful life together. He could almost feel her touch now. As the priest had pronounced them man and wife, the feeling of goodwill radiating from their guests standing in the pews was almost palpable.

Later in the day they had both sneaked hand in hand up to the bridal suite, just to take a few minutes out for each other from the madness going on downstairs in the reception. Sitting under the canopy of the chintz drapes on their four-poster bed, they couldn't help talking over each other in excited bursts about how fantastic their day had been so far. He could remember looking into her eyes, deep into their depths and she had gazed right back at him with that same intensity. This was to be the start of the rest of their lives. They hadn't needed to say anything; they just sat like that for a moment, taking it all in. It had probably lasted only for a few seconds but it had felt timeless, it would always stay with him. That feeling of pure joy – yes, they had once been happy.

15

Friday couldn't come fast enough for Zoe. She'd had Emma's dress hanging on the outside of her wardrobe all week and every time she looked at it she got butterflies in her tummy. When the day finally dawned, she was excited about seeing Steve again but nervous too. She just wished she could relax and enjoy it but instead she was obsessing over every detail. Hair up or down? She had finally decided on up. Should she wear a necklace or just leave her neckline bare? In the end she chose to wear a simple silver chain that trailed downward to form a knot just below her collarbone. Would he make sure to introduce her to everyone? What if he left her standing on her own all night?

She got dressed in the lace gown she had borrowed from Emma. When she put it on it made her feel fantastic once again. The bodice of her dress fitted perfectly over her breasts before it gently fell away, skimming over the areas she didn't want attention drawn to. Not trusting the hairdresser not to do something overly fussy, she had done her own hair by twisting it into two rolls on each side of her head using Kirby grips to pin it all into place at the back. When she looked at herself in front of the mirror, she felt good. She just prayed Steve would like it.

Bang on eight o'clock she heard her buzzer go. She hurried out and opened back the door to see Steve standing there dressed in a tuxedo with a tall bunch of gladioli in his arms.

"Hi, there!" He smiled and handed her the flowers. "You look stunning, really beautiful." He stood back, admiring her.

"Why, thank you! You're not looking too bad yourself!"

His tall stature suited a tux, his broad chest filling the jacket handsomely. He was cleanly shaven and his usually messy hair had been brushed back. His eyes twinkled and she had to do everything in her power not to jump on him there and then.

"Are you sure I look okay – I always feel a bit funny in these things?" He started tugging at the neck of his shirt. "I think after the years of wearing a suit in the bank I have a phobia of the things now."

"Well, I must say it suits you. You look very handsome."

* * *

As they walked into the room, Steve nodded and greeted people he knew standing at the bar. He was proud to have Zoe on his arm. He knew some of the people were looking at her as they tried to work out who she was. He led her over towards a group of men and women. Zoe saw a waiter go past with a tray of champagne – she grabbed two glasses and handed one to Steve before taking a long sip from hers. She barely knew him and here she was about to meet his friends.

"Well, you're a dark horse, Steve – are you not going to introduce us?"

"Barry – this is Zoe. Zoe, these are some of the other stand-holders at the market." He named each person as she shook hands with them one by one.

"So, Zoe, how long have you two been going out together?" a lady he had introduced to her as Yvonne enquired.

They both squirmed awkwardly and she could see Steve's cheeks go red.

"We're not . . . well . . ." he looked at Zoe, "not yet anyway."

"Oooooh!" one of the other women said.

"I mean, we haven't known each other very long."

"I see. Well, how did you meet?" She continued her line of interrogation even though she could see they were both wriggling in front of her.

Zoe jumped in to save Steve who was going redder by the second. "It's a long story."

He flashed her a grateful smile.

Finally they were saved by the gong calling everyone to take their places for dinner.

"Phew!" Steve sighed as they took their seats, which were thankfully on a different table to the group that they had just walked away from. "Sorry about that – Yvonne is forever trying to set me up with her friends. And she's so nosy – she just keeps digging until she finds out all the details."

"I can see that!"

Knowing that they would be serving the most discerning of customers, the hotel had prepared a wonderful banquet featuring the best of Irish produce including crab-cakes, duck and turbot, finishing with a dessert of pear-and-almond tartlets. Zoe was grateful that her dress was an empire line and would hide her stomach, which had grown after all the rich food that she had eaten.

After the plates had been cleared away it was time for the annual award ceremony. Zoe was surprised to see Steve had been nominated in two categories – one for 'Best Cheese Producer' and the other for the 'Best Artisan Producer'. He blushed when she asked him why he hadn't said anything about it.

"Ah, you know yourself – these things don't really mean anything. It's just hours of boring speeches and clapping hands on cue while some fella in a fancy suit presents a bit of crystal."

"Stop being so modest!" Zoe chided as she rubbed his arm affectionately.

Although he didn't win the 'Best Artisan Producer' award, he did receive a runner-up prize for his oak-smoked cheese. Zoe clapped enthusiastically as he went up on stage to receive it.

"I'm very proud of you," Zoe whispered when he returned to his seat and although she knew he was embarrassed, she could tell he was delighted at having won.

Once all the awards were given out, the tables were cleared away to make a dance floor and the band started.

"Here, let's dance," Steve said, and he led Zoe onto the dance-floor.

As he took her in his arms, Zoe was surprised to find Steve was a good dancer. He twirled her around the floor to sounds of the old Rat Pack, moving with ease and confidence.

"I wouldn't have had you down as a good dancer!" Zoe whispered in his ear.

"I'm full of surprises, me!"

After a while, breathless from all the dancing, they sat down for a bit.

He leaned in towards her. "Here – why don't we get out of here? It's stuffy anyway. I hate all this pretentiousness."

"Do you not want to stay till the end?"

"Nah – we'd only be attacked by Barry and Yvonne again anyway."

He led her by the hand as they left the room and stood outside in the evening air.

"That's better," he said, loosening his bow-tie. "Here, you look perished – put this around you." He placed his big jacket around her shoulders.

They were alone. The full moon cast silvery shadows across the lawn.

"Zoe, I just want to say thank you for coming tonight. I really enjoyed it."

"I'm glad I came too."

"I feel like I should do something romantic like you see in the films."

"Like what?"

"I don't know – point out the stars or something."

Zoe giggled and he took her in his arms. He leant in so that she could smell the champagne off his breath and began to kiss her slowly. She had been wondering how long more she would have to wait but now that the moment had arrived she savoured it. His lips felt so good against hers, like they had known each other for years. As they kissed deeply, she knew where he would be staying tonight.

16

Adam strolled down Grafton Street towards the pub where he had arranged to meet his brother Rob. After a long day in work, he wasn't in the mood for another evening in the house on his own, with only his feelings for company and too much time to think. Thinking wasn't good. So he had emailed Rob at work and they had arranged to go for a pint.

It was the time of the day where the street underwent its transformation for the night. He walked past shop fronts pulling down their shutters, flower sellers tidying up their stalls, while bars and restaurants set their tables and put out their chalk-written menu-boards, readying themselves for the evening trade. Crowds of shoppers gathered around a tinfoil-clad street artist pretending to be a statue. His audience took up the width of the street, forcing people to walk around. Adam kept on walking, weaving left and right through the hordes of people coming at him like shoals of fish.

Rounding a corner, he walked down Castle Street. Its narrow paths were crowded with gangs of smokers standing outside so he turned onto a quieter cobble-locked side-street where crowds were sitting along the outdoor terraces under café-bar awnings, friends laughing and joking.

He caught sight of a man standing under a shop front wearing heavy-set frames with a huge bouquet of blush roses in his hands. He was checking his watch and his eyes darted around the street. The woman he had obviously been waiting for came up moments later, surprising him from behind by putting her slender arms around his waist. He watched as he swung her around to face him. As they embraced and smiled fondly at one another, they were unaware of the man standing watching them only a short distance away. It was the look in their eyes that did it. It caught him off-guard like a blow in the pit of his stomach. Emma used to look at him like that. They used to do this. That couple used to be them. He stared over at them, happy in each other's arms, chatting animatedly, oblivious to the street life going on around them. They were the centre of each other's world. 'I used to have that too!' he wanted to shout over to them out of sheer petulant rage. '*That used to be me!*' He watched them walk off then, the man's arm draped lazily around his lover's shoulders.

* * *

They used to meet in town every Friday evening after work; it was something they had always done. Friday was their night. The streets were always alive with suits filtering out of offices, relieved to be escaping work for the weekend. You could almost feel the infectious excitement in the air. A stressed Emma would hurry out of A1 Adverts flustered and apologising for being late. She would complain that A1 was sucking the life out of her and how Maureen had landed her with something that was so urgent that it had to be done '*now*' just as she was about to leave the office for the weekend. But no matter how bad her humour was, she would always light up as soon as she saw him. He knew how to make her smile and lift her out of any mood.

They would have a table reserved, usually in a new restaurant that they had read about in the Sunday papers and they had been dying to try. They would start by ordering a bottle of red wine, instantly helping them both unwind from the pressures of their work. The heavy clunking sound it made as it poured out of the bottle was the sound that said the weekend was here. They would take their time poring over the menu, trying to guess what the other was going to order.

After dinner they would normally stroll hand in hand up to their local, Brown's on the canal, to meet the rest of the gang: a mixture of his and her friends. There was always someone there. In winter they would try to get the seats closest to the turf fire and in summer they would sit outside on a wooden picnic bench overlooking the lock gate until it began to get chilly and they would move back inside. More often than not, whoever was left at the end of the night would pile into a taxi and head back to theirs in Rathmines for another bottle of wine.

The next day neither would have the energy or the inclination to move very far and it would be spent hung over, snuggling on their sofa, eating crisps and chocolate, watching old films like *Breakfast at Tiffany's* or *Chitty Chitty Bang Bang* which they knew off by heart. They were always happiest when they were in each other's company. That was their routine, as comfy as old slippers, but that was them.

*　*　*

Adam made his way towards the back of the dimly lit pub, which was quiet enough that evening, but then again the good weather meant most people chose to sit outside. They found a quiet alcove and Rob ordered pints for them both. They sat in and sipped the creamy heads on their pints.

"So how are you? How're things in work?" Adam asked.

"Good, y'know, busy so can't complain. How about you?"

"Yeah, same old, it's grand."

"And how's Emma?" Rob knew when his younger brother rang him to go for a pint it was usually because he needed to talk.

"Good." He paused. *It's fucking shit.* "Well, as good as can be expected, I suppose." He took a slow sip of his pint and placed the glass back on the table.

"Yeah?" Rob said.

The silence sat heavy in the air between them.

"I don't know if we're going to get through it, Rob," Adam blurted out.

"Hang on – what are you saying things like that for?"

"I'm serious, Rob. I don't know if we've much of a future left together. She stays holed up in her room whenever I'm in the house. She won't speak to me. It's as if she can't bear to be around me."

Rob was taken aback by his brother's admission; he'd had no idea things were so bad. "Jesus, I had no idea!" He took a swift intake of breath before adding, "Jesus, sorry, bro'. I didn't know it was that bad."

"Sure, you weren't to know."

"Has it been like that since you came home?"

"Uh-huh." Adam nodded his head.

"Fuck. Look, I don't want to say some shit like 'give it time' or 'time is a great healer', but I, well . . . I don't know what to say. Sorry."

"I'm trying, I really am, but she doesn't seem ready to move on and I know this is awful but . . ."

"But what?"

"I'm starting to lose patience." He lowered his voice, shamed by his own admission.

"Look, I don't know what to say," said Rob. "I hate all this shit, y'know I do, but you and Emma, well, you've been through a lot . . . so give it time, yeah? You can't just expect her to forget what happened, Adam." Rob whistled softly. "Whoooah there – Jesus, listen to me, I sound like Jeremy Fucking Kyle!"

"I know, I know, you're right. It's just I don't even know if that's what she wants any more."

"Jesus, I don't know – just talk to her or something."

"Yeah, you're probably right – I think we need to have it out."

"Look, I'm sorry, I'm crap at all this."

"Yeah, I know you are!" Adam laughed at his brother who was shifting uncomfortably in his seat.

"Fuck off, you!"

The conversation changed to the steadier ground of Leinster's chances of winning the Heineken cup and eventually, after midnight, Adam called it a night and went home.

17

Adam woke abruptly and bolted upright in his bed. His mouth was dry. Panicking, he tried to take in great gasps of air against the will of his constricted throat. He started to cough and splutter as the air made its way deep into his lungs. Lying there, at last still, he kept on breathing.

He was covered in sweat and his heart was rattling wildly against his ribcage. It was always the same dream.

He put a hand down to feel the sheets underneath him. They were damp and cool to the touch against his flushed skin. In the darkness he automatically felt blindly over to the other side of the bed but then he remembered. He turned back and looked at the clock sitting on his locker: its illuminated red LED display told him it was only 5.44 a.m. He groaned; his alarm wasn't due to go off for at least another two hours. Knowing that he wouldn't be able to go back to sleep now, he threw his legs over the side of the bed and got up instead.

Switching on the side-lamp, he took his dressing gown from its home, hanging on the bedpost, and wrapped it around himself tightly, swathing his body against the early-morning coolness of the house. He looked at the damp imprint that he had left on the sheets. He pulled them off the bed to leave the bare mattress exposed and bundled the pile into the laundry basket in the en-suite. The bathroom tiles were a welcome coolness against his feet. Tugging on the cord on the shaving light above the bathroom mirror, he lit the bathroom in an eerie glow. He was almost frightened by the pallor of the man staring back at him: the lines were deeper, the circles blacker than ever before. He pulled the cord down, cloaking the bathroom in darkness once again.

Tiptoeing out onto the corridor, he glanced at the door behind which she lay sleeping. Or maybe she wasn't sleeping, he thought. He stood briefly in front of it, before continuing past.

He crept downstairs and went into the kitchen. He flicked the switch on the kettle and waited for it to boil. It seemed unnaturally loud against the stillness of the house. He made himself a cup of instant coffee with two sugars and no milk and some toast. Sitting down at the table, he flicked through the sports section of yesterday's broadsheet to pass time.

A while later, he rubbed his head and looked at the clock on the wall: it was just after seven. He supposed he might as well go into work early. At least then he would be gone before she woke. He would be doing her a favour, he thought to himself, by saving her the hassle of avoiding him for once.

As he left the house, the sun was starting to rise, filling the sky with its awesome red glow. The grass was bent double under the weight of its dewy cover. He cycled along the canal bank, its body of water still save for the odd ripple from life carrying on underneath its surface. His head was spinning with fragments of his dream. Fragments were all he was ever left with when the night was over. Fragments of frost-covered trees, a watery sunlight, his car, his hand on the grey leather of his steering wheel. It was always the same, it wouldn't leave him.

They needed to talk. He couldn't do this any more, live in this void of despair, it was smothering him whole. Things had gone on like this for too long now and there was an ocean between them. One of them had to do something. He decided he would cook her dinner that night and then he would broach it with her. His stomach was somersaulting even just thinking about it.

* * *

That evening Adam set the table with the Newbridge canteen that they had received from his Great-Auntie May as a wedding gift. If the truth were told they had never so much as taken it out of its polished wooden case before now – it was far too formal for the pair of them but he felt he wanted to make a special effort for tonight. He was following a recipe for slow-braised beef and he studied each line thoroughly in case he missed a bit. He was measuring the ingredients precisely because he wasn't confident enough to throw a cup in here and a spoon in there *ad lib* – if it said fifty grams then fifty grams it was, no more or no less. He had bought a big sticky pecan-nut tart in an artisan bakery that had set him back more than the beef and ingredients for the starter and mains combined, but it was Emma's favourite dessert and he wanted everything to be just right. He knew it was cringey but he just wanted her to remember what they had once been like and, if she could remember that feeling, well then, maybe there was a glimmer that they could save their marriage.

He set the table with the runner and place mats, the way they did it whenever they had people over for dinner. He had a bottle of Sancerre chilling in the fridge and a Montepulciano on the worktop in case she would prefer red. The starter he had prepared was a Caesar salad with no Parmesan or anchovies, because that was how Emma preferred it. Now all he had to do was get changed and wait. He had emailed her at work a few hours ago to ask her to come home early that night but she hadn't even bothered to reply, let alone ask why. But he still held out hope that she would come soon. He had been thinking about it all day, playing over and over in his head how he hoped the conversation would go.

By half past eight there was still no sign of her. The beef was well braised at that stage so he lowered the temperature of the oven and waited. Quarter of an hour later he checked on the beef again which was now way overdone. Frustrated, he turned it off and just let the dish sit there.

At a quarter past nine he opened the bottle of wine in the fridge and poured himself a large glass. Eventually just after half nine, he heard her key in the lock and started.

"Hi, Emma!" He swung his head around the door into the hall.

"Hi." She was purposely monosyllabic.

"You're working late?"

"Yeah."

That was as much as she was offering by way of an explanation.

"Come in, I've made dinner."

"Well, I'm not that hungry."

"Oh right – well, sure the beef is probably inedible at this stage anyway." He laughed nervously, alone.

She followed him into their kitchen, her cool eyes taking in the set table. There was the unmistakable smell of burnt meat. He hurriedly poured her a glass of wine in case she decided to go back upstairs. He needed to keep her here.

He cut her a slice of the tart and put it in front of her.

"I said I wasn't hungry." Her tone was terse.

"Sorry, it's just it's your favourite, that's all, I thought you might like . . ." He trailed off. She wasn't even listening.

"Emma – we need to talk," he blurted out.

Emma looked down at her fingers wrapped around her

glass and felt them tighten automatically. "I already told you, I don't want to talk about it," she said coolly.

"Emma, please just hear me out. Can you just sit down for a minute?"

Amazingly, she did as she was asked and took a seat on one of the high stools at their breakfast bar. He knew he had only a short period of time to say what he wanted to say so he came straight out with it.

"We can't keep on living like this, Emma."

"Like what?"

"Emma, please, I'm begging you, don't make it any harder for me than it already is. I'm just asking to talk to you."

"I've told you before I don't want to fucking talk about it!"

"Look, I'm worried about you. Maybe you need to see someone?"

"Like who?"

"A counsellor or a doctor – I don't know – maybe just someone to talk things through with."

"Oh and talking is really going to fix things, is it? Now why didn't I think of that?"

"Emma, please – there is no need for sarcasm. I'm trying to help you here."

"Well, don't bother!" She practically spat the words at him.

"Emma, we're going to have to talk about things sooner or later – it's sitting between us like a gulf. We can't just keep ignoring it."

"*Ignoring* it? Who's *ignoring* it?" She was shouting now. "If anyone is *ignoring* anything, it's you! Should I just be like you and forget everything that has happened and get on with my life – go back to work straight away, go out drinking every night and think everything will be the same as it was before? Is that what I should do?" She was roaring bitterly at him, her voice full of contempt.

Adam felt as though her words had pierced through his skin and into his chest.

"I haven't forgotten," he said.

"Really? Well, you're doing a pretty damn good job of pretending that everything is normal!" She practically said the words as if they were on fire in her mouth. They fell out on top of one another, landing like hot coals on Adam.

"Emma, it's been over a year now."

"Oh and after a year I'm meant to be feeling okay again, am I? Is that the magic number?"

"I didn't say that." He lowered his voice. "I just thought . . ." He trailed off. "Emma – it's hard, it's a bloody nightmare, but sooner or later you're going to have to realise that life goes on. Whether you like it or not there will come a time when you have to move on."

Emma was stunned as she tried to process the words that Adam had just uttered. They hit her with an almost physical force. She felt winded, as if Adam had just put his mouth over hers and sucked every last breath of life from her lungs or punched her in the chest so hard that she couldn't breathe. Had he really just said what she thought he did? She looked at him in disbelief and Adam knew instantly that he had said the wrong thing. He could see the anger infused with hurt washing over her face, working its way down from her forehead to her mouth, like a venetian blind being shut. *Fuck*. But it was too late, he couldn't take it back.

"Well, I don't *want* to move on, Adam!" she screamed. Her face was red, her eyes wide. Her face was consumed with hatred and anger and it was all directed at him. "How dare you!" Her voice was shrill but trembling, the pitch of her voice rising rapidly. "I cannot believe you just said that!"

Never in all their years together had he ever seen her react like this. Never. *Oh, Sweet Jesus*. Her face was contorted in such rage that he didn't dare answer.

"Time to move on? Do you think I am supposed to just forget everything?"

"No . . . I . . . Oh God, Emma, I'm sorry. That wasn't what I said . . ." Adam buried his head in his hands.

She grabbed her bag off the worktop and ran out to her car. Somewhere on the periphery she could hear Adam calling after her but she wasn't looking back. She jabbed her keys into the ignition and somehow managed to start the car.

She drove on autopilot for a few moments until she felt her mouth water and a rush of nausea forced its way up her throat. She pulled the car over to the side of the road and brought it to a sudden halt, causing another car to swerve out of the way to avoid her. She could feel the sick making its way up her throat. She swung the car door open and leant over, retching onto the road below her. No sooner had she sat back in the seat than she could feel her mouth fill with saliva again. *Oh Jesus.* Emma watched as vomit was projected from her mouth onto the road again.

She sat back into her seat and waited for her body to cool down. She wiped the beads of sweat off her forehead and searched inside her tote for a tissue to clean the spittle from her mouth. She looked at the ground beneath her which was splattered with the liquid that she had spewed up. She closed the car door again and breathed in deeply in an effort to calm her body.

* * *

Emma drove aimlessly around south County Dublin for hours. She had gone through roundabouts, traffic lights and driven down roads she didn't know until she eventually found herself in Dun Laoghaire. She got out and walked the length of the pier and wondered what would happen if she just kept walking until she fell off the end of it. It was tempting to think that with just a few short steps she could be free from all of this. It could all be over. But she knew in her heart and soul that she would never have the balls to do it. She watched a passenger ferry set off majestically on its voyage overseas before she turned around and walked back to her car and sat inside it in the darkness thinking through it all. She was reeling; she couldn't believe Adam could be so callous and have such a lack of awareness of her feelings. After all they'd been through together, she had thought that he knew her better than that. Her chest ached and she was almost certain it was physical; it felt as though her ribcage had been crushed inwards and she found it difficult to draw breath. The ever-present questions kept looping inside her head: *Why, oh why? Why them? How had this happened? It was too cruel.* The injustice goaded her. She felt the warm tears flowing uncontrollably down her face until she could taste the salt in her mouth.

18

Adam sat on his own at the kitchen table. All he could do was sit in stunned silence and let the thoughts and the fear play over and over in his head. He was utterly deflated, all his hopes of having a heart to heart had been quashed before he had even got started. *How have we ended up like this?* He was racking his head for something. Anything. He needed something to cling onto that would make everything okay. He was at the end of his tether. His wife didn't want to be around him, couldn't bear to be around him, as if she resented his very presence in her life. She had effectively shut down on him. He wasn't sure where they went from here. He wasn't religious but he even found himself asking God for an answer. He needed bloody divine inspiration because he didn't know what else to do or what more he could do. He had apologised to her over and over, he had tried to talk it through with her, tried to put himself in her shoes. But it wasn't easy for him either. He couldn't undo what had happened, there was no 'undo' button in life. They either moved on or . . . well . . . he wasn't sure what they would do.

Her words had cut deep; his way of dealing with things was to keep busy, bury his head in work, watch TV, go for a run, meet people – anything at all to take his mind off what had happened – but it didn't mean he had forgotten! He knew he had effectively shut down that part of his brain because it hurt too much but there wasn't a day that went by that he didn't think about what had happened, no matter how often he wished to forget. He was angry now and thinking of all the things he wished he had said. It wasn't easy for him either. It wasn't his fucking fault! Why did she blame him? It was all swirling around in his head. He felt as though he was competing against an egg-timer and his side of the sand was running out rapidly.

The reality of how desperate things were between them had begun to hit home and it both frightened and angered him. He felt like he was banging his head off a brick wall. Emma was his *wife*, they were best friends, he should be able to talk to her. Did she really think she was the only one hurting? He had a right to be upset too – didn't his feelings count? Well, fuck that, there was only so much grovelling he could do. He grabbed his jacket off the coat stand in the hallway. He was going out and he was going to get slaughtered.

He walked to the top of the road and flagged a passing cab. As he sat back in the taxi, he was already starting to feel more relaxed, now that he was out of their house.

When he arrived into the pub, the usual crew was there. He nodded at them all before heading straight to the bar. He needed something stronger than his usual beer so he ordered a double Jameson and Coke. He inhaled the vapour of the whiskey while still standing at the bar, before taking a long sip, allowing it to flow straight back, feeling it burn its way down his throat. He instantly felt warmer, *happier*, as he made his way back to the gang.

They were all well on, having been there since after work

and he was playing catch-up. He had finished the Jameson five minutes later and went back up and ordered the same again plus a round of Mickey Finn's for everyone. A cheer rose up when they saw him returning with the tray of shots. It was a cue to play their usual game where the last person to knock back the shot had to buy another round of shots for everyone. As this game had no discernible end-point everyone ended up in a right state but that was exactly how Adam wanted to feel. He wanted to get shit-faced and forget his own name, where he lived, what had happened, and mostly he wanted to forget that he was married.

* * *

Two hours later and Adam was in a worse state than any of them. He was feeling buoyed up and merry when he went for a wander around the pub. He saw some of the lads were huddled in together talking about something before they all threw their heads back at the same time, exploding in laughter. That was where the *craic* was at.

He made his way over and listened to his mate Tim recount how he had been chatting up an air-hostess on a flight from London recently. As they descended into Dublin, he had asked her what her plans were for later.

"So she was there writing down her number, chatting away, and she goes to open the door and the next thing there's a fucking humongous yellow slide blowing itself up right outside the door! She had forgotten to cross-check the door! So she roars '*Oh fuck*!' and you should have seen the looks on the faces of the other passengers! So as soon as they deflated the bloody slide, we all had to stay in our seats until airport security came on board and she was escorted off the flight. And that was the last I saw of her!"

They tilted their heads back and roared with laughter again.

He tried to keep up with the conversations going on around

him but he found he wasn't able to hear as well as he normally would. It was as if he was listening to everyone at the end of a long tube. He couldn't talk and found it hard to follow what people were saying so he just stood there smiling to himself at Tim's story. He needed to use the bathroom. He squinted his eyes and scanned the bar and eventually he saw a green neon sign down the back of the pub. It was like a beacon. He stumbled from side to side as he made his way down towards the back of the packed pub. "Shorry, mate!" He was aware that people were looking at him and clearing out of his way, in case he should fall on top of them. "I's okay!" He tried to tell them but the words wouldn't come out properly. "Shorry, there!" He tried to straighten up but his body wouldn't listen to his brain's commands – he was too far gone at that stage.

Once inside the single cubicle, it was a relief to have some quiet from the noise outside. He sat on the toilet bowl for an age as his head spun round and round and sloshed from side to side like he was sitting in the middle of a tippy boat. He tried to steady himself but he needed to close his eyes for a minute.

Sometime later there was a loud rapping on the toilet door. He opened his eyes to see he was still sitting on the toilet bowl, trousers gathered around his ankles. How long had he been here? He must have fallen asleep.

He held onto the toilet-roll holder to get his balance as he hauled himself off the toilet seat, then using one hand he bent down to pull up his trousers. He did up his fly and buckled his belt and, sliding the flimsy brass latch across, he went outside. He scanned the blurry queue of angry male faces. *"Shhorry. Fell shleep,"* he mumbled to the waiting crowd by way of explanation. He stumbled back into the bar, bumping and apologising his way down to the lads.

Zoe and Steve came out of Figaro restaurant hand in hand. They'd had a delicious meal and were both stuffed. She had been dying to try out Figaro's menu since she had read a review about it in a magazine a few months back, so when Steve suggested they should go there, she was delighted. The menu had certainly lived up to the review – there was an eclectic mix of dishes, including ostrich meat and shark as well as more local favourites like organic Wicklow lamb. Steve was far more adventurous in his tastes than she was and he had ordered the wild boar, while she went for the safer option of Wagyu beef.

Since the ball, things had been going well between the couple. They saw each other most evenings, when Steve would call in on his way home from whichever market he had been at earlier that day. He always brought Dave with him and Zoe had bought a little wicker basket for him to sleep in, for whenever he stayed over at her place. She had also made him a cushion for inside it from a remnant of some blue gingham fabric they had been using at work. She had stuffed the fabric with some foam before sewing it up. But Dave had chewed up the cushion within hours of Zoe giving it to him, shredding stuffing all over her apartment. So, lesson learned, Zoe now lined the basket with a towel.

"Fancy one more?" Steve asked, draping his arm lazily around her shoulders as they strolled along. They had shared a bottle of red wine with their meal and he fancied another one before they went home.

"Sure!" Zoe said. "There's a lovely pub which I go to sometimes, it's really cosy and it's only a short walk up the canal. How about there?"

"Sounds good to me."

They chatted easily as they walked along. There was a bitter wind blowing and Steve pulled Zoe in tighter against him. Their height difference meant Zoe's head fitted snugly under his arm.

As they approached the pub, they could see a man stumble as he made his way out the door. They both watched the guy, who was as drunk as a lord, but as they got closer Zoe exclaimed, "Is that Adam?"

"Who's Adam?"

"My best friend Emma's husband!"

"Oh yes, of course," Steve mumbled, abashed. She had told him all about Emma and Adam.

"Adam?" Zoe said at they reached the guy who was finding it hard to walk straight.

"Huh?" he said, looking up and taking a while to register who had been calling him.

"Are you okay, Adam – you're looking a bit the worse for wear?" Zoe asked, her voice full of concern.

"S'hure, Zoe, I'm grand." He tried to speak clearly but he was finding it difficult. "Jusht heading home now."

"Right," Zoe said doubtfully, as she and Steve watched Adam stumble away.

"Jesus, that fella will go into the canal if he's not careful. I'll flag a taxi for him," Steve said.

"Good idea," Zoe said gratefully.

Zoe tried talking to an incoherent Adam while Steve kept an eye on the passing traffic. Taxi after taxi went by them with their roof lights off until finally Steve saw a yellow light in the distance. He stuck out his arm and waved at the driver who pulled up at the path beside them.

"Can you give this friend of ours a lift?" Steve asked, smiling at the driver.

The driver looked hesitant about letting Adam into his car when he saw the state that he was in.

"Don't worry, I'll pay for it," Steve said, taking out a twenty-euro note from his pocket and handing it to the driver.

"Well, he'd better not get sick in my car," he said grumpily. "I'm fed up of cleaning the cab after drunken passengers vomit on the seats."

"Not at all, he hasn't had that much to drink," Steve lied even though they all knew Adam was plastered.

"Where am I taking him?"

Steve looked to Zoe.

"Sorry, yeah – it's 59 Cherry Tree Road, Rathmines."

They helped Steve into the back of the car and watched the taxi as it pulled away.

"He'll have some head on him tomorrow!" Steve said, trying to sound light-hearted. He knew Zoe was disturbed about her friend.

"He sure will," Zoe replied distractedly. She was deeply worried. She had never seen Adam so drunk in all the years she had known him. Sure, he enjoyed a few drinks like anybody, but he never normally went overboard like he had obviously done tonight. She knew things were hard for him too and he was going through a lot but she had already tried talking to Emma about it and she hadn't got anywhere. They went into the pub, Zoe vowing to talk to Emma about it again.

19

The next morning Adam was woken by his screeching alarm clock. He didn't dare open his eyes – instead he felt blindly over to his locker to shut the blasted thing up. He drifted off to sleep again and later woke with his heart hammering. He looked at the clock. The red display told him it was 9.03 a.m. *Shit, I'm late.*

He was dying. His head was thumping and his throat was dry. He reached over to his locker for the pint of water that thankfully he had somehow remembered to bring up with him. He gulped it back, leaving only a dribble to run back down the side of the glass. He looked down at himself: he was still in his jeans and T-shirt from last night. *Look at yourself! You're a disgrace.* He lay back and kept still, not daring to move as every part of his aching body screamed in punishment at the amount of alcohol he had consumed the night before, physically telling him he had overstepped the mark.

He forced himself to get out of bed and stand up. But his head was spinning so he sat back down again for a few minutes to steady himself before making his way into the shower. As he stood under the water, every nerve-ending in his body was on a go-slow, his skin almost numb as the droplets danced along his body. When he got out of the shower he felt feverish and thought he might get sick so he opened the window and lay back on the bed until his stomach settled.

He got up at last and dressed slowly and torturously. He walked past Emma's bedroom door and didn't bother to check if she had come home last night. He'd had enough of the anger and hatred she had for him so he kept on walking.

He cycled into work along the well-worn tow-path, forcing himself to breathe the fresh air deep into his lungs to sober up. Although he was feeling like death, it was almost a relief to be going to work; the routine of his job was a welcome escape from his home life. He was respected; people cared what he thought and valued his opinion. They didn't use every excuse to keep away from him or deliberately avoid him. Nobody treated him like he was invisible there.

He sat at his desk in Parker & Associates, just staring at his screen. Being hung over didn't help, but no matter how many times he tried to give himself a shake or reprimanded himself for not concentrating, he still couldn't get what had happened with Emma last night out of his head. He had been in denial for too long now and last night it had really hit home just how bad things were between them. There was nothing left there any more and he didn't know how to get it back. Or even if they would get it back. He felt panicked now; everything was dangerously off track, spiralling out of his control.

* * *

Emma lay still, wondering what time it was. Light was showing around the narrow gaps of the window shutters and was the only wash of light able to enter the room. She lay there with the duvet pulled right up underneath her chin. She stared up at the ceiling; she knew every inch of it, every paint splodge that shouldn't have been there, the cracks in the cornicing and the wispy cobwebs that were getting bigger in the corner. She was too upset to go in to work that day but her mind wouldn't allow her to sleep, as it ran over last night's events; it was running and racing and competing with itself in its thoughts. It chased thoughts like a dog chased its tail.

Earlier that morning she had lain there as Adam's alarm repeatedly went off but he had continued to sleep through. It had enraged her how he was able to sleep through that high-pitched beeping. She'd heard him stumbling in sometime after one as she lay in bed. He'd plodded up the stairs and then had gone quiet and she'd thought that he had finally gone to bed, only for him to resurrect moments later as he staggered along the landing.

Eventually, after the alarm had been blaring on and off for ages, she'd heard him moving around the house: getting out of bed, showering, dressing, plodding downstairs, banging around in the kitchen, before finally banging the front door closed. Even just hearing him moving about was enough to make her body go rigid with tension; everything he did, every move he made, every footstep, every cupboard door banging, made her angry. How could he have said those words last night, how could he tell her it was time to move on? How did he not feel like she did, the hurt, the anger, the injustice all rolled into a sickly ball?

Sometimes, when she looked at Adam now, it was like looking at a stranger. How could he just get on with life like nothing had ever happened? How could he do that – just pretend that everything was normal? It wasn't unusual for her to wonder if she even knew this man any more. Maybe she had never known him?

Now she lay in bed thinking, the anger building inside her. She resented how his life could still go on whereas hers had all-but-in-body ended *that* day.

She needed to see his face so she slid open the drawer on her locker and took out the book where she kept the photo, but looking at him like that wasn't enough. She desperately craved more, she *needed* more, something to touch physically, to hold onto tight and never let go. She slotted the photo back in between the pages of the book and closed it again. The tears began to spill down her face and she wondered when they would ever stop. She had cried so many tears over the last year she thought she would have no more left, that her body should be depleted of its tear reserves at this stage, but there was always more to replace the ones she had freshly cried. Her eyes were red and swollen and her cheeks were patchy and stingy from the salt.

She felt exhausted but her mind was too alert. She reached into the drawer and took out the plastic vial. She took off the cap and shook out two tablets. She swallowed them back without the need of a drink and waited for sleep to take her.

20

That night Adam tossed and turned and eventually, exhausted and worn out from his nightly battle, fell into a deep sleep but he had only brief peace before he found himself back in the dream again. He was driving down the road he knew so well. His arm was stretched out onto the grey leather of his steering wheel. The white winter sunshine glared in through his windscreen, flickers of trees and leaves passed in front of his eyes. Frost wrapped the blades of grass on the ditch in its chilly coat and in places there was the sheen of ice on the road. He passed the farmhouse with the red door and its chickens roaming around amongst bits of old farm machinery and scrap lying idle, having been discarded in another era. He rounded the bend and was gently pulled to the left as the car hugged the curve of the road. Ahead of him a car zipped through a crossroads at speed though it didn't have right of way. Christ! If he had reached the junction a few seconds earlier the idiot would have hit him! Crossing the junction he heard the roar of acceleration. He looked to his left. Oh shit, it was coming straight for him! *Why wasn't he waking up? He normally woke up at this stage.* He waited for what felt like an eternity for the bang. And then it came louder than he had expected: the awful sound of metal crashing upon metal. Simultaneously, he fell forward onto a hard cushion of air and then backwards as instantly. His car was spinning now, his tyres locked, sliding along the icy surface, and he had no control. He was tossed high up in the air, turning over and over like a leaf blowing in an autumn gale and then he was tumbling down, falling, falling. *Bang.* Twisted metal crumpled in around him as shards of silvery glass rained down over his body. Then there was just silence. Deafening, thunderous silence.

When he came around, he didn't know how long he had been there or indeed if he was dead. Every part of his body was roaring in pain. *Is this what death feels like?* He was cold, so, so cold and his clothes felt damp and sticky against his skin. There were voices somewhere and he thought they were calling to him but he couldn't answer. He opened his eyes and looked squarely at the man who kept shouting at him, but it was easier just to close them back down again. He could still hear him, roaring at him now, demanding his attention and he wanted to tell him to fuck off. He just wanted to rest for a while but the stranger wasn't getting the message. He tried to turn his head to check on Fionn but a steel prop was pressed against the side of his face so he couldn't move. The wreckage of steel had anchored him to his seat. He tried to talk to Fionn – *It's going to be okay, son, you're okay* – but no words left his mouth. *Am I dead? Maybe this is what it feels like.*

He could hear a brigade of piercing sirens that were getting louder and higher until they were on top of him, deafening him. He wished they'd go, it was tiring him out. He needed to rest. Then there was a sawing noise cutting so close to him that he could actually see the sunlight gleaming off the blade. He felt tugging as the reverberations from the cutting vibrated through his body until eventually the rays rushed in and blinded him. And then he was being lifted up and laid down. *Maybe now I'm dead?* They were trying to talk to him but he didn't want to talk. They strapped him in and then he was travelling with the siren chasing him. *Fionn. Did they remember to bring Fionn?* He had to close his eyes again, he was so tired.

Part II

21

November, 2009

Jean McParland stumbled sideways, free-falling. She scrabbled to try to grab onto the locker to break her fall but missed it and kept careering forwards, waiting for her head to smash off the wall at any second. Finally it came. She heard the smash of bone against concrete as she tumbled forward, her forehead hitting off the wall. She rebounded again as she fell so that her skull bore the brunt of it this time. She lay slumped on the floor, momentarily stunned, her head looking down on her own body from an awkward angle as she tried to figure out what had just happened.

Almost instantly the pain began to radiate from her skull down through her body and she thought she might be sick – she wasn't sure if it was from the shock or the bang. The 'Hello Kitty' posters looked blurry above her on the wall from where she was lying between the radiator and the plastic-pink doll's house. She could hear Chloe's small voice whimpering in fear.

"Shut the fuck up, y'little bitch, or you'll be fucking next for a slap!" he roared at her terrorised daughter.

Chloe stopped crying immediately, afraid that she would be

next for the brutal treatment. Jean went to shift herself upright in a half-sliding manoeuvre against the wall but her head was spinning so she lay where she was for a few minutes longer. He was standing over her now, looking down at where she was lying on the floor. She swore she could see hatred in his eyes.

"Please, Paul," she begged with her hands covering her face.

He turned and walked calmly out of the room and slammed the door behind him. It wasn't until they heard the car engine that either of them dared moved. Chloe rushed to help pull her up onto her feet.

"Are you okay, Mam?" Chloe was sobbing. "I'm so sorry, Mam, I'm sorry for fighting with him. I should have just given it to him."

"It's not your fault, love. I'm okay, I promise. It's just a bump on my head." She put her hand to her head and already she could feel the swelling grow. Everything was swaying before her eyes but she forced herself to act normally for her ten-year-old daughter's sake. She sat on the edge of the single bed to steady herself.

"I'm scared of him, Mam – I wish he'd just go away and leave us alone."

"I know, pet. I know. Come here." She hugged her daughter in her arms so that Chloe wouldn't see the tears that were streaming down her own face. She was scared too. That was the first time he had actually hit her. God knows he had come so close to it several times before but never before had he actually done it. *Her son had hit her.* She was left reeling with the shock of it all.

"How about you sleep in with me tonight? We can cuddle up together and watch a film in bed. How about that?" She knew it was safer to have Chloe sleep beside her as she couldn't predict what kind of a mood he would arrive home in. She had seen his Jekyll and Hyde behaviour before – he could either be a total monster or else he act like nothing had happened just hours earlier.

Chloe nodded her head emphatically, relieved that she wouldn't have to go to sleep on her own. At ten years of age, she was at that stage where she didn't usually like her mother fawning her with affection but tonight she was vulnerable and upset and was happy to let her mother take care of her. Thank God Kyle was at a sleep-over in his cousin's house, Jean thought to herself. It was one less thing to worry about.

Jean was still trembling as she set up the DVD player while Chloe chose what DVD she wanted to watch. She picked *Shrek*, one of her favourites. Jean sat up against the wooden headboard with her daughter's head resting on her chest as the colours danced from the screen to the wall. Chloe was sucking her thumb, which she did only when she was really tired, and had the duvet pulled right up under her chin while her mother stroked her hair softly. Jean watched her daughter's eyes repeatedly grow heavy and the lids begin to close before she would open them wide again as she tried to fight the tiredness. Eventually she gave in and dozed off in her mam's arms.

Jean lowered the volume so that she was watching the rest of film in silence, as her daughter slept peacefully in her arms. Her head was pounding. She listened to every sound, to see if it was Paul coming home, and she had her phone in her hand just in case. Every sound she could hear outside caused her to tense up with fear in case it was him. She couldn't fall asleep, she was too scared of what might happen if she did, so instead she stayed there staring at the ceiling all night watching Chloe's chest rise and fall in shallow beats.

When morning dawned, Jean was relieved to find that he hadn't come home. It wasn't unusual for him to stay out all night, but there was always the lingering worry of what he was up to. Chloe was still asleep beside her; the poor mite was exhausted by the events of the night before. She managed to wriggle her way out from underneath her and went into the bathroom. She took two more Paracetamol but they didn't seem to be shifting her headache. When she looked in the mirror, the damage was plain to see. It was far worse than she had thought. Her whole left eye was inflamed in an ugly mass of blue-black tissue. How was she supposed to hide that? She splashed cold water on her face before dabbing it dry with a towel. Her sister Louise would be calling to drop Kyle back later on that morning; she would be wondering what had happened. She tried to dab some foundation over the skin to conceal it but it was painful under her fingertips. She persisted, trying to layer concealer, foundation and powder, but no matter what she did the bruising still came through. She knew she was wasting her time; no amount of make-up was going to hide it. She racked her brain to come up with a decent excuse, one that wasn't the usual one women used about walking into doors. She decided to say that she slipped on the floor in the kitchen after she had mopped it and fell against the kitchen table. She would blame her flip-flops. Yes, that was it. They were lethal on wet surfaces, everyone knew that, and in fact she *had* nearly slipped on several occasions in the past when she had been mopping the floor so it was a very easy thing to do. The more she thought about her story, the more she began to believe it herself.

When Chloe woke up, she padded into the kitchen where Jean was seated at the table with a cup of tea. She was startled by her mother's face.

"Your face looks really sore, Mam!"

"Oh, it looks worse than it is," she brushed her off.

"Are you sure?"

"Of course I am!" Her tone was upbeat. "Now, do you know what I'm in the mood for?"

"What?"

"How about pancakes?"

"Pancakes?" Chloe's eyes were wide with excitement.

"And maple syrup!"

"Oh yes, please, Mam!" Chloe squealed at the rare treat.

Jean moved around the kitchen mixing eggs, milk and flour before pouring some of the batter into a heated frying pan. She turned the pancake over and as soon as it had browned, she flipped it out of the pan and onto a plate. She squirted maple syrup in lines across it and served it up to Chloe, then set about cooking more and piling them up on a heated plate.

"He's not here, sure he isn't, Mam?" Chloe asked through a mouthful of pancake.

"No, love, he didn't come home last night."

"Good – I hope he never comes home."

"Chloe!" Jean was taken aback with her daughter's forthrightness. "You don't mean that!"

"I do, Mam!" She defiantly shook her head, her brown eyes wide and serious. "Every time he goes out, I hope he never comes back."

Dear God, thought Jean. She had no idea her daughter was that scared of him. *In her own home.*

"It'll be okay, love."

"Will it, Mam? Because he just keeps getting madder and madder."

She was only ten years old but already she had seen so much and was speaking more sense than Jean ever could.

"I'll talk to him, love, okay? Don't be worrying about things." She took a deep breath. "Now, y'know your Auntie Louise will be dropping Kyle home later?"

"Yes?"

Chloe was smart; Jean knew she would have to tread carefully. "Well, she'll probably be wondering what happened to my face, so I was thinking it might be a better idea to say nothing to her about last night?"

"Why not, Mam?"

"Well, we don't want to worry her. I'll just say I slipped after mopping the floor."

"Mmmh," her daughter said, giving a half-hearted reply, and Jean could see she wasn't really buying into it.

"Please, Chloe, we'll just keep it between ourselves, yeah?" Her voice was desperate.

Chloe looked up at her and Jean begged her with her eyes.

"Okay, Mam, if that's what you want."

"Thanks, love. Did you have enough pancakes? Will I put on another batch?" She was disgusted with herself – trying to butter up her own daughter.

She was dreading facing her older sister. She considered getting Chloe to tell her that she was sick in bed but she knew she would insist on coming up to the room to see how she was, so she would see her either way.

Chloe sat chewing away on her pancakes in small bites while Jean played around with the one on the plate in front of her.

Soon after she could hear the heavy engine of her sister's black Range Rover SUV pulling up beside the footpath outside the house. A gang of teenagers began to circle around it before Louise had even had time to step out of it. They eyed up Louise as she climbed down from the jeep. It looked completely out of place in the forlorn council estate with its graffitied walls, boarded-up houses and foot-high weeds shooting up through the cracked pavements. Louise looked nervously at the teenagers and held her Louis Vuitton tote tight to her chest. Kyle hopped out of the back seat and came running up the path ahead of her.

Although the sisters were separated by just two years in age, Jean and Louise's lives couldn't have turned out more differently. Louise was the wife of an adoring husband who was always whisking her off for romantic breaks or giving her thoughtful little gifts such as flowers or jewellery. He was a senior partner in one of Dublin's leading accountancy firms, which allowed her to be a stay-at-home mum to their two boys, Ronan and

Seán. They had built a huge seven-bedroomed house in the country on acres of land, with its own stables and paddocks and Louise had kitted it out with luxuries that Jean could only dream of, like a mahogany walk-in wardrobe, a kitchen island that was as big as Jean's entire kitchen and a bright and airy living room with floor-to-ceiling-height glass. Louise had employed a designer to choose the wallpapers for the feature walls and complementary fabrics for the curtains and cushions. The house wouldn't look out of place in an interiors magazine. Louise and her family were living the country dream. It was in stark contrast to Jean's three-bedroomed house down the back of a tough local-authority housing estate.

Kyle came in the door. He dropped his bag on the floor and stared at his mother. "What happened to you?"

"Well, hello to you too! Did you have a good time? I hope you were good for Auntie Louise?"

He nodded his head.

"Jesus, Jean, what happened to your face?" Louise's eyes were riveted to the bruise on her younger sister's face. It looked tender and, judging by how she winced every time she made a facial expression, it was painful.

"Oh that? It's nothing!" she replied, trying her best to sound nonchalant. "I was stupidly mopping the floor yesterday in my flip-flops and I slipped and fell against the table. No matter how many times I tell myself never to mop the floor in flip-flops, I never learn, and I ended up with this shiner!" She forced a smile on her face to sell her story.

"My God – that is some bruise!" Louise leant forward to take a closer look.

"It looks worse than it is," Jean lied, because it was bloody sore, as was the egg-shaped lump on the back of her head.

"You gave yourself some bang."

"Bloody flip-flops, you know how slippy the things are."

Something in Jean's eyes wasn't quite right and Louise looked over at Chloe for confirmation.

C'mon, Chloe don't let me down, Jean begged silently.

Chloe sat at the table, saying nothing. Her expression gave nothing away. Jean thanked her inwardly.

"You should get that seen to," Louise continued.

"Sure they can't do anything about a bruise, I'll just have to hide under a pair of dark sunglasses for a couple of days." She laughed, trying to make light of the situation.

"I suppose you're right," Louise said somewhat hesitantly. She looked at the lines on the face of her younger sister, her grey pallor, her brown velour tracksuit, her lank hair pulled back. She was stick-thin from years of worry. You would never think she was the younger one of the two of them.

"Are you sure you're all right?"

"I'm grand, it's just a bruise. I'd hate to see the fuss if I really injured myself."

"Mmmh . . . well, are you sure you're okay?"

"I'm fine, Louise, stop worrying. Will you stay for a coffee?"

"Sorry, love, I have to pick Seán up from karate in five, but if you need anything just give me a ring, yeah?"

Jean let out a huge sigh of relief as soon as she closed the door behind her sister and from the window watched her pull off from the kerb. Chloe and Kyle had moved to the sitting room to play on the X-Box. They were twins and were as close as they came. She could hear Chloe's animated voice talking to Kyle so she moved towards the door so she could hear them better. Their backs were to her and their faces were concentrating on the graphics on the screen.

"He just started screaming because I wouldn't give him my money and then when Mam came up he pushed her and she banged her head and now she has the bruise."

"You should have just given it to him, Chloe."

"I wish I did because it's all my fault that Mam hurted herself."

"Where is he now?"

"Dunno." She shrugged her small shoulders. "He didn't come home. I hope he's gone away forever."

"Me too."

They continued playing their game, as if it was the most normal thing in the world and Jean felt her heart twisting with sadness. She was supposed to be the adult here, she was meant to be in control, but this whole situation was her fault and it was now starting to affect Chloe and Kyle. *How could he try and take her pocket money from her?* She was only ten years old for God's sake! She was saving it for a trip to the toy store that Jean had promised her.

She went into the kitchen and sat at the table drinking a cup of tea. She knew she needed to do something but she hadn't told anyone about the nightmare that was her daily life. No one knew of the constant terror that followed her around, the anxious waiting and wondering what kind of a mood he would come home in. And now that the line had been crossed into violence, what would come next? She constantly lived in fear in case the smallest thing set him off into a rage. He could have killed her last night – her head had missed the edge of the radiator by millimetres, but what was worse was that Chloe had seen the whole thing. What kind of an environment was that for the twins to be brought up in?

After dinner there was still no sign of Paul and she didn't know if that was a good or a bad sign. On the one hand it would give him more time to calm down but on the other he could be building up into a rage again and could fly through the door in a mood worse than when he had left. That was the thing with Paul – he was completely unpredictable.

Later on, after she had put Chloe and Kyle to bed and gone

back down to watch TV, she heard his engine revving outside the house. Automatically her breathing quickened and she prayed he would be in good form. She heard him come through the door and walk straight into the kitchen. He was opening the fridge and then she heard plates banging. He walked out of the kitchen and straight past the sitting-room door and continued upstairs. *Please leave them alone.* She was relieved when she heard him go into his bedroom but minutes later the sound of dance music was pumping throughout the house. She really didn't want to have to confront him.

The sitting-room door opened inwards and Chloe's small face appeared around it.

"Mammy!" Chloe started to cry.

"Come in, pet, what's wrong with you? Is it the music?"

She wouldn't say and just buried her face in her mother's lap, sobbing.

"What is it, Chloe – has he been in to you?"

She shook her head.

"What is it, Chloe – come on, love, you can tell me."

"My bed is all wet." She looked at her mother with shame in her eyes as her face convulsed in tears.

"Oh love, it's all right, these things happen."

She hadn't wet her bed since she was being toilet-trained at the age of two.

"I'm sorry, Mam."

"Don't be silly. C'mon and we'll get you changed."

Afterwards, Chloe didn't want to go back to her bedroom so Jean let her snuggle up onto her knee on the couch. Soon after it was Kyle's turn to come down to the sitting room.

"I can't sleep, Mam, the music is too loud." He rubbed his sleepy eyes as they adjusted to the brightness of the room.

"I know, love, I'm sorry." *Sorry for being too scared to do anything about it.* "Sit down here with myself and Chloe."

Later she sat upright on the sofa with her two children lying on either side of her in sleeping bags as they eventually nodded off to sleep. She watched the hours change with the small hand on the carriage clock, the music still blaring down from upstairs until she drifted off in a hazy sleep at some point herself.

22

On Monday morning Jean busied herself with the morning routine of buttering bread and packing lunchboxes for Chloe and Kyle. They ate their cereal with painstakingly small mouthfuls while she looked on in exasperation.

"Hurry up, you two – we're going to be late."

They looked up at her but continued to chew at a frustratingly slow pace. When they finally finished, they all bundled into her car. They were just reversing out the drive when Chloe realised she had forgotten her PE kit. Jean sighed wearily before getting out of the car again and letting herself back into the house, running around frantically trying to locate her daughter's tracksuit and runners. She ran back out to the car and they set off on the school run. She dropped them outside the school gates, giving them each a kiss as they hopped out.

Although it was only nine o'clock she was already exhausted. She hadn't slept a wink after Paul's antics over the weekend. She looked at herself in the rear-view mirror. The swelling in her face had now turned to a dirty yellowy-green colour but at least it was starting to fade. She had masked it as best she could, using layers of carefully applied concealer and different shades of foundation but if anyone in work asked what had happened, she would tell them the same story as she had told Louise. She locked her car and, taking a deep breath, made her way into the small solicitors' office where she worked as a legal secretary.

As expected her colleagues looked at her face with concern but her recounting of the story to Louise at the weekend had served her well and she told the story like it was real and even managed to throw in a laugh at her own stupidity. She knew they bought it.

She sat down in front of her computer and got stuck into the cases she was working on. Her desk was a mass of paper – she had several letters to type, she also had to serve the proceedings for a family dispute. Plus she needed to do the preparation for a High Court case for her boss Sheila by this evening. Normally secretaries didn't get involved in that sort of work but the partners had grown to trust her over the years and had been giving her bigger and bigger projects until now she was often doing the work of the solicitors herself. She liked the fact that they knew she was capable of the extra responsibility so she gladly took it on, plus it was break from the tedious administration side of her job.

When the rest of the girls were going out for lunch she declined because she wanted to get through all the paperwork on her desk. At half three, just as she was putting her signature on yet another notice letter, her mobile on the desk beside her started to ring. The number of her neighbour Rita Maguire flashed up. She knew immediately something was up at home so she excused herself from the office and stepped outside to answer it.

"Rita – is everything all right?"

"Jean, I'm sorry for ringing you in work again but it's Paul."

Jean felt her heart sink. She knew where this was going. "What's he done now?"

"He's gone and locked the other two out again, I saw them out my window – standing shivering outside in the garden, the poor things."

"Oh God, are they okay?" *I'm going to kill him.*

"They're grand, don't worry, they're fine. They're over here now, having a cup of tea and some bread and jam with me."

"Right, I'm on my way."

"You take your time, love. Sure amn't I glad of the company?"

"Thanks, Rita, I'll be there as quick as I can."

When Jean hung up she was trembling with rage. Enough was enough. This was the third time in the last month that he had locked them out after they had come home from school because he wanted the house to himself. Effectively he was barring them from their own home and it wasn't on. She went back into the office and a sea of heads turned to look at her but she kept walking past her desk and knocked on the glass pane of Sheila O'Malley's office.

"Come in!"

"Hi, Sheila."

"Jean, is everything okay?"

"Look, Sheila, I'm really sorry, but there's a family emergency. I have to leave early."

"But what about the Gallagher case – you were meant to be preparing a summary for the court case tomorrow?"

"I'm really sorry, Sheila, it's halfway there. I know that isn't good enough," she lowered her gaze, "but I really have to go."

"Jean, this is the third time this month you've had to run home for a *'family emergency'*." She said the words with emphasis to imply that she didn't really believe her.

"Sheila, I'm awfully sorry, I really am – I know this isn't acceptable – but I have to go." She couldn't meet the other woman's eyes.

"You're right, Jean, it *isn't* good enough – do you think I can stand up before the judge, in front of the senior counsel and whoever the hell else in the High Court tomorrow and tell them my summary is half-ready? You can be bloody sure I can't!"

Jean squirmed awkwardly in front of her boss. She knew everyone outside would be able to hear the exchange.

"Well, you'd better go then if you have to go," said Sheila curtly. "But we'll talk about this tomorrow."

"Thanks, Sheila," she mumbled before leaving the office. She could feel her cheeks burning and she knew her colleagues would all have been earwigging and trying to figure out what had just gone on.

* * *

When she rounded the corner to the road where she lived, she saw Paul's car in the driveway. She parked on the road outside and got out quickly. She knew the twins would be okay with Rita for a few minutes longer. She was livid; she needed to speak to him now. She let herself in and stormed into her living room, where Paul was sprawled out on the couch watching some daytime TV show about police chases. She walked straight over and turned it off.

"What the fuck d'you think you're doing?" he roared at her, rising up from the sofa.

"I could ask you the same question – what do *you* think you're doing? This is *my* house, Paul – *my* house. As it is also Chloe and Kyle's! How dare you! How dare you stop them going into their own home!"

"Ah, would you ever fuck off!"

"No, Paul, no, I won't. This is the third time this month you've done this, left your brother and sister sitting on the doorstep on a bitterly cold day and left me explaining to my boss yet again why I have to run home. Well, that is it. I won't tolerate it any more. Are you listening to me, Paul – that is the end of it!"

"Whatever." He got off the couch.

"Come back here, Paul! *Paul!*"

She was screaming now she was so infuriated but he ignored her and walked out the front door and got into his Honda Civic. He had modified the white Honda Civic Type R so that the modifications were worth more than the car itself. You could hear the sound of the chrome exhaust pipe as it roared before he got near the house and the gears hissed into action when you changed them. He had got the windows tinted, bucket seats fitted, and had recently had enough cash to have a spoiler moulded onto the back. Jean didn't know how he paid for it all and she wasn't sure she wanted to.

His indifference enraged her. She just didn't seem to be able to get through to him. No matter how much she shouted and screamed and ranted and raved, he didn't pay any heed to her. He didn't respect her authority any more; he hadn't done for a while now. The last time he had done this, she had tried getting through to him by taking away the one thing he loved: she had hidden his car keys as punishment but he just went and took her car instead even though he wasn't insured to drive it.

Of course she knew it was her own fault that Paul was like this. Coming from a broken home and not having his father in his life were bound to have an effect. She knew what the child psychologists and parenting books would say. She had let him down over the years and it was payback time now. Her son had so much anger built up inside and she was his target practice. But over the last year Paul's behaviour had gone from bad to worse. He was out of control. He lay around the house all day; she had given up on asking him to get himself a job. Then he would go off at night in his car to God only knew where. She had asked her own father, who Paul had always been close to, to have a word with him but to no avail. He wouldn't listen to anyone; there was no getting through to him. She was at her wits' end and, what was worse, the effect it was having on his younger brother and sister broke her heart. They were afraid of his mood swings and what they would face each day. Chloe would be watching a cartoon in the sitting room and Paul would just walk in and switch channels and the sad thing was she didn't even dare challenge him on it any more. He terrorised the whole house. One wrong word and he would rise up, like a lion awakened – it could be something simple like asking how he was that day or serving him his dinner slightly burnt.

Jean went across the street to Rita's house. The woman was in her mid-seventies and lived alone. She had been widowed young and all her children had grown up and moved on. She loved making a fuss of Chloe and Kyle and often gave Jean a hand to keep an eye on them if she had to go out somewhere. Jean didn't know what she would do without her. She let herself in through Rita's back door.

"Hi there, Rita."

"Come in, love, they're in here."

The twins were seated around Rita's kitchen table eating freshly baked Madeira cake and washing it down with cups of tea.

"Hi, Mam!" said Kyle.

They both smiled up at her and Jean felt her heart twisting with guilt for them again.

"Will you have a cup yourself, love? God knows you could probably do with it – you look exhausted!" She eyed Jean's bruised face but made no reference to it.

"I'm okay, thanks, Rita – are you two ready? We need to get cracking on your homework."

The disappointment on their faces at having to leave Rita's homely kitchen and the feast in front of them was obvious.

"C'mon," she said firmly so they knew there was no point protesting.

As Chloe and Kyle walked ahead of her over to their house, she stood on the step with Rita.

"Thanks again, Rita."

"Will you stop – sure isn't it nice for me to have their company for a while?"

"No, I mean it, Rita, thanks for keeping an eye out for them."

"Well, y'know how fond I am of the pair of them and they don't stay small for long – don't I know it from all of mine?"

Jean smiled at the older woman whose lined face was the very essence of human kindness.

"Look, Jean, is everything okay? I'm not prying and you can tell me to mind my own business if you think I am but . . . well . . . just with Paul?"

"I'm doing my best, Rita."

"Heavens above, I know you are, love, I know you are. That's not what I meant! It's not easy on your own – but just give me a shout, any time, if you need anything, you know where I am."

"Thanks, Rita. For everything."

* * *

When Paul came home that evening he was his usual gruff self. He ate the dinner put in front of him without so much as a thank-you. Of course Jean knew better than to expect an apology for what had happened at the weekend or even today. And she was too worried about Sheila's parting words to push things further with Paul. Sheila's 'We'll talk in the morning' had seemed ominous.

* * *

The next morning, as Jean walked into the office, she braced herself to face her boss. Knowing Sheila, and knowing she'd had even more time to stew, she knew she would be in for a severe telling-off. Oh well, she would just have to grin and bear it, she thought to herself. She sat down at her desk and, while the rest of them chatted about last night's *Coronation Street*, she kept her head down and tried to finish off the summary for Sheila's case in the High Court in the afternoon; she hoped it might appease her a bit. As she typed out a list of precedents she could feel a presence and she looked up to see Sheila standing at the side of her desk.

"I'm just finishing off that summary for you, Sheila. Sorry, I know I'm cutting it fine but I should have it for you within the next hour."

"There will be no need, Jean –"

"No, honestly, I'm almost done now."

"No, Jean, I don't think you understand. We need to speak with you in my office."

Jean wondered who the 'we' were? She began to feel flustered and her heart was beating wildly. She walked behind Sheila and made her way into the office to see the managing partner, Billy Walker, already sitting there waiting for her. Sheila shut the door behind them before taking a seat alongside Billy so that the desk divided them from Jean. Jean knew things were serious if Billy was here.

"Jean, firstly I would like to thank you for coming in to see myself and Billy." Sheila was being overly formal. "Now . . ." She cleared her throat before proceeding "The last few weeks, Jean, have seen you need to leave work early on three separate occasions."

"Sheila – and Billy – again I apologise, I admit I haven't been very professional over the last month or so but . . ." she lowered her voice – it killed her to bring her personal life into things, "well, I'm having some family difficulties at the moment."

Silence descended upon the room.

"Jean, we don't wish to delve into your private life but we need someone who is reliable, not someone likely to have to run home after only starting work five minutes beforehand. We have clients' deadlines to meet, legal deadlines that have to be fulfilled. You of all people will understand that."

She found herself nodding in agreement.

"Now, we both know you are a very valuable employee, in fact you are our most capable secretary, but your behaviour over the last few weeks has left us with no option and it is with great regret that we have to inform you that unfortunately we will no longer be able to keep your position open for you. Jean, I'm sorry but we have no choice but to let you go."

Jean felt as though this was all being said to her from afar. She was being fired? She hadn't been expecting that – she thought she was in line for a warning at the most. A warning – she would have understood that – but surely they were overreacting by firing her? In fact, they couldn't. Legally, they wouldn't be able to do this. There had been no written or even verbal warnings and a solicitor especially would need to be seen to be going through due process.

These thoughts flew through her mind. Then, "I understand," she found herself replying although she wasn't sure why. She only knew she had no energy left for a fight of this kind. And she knew in her heart that, inevitably, there would be more crises with Paul in the very near future.

They nodded at her, obviously relieved that she seemed to be taking it without protest.

"Now we will of course pay you one month's notice and we'll give you a good reference."

"Thank you," was all she could think of to say. She stood up to go, and let herself out.

As she walked back to her desk, she was stunned. Why had she been so complicit in all of this? As usual she had done what she was told. When was she ever going to learn how to stand up for herself? But instead she found herself standing at her desk packing up her things.

She went home a broken woman. She tried her best to hold back the tears but she was devastated. Her work was important to her; it was the one thing that gave her a sense of self and made her feel like she wasn't just scrounging off the state. It afforded her a small bit of independence, things like having her car or being able to buy little things for the kids. It was only small money but it meant so much for her to have it. Plus the routine of going into an office every day and not just meeting the same depressing faces from the estate did her good. She knew if she sat at home all day long, looking out the windows, the hopelessness would eventually get to her. But it went beyond her own personal reasons – she had desperately wanted to save up enough to get Paul out of the estate; she was trying to save up to rent a house in the town and to take him away from all his friends and the trouble. That was her goal, to get out of the bloody hell-hole where they were living. Without her job, she knew her future was bleak. All her dreams of giving her children a better life had just been wiped out. She didn't know how she would ever get out of the poverty trap now.

23

Ballydubh Village, 1991

Jean had met Gavin Grimley when she was just fifteen years old. She vaguely knew who he was; he was one of *them*, the gang of lads that hung out on the wall outside the school. She and Louise had to walk past them every day on their way home. She knew their faces – they had been a couple of years ahead of her in school, but one by one they had all dropped out. They had never bothered to look for work, it was easier just to draw the dole. They now filled their days hanging around the town and would always be waiting on the school wall at the end of the day. They would shout down at the sisters from where they sat on top of the railings. Sometimes they would even throw things at them, but never anything that would hurt, just random objects like sweet wrappers or pieces of paper. They always singled Jean out because they knew they got the best reaction from her. They would make a comment about how she looked or what she was wearing, anything at all that they knew would embarrass her. She was painfully shy and her cheeks would go bright red until her whole face felt as though it was burning up to match her wine-coloured gabardine. Her reaction egged them on even more. She wished they would leave her alone, she didn't want their attention. Louise would tell her to ignore them, that they were just looking for a reaction, but she couldn't help it. She felt as though Louise thought it was her fault, that she was drawing it on herself. She began to dread their journey to and from school and, if for some reason Louise wasn't able to walk with her, she would lower her head and quicken her pace almost into a run until she was past them.

When Louise went to university, Jean knew she would have to walk home alone every day so she began to heed Louise's advice and tried to act cool as she walked past them, pretending not to hear them when they shouted at her. On the first day she tried it, they kept on shouting but on the second day, the shouts were fewer and by the end of the week they never shouted again. She was amazed when this had the desired effect. She slowly began to get used to them and, although they would watch her and take a drag on their cigarettes as she passed, for the most part they left her alone.

One day just after she had walked by them, she heard heavy footsteps running behind her. She felt her blood run cold; there had been no one else on the path but the boys. She swung around in panic and immediately saw it was one of them. He was dressed in baggy jeans with a hoody pulled up over his head. She tried to break into a run but found herself rooted to the pavement, her legs were frozen in fear.

"Hi, there." He came up beside her and slowed down to walk on the path next to her. "Sorry, didn't mean to scare you." He pulled down his hood.

He was smiling and he didn't seem like he was going to hurt her.

"You didn't," she lied. She felt a bit silly now.

"Where are you going?"

"Home."

"Can I walk with you?"

"Why?"

"Because I like you."

Jean was startled by his forthrightness. This was the same boy who had tormented her since the age of fifteen and now he was telling her he liked her!

"But you always tease me and shout!"

"Yeah, sorry about that. It was only a bit of fun. What's your name?"

"Jean."

"I'm Gavin."

They walked the rest of the road in silence. Jean didn't know what to make of him. She wondered if it was a dare from the lads and tomorrow she'd be the subject of more ridicule. When they reached the top of her road, she told him he had better go. She didn't want her mother to see her with him. She knew she'd be in trouble.

The next day, the lads had stayed quiet as she approached and Jean inwardly said a prayer of thanks that she wasn't going to be mocked for having fallen for one of their stupid pranks. When she walked through the convent gate, Gavin hopped off the wall and walked up beside her again. He continued doing the same thing each day, until it became a daily routine that he walked her home.

When it became clear he wasn't trying to cause trouble for her, she began to lower her guard with him. She was surprised to find herself thinking that he was a nice guy; he was completely different to what she had thought. Plus, because she was so shy, she didn't have too many friends in school, so she enjoyed their chats. As she talked to him and got to know him she learnt that he was from the town. He was very open with her and he told her that his mother was dead and he lived with his father who had hit the drink very hard after his mother had passed away. He wasn't violent or anything but he was just buried under his grief. Jean was shocked by his story and felt so sorry for the childhood he'd had but he just shrugged his shoulders at her and said "That's life!"

As he told her more about himself on their walks she couldn't help but compare his upbringing to her own. While she had two loving parents, breakfast served before school every morning, a clean pressed uniform laid out, warm soup waiting on the cooker in the evenings, piano lessons, speech and drama and ballet and hopefully, if she did well enough in her Leaving Cert, university next. Gavin didn't have any of that. He was only two years older than her but he had grown up years ago. However, he didn't want pity. He accepted that this was his lot and just got on with it.

Soon she found she loved being around him. When she walked out of the school every evening she was so excited. Her heart would leap when she caught a glimpse of him waiting for her outside the gate.

She dared not tell her mother or Louise; she knew what they thought of the Grimleys. She had heard her father talking about how he had seen Gavin's father falling out of O'Looney's pub and her mother would tut and say that that he had "never got it together after his wife had died" so she knew they would never approve of their friendship.

Soon after, the daily walk from the school to her house became too short and she longed for more time with him so they began to take a detour and go down to the weir on their way home. They would sit and watch the rushing water until Jean would look at her watch and know her mother would be starting to wonder where she was.

One day out of the blue as they sat on the meadow grass, their voices drowned out by the rushing water, he had leaned over and kissed her. It was the first time she had ever kissed a boy and she could have sworn she had been lifted off the ground. She wanted more and they had kissed deeply for hours.

Pretty soon they started to climb over the old stone wall to the weir every day. When the summer came, she would fling off her gabardine and roll down her long wool socks. She would loosen the knot in her tie, undo the top button of her blouse and run through the grass until they reached their spot near a big ash tree. He would sit back against it and she would lean back into his arms. He would stroke her hair or plant delicate kisses along the skin of her neck, so light that they caused the hairs on her skin to stand up. They would pick blades of grass and split them down the centre. She felt so comfortable with him. He understood her and he was the only other person who she had ever opened up to outside of her family.

As the exams drew closer, she began telling her mother she was staying back after school to do supervised study just so she could have an extra two hours with Gavin. She knew she was way behind on the amount of revision that she needed to have done at this stage but she still couldn't bring herself not to meet him every day. She cringed inwardly whenever she heard her proud parents telling friends and family how she "had the head down" and was "working very hard" and that they were "expecting great things from her" – it just made her want to run out and escape and to spend even more time with Gavin. It was a vicious circle. She had such a mountain of revision that she needed to do, she didn't even know where to begin. She felt the pressure building inside her and the more she avoided it, the harder it became. She began to block it from her head and pretend it wasn't happening.

The weeks went on and soon it was the night before the Leaving Certificate. The first exam was English Paper I and, as she opened her copy of *Othello*, she began to panic when she realised that she didn't have the first idea what the play was even about. She had been in class but had been too busy daydreaming, as evidenced by the pencil scrawls that littered every page. She tried to remember what her teacher had said about the characters of Iago and Desdemona. She knew one of them was meant to be evil but for the life of her couldn't remember which one. She knew there was no way she would even be able to blag her way through this. She slammed the text book shut. It was too late; the volume of work to be done at this stage was insurmountable.

* * *

Jean climbed out of her bedroom window and ran down the road into town. She knew which house belonged to Gavin because he had pointed it out to her before. She knocked on the door with the paint long since cracked and faded and prayed he was home. She was relieved when it was opened to see him standing there.

"Hey, what are you doing here? Are you okay?" He was surprised to see her. She had never been to his house before.

"No!" She began to cry. "I've left it too late to study, I can't take anything in. My mam and dad are going to kill me."

"Hey, it's okay!" He wrapped his arms around her and brought her inside.

Jean stepped inside into the hallway and took in the gloominess of the room. She tried not to look shocked by the state of the house. The wallpaper was coming unstuck from the wall in parts and the ceiling was stained with black mildew spots. The brown swirly carpet on the floor was filthy and as Gavin led her upstairs to his room Jean noticed the stair rail was covered in a layer of dust. She quickly removed her hand. As she followed Gavin into his room, she was hit by the stale air. Even his room was grimy. She sat on the edge of his bed, amongst piles of CDs and clothes strewn about the floor.

"C'mon, you're going to be fine." He rubbed her shoulders "You're really clever."

"No, I'm not."

"Yes, you are. Some of things you tell me – like that time we were sitting out in the rain and remember there was thunder and lightning and you told me that you could calculate how far away it was from us?"

"But that's not going to pass my Leaving Cert for me, is it?" she wailed. "Oh I'm in such deep shit. I'm not going in tomorrow."

"You have to go!"

"I don't!"

"At least give it a go – it might all start coming back to you again once you get in there."

She looked at him doubtfully.

"Please, Jean, you have to – your parents will freak if you don't go in. Then they'll find out about us and they'll stop us being together."

The thought of not being able to see Gavin frightened her. She knew he was right; if she didn't do her Leaving Cert, her parents would leave no stone unturned until they found out what was wrong. She could see it now; she would be wheeled into counsellors or brought to the best education advisers money could buy. It would just make everything a million times worse.

"C'mon, do it for me. Please?" he begged.

"Okay, only for you – I'll give it a try."

"That's the girl!"

He walked her back down the stairs. As she passed the sitting-room door, she could hear loud snores, presumably coming from his father. At the top of her road he gave her a kiss on the forehead and told her he would be waiting for her after the exam finished.

* * *

While all her classmates had chattered nervously outside the exam hall saying that this year it had to be "Yeats because

Clarke had come up for the last four years in a row" and that "the character sketch better be based on Iago", Jean hadn't joined in. She had kept to herself because she didn't have a clue what they were even talking about. They had looked at her and assumed she was just quietly confident.

With trepidation she turned over English Paper I. All the words in black print looked jumbled together. Phrases like *'Compare and Contrast'* and *'Give an Account of'* jumped off the page in front of her. She told herself to calm down and to breathe deeply. She read the questions and read them again but she couldn't think of anything to write. Whatever bit of knowledge she had retained from class, that she was hoping would get her through, was still locked inside her head. She looked around the exam hall at the heads buried in concentration. Hands were writing furiously trying to get hurried thoughts onto the paper in case they were forgotten again. She wrote her name and exam number on the top, hoping that that might quick-start her memory, but nothing was coming.

Someone coughed she could hear the heavy footsteps of the invigilator as he wore a path up and down the hall. He stood beside her breathing heavily and she could tell he was looking at her empty answer book. She kept her head down and pretended she was just reading the paper again. She looked up at the black and white clock on the wall and watched the hands moving around. *Tick, tick, tick.* She knew she was obliged to stay for the first half an hour and after that she could go. She watched the hands turning around until they read ten o'clock. She shoved back her chair, causing a screech along the floor tiles. A sea of heads turned to stare at her. She got up from her desk and walked up towards the invigilator and handed him her paper. She could see the looks of confusion on her classmates' faces as they wondered where she was going: *She's only been here half an hour – she couldn't be finished yet!* She could see them looking at each other, amazed.

Jean was one of the top pupils, she was one of the ones that should be there right until the last second frantically trying to scribble down every last bit of knowledge onto the paper before she was forced to stop.

As she walked towards the door Jean could feel ninety pairs of eyes boring holes in her back. When she got outside she cried. *Her life was over, she had just ruined her life.* She was forever being told that the Leaving Cert was the most important exam of her life and it would determine her whole future. She went outside into the yard and through tear-filled eyes could make out Gavin's outline as he waited for her on top of the railings like he did every day. As he climbed his way down, she ran up to him and flung her arms around his neck. She was relieved to feel his strong arms around her, tight and reassuring.

They walked hand in hand and climbed over the stone style and walked down to the weir. She sobbed as he held her tight in his arms. She started to kiss him, hard and passionately. She wanted to feel his skin, she needed to be close to him, closer to him than she had ever felt before. She took off his T-shirt and lay on his bare chest in the heat of the June sun. They fumbled with each other's clothes until they were both half-naked and he was lying on top of her. Then he entered her and she felt a sharp stabbing pain momentarily.

"Are you sure you're ready?" he asked, feeling her body tense.

"Uh-huh," she nodded.

He moved inside her, their bodies united. She had never felt closeness like this.

"I love you, you know?" he said.

"I love you too."

* * *

They lay there together in the heat of the sun for hours until Jean checked her watch and knew her mother would be waiting for her at home to hear how the exam had gone.

Gavin helped her back over the wall and she jumped onto the path below. He walked her to the top of the road and they kissed goodbye. She loved Gavin Grimley and he loved her, that was all that mattered. She couldn't believe she had just had *sex*. She tidied herself up and smoothed her hair so her mother wouldn't become suspicious and walked on cloud nine back to her house.

As her mother fussed and fawned over her, serving up her favourite dinner of lasagne, followed by home-made chocolate brownies, Jean knew she couldn't do it to her. She couldn't shatter the high hopes that she held for her so she lied and told her that it had gone well, a bit tricky in parts but otherwise okay. She didn't have the guts to tell her that actually she had handed the paper back to the invigilator as blank as it had been given to her in the first place. She was amazed at how easy the lies came. She knew the truth would come out eventually but she would get a plan together by then.

* * *

By the end of June, Jean's period was overdue by a week or so. She tried not to think about it. She pushed it out of her head. She was irregular anyway. Now that school was finished, she had loads more time to spend with Gavin. They spent long endless days by the river in each other's arms talking about what they would do in their future together, making up scenarios about where they would live and what they would work at.

By the middle of July, before Jean could even get out of bed in the mornings, she had to rush to be sick. She felt wretched; she was pale and drawn and was constantly exhausted. She couldn't stomach the dinners her mother prepared for her; even the smell of her favourites were enough to send her running to the bathroom to throw up again. Her mother, worried that she had a vicious stomach bug, insisted on bringing her to Dr

Thornton. Jean tried to tell her she was fine but she insisted they were going and that was the end of it.

Jean couldn't make eye contact with Dr Thornton as her mother outlined her symptoms. When he asked Mrs McParland to step outside because he wanted to have a word alone with Jean, her mother began to protest but the doctor stayed firm and an annoyed Mrs McParland found herself sitting outside in the waiting room.

"Now, Jean, nothing to be frightened about, I just want to ask you a few questions alone if that's okay?"

Jean nodded.

"So when did you have your last period?"

"May or June."

He looked up from where he was scribbling his notes. "Can you remember which?"

"End of May maybe."

He began to write again. "Now please don't be offended but I have to ask the question – is there any possibility that you might be pregnant?"

Jean said nothing. She felt her eyes getting heavy as they filled with the weight of tears which overflowed and spilled down her face. She tried to wipe them away but they still kept coming.

"It's okay, Jean, it's going to be okay. I'm going to get you to do a pregnancy test just to confirm, okay?"

She nodded, incapable of speech.

"There's a toilet in there and I want you to get a urine sample for me." He handed her a brown plastic vial.

Jean sat on the toilet knowing what was going to happen. She knew she was pregnant; she had known it since she noticed her period hadn't arrived in June. She knew she would come out and hand this jar of piss to the doctor and he was going to tell her that she was pregnant and her life would be changed forever. She knew her mother was going to hit the roof, that was a given. She didn't know how Gavin would react, she hadn't told him her period was late. Would he stick by her and tell her they would raise the baby together? Or would he do a runner like the nuns in school and her mother had always warned about when young girls got pregnant? She considered staying in the small toilet cubicle forever where she could be protected from all their reactions. There was a soft knocking on the door.

"Jean – are you okay in there?"

"Yes, I'm coming now, Dr Thornton." She did up her jeans and went back out to the surgery and handed the vial to him.

She didn't watch as he went about the test. Instead she prayed that maybe it was just a bad bug she had picked up after all, like her mother thought.

The minutes ticked by, then she became aware that he was checking the test.

"Jean . . ."

She looked up and met his eyes.

"It's positive."

She was pregnant. Her life was over.

Her mother had been called back into the room then and Jean felt as though she was watching all of this from above. As Jean was incapable of speaking, Dr Thornton had broken it to her mother that her seventeen-year-old daughter was actually not sick at all, just pregnant. Jean watched her mother's face crumple as the shock took hold and she looked at her daughter for confirmation that it was true. But instead of shouting and screaming like Jean had thought she would, she remained silent which unnerved her. She almost wished she was angry.

"You couldn't be – are you sure?" was all she could muster up.

They left the surgery and a stunned Mrs McParland drove home with her daughter in the passenger seat, clutching a bundle of leaflets all offering advice on how best to deal with a crisis pregnancy. Every so often her mother would ask a question. "But how? Who? Where?" but Jean stayed quiet.

Later that evening, when both had had time to digest the turn of events, Jean told her mother everything, from how she met Gavin, to her appalling Leaving Certificate. She watched as each confession broke another piece of her mother's heart as she realised that her daughter's future had been dramatically altered from the path she had hoped and dreamed for her. Even though she had been bright in school, Úna McParland had never gone to university herself; her parents could never have afforded it in a million years. She had a tough childhood, helping out on the farm early in the morning before school and afterwards every evening too. She had left school at the age of twelve to work in the local sewing factory. Most of the girls in her class had done the same thing; it was only the privileged few, the daughters of doctors or solicitors in the town that had gone on to secondary school. That was why she had wanted so much more for her daughters, she had made it her life's work to make sure they had everything that she didn't have and now her youngest daughter was about to go down a radically different path despite everything she had done for her. Úna had not seen it coming.

As expected, her father had hit the roof when he was told that evening, but Úna had begged him to stay calm and pointed out that his reacting like that wasn't helping anybody.

Louise came in from college a while later, in her long skirt and granddad-style cardigan – she had recently become a convert to the grunge look. When her mother had told her about Jean, she had looked at her little sister with a mixture of disgust and pity. Later, when they were alone, she had cornered her. "How could you be so naïve – have you never heard of a condom? All teenagers have sex nowadays but they use protection for God's sake!" she said angrily. It was Louise's reaction that had hurt the most. She had always looked up to her older sister.

Over the next couple of days her family discussed what Jean

was going to do, but she wasn't included in the plans. She tried telling them that Gavin was a really good guy and that he loved her and it wasn't his fault that his dad was an alcoholic. She told them that she and Gavin would raise the baby together and that she knew Gavin would stick by her even though she hadn't even told him yet that she was pregnant, but her parents forbade her to go anywhere near him ever again. She listened as they planned her whole life out for her. She was going to take this year off and have her baby, then she would go back and repeat the Leaving Cert the following year and go on to university. Úna would take care of the baby. They never asked her if this was what she wanted.

24

As the weeks went past, Jean missed Gavin desperately. Her mother stuck to her like glue and Jean found it impossible to sneak off and meet him. She had no way of communicating with him and she was worried about what he must be thinking of her, when all of a sudden she didn't show up to meet him. She had just vanished on him and he didn't even know she was pregnant. It didn't help matters that his dad didn't have a phone in the house so she couldn't even ring him when she was at home alone. She begged to be allowed go for a walk on her own, but her mother refused saying she couldn't be trusted and that if she really wanted to go for a walk, she would happily go too.

One day her mother accompanied her to Dr Thornton for one of her antenatal check-ups. After an hour Úna looked up from the magazine that she had been licking and thumbing for the umpteenth time and sighed. The waiting room was still packed – there were still nine people ahead of them. She knew it would be hours before Jean would been seen and, sighing heavily again, she put the magazine down and said she was going off to get a few messages and would be back shortly.

Jean knew this was her one and only chance. Gavin's house was located two streets behind the surgery. She knew if she hurried that she could be there and back in a matter of minutes and her mother need never know. She had butterflies in her tummy just thinking about seeing him again. She waited for a few minutes after her mother had gone, before getting up and telling the receptionist that she needed some air. Taking in her growing bump, the receptionist smiled at Jean sympathetically and told her to take her time and she was sorry they were running behind schedule.

Once outside the door, Jean looked left and right to make sure there was no sign of her mother before she tore down the street and around the corner to Gavin's house. She knew people were looking at her but she needed to get there fast, she didn't have much time. She prayed he was at home. She pressed the bell and stood on the step and waited anxiously. She strained to listen for anyone coming to the door but she was met with silence. *Please be here, Gavin. Please.* She pressed the bell again and pounded on the door with force and waited a bit more but there was still no reply. She felt cheated that he wasn't in; this was the first chance she'd had in months to see him and likely the only chance she would get for months again. She turned around defeated and walked slowly back towards the surgery. She had just rounded the corner back onto Market Street when she heard her name being called.

"Jean!"

She swung around to the familiar voice, the voice that instantly comforted her and told her things would be okay.

"Gavin!"

They ran towards each other on the street and embraced, momentarily forgetting they were in Ballydubh village where people weren't used to this kind of carry-on. People were stopping in the street to look at the pair of them. Gavin took a step back as he noticed Jean's bump.

"You're not . . ." he lowered his voice, "pregnant, are you?"

Jean nodded. She watched his excitement at seeing her wane before her eyes as the shock took over. They were starting to attract the attention of the town busybodies so Jean pulled him down a side street.

"Jesus! Why didn't you let me know?"

"My parents won't let me out of their sight. I've been trying to think of ways of getting to see you but they're all over me."

"But I posted a letter to your house! Did you not get it?"

"No! I never got it!" she cried angrily. "I bet my mam opened it before it got to me. I can't believe she's reading my post too!"

"I thought you just didn't want to be with me any more. God, I've missed you so much." He hugged her tight.

"I haven't much time, I'm supposed to be in Dr Thornton's waiting room for my check-up – if Mam finds me here she'll kill me."

"Come away with me."

"What?"

"Yeah, you and me . . . and now our baby. Jesus, I can't believe you're having a baby!"

"Really?" Jean's eyes had lit up. All she wanted was to be with Gavin and get out of this godforsaken town.

"Yeah, I'll find us somewhere to live, I'll get a job. We can be a family!" His idea was starting to gain momentum and he was being carried away by his excitement.

"Meet me at midnight tomorrow night, down by the weir. We'll go away together, miles from here. I'll have everything organised. I have some money saved –"

"I have some put away at home – I'll bring that."

"Great!"

She kissed him on the lips and ran back to the surgery with a huge smile all over her face.

"Where were you?" Her mother, who was already back, asked with a face that would turn milk sour.

"Sorry, Mam, I just needed some air. I felt faint."

"Well, you look perfectly fine to me."

"That's because I just had some air."

"Don't use that tone with me, young lady!"

Jean was going to reply but she bit her tongue. Tomorrow she would be free from all of this. In little over twenty-four hours, she and Gavin would be together again.

* * *

The next night, Jean sneaked out of her bedroom window and tiptoed down the garden path. She held her breath, praying the neighbour's dog wouldn't start barking and blow her cover. As soon as she was away from her house, she started to run. There was a full moon out, lighting the path for her. All she had managed to bring was a backpack with a few of her clothes, some toiletries and a photo of her family. She was beyond excited at the thought of her and Gavin running away together, setting up a new life for themselves and becoming a proper family.

They hugged as they were reunited. Gavin told her that he had managed to find an abandoned shed that they would stay in until morning but he assured her it was only for tonight and that tomorrow would be different. Jean was so buoyed up that she didn't care that they would be sleeping in a shed. Luckily it was a mild October night and the winter frost had yet to bite. As they lay there in each other's arms, under the moonlight, she couldn't help but think how romantic the whole thing was; they would be telling their baby this story in years to come.

At first light they got on a bus to Cork. They both slept the whole journey long as neither had slept properly in the shed. They didn't wake until the driver turned off the engine. Looking out the windows, they realised they were in the terminus. They got off the bus and took their bags out from the hold. Gavin had the name of an auctioneer who let houses and they asked a man for directions before setting off.

The city was coming alive for the day ahead. Traffic filled the quays, the pavements were filling up and shops were opening up. Jean looked around in excitement; she couldn't believe they would be living in a city. She had been living in the small village of Ballydubh her whole life, but this place was so alive and vibrant that it seemed like another world altogether.

25

John Grace had looked at the young couple sitting across the desk from him with raised eyebrows. They were a very young couple, he thought, hardly out of their teenage years with all their worldly possessions on their backs. And her pregnant! He knew something wasn't right but it wasn't his place to say so. After all, he was just an auctioneer – he was in the business of renting houses, he wasn't bloody Social Welfare. It wasn't his business to be sticking his oar in and wondering what folks were up to. He gave them brochures of all the houses and apartments that he had on his books but when they turned them over and saw the rents, he thought that the young fella was going to pass out. Then, when he had happened to mention the fact that you had to pay a month's rent in advance plus another month as a deposit, you'd think he had told them the sky had fallen in! And then of course the girl had gone and started to get upset. He was beginning to feel like the inn-keeper that turned Mary and Joseph away. It was pretty easy to guess that their finances were pretty dire. So much for a handy commission, he thought grimly. Then he remembered the bedsit that was adjoining his own house. His mother had lived in it until she died last year and he had never done anything with it after that. He knew it was hardly in a fit state. By now the place was damp and teaming with mildew but, sure, as his mother always said, beggars couldn't be choosers, now could they?

As he showed them the dark one-roomed bedsit, he couldn't help thinking that it was worse than he had remembered – if that was even possible. It had been nearly a year since he had set foot in the place and he was greeted with a pungent odour as soon as he opened the door. There was a flowery settee against one wall, a double bed against the back wall and a small circular table and chairs stood in the centre of the room. There was a battered TV set with a faux wooden surround. John tried to remember how long he'd had it – it must be at least twenty years old but sure it worked grand. The floor was covered in grey stripy linoleum throughout and the walls were papered in ruby-red velvet-effect wallpaper. His mother had taken a fancy to it a few years back and had gone wild with it. She'd had the entire place covered in it. All her old ornaments and china figurines stood on every space; he had never got around to tidying the hideous things up. He thought up a figure in his head for the rent, enough not to scare them off completely but sufficient for it to still be a nice little earner for him; he wouldn't get *too* stuck into helping them out.

* * *

Jean blinked back tears as she watched Gavin shake hands with John Grace as he handed over three quarters of all their money for the deposit and first month's rent alone. She didn't think she had ever seen anywhere quite so awful – granted she'd had a pretty sheltered upbringing but this place was dire. She knew John Grace wasn't doing them any favours on the rent either but, as Gavin kept on telling her, they didn't have any other option. For some reason she had thought they would be able to afford somewhere a bit nicer, a proper home, small but cosy, but she had underestimated rental costs. She tried not to let her disappointment show.

While Gavin signed the lease, Jean stayed standing. She was afraid to touch anything in the place and there was no way she was going to sit on the furniture. As soon as John Grace had gone, she set about cleaning straight away. She put on rubber gloves and wiped away layers of greasy dust that had built up over years. She swept away wispy cobwebs from the ceiling but, no matter how much she sprayed her deodorant, she couldn't mask the musty smell. She was sure she could still smell the old woman who had died here. She shivered at the thought.

She thought about home as she cleaned. Her family were probably in a panic now that they had realised she was gone. She didn't want them worrying about her; she just couldn't live there any more. She would ring them in a few days to tell them she was okay when hopefully they would have calmed down.

After they had bleached and dusted the place as best they could, they sat back wearily onto the settee, which they had now covered with throws which Gavin had gone out and picked up cheaply in a discount homewares store on North Main Street. This was their first night together in their own place and already the excitement of living together was starting to pall. They had only ever spent short amounts of time with each other but here they were playing house. It was odd deciding what to watch on the TV, when to go to bed or asking what the other wanted to eat. They had bought a small few bits to eat in a supermarket and Jean was shocked at how much everything cost. She began to fret that their money was being swallowed up rapidly but Gavin told her not to worry and that first thing in the morning he was going out to look for a job.

That night as she listened to him snoring gently beside her in the bed, a tear rolled down her face.

* * *

Days went by with Gavin trawling through the job notices in the windows of the employment office. He soon realised that jobs were not as easy to come by as he had hoped. The building sites didn't want to know him as he was too young and anyway, even if they were to overlook his age, his scrawny body didn't look like it would be capable of the heavy work. He spent an entire day walking to all of the factories but none of them were hiring at the moment. He tried shops and offices but they all wanted people with experience.

He knew he needed to get something fast. They were down to their last twenty pounds and the rent was due again at the end of the week. He couldn't draw the dole because Jean wouldn't let him sign on in Cork for fear that it would flag their whereabouts with the authorities. She was paranoid about going to the Social Welfare office even just to enquire about their entitlements in case they would trace her back to her parents. She wouldn't even go to a doctor down here for her check-up in case the doctors had been alerted to her being missing. Gavin himself thought she was over-reacting but she was insistent so he had no choice but to try and get a job somehow. He could see she was getting more upset by the day and he knew she was having second thoughts about running away together. And even though she denied it, he could hear her crying at night. She was nearly now in her third trimester; she was getting bigger and wasn't as mobile as before. Gavin could see she longed for the comforts of her old life and the novelty of them running away together had quickly worn off. He was trying his best to be positive but it wasn't enough. He knew that John Grace would soon be looking for next month's rent and Gavin knew that his type would have no qualms about throwing them both out onto the street whether or not Jean was pregnant. Gavin didn't want to admit to Jean that he was actually really worried, so he kept on saying that everything was fine and he hoped she believed him.

26

November, 2009

The music boomed down from the stacked speakers and echoed around the vast concrete warehouse. Beams climbed up the high walls, climbing higher still so that they illuminated the cracked windows running along the top before running back down to the floor again, scattering coloured shadows around the space. All the bodies faced forward, dancing together, covered in sweat, and their heads tilted upwards in a kind of intimacy. The blinding halogen light made the DJ appear like God above them. Someone had managed to climb their way to the top of the speakers and was now frenetically moving to the music from way up over the crowd.

Paul could feel the music reverberating from the speakers, rebounding off the floor and up through his feet, until it was like electricity, coursing through his body from the tips of his toes, travelling up his legs, pulsing around his veins and vibrating through his bones. His two hands were raised above his head as he thumped the air to the beat of the music. The music slowed; then briefly speeded up, before slowing down again as the DJ played cat and mouse with them. Then finally after he had teased them for long enough, he roared *"One! Two! Three! Are you ready?"* He spun his two hands on the decks sending the tempo faster, the music getting louder. *"Here! We! Go!"* Paul could feel the rushes building and radiating across his body to the beat of the music. When finally it reached the climax, a cacophony of foghorns blared. Paul felt as though every nerve-ending in his body was exploding in small pops of blissful euphoria like a flower bursting through its bud. He felt weightless as he floated on the sound waves being carried along by the volume of the base drum pounding.

He loved everyone. *Loved* them. Every single person in the warehouse was the best person in the world. Everyone in this room was fucking deadly. They were all rolled into this ball of love together, united on a higher plane.

A girl wearing red sequined hot pants and a white bikini top displaying a toned, tanned midriff was walking towards him. She had a pink cowboy hat on her head and a purple feather boa around her neck. She went behind him and wrapped the boa around him before putting her two hands around his neck. She began to massage his shoulders and tickled his back by running her fingertips in light feathery movements up and down his spine. He felt the rush building inside again. He swung her around so that she was in front of him and cupped her head in his hands. He leant down and kissed her dry lips. Her mouth tasted like chewing-gum.

"You're fucking ace!" he shouted at her.

"What?"

"I said you are fucking ace!" He roared back again. He wanted her, he needed to touch her. His hands reached out and started feeling her body, moving up over her breasts. She threw her head back laughing, her mouth wide open to reveal small gappy teeth. She jerked back upwards again before pulling away from him. He watched her as she walked off on her path through the crowd, kissing strangers as she went. He was left

standing, swaying gently as the music softened into a trance. His hands fumbled with the small plastic bag full of pills. He used to eat ten-penny mixes from bags like this. He swallowed two instantly and waited for the warm feeling until he could feel it rise up inside him, building from his core, radiating out to the tips of his fingers, skin, toes, until every part of him tingled in pleasure, alert and alive. His white T-shirt was stuck to his skin, transparent with sweat. He took off his top and threw it aside. He was thirsty and grabbed a plastic pint glass of water from where they were lined up on a table, gulping it straight back; he took another one and poured it over his body to cool himself down. His heart was thumping and his breathing rapid. All the while his foot kept tapping out the beat. He continued dancing bare-chested, pounding out each beat as if it were physically in the air in front of him. He danced for hours, never wanting this to end. He wanted to stay like this forever; feel like this forever.

After a while the music stopped. The lights were coming on. He could see forlorn faces. They all felt it. He searched out their God up high and begged him with wide eyes not to stop but already he was packing up. The lights illuminated bay upon bay of empty racking and for the first time he saw how vast the place was.

Despondent bodies began to filter out of the warehouse, subdued and exhausted from hours of hardcore dancing. It was raining and the droplets felt cool as they danced along his bare skin. The chemical high from before was rapidly evaporating as bare-chested men and semi-naked women stood huddled around outside with vacant faces and dilated pupils as the fear began to ascend, disenchanted that it was all over and now they were faced with reality again. The amphetamines were still racing around his body but the warm feeling had worn off; he needed something to replace this awful sinking feeling. He saw the girl that had kissed him earlier on; she was shivering in the moonlight. She looked older than she had inside. She was more wrinkled and instead of looking toned, now she just looked bony. He watched her angular body, with its bones jutting out all over as she stood taking long drags from her cigarette, exhaling grey plumes onto the night air. He could now see her teeth had yellow pockets in between. He had to get away from her. She was bringing him down. He needed to escape from everyone here with their empty faces. He whistled to the lads and they all headed over to his car. Aido asked three girls who were standing nearby in the rain if they wanted to go to a party. They shrugged their shoulders and, with no better offers, squashed in on top of the four lads sitting in the backseat of the small Honda Civic. He had to get out of there.

He drove fast, speeding along the main road. The roads were empty, with only the silvery glow of the moon keeping them company. They turned off that road after a few miles, branching onto back roads, pot-holed country lanes.

"*Da, da, da, da-da!*" Aido was humming a tune from the rave in the passenger seat beside him. He tapped his foot to the beat. "*Da, da, da, da-da!*" He kept going, repeating the same five notes on loop until Paul felt as though *Da-da-da* was boring holes in his skull and drilling into his brain. "*Da, da, da, da-da!*"

"Would you ever shut the fuck up!"

"Jesus!" Aido let out a low whistle. "Relax the fuck, Paul!"

The car descended into silence again as Paul drove faster. He swung around a corner onto the other side of the road. His passengers all swung with the gravity to the right and then back again. One of the girls started to laugh, high-pitched and squealy. It drilled through Paul's skull. Eventually he pulled up outside his home.

He let them in the door. The house was in darkness so he turned on all the lights. He walked over to the CD player and took out the CD in it that belonged to Jean, flung it onto the floor and put in his own CD of trance music. He left them all there in the sitting room while he went up to his room to get some gear. He needed to get rid of this feeling. He snorted line after line of the white powder until the membranes of his nose were tingling and his gums numb from where he rubbed it on directly. The cocaine gave him a different buzz altogether, the feeling of euphoria was gone – instead he felt alert and his heart was thumping in his chest.

He could hear the others laughing and shouting in the sitting room. What the fuck were they laughing at? The girl with the laugh let out another squeal before her and Mick descended into fits of laughter again. He wondered what was so bloody funny. Were they laughing at him? It better not be about him because it was his bloody house and no one would laugh at him in his own house.

He went back down to the sitting room and threw himself into the centre of the couch between two of the girls. He felt a hand move along his leg and when he looked to find out whose hand it was, the girl smiled at him. Her eyes were half closed and Paul knew she was in her own world. Her hand moved further along the top of his thighs towards his crotch and he felt himself instantly harden. He needed to release it. He looked at the faces in his own sitting room and pulled the girl up and led her into the kitchen.

He sat on one the wooden kitchen chairs and undid his fly. He kicked off his trainers, unbuttoned his jeans and pulled them off together with his boxers, throwing them onto the floor. Wearing only his socks, he guided her down on top of him. She swayed backwards unsteadily for a few moments so he had to hold her. He lifted her dress so it was above her waist and moved her tight lacy thong to the side and seconds later he was in. He gripped her hips and moved her up and down on top of him, until she was grinding against him. He looked up at her; her eyes were closed now. He started to go harder, pounding away on the verge for an age until finally he felt himself explode inside her. He sat back into the chair and she slumped forward so that her head was hanging over his shoulder. He held her back out from him by her two shoulders and shook her.

"Fucking hell – wake up!"

She opened her eyes, smiled at him before closing them down again and slid back into her trance. He got out from underneath her and stood up while she slumped back down on the chair. *How could she sleep through that?*

He lit himself a cigarette on the gas cooker and stood looking at her where she slumped on the chair, her skirt still above her waist so that everything was on show. *Served her right, the stupid bitch.*

27

Jean had woken up to the sound of shouting coming from her living room. She'd quickly sat up in her bed and listened, to try and figure out what was going on. It was followed by someone roaring in laughter, then more shouting and screeching. The light from the hall was flooding under her door and illuminating her bedroom. It was Paul. Her clock said it was 3.05 a.m. *This isn't fair,* she thought. Whatever about her not being able to sleep, Chloe and Kyle had school in the morning.

She'd sat there contemplating what she should do, hoping the noise might die down by itself but when it became clear that that wasn't going to happen, she got out of bed and wrapped her terrycloth dressing-gown over her pyjamas, before making her way down towards the noise.

Bracing herself, she pushed open her sitting-room door. Her eyes had to adjust to the light as she took in a crowd of teenagers sprawled across every conceivable space in her small sitting room. The air was heavy with thick white smoke and cans were littered around the floor and coffee table. As she took in the torn pieces of white paper, ripped cigarette boxes and tinfoil strips that were strewn everywhere, she could feel the rage starting to build inside. How dare he! She scanned the unfamiliar faces that didn't even look up at her. No one seemed to register her standing there and if they did, they weren't too perturbed by her presence.

"Where's Paul?" she asked a girl who was closest to her but she just shrugged her shoulders at her. *She probably doesn't even know who Paul is*, thought Jean. She looked at the vacant faces to see if there was anyone she knew but she had never seen these people before.

She stepped over legs and strung-out bodies, walked over and switched off the CD player, instantly bringing the room to silence before going into the kitchen. She stopped in the doorway and took in the sight of her son standing over beside the cooker. His back was towards her and he was bent forward onto the worktop in the process of snorting a line of cocaine. A girl sat slumped on one of the wooden kitchen chairs. Her skirt was pulled up over her hips so she could see her little thong and much of her pubic area.

"What do you think you're doing?"

He swung around at the sound of her voice, his eyes blazing and his teeth bared.

"This isn't on, Paul. This is my house – Chloe and Kyle have school in the morning!"

"Fuck off!"

"Paul, I'm serious, I want all your friends out of the house immediately."

The girl on the chair suddenly began to sway and Jean rushed over to steady her. She opened her eyes momentarily, before smiling at Jean and shutting them down again. She was out of it.

"No one's going anywhere!" he roared at her.

"Paul, please, I'm asking you – just tell everyone to go home. The party's over."

"No, it's fucking not, you stupid bitch! Who the fuck do you think you are, trying to tell me what to do?"

"I'm your mother, Paul –"

"No, you're bleedin' not! You're nothing to me!" He lunged forward so that before she knew it, she was lying on the ground and he was on top of her, thumping her in the head. She could hear herself screaming at him to stop from afar, *"Stop it, Paul . . . please . . . stop!"* She screamed for help, *anyone*, but the swaying girl merely opened her glazed eyes again and stayed slumped on the chair.

Through swollen eyes she saw Chloe and Kyle come into the room, the fear written all over their small faces. Mercifully Paul stopped punching her when he saw them and Jean thanked a God she didn't believe in. She tried to speak to them to tell them it was okay but the words wouldn't come out and instead she had to spit out a mouthful of blood. She watched the blood, mixed with spit, pool on her beige kitchen tiles. Chloe and Kyle both turned and ran out of the room and Jean prayed they would just stay in their room, out of his way until he had calmed down. She reached upwards to grab onto the edge of the table and managed to pull herself up onto her feet. Her head was spinning and she had to hold onto the table to keep steady. Through slitted eyes she saw ruby-red trails of blood were staining her pyjamas. Paul was standing holding onto the sink with his back to her. Using the wall as an aid, she managed to feel her way quietly over to the door; she had to get away from him. She had just put her foot onto the wooden floor in the hallway when she heard heavy footsteps behind her.

"Where the fuck do you think you're going?" he roared.

"Paul – stop – I –"

He grabbed hold of her wrist and swung it back until she heard it crack. The pain seared through her arm. The thumps rained down on her again, heavy and fast, as she slid onto the floor, putting her hands over her head to protect herself until she thought she was going to pass out. She didn't know how long the beating went on for.

Finally she heard a noise coming from behind the door.

"Stop what you're doing! Gardaí Síochána. Stop!"

Someone finally pulled him off her. A woman's voice could be heard talking softly to her but Jean couldn't make out her face through eyes that were almost closed now.

"You're okay now, it's okay. It's all going to be okay."

The woman helped her up and sat her at the table and Jean realised she was a Garda. She began to cough and had to spit out another mouthful of blood. She could hear the Gardaí ordering everyone out of the house. She watched as Paul was put into handcuffs and led away. The girl who had been strung out through Jean's ordeal came to, looked at the scene around her and just walked out, oblivious to what had just happened in the same room as her.

"Don't worry, the ambulance is on its way," the female Garda reassured her. "I think your wrist is probably broken and we need to get those cuts looked at – you might need some stitches."

She went to the fridge and Jean could hear her rooting around in the freezer.

"Here, put this on it." She held a bag of frozen peas wrapped in a tea towel up to Jean's head.

And then the tears started as the shock began to subside. Jean hadn't cried in years but they were flowing freely now; the worry, the fear for the last few months, the relief that the Gardaí had come when they did, the kindness of the woman looking after her – it was all released.

"It's okay, you get it all out," the Garda said, holding onto her shoulders. "It's not the first time, is it?"

She shook her head, her whole body heaving with sobs. She registered the small outlines of Chloe and Kyle as they appeared around the door before they ran over and put their arms around her. She tried to hug them as best she could.

"How did you know to come?" Jean asked the Garda.

"This brave little man here gave us a call." The Garda smiled at Kyle.

Jean looked at the shy face of her ten-year-old son and felt a horrible mixture of deep gratitude and guilt; he shouldn't have had to do that.

"I'm so sorry!" She began sobbing louder until Kyle and Chloe joined in and the three of them huddled together crying.

"Now, have you anyone who can come and look after these two while you're gone to the hospital?" asked the Garda.

Jean didn't want to call Louise, she really didn't want to do that, but she didn't exactly have many options. She nodded meekly.

"I can call my sister."

The game was up; she knew she could no longer hide the truth from Louise.

* * *

The hospital put seven stitches in the wound above her eyebrow before bandaging it with a large gauze pad that stretched halfway across her forehead. They gave her drops to take down the swelling in her eyes so she could see out through them again and her left wrist was put into a cast all the way from her forearm down over her hand.

When she finally got back home after seven in the morning she was exhausted by the night's events. Her bruised and battered body was weary. She rang the bell and Louise ran out into the hallway to let her in. She threw her arms around her younger sister. They walked in silence into the sitting room where Louise had been waiting up for her with only the lamp lighting up the room. Jean noticed the room had been tidied up from its earlier state but it still reeked of stale smoke and beer.

"Why didn't you tell me?" Louise started to cry.

"I'm so sorry, Louise, I couldn't – I just couldn't bring myself to say it."

"I'm so sorry! I knew something was up the other day. I knew something wasn't right, I just knew it, but I went off and left you. He did that too, didn't he? That bruise over your eye last week, that was him, wasn't it?"

Jean nodded.

"God, Jean, I'm so, *so* sorry. I let you down. You must have been so scared!"

"Sure, what are you sorry for? I should have told you but it's hard, you know, to admit your own son has done that to you. I just don't know what has come over him . . . the last few months, it has been like living with – a – a time-bomb."

"I wish you had told me, I could have helped you out, got Brian to talk to him or something?"

"I think he's beyond talking to at this stage."

"Jesus Christ, he could have killed you – that wound over your eye and your wrist – how could he lay a finger on his own mother? How could he do that to you?" The anger in Louise's voice was unmistakable.

Jean stayed silent; she was wondering the same thing herself. They stayed like that, looking at each other.

"How are the other two?"

"They're fine – they were a bit upset when you left but they're fast asleep now."

"Thanks."

"What are you going to do?"

"I don't know, I really don't know," she sighed.

"Hopefully getting the Gardaí involved now will have given him the wake-up call he needs."

"I hope you're right." *I really hope you're right.*

After they had talked it out, Jean tiptoed into the bedroom that Chloe and Kyle shared. Although it was nearly time to be getting up for school, no one would be going to school today. Their room was divided in two by an invisible line down the middle so that only they knew where it was. Their peaceful faces were lost in the land of slumber and showed no signs of their fears from earlier on. She hoped they were dreaming sweet dreams. She felt a pang of guilt for what they had seen that night. They must have been scared out of their minds, especially if Kyle had rung the Gardaí. How brave he had been! She gave them both a kiss on their foreheads before creeping out again and shutting the door quietly behind her.

Jean hadn't realised how difficult things would be with only one functioning hand so she was glad Louise was there to help her to get ready for bed. Louise tucked her younger sister up, making sure she was comfortable, before heading home herself to get her own two ready for school but promising she would be over again later on.

When she was finally alone, an exhausted Jean fell into a deep sleep; nights of broken sleep full of raging fears and worry had finally caught up with her. She didn't wake until she heard her doorbell ringing. Her head was thumping. She looked at her cast momentarily before it all came flooding back to her. As she got out of bed, her whole body felt stiff and achy. She made her way towards the door. She caught sight of her reflection in the hall mirror. *Jesus.* She was startled by her bruised and swollen face and the white bandage across her forehead. Through the glazed panes at the end of the hall, she could make out the shape of the two Gardaí from last night standing on her doorstep again. She pulled back the door to them.

"How are you this morning, Jean?" They both smiled kindly at her.

"I've been better."

They both nodded at her. "Of course."

"We didn't really get a chance to introduce ourselves properly last night. I'm Garda Lisa Jones and this is Garda Terence Fingleton. We just want to have a talk about the events last night, the lead up to it etcetera."

"Sure. Will we go into the sitting room?"

They sat beside each other on the sofa while Jean sat gingerly into the armchair.

"Now, there's no need to worry," said Terence Fingleton. "Paul is sleeping it off in a cell but we need to ascertain what exactly happened last night."

She relayed the story as best she could remember but it had all happened so fast she wasn't sure if she was recalling everything exactly as it had unfolded. They nodded sympathetically and took notes as she spoke but for every word they wrote down against her son, Jean felt a stabbing in her heart.

"What we need to determine is where you want to go from here?" said Lisa Jones.

"How do you mean?"

"This can't continue, Jean," Terence Fingleton said. "He savagely beat you last night, you're lucky the damage wasn't more serious. He has done it to you before and, in my experience of situations like this, I would say there is a pretty high risk he will do it again. For the sake of your two younger children . . ."

"It isn't a good environment for them to be living in, Jean," Lisa Jones interjected. "And they could be in actual danger."

"I know."

"So what we need to ask you is –" Terence Fingleton looked at his colleague before continuing, "whether or not you intend to press charges?"

She was horrified at what they were suggesting. "Against my own son?"

"Jean, I realise this is hard for you but domestic violence is a crime like any other. The sad part about it is that it is usually someone we love that is the perpetrator, which leaves the

victim in a very difficult and emotionally conflicting position –
but that doesn't mean it should go unpunished."

Jean zoned out on what they were saying. All she could think
of was they wanted her to Judas her own son.

"Of course we are very sensitive to these matters and we
have dealt with similar cases in the past. Now, granted, the
usual cases are husband and wife rather than mother and son,
but we have very experienced staff who are available should
you require their services."

"I can't."

"Can't what?"

"I can't do that to my own son. I just can't do it."

"Jean, I would strongly urge you to consider it. You are not
to blame here. He has committed the act, not you."

He wasn't like that, she wanted to tell them. Paul was her
son, *her baby*. It wasn't black and white like they were suggesting.
What had happened to her baby boy who had been the light of
her life, her firstborn that had filled her with such pride? When
he was a boy, he had been sweet and gentle, constantly giving
her kisses and cuddles. She still had his artwork from primary
school, scrawly drawings with childish handwriting "*I love
you, Mammy*" with hearts falling in an arc from a small stick-boy
towards his mother. He used to be great helping her around the
house, cutting the grass for her or watching the other two. In fact
she had relied on him, he was the man of the house, he took
pride in helping her out and they had a special bond, a
different bond than that she had with Chloe and Kyle. He was
older than them by a good few years so had an understanding of
the situation. Maybe it was her own fault because she had been
unconsciously treating him as an adult for years. They had a
special trust but recently he seemed to have replaced their
closeness with resentment and anger. She still could only see
Paul as her son and it was her job, as ever, to protect him.

She stood up and they took this as their cue to go.

"Okay. Well . . . ultimately, Jean, it is your decision. If you decide not to pursue things any further, he will be cautioned and released today and hopefully that will be enough for him."

"It's okay. I just want to leave it for now." She could see it in their eyes: they were judging her.

"Well, it's up to you how you handle things from here but please be aware that we are obliged to inform social services about Paul's behaviour due to the fact that there are children living here who may be in danger."

"I see," Jean said.

"In the meantime please don't be afraid to ring the station if you run into any more problems with him."

"Okay, thanks." She just wanted these people gone from her house.

She showed them out and stood at the door watching the squad car as it drove off and made its way towards the top of the estate. Litter swirled along the green, dancing in the wind before it got caught in the wire fence at the edge of the estate. She shivered and went back inside and closed her door to shut out the cold air.

28

November, 1991

Jean bundled herself into the phone box and slotted in the coins and dialled the number of her home. It was her mother who picked up.

"Hello?" Jean could hear the tiredness in her voice and her heart ached with regret.

"Mam, it's me."

"Jean, oh Jean, love! Where are you? Are you okay?" She started sobbing hysterically down the phone.

"Mam, I'm fine, please, don't worry. I needed to be with Gavin. We're a family now." The guilt began to rise inside her.

"Jean, please come home!" her mother wailed.

Jean had never heard her cry like that before.

"Pleeeease, Jean. I-I'm so worried, I haven't slept since the night you left. Y-y-you're pregnant, you're not in any condition to be running off around the country. Come home, love, we'll talk it out, we can sort it out. We were probably a bit too hard on you, I can see that now, but if you just come home, we'll work it out."

Jean would have liked nothing more than to tell her mother

176

where she was and have them come and collect her and take her home. She wished desperately she could say she was coming home, get on a bus back to Ballydubh, run through the kitchen door and put her arms around her mother and sleep in her own bed, but she had to be an adult now, she was going to be a mother in a matter of weeks, she needed to grow up sometime.

"I can't, Mam." She started to cry too.

"Please. Jean, I'm begging you – for your sake and the sake of your unborn child – you're only *seventeen*, you need your family around you, love."

"I'm sorry, Mam, I'm so, so sorry. I love you all. I really do." And then she hung up on her mother.

Her body heaved with sobs as she stood in the Perspex phone booth, tears streaming down her face until an angry-looking woman rapped on the door and told her "Get the fuck out of the box if you're not using it!' Jean wasn't used to people speaking to her like that and the woman just made her feel even more wretched.

She ran down the street with tears blinding her vision. She didn't feel ready for this; she had made a mistake, she wanted to go home. She needed her mother, someone who knew what it was like, someone who would take care of her. She was frightened, alone and scared. She came up to a bench overlooking the river; she sat down on it and cried. She loved Gavin but, in the harsh light of reality, their dreams of running away together now seemed ill thought-out and immature. How were they going to afford a baby when they couldn't even feed themselves? She had never even held a baby before, she was the youngest in her family, she had never had younger brothers and sisters or even small cousins to practise on. Then there was the birth. She was scared and she didn't know what to expect and the more she watched her bump grow, the more the fear inside took over. *How was she actually meant to get it out?* But she was too embarrassed to talk to Gavin about it. She knew he was trying hard to sort them out and provide for them but as the weeks went on she was becoming disillusioned by his attempts and now he was starting to grate on her.

She sat there alone for a few hours, just watching life around her. She knew she had to stop feeling sorry for herself – this had been her choice as well but she hadn't known it was going to be this hard. She had to keep telling herself that she wasn't a baby any more; she was going to *have* a baby. She had made her bed, now she would have to lie on it.

Almost as if he could read her thoughts, when Gavin came home that evening he had a bouquet of bright, unnaturally coloured carnations in his hands for her. She groaned inwardly because they couldn't afford flowers. Flowers meant they went without a meal because their finances were so bleak but when he announced that he had managed to get a job in a pub, she jumped up and hugged him. He told her how he had been calling into every bar and pub in Cork City but no one had any work. He'd almost walked past a tiny pub, dismissing it as too small, but he said he'd try anyway. There had been an old man, about eighty Gavin reckoned, sitting on a stool behind the bar with a few old men with caps on sitting up on stools at the bar. They all turned to look at him and he was about to walk back out when the old man asked if he was all right. He mumbled that he was just looking for work but that he could see they probably didn't need anyone. He turned again to leave but then the old man said he was getting too long in the tooth for running the pub himself and was looking for someone to come and do the evenings for him. He told him he could start tomorrow night.

Jean jumped up and down and hugged him. She didn't care that this meant he would be gone every evening; she was just so relieved that he had a job.

From then on, Gavin headed off to work every day from

four to close which was usually the early hours of the morning. The work itself wasn't too hard – basically, he was serving the same few elderly men that had been coming into the pub, some every day, for the last forty years. For them it was more a social outlet than for the drink. Gavin soon learnt that the majority of them were widowers or bachelors who had never married. He grew to know them and their stories and they warmed to him too and would slip him the odd fiver here and there which he promptly gave to Jean to save up for the baby. He would come home and climb into bed beside her and sleep until lunchtime before getting up again to get something to eat before heading off on his bike to the pub.

He worked all the hours he could get and so Jean spent most of her days alone. She would usually walk into town, picking up tiny fleecy baby outfits in expensive boutiques to look at them before putting them back down again because they couldn't afford them. Sometimes she would ring her mother or Louise just to talk to them and hear their voices, but no matter how many times they asked, she would never tell them where she was. They would cry and beg her to come home, telling her over and over that they were worried about her and that the way she was living was no way to bring a baby into this world, but she wouldn't change her mind, not now, not after all Gavin had done for them. He was working so hard to make a life for them together, to take care of her and their unborn child. She didn't admit to them that she had the same fears as they had; how *were* they going to manage? Was she going to be on her own all day with the baby while Gavin worked? Would he be around to help? But even though she was scared about what lay ahead for them, she couldn't throw that all back in his face, not now after all he had done for her.

29

The stress and strain of the final months of pregnancy began to take its toll on Jean; money worries, doubts over how they would cope when the baby was born and even fears about what to do with a baby were continuously on her mind. She wasn't sleeping well at night and she was constantly tired and pale. She desperately wanted her mother near her; she needed her reassurance about what lay ahead. She would pluck up the courage and dial the house phone. She longed to say the words "Mam, I'm sorry – I want to come home" but the words would never come out. Sometimes she didn't say anything at all. She would hear her mother's soothing voice at the other end of the line saying "Hello. *Hello?* Hello, is there anyone there?" and she would hang up the phone again with tears streaming down her face.

One chilly February day, she sat shivering in their bedsit. The rain was coming down in icy sheets outside the house. It was a grey and bleak day. They had only storage heaters and as they couldn't afford the cost of them they didn't use them so the place was permanently freezing. The paper-thin walls had no insulation and you could feel the draughts coming through the sides of the windows. She walked around tidying up the bedsit, wearing a hoodie and a large woolly jumper belonging to Gavin over it, but no matter how much she moved or how many layers she put on, she just couldn't get warm. Gavin had already gone into work for the evening. She tried to read her book but she just couldn't get comfortable – her bump was heavy and awkward and was starting to weigh down on her now. She got up to make herself yet another cup of tea to keep her hands warm when she felt a pain across her whole bump. She had to lean forward and hold onto the side of the cooker until it passed. The same thing happened again some minutes later. The baby wasn't due for another few weeks yet, she told herself, it was too early for labour pains, but soon she was caught up in waves of agony and she knew that the baby was on the way.

She threw on a raincoat that was hanging on the back of the door and made her way to John Grace's front door, picking a path through the puddles. She knocked hard but he wasn't home. The lights were all off and his car wasn't in the drive. The rain was pouring down on her now. She had to lean forward and place her palms flat on to the panels of the front door to steady herself as another contraction gripped her. She knocked harder still, willing someone to answer but there was no one there. She knew she would have to walk to the telephone box down the road.

Her steps were slow and clumsy as the pressure became unbearable. She kept having to stop as another contraction took hold. Passing motorists splashed the pools of water from the side of the road up onto the footpath so that muddy trails of grit were running down her face as she bent to endure the contractions. Finally a car, seeing the hunched-over figure out on such a night, knew something must be up and pulled up on the path beside her. The driver asked if she was okay and then, when he saw her bump and the agony on her face, he told her to get in and said that he was taking her to the hospital straight away. Jean couldn't even answer this stranger. He told her it was okay, he was a father of three himself. Jean knew from his kindly eyes that she could trust him. He brought her into the hospital and handed her over to the nursing staff. She didn't even get to thank him.

She was led straight to the delivery room. The midwives looked at her, full of pity, a young girl drenched with rain and her eyes full of fear and terror. The contractions were coming thick and fast now, one on top of the other, there was no let up. They would start off down low before gripping her abdomen like a vice and then wrapping around into her back. She tried to tell the midwives to ring Gavin but they told her there wasn't time and that it was time to start pushing the baby out. She felt the pressure bearing down on her and the urge to push became overwhelming. She summoned up all her strength and pushed her baby out into this world.

"It's a boy!" she could hear them telling her from afar and then she heard the primal infant cry as they placed her newborn son in her arms. She looked down at him with his tufts of dark hair, looking so much like his father. He was small but perfectly formed, with the most beautiful little fingers and toes. She couldn't believe that this tiny little being, this small bundle, was hers.

* * *

A while later, when she was back in the ward, Gavin's head appeared around the curtain of her cubicle.

"I'm so sorry, I'm so sorry!" he panted. "I only just got the call and I came as fast as I could."

He stopped in front of her in awe of their tiny baby in her arms.

"Do you want to hold your son?"

"A boy?"

Jean nodded and placed the towel-wrapped baby delicately into his arms.

Gavin stared at him in wonderment, taking in every detail on his small scrunched-up face and his pouty lips.

"He's perfect, isn't he?" Jean asked.

"He is that all right." He couldn't take his eyes off him. "What are we going to call him?"

Jean went silent.

"What?"

"Well, I was hoping – if you wouldn't mind – I'd like to call him Paul, after my dad." She lowered her gaze and felt the familiar pang of longing for her family. There was an unmistakable sadness in her eyes.

"Sure, of course, pet. Baby Paul it is."

* * *

In the weeks that followed, Jean was snowed under by the routine that her new baby demanded. It was a never-ending conveyor belt of nappy changes, four-hourly feeds and winding. Sometimes it felt like she had just put Paul to sleep after the last feed by the time he was awake and grizzling again. She would look at the clock in disbelief but it would indeed be four hours later. She would sigh before lifting him from his crib and the cycle would start all over again. In the evenings he would cry so hard his whole body would tense up and his face would turn purple because he was screaming so hard. He just wouldn't settle no matter what she did – she tried burping him, walking with him around the room, rocking him in his crib or singing to him – but nothing she did would ease his distress. Jean herself would begin to get upset because she felt like such a failure watching her son in pain and not knowing what to do to help him. Then John Grace would bang on the wall and roar at her to "Shut that bloody child up!" She was starting to feel trapped, as if the four walls with the velvet wallpaper were coming in around her. Sometimes the crying felt as though it was drilling into her brain and she didn't think she could stand it any more. And because Paul was still so small and the weather so bitter, she didn't want to risk taking him outside until he was hardier so she was confined indoors most of the time.

The days dragged with no one to talk to but her baby son and she longed for other company, but then he would look up at her with his innocent blue eyes and she would feel guilty for her thoughts.

Now that Paul was here, neither could believe how much having a baby ate into their already limited finances. Gavin was working more than ever to pay for the nappies, formula and clothes for him, plus it was one of the harshest winters on record and they needed to have the heat on constantly. He would reassure Jean with a kiss every day that it was just for a few months and, when summer came, he would be at home more to help her – but the weeks seemed endless to her.

Gavin would come home in the early hours of the morning and, no matter how quiet he tried to be, inevitably in the one-roomed bedsit he would wake Paul, always after Jean had just settled him. Gavin would collapse into bed exhausted, leaving Jean to get up again to see to the baby. Then in the mornings she would be busy looking after Paul while Gavin slept late.

She had phoned her parents from the hospital the day after Paul was born to tell them that she'd had a baby boy and that they had named him Paul after her father. They had begged her to let them come and visit, promising that they wouldn't put any pressure on her to come home, that they just wanted to see their grandson and her, just to make sure they were both okay. She had asked Gavin what he thought but he told her it wasn't a good idea, that once her parents knew where they were living that would be it. So even though it broke her heart, she stood firm and refused to allow them to come to see her. She missed her mother desperately – she needed her help, she had so many questions about Paul that she wanted to ask. Was it normal for him to cry this much? Was there something wrong with him? She felt so alone.

One evening when Paul was a month old, he started his usual evening screaming but this time his hair was damp with sweat and his body felt hot to the touch. Jean began to worry. She stripped him but nothing was calming him.

John Grace was knocking on the paper-thin wall next door, shouting *"For the last time, would you ever shut that bloody child up!"*

She began to panic because she didn't know what to do. She didn't know if he had a pain or if he was sick, she didn't even have a thermometer to check his temperature. His crying had a shrill, high-pitched tone to it and, as his screams began to get higher and more agitated, Jean panicked. The sensation that her baby was distressed and nothing she was doing was helping him was overwhelming, until eventually she was crying with him.

And that was it; she snapped. She'd had enough; she couldn't take any more of this. She wrapped her baby in two blankets and put a woollen hat on his head before putting him into the buggy. She grabbed her bag and coat and ran down the road to the phone box, pushing the buggy in front of her. She dialled her parents' number.

"Hello?" she heard her mother's voice answer sleepily and her father asking who it was in the background.

"Mam, it's me."

"Jean, love, are you okay?"

"Paul has been crying all evening – I don't know what to do!" she sobbed.

"It's okay, love, it's okay. Where are you? We need to help you."

"I'm in Cork."

There was a short silence. Jean guessed her mother had

expected her usual refusal to say where she was and was taken aback when she told her.

"Tell me exactly where you are, love. We're coming to get you right now."

Instantly Jean felt as though a weight had been lifted from her shoulders. She gave her mother the address and said goodbye. Then she replaced the receiver with a shaking hand and stepped out of the phone box. She took a deep breath in the cool air and exhaled, watching the plume of white air form in front of her. It was going to be okay. She pushed the buggy back to the bedsit. As she sat waiting for them, for the first time all evening, she noticed there was silence. Paul had stopped crying.

*   *   *

It was a tearful reunion for the McParlands. Jean fell apart as the tension of months of trying to hold it all together was released. Úna and Paul peered into the cradle at their little grandson, looking so contented as he slept, showing no signs of his marathon crying session from earlier on. They were appalled by the conditions that Jean and Gavin has been living in. They had known things were bad but they had no idea just how bad.

When Gavin finally came in the door from work after three in the morning, he was shocked to see Jean's parents there sitting on the flowery settee. He knew them to see but he had never even spoken to them before. The look of contempt and anger in their eyes was unmistakable. Gavin felt as though they all wanted to attack him.

"What's happened? Is Paul okay?" He looked at Jean for answers.

She nodded and dried her eyes with a tissue.

"I can't take it any more, Gavin."

"*What?*"

"This!" She gestured around the bedsit. "You being gone the whole time, me left on my own looking after Paul with him screaming the place down every single evening. I just can't take it any more."

She could see the hurt register on Gavin's face. She felt as though she had betrayed him.

"I thought this was what you wanted?"

"I do, Gavin, I did – I love you but I can't live like this."

"Christ almighty, I have been working my ass off just to pay the rent, the bills. Do you think I enjoy being away from you and Paul the whole time? We're parents, we're grown-ups now, that's life!"

Mr and Mrs McParland sat with their eyes looking at the floor. They said nothing; this was up to their daughter.

"Well, I can't do it any more," Jean said quietly.

"So what are you saying?"

"I want to go home."

"You're leaving me?"

"No – I want you to come too."

"I'm not going back to that shithole!"

"Please, Gavin!"

"No fucking way am I going back there!" He looked at her and shook his head before walking out and slamming the door behind him so hard that it rattled against its thin frame.

"Would ye ever keep it down in there!"

John Grace banged on the wall again and Mr and Mrs McParland looked at each other in horror, wondering for the hundredth time since they had arrived here how their daughter ended up in a place like this.

They all sat in silence for a while until eventually Úna plucked up the courage and asked Jean softly what she wanted to do, saying that either way it was her decision and they would support her.

Jean was torn, she hated having to choose between the people she loved like this but she was at her wits' end. Her mind was made up.

"I'm coming home, Mam."

They helped her pack up her small amount of belongings. They wrapped Paul up in warm clothing and put him into the car while she finished off inside. She wrote a letter for Gavin, telling him that she was sorry but that she needed to be close to her family. She told him that she still loved him very much and begged him to reconsider and come home with her, that they would work something out together. She placed the note on his pillow and then closed the door behind her for the last time.

30

When Jean arrived home into the familiar house of her childhood, instead of feeling sad all she felt was an overwhelming sense of relief. It was bliss when her mother tucked her up that first night under a mound of blankets and duvets, with her bed already warmed with a hot-water bottle.

Her parents' house was warm and comfortable and didn't smell of dampness. The little things that she had taken for granted before now seemed like great luxuries. The feeling of soft carpet underneath her feet made a welcome change from the sticky lino in the bedsit with holes that were worn through to the concrete floor below. As did not having to wear layers of clothing just to keep warm. She knew it was a much better place for Paul too who seemed calmer from the moment they had arrived.

She rang Gavin in work the next day but the man who answered told her gruffly that he hadn't shown up for work.

"I had a funeral on today," he complained to her. "That fella will hear it from me now when he shows his face and you can tell him that too if you see him!"

She left her number and told him to call her or get Gavin to call her if he showed up. She was worried about him now on his own. They didn't know anyone else down in Cork. She plucked up the courage and decided to ring John Grace to check if he had seen him but he said there was no one there and that after the racket they had made the other night he was glad of the peace and quiet over the last few days. She hung up on him.

She went back into the kitchen, sat at the kitchen table and put her head in her hands. Her mother was holding Paul in her arms singing a lullaby to him. She looked up at Jean.

"Any luck?"

"No, he hasn't shown up for work and John Grace our landlord hasn't seen him. I'm really worried about him, Mam."

"Give him time, love, I'm sure he's okay – he probably just needs a bit of space, a bit of time to think."

"I feel so guilty, Mam, just leaving him like that – walking out the door with our son after all he has done for us!"

"There, there, love, I know it's difficult for you but you need to put yourself and baby Paul first. You couldn't stay in that place with a baby, Jean, c'mon! Sure the damp alone would have had you running in and out of hospital with him. And him weeks early and everything! It's no way to raise a child."

She looked over at Paul snoozing in her mother's arms and, granted, he seemed like a different baby since she had come back home. She didn't know if it was because of the comforts and warmth of where they were or if he could sense that his mother was more relaxed, but all Jean knew was that he didn't scream any more. She lifted him out of her mother's arms and smiled down at his gorgeous plump face. He smiled back at her.

"Did you see that, Mam? Paul just smiled at me!"

"Well, would you look at that! There's nothing like those

first smiles – I remember when you and Louise first smiled at me, I thought I might just burst with happiness."

Her mother busied herself making Jean a cup of tea and serving up a plate laden with cream cakes. Having full presses was another thing Jean used to take for granted but now she could really appreciate it.

* * *

The days went on and she didn't hear from Gavin. She had tried the pub on several more occasions and also John Grace, who was now losing patience with her, but they hadn't seen him or heard from him.

One day when she was up changing Paul's nappy she heard the doorbell go downstairs. Her parents were out at the time. She cursed inwardly as she tried to change Paul's nappy as fast as she could while he kicked his legs in the air and gurgled up at her. She picked him up and went down the stairs. When she pulled back the door she was shocked to see Gavin standing there. She threw her free arm around him in relief as her eyes pricked with tears.

"I'm sorry, Gavin – I didn't run out on you, I just couldn't take it any more." She sobbed into his shoulder. "But I've been trying to ring you. Honest I have. I phoned the bar – I even phoned John Grace every day!"

He reached out, took Paul in his arms and smiled down at his baby son who had got so much bigger even in the short while that he hadn't seen him. His pudgy fists thrashing about, Paul beamed back up at him.

"It's okay, I'm not angry with you." He looked at her. "I was angry – I was raging for a few days but I've calmed down now and I've had time to think and see it from your side. I know I was always working – I didn't have much choice but it can't have been easy being on your own all day with a new baby."

191

"Here, let's go inside, it's freezing out here and I don't want Paul to get a cold."

"What about your parents?"

"They're not here but don't worry. They've been great, really they have. They're not shouting and screaming at me like I thought they would, they've just been really supportive. And they *love* Paul – you should see my dad with him – he ooohs and aaahs over him – Mam says he was never like that with me and Louise." She paused and put her hand on his arm before leaning in towards him. "I'm so glad you're here, Gavin."

When her parents came home they were shocked to see Gavin in their living room. For their daughter's sake they tried to act calmly and not let their disappointment show. After all, he was Paul's father but, deep down, they had both been secretly hoping that they had seen the last of Gavin Grimley. They left the two of them alone to talk things out, praying that he wouldn't talk Jean into leaving home again. They were relieved when a couple of hours later they heard Jean letting Gavin out the front door. She came back into the kitchen and told them that he was going to stay with his father. They both breathed out a sigh of relief.

31

Gavin let himself back into his father's house, pushing back the heavy door. He was met by the stale air. He had never noticed it before. He made his way in to his father who was sleeping off the excesses of a bottle of whiskey in his armchair. Gavin couldn't believe the state he had got himself into. He seemed to be wearing the same filthy clothes since the day Gavin had left and he smelt dirty.

When he woke and saw Gavin there, he didn't seem surprised to see him. It was as if he hadn't even noticed that his son had been gone for the last few months. Gavin tried talking to him but he didn't seem to register him sitting there, he was so caught up in his own drunken haze.

The house was filthy, the kitchen had used plates and cups piled high, the curtains were closed and Gavin wondered if they had ever been opened since the day that he left. He walked back out and went up to his room. He couldn't believe he was back in this shithole.

* * *

Gavin knew he would need to get another job. He tried the village pubs first as that was what he had experience in and was offered a job in O'Casey's Pub. It was a lively place where all the young people in the town went. The place was literally heaving with people every Thursday, Friday and Saturday night and they had a DJ playing. It was worlds away from the place where he'd worked in Cork. Here there were four barmen on a shift, all young fellas like himself. The queue for the bar was always ten deep, with people ordering pints and shorts. The barmen were allowed to drink a few pints on the job as well – as long as they weren't falling around the place no one minded. At the end of the shift they would all sit down and drink a few nightcaps before heading off for home. Sometimes a few girls would stay back too and they would have a right laugh playing drinking games as the girls flirted to get more free drink. He loved going to work; there was always banter and *craic*.

He would call over to see Jean and Paul each evening on his way to work but he never felt as though he could fully relax in the McParland household. They watched his every move, waiting for him to make a cock-up before they would pounce on him. Of course Jean assured him that they weren't but it was clear as day in the looks he would get from Úna and Paul. They would look over his shoulder as he played with baby Paul; if he swung him in his arms they would tell him "Be careful with him!" or if he heated a bottle for him, they would double-check it again to make sure it wasn't too hot. They didn't trust his judgement or didn't seem to see that he was trying his best for his son. Some days if Paul was overtired, he wouldn't come to Gavin and he would scream crying if he tried to pick him up. Jean's parents would hurry over and take him out of his arms and of course he would instantly quieten then. He felt like roaring at them *'He's my son for fuck sake – I've a right to hold him too!'* but instead he internalised it and it went with all the other put-downs and the 'not feeling good enoughs'.

Jean never spoke up for him and Paul wondered whether she just didn't notice or if she was afraid to speak up against her parents, but either way it infuriated him how she could be so oblivious to it all.

He knew something had changed between them since they had come back to Ballydubh. Although he would never admit it, he resented the fact that she had chosen her family over him. He had been willing to give it all up for her but when push came to shove, she hadn't been willing to do the same for him.

He had asked Jean several times to come out with him to O'Casey's when he had a night off. He had told her it was a great spot but she rarely came; she wasn't one for drinking and found the crowd that frequented O'Casey's raucous. It was only then that Gavin realised that they were essentially different people. Sometimes she seemed so innocent to the ways of the world. How had he ever thought that she would be able to survive on her own in Cork without the back-up of her family? He'd had to do it for years since his mother had died but Jean wasn't tough like him.

He saw her as 'one of them' now. Her mannerisms were the same as her parents' and the way she would ask her mother first if there was a decision to be made about Paul drove him demented. 'Should I put a cardigan on him, do you think, Mam?' she would ask her mother instead of asking him, as Paul's father, what he thought. He couldn't even remember the last time they had been intimate. The only time they would get alone together was if they brought Paul out for a walk. Gavin knew she was a great mother to Paul – she would cuddle and kiss him and they had a bond like no other – but he found himself looking at her and wondering how they had even been together.

32

As the years went on, things stayed the same. Gavin would call in for an hour on his way to work in the evenings. Jean's parents would mumble a greeting to him and he would grunt one back, even though they despised each other. He knew the McParlands looked down their noses at him; their feelings hadn't thawed with time. But he didn't really care what they thought. Paul was old enough now to play with him and he would come running up to him as soon as he came through the door. He loved the rough-and-tumble play with his daddy.

When Paul started in primary school, Jean had got a job in the mornings in a solicitor's office in town, doing a bit of admin work. She seemed to like it and they were impressed with her aptitude so they had begun to give her more work on higher-profile cases and trust her with more complex issues. They suggested she should study a legal course part-time and said that they would even pay for the course but when she reluctantly told them she didn't have a Leaving Cert they had been shocked and never brought it up again.

* * *

One night Gavin came home from O'Casey's feeling warmed up by the couple of whiskeys they'd had after work. "Hey, Dad!" he shouted in to his father. He didn't respond so Gavin went into the dark sitting-room to check on him. He saw he was fast asleep in his armchair. Gavin stumbled over an empty bottle of whiskey that he had left on the floor and sent it clattering across the bare floorboards until it careered loudly against the radiator. He picked up the bottle and went up to bed.

When he got up around lunchtime the next day he went back into the sitting room to see if his father had even moved since the night before. When he saw him in the exact same position, his arms resting at the same angle, his mouth half-open the same way as when he saw him in the dark the night before, he knew something was up with him. His heart somersaulted and he ran forward and put his hand on his father's arm which was cold and stiff. He tried to pull him forward and listen to see if he was breathing but there was nothing. He realised then that he was dead. *No, Dad, please don't be dead!*

On autopilot he phoned Dr Thornton who hurried over and, using his stethoscope to listen, shook his head. "I'm sorry, Gavin, he's gone," Dr Thornton lowered his head.

Even though they hardly had anything remotely resembling a father and son relationship, Gavin was acutely aware that, apart from Jean and Paul, his father was all he had left in the world. They had long since lost touch with his relatives on his mother's side and his father had been an only child like himself. The loss brought back all the old feelings of when his mother had died when he was only seven years old, old enough to understand what had happened but young enough still to need her desperately. The anger and grief he felt overwhelmed him.

He got through the next few days and the funeral in a blur. Jean was by his side throughout and she even stayed over in the house with him so that he wouldn't be alone. She held him as he cried at night and they had a togetherness again that had gone missing years ago.

He went back to work the week after the funeral; he needed the distraction. For every pint he drank behind the bar, he would sneak a quick short as well. Pint, short, pint, short. Alcohol was the only thing that allowed him to forget. If anyone noticed, no one said anything to him because they knew he was grieving. But, before long, he couldn't get out of bed in the mornings without taking a quick swig of whiskey to knock the edge off the pain and get him through the day. He told himself that it was only temporary to help numb the pain of his father's death. An image of his dead father sitting in rigor mortis in his armchair with an empty whiskey bottle beside him would flash into his head and he would push it out again. He wasn't like him, he told himself, and he could control it. He would stop soon.

Jean began to worry about how he was coping. Some days he seemed to be dealing with it quite well and other days he would go to pieces. So that he wouldn't be alone, she decided to move in with him with Paul. He was delighted at first but once Jean was in the house it became harder to hide his drinking from her. At least in work he could drink all he wanted – it was a pub for God's sake, he was supposed to drink – it wasn't his fault that his job involved so much drinking. Of course he did try to stop, especially for Paul's sake – he didn't want Paul growing up the same way as he had – but he couldn't help it, he needed it to get him through the day.

* * *

One day after he had collected Paul from school, he went up to the bedroom and gulped back an entire naggin of vodka in one go. Instantly feeling warmer, he came back down to his son who wanted to go outside to play. Outside, the fresh air hit him and as he swung Paul around he started to feel dizzy.

"Faster, Daddy, faster, Daddy!" his son roared.

"You want to go faster? Okay then, you asked for it, matey!"

He spun and spun in rapid circles, the trees whizzing past his eyes and the sound of his son's infectious giggles filling the air until he found himself careering headlong into a spin that he couldn't stop, until eventually himself and Paul both came crashing down against the garden fence. He managed to protect Paul from the fall, taking the brunt of it himself, but Paul had got a fright and began to cry. When Jean had come in from work, Paul relayed the story to her as she cuddled him in her arms. Gavin told her they had just tripped up over a rock in the grass but it was a wake-up call for him. He swore he was never going to touch a drop again. For Paul's sake.

He took the bottles from his hiding-place in the wardrobe and poured them down the sink. He resisted temptations all around him in O'Casey's and was the only person sober in the place.

* * *

Paul was six years old when Jean sat Gavin down and announced that she was pregnant again. He was dumbfounded. For a start he could count on one hand the number of times that they had slept together in the last year. He normally came in so late that he automatically slept in the spare room so as not to wake her. He had asked her how she had let that happen and she had got really upset with him and stormed back to her parents with Paul in tow. He had reached for a bottle of whiskey again and, as he gulped it back, with every sip he wondered what the hell he was going to do now? It was hard enough providing for Paul but now, if there was a second baby on the way, how were they meant to afford it?

He knew his reaction was out of line so the next day he had swallowed humble pie and called over to the McParlands to apologise to Jean. He told her that of course he wanted this baby and that they would figure it out. They made up and Jean came back home. He made a promise there and then to himself to stop drinking. With a second baby on the way, they couldn't afford it for a start. But within three days he had succumbed to the pressure of the lads as they stayed back after hours in O'Casey's.

* * *

As the weeks of her pregnancy progressed, Jean was beginning to put pressure on him to get a more agreeable job with regular hours so that he would be at home more in the evenings to help out with Paul and the new baby that was on the way. She would give him the newspaper every day with jobs already circled and then she would ask him what ones he had applied for. He could feel the pressure mounting on him. He tried fobbing her off, saying that what he had was the best for everyone because he would mind the children when she was in work and be with them all day and that if anyone should change their job it should be her. She got upset with him, asking him why he was being so difficult, but he just couldn't contemplate leaving O'Casey's. It was the only thing that kept him going. It was the one place he could drink freely, no one noticed if he took an extra shot of whiskey or had a double vodka on the go. It was acceptable to drink there. If O'Casey's was gone, then he would be too.

* * *

At Jean's first scan the ultra-sonographer had probed around her belly for longer than normal.

"Is everything okay?" Jean had asked worriedly.

"Mmmmh . . ." The ultra-sonographer stared intently at the screen.

"What is it?" Gavin asked, scared.

"Don't worry, everything is fine, guys, but . . . well . . ."

"*What?*" Gavin demanded.

"Well, you're actually having twins!"

Gavin felt the blood drain from his head.

"Oh my God! Did you hear that, Gav – twins! That is unbelievable!"

He looked up at Jean and the ultrasound technician who were smiling wildly at one another as if this was the best news in the world.

"Is there a history on either side?" she asked.

"Not that I know of!" Jean replied, laughing.

He began to sweat; a mixture of water and vodka came out through his pores until he could smell the salt on his skin. *What the fuck? Twins! Jesus, things were bad enough as it was – he was barely getting used to the idea of another baby being on the way but twins! They didn't even fucking run in the family!*

He felt as though the walls were closing in around him. The pressure was unbearable. He looked at the two of them grinning at him like a pair of Cheshire cats. He looked at the door, which had a porthole window and, although he didn't know why, he suddenly found himself bolting out of the room. As he ran through the hospital corridors, trying to avoid bumps large and small, he could hear Jean's voice calling behind him but he had to get away.

33

A letter arrived on the doormat a few weeks later, with a postmark from Spain. It was from Gavin, explaining why he had left and that he was sorry but that they would all be better off without him. There was no return address. Jean ripped the paper into shreds and threw it onto the fire and watched it until the paper had singed and eventually dissolved in the heat of the flame.

Initially she was shocked at how Gavin had just walked out on her like that. How can you think you know someone only to discover that you never really knew them at all? But as the shock began to subside, she became angry. She never in a million years would have thought he would do that to her. Never. Her parents had been right about Gavin all along. She knew that if he ever so much as showed his face back in Ballydubh again, she would run him out of the village herself.

She moved back home with her parents once again. They stepped in as best they could but Jean knew they were bitterly disappointed in her. They had got over the fact that she had fallen pregnant with Paul, these things happened, people made mistakes, but to do it again, a second time – well, they had no understanding of how she could let it happen again and to be carrying twins was a whole other ball game. They knew the town gossips were having a field day but at the end of the day she was their daughter and they would do the best they could to support her.

It broke her heart how Paul, who was old enough to understand that his father wasn't around, asked where he was constantly. He was only six years old and he couldn't understand why his dad wasn't waiting for him outside the school gate like he used to. She tried to keep it together for his sake and for the sake of the two little babies growing inside her who were now starting to make their presence felt with small kicks and wriggles inside her rapidly growing tummy.

A few months later, Jean gave birth to a boy and girl. She named them Chloe and Kyle.

The first few years were tough. Jean had her hands full with a seven-year-old boy and newborn twins. Her parents tried their best to help out but the house wasn't big enough for all of them. Jean returned to her job in the solicitor's office in an effort to pay their way while her parents minded her three children. They brought Paul to school in the mornings and she collected him on her way home from work in the evenings. But Úna and Paul found themselves resenting the fact that although this was the period of their life when, having reared their own kids, they should be winding down and starting to live their lives again, instead they were back in the baby stage. Jean could sense that they were growing tired of having the house overrun by three small children so it was a relief for all concerned when Jean managed to get a council house in a village nearby. They would still be close enough to help out but they would have their house back to themselves again.

The house that Jean was given was basic and in many ways the leaking windows and lack of proper central heating reminded her of the bedsit in Cork, but it was a roof over their heads and it was a relief to be out of her parents' hair. At least now if the twins cried during the night, she didn't feel under pressure to keep them quiet, or when Paul was tearing about the place pretending to play cops and robbers she didn't have to keep on telling him to be quiet.

She set about putting her own touches to her new home. Paul chose a cornflower blue for his room and she put a sunny yellow in the twins' room. Her dad helped her to paint the walls. He pulled up the ancient carpet and put down some semi-solid wood flooring, he sealed the leaking windows and hung pictures and photo-frames around the place. They gave her their old sofa and she decorated it with throws and cushions. For the first time in her life she felt as though she was finally taking control of her own life. For years she had been doing what her parents told her to do, then she had let Gavin take charge. Now it felt good to have her own independence, to do the things she wanted, to be a mother in the way she wanted without her own mother looking over her shoulder. In fact, she found it was quite liberating.

34

As the months after Gavin had left went by, Paul began to mention his daddy less and less. Jean was relieved that he didn't seem to be as upset as he first was. He loved his new school and was doing well. His teachers were happy with his progress. He still asked for his dad occasionally, usually after he heard other boys in his class talking about the things that they did with their dads. Her heart would break for him. It was different for Chloe and Kyle. They had no memory of Gavin so in some ways that was just the way things were for them, they didn't know any different. But Paul had memories of his father, he knew what it was like to have a dad and to have him taken away. She didn't know if it was because they had been together for seven years on their own or for what reason but she had a special bond with Paul, different to the bond she had with the twins. They had been through a lot together and she knew she treated him differently to the other two because of that. She relied on him. He would keep an eye on the twins if they were outside playing and he helped her do little jobs around the house. She called him her 'big strong boy' and when she said that to him, his face would burst with pride. She would let him stay up after the twins had gone to bed at the weekends and they would snuggle up together and watch a film with bowls of popcorn and goodies. It was their special time of the week together and they both looked forward to it.

Every year on Paul's birthday, Gavin would send him a card with money in it. But there was never anything for the twins. She assumed it was because he didn't know their birthday. She had heard through people in the town that he was running an Irish bar somewhere in the Costa Del Sol and she had remarked that it was very apt with more than a hint of bitterness.

But as the years went on Jean couldn't help but notice that the absence his father was having a huge impact on Paul. When the boys in his class realised that he came from a broken home, they had started bullying him. Jean had tried talking to his teachers but they didn't take it seriously and told her that that was just "what boys did" – they were just "playing". But she knew it wasn't right for a ten-year-old to come home from school with a black eye or ripped uniform; that wasn't "playing". She had tried to teach him how to stand up for himself but he was embarrassed and would tell her to leave him alone. She asked her father to have a chat with him but Paul had pretended that everything was fine. She had wished his father was still around to help him. Chloe and Kyle had each other but she couldn't help thinking that poor Paul was on his own.

The bullying had marked a change in Paul. No longer was he her sweet innocent son. He had grown up, almost too soon, and was tougher now and less inclined to let his feelings show. Whereas, before, he would walk up to her openly and put his arms around her, now he put on a brave front and he wouldn't show her any affection. Then he made new friends in the estate, friends that were a little older and from similar backgrounds as himself so he wasn't laughed at by them for not having his father around. His new friends were in the classes above him and as soon as the bullies saw who their victim was now hanging around with, they left him alone. The new friends became a shield around him.

Jean didn't like these boys. She knew their faces from where they hung around the estate every day, messing and smoking, but there was no doubt that Paul had seemed happier since he had made friends with them. For the first time in two years, he was sure of himself – a new-found confidence that Jean didn't want to take away from him, so she knew she had to tread carefully. She tried her best to distract him from his new friends but he wasn't having any of it.

Things began to go downhill. At eleven years of age she had smelt cigarettes on him, at twelve he had stumbled in drunk. It became a daily battle to get him to go to school and keep him in there. Whereas once he had excelled, now in secondary school Paul was one of the troublemakers. She was forever being called in to discuss his behaviour and Jean had to beg for second chances from disgruntled teachers. She knew he was doing drugs at fourteen; he would come home with his eyes rolling in his head and his tongue bulging in his mouth. He brought girls up to his room and no matter how Jean tried to stop him, he wouldn't listen to her. He would lash out in temper, kicking holes in the door or the wall or throwing her belongings on the floor. One time he had flushed her phone down the toilet because she wouldn't give him money. He was finally expelled at the age of fifteen. Jean didn't blame the school, she knew there was nothing they could do for him any more, but it now meant that he was at home all day with time on his hands and his temper seemed to grow. She began to fear his outbursts. She was afraid to be in her own house and it was her own fault for giving in to him over the years. It was as if he blamed her first for his dad leaving and second for being bullied at school, and her guilt meant that she made excuses for him. But he was out of control. She knew she had no one to blame but herself because when his behaviour had first started getting out of hand, she hadn't stood up to him. She hadn't challenged him on it and now she was paying the price.

35

November, 2009

When Paul came home from his night in the Garda cell, Jean was shocked at how calm he was. She had expected him to storm straight into the house and go ballistic but yet again her son surprised her by acting completely the opposite to what she had feared. While he didn't talk to her, he did stay out of her way up in his room. There was no music blaring and no shouting at Chloe and Kyle. Jean was dumbfounded by his behaviour but maybe the stint in Garda custody was the wake-up call that he had finally needed. When he was hungry that evening he didn't come in like he usually would and demand that she cook something for him, he just went and made it himself. Even the twins were gobsmacked and they all looked at one another with surprised faces.

When Louise called over to check how she was doing, she told her sister about the complete change in his personality. They both hoped it was a lesson learnt for Paul. He went out quietly that evening and Jean prayed he wouldn't come home in a state. She knew he could be fine when he was sober but under the influence of drugs and alcohol there was no telling what he would do.

She didn't even hear him come home that night. Usually he would come in slamming doors and turn up the stereo but she hadn't heard a sound last night. As she was getting breakfast ready for the twins the next morning, Paul stuck his head around the kitchen door and asked if she wanted anything in the shop. She was stunned by the gesture; it had been years since he had done anything remotely like helping her. She longed to walk up to him and draw him close into a hug and tell him that she loved him, but she knew that would be pushing it so instead she replied that she was okay for everything but thanks for the offer. When he left she let out a long sigh of relief. *My son is back*.

The atmosphere in the small house perked up instantly. Chloe and Kyle didn't seem so weighed down with worry and fear, and Jean could relax a bit more now that she knew Paul wasn't going to descend upon them all in a vicious rage. The Gardaí had rung to check how things were since he had been released and she was glad to report that things were great, in fact better than they had been in a long time. Imagine if she had listened to them and pressed charges like they had wanted her to do! Of course she was very grateful that they had stepped in when they did but all that was required was a caution and he was back to his old self again. Her son had learnt his lesson; he wasn't a violent man like they had made him out to be.

For the first time in weeks, she began to sleep at night without fear. Chloe and Kyle began to do better in school; the combination of being able to get their homework done in peace and getting a good night's sleep had worked wonders and made Jean feel awful because it was only now that she was realising just how badly they had been affected by Paul's violence.

Paul seemed to have a new-found respect for her and her house and no longer saw it as his own stomping ground to invite his friends over and do whatever he wanted. Whatever they had said to him in the Garda station, it had worked.

She stopped making excuses when her mother or Louise suggested calling over to her – she was no longer afraid of what state Paul would be in. He began to talk to her again – granted, there was no in-depth conversation, only greetings like 'Hi' or 'See you later' but it was a start. She hoped that maybe he was finally beginning to grow up. He still went out with the lads to God knew where and she was pretty sure he was still doing his assortment of drugs but, if he was leaving her and the twins alone, she was going to leave him alone.

36

December, 2009

Saturday morning was the one morning of the week that the Kinsella family all sat down and ate breakfast together. Morning time on the weekdays was a blur of trying to coax the girls to sit down to eat a few bites of breakfast cereal while Nora flustered around making lunches, finding missing school-ties and packing schoolbags that she had been promised were already packed. Her husband Pat was usually on the road early every day to beat the commuter traffic from their County Wicklow home into Dublin City Centre. But on Saturday mornings they normally all sat down together and had big blow-out late breakfast. Of course it was Nora who was left cooking the fry, flipping pancakes or pouring maple syrup over the waffles, but it was as much a treat for her as it was for the rest of the family. The three girls were seated around the breakfast table whilst Nora tossed the eggs over in the frying pan.

"I no want guggy-egg," Emily, the three-year-old, roared at her mother.

"No guggy-egg, love – I'll make it hard, so."

"But *I* want guggy-egg!" Katie, her four-year-old daughter, protested.

"All right, here you go then," Nora said in exasperation as she walked over to the table with the frying pan and placed the egg onto Katie's plate before bring the pan back over to continue cooking Emily's egg. Nora knew Katie was just doing it to be difficult – whatever her sisters did or wanted Katie had to do the opposite.

"What way do you want your egg, Orla?"

Orla was six and was a mini-adult in comparison to her two younger sisters.

"Guggy-egg is for babies, I want it hard."

"No, it's not!" Katie whined. "Mammy, tell her it's not!"

"Orla, guggy-egg isn't for babies – stop winding Katie up!"

"Ha!" Katie said goadingly to her sister.

"Now that is enough, the pair of you!" *Jesus, Sweet Mother of Divinity, why do I bother at all with family breakfasts? They aren't worth the stress!*

"But I need soldiers, Mam!" Katie was looking at the lonely egg on her plate.

"Right, sit back down. I'll put toast on for you now."

"I want soldiers too!" Emily was roaring again.

"Emily, I can hear you perfectly well – there is no need to shout."

Nora popped bread into the toaster and wondered how she would get through the day. It was only eight o'clock and already she was worn out from the demands of her daughters. And Pat was enjoying a lie-in as usual. It irked her that, even though she was up early with the kids all week, just because he went out to work he automatically felt entitled to his weekend lie-ins. It didn't matter to him that her job as a stay-at-home mother didn't operate from Monday to Friday with the weekends off and an hour-long lunch-break. In a few minutes she would shout down the hall to wake him up and he would wander into the kitchen with a big sleepy head on him and have his 'family breakfast' served up to him on a plate. She sighed and opened the fridge door and a carton of milk that had been hastily stuffed onto the edge of one of the glass shelves fell out and spilled all over the floor.

"For Christ –" she shouted but, when she saw her daughters looking at her wide-eyed, fearful of the tone of her voice, she stopped herself in her tracks. "Who left that there?" She took a deep breath. *Patience*, she reminded herself, *patience*. She knew already that today was going to be trying.

She had bent down on her hunkers and was looking into the cupboard under the sink for kitchen-roll when suddenly there was a huge screech from outside. Its pitch sent a chill down her spine. *What was that?* It was followed instantly by the sound of metal crashing upon metal. She felt goose-pimples rise on her skin. *Sweet Jesus.* She looked over at the three girls who now, instead of being frightened by her, were frightened instead by the noise coming from outside.

She hopped up and looked out the kitchen window. Her eyes scanned the garden as she saw clumps of leafy green foliage scattered all around the grass. *The hedge, there was a hole in the hedge. What had happened to the hedge?* Then she noticed the trampoline had been upended and was turned upside down, lying on the opposite side of the garden instead of in its usual spot. Deep ugly brown track-marks now divided the green lawn in two. Her eyes followed the tracks until they rested upon a car lying on its side. *A car!* It all seemed so out of place. *Why was there a car in their garden?* She could hear a commotion coming from the road.

"Pat! *Pat!*" She shouted down the hallway of their bungalow towards their bedroom. But he was already running towards her; he had heard it too. He ran past her and the girls and out the back door. The four of them followed in haste behind him. They all stood momentarily on the doorstep, just surveying the sight before them, trying to process what they were looking at.

Pat sprang into action. "Get the girls inside, Nora! Quick, call an ambulance!" he roared at her.

And at last she realised what was happening and ushered the girls back into the house. Her daughters looked at her for explanation, their small confused faces trying to make sense of why their dad was shouting and why there was a car lying sideways in their garden. She hurried them into the playroom and told Orla to put on the *Peppa Pig* DVD for the girls. Emily was thrilled by the impromptu viewing of her favourite cartoon without even having to ask for it. She started jumping up and down, repeating giddily, *"Peppa Pig! Peppa Pig!"* Orla was about to protest, probably something along the lines of her not wanting to watch *Peppa Pig* and how it was only for babies but something about her mother's voice and demeanour told her to do as she was told. She led her younger sisters into the playroom and turned on the TV for them.

Nora fumbled with the phone, trying to dial 999 while simultaneously peering out through the frosted glass in the side panels of their door.

"Hello, yes . . . There's been a bad accident. At the crossroads on Newtown Road – a car has gone off the road and tumbled into our garden. I'm not sure how many are in the car." Her voice was trembling. They took her address and said they would dispatch an ambulance and the fire-brigade.

She ran back out to Pat who was trying to peer into the car through the shattered front windscreen but the millions of small cracks made it impossible.

"They're on their way," she said.

He ran around to the back of the car, where the back window had fallen through and peered in.

"There's a baby in there, Nora. Holy Jesus!"

Feeling utterly useless, Nora willed the emergency services to hurry the hell on.

She watched, fearful that the car might explode or something, as Pat tried to climb up the undercarriage of the car so that he could look in through the side window.

"It's a man. There's a man in the driver's seat!" He started shouting into the car. "Hey, can you hear me? The ambulance is on its way. Can you hear me? What's your name?" Pat watched the man's eyelids flash open for a second before closing again. "You're going to be okay, just hang in there."

Eventually sirens could be heard in the distance, getting closer. The fire-brigade arrived first and mobilised themselves into action immediately. They cut through the roof of the car as if they were opening a tin of bins. The ambulance pulled up swiftly after. One crew immediately began trying to free the baby and another began to remove the man. Both were removed gingerly and placed on stretchers. And then the ambulance sped off in the direction of Dublin County Hospital.

Nora and Pat were guided back into their house by a Garda who had arrived on the scene also. He told them to sit down and made them sweet tea as if they were guests in their own kitchen. They all sat in silence for a while before he asked them for their version of events. They tried to tell him what they knew but the shock made it seem surreal and they weren't sure if they were making any sense. Eventually the Garda left and told them they would let them know as soon as they had any news on the victims.

Later on some of the neighbours had called around and they all sat huddled together around the rectangular table, adding in their pieces of the story. Nora and Pat soon learnt that there was another car involved too but it was a hit-and-run. It had gone into the ditch in front of the McDermotts' house but had reversed out and driven off before anyone had time to stop it or get its number plates. They shook their heads in despair as to how anyone could be so callous. The neighbours would fall silent as they all prayed inwardly for the man and the baby before someone would speak up again as they tried to process their disbelief at what had happened on their quiet country road that morning.

When the Gardaí phoned later that afternoon, they learnt the worst. The baby had died at the scene. It had been a baby boy, only six months old.

"Oh, dear God! In our garden!" Nora found it hard to take. She felt the blood drain from her head and her legs felt weak beneath her. She had to sit down on a chair and catch her breath. Although it was a baby she had never known, she was a mother herself so she could only begin to imagine what the parents were going through. The man was in a coma in intensive care but his condition hadn't deteriorated any further which they were hoping was a good sign. Pat had asked the Gardaí what had happened, what had caused the accident, but they weren't inclined to comment until their investigations had been completed.

That night as Nora tucked her three white-haired angels up in bed, she hugged them all so close that they tried to wriggle away from her arms in laughter. She was grateful that they didn't seem to pay much heed to that morning's events. Orla had asked what had happened and they had explained to her that there was a car-crash but never mentioned that there were people involved and she didn't ask. She seemed more concerned by the fact that their trampoline had been uprooted. How blessed Nora felt to be able to hold her daughters. To think that only that morning she had been groaning inwardly, losing patience at their ever-increasing demands! What that baby's parents wouldn't give for that! They would never get to experience it now. And what would have happened if the children had been playing in the garden at the time? Her blood ran cold at the thought. You really had to cherish each and every day, she thought.

Once the girls were asleep she went back out to her husband. He wasn't normally one for affection but he wrapped his arms around her so that her head was buried into his chest. She didn't need to be able to see his face to tell he was crying. The reminder of the fragility of life that day had shaken them and they both knew that they would never be the same again. She said a prayer for the family of the baby boy, people she didn't know but that were now living through every parent's worst nightmare; she prayed they would have the strength to get through it.

37

The first thing Jean noticed when her son walked into the kitchen was a large gash right above his left eye. He was also limping badly and grimacing at each step he took. She got a fright and instantly rushed over to attend to him but he pushed her away and sat down.

"What happened to you?" she asked worriedly.

"Leave it, Ma, will you!"

"That is some gash, Paul – you need to get that seen to." She looked down at his leg where it was swollen to twice its size. "Jesus, Paul, it looks broken. I'm taking you to the hospital."

She flustered around the place, moving papers and pushing jars to find her keys.

"Not now!" he said, raising his voice.

He looked out of it and Jean wasn't sure if it was because of the pain he was in or for other reasons so she backed off. She placed her keys back down on the counter. On the one hand he looked to be in tremendous pain but still he was insisting he didn't want to get it looked at.

She went out to the hallway and through the glass panels of her front door she saw that Paul's car was completely crumpled on one side. The metal was raised and folded and the white paintwork scraped off to reveal the tin underneath. She realised what had happened. She went back to the kitchen.

"I saw your car!"

He said nothing.

"What the hell did you crash into?"

"Ah Ma, stop, would you just give over, you're wrecking me head!" He hopped up from the chair, taking a sharp intake of breath, then hobbled in obviously excruciating pain upstairs to his bedroom.

She wondered what had happened and what trouble he had got himself into now. And worse – what kind of a state had he been in at the time? Suppose he had been driving faster? He was lucky he wasn't killed. She shuddered at the thought. Her heart lurched as she realised it could have been very different; at least bones would heal. She would allow him sleep off the effects of last night and then she would insist that they go to the hospital and get the wound and his leg treated.

She turned on the radio and went about the kitchen doing her chores. She cleaned out the fridge, throwing away a load of out-of-date yoghurts that Kyle had begged her for the week before but hadn't eaten. She shook her head despairingly; she couldn't afford to be throwing out food like this. She made a note to herself to tell Kyle later that the next time he begged her to buy him something in the supermarket he had better eat it. She cleaned down the counter-tops and swept and mopped the floor. She had to stop for a minute to flex out her wrist – she had only just got the cast off and, although the break had healed well, it tended to get sore if she did too much with it. She listened to the songs on the radio – it was one of those eighties hours. She sang along to A-Ha's 'Take on Me'. She remembered how she had thought that song was the best song ever when she was younger. She had bought the record and everything and had the band's posters all over her bedroom wall.

Then the serious tones of the newsreader could be heard as he broadcast the lunchtime news and the events that had taken place overnight.

An earthquake measuring Force 7 on the Richter scale had hit Chile; the workers of Aer Lingus were going on strike on Monday; a baby had died after a serious road-traffic accident in Newtown Village and the male occupant in the car was in a serious condition in Dublin County Hospital. The Gardaí were appealing for witnesses.

She knew that road well. It was a peaceful country road but all it took was for someone to hit those bends at speed and they could easily be gone – and there was one blind junction where there had been more than one accident in the past. Her heart went out to the family – to lose a child like that was every parent's worst nightmare.

Jean then set about dropping the twins to their Saturday activities: Chloe was going to her horse-riding lesson and Kyle was going to soccer practice. She was grateful to her parents who paid for their activities since she had lost her job – it would have broken the kids' hearts if she'd had to tell them that she could no longer afford it. Plus, she hoped it would give them an interest and a broader outlook on all the possibilities that life had to offer, and maybe stop them going down the same road as Paul. She wanted them to make something of themselves, be comfortable financially and not to make the same mistakes that she had.

When she got back to the house, she went up to check on Paul. She pushed back the door to his bedroom, cursing silently as it creaked, but he didn't wake. He was still sleeping off the effects of whatever was in his system.

It had been months since she was last in his bedroom and

she nearly gagged on the stale smell of smoke and overflowing ashtrays that littered the place. Posters of half-dressed pin-ups hung on the wall now – they hadn't been there the last time. She looked at the rise and fall of his chest. The gash on his head wasn't bleeding but it was gaping and could probably do with a stitch before it got infected. She couldn't see his leg and she didn't dare pull the blanket back to take a look. She tiptoed back out of the room and closed the door gently behind her. She would wait until he woke up.

Jean had half an hour to spare before she had to pick up the twins. She sat down with a cup of coffee and a digestive and switched on the TV. The news was on and they showed the mangled car involved in that crash on Newtown Road being lifted up by a tow-truck. She dunked her biscuit in her tea and tutted at the wreckage. *The poor baby didn't stand a chance*, she thought. She watched the Garda appeal for witnesses to the horrific hit-and-run.

Her blood ran cold. She hadn't known it was a hit and run. Jesus Christ. She thought about Paul: his crashed car, his wounded forehead and most likely broken leg and his reluctance to get them seen to. *No*, she told herself. *Don't be silly. Stop over-reacting, putting two and two together and getting twenty-two*. Paul wouldn't do that. He might be capable of a lot of things but he would never crash into another car and leave the scene of the accident. *Would he?* No matter how many times she tried to suppress the thoughts, they kept popping up again like one of those pop-up games that the kids had when they were babies that no matter how many times you hammered down the shapes, another blasted one would always pop up again. The doubts kept niggling at her and for some reason she just had a bad feeling about all of this. She really hoped she was wrong.

Almost on autopilot she got up and went to collect Chloe and Kyle. She walked past the wreck of Paul's car. She stood momentarily and surveyed it. It was damaged but not nearly to the same extent as the wreckage of the other car that had been on the news. There was no way it had been Paul's car. Sure he had driven it home. If it had been Paul's car, it wouldn't have come out of the crash with just a crumpled front bumper. She felt better as she drove away. She would talk to Paul about exactly what had happened. She was sure it was nothing major but she would have to broach it with him. She needed to make the point that, if he was driving under the influence of drink or worse still drugs, even if he had a lucky escape this time, he mightn't be so fortunate next time. He was going to have to cop himself on.

* * *

Chloe and Kyle hopped into the car and immediately started chatting to her, Chloe regaling her about how high the jumps were and Kyle about how he had scored the winning goal. They were both buoyed up and excited and she wanted to hug them close. She knew they were at that age where their childhood innocence would soon disappear. She wanted to keep the fragments and savour their excitement at small things for as long as she could because, as she had seen with Paul, in the blink of an eye they would grow up.

When she pulled up in the driveway and they saw Paul's car they both looked to her for an explanation.

"Oh, I think he just hit off something last night."

They both looked confused by her brief explanation but knew by her tone that they shouldn't push it any further.

When Paul finally got up the twins had gone to bed. Jean was glad because at least it would allow her to ask him without them overhearing. He hobbled into the kitchen, barely able to walk, his face etched visibly with pain at every movement.

"Have you any painkillers, Ma?"

"Sorry, love, only Paracetamol and I think you need something stronger than that – look, I really think we need to get that leg looked at."

"Not now. Just leave it, yeah?"

"But, Paul, you could really do serious damage. What happens if it doesn't set properly or if that wound gets infected? Jesus, you could get septicaemia in that!"

He was about to argue back but he let out a groan of agony instead. "In the morning," he said with a grimace.

* * *

The next morning, on their journey to the hospital, Paul became increasingly agitated and wound up. She put it down to the pain but when he kept telling her what to say and what not to say, the niggling worries about that hit-and-run on Newtown Road began to bother her again. He told her that she wasn't to mention anything about a crash; he had just fallen over at home. And she was to say it happened only last night, she wasn't to mention anything about Friday and if anyone did ask her where he had been on Friday night, she was to say that he was at home with her.

She looked at her son, deep into his blue eyes, and she knew.

38

Jean was thankful that she didn't have to lie to anyone at the hospital because she wasn't sure if she would be able to do it. No one had batted an eyelid at their circumstances and whatever story Paul had spun them, they believed it and assumed it was just your run-of-the-mill domestic accident. Although the sweat was pumping out through her pores, Jean sat shivering in the waiting room. She rubbed her arms to get warm and tapped her feet. How could he do that? *A baby had died.* And a man was seriously injured. That poor family torn apart because of *her* son. *Jesus Christ. Jesus fucking Christ. What the fuck was she meant to do now? Paul was her son, her firstborn baby, but he had gone too far this time.*

When he came back out to her with his leg in a plaster-of-Paris cast, balanced on crutches with his bandaged forehead, he smiled at her. It was the first time he had smiled at her in years. Just days ago she would have begged the gods up high to let her son smile at her but now, under these circumstances, it made her feel ill. She could have sworn there was a tinge of relief in it – she wanted to go up to him and wipe it off his face.

Slap his face hard and scream at him. *How could he have done that?*

They walked in silence back to the car. The news came on the radio and said they were still looking for witnesses to the crash. They were appealing again to anyone who knew anything or anyone who might have seen a white car in the vicinity. Paul leaned forward and turned it off. They both sat listening to the squeak of the wipers going back and forth.

"It was you – wasn't it?" Jean turned to him.

He didn't answer her but he wouldn't make eye contact with her. That was all the answer she needed.

When they got home, Paul went up to bed. She busied herself in the routine of making a snack for Chloe and Kyle but she couldn't stomach anything herself as the worries kept on circling around and around in her head. What should she do? On the one hand, she knew she should report him to the Gardaí. Somebody had died. But he was her son. She couldn't be a traitor to her own son, could she? She was the reason he was like this. It was her fault; he had a difficult upbringing and she needed to take her share of the blame on board.

She watched the other two innocently eating their tea, oblivious to the dilemma she was faced with. She opened a bottle of wine and they looked at her – she rarely drank but she needed something now. The heavy noise it made as it filled the glass calmed her. The stress was taking its toll; she was only in her thirties but she felt in her eighties. She wished she was that age – at least she would be close to death's door.

Why did this have to happen? Why her son? He had a tough enough life as it was and just as she finally felt she was getting through to him! If she let him down again, that was it, his life would be over. He would probably get a long jail sentence: driving under the influence, dangerous driving, failing to stop – the list of possible charges was endless. He would probably get life imprisonment. No judge would have sympathy for him.

They would look only at the black-and-white hard facts of the case. They wouldn't care if he was bullied in school or had a tough childhood or that his dad had walked out on him when he was small – none of that would matter in a court. This was the one time in her life that she could do something to protect him. But on the other hand a baby had died. *A baby!* She thought back over all the times where she had failed him: letting his dad walk out like that, the bullying in school, maybe she had been over-reliant on him, he'd had to grow up too quickly, he didn't have the childhood that the other two had. Every mother was hardwired to protect their child. The protective instinct was present as soon as he had been placed in her arms. No matter what, he was still her son, he always would be. Her mind was made up; she wasn't going to let him down again. She couldn't do that to him.

39

It had been Aido's birthday. He had a free house for the weekend, so they were heading over there for a session. They all sat around the living room drinking from tins of beer.

"All right, boys!" Paul came through the door, grinning at the lads.

"Jesus, where the fuck were you?"

"Patience, J, *patience* – all good things come to those who wait. Did your ma never tell you that?" He piled his tray of cans on top of the rest.

"Here, dish it up the fuck, would you? We've been waiting long enough!" J was irritated.

Paul took a small bag full of white powder from inside his jacket and threw it onto the table. J sat forward and immediately started untying it.

"Hold on a sec, what do you say?"

"Cheers, Paul."

"Louder."

"For fuck's sake – *Cheers, Paul!*"

"That's better – after all I do for you! I thought the pigs were onto me."

"What d'you mean?"

"There was a copper car behind me most of the way back here, so I pulled in to a garage but he kept on going."

"Ha, ha!" laughed Aido.

J proceeded to tip some of the cocaine onto the glass coffee table. He measured it out with a card before chopping the powder into individual lines, using the card to even them up. He took a fifty out of his pocket, rolled it up and began snorting up his nose before passing it on to the rest of the lads.

They knocked back tins and snorted line after line of cocaine until eventually they could no longer feel the insides of their noses. Paul was starting to feel good about himself. The stereo was pumping out the lyrics of Dizzee Rascal. He paraded around the living-room floor like it was him on stage. He stepped over the legs of the lads who were sprawled around the floors as he waved his arms and synched his lips to the music. He knocked over a half-drunk can that had been sitting on the floor and watched as it spilled out, forming a foamy pool across the carpet. He stepped over it and kept on dancing.

"Here, give us some more of that Charlie, J!" Paul said as he plonked down on the sofa again.

"Fuck off, you, get yis'er own!"

"What the fuck are you saying, and me after buying it for you?" Paul's eyes grew wide and angry.

"I'm only buzzin' off, ya' muppet ya! Here!" He slid the bag of white powder over to where Paul was sitting.

They sat around all night, drinking tins and hoovering up the last of the cocaine until the sun started to come up outside. Some of the lads had started to doze in their chairs. Someone was snoring in the corner. But Paul wasn't feeling sleepy; on the contrary he had never felt more alive. He was feeling thirsty but there was no drink left. The stereo was still blaring away and the room reeked of stale beer.

"Here, who wants a race to the shops? C'mon, me and Aido against J and Noel!"

"You're on!"

They went outside into the cool morning air in their T-shirts but they didn't feel the chill. J and Noel got into one car, while Aido got into Paul's passenger seat. When he turned the key in his ignition, the rest of the song from where the CD had stopped last night started up again but the beat was too fast and too loud now so he lowered it rapidly. He lit a cigarette and put it between his lips, then reversed at speed out of the driveway so the tyres screeched. He could see some of the neighbours coming to their windows to see where the racket was coming from. He gave them the finger out the car window and made the engine rev even louder.

He drove along with the window down, letting the chilly morning air into the car. The lads were following behind and as soon as they got out of the estate they tried to take him on the outside. He swerved across the road to block them. Aido turned the mirror around to see them and started laughing. When the road widened, he moved to the left but when J went to overtake again, he moved out right across the road to block him. But J bounded back to the left, managed to undertake him and moved ahead. Paul pressed his foot to the floor to catch him. They came up to a bend and Paul went up the inside. It was tight. He didn't know if he was going to get through. Aido looked over at him but there was nowhere else to go. His car was inches from J's wing. At the last minute, he got through. J swerved to the right, into the path of an oncoming driver who swerved to avoid them both.

"Fuck, that was close!" shouted Aido.

Paul's heart was thumping; the adrenaline was rushing through his veins. J was chasing close behind him now, sitting on his bumper. He zigzagged to the left and right, J trying to overtake. They bounded left then right and left again. They came up to a wider part of the road and J moved out to the other side so that they were neck and neck, taking up both sides of the road.

"Here we go! *Woo-hoo*! Floor it, Paul, c'mon!"

He pressed his foot down on the accelerator. The wind coming in through the window filled his ears from the speed. Their car moved marginally ahead before J's caught up again.

"C'mon, Paul! *C'mon!*" Aido was roaring in his ear. "*C'monnn!*"

His foot was to the floor but J's car shot ahead, Noel raising his fingers in a mocking L-shape to them as they passed.

The trees whizzed past as he tried to catch up. He tapped his jittery fingers on the steering wheel. They came up to a crossroads with a stop sign. J drove straight through, he wasn't stopping. There was no visibility right or left and Paul hesitated instinctively, his foot coming up off the floor. Then he accelerated out onto the junction at precisely the same moment that a silver Volkswagen came through from the right. He spun his wheel and swerved but it wasn't enough and he braced himself for the impact, waiting for the bang. Then came the sound of crumpled metal as he careered into the rear left-side wing of the other car. Their car skidded along for what seemed like an age but it was probably only seconds before they slid into a ditch and next thing he saw was a grass verge outside his windscreen.

Paul sat in the seat, too stunned to move, his whole body shaking uncontrollably. His chattering teeth felt as though they were banging off his brain.

"Jesus Christ. *Jesus Christ!*" Aido kept repeating. "*Jesus fucking Christ!*"

"*Shut up!*" Paul shouted back at him. "*Just shut up!*"

Automatically he put the car into reverse, a savage pain shooting up his left leg as he did so, but it wasn't moving. *C'mon.*

He tried again with heavy revs but he was wedged up onto the bank and the wheels were just spinning, going nowhere. *C'mon the fuck!* He knew they only had minutes before the police would be here.

"*Get out and push!*" he roared at Aido who did as he was told and hopped out of the car.

As Aido used all his strength to push the car down off the ditch, he revved the engine. In the distance they could hear sirens. Paul revved the engine harder, battling against the pain in his left leg. The sirens were getting closer but his car wasn't moving.

"*C'mon, Aido!*"

He watched as Aido's face turned purple from exertion until at last the car started to budge. Aido jumped back in as Paul put his foot to the floor and they screeched out of there. His car was rattling and pulling to the left as he drove. He glanced back in his mirror to where the crash had happened but he couldn't see the other car, just the road blackened with curved tyre tracks.

40

Jean tossed and turned all that night. She tried to justify her decision, she tried to tell herself that it was the right thing to do, but it still didn't sit easy with her conscience. She told herself that she was doing what any mother would do but why then did she feel so physically torn apart? She wished she could just be morally weak like so many people on earth and look after her own first and let everyone else sort themselves out but then an image of the dead baby would come into her head, just staring at her, and she would start to sweat and her resolution didn't seem so right any more.

She thought back to when Paul was born and wondered, if she had known then what she knew now and how he would break her heart, would she do it all again? How does an innocent bundle who snuggles in your arms, depending on you to answer its every need and filling you with pure joy, grow up into a person that you still love and adore but do not necessarily like? How does that happen? It was hard to believe that an innocent newborn would ever be capable of any wrongdoing; could it be that a life of hardship was already mapped out for them? How she wished that he could have just stayed that tiny sleeping bundle in her arms, never having to grow up and face the big bad world. The sad thing was that he was still only a child; he was only seventeen years of age with his whole life ahead of him.

She thought of Paul at the same age that the baby had been, six months old, laughing and clapping and starting to express his personality with new high-pitched gurgles. She had to get out of bed and run to the bathroom to be sick. The cool tiles were a welcome relief as she sat on them, her back resting against the bath-tub, the room illuminated in silver moonlight. She stayed there all night sobbing. She knew that in the morning she would have to do the most difficult thing she had ever done.

* * *

At first light the next morning she rang the Chief Superintendent in Newtown Garda station and told him everything she knew. As it all spilled out, her heart felt as though it was being twisted and wrung out with guilt. She knew she had a few minutes before their world was to be shattered apart. She opened the door to Paul's bedroom and watched him breathing. She walked over and sat down on the side of the mattress and stroked his hair, the skin on his cheek smooth under her fingertips. His eyelids flickered momentarily, registering her touch, but then relaxed back to sleep again. It had been so long since she had touched him; she wanted to remember every piece of him. She could hear the rain pounding on the roof outside, hopping off it in staccato beats. She sat stroking his face until the doorbell sounded and it was time. She took a deep breath and left the room, racked with painful guilt for what she was about to do to her own son.

Her greetings to the Gardaí were monosyllabic. They went into the kitchen and they took her statement. She told them the whole story from the beginning, what she knew of it anyway.

They asked her for his car keys and she watched as they drove the car up onto a pick-up truck to take it away as evidence.

They asked her where he was and she wanted to scream to him to run and make a break for it, to run away from it all, but she gestured to his bedroom before breaking down, convulsed in grief, knowing their lives were forever going to be different from this moment onwards. She heard his startled wakening from the hallway, she heard them read his rights, she heard the click of handcuffs and bedroom door belonging to her two younger children opening and their sleepy heads appearing, wondering what on earth was going on. She hadn't known what to expect, maybe some resistance or that he would put up a fight, but she watched her son crying as he was brought out of his bedroom in handcuffs. He looked smaller, as the inches of his macho bravado had gone. An image of him on his first day of school flashed into her head. *Her son.* She walked up to him and squeezed his hand and whispered, "I'm sorry. I love you." She could see the tears in his eyes and there was unmistakable fear within their depths. He looked like the boy that he was. She watched as they pushed his head down into the back of the squad car and then drove slowly out through the estate. She felt her legs get weak and somehow she found her way to the floor. The confused faces of Chloe and Kyle, her own despair. They huddled together heaving in grief. Her heart felt as though it had been knifed in two, split down the middle and left exposed. This was the ultimate betrayal.

41

The first time Jean had been to visit Paul was one of the most difficult and emotionally draining days of her life. To see her son behind prison walls was devastating. He was allowed visitors for half an hour every Saturday.

On her first visit, she was shocked by the security procedures and searches she had to go through just to see him. She had only ever seen this sort of thing on TV. She watched as other people went through the screening rituals, like it was so normal to them. It seemed like water off a duck's back to some of them, but it dawned on her that maybe they had been coming here for years. Once she was led inside, it was like another world entirely. Life, albeit of a different kind, still carried on behind the old stone walls.

She had been shown to a small table where she waited for him to appear. As she looked around the room, she saw women with small children running around their feet, there were older people visiting adult children, people of all ages and all types. One particularly well-dressed lady caught her eye. She was dressed immaculately in a full-length fur coat and jewels that you just knew cost obscene money. A man of a similar age was led in to meet her and she wondered what their story might be.

Eventually she saw Paul being led into the room by an officer. Her heart lurched and yet again she wondered how had she let everything go so wrong that her son had ended up here? She felt the tears filling her eyes but she forced them back. She needed to be strong for him. After all, he was the one having to spend his time locked up here; she could still go home to her comforts, to freedom. The case had yet to go before the court so they still didn't know how long his sentence would be but she knew that the judge would look upon it severely, a hit-and-run would never be shown any leniency.

"Hi there," she said, her voice shaky as she forced herself to act as normally as she could for Paul's sake.

"Hi, Mam." He looked up at her with those large blue eyes that made her melt when he was a baby. For the first time in years there was no anger in them.

"So how are you getting on?"

"I'm having a real laugh." Although he was sarcastic, he was smiling at her.

"Are they feeding you okay, looking after you okay?"

"It's all grand – except obviously I can't leave, but there are a few lads the same age, so we hang out together."

"Well, that's good, love." Jean tried to hide her doubt and anxiety. Of course she wanted him to have friends but not the same sort of friends that he had on the outside. How would he ever break the cycle if he kept on meeting the same sorts?

"Look – I'm sorry, I really am," she said.

"I know, but what could you do? I'm not angry."

He was being civil, acting like an adult, and it felt strange to her. Strange and good.

They chatted until a guard came up and told them they had only five minutes left so it was time to start wrapping it up. Jean couldn't believe the visit was nearly over already.

"Chloe and Kyle said hi. And Nana, Granddad and Auntie Louise."

She didn't want to bring the twins to visit him, she didn't want them to see the bleak inside of a prison, she wanted them to stay as carefree and innocent as they could be in the circumstances.

He said nothing.

They chatted generally until a guard came up again and told them their time was up.

"Okay, well I'll see you next week, yeah?" Her voice quivered.

"Thanks, Mam."

She could see tears in his eyes. He wasn't the big macho man full of bravado that he pretended to be, he looked vulnerable instead. She leant forward and wrapped him in her arms, his head pulled in tight against her chest. She wished she could keep him there. Soon though he was being pulled away from her.

"I'd better go, Mam."

"I love you," she mouthed at him, before convulsing into tears.

She had gone home and fallen to pieces. She knew she had no right to grieve in comparison to the family that had lost their baby but in some ways she couldn't help but think that she had lost her son too. Yes, he was physically present in the world, but thirty minutes a week across a table supervised by guards for God only knew how many years was hardly a great way to see your son. And he was still so young; it was all such a waste. What if she had done things differently? If she had acted sooner or stood up to him earlier, might things have been different? She knew he would never be the same again, how could he be after spending time in a place like this? She knew he would emerge, with that exterior people seemed to have when they came out of prison, as if they were now hardened to the world.

Her family had rallied around ever since she had phoned

them to say that Paul had been arrested for his involvement in the hit-and-run. They had been stunned and equally devastated by the news. Although he had been out of control over the last few years, they knew the real Paul underneath: the smiling baby, the good-natured child. They also found it hard to accept that this was his fate and they couldn't do anything to help him now. They blamed themselves for not acting sooner. Louise had said that if she had known that Jean was saving up to move out of the council estate, she would have just given her the money. But there were so many 'if onlys'. Jean tormented herself with them, but they had to accept that hindsight wouldn't help any of them.

They had insisted there and then in giving her the money to rent a house in the town and to get the hell out of the estate. They knew it wasn't the solution to Jean's problems but, if it prevented the twins from going down the same route as Paul, it would be worth it.

Jean was relieved to finally be able to leave behind the estate so full of bad memories. Every time she looked out the window at the graffiti, the gangs of teenagers younger than Paul, starting out on the same road that he had gone down, she feared that might happen to Chloe and Kyle too. They were at an impressionable age and she knew she had just a year or two before they would want to be hanging out with their peers.

She was looking forward to the fresh start in their new home; they all needed it after everything they had been through.

It was emotional boxing up all of Paul's clothes and belongings and wondering when he would get to use them again. She would come across family photos of him that she hadn't seen in years and his smiling innocent face would tear her apart. There were a few from his eighth birthday party with big gappy teeth and freckled cheeks as he blew out the candles on his cake. She was glad she had happy memories though; glad she didn't know then all the pain that lay ahead for them.

On the day of the move Rita from next door had come over with a small present and some sweets for the twins, saying that she'd miss seeing them both about the place. Jean promised her she would keep in touch and that they would call in to see her frequently and take her to see their new home. Rita had been so good to her over the years.

The new house was a world away from the house with the leaking windows that were always full of condensation running down the insides. It had all the mod-cons like a dishwasher and a tumble-dryer, luxuries she could only have dreamed about before, but Louise had insisted that they pay the bit extra and have somewhere decent for her and the twins to live. The twins each had their own bedroom for the first time in their lives and she even had an en-suite bathroom with an electric shower. She had to swallow back when she thought about Paul and that he didn't have a room here. The house was closer too to the twins' school; they would now be able to walk every day instead of having to get the bus. There was also a good secondary school nearby.

Although Jean was grateful to her family for all they had done for her, she still wanted to be able to pay her own way so she was back looking for a job. She was lucky that she had a lot of experience from her last job, plus they had given her a good reference, which she supposed she ought to be grateful for under the circumstances. She had a few interviews lined up, all with local firms so she prayed she would get one of them. She knew she had to keep busy, it was the best thing she could do. Although the last couple of months had definitely been the toughest of her life so far and her heart had been broken in two, she could see a glimmer of light again.

Part III

42

Emma had been out Christmas shopping with Zoe when she got the call that would forever change her life. Ironically, it was her first day to leave Fionn since he had been born six months before. She hadn't wanted to leave him and had hummed and hawed about whether or not to go but, with less than two weeks left before Christmas, she needed to make a start on her shopping. She knew that by having a baby in tow she would get nothing done, between trying to manoeuvre a buggy around shops that were thronged with people and stopping for bottles and nappy-changes, so reluctantly she had left him at home. Adam had practically pushed her out the door, telling her that he'd be fine and he was looking forward to having his son to himself for the day. So with trepidation and a long to-do list, she had kissed Fionn goodbye on the top of his silky head and pecked Adam on the cheek, making him promise to call her if he wasn't sure of anything. *Anything at all,* she had reiterated and Adam had laughed at her and gently propelled her out onto the doorstep.

Sitting on the bus into town, she had stared at her phone,

waiting for Adam to ring. After half an hour of that, she rang to check things were okay. He had told her to stop worrying, that things were fine, all under control and to enjoy the day of shopping.

She had met Zoe then and relaxed into it. They had strolled down Grafton Street where a crowd had gathered around a group of carol singers collecting for charity. They stopped to listen to the spectacular voices as they lifted upwards for the soprano notes of 'Oh, Holy Night'. The street lights were switched on and swags of ivy adorned with red bows hung from the buildings on either side. Even the lampposts had garlands wrapped around them so they looked like giant candy-canes. The shop windows were all embellished with festive sparkles of red, gold, silver and green, some with traditional snow scenes with slow-moving Santas and elves busy at work. It was hard not to get caught up in the atmosphere.

They trailed around a few shops, trying on clothes, which was a novelty for Emma who hadn't had much opportunity to buy clothes since she was pregnant. She couldn't walk past a baby boutique with a washing-line of miniature outfits hanging in its window. When she came across a ridiculous plum-pudding outfit, complete with a hat that had a holly leaf on top, she couldn't resist buying it for Fionn.

As they strolled along side streets, peering in through the windows of the antique jewellery shops, her eye was taken with a vintage chronograph watch with a silver face. It had a manual wind and a brown leather strap. Knowing it would be perfect as her Christmas present to Adam, she had gone inside to look at it. She ran her fingers over the leather strap, softened by years of wear, and when she turned it over she saw it was engraved with the initial 'A'. *An 'A' from times gone by,* she thought sadly. She took it as a sign. She waited while the shop assistant wrapped it for her. She couldn't wait to give it to Adam.

When the shops started to get crowded they decided to treat themselves to a glass of wine over a leisurely lunch. They took seats in the noisy bistro, the floor around their feet covered with their shopping bags. Emma had ordered a goat's cheese salad and Zoe had gone for a panini. They were sitting back, satisfied with their purchases and sipping their Pinot Grigio, when her phone rang.

It was her mother. She mentioned something about a car accident. And Adam. And Fionn. Emma couldn't process all those words together. Her world stopped, she could hear her mother still talking to her at the end of the phone but she couldn't answer. Nothing would come out of her mouth. She zoned out from the chatter in the bistro, still going on around her. Zoe had grabbed the phone from Emma's hand and, when she hung up, her face was ashen. She hopped up and steered Emma out of the restaurant, hailing a passing taxi to bring them to St Mary's Children's Hospital telling the driver it was an emergency and to hurry on.

Zoe using the word 'emergency' had startled Emma. *Was it an emergency?* She felt she was watching all of this from above. Only for Zoe, Emma didn't know what she would have done.

The taxi had overtaken slow drivers and broken red lights so that only minutes later he was dropping them off outside the hospital. Emma's dad met them in the entrance foyer and Emma realised that he had been waiting for her. He wouldn't make eye contact with her but she could tell instantly from his red-rimmed eyes that he had been crying. She remembered thinking how strange it was because she had never seen her dad cry before. He pushed open a door and guided her into a small room with just a laminate-topped desk, a chair and a trolley. Emma had wondered how he had known the room was there or even how there was no one in it.

Then he said the words that shattered her from within, piece by piece: *Fionn was dead.*

Her chest had tightened until her lungs wouldn't allow her take in any more air. The voices around her became loud and jumbled and her sight became a blurry vision of thick yellow and black stripes. She felt herself sliding away. Her mind left her body, floating upwards, and her feet deserted her until next thing she knew she was falling to the floor.

When she came around they were still in the room and she was lying on the trolley. They asked her if she wanted to see him. She nodded her head. It was an automatic response but what she meant was that she wanted to see him as she had seen him that morning, smiling and pudgy and happy, but she couldn't get the words out and they had guided her into a darkened room and placed the delicate body of her baby in her arms. Then they had backed out of the room, closing the door behind them, leaving her alone. It was all wrong. She just stood there for a while, not sure what she was meant to do or even what was happening. She hoped that maybe they had made a mistake and that he really was just sleeping. She stroked the smooth head of her baby. He looked like he was just sleeping.

After a while she sat back into a rocking chair that was in the room, just staring at him. He was perfect; the only mark on his delicate skin was a small purple bruise over his left temple. *Was he really dead? Were they sure? Didn't doctors sometimes get these things wrong?* She stroked his face, which was soft like a peach; it was still warm to the touch but she knew it was not warm enough.

She whispered into his ear the stories she used to make up about farm animals, while she brushed his downy hair back and forth, using her fingers. She sang the lullabies that had soothed him and she told him how dearly she loved him.

The doctors had come in after some time and told her it was time. It had taken a while to register. Time for what? Then they explained that it was time to say goodbye. *How was she meant to say goodbye to her son?* She didn't want to leave him go, her baby boy. She was overcome and had heard herself screaming. She didn't remember much after this. She assumed they had sedated her.

* * *

The next few days were a blur of heavy medication, awakening and remembering the awful truth, being overcome with grief and then more tablets. The days blurred into night and back into day again but the change in light didn't register with Emma. She felt black permanently. It was too awful a thing for a person to take in, so she couldn't, and instead stayed within her own world inside her head. Concerned faces came and went from her bedside. She had been plied with sleeping tablets by the familiar face of her childhood doctor and these allowed her to retreat back into her place of deep sleep, away from all the worried faces and the horrible physical pain in her chest. Each time she woke she had a blissful few seconds before she remembered what had happened and then her world crashed down all around her and she would relive the horror again.

It was like a cruel trick every time. And then someone would give her a tablet and she would sleep once again.

43

It had taken them nearly three years to get pregnant. Emma had been broody for a long time before she got married. She had wanted a honeymoon baby and had naïvely thought it would be that easy. She had assumed that she would decide the time and a baby would duly oblige her.

She had done all the preparation. She had done research on what were the best days to conceive, she had started taking her prenatal vitamins and folic acid several months before the wedding. She was ready.

When they first started trying to conceive, she had assumed that after giving her body a month or two to adjust to coming off the pill it would simply be a case of 'wham, bang, thank-you, ma'am' but she soon learnt it wasn't that easy for everyone.

After the first year of trying went by and nothing happened, she began to despair. Emma had never for one second envisaged that she would be in this situation. She had spent most of her teenage years, and her twenties too, praying she wouldn't get pregnant and it had all been a waste because here she was in her thirties, desperate for a baby, and couldn't get one.

It was made worse by people forever asking when they were going to start a family like it was something that they had control over. They would say things like they had been married now for quite a while and surely they would be hearing the pitter-patter of tiny feet soon – or that they shouldn't leave it too long, time was ticking and all that. Or the worst were the women who already had children who intimated that women like Emma were selfish for putting their careers first by waiting so long to have kids. Their insensitive comments cut to the bone and would leave Emma biting her tongue in rage.

She had bought sticks that pin-pointed when she was ovulating and her whole bookshelf was stuffed full of fertility books. But it still wasn't happening for them. So she researched some more and clung to any new nugget of information that she heard would improve their chances of conception. She had changed both their diets: leafy greens were in, alcohol was out. She examined her discharge with a new level of interest. She had become a pregnancy-test addict; instead of shopping for new face creams like she used to, now when she was in a pharmacy she would wander straight to the shelves that had the pregnancy tests to see if there were any new products on the market since she had checked there last month. She knew every brand there was and could even rank them in order of their level of detection. Before she got out of bed every morning, she would reach out to the bedside locker to feel for her thermometer so that she could track any temperature shifts which might indicate when she was ovulating. Days were counted down each month until they reached the all-important ovulation days and then sex was almost timed to the hour. Then the days were counted afterwards to see how early she could do a test. She could divide every month in two: there were the days before ovulation and the days of waiting after. No matter how many times she warned herself not to get her hopes up, she couldn't help it, and whenever her period arrived she would feel wretched, as a black cloud descended over her. She would spend the next few days in a deep depression until she pulled herself together with the hope of another month. She had become obsessed with trying to conceive.

It was made worse by the fact that all around her people seemed to be getting pregnant by just mentioning the word 'baby'. Women who she worked with, relatives and friends, the lady who worked in the deli beside the office – it seemed like everyone was pregnant except her and if she heard one more throwaway remark about how "it happened first time" she thought she might either hurl herself at the person in a fit of rage or dissolve on the ground crying – she wasn't sure which. She constantly found herself asking why them? Why were they having such difficulty conceiving a child when every schoolgirl just had to look at a sperm and could get pregnant? Or she would see mothers who sat around drinking in the pub all day and letting their kids entertain themselves and she would have to stop herself from walking up to them and telling them they didn't deserve to be parents. She felt as though she was going round the bend from the whole ordeal. She had always been in control of every aspect of her life and she felt panicked by the fact that this was the one area she had no control over, no matter what she did.

Adam had been terrific throughout; he was her rock even though she knew that some months it must have been like living with a time-bomb. He never complained, although he must have been feeling a bit taken for granted in his role as a sperm-donor. Whenever she was feeling low, he encouraged her to keep going.

It was Adam who had suggested that after two years of trying with no success they should go to their doctor. He had finally said the words she had been dreading. For so long she had managed to convince herself that they were okay, that they didn't have a problem. She had felt defeated. She was always able to sort out her own problems; she didn't like having to resort to anyone for help. But she'd been in denial for too long and she knew he was right. So, despondently she had agreed with him that it was time to hand control over to someone else.

The first doctor they had gone to see was from a different generation. He was reluctant to refer them for tests, fobbing them off with the line that they were "still young" and "had only been trying for a few months". *Only a few months?* She had shown him her ovulation charts and he had taken them in hand and peered at them over the rim of his glasses like she had just handed him some new-aged mumbo-jumbo that he had no time for.

They came out deflated. It had taken a lot of courage to get to the point of telling someone about their problems but they were just back to square one again. So Adam had suggested that they should go to a different doctor. They had chosen a female GP this time and, in contrast to the first doctor, she listened intently to what they were saying, taking notes all the while. She took them seriously and had immediately referred them for tests at a fertility clinic but warned them that the clinic was located in Dublin Maternity Hospital. Emma had to smile at the irony of this – talk about rubbing it in.

A month later, as Emma walked down the corridors to her appointment, she couldn't help staring at the massive bumps on the women all around her. She was fascinated by them all. Some were perfectly rounded like basketballs that were somehow attached prosthetically onto the women's abdomens, while some were just massive. It was amazing how big they actually got. She watched as one heavily pregnant woman struggled to get off a chair until her partner eventually gave her a hand up; she hoped that she and Adam would be in that situation some day. Another woman sat stroking her bump absent-mindedly while flicking through a magazine, oblivious to the strange woman who had fixated her gaze on her. She wouldn't allow herself to get upset; she told herself that she would be back here soon with a bump big enough to hold a baby elephant.

Once inside the clinic, she was greeted by a very cold-looking female doctor and Emma couldn't help wondering how someone with the bedside manner of a fridge ended up in a job like this. After she had poked and prodded Emma and performed a battery of tests on her, she sat her back down and informed her that everything looked perfectly healthy. She actually seemed like she was peeved that Emma was wasting her time and when she told Emma to "relax" and that "she was still very young", Emma could have screamed. Two years was a long time to keep having your hopes torn apart each month. She had expected more understanding from a fertility clinic.

Adam's sperm analysis had come back fine. His 'swimmers' were deemed healthy and his sperm count was actually above average. The clinic had termed it 'unexplained infertility'. But instead of feeling relieved that physically everything was all right with the two of them, she didn't, because she still was none the wiser as to why they hadn't conceived yet. It was beyond frustrating. At least if there was a problem with one or even both of them they could pin-point it and then hopefully solve it, but now they were on their own again ploughing on through the dark, wondering if they were casting a net into a pool that didn't have any fish in it or even if they were casting a net at all.

And then in September she had felt the familiar cramping before her period was due and, utterly deflated, she prepared herself for yet another month of coming to terms with the fact that she wasn't pregnant. That was it, she had thought, she couldn't go through any more of this. She felt exhausted and worn out by the whole ordeal. When she realised that her period was two days late, her hopes had started to rise but she cautioned herself to stop with the false hopes. She had reluctantly done a pregnancy test but nothing showed up. She felt like kicking herself for being that stupid. Why did she keep on putting herself through it? Would she never learn? She picked up the stick, ready to throw it into the bin, but then she noticed something that wasn't there a few seconds earlier. A very faint trace of a pink line had appeared beside the control. The more she stared at it the more she wasn't sure if it was her eyes playing tricks on her or if there were actually two lines there. She wanted this so badly, was she starting to imagine things now? She looked at the stick again and there definitely was a second line. She immediately unfolded the information leaflet that came with the packet, even though she already knew it word for word anyway and, yes, according to it she was finally pregnant. She was pregnant. She clutched her tummy as tears of relief and joy fell down her face. It was so hard to take in; she was going to have a baby! *They were going to have a baby.*

She waited for Adam to get home from work. She didn't want to tell him over the phone but the excitement was killing her. When she finally heard him coming in the door, she tore down the stairs and thrust the stick into his hands. He had taken it from her, trying to comprehend what was going on, and then he looked at it.

He stared at it, his eyes wide with hope. "So does this mean we're . . . *pregnant?*"

"*Adam White, we are having a baby!*" she had screamed.

He had picked her off the ground and swung her around in circles like a child before gently putting her down again.

"Sorry! I probably shouldn't have done that. I just can't believe I'm going to be a father!" He had said it over and over in shock and disbelief. "I'm going to be a dad! I'm going to be a dad!"

"No, no, rephrase that, you're going to be a *great* dad!"

"God, I hope so." The weight of the responsibilities that came with being a parent suddenly dawned on him. He felt daunted but excited at the same time.

"Don't worry, you'll be fine, we'll be fine," she said. "This baby is going to be so loved!"

"Do you feel any different?"

"No, not really, just a bit tired but I thought that was just because of work and the pitch for the Freeman campaign. I thought when you were pregnant, you would feel it, y'know? But I feel exactly the same!"

"Well, that's a good thing. God, I just want to run out and tell the world!"

"We can't tell people yet!" she said quickly. "You know what they say about the first twelve weeks . . ." Emma's stomach did a somersault. She felt anxious even just thinking about it, as if by having bad thoughts she would automatically bring that fate on herself. "We should wait. I don't want to jinx it."

"Okay then, I won't breathe a word." He laughed at her before hugging her close again.

It was supremely difficult to keep it secret from their families and friends, especially from Zoe. Emma felt so guilty; she normally told Zoe everything. She was so afraid of tempting fate that she didn't want to risk it, but she was rapidly running out of excuses as to why she wasn't drinking or why she was too tired to go shopping after work like they normally did.

The first twelve weeks were a nightmare. Morning sickness had kicked in the week after the test and the novelty of being pregnant had quickly worn off. From the moment she woke up in the morning she could feel her stomach churning and she would have to run out of bed to be sick. She spent a good bit of time in the toilets in work and even had to dash out of a client meeting. It only took something small like the smell of pesto or an overpowering perfume and she would feel nauseous. Her boobs felt as though they were on fire and her nipples permanently stood to attention. Plus she was utterly exhausted; she was asleep on the sofa before nine every night.

It felt as though the weeks were dragging on and on. As she

anxiously counted them down, she crossed them off the calendar, longing just to get to week twelve. Week twelve was the magical week where she could finally relax, but she wondered if her worries would stop there or if there would be a whole new set of worries to replace them.

When the twelfth week of Emma's pregnancy finally arrived, they made their way nervously to the hospital for their first scan. That morning before their appointment, Emma couldn't stop imagining all kinds of awful scenarios. No matter how many times she tried to force them from her mind, they would pop back in again. *What if there was no heartbeat? What if the baby had stopped growing?* Or the most ludicrous was: *What if she had just imagined the whole being-pregnant thing in the first place?*

The doctor had tucked some tissue into Emma's waistband and then spread the cool gel on her tummy. They didn't dare breathe as they watched the grainy image appear on the screen beside them. They looked anxiously at the doctor's face and back again to make sure everything was as it should be. As he moved the probe across her abdomen they saw a dark outline appear on the screen. It was their *baby*. It had quite a large head, a long bony spine and little arms and legs that moved in rapid jerky movements. It was tumbling around the place in its own little world, oblivious to the people watching in from the outside in amazement. She couldn't believe how much it was moving and yet she couldn't feel a thing. He let them listen to the heartbeat, which was rapid like the sound of horses galloping over arid land.

"Congratulations, guys, everything looks perfect. Your baby has a very strong and healthy heartbeat." He zoomed in on the heart and they watched the tiny organ pulsing away with life. Emma felt a tear roll down her cheek in awe of the moment.

"Would you like to know the sex?" the doctor asked.

"No!" Emma said. "We want it to be a surprise," she added quickly.

"Okay, well then you'd better look away for a minute while I check the leg measurements."

They laughed as they turned their heads to the side while the sonographer had a detailed look at that area.

Coming out of the clinic they had both been overjoyed and so proud of their baby for growing so well and for being strong. Adam had squeezed her hand tight and they had laughed at themselves – if they were this proud already, imagine what they would be like when the baby was born? They were relieved that they could now start to relax and enjoy the pregnancy.

Emma had said that they were finally able to start telling people. They had made the trip around to the houses of their parents to announce the news. As expected they had all been overjoyed, Emma's parents having long suspected that they had been having difficulties because they knew how set on having a baby Emma had always been.

Then they had driven over to tell Zoe and she had cried, which set Emma off again too.

"I can't believe I'm going to be an aunt!" she had said over and over.

Emma didn't bother pointing out the obvious that, technically, she wasn't but she would be as good as an aunt to the baby.

* * *

The pregnancy had seemed to stretch on forever. Emma, an impatient person by nature, wanted to hold her baby now. Now! She reckoned nature was flawed. Why did it need to take forty weeks? Surely the process could be speeded up into four weeks? She watched what she ate – lots of fruit and vegetables and red meat to keep her iron levels up – she did yoga twice a week and tried to walk most days. She looked forward to every scan and getting a glimpse of the wonderment that was taking place inside her, like a child waiting for

Christmas. She had felt the first movements, like little flickers of a taut elastic band being stretched, and then those movements getting stronger until they were full-blown kicks.

Once she reached the twenty-week mark, she consoled herself that she was halfway there, but if the second half was as slow as the first half then she was in trouble. And if she had thought her worries would ease after the first trimester, she soon learnt that they were only just beginning. *Was the baby moving enough? Why was he or she gone so quiet? Had she felt kicks yet this morning?*

As she got bigger and her baby's space became more confined, she could feel the head move underneath her hand if she pressed into her side and sometimes when she was lying in bed at night they would watch as her bump raised itself into a point as their baby stretched out its elbows or knees, they weren't sure which.

Like all eager first-timers they had everything bought and ready to go – the buggy, a cream wicker Moses basket – and her hospital bag was packed. Drawers already overflowed with cream, white and yellow Babygros. Tiny knitted cardigans and bootees hung waiting in the wardrobe and although it would be a while yet before the baby would sleep in his or her own room, a polished mahogany cot stood in the centre of the decorated nursery. Adam had attended all the antenatal classes with Emma. She'd had a list of questions about what to expect in labour and Adam had taken notes when the midwife giving the classes told them about the main signs of labour and how far apart the contractions should be before they should go to hospital. Eager for information, they had read all the pregnancy books and researched the parenting forums to try to learn what lay ahead of them in the coming months.

She counted down the days until she was due to go on maternity leave. She was big and awkward, the size of a small house as she kept telling people, and her bump sagged down from its weight. She wasn't sleeping well at night either. A combination of her sheer size and a mixture of excited nervousness made her tired. Her brain didn't fire as quickly as she was used to and she wasn't able for the fast-paced environment of A1 Adverts, the endless standing up presenting pitches and pandering to their clients' needs. She had other things on her mind now. So it was with relief when her last day in work finally came around. Emma packed up her desk, accepted a small presentation from Maureen and her colleagues, and ran out the door as fast as her swollen legs would carry her.

Adam had been waiting for her outside in his car as he had done every day for the last few weeks as she began to get too big for the rush-hour squash on public transport where people would avoid making eye contact with her so they wouldn't have to offer her their seat. She threw her handbag into the back seat of his car because there was no room for both her and it in the front.

She had lowered herself into the car when she suddenly felt tightness all across her bump.

"*Ooooooh!*"

"What's wrong?" Adam had looked at her worriedly. Every twinge he greeted with concern these days.

"Nothing, nothing. I think I just pulled something getting in the car there."

"Jesus, don't do that to me! I'm a bag of nerves as it is."

They drove along and she chatted about how much she had planned to do to pass the time for the next two weeks until her baby was due. She was convinced that she would go overdue, first-timers usually did she was reliably told by her doctor. Her to-do list included giving the house a good clean from top to bottom, going to get waxed so that her lady-bits were looking good for everyone that would be seeing them in the hospital and meeting some friends for lunch – plus she had a stack of books on her bedside table that she wanted to get through.

"What about relaxing like you're supposed to be doing?" Adam asked.

"I'll have loads –" She felt her whole bump tighten again and she took a sharp intake of breath. "*Oooh!*"

"What is it?" Adam looked at her in panic.

"Jesus, I don't know but it's bloody sore. I thought Braxton Hicks contractions were meant to be painless?"

"You don't reckon it's the baby, do you?"

"But I'm not due for two weeks yet!"

"Yeah but maybe it's coming early?"

"Nah –" But before she could finish, she was gripped with pain again. "Fuck, Adam, I think maybe you're right."

"What will I do?"

"I don't know. Start timing them or something!" she snapped.

Almost immediately the contractions had started getting longer and the time between them shorter.

"Emma, the last two were six minutes apart."

"Jesus, I thought they were meant to start off slow!" she said through gritted teeth. She was just getting over one before another would rise through her again.

Adam felt utterly useless. He was driving around in circles, not concentrating on where they were meant to be going. "Remember your breathing," was all he could think to say but Emma's glare told him she didn't find it helpful. They pulled over to the side of the road and, as the contractions started coming closer together, she would grab the dashboard with a white-knuckly grip until it passed. He desperately tried to remember what they had told him in the antenatal classes about when they should go to the hospital – was it when there were ten minutes or five minutes between each contraction?

"*I think we need to get to the hospital!*" Emma said through clenched teeth before she grabbed hold of the dashboard again as she got caught up in another wave of pain.

"Okay, okay." He tried to pull himself together. He got his bearings, took a deep breath and made for the maternity hospital on the other side of the city. The rush-hour traffic inched forward before coming to a frustrated stop once again. When Adam looked over at Emma he realised he didn't have the luxury of time so he cut into a bus lane and zipped up one-way streets. It was the kind of driving the ten-year-old boy in him had always fantasised about but now that he was doing it for real, in these circumstances, it wasn't fun. He felt powerless and scared.

Outside the hospital Emma tried to walk out of the car but she had to double over in agony. A porter spotted what was happening and rushed over with a wheelchair and they sped off in the direction of the labour ward, leaving Adam frantically running behind.

"I forgot my overnight bag!" she wailed at no one in particular when they reached the labour ward.

"Don't worry about that, we have everything you'll need here," a kindly midwife called Jenny told her. "Now I need to examine you, Emma, okay?"

Emma grimaced as the midwife did an internal examination and prayed she would remove her hand in time for the next contraction or she didn't think she could cope.

"I need an epidural!" She looked at Jenny desperately. For the first time Emma understood the power that drug lords held over their addicts. She was totally at the mercy of this woman: she had the drugs and Emma needed them. Her fate was in her hands.

Jenny removed her hand. "Emma, love, you're almost fully dilated. I'm afraid it's too late for that."

Emma felt her world had ended and she zoned out on what Jenny was saying as the realisation hit her that she was going to feel every inch of her vagina stretch to allow her baby to pass through. She didn't know if she could do it. She couldn't handle any more of this, she was afraid the pain might actually kill her.

But almost as if she could read her thoughts, Jenny said, "Now don't worry, women the world over do this day in day out and most do it more than once, so you can do it and you will be okay. Do you hear me?"

Emma nodded vigorously at Jenny. She had no choice but to put her trust in her. She felt the pressure of her baby bearing down on her and she knew she couldn't hold it back.

"Now what I want you to do is listen carefully to everything I say," said Jenny. "When I say push, I want you to push with all your strength, right down into your bottom. If you feel like you're going to do a poo, that's good because it means you're pushing properly. When the head is crowning I will instruct you to take short pants. If you keep your eyes on me and listen, we'll be fine. Yeah?"

Emma was nodding.

"Now then, Adam, I want you to grab hold of one of Emma's legs here and I will take the other."

Adam looked like he was almost about to faint. The blood had drained from his head. He wasn't expecting it today – even though he'd had eight and a half months to get used to the idea, it was still a shock that it was happening now.

"Okay, everyone ready? Now on the next contraction I want you to push, Emma. *Push*!"

Emma summoned up all her strength into pushing; she just wanted it over with at this stage.

"*Grrrrr-ahhgggggh!*" She breathed out.

"And again, come on, Emma, come on, Emma, come on, Emma!"

"*Grrrrrrrr-ahhggggggggggggh!*"

"And again, one big push, Emma!"

For fuck sake, would they not allow her catch her breath at least?

"*Grrrrrrrr-ahhhhhhhh!*"

"Good girl, Emma, that's it. Keep it coming."

"*Aaahhggggggggggggggggh!*"

"Good girl, well done. I can see the head. Do you want to touch it?"

She shook her head emphatically and Adam thought he might get sick.

"Okay, now just pant for a few moments like this . . ." She blew gentle little streams of air.

Emma let her body recover for a few seconds before Jenny was back at her again.

"Now one more really big one this time and the head should be out."

"*Grrrrrr-aaaaaaaaaaaaaahhhhhhhhh!*"

"That's it, that's it. There you go, well done."

Adam looked down at what looked like anything but a baby. It was covered in blood and vernix with a scrunched-up red face. Only the matted hair gave away the fact that it was a baby.

Emma caught her breath.

"Now for one final big push and you should be holding your baby, okay?"

"*Grrrrrrrrrr-aaaaaahhhhh!*"

She felt the baby slither out of her body. And when she opened her eyes, miraculously there was small, wrinkly bundle on her chest, his skin red from his entrance into the world. Of course she knew that she was having a baby but it was still a shock to see one actually lying on her chest.

"It's a boy!" Jenny announced and then their baby stretched his lungs and gave a good hearty cry. "Oh, that's a good cry! Well, little man, you were in a hurry, weren't you?" Jenny cooed as she took him over to be weighed. "We don't normally see first babies come this fast!"

A boy! Shock was being heaped upon shock. Emma had been sure that she was carrying a girl. Everyone had commented on her neat bump and she was sure it was a girl.

She tried to get her head around the fact that three hours ago she had been packing up her desk in work and here she was now holding her baby in her arms. She was stunned by the speed of it all. It was almost like he was saying 'Okay, you've done that job, now it's time to have me'. She looked at his dark tufts of hair and a face so familiar, just like Adam's.

They had listened in amazement to the strength of his cry, a primitive animal sound roaring through an O-shaped mouth and watched as his pink hands furled and unfurled like a peony rose, in complaint about having been disturbed from the comforts of what had been his home for almost the last nine months. They named him Fionn.

* * *

When Adam had gone home later that night, Emma had pulled the curtain across her cubicle to give her privacy from the rest of the ward. It was the first time that she was alone with her baby. She had found herself staring in wonderment at the contented little face sleeping peacefully beside her, almost forgetting about the pain of the delivery. Already his face was less mushed and had opened up more, to reveal long eyelashes and pouty lips.

He was feeding like a dream. He was a hungry baby so she found it hard to keep up with his suckling demands, but she knew she should be grateful that he was like this when she listened to other women in her ward as they struggled to get their babies to latch on. She looked down at him when he fed from her breast, his rosebud lips attached to her and his blue eyes open wide, staring up at her contentedly. It was an indescribable closeness that she had never experienced before. He was so utterly small, so totally dependent on her.

In the days that followed Emma was detached from the tedious reality of everyday life and existed only in her own bubble of bliss with Fionn. When she had been pregnant everyone had told her how her life would be changed forever but nothing could have prepared her for the intensity of this feeling. She was buoyed up high on a wave of euphoria. She felt there was a beam radiating from her heart, directed into the cot of her infant son beside her. She would just breathe in his warm milky scent and, if she was a comfort to him, he was as much to her. Hours flew past just staring at him and then she would wonder where the time had gone to. The sound of his cry made her milk leak and tore at her gut, making her physically upset too so that she had to react immediately and do everything in her power to attend to his needs. She was convinced too that he was smiling up at her and even though the books said it was just wind, she liked to think that he was.

* * *

Adam had missed them both dreadfully while they were in the hospital and he couldn't wait to take his baby son home so he could get to know him too. The day he came to collect them, he was beaming with pride and excitement. He ensured the car-seat had been fitted correctly and they drove the slowest journey of their lives that day with Emma sitting in the back with their precious cargo.

He'd had flowers and balloons waiting when she walked into their hallway and told her to go upstairs to their bed for a much-needed few hours' sleep while he minded Fionn. He had sat in their living room as his three-day-old son lay sleeping in his arms, too afraid to move in case he woke him.

So he just sat there, staring at him, thinking about how much lay ahead for them. He swore he would be the best father he could be. His love for him was almost physical and he knew from that point on he would lay his life down for this baby even though he had been in his life only for a few days now. He also knew that forever more he was vulnerable as a person; how would he ever cope if anything should happen to his son? It was as if his Achilles' heel had been exposed for the world to see. He would do anything to protect this little person that he had been entrusted with. It was exhilarating but breathlessly terrifying at the same time.

44

It was days after the accident before the numbness began to subside and the awful aching took over her whole body. Emma ached so much to hold her baby that it felt like an elephant was compressing her chest. Sometimes the weight of her longing made it difficult even to catch her breath.

The fogginess of the drugs was beginning to clear and her mind was starting to process thoughts. She had so many questions that she needed answered. What had happened for a start? They had tried to explain it to her. They said something about a driver not stopping at a junction and hitting Adam's car on the rear left wing where Fionn had been strapped into his car seat. Adam's car had tumbled off the road and landed in the back garden of a nearby house. But to her it didn't explain anything, instead it just threw up more questions.

She had asked if the other driver had died. She had wanted to hear that he was dead too, tit for tat, a life for a life. He had wiped out her family with his carelessness and he should have to pay. But he hadn't even stopped at the scene. They were still trying to track him down. She was so angry, like a force had gripped hold of her body and wouldn't let go.

Someone had asked her if she wanted to go and see Adam. He was in Dublin County Hospital. And it was only then that she remembered Adam. *Adam had been in the crash too.* They had tried to persuade her, especially her in-laws, saying that it would do him good to hear her voice but she didn't want to go. They persisted with asking her daily if maybe she felt up to visiting that day and she would shake her head. There was only so much her mind could deal with. She couldn't even contemplate what had happened and she wasn't able to process the demands being made of her.

She missed everything about Fionn, every part of his perfect babyness. His satiny hair, his plump newborn skin, his scent. His fingernails, his long toes, his rounded tummy. His neck folds that began to smell when milk got trapped within them. The way his joints were swallowed up with baby-fat. His defined chin. His sticky-out ears. She couldn't believe all of those parts of him that she had loved so dearly were gone. *He was gone.* She couldn't accept that she would never again hear his gurgling high-pitched squeals coming over the monitor in the mornings. She had been able to identify each syllable and, when he uttered a new one, she instantly recognised it as that, as if all his sounds were automatically programmed into her brain.

Sometimes the anguish and pain felt so sharp and overwhelming that she felt she might die too.

All she had been left with was a bag containing his "effects" as they had termed it. She didn't like that word; it seemed so clinical, so impersonal. The bag had the Babygro that she had dressed him in that morning, his white cotton vest and his soother. All those inanimate articles survived without a mark but Fionn didn't. She had slept with the Babygro placed under her cheek every night since; it was damp from her tears. She would bring it up close to her nose and breathe him in. She couldn't bear to wash it and wash away the scent of her baby. They had asked if she wanted a lock of his hair in the hospital and initially she had said no. She couldn't accept that this was all she would be left with and somehow felt by accepting this piece of hair she was accepting what had happened. She hadn't wanted them to touch him, not even a hair on his head, but her mother had told her that she might regret it so they had kept a piece anyway for her and now she was glad she had that small piece of him because as the reality dawned that he wasn't coming back, it was all she had left.

Sometimes she woke in a panic because she could not remember his face, exactly how it was. It was as if her brain wanted to torment her and purposely block out the very pictures she wanted to remember. She would beg: *Please let me remember his face. Don't take that away from me too.* Some parts of him would be wrong, the smile wasn't quite right or the eyes were different and she would look at the photo again to be sure but even that didn't capture him whole. It was missing his essence. She couldn't breathe when this happened and became filled with fear and panic. All she had left were the memories and if they were gone too then she would have nothing.

The room which had once been a sunny nursery, decorated with cream walls and white billowing curtains, now had an empty and dark feel to it even when the sun shone in through the window. His teddies sat in an orderly row on the shelf. She would go in there just to sit and remember, desperately trying to smell the sheets in his cot or anything that might still have some trace of him but as the weeks went on, his smell became less and she desperately clutched for something else. Babygros and vests stayed folded in the drawer, bibs and muslin cloths too. Tiny socks would no longer fall off tiny feet. Blankets with no one to wrap still lay in the cot along with a comforter that comforted no one.

45

The voices surrounding him had finally gone quiet. Sometimes they just kept talking – talking to him, talking about him, talking to each other, always talking and not allowing him to rest. Between the voices and the machines that bleeped all day long and the rumble of trolleys being pushed along the corridor, he felt like shouting at them all to shut up and leave him in peace. The fragments flickered past his eyes. He tried to summon the will to force them open. He felt his muscles twitch from the exertion. *Almost there.* He tried harder still. He felt pain. A deep pain that couldn't be isolated to a particular region because it was all over. It was as if every nerve ending and synapse was on a heightened state of alert, rapidly transmitting the pain until it radiated throughout his body. He didn't know what was going on. He forced his eyelids open even though they stung as he did so. The room was too bright, sunlight reflecting off whiteness. He saw a woman rush towards him. *Don't touch me.* He wasn't sure he would be able to cope with the pain if she touched him. He closed his eyes again and braced himself.

"Adam, Adam, can you hear me?" the woman asked softly but there was an urgency in her voice. "Adam, come on, love, I know you can hear me. *Adam.*" She wasn't giving up.

He opened his eyes again.

"Adam!" Her face lit up. "Oh Adam, you're awake! Thank God! Thank God!"

He looked around and took in the cream-painted steel bed frame, the equipment and wires and bandages, the white plaster cast on his left hand and the woman. The woman he knew, he tried to place her. He looked around to see a circle of familiar anxious faces. He searched for the people that he wanted to see but couldn't find them. The faces began crowding in on him and he wanted to back away but he couldn't go anywhere with the amount of tubes, wires and bandages that were tying his body to the bed. The woman reached out to grab his hand. *Ouch.* The pain radiated throughout his body. She bent her head into his arm and started crying and for the first time he noticed they were all crying. He was confused and bewildered by their actions.

"Adam, it's me – your mam. Dad's here too and Rob. You're in Dublin County Hospital. You probably don't remember, Adam, but you were in a bad accident. That's why we're so relieved to see you awake."

"Where's Emma?" His voice was weak and it took all his strength to get the words out. "Where's Emma?" he repeated, wondering if he was making sense.

No one answered.

"Where are Emma and Fionn?"

"She's not up to it, Adam, she's not feeling too great herself."

Oh shit, was she in the accident too?

"Is she in the hospital?"

Maybe they would let him go see her.

"No, Adam, no, she wasn't involved in the accident thankfully."

"Is she minding Fionn?"

"Well, now that you're awake, I'm sure she'll be here later." His mother had tears in her eyes and she was stroking his hand.

At least she knew who Emma was; that was something. He felt rushes of thoughts pound his brain, making everything confused.

"And Fionn, where is he?" he demanded but the tone he was using in his head didn't match up to the feeble croak that came out instead.

He saw her eyes dart manically towards his father.

"Do you think he remembers?"

"I don't know, I just don't know."

I can hear you, you know!

Joe White took a deep breath. "There was a bad accident, son." He paused. "Now Emma is okay, she wasn't involved and she's at home, she's . . . fine . . . but Fionn . . ." He took a deep breath before continuing. For Joe White this was the worst thing he had ever had to go through in his life. He had just lost his grandson, almost lost his son, and now he had to deliver this devastating news and watch him fall to pieces.

"I'm afraid, Adam, Fionn didn't make it . . . he . . ." his voice broke, "he died at the scene." His dad lowered his gaze. "I'm so, so sorry. Truly I am."

Fionn didn't make it. Didn't make what? He tried to process the information as it was presented to him. He looked at his mother for answers but she had dissolved into big heaving sobs, rocking her whole body and shaking her head.

Adam instantly felt the most acute physical pain right in centre of his gut. It was different to the other pain, it went much deeper. It was all starting to make sense to him now. The hospital, the tears, the worry on everyone's face, the tubes, the wires and the pain all over his body. He felt his chest tighten and instantly an alarm was triggered. Hysteria broke out in the room; he could hear his mother screaming, his father shouting for help. Doctors came piling in from nowhere, pushing his family back. They flicked switches, changed settings until the alarm stopped again. They gave him some tablets to help him sleep and he drifted off on a high-up cloud.

The next time he woke he had a few seconds to process everything before he remembered what had happened. They had said his baby son was dead but he had been in the crash too and he was still alive. Surely they had got things wrong? He forced himself to try and remember the exact sequence of events but he could only recall bits of it. He racked his head to recollect what had happened, anything at all that would give him some answers but he could only remember driving along in his car. That was it. He couldn't remember more after that. He needed to talk to Emma; she would know what was going on.

"Where is Emma?"

"She's not doing too well, love, she's at home at the moment. I'm sure she'll be in when she's up to it," his mother reassured him, rubbing his hand.

Jesus Christ. Did they not understand? *He needed to see her.* He wanted answers.

"I have to see her. I need to talk to her!" He tried to sit upright in the bed but the tubes kept him pinned down.

"You can't go anywhere, Adam – you're still in a serious condition. You shouldn't go upsetting yourself, love, it's not doing you any good."

"I need to see him." He couldn't believe all of this until he saw with his own two eyes.

"Who, Adam?"

"Fionn, of course."

"You can't, Adam."

"Why not?"

272

"Because, well . . ."

"Why not?" He was becoming agitated.

At this stage his dad had interjected, "Because, Adam, Fionn has already been laid to rest. I'm sorry, son."

His mother started dabbing at her eyes with a tissue.

They had already buried Fionn. *Without him?* He didn't even get to say goodbye. That couldn't be right surely? He closed his eyes shut again to allow his head to think straight. Was he just imagining all of this? He thought he would wake up now any minute and breathe a sigh of relief about all of this but when he opened his eyes they were all still there and the room was full of brightness with sharp edges and vivid colours and he knew it was too real to be a dream.

"Was Emma there?"

"No, love, I'm sorry, she wasn't up to it at the time."

The frustration of the situation overpowered him and he started to cry big heaving sobs.

"Why did it have to be Fionn? *Why?*"

His mother sat holding his hand, crying with him. He was blistered with grief; it pained him no matter how he moved or what he did. It was everywhere.

"I don't know, love. I don't have any answers for that one. Life isn't fair. He was too good for this world."

'Too good for this world' – what a ridiculous thing to say, Adam thought. His heart ached for Fionn. Their poor baby had been lowered into the cold ground without his parents at his side. It was wrong. He needed to see Emma. He had so much to ask her, so many questions. *Why wasn't she here? How was she coping? Was she going through her own personal hell like he was? Why didn't she want to see him? Did she blame him?*

He drifted in and out of consciousness and every time he woke he remembered the awful news that his son was dead. It all came back to him, the grief flooding down over him, no matter how much he tried to digest it, more pain washed down until he felt as though he was drowning. Sometimes it was easier to stay asleep than deal with the pain and the worry etched on the faces of his family watching him from his bedside.

46

Every day when Emma woke, she had a few seconds of bliss before the nightmare was remembered again. The tablets she had been prescribed helped her sleep a deep sleep where dreams couldn't find her but there was no tablet to ward off the reality of morning.

The reality of her loss. The reality of having to bury her little son. The same priest who had christened Fionn only three months earlier had called to the house to discuss the funeral arrangements. He had gone upstairs and tried to console Emma but he had left her soon after, knowing nothing he could say would offer comfort to this particular mother faced with burying her baby. So he had gone downstairs and spoken to her parents instead.

Emma hadn't been able to face the funeral. How was she supposed to do something like that – a mother, bury her own child? The baby that she had carried for almost nine months and had then lived for only six? Her mother had begged her to go, telling her she would regret it, that it might even help her deal with events. And Emma had wondered if her mother was really on the same planet as her at all, did she even know what had happened to her grandson only days earlier? Sitting in a church and watching her son's coffin being lowered into the ground was not going to help her grief. So she had stayed in her bed and the faces emptied out of her house until it was just Zoe left sitting with her and her son had been buried without either of his parents present.

Then the day came when Emma heard the phone ringing and people shouting, loud happy shouts. She heard someone say that Adam had come round. *Adam*. Her husband. They quickly bounded up to her bedroom and relayed what she had already heard. Adam had just woken up from his coma. They asked her if she wanted to visit him, they were all heading to the hospital straight away. He was asking for her, they had told her, but she had said 'No' and turned over onto her side so that her back was to them.

She had heard they had tracked down the driver of the white car. A seventeen-year-old male off his head after an all-night drink and drugs bender. It just made Emma angrier – his actions had ruined her life, she would never get her baby back. His mother had called over to apologise in person for her son's actions but Emma didn't want to see her. She was too afraid of what she might do or say. So she had stayed in her room and her parents had spoken with the mother downstairs. They had relayed it back to her that she was so sorry for what her son had done and that she was devastated beyond words that he was to blame for something so tragic. But, for Emma, no matter what words of comfort the woman offered, she still had her son. She'd had seventeen years with him, Emma had only had six months. She knew it would go through the courts and they would serve an appropriate punishment, but that would never be enough. It just served to heighten the sense of injustice that she felt.

* * *

They said when you lose a child that a part of you dies too. But Adam wished he had died instead of being in the half-limbo state he now existed in. He was in a numbed trance, with all his senses muted except for the awful feeling of loss that he had to bear. To outlive your own child was the cruellest blow a parent can suffer; it was a reversal of the natural order and he was left flailing in despair.

The hospital had sent a bereavement counsellor to his bedside to talk it through with him but he had pretended to be asleep and ignored further efforts at contact.

Everyone said how lucky he was to still be alive – he had been "minutes away from death" they told him. His crushed pelvis had perforated the surrounding blood vessels causing massive internal bleeding and his body had gone into shock. They'd had to perform major surgery on him, piecing his shattered pelvis back together but he wished they hadn't bothered. He had broken his arm and his collarbone too and his skin was sewn together in a patchwork of coarse black thread. His mother in her Catholic zeal kept on saying that it was his Guardian Angel that had been watching over him: "Blessed he was, blessed." But he didn't feel blessed, how could he? On the contrary, life hadn't done him any favours. His son was now dead. That wasn't very "blessed", was it?

He had so many questions to which there were no answers. Why their car? There were literally hundreds of cars driving up and down that road all day every day – why couldn't it have been someone else's car? Or why couldn't it have been him instead of Fionn? If he had died instead, he knew that Emma would do a good job of raising their son on her own. What if they hadn't gone? He was only calling to visit his parents, hardly something he needed to do. He shouldn't have gone anywhere. If he had left a little later or earlier or if he had driven fractionally slower or faster, the other car wouldn't have met his at that instant in time. What if Fionn's seat had been on the opposite side of the car? Why couldn't the car have hit them from the other side? What if he'd had an SUV – nothing would have touched him in that. What if the council had gritted the road? What if the sun wasn't glaring? *What if? What if? What if?* The words tortured his every thought until he couldn't bear them any more and his brain would shut down again.

He had gone over the journey that morning so many times before. He knew the Gardaí had arrested some little seventeen-year-old boy racer, but was some of it his own fault too? The post mortem had said that Fionn had died from trauma to the head, most likely caused by the impact from the car crumpling around him, but Adam was starting to doubt himself and wonder if he could have done something more to prevent his death. When Emma had been pregnant he had spent so much time researching the technical specifications for infant car-seats; which one had the best safety record and which was ranked highest by the experts and he thought he had followed the instructions on how to install the seat carefully, but maybe he hadn't? He had heard the statistic that eighty per cent of all car-seats are fitted incorrectly. Maybe theirs was too? Did he have the car-seat mounted into the iso-fix system properly? Had the straps been tight enough?

He couldn't believe that he would never see Fionn again. He had loved every hair on his head, his Buddha-like tummy, his long toes with their jagged toe-nails because they had been too afraid to cut them. How he giggled infectiously if you swung him in your arms or bounced him on the bed. How he opened his mouth for more spoonfuls of baby rice. How he had started rolling over a few weeks before or how he had found his voice and now shrieked at everyone all day. He had bored the lads to tears with tales about his toxic nappies that always managed to leak out the sides. Fionn had sat up on his own for the first time only that week, his muscles finally strong enough to hold him. Adam had been so proud – as if Fionn was the first baby to sit up – because his son was another step closer to his independence. The unjustness of the situation made him so angry that he wanted to hit out at something or someone.

Things were made worse by the fact that he still hadn't seen Emma; she was the one person he really needed to see. His heart had risen when he saw her family coming through the door of his room but, when she hadn't been with them, it had sunk back down lower than before. Every day he hoped he would see her face coming through the door. He knew she wasn't coping too well from what her parents had intimated. It was the not knowing that was the hardest. If he could just see her, they would get each other through. He needed to see her.

The next few weeks were spent in a blur of painkillers, physiotherapy and strengthening exercises. He faced a daily endurance test with the pain. The doctors were stingy with their doses of morphine so that he wouldn't become addicted.

It was six weeks after the accident before he took his first tentative steps on a Zimmer frame. The exertion wore him out after only travelling a few metres. It was gruelling but he was determined to get back on his feet properly so he persisted in his daily exercises until his face was bathed with perspiration. At his check-ups the doctors had said that the physical breaks were healing well but he was tormented with re-occurring flashbacks as he desperately tried to remember what had happened. Random scenes that he could put no order on constantly flitted through his head.

The weeks went on and Emma never came to see him no matter how much he asked after her. No matter how many people he told to pass on the message to her that he needed to see her, she still didn't come. He had tried phoning her a few times but she never answered. All anyone ever said was that she "wasn't up to it". He was beyond worried about her at this stage. So he persevered with getting back on his feet again so he could be well enough to get out of there and go home and be with Emma.

47

Emma still couldn't bring herself to wash the Babygros that had been in the laundry basket since the day Fionn died or the blankets from his cot. Her mother had packed away things like the buggy, the steriliser, monitors, bottles and toys but the absence of these reminders wasn't going to help her forget what had happened. Not being able to hold Fionn caused her to physically ache. It would overcome her whole body and on these days all she could do was stay in bed because she couldn't face the world.

Life still went on around her; the days rolled into night, Christmas passed unmarked, people went to work, children went to school, cars still went up and down the road, the post came through the letterbox and visits from concerned friends and relatives became less frequent. She felt like screaming at the world to stop. How could everyone just carry on as normal after all that had happened? But her grief was hers alone and, although people sympathised, they could never begin to imagine the pain she was feeling.

Then the seasons moved along too, the snowdrops had

braved the January frost to be pushed out by the daffodils in late February. The evenings got longer and brighter and then one day Adam came home. He just walked in through the door of their house and appeared in front of her in their living room as casually as if he had only popped out to the shops for milk. Seeing him there had startled her. She had felt the room close in around her as if she was a character painted onto the side of a spinning top. She reached forward and held onto the edge of the fireplace to steady herself. She just stood staring at the man, holding himself up on crutches. He was like a complete stranger to her; a memory from a different life. Looking at him was like looking at a living memory of Fionn, it was more than just the similarities in their look, their dark hair and pointed features; he was living proof that there had been an accident. While he stood in front of her the evidence was there in his repairing body. You couldn't shut it out or deny it. He had been the last person to see her son alive, he had been driving the car when he had died and when she looked at him this was all she could see.

"Emma, it's okay, I'm here now."

Adam was shocked by his wife's appearance. She was a shadow of her former self. Her usually slight frame was now gaunt and her eyes were hollow with blue-black circles underneath. They were vacant, as if nothing existed behind them. Her hair looked as though it hadn't been brushed in weeks; her soft curls now were matted and frizzy.

"I'm so, so sorry, for everything . . ." He trailed off. "Look, we need to talk. I've been worried sick about you."

He took a deep breath and took a step towards her on his crutches. He wanted to wrap her in his arms and look after her. He wanted to tell her that he was here for her now and that they would get through it together, but she stepped back away from him and slid wordlessly out past him. She went upstairs to their bedroom, leaving him standing in his own living room staring after her. He wondered whether he should follow her up or just stay where he was. He hadn't known what to expect from Emma but it certainly hadn't been a reaction like that. He realised that things were much worse than he had thought. He now understood what his family had tried to tell him in so few words. It was as if the old Emma had departed when Fionn had died. He had been waiting for so long, working so hard at getting better so that he could come home and be there for her, but it was like she didn't even know who he was and what was worse was that she didn't seem to care who he was. He had built it up so much in his head, imagining the scene. He had thought that as soon as she had seen him he would be able to lift her out from beneath the mountain of despair that she had been sinking under and they would get through it together. Over the last few months, all his energies were focused on getting strong enough so that he could help Emma; it was all that had helped get him through and kept him going. It had become his mission.

He tried not to feel disappointed; this was her way of dealing with her grief, he reminded himself. Why had he expected that once she saw him everything would be the same as before? How could he have expected her to still be that same person? He needed to be the strong one here. He knew it wasn't going to be easy but at least he was here now and he was going to do everything in his power to help her through.

He glanced around the strange but familiar room, unsure as to whether he should sit down on his own sofa that still had his shape moulded into its cushions. There were books belonging to him on the shelves and his CDs were stacked in the rack, there were even photos of his graduation and of him in his morning suit on their wedding day on the mantelpiece. Everything in this room was recognisable so why did he feel he was a visitor in his own home?

He walked out through the hallway and into the kitchen.

Normally you had to squeeze past the buggy to get to the kitchen but there was an empty space where the buggy used to be. He had to swallow back hard.

His eyes took in the kitchen which looked different since he had last been here. It looked barer somehow and then Adam realised that all the baby paraphernalia that had been sitting cluttering the worktops was now missing. The high chair was also gone from the end of the table. He noticed the pots growing herbs on the kitchen windowsill had all died, their shrivelled brown leaves now clinging desperately to the stalks. Everywhere he looked a different memory lay in store. He could feel his chest tighten, the familiarity was painful. In the hospital he had been spared the constant reminders of life when Fionn was in it but here they were everywhere.

As he looked around the kitchen, he could recall the morning of the crash with clarity. He had strapped Fionn into his high seat to give him his breakfast. Fionn had smiled and screeched at him and kept his mouth open constantly for more cereal. He had slapped his two palms down on the tray, causing his cup to fall off, and then he had leaned over the side looking at it on the floor. When Adam had picked it up for him, he had giggled. He saw it as a game and continued slapping the tray so that Adam would have to pick the cup up for him again.

After breakfast he had cleaned him up and got him dressed and decided they would call over to see his parents. They loved having any opportunity to spend some time with their grandson. He had packed up Fionn's bag with a spare set of clothes, nappies, wipes, barrier cream, bottles; he had hoped he wasn't forgetting anything. He dressed Fionn in his snowsuit to protect him from the chilly winter morning and strapped him into the car. The white sunlight flooded in through the car windows. He had driven slowly, leaving the city behind and within minutes was out in the countryside amongst frost-tinged trees and ditches. He passed by a farmhouse with red sash windows and wrought-iron gates marking the start of a narrow path leading to the front door. He hugged the bend of the road as his body pulled softly to the left with the car. Right ahead was a crossroads and a car shot through it at speed, startling him. He reached the crossroads as a second car tore out from the left.

And then Fionn died.

48

As soon as Adam came home, the faces disappeared just as instantly as they had arrived. Emma's mother, who had more or less moved in to take care of her in the aftermath of the crash, said that they needed their own space and so she had gone home to her own house. She gently told Emma that she and Adam had to get on with things themselves as a couple. But Emma didn't feel like part of a couple; she barely knew the man who was now back in her house claiming to be her husband.

She stayed holed up in her room because she couldn't bear to look at the constant reminder that was Adam. Looking at him alive was just too raw; she knew it was wrong but she wished it was him instead of Fionn. The unjustness of it all made her so angry. She couldn't talk to him; she couldn't find words because her head was spinning with grief. He had been the last one to see him alive, he had been driving the car for Christ's sake, and she resented that. He kept persisting with her, sitting by her bedside, trying to talk to her about Fionn, trying to get her to open up, telling her he was worried about her or asking if he should he get someone to come and talk to her. She never responded. When that didn't work he would switch to mundane topics and have a running monologue with himself trying to fill the silence with words. He would ramble on about the weather or about some news story about fraudulent bankers or whatever project he was involved in at work. His chatter grated on her. How dare he just come back here and try to act like things went on as normal! She couldn't bear to say Fionn's name, she feared that if she said it she might choke on the word like a lump stuck in her throat. Every time Adam mentioned his name she wanted to scream at him to stop, it was too painful to hear it out loud, a name that still existed but the person gone. How can a name exist for a person no longer there? The hollowness of hearing his name was too awful and it just tore at her chest, like a knife darting against her flesh.

* * *

The painkillers that Adam had been prescribed were no match for the morphine that he had been given in hospital. Every day was a daily battle against the pain. Nevertheless, there was something he had to do. His stomach was knotted together and he broke out in a sweat with dread whenever he even thought about it. But he still found it hard to believe or accept what he was being told; he needed to see it for himself.

He went through the turnstile of Primrose Cemetery and felt ashamed that he didn't even know what direction to go in. He didn't know where his own son was buried. He staggered along the twisting path on his crutches. Some graves were decorated with coloured pebbles; others were neatly sown with grass. Some were carefully maintained, more lay weedy, with cracked yellowing plastic crosses that once contained vinyl flowers. There were large, leaning headstones from days gone by. As he scanned the names and ages on the headstones, all belonging to people who had lived good long lives, it was another painful reminder that Fionn was taken away too early.

Birds could be heard tweeting their morning song on the crisp, sunny air and that almost seemed to be a mockery of how he was feeling inside. He made his way towards the newer plots at the back of the cemetery and suddenly he was faced with a small white marble headstone which had Fionn's name on it.

He moved forward and read the inscription:

Here lies Baby Fionn White
Born on June 6th 2009
Died tragically on December 14th 2009
Always remembered by his loving mammy, daddy,
grandparents, aunt and uncles.
Rest In Peace, Angel.

He wondered who had organised the headstone. Weeks of holding himself together made it suddenly hit home. *Fionn was gone.* He was lying here underneath this cold earth – his baby, his baby son. It was all he could do not to put his crutches aside and start scraping at the earth to dig him out and hold him again in his arms. His arms ached to feel his full weight. He'd had such a short time in this world.

He fell down onto his knees and hammered the gravestone with his fist repeatedly until it began to hurt. He stood back up and kicked a wreath that lay on the grass so that it flew up into the air over his head with the flowers falling off before it landed back down again. How dare this happen! What the fuck had he ever done to deserve this? It wasn't fair! If there was a God in this world – and he strongly doubted it – how could he let such a cruel thing happen? Someone had said to him that it was the circle of life, but how could it be when Fionn didn't even get past his first year?

"I'm so sorry, son," he sobbed over the grave. "I'm so sorry I couldn't do more for you. I'm sorry I even brought you out, we didn't need to go, we could have just stayed at home and then you would still be here with us today." His whole body heaved with the force of his tears, his shoulders jerking up and down. "If I could turn back the clock, just to hold you for five more minutes, that's all, just to hold you in my arms again and tell you I love you, I would. I'll always love you, Fionn."

When the tears finally stopped, he sat back, worn out, and rested against the headstone. Had he really done his best? Could he have acted faster? Could he have pulled them out of that spin? Had the impact of the crash killed Fionn or had he died when they tumbled into the garden? There they were again, the 'what ifs' tormenting him.

He pulled himself up and stood breathing in the chilly air in the lonely graveyard before hobbling on his crutches up to the top of the cemetery.

* * *

As the weeks went on, Adam soon realised things were not good with Emma at all and they didn't show any sign of getting any better. She stayed in her room whenever he was in the house and when he tried to talk to her, she didn't talk back. It was as if she was looking straight through him, like he was opaque and she couldn't see him standing there in front of her. He felt like shaking her by the shoulders to tell her it was him, Adam – her husband was back. *Did she not remember?* She went around like a zombie, oblivious to life around her. He felt like he was in her way and maybe she needed some space so, not knowing what else to do with himself, he decided to return to work.

After being off for four months, the office had seemed very different even in that short period of time. Firstly, there was a new receptionist, a mad little thing called Jo who seemed to have the entire male workforce in the company wrapped around her finger. Then everyone was busy working on a new project; the project he had last worked on had long since been completed.

His first day was awkward for everyone. People didn't know what to say to him when they saw him first. He still limped slightly but every day his muscles were getting stronger. He covered up his scars by wearing long-sleeved shirts and jumpers. His colleagues had taken it in awkward turns to come up to him with a mumbled "Sorry for your trouble" before quickly running away in case he fell apart in front of them. He almost wanted to tell them that their words didn't cause the memories to resurface because he constantly thought about what had happened. He knew they were wary about what they said in front of him. They carefully chose topics of conversation and those who had kids didn't talk about them. It had taken a while for people to relax around him but, after a few weeks, they gradually began to treat him like they always did. They included him in their chats and jokes or they asked him if he wanted to go out for drinks which he never did because he would always hurry home to Emma. Though he didn't always find her there.

He was surprised to find that work was actually a welcome distraction; it was a relief to be able to go in there and escape his house every day. He was distraught with worry about Emma's state of mind. He didn't know what was going on inside her head. He desperately wished she would just talk to him. He had tried everything. He didn't want to worry his family by telling them what was going on – they were already devastated after what had happened, they had been through so much as well. So he said nothing, and as far as everyone was concerned they were working through their grief together.

The nightmares tormented him on an almost nightly basis; they were becoming more and more frequent. He was finding it hard to go to sleep at night out of fear for what lay in store for him but inevitably he would drift off at some godforsaken hour only to wake in a sweat moments later with fragments of what had happened spinning around inside his head.

49

A few months after Fionn died, Emma had received a phone call from some poor intern in the Human Resources department of A1 Adverts who had been tasked with giving her a call. Emma could tell that the girl on the other end of the phone, who sounded young, and who stuttered and stammered as she spoke, was obviously embarrassed at having to make the call that no one else had wanted to make. She tried her best to delicately ascertain when, if ever, Emma might be planning on returning to work. Emma had completely forgotten about work. It just hadn't even entered her head that they might be wondering what her plans were now that a few months had passed since the accident. No matter how much she wished it wouldn't, everything still moved on.

At first she had been horrified at the thought of getting up and carrying on as if her life was normal when it wasn't. She felt as though Fionn would think she was already moving on, that she had already forgotten about him. Everyone was telling her the best thing that she could do was to keep busy and get some routine back into her life but she knew in her heart and soul that it still wouldn't stop her thinking about him every minute of the day. However, the more she thought it over, the more she realised that no matter how many times she relived what had happened, it wouldn't change anything – it wouldn't bring him back – so with an overwhelming feeling of guilt, she reluctantly had phoned the intern back and told her she would be back the following Monday.

When Emma had gone in the door on her first day back, she couldn't help but notice that people didn't make eye contact with her. When she spoke they would start shifting nervously and would lower their gaze to the floor. As she walked down the corridors she could feel eyes on her back and whispers crept around the office that she was back. She had met with Maureen in her office. She started by telling Emma that she was truly sorry for everything that had happened. Emma was used to hearing these words from people so she put on her strong face which seemed to make Maureen more relaxed. She told Emma to take her time and if there were days that she just wasn't feeling up to it not to worry about coming in, but Emma could see she was more than a bit relieved to see her. She briefed Emma on which campaigns they were preparing pitches for, which had recently been won and were now in the production stage and those that were starting on further phases. Emma could see there was a lot on.

Although everyone had warned her to ease herself into it gradually, Emma threw herself straight in. Instead of dodging the new client enquiries like the rest of the overworked campaign managers, she was now glad to take on more than her fair share of work. Whenever Maureen tried to suggest that maybe it was a bit too much for one person and that she would divide it up amongst the rest of her colleagues, Emma would shake her head, so reluctantly Maureen left her alone. She threw herself into preparing the pitches and winning business for A1.

The funny thing was that when Fionn was born, she had lost all interest in her job, she hadn't wanted to return to work, she had considered being a stay-at-home mum but they had a large mortgage as a result of buying their home at the height of Ireland's property market and she'd had no choice but to return to work. Now here she was a few months later, broken emotionally and using work as a crutch to escape the sadness of her life.

She stayed later than everyone in the evenings, even Maureen, and she worked through lunch most days but although people had said that the best thing she could do was to keep busy, it didn't help her to forget. Of course getting up in the mornings and leaving the house every day helped lift some of the blackness, but she thought about Fionn constantly.

Looking at Adam now was like looking in a mirror of the grief she was trying to hide from. She knew she needed to face him sooner or later but she couldn't look at him without it dredging up all the hurt and upset and resentment that he was just getting on with his life. That wasn't right. She was living day to day, not daring to think ahead about their future, but she couldn't ignore the tell-tale signs that life was running on all around her; winter changed to spring and spring to summer.

Emotionally she had been through her very worst nightmare, everything else was secondary. Her mind had shut itself off, and made her immune to anything which would hurt her, in order to protect her, like a ship seals off compartments to stop it sinking. Her senses had shut down. She was a shell of a person going through the motions, unable to make a decision, living from day to day, drifting along in the ebb of life because if she thought too far into the future, the thought of living an entire life without her son was overwhelming. So she lived from day to day; then days turned into weeks, and weeks to months and somehow that got her through.

* * *

Adam still bore the physical scars from the accident. He had a long lumpy keloid scar running down the front of his left shin from where he had broken the bone quite badly and one on the inside of his wrist which if he didn't wear long sleeves tended to draw people's eyes, but he was limping less now and his daily cycle to and from work was helping the muscles regain strength. It was the mental scars that were proving the most difficult to heal.

The dream was re-occurring on a nightly basis, hunting him down during the small hours of the morning. The ordeal was played out over and over in his head, night after night. Even when he was in an alcohol-induced sleep it still managed to find him, he had no escape. He could see the silhouette of trees shining in through his car window as he drove along on a crisp sunny morning. There were the trees, the branches covered in frost, the white sunlight cutting through the sky, the farmhouse with its red windows and wrought-iron gates. There was the bend in the road. The crossroads. Adam would wake up in a panic, soaked with sweat. He felt empty, alone and fearful. Things were bad enough without nightly reminders too. He was becoming too scared to sleep and he was exhausted. He would drink endless amounts of coffee in work, just to get through the day but it gave him a nervous energy, he felt jittery and restless. His foot or fingers were always tapping. Tell-tale bags had formed under his red-puffy eyelids, his skin was ashen and he couldn't keep the weight on him.

For some reason Adam didn't feel entitled to grieve. Although he had lost his child too, so much focus was on Emma as the mother that people expected him to be the strong one. They assumed he should be the one helping her through her grief and supporting her. It was as if she had a monopoly on the grief. He was expected to be a man, to be stoic and strong. He wasn't allowed go to pieces. But it wasn't easy.

He had no doubt but that Emma attached some of the

blame to him and he could understand it. Who knows, he might have done the same himself if the roles were reversed? He knew it wasn't her fault; she needed to blame something, to lash out at someone. When she looked at him, he knew that was what she was thinking; he could see it in her eyes. What if he had been driving slower? What if he had left the house a minute later or didn't decide to go to see his parents that day? He constantly wondered the same thing himself. And so the weight of his own guilt and Emma's blame, while never actually voiced, stood between them, growing by the day until the wedge grew so wide that they were where they were today. He couldn't help getting more and more frustrated by her behaviour. It wasn't his fault, he wanted to shout.

And then one day, Emma had come into the kitchen in her work suit. He had been amazed to see her properly dressed and not in her pyjamas. Her hair was done, she still looked pale and tired but he could see pieces of the old Emma that had been missing for months now. She didn't look at him, she had just grabbed her bag and walked out the door, but it was a start. He stood watching after her in disbelief and hoped that she might finally be starting to heal but his hopes had been short-lived. She worked all the hours possible so she was never at home. He barely saw her and when he did see her, she still wouldn't talk to him and continued to act like he wasn't there.

Recently things had gone from bad to worse between them; he hadn't even seen her this week. He knew he should be helping her; he was trying to be understanding of what she was going through but instead he just felt angry. He was rapidly losing patience and he didn't know how much more of this he could take. He was tormented too – why couldn't she see that? She needed to stop blaming him and accept that nothing would ever bring Fionn back.

* * *

When Fionn's first birthday came around, she didn't know quite how she was going to get through it. It should have been a happy occasion: a party, a cake, new toys, maybe his first taste of chocolate, he might have been walking or he might not. She felt robbed and cheated and so angry for losing out on all of this. Her mother had tentatively suggested that it might be a good time for her to visit the graveyard but she had never been able to get the courage up to go there. She couldn't bear the thought of him lying there cold and alone, her baby. Her mother felt it would do her good but she wasn't able to face it. So on Fionn's birthday she had tearfully written him a card, filling it with words trying to express just how much she loved him and missed him and was sorry for everything that had happened. She held onto it for him, she would take it to the grave someday, just not yet.

Part IV

50

January, 2011

From the kitchen Emma heard the doorbell sound. She opened the door to see the postman standing there. The long evenings had started to come in and dusk was falling. A rush of leaves swirled up at her feet. He had a parcel that she had to sign for and a letter. She thanked him and closed the door. The parcel was for Adam so she left it on the hall table for him. She looked at the address on the letter through the cellophane pane of the envelope. *To the parents of Fionn White.* She felt a lump in her throat. Emma opened the white envelope – normally these letters were reminders about his vaccines or from a PR company trying to sell her something for the milestone that he should be at now if he were still alive. She knew she should probably throw these things into the bin but for some reason she never could. She still hadn't been able to summon up the strength yet to ask them to take his name off their databases. But this letter had the red ink of the state harp on it. The gummed seal tore in parts so she stuck her finger inside and pulled it along to open it. She unfolded the white paper and read down through the letter.

The text began to dance before her eyes. It was Fionn's death certificate. There it was in black and white on paper. She looked at the shortness of his life written in front of her: *Date of birth June 6th 2009; Deceased December 14th 2009*. Six months old. Just six months. There it was in black and white in front of her – he was no longer considered to be a person of this world. The finality was overbearing.

She felt her knees buckle beneath her and she reached out to grab onto the post of the staircase. She used it to guide herself downwards so that she was sitting on the bottom step. Just as she thought she might be starting to heal, taking tentative steps forward, this had come and knocked her off balance again. She wasn't expecting it; it was like a below-the-belt punch coming at her, leaving her reeling in its wake. She needed to see his face as if somehow by looking at him it would confirm that he had been a real person. She ran upstairs and into her bedroom. Pulling out the drawer of her bedside table, she reached for his photo. The smiling baby staring back at her, so happy and full of life, was so at odds with what had happened. Sometimes she still couldn't believe this had happened to him, that he was gone and never coming back. The pain tore at her chest. The unjustness caught her again as it always did and she felt the sting of tears building up behind her eyes before spilling down her face. Would she ever get over how unfair the whole thing was? If only she had control, could turn back the clock. It was unfair that they didn't get a second chance. She screwed the lid off her tablets, swallowed two back and waited for the heavy sensation to come and numb the pain.

* * *

When Emma woke again everything seemed blacker. The room was still cloaked in early-morning darkness but nothing was as dark as how she was feeling inside. Today was one of those days that felt as though someone had turned out all the lights.

It had been a while since the blackness had descended upon her with such strength but now it felt like it was smothering her until she could no longer breathe. She knew Maureen would understand if she didn't go into work today.

She fell back asleep and managed to sleep right through the day and was only woken by the doorbell ringing. She opened her eyes and remembered where she was. The clock on her locker told her it was after six in the evening. She lay there hoping that whoever it was would go away but they were persistent so she dragged herself out of bed and trod downstairs to answer it.

"Hi there," Zoe said softly as she opened the door. "I rang you in work and they said you hadn't come in today, so I thought I'd stop by and see how you're doing?" She took in Emma's red-rimmed eyes and stained face. "Aw pet, today's a tough one, isn't it?"

Emma let her in silently and Zoe followed her into the living room. She sat on the couch beside Emma and encircled her in her arms.

"His death cert arrived today." The tears built up inside and spilled down Emma's face again.

"Oh Emma!" Zoe hugged her tight. She felt a bit puzzled. How could the certificate have taken a year to come, she wondered. "There, there, pet. It's okay, it's okay."

Emma's whole body shook with tears until her cheeks stung and her nose was running, streaming with watery mucous.

Zoe felt wretched watching her friend in this state. She was useless to her; nothing she could do or say would change anything.

"I just miss him so much, Zoe. It never gets easier. People keep telling me that time is a great healer but it isn't – the pain never goes away. It's always there, constantly, and I'm so tired of crying. I'm just so tired."

"Oh God, Emma – I'm so sorry."

"It's just . . . so . . . so . . . final."

Zoe rubbed her back while Emma cried hard.

A while after, Emma said she was exhausted and wanted to go back to bed.

Zoe helped Emma into bed and watched as she fell asleep instantly, worn out from all her tears. She stayed there stroking Emma's hair softly. It was painful watching her friend fall apart and knowing there was nothing she could do for her. So much time had passed but it was all still so fresh. While Emma snored gently, Zoe tiptoed quietly out of the room.

* * *

Just as Adam was dismounting his bike, he saw Zoe letting herself out their front door.

"Hi, Zoe."

"Hi, Adam," she said somewhat awkwardly. "I just called in to check on Emma."

"How is she?"

"She's not too good actually. You see, Fionn's death cert arrived in the post today. She's taken it pretty badly."

He took a sharp breath. "Jesus!" His eyes widened in horror. "Oh God, Zoe, I wanted to spare her that. I asked them to address it to me."

"Why did it take so long to come, Adam?"

"It was just a copy, Zoe. Em's parents mislaid the original in the months after his death and I only recently steeled myself to send for another."

His eyes began to brim with tears and he had to do everything in his power to keep it together.

"I'm sorry, Adam, I really am. I can't imagine what you're both going through." The man standing before her, the man who used to be tall and strong, now was broken.

"Is she in her room?"

She nodded. "I'm worried about her, Adam. She's in a bad way up there."

"Well, she won't talk to me. It's still as if she can't bear to look at me or she blames me or something. When she looks at me all I can see is contempt in her eyes."

"It's not easy for her."

It's not easy for me either.

"I know but she just keeps pushing me away. I just want to get inside her head to understand exactly what is going through her mind about me. Surely by now she should be coping better."

"I really don't know what to say, Adam. I know you don't want to hear it but be patient with her, it's still quite soon. And today is bound to be another setback."

"Yeah, I suppose you're right." He let out a heavy sigh.

She nodded and turned away. He watched her walk off into the dusky evening.

Adam let himself into the house and picked up the white letter that Emma had left on the hall table. He unfolded it. *To the parents of Fionn White.* That's why she had opened it. He had asked them to address it to him. He stared at the text. That was it: Fionn was gone. A piece of paper was all they were left with. He stood and broke into sobs as the grief flooded down upon him. He longed to hold Emma and to have her hold him back. He missed the closeness of his wife.

He climbed the stairs and stood outside her door. He had long since given up calling into her but he needed her right now. The lights were off and he could hear from her slow and heavy breathing that she was sleeping. He tiptoed across the floorboards. In the darkness, he looked down at her. Her hair was fanned out on the pillow around her. He reached out to touch her skin; his fingertips stroked its softness while he brushed the strands of hair back off her face but she didn't wake.

Adam slept fitfully that night. When he finally drifted off, the dream was back again with terrifying force, menacing him in the darkness, looming over him like a spectre waiting until he went to sleep to appear. It was all disjointed. Driving along.

The sun. The blinding sun. The frost-tipped hedgerows. Trees. The house. The gate. The bend. The crossroads.

His body bolted upright as beads of sweat ran down his bare chest. He tried to catch his breath as he sat trembling in his own bed.

He saw every hour change on the clock. His mind was whirring with activity. His world had been thrown upside down and it never got any easier. Today was another hurdle, another painful reminder when he had hoped things might be starting to get easier for them. He was free-falling and life felt out of his control. And he had lost his wife too. The one person he should have been able to count on kept pushing him away. He felt so powerless. Where could they go from here? He was slowly going around the twist from her torturous ignoring of him. She didn't want him around her. She didn't want him any more. Months of anxious worry were climaxing to realise his worst fears.

51

Zoe went home and poured herself a large glass of wine. She needed it. It had been awful seeing her friend and knowing there was nothing that she could do or say to help her. She had thought Emma was finally starting to take baby steps forward but the arrival of the death cert had been a major setback. Then there was Adam too, he had seemed devastated when she had told him. She phoned Steve and he insisted that he and Dave would come straight over to her. When he came into her apartment, he wordlessly wrapped her in his strong arms as she sobbed into his shoulder.

It felt like Zoe had known Steve for years. Of course she knew it was a time-old cliché but since the day she had met him he had felt like an old friend. They never had any of that awkward conversation-making or running out of things to say to each other – they had always chatted openly and easily. She was amazed at how quickly they had fallen into a routine. He would call into her a few evenings during the week and then she would join the thousands of others making the mass exodus out of the city on a Friday evening where they would spend the weekend together holed up inside Steve's seaside cottage. He would have a huge feast waiting for her when she'd get in the door. Rack of lamb, chunky vegetable soup or steak and homemade chips – always followed by a delicious homemade pudding. She joked to him that he was having a detrimental effect on her waistline but he loved cooking things and getting her to try them out.

Steve was good and steady, dependable. In his own way he was romantic too; he would pick wild flowers for her or if he spotted something quirky at a market, he would buy it for her as a surprise. She and Dave often went along to markets with him where she watched him at work in his stripy canvas apron, strolling around offering people samples. She was amazed to see he had a lot of repeat customers that came to the market on the same day every week just to stock up on his produce. He would be selling a loaf of bread and then he would suggest they try some of his relishes or jams, and because of his friendly nature no one seemed to refuse; he was a natural people person. And what was great was that he was in his element, there in the outdoors with people, doing what he loved. It made Zoe think twice about all the years of being stifled by her own job. Steve had balls, he had followed his dream, and there was an awful lot to be said for that.

Dave was doing well too. He was growing into a wiry young dog, always leaping up and running wild around the place. They would usually go for a long walk along the beach on Saturday morning with Dave running off ahead of them chasing the sticks they threw, before sprinting back again with the stick firmly gripped in between his teeth. They would try to prise it from his mouth but he wouldn't let it go so they would have to find another one to throw for him. Then he would act brave and chase the waves as they lapped the shoreline, but when they broke and washed out across the sand towards him, he would run back scared. Steve and Zoe would be helpless with laughter. It was still hard to believe that it was all down to Dave that they were together. It definitely was fate.

After a long walk on the beach, they would come back up to the cottage, Dave shaking sand everywhere while Steve would feed her some more of his treats. He would light the fire and the two of them would cosy up on the couch, reading or watching a film, sometimes sipping a glass of red wine. They felt as comfortable in silence as they did talking. She hadn't felt this relaxed since she didn't know when. She felt as though she belonged there and it had been a long time since she had felt like that. Even as a child she had never felt as though she truly belonged because she had been passed around so much. If you had asked her a year back if she could have ever envisioned being contented by such a lifestyle she would have laughed. She had always loved the hustle and bustle of city life, but she was surprised to find she enjoyed the quiet contentment of spending time with Steve in his remote cottage.

She had even worked herself up to tell Steve about her childhood and her mam but instead of being horrified like some of her exes had been, he took it all on board and listened. He didn't offer platitudes or sympathy and she had found it much easier to open up to him than she had anyone else before. When she had told boyfriends in the past about her upbringing they would start with the 'poor you' routine and, inevitably, even if they didn't mean to, they would start treating her differently. It would make her feel guilty then about the fuss they were making and she would wonder if they were with her because they felt sorry for her or because they genuinely liked her? But it wasn't like that with Steve.

When they went to bed together that night Zoe, worn out from her tears and worry about Emma, fell asleep as soon as her head hit the pillow. Steve wrapped her close in his arms and spooned her from behind as Dave snored gently on a rug on the floor beside them.

52

After hours of tossing and turning, Adam got out of the bed and walked over to the wardrobe. Reaching up to the top shelf, he pulled down his holdall. He packed it with most of his clothes and threw in some toiletries. He reached into the wardrobe and took out a pair of trainers and the shoes he wore to work and took some suits and put them into a bag. He looked at a photo of himself and Emma and Fionn that hung on the wall. He took it off the hook and held it in his hands. He stared at it briefly before packing it in with the rest of his belongings.

He knocked on the bedroom door where Emma was. As usual there was no greeting. She was lying in the darkness. He wasn't sure if she was asleep or awake. He switched on the light and saw she was awake but she didn't look at him, instead her two eyes stared straight ahead.

"I saw the death cert."

She said nothing.

"Emma, I'm sorry – I don't want to cause you any more pain but I'm at my wits' end. I can't take it any more." He took a deep breath. "I think it's for the best if I moved out for a while. Maybe just give you some space?"

Her expression remained impassive, giving no sign of how she was feeling or even if she was listening to him.

"Right. Well, I'll be in Rob's if you need me."

He lifted the holdall over his shoulder and closed the door behind him.

* * *

Emma listened to Adam's footsteps as they made their way down the stairs, across the floorboards in the hall and then the sound of the swooshing of their heavy front door closing. She wanted to react somehow but felt paralysed by her grief. She couldn't move. She listened to the stillness of the house; it was still dark out. She shook out a couple more of her tablets, swallowed them down and fell into a deep sleep.

When she woke again, she still felt exhausted. She had slept too deeply and it took a while for the tablets to wear off so she felt like a zombie detached from the world going on around her. And then she remembered Adam was gone. She felt numb. She couldn't even get out of bed. She just wanted the pain to go, just to leave her in peace even for a few moments.

She couldn't compete any more with the fight and struggle to live her daily life. She just wanted to be asleep again and not wake up to her horrible reality. She swallowed back some more tablets, but they weren't working any more – sleep didn't come so easily now. She opened up her drawer and took out the photo and stared at the familiar face of her baby boy. She tipped more tablets into the palm of her hand, looking at them momentarily before stuffing the fistful into her mouth and washing them back.

She lay back down and waited, but they still weren't working. She dragged herself out of bed, went down to the kitchen and pulled open the press above the fridge where they kept their alcohol. She reached up for the bottle of vodka that had been there for years, probably left over from some house party. She unscrewed the cap and watched the liquid slosh into a glass. She put it up to her lips but the alcohol stung her gums and made her grimace. She opened the fridge and found a carton of orange juice. She poured it on top of the vodka before knocking the whole mixture back. Within minutes she began to feel relaxed and subdued. She brought the bottle back up to the room with her.

She tipped out another few tablets and washed them down with the vodka. She was able to drink it neat this time; it didn't taste as bad now. She felt the familiar deadening of all her senses, the sounds from outside the house got further away. It was harder to see. She didn't want to move, she just wanted to lie there. She gulped back some more vodka and closed her eyes, enjoying the sensation of peace and deep relaxation until she was far away from all the heartache that was her life.

53

When Rob had heard his doorbell go in the early hours of the morning, he knew it was something serious. He had been dumbstruck to see Adam standing on his doorstep with his holdall on the ground at his feet. Seeing the dishevelled state that his brother was in was frightening. Adam was a shadow of his former self. His gaunt face was now creased and lined and the dark circles under his eyes showed a frightening depth. He ushered him in but Adam was barely able to speak.

Rob could make a good guess at what had happened, but he could hardly believe it. He had known things were bad between them but he had never thought that Adam would actually *leave* her. His brother adored Emma, he always had from the day he met her – they were the couple he always looked up to, his benchmark for an ideal relationship. They were the one couple he would never have imagined splitting up. They were good together, each still an individual but complementing the other.

He hoped that his brother just needed some headspace for a couple of days but he wasn't so sure and Adam didn't seem to know himself.

Adam sat in stunned silence on Rob's settee. He had been in denial for so long and he still couldn't believe it had actually happened. He had just got up and left her. He hadn't planned it. It hadn't been premeditated; he just literally had had enough. Seeing Emma's lack of expression had hurt. Deep down if he was honest some part of him had hoped it would have been enough to snap her out of the despair and to bring her back to him but nothing was giving. He had hoped that she might have sat up and asked him to stay, that she would say that she did still need him but instead her face had shown no reaction, as if she really couldn't care less or wasn't even registering what he was saying to her. As if he was a complete stranger to her.

He didn't know how long he was going to stay with Rob – it could be a few days, it could be months or maybe they would never work it out. All he knew was that he couldn't stay there any more.

54

Zoe dialled Emma's mobile number yet again but it just rang out and went to her voicemail. She had been phoning her and leaving messages for hours now and for some reason it made her feel uneasy. When she told Steve that she was worried, he said he would drive her over there. Emma had been very low over the last few days. She couldn't explain why but something told her she should just go and check on her friend. She had tried ringing Adam to make sure that everything was okay but she hadn't managed to get hold of him either.

When they arrived outside Emma's house on Cherry Tree Road, Steve stayed in the car while Zoe walked up the path and pressed the bell. She noticed Adam's bike wasn't there. Normally it was chained to the railings whenever he was at home. She waited for a while before ringing the bell again but no one was answering. She began to feel stupid then. Emma had probably just gone out. Or she might be asleep, in which case Zoe really didn't want to wake her. She rang Emma's mobile again but there was no answer.

She turned around and got back into Steve's car, cursing

herself for overreacting as usual. Steve was just reversing out the driveway when Zoe noticed that the bedroom light upstairs was on. Surely if Emma was asleep she wouldn't leave the light on? She asked Steve to stop the car again. She jumped out and ran back to the front door. She started ringing the bell again and pounding on the knocker but there was no answer. She couldn't explain it but she knew something wasn't right.

Steve joined her and they both went around to the side of the house and scaled the locked wooden gate before hopping down onto the patio. They tried the back patio door but that was locked too.

Zoe knew that Emma sometimes left a spare key in the shed. She swung back the creaky wooden door and went into the cobweb-covered shed. She went over to a frame of shelves and looked under the usual flowerpot but there was nothing there. She began to search under and inside other flowerpots and containers but she couldn't find it anywhere. Steve was just about to pick up a hammer and use it to break the glass door, when Zoe found the key wedged behind a box of tools.

They hurried to the back door. Zoe fumbled with the key in the lock for a few seconds before it clicked open. They let themselves in.

"Emma?" Zoe shouted. "Are you here, Emma? Emma, are you okay?"

She bounded up the stairs and pushed back the door to Emma's bedroom. She saw her friend lying there on top of the duvet cover, white froth coming from the side of her mouth.

Steve came into the room behind her. "Oh, *shit!*"

Zoe ran over to her and instinctively lifted her head in her hands before remembering hearing that you shouldn't move the person, or was that for people that had a physical injury? She couldn't remember, so she removed her hands and watched as Emma's head flopped backwards onto the pillow again. She observed the bottle of vodka and a brown plastic vial with a pharmacist's label.

"Emma, what have you done to yourself?" she whispered.

Steve put his head down onto Emma's chest. "She's breathing but it's very shallow."

Zoe jerked into action immediately and frantically tried to dial 999, her fingers clumsy and awkward on the vinyl buttons. An engaged tone.

"Shit, Steve, what's the emergency number from mobiles?" Her mind was blank and wouldn't allow her remember what she needed to.

"112."

This time a voice answered, "Hello, Emergency services, how may I direct your call?"

"It's my friend, I think she may have overdosed on some tablets, she's comatose here, she's – she's frothing at the mouth."

"Is she breathing?"

"Yes – but it's very faint."

"Okay, now give me your address and I'll send an ambulance over there immediately."

"59 Cherry Tree Road, Rathmines, Dublin 6. Please hurry."

She looked at Emma where she was lying splayed on the bed. She didn't know whether they should be shaking her or doing chest compressions like they did on medical shows or if they should just leave her alone altogether. All the medical advice she had ever heard was jumbled around inside her head, none of it helpful or any use in this situation. She willed the ambulance to hurry up. Every minute felt like an eternity.

Eventually they heard a siren blaring in the distance so Steve ran down the stairs and out the front door onto the road so that he could flag the ambulance down and hopefully save time.

The paramedics stormed up the stairs and within seconds they had lifted Emma gently off the bed and placed her still body onto a stretcher. They carried her downstairs and put her into the back of the ambulance. They allowed Zoe to come in the back with them and Steve said he'd follow behind in his jeep. One of the paramedics hooked Emma up to some machines and then they sped off.

On the journey to the hospital, they worked on trying to stabilise Emma. They asked Zoe questions such as "What's her name?" and "What medication was she on?" and "Has there been anything out of the ordinary with her behaviour in recent times?" Zoe wasn't sure where to start with this one. Should she go over everything that had happened in the last year – the accident and losing her son? As the ambulance whizzed down the road she could only see bits of the journey through the small portholes with an orange tint so people couldn't see in. She knew people were probably looking at the ambulance wondering who was behind its doors – she did it herself all the time to pass the time in traffic – and now that it was her best friend she wished she could swap with them and be the ones sitting at the traffic lights with the idle thoughts.

As soon as they arrived at the hospital, the back doors were thrown open and they flew off through double doors with Emma's stretcher. Zoe followed them but was told she had to wait outside the A&E.

Even though she had given up smoking years ago, Zoe desperately needed one now. She went outside and found herself asking an old man for a cigarette. It was a short, stubby green Major but beggars couldn't be choosers. She inhaled deeply, feeling the smoke catch the back of her throat; she had forgotten how strong they were.

Steve came up beside her moments later and put his jacket over her shoulders. "Here, put this on – you'll catch your death."

Zoe remembered Adam. She needed to tell him. She took out her mobile out and dialled his number.

"Adam – it's Zoe."

318

"What is it, Zoe?" He sounded apprehensive.

"I'm at the hospital, Adam. It's Emma – I found her – look, Adam, it seems she's taken an overdose."

He didn't respond.

"Are you there, Adam?" she asked urgently.

"Jesus Christ – an overdose of what?"

"Vodka and some sleeping tablets, I think. She's in Dublin County Hospital."

"I'm on my way."

While Zoe and Steve waited outside for Adam to arrive, she dialled Emma's parents' number.

She was relieved when Emma's dad picked up. She was afraid that news like this would break her mother altogether.

"Peter – it's Zoe."

"Zoe? Is everything okay?"

"No – it's Emma – she's in the A&E in Dublin County Hospital. It seems she's taken an overdose."

* * *

Emma parents, who lived only a short distance from the hospital, arrived first. Her mother had red-rimmed eyes and her father was ashen. They were back at the same hospital they had been in when they had lost their grandson. They weren't able for this. They had aged a shocking amount over the last year, more than they had in the last ten years; the rollercoaster of human emotion was too much at this stage of their lives. They were in their sixties, life was meant to be winding down for them now – instead they found themselves living through their hardest years.

"Do you know what happened?" Peter Fitzpatrick seemed to be the only one capable of coherent speech.

"I called over to her – and found her lying there. Her sleeping tablets and a bottle of vodka were beside the bed."

"Oh God – I – I –" Her mother broke down.

"She's going to be okay," Zoe tried to reassure her. Jesus Christ, she prayed she would be all right! "Emma is strong – she's a fighter."

"Can we see her?" Emma's dad asked as if she was the authority for the hospital.

"I don't think so, they told me to wait here. They're treating her at the moment."

"What about Adam? Where was he?"

"I'm not sure but I rang him too – he's on the way."

After a while they begged the hospital staff to tell them what was going on but were told only that she was being treated and they wouldn't know anything for a while.

They sat in anxious silence, praying that she would be okay.

55

The drive to the hospital in the darkness had seemed to take forever. Rob drove as fast as he could and luckily the roads were clear from traffic at that time of night. They sat in silence as the thoughts whirred around inside Adam's head. It was all his fault. He shouldn't have left her. It was stupid and selfish to walk out on her like that; he knew she was at a low ebb and he had just walked out on her. He would never forgive himself. Thank God Zoe had found her. What if she hadn't? Well, it didn't bear thinking about. What the fuck had he been thinking? She needed him more than ever and he had just walked out like that! He had pushed her over the edge. This whole mess was his fault. He could imagine her lying there barely breathing. What if she died? He couldn't do this again. He couldn't go through all of this again. He couldn't lose her too. He wasn't religious, but he prayed and begged God on that car journey to spare her.

As they pulled into the car park, the sight of the hospital brought it all back again. The awful ache in his chest, the feeling of life closing in around him; he could nearly feel the pain in his pelvis again as it had mended itself back together.

He sat in the car and wondered if he would even have the strength to get out of it but Rob, seeing him shrink back, held out his arm and pulled him out. As the two brothers walked towards the doors, Adam thought he might collapse. He wasn't able for this, but Rob gripped his arm tighter and pushed him on.

In the thronged waiting room, Emma's parents, Zoe and her boyfriend came to meet them. He didn't know what to say to them. Did they know that he had walked out on her that morning? Did they know it was all his fault?

"I'm sorry!" He broke down.

Emma's dad put an arm around him. "You're okay, it's not your fault!"

"It is – I left her this morning."

"What do you mean?"

"Adam, what happened?" his mother-in-law begged.

"I couldn't take it any more. I just couldn't do it. I don't know what came over me but I just walked out. I'm so sorry." His voice dissolved into a whisper.

It all started to make sense to everyone now.

"It's okay, Adam – it's not your fault. She was very fragile anyway." Peter Fitzpatrick patted him on the back.

"How is she?" Adam somehow managed to ask.

"We're not too sure," said Zoe. "We're just waiting to hear. Here, sit down." She cleared off an ancient copy of *Hello* magazine with a ripped cover and patted a seat for Adam.

They all sat down again.

"Adam, you haven't met Steve properly, have you?" said Zoe.

Adam vaguely recalled meeting him in his drunken state when Zoe and Steve had to put him in a taxi home.

They mumbled greetings to one another.

They all sat around, each transfixed by their own thoughts, oblivious to the hustle and bustle around them. No one spoke for long periods and then, when someone did open their mouth, it seemed too loud and incongruous so they just shut

322

up again. Emma's father kept on clearing his throat as though preparing to break into song – then he would get up off his chair and pace nervously around the room before sitting back down again. Emma's mother looked as though she was saying a novena; her face was deep in pious concentration. Everyone else just sat still and either stared straight ahead or at the ground.

Adam sat and ran over the same internal monologue that had been running through his head since Zoe had first phoned him. He shouldn't have left her, he should have got her help – that was what she had needed, why hadn't he been able to see that? He would give anything to be able to turn back the clock to this morning. He needed to talk to her and tell her that he still cared, he was sorry, he loved her. He hoped it wasn't too late, because he couldn't bear that again, he could not lose another person in his life. He wasn't tough enough to withstand that. He wished someone would tell him how she was doing.

Peter eventually approached a passing nurse.

"I'm Emma Fitzpatrick's father – do you have any news on her?"

"I'm afraid I can't discuss that with you but the doctor will be with you shortly."

Peter had to use all his inner restraint to keep from shouting at her just to tell him what was happening.

He went back to the others.

"Bloody won't tell me anything, she's my daughter for Christ's sake!" he bellowed at no one in particular. He sat down momentarily before getting up just as quick. "I'm going out for some air."

He left and the others sat waiting again.

Eventually a man in a white coat came through the door to the A&E and approached them.

"Are you the family of Emma Fitzpatrick?" He looked around at the grave faces. They all nodded their heads at him, each too afraid to speak, each feeling their hearts lurching in their chest.

What was he going to say? What was he going to tell them? Please let her be okay, please!

The doctor went to sit down.

Dear God, no, this wasn't a good sign. Adam thought he was going to be sick; he had broken out in a sweat and his mouth was watering.

Emma's father arrived back at that instant.

"Well, can you tell us how she is?" he demanded.

"I'm Dr Jacobs. The good news is Emma will be okay."

They each internally said prayers of gratitude, some to God, some to no one except in a dialogue with themselves.

"She is still quite heavily sedated but we would expect her to come round later this evening," the doctor went on. "We've given her flumazenil which is an antidote for the diazepams she overdosed on. She is on a ventilator to help with her breathing and appears to be responding well. Normally diazepams on their own don't cause unconsciousness but in Emma's case she combined the tablets with alcohol, which can prove fatal. There was quite a high level of alcohol in her bloodstream – she is very lucky. We're hoping that she may be off the ventilator by this evening. We'll try to move her to a ward as soon as possible but, in the meantime, you're welcome to go and sit with her in A&E if you'd like. Only two people at a time though."

Adam went first, Emma's parents deciding to wait and go in together. He followed the doctor through the swing doors with round portholes and down a corridor lined with patients on trolleys. Doctor Jacobs pulled back some curtains around a cubicle and ushered him in, then left.

Emma was lying on a trolley hooked up to wires and machines. It was all too familiar. Adam sat down on the chair and took her hand in his and was surprised by the familiarity of her touch. Then the tears rolled down his face. They kept on coming, tears for Emma, tears for Fionn, tears for their marriage, tears for their loss, tears for the last few months of heartache and

324

separation, tears for the fact that he had left Emma to handle her grief alone, tears because he wasn't there for her, tears because she had needed someone to blame and unfortunately that person had been him. How did it come to this? How did he let this happen? The tears would not stop spilling down his face.

"Emma, I'm so, so sorry," he mumbled. "So sorry. I love you, so, so, much, I really do. I need you – just you work on getting better and when you're ready to wake up I'm going to be here with you. Do you hear that? I'll be right here by your side. I won't leave you like that again. I know I've let you down but I'm going to make it up to you, just you wait and see. So I hope you're listening to me and getting stronger, do you hear me? I'm so sorry for everything you've had to go through for the last few months, I truly am. Just you work on getting better."

He stared at her as she slept. She seemed so peaceful, so far removed from the horror of the last year.

* * *

Later that evening they took her off the ventilator and were relieved to see her breathing well on her own. They then moved her to a private room where Adam sat with her all night, with Emma's parents relieving him for short spells.

Eventually, the next morning, he saw her eyelashes flicker and her eyes widen. She looked around the room before closing her eyes again.

"Emma, Emma, you're awake!"

She went to speak but couldn't get the words out.

"You're okay, don't worry," he said, "it's going to be okay. Do you hear me?"

"Where am I?" she finally croaked.

"You're in the hospital but it's okay, you're going to be fine, just fine. I love you, Emma, and I'm sorry, I really am, for everything."

She lay there, looking around the unfamiliar room and tried to straighten out her thoughts to make sense of what was going on. Her head was pounding and the bright room made the pain behind her eyes worse.

"How are you feeling?"

"I've been better," she whispered.

She drifted back to sleep and Adam quietly slipped out to tell the nurses and phone the Fitzpatricks. Then he went back to her bedside, brushing back her curls behind her ear soothingly, wondering if the worst was over and his wife had truly come back to him again.

56

The next morning Emma was feeling brighter. Her head still felt fuzzy and she was exhausted but the awful weight of sadness that she had been carrying around for the last few months didn't seem as heavy any more.

She had overdosed because she wanted to forget; she was in so much pain and torment that she had wanted to feel numb and the alcohol allowed her to do that and the tablets helped her sleep and the next thing she knew she was forcing them down her throat. She hadn't wanted to kill herself; she just wanted not to feel any more. She had hit rock bottom but it was as if a hole had been cut through the numbness that allowed a small chink of light to shine through. She felt embarrassed for all she had put Adam and her parents through; they had suffered so much without her adding to their woes. For the first time she noticed that her parents were starting to look old. Her mum seemed small and frail, she had let the colour grow out of her hair so it was now silvery grey and her dad looked smaller than she had remembered as a child. They had aged so much in the last year. God here she was at her age causing them all this trouble and worry, more than she had ever caused as a teenager.

Adam was still at her bedside when she woke and she felt content just having him present again, knowing he was beside her. For the first time since the accident, it was as if she could see him as her husband again, the way she used to see him. She could finally see past the fog and she might just be able to get through it.

* * *

While Emma slept peacefully, Zoe came in to visit that evening.

"Hi there," she whispered to Adam "How's she doing?"

"She's good, she's sleeping a lot but the doctors said that's to be expected – she's sleeping off the excess tablets. It'll be a few days before she'll be back to full strength but they reckon she should be able to come home tomorrow."

"Oh thank God!"

"I'm going to be there for her now – help her recover, be there for her properly this time. I've let her down. I'll never forgive myself for just thinking about myself and how I was feeling –"

"Don't be so hard on yourself – you've been through as much as she has, Adam! It was bound to take its toll on your relationship but at least you're going to work through it together."

"I know this might sound weird but it's as if she finally sees me again? Since the accident she just looked through me but now it's different."

When Emma woke later, she was surprised to see Zoe sitting there with Adam.

"How are you feeling, darling? Look who's come to see you!" Adam said.

"Hi, sweetheart. How are you feeling?" Zoe asked.

"Zoe," Emma said, smiling at her.

"I'm going to grab a coffee in the canteen, okay?" Adam wanted to leave the two of them alone. He knew they had some talking to do.

"Fine." Zoe smiled at him as he left. She turned back to her friend. "Emma, thank God you're okay – I – I got such a fright." Zoe's eyes welled up with tears just thinking about it.

"I'm sorry, Zoe – for letting you find me like that, for putting you through that – seeing me in that state. I'm so embarrassed."

"Don't be embarrassed for God's sake! Just promise me you will never, *ever* do anything like that again."

Emma shook her head. "I can promise you I will never touch the things again."

"So how are you feeling?"

"A bit better today, thanks, but still so sleepy – I just keep drifting off but at least the pounding headache has gone. But it's so strange – it's like I've finally came back to reality, y'know? For months I've just felt numb but it's like someone has shaken me by my shoulders now and said wake up. The last year has been a complete nightmare and it's only now I'm coming out of it. I think I might be okay – it doesn't seem so hopelessly bleak now."

"Oh Emma – thank God. And Adam, how are you finding things with Adam?"

"We're doing all right. We've talked – like, properly talked for the first time since it all happened. I think we're going to be okay."

"That's good. You and Adam need each other – you're good together."

"I think you're right." Emma smiled sleepily at Zoe as she drifted off again.

57

Zoe finally felt ready to bring Steve to meet her mother. It was the first time she had ever brought a man to meet her family. She had met his family only weeks after they had first met because he couldn't wait to introduce her to them. He was the second eldest of a family of seven children and his upbringing had been so different from hers. His family was very close – they were not just siblings, they were friends. It was a busy farmhouse full of energy and even though Steve said they argued constantly, you just knew at the same time that they all looked out for one another.

She had been so nervous before she went but she needn't have worried; they had welcomed her in with little fuss as she took a chair at the already full kitchen table while the TV blared some football match in the background. His mother had left pots of potatoes, bowls of carrots and peas, a roast chicken and a huge pile of knives and forks in the centre of the table and told them to "dig in and help themselves". Everyone dived in and it was then that the noise level went up a gear as every voice struggled to be heard and they all talked over one another. It was so strange for Zoe – as an only child she had never seen anything like it. It was the type of family that she had always yearned for.

She was surprised that she didn't feel nervous about bringing Steve home but she knew that he accepted her for who she was, he didn't judge, and if her mother was having a bad day he probably wouldn't think anything of it.

Zoe's mother could be one of two ways; on a good day she could be on a high, gushing and welcoming, running around making tea and apologising because she had "no cake but she did have biscuits, chocolate-covered Rich Tea in fact", but on a bad day she could literally let you in the door without any greeting and you would spend the next hour sitting in silent discomfort, which she seemed to be unaware of. You never knew what you were going to get when you knocked on the door and that was why Zoe didn't visit as much as she ought to. The worst moodswing though was when she was on one of her rants against men. She still hadn't moved on from Zoe's father walking out the door on her. She was blindsided by anger and hatred and felt that all males on the planet were like that. She didn't leave the house too often and had few visitors – mostly just the community nurse who checked on her daily, and her brother and sister-in-law who were good to her. She preferred it that way, she got angsty being around people for too long.

Zoe had rung her mother first to tell her that she would be calling and that she would be bringing someone too. The news wasn't greeted with a reaction either way.

* * *

Zoe opened back the rusty half-height gate with difficulty. The long grass obviously hadn't been cut since the last time she had got a gardener to come out and tidy up her mother's weedy overgrown front lawn. The lichen-covered concrete-slab footpath had weeds shooting up through the cracks. She made a mental note to give him a call again. The front garden wasn't that big, certainly not how Zoe had thought of it as a child, but her mother didn't bother with it.

She stood with Steve by her side and rapped the brass salmon-shaped knocker on the teak door.

Her small thin mother answered the door in a hairy bottle-green cardigan that Zoe could remember her wearing when she was a child. There was more grey in her hair now with just a bit of auburn left at the ends in the few months since she had last seen her. She had obviously decided to give up colouring it. From looking at old photos of her from her twenties and thirties Zoe knew her mother had once taken a pride in her appearance. Zoe felt guilty then. She knew she really should visit more often.

"Hi, Mam, this is Steve."

"Pleased to meet you," said Steve.

"Steve." She pondered the name abstractedly. "Well, come in, don't stand outside in the cold."

She showed them into the 'good' room, although it was a long time since it was 'good'. It was a dark room with net curtains hanging inside the bay window and gold-sheen wallpaper. They sat down on the blue floral-patterned settee that clashed wildly with the orange shagpile carpet.

"So, Zoe – how have you been?"

Her mother was being overly formal and polite but Zoe supposed it was better than shouting at Steve because he happened to be male.

"Good thanks, Mam, busy in work."

"Oh."

"I brought you a few bits." Zoe opened a bag full of groceries including a cake, biscuits and some essentials like milk, tea, butter, coffee and bread because it was hit-or-miss whether her mother would actually have these.

"Thank you, Zoe." She made no effort to take them from her daughter.

Zoe took the initiative and packed away the milk and butter in the fridge, throwing out some out-of-date cartons and butter. She put the kettle on and called Steve to give her a hand to make the tea and slice the cake.

The gold-plated clock on the mantelpiece chimed as they sat drinking their tea and eating an M&S sponge cake in silence.

"Will I put on the TV for the two of you?" her mother asked her as if they were ten years of age.

"Sure, go ahead."

She turned on an old episode of *Murder She Wrote* and they watched Jessica Fletcher solving the puzzle again.

"How's Uncle Ed and Aunt Lydia?" asked Zoe.

"Good."

"How is Ed enjoying retirement?"

Her mother didn't answer, her eyes fixed on the TV screen.

Zoe checked her watch. She knew that after an hour they could go but there still was a good twenty minutes left.

After some general chit-chat, mostly on Zoe's part, and a few polite questions from Steve which didn't elicit any response from her mother, Zoe stood up and excused herself with promises that she wouldn't leave it so long the next time and she would call in again soon.

"I think he's very nice," Zoe's mother said out of the blue as they walked out into the hallway.

Zoe was amazed to get this seal of approval from her mother. They kissed goodbye and Zoe hugged her mother tight before they went back out across the broken footpath and stiff gate and got into Steve's car, her mother waving at them from behind the net curtain.

"Well, go on, you can be honest. Was it awful?" Zoe asked as Steve pulled out onto the road.

"Don't be silly Zoe, she was fine."

"She's bats, isn't she?"

"Not bats. Well, maybe a little . . . *detached*."

"*Detached* – mmmh, I like that description. I must remember that one. At least she liked you."

"How did you come to that conclusion considering she never even spoke to me?"

"She does that to everyone. But she said you were nice – that's a ringing endorsement if I ever heard one."

"Maybe we should go over again in a few weeks?"

"Really? You wouldn't mind?"

"Of course not, I could even sort out her garden – I'd say the neighbours are going mad – she's ruining the manicured gardens of suburbia."

And then Zoe knew it. He was 'The One'. He accepted her for who she was, her baggage, her strange mother and all. He didn't bat an eyelid.

"Look, I don't know if now is the right time but, well . . . I was wondering if . . . you want to move in with me and Dave?"

Her face lit up. "Really?"

"Well, yeah. You stay over every weekend anyway and I know it would be a bit of a commute from my house into the city every day, but I love being with you, Zoe, and I want to wake up beside you every day."

"And you won't mind sharing your bed every night?" she teased him gently.

"Who said anything about sharing a bed? You'll be taking the spare room!" he mocked.

For the first time in her life, Zoe felt safe and secure.

58

The day flew past in a whir of different family members visiting and chatting and it was only when they were finally on their own that Adam dared broach the subject that each of them knew had to be talked about sooner or later. They couldn't avoid it forever.

"Why did you do it, Emma? I couldn't have coped if anything had happened to you."

"I was so tired, Adam. I couldn't sleep, the pain was awful. It just all got too much, you know – I didn't mean to, I just wanted to escape my own head. I was so low, I felt so alone, I had lost Fionn and then you, and I just felt so worthless and full of self-hatred. So I was taking my tablets but they weren't helping at all so I drank the vodka and then I woke up here . . . I'm sorry."

"I'm sorry too. I let you down – I just couldn't take it any more."

"I know, Adam. I understand now. I locked you out and left you alone when you needed me. I didn't see your suffering, only my own. I just want to say now that I love you, I always have. I know it may not have seemed like it, the way I've been treating you, but I just hope you will be able to find it within your heart to forgive me . . ." She trailed off.

"There's nothing to forgive." He leant his head down to rest upon her chest.

They lay like that for a while before Adam spoke again.

"Emma, I still miss him desperately. It hurts so bloody much."

"I know," she said in almost a whisper.

"I keep going over and over what happened and just wondering if I had done anything differently, would things be different now? If I had braked coming up to the crossroads after seeing the first car go through . . . or if I had gone through faster. It drives me mad, all the endless combinations and permutations of scenarios and wondering what might have been."

"Adam, love, it wasn't your fault – I keep thinking the same thoughts myself – what if I hadn't gone out that day, what if I had stayed at home – but all they do is send you doolally and drive you demented."

This was the first time she had ever said this and the weight of what she was saying was felt by Adam.

"I'll never know if I could have done more, Em. But it all happened in a moment. There was no time to react."

She remained quiet; it was hard to hear what happened. It felt like an open wound just discussing it, she had to take it slowly and let each piece of hurt settle in before she could discuss it some more.

"There was nothing you could have done," she said then. "It was just chance. We were just so, so, unlucky, weren't we?" The unjustness of it all hit her again, a wave of unfairness washed up her body and she felt the anger rising after it once again, until it caught in her throat and tears began to flow.

Adam rubbed her hand.

"Do you think we'll ever be the same again?" she asked.

"I can't say that, Em, I don't know. Probably not, if I'm honest. Sometimes I miss him so much it feels like a physical longing to hold him, or I can't breathe with grief if I think about him."

"Me too – some days I couldn't even get out of bed with the pain. That's why I was so distant from you, because when I looked at you I saw Fionn. You were a constant reminder of him and it was too painful to be around you. I'm so sorry, but he looked so like you, you know."

"I know."

* * *

The next morning a counsellor came around to speak with Emma. Adam left them alone and went to get a coffee. He sat in the coffee dock with a few other lonely souls flicking through magazines. He mulled over the events of the last few days which seemed light-years away from what went before. The grief that had pushed them apart had now drawn them together again.

The counsellor was satisfied that, after all Emma had been through, she had reached rock-bottom and with Adam by her side she would now start to heal. He had advised them to seek couples therapy or even go alone to get help with their bereavement.

Her doctor was happy with her recovery so he allowed her to be discharged. Together they went back to their home.

* * *

It felt strange being back in their house. Emma felt as though she was looking at it with fresh eyes, new eyes, almost like the first day that they had got the keys and moved in here.

They went to bed together that night and slept wrapped in each other's arms – once a familiar routine, they slotted easily back into it again. The touch of his skin was still the same and she was surprised at how much she had missed it.

Adam lay awake for a long time, while Emma still under the influence of her tablets, slept heavily beside him. It was a new beginning for them.

Epilogue

In a garden children ran and played, a mother brought out a homemade birthday cake with lemon buttercream icing in the shape of a butterfly. She bent down to light the four candles but had to do it a few times as the flame kept being extinguished by the gentle breeze. Then the children and adults all stood dutifully around the table while her four-year-old daughter beamed as everyone sang 'Happy Birthday'. When it was time for the little girl to blow out her candles, her brother barged in to do it for her.

"Let Ava do it herself, Jonathan!" the mother chided.

"She's not able to – I have to show her," her bossy older brother replied.

Ava let her brother show off to the crowd as he helped her blow out the four candles with over-exaggerated breaths. The cake was cut and served up to everyone. The children had to be harangued to pose for some photos and shouted 'cheese', revealing big toothy grins before running off again, weaving in and out through the other guests like a train as they chased each other with the younger children trying to keep up with the older ones. They zigzagged around sun chairs, prams, buggies and babies sleeping in their grandparents' arms and a long wooden table laden with treats, leafy salads and bowls heaped with ripened fruit, a jug of homemade lemonade and a cake stand stacked with pink and yellow cupcakes. White, willowy butterflies flitted through the hot air and honeybees could be heard buzzing about their work.

A man with a newborn in a sling was feeding some bits of burger to a chocolate-brown dog while chatting to the host who was turning sausages over on the barbecue, the smell of charred meat wafting in the summer air. Chinese paper lanterns hung from trees billowing in the breeze.

The mother returned inside to the welcome coolness of the house to get more food. She opened the fridge, took out a bag of salad and shook it into a bowl before tossing it around with some balsamic vinegar and olive-oil dressing. She grabbed a packet of ice-creams and a bottle of chilled white wine and put them onto a tray with the salad. Passing back out through the hallway, she glanced at a photo in a silver frame of a baby lying on his front, body raised up by his arms, his smile beaming at the camera. She stood momentarily just looking. She smiled wistfully at the photo of her baby. It was just like he was smiling back at her. At moments like this her heart literally ached with wishing she could hold him in her arms again and he could be included in the celebrations, running around with all the other children.

"Mammy, mammy, where are the ice-creams! We all want the ice-creams! We are soooo hot and hungry!" the birthday girl exclaimed dramatically from the doorstep. Her mother snapped back into the present, to where she was needed.

"Coming, love, I'll be there in a second."

Balancing the tray in one hand, she kissed the tip of her index finger and planted it firmly against the glass of the smiling baby before walking back out into the garden.

POOLBEG WISHES TO

THANK YOU

for buying a Poolbeg book.

If you enjoyed this why not
visit our website:

www.poolbeg.com

and get another book delivered straight
to your home or to a friend's home!

All books despatched within 24 hours.

POOLBEG

WHY NOT JOIN OUR MAILING LIST

@ www.poolbeg.com and get some
fantastic offers on Poolbeg books